THE WORLD'S CLASSICS

THE PATHFINDER

JAMES FENIMORE COOPER (1789–1851) grew up at Otsego Hall, his father's large estate at the foot of Lake Otsego amid the newly developing farmlands of New York State. A son of the region's dominant land developer and politician, Cooper absorbed memories of the Iroquois Indians' habitation of his family's lands. At an Albany school for patricians' sons, he heard legends of the nearby battles of the two wars which had brought the new American Republic into existence: The French and Indian, or Seven Years War (1756–63), and the Revolutionary War (1776–83). After two years at Yale College, Cooper spent five years at sea, married into a prominent Westchester County family of former loyalists, and began the life of a gentleman farmer on family lands. Although literary and family legend contends that Cooper began writing his first novel *Precaution* (1820) in order to outdo a contemporary British woman novelist, recent research suggests that the loss of the Cooper family wealth had made a profitable career necessary.

Cooper's second novel *The Spy* (1821), a patriotic but politically complex novel about the Revolutionary War, was an immediate success. In *The Pioneers* (1823), Cooper introduced Natty Bumppo (Leatherstocking) and Indian John (Chingachgook), the paired heroes of the five Leatherstocking Tales, which would include *The Last of the Mohicans* (1826), *The Prairie* (1827), *The Pathfinder* (1840), and *The Deerslayer* (1841). *The Last of the Mohicans* secured Cooper an international reputation as a major writer of historical romance, America's counterpart to Sir Walter Scott. Testimonies to the lasting power of Cooper's fiction have been written by novelists as diverse as Balzac, Melville, George Sand, Joseph Conrad, and D. H. Lawrence.

WILLIAM P. KELLY is Associate Professor of English at Queens College and the Graduate Center, City University of New York. He is the author of *Plotting America's Past: Fenimore Cooper and the Leatherstocking Tales*.

Oxford University Press, Walton Street, Oxford OX2 6DP

Oxford New York Toronto
Delhi Bombay Calcutta Madras Karachi
Petaling Jaya Singapore Hong Kong Tokyo
Nairobi Dar es Salaam Cape Town
Melbourne Auckland

and associated companies in
Berlin Ibadan

Oxford is a trade mark of Oxford University Press

British Library Cataloguing in Publication Data
Data available

Library of Congress Cataloging in Publication Data
Cooper, James Fenimore, 1789–1851.
[Pathfinder]
The pathfinder, or, The inland sea/James Fenimore Cooper:
[edited by] William P. Kelly.
p.   cm.—(The World's classics)
Includes bibliographical references.
1. United States—History—French and Indian War, 1755–1763—
Fiction.   I. Kelly, William P.   II. Title.   III. Series.
PS1410.A2K4   1992   813'.2—dc20   92–144
ISBN 0-19-282956-4

Printed in Great Britain by
BPCC Hazells Ltd.
Aylesbury, Bucks

THE WORLD'S CLASSICS

JAMES FENIMORE COOPER

The Pathfinder

OR THE INLAND SEA

Introduction and Notes by
WILLIAM P. KELLY

Oxford   New York
OXFORD UNIVERSITY PRESS
1992

CONTENTS

ACKNOWLEDGEMENTS

THE text of this edition was established by Richard Dilworth Rust. It is from *The Writings of James Fenimore Cooper*, edited by James Franklin Beard (Editor-in-Chief) and James P. Elliott (Chief Textual Editor), sponsored by Clark University and the American Antiquarian Society, assisted in part by the Program for Editions of the National Endowment for the Humanities, an independent federal agency, and published by the State University of New York Press. The Cooper edition is approved by the Center for Editions of American Authors of the Modern Language Society of America. The University of North Carolina at Chapel Hill is the volume sponsor of *The Pathfinder*.

I would like to pay particular thanks to Marybeth McMahon, who wrote the essay on the historical context of *The Pathfinder* which appears in this volume, to John McWilliams, who prepared the chronology of Cooper's life, to Dever Powell, who researched many of the Explanatory Notes, and to Beth Stickney, who assisted in the preparation of the Select Bibliography.

W. P. K.

INTRODUCTION

THIRTEEN years after James Fenimore Cooper concluded the Leatherstocking Saga by laying Natty Bumppo to rest in *The Prairie* (1827), he resurrected the scout in *The Pathfinder* (1840). That decision marked a significant shift in Cooper's career. With the publication of *The Spy* (1821), *The Pioneers* (1823), *The Pilot* (1824), and *The Last of the Mohicans* (1826), Cooper had established himself as the preeminent American novelist, the first to enjoy an international reputation. Capitalizing on that status, he left the United States in 1826 for an extended residence in Europe. During the early years of his stay he continued to write American historical romances, most notably *The Prairie* and *The Red Rover* (1827). But in 1832 he published *The Bravo*, the first of a series of three novels set in the European past. Cooper had come to see himself as a spokesman for republican principles, and in these novels he addressed what he took to be an oligarchic threat to the nascent democratic movements of Europe.

Cooper's European novels failed to win a popular audience; more important, they prompted American critics to challenge his national loyalties. Stung by their charges, Cooper responded in kind, denouncing his critics and instructing his countrymen in sound republican practice. Cooper's condescension exacerbated the conflict and further alienated him from his readers. Thoroughly disillusioned by the course of American democracy and entangled in a series of largely futile lawsuits with the Whig press, he publicly abandoned his literary career. That pledge, announced in *A Letter to His Countrymen* (1834), did not silence Cooper—he produced several volumes of social criticism and travel writing during this period—but with the exception of *Homeward Bound* and *Home As Found* (1838), two thinly veiled social satires, Cooper ceased to write novels.

The publication of *The Pathfinder*, then, marks not only Cooper's return to the Leatherstocking series but also the abandonment of his self-imposed literary exile. Rather than

stridently assailing the mendacity of contemporary life,
Cooper calls his readers back to the colonial setting of *The
Last of the Mohicans*. Here Natty and Chingachgook are
again in their prime; the French and Indian Wars once
more imperil the New York frontier. For Cooper, *The
Pathfinder*'s nostalgic appeal was personal as well as
cultural. His youthful experience as a midshipman on Lake
Ontario informs both the novel's setting and its major
incidents. In her account of her father's return to the
Leatherstocking series, Susan Cooper recalled that his
naval memories were especially dear to him. He had long
hoped to recover that experience in a novel, she tells us, and
'more than thirty years' later the young midshipman, now
an experienced writer, determined that his next work of the
imagination should be connected with that ground'.

Contemporary reviews of *The Pathfinder* were mixed; the
partisan journalists of the period were not quick to abandon
a quarrel. But most of his critics did note with pleasure the
renewal of Cooper's historical interests and welcomed him
'back to his old ground'. In a memorial oration delivered
shortly after Cooper's death in 1851, William Cullen
Bryant was particularly alert to the shift in direction *The
Pathfinder* represented for Cooper's career. American
readers, Bryant wrote, had come to perceive Cooper

as a controversialist, acute, keen, and persevering, occupied with
his personal wrongs and schemes of attack and defence. They were
startled from this estimate of his character by the moral beauty of
that glorious work—I must so call it; by the vividness and force of
its delineations, by the unspoiled love of nature apparent in every
page, and by the fresh and warm emotions which everywhere gave
life to the narrative and the dialogue.

Many of his twentieth-century readers have characterized
Cooper's return to his 'true ground' in *The Pathfinder* and
The Deerslayer (1841) as regressive. In what is surely the
most influential essay ever written about Cooper's fiction,
D. H. Lawrence described the Leatherstocking Tales as 'a
decrescendo of reality, and a *crescendo* of beauty'. Beginning in
the 'actuality' of *The Pioneers*, the series progressively yields,

Lawrence argued, 'a wish-fulfillment vision, a kind of yearning myth'. By restoring Natty to life Cooper imaginatively banishes the contentious democracy of the 1830s and escapes into a pastoral world of beauty and memory. *The Pathfinder* does subordinate the social concerns of the first three Tales: Cooper is less explicitly concerned with the dispossession of the Indians, the destruction of the wilderness, and the basis of social order on the frontier. History itself recedes; its role as informing context is commandeered by the primal beauty of lake and forest. In none of the earlier Tales do the affairs of men seem so inconsequential and the power of nature so great. Ontario and its forests enfold and dwarf Cooper's characters and the political interests they represent.

The weight of ideology has eased. Unlike the native spokesmen of *Mohicans* or *The Prairie*, *The Pathfinder*'s Indian characters do not deliver impassioned orations assailing European imperialism and the disruption of tribal life. They are narrative props whose machinations advance Cooper's plot. Chingachgook himself has been marginalized. Absent for long stretches of the novel, consigned almost exclusively to scenes of battle and martial display, he has none of the elegiac power he possesses in *Mohicans*. In his preface Cooper acknowledges a shift in emphasis by arguing that: 'The Indian character has so little variety, that it has been my object to avoid dwelling on it too much, on the present occasion.' This assertion represents a dramatic retreat from the first three Tales, where Cooper insisted on the distinctive tribal natures of the Delaware and the Iroquois. More important, it signals an abandonment of his use of Indian characters to address the destructive consequences of the westward march of American civilization.

Natty too has undergone a change from the first three volumes of the Tales. In *The Pathfinder* his character and commitments are more idealized; his distance from social and political concerns more pronounced. Even though he speaks more frequently here than in any of the other Tales, he rarely concerns himself with civilization and its destructive course. To some extent, Natty's turn from public to private discourse is the inevitable consequence of Cooper's decision to portray him in the grip of the 'master passion'. But Natty's courtship of Mabel Dunham is futile from its beginnings. Indeed, the principal narrative thrust of the novel involves Natty's recognition of his unsuitability as Mabel's lover. For Lawrence, Mabel's rejection of Natty and his subsequent departure for the forests is itself a form of wish fulfilment, an emblem of Cooper's longing to 'turn his back on white society', to abandon domesticity, and to pursue 'the onward adventure of the integral soul'.

More striking still is the absence—for the first time in the Leatherstocking Tales—of a pair of upper-class characters whose marriage is meant to resolve the conflicts of the novel and to transmit Natty's values to a new generation. The union of Mabel Dunham and Jasper Western, which does conclude *The Pathfinder*, is an appropriate one, but it lacks the cultural resonance of earlier marriages in the series. Mabel and Jasper secure neither Natty's legacy nor the progressive direction of American culture. They return to New York, where Jasper becomes 'a successful and respected merchant' and Mabel 'the mother of several youths'. In the novel's final pages Mabel journeys in middle age to the Mohawk Valley, where she sees Natty on a distant shore. When she inquires about him, she is told that 'he was the most renowned hunter of that portion of the state . . . A being of great purity of character, and of as marked peculiarities, and that he was known in that region of the country, by the name of Leatherstocking'. Mabel remains on one side of the Mohawk and Natty on the other. They do not speak; the gap between them is unbridged.

But although *The Pathfinder* unquestionably marks a shift in Cooper's narrative practice, it is nevertheless a sequel. Cooper chose to resume his career as a novelist by returning to a story whose conclusion he had already written. *The Pathfinder* carries with it, therefore, a good deal of narrative prehistory. We know that the Natty of *The Pathfinder* will become the exile of *The Pioneers* and *The Prairie*, and that the pristine wilderness of Ontario will fall to the wanton axes and ploughs of settlement. Furthermore, we know from *Home As Found* that Templeton, the frontier village delicately balanced in *The Pioneers* between order and anarchy, will become the domain of pugnacious levellers. Natty's memory survives there, but only as a cruel measure of loss. Visiting the site of Natty's hut, John Effingham, the novel's aristocratic hero, mournfully concludes that 'the days of the Leatherstockings have passed away. He preceded me in life, and I see few remains of his character in a region where speculation is more rife than moralizing, and emigrants are more plentiful than hunters.'

In short, Cooper's decision to return to the Leatherstocking series involves us in a complex exercise of intertextuality in which reading is neither innocent nor discrete. That is not to argue that *The Pathfinder* cannot be profitably read in isolation from the other volumes of the series, but rather to suggest that a full appreciation of Cooper's intentions is dependent on context. Read from the perspective of the preceding Tales, *The Pathfinder* does not invite our indulgence in escapist reveries but demands instead our participation in Cooper's twenty-year meditation on the course of American democracy.

In the first three Leatherstocking Tales—and throughout his writing in the 1820's—Cooper advances a remarkably balanced critique of American culture at the dawn of the Jacksonian era. He celebrates the rising glory of America in conventional terms: an independent people march ever-westward, preparing the way for unprecedented achievement. But he cautions that America's present security and its future glory are precarious; that progress depends on defusing the disruptive tensions inherent in national experience. For Cooper, the frontier suggests space and abundance, but it evokes as well the spectre of social fragmentation and unbounded greed. Democratic principles promote the elimination of arbitrary barriers but threaten to enshrine the lowest common denominator as a standard of national value. Cooper pays homage to America's revolutionary and republican heritage, but also points to the destruction of the wilderness and the annihilation of tribal cultures. He assails a slavish dependence on European canons of judgement but charges cultural nationalism with the dilution of standards. Throughout the twenties he remains committed to republican ideals—to what he called in _Notions of the Americans_ (1824) 'the improvement of the species in the mass'—yet he is keenly aware that such a process might well yield a tyranny of the majority and the ascendancy of the mediocre.

Crucial to Cooper's vision is the emergence of a natural aristocracy whose claims to leadership are based on merit rather than birth. He believed that such a class could act as a kind of social leaven, securing order and preserving democratic principle, while simultaneously elevating American standards. In each of the early Tales, Cooper invests his hope in a young male character bound both to Natty and to civilization. Oliver Effingham in _The Pioneers_, Duncan Heyward in _Mohicans_, and the aptly named Duncan Uncas Middleton in _The Prairie_ are direct descendants of the middling heroes of Sir Walter Scott, but they are charged with a more complex task. Scott's heroes are primarily passive figures who stand between zealots of the old and new orders. They balance the conflicting claims of progress and tradition by speaking for stasis and moderation. Cooper's heroes share this commitment, but they lack the resource of an informing social tradition. Theirs is a fluid world in which the competing demands of order and freedom are announced against the backdrop of the frontier. They must balance the rapacious greed of the settlers with Natty's respect for nature, and in so doing, point the way toward ordered development. Their ascendancy in the final chapters of their respective Tales by no means suggests the elimination of social tension; those pressures retain their ominous force. Effingham, Heyward, and Middleton are, however, emblems of Cooper's hopeful commitment to America's experiment in self-government.

The social criticism Cooper wrote in the 1830s provides ample evidence of his retreat from that optimism. Returning home after seven years in Europe, Cooper was appalled by what he took to be a decline in national values. He was convinced that democracy had not yielded 'the improvement of the species in the mass', but had instead spawned a meretricious culture anchored to the standards of its lowest classes. In satires such as *The Monikins* (1835) and *Home As Found* (1838)—and more directly in *The American Democrat* (1838), a social tract he vainly hoped would be adopted in the public schools—Cooper inveighed against the arrant philistines and hypocritical levellers whom he accused of subverting republican principles. In particular, he mourned the disappearance of the yeomen villages he had idealized in *The Pioneers*. Constant social flux, he argued, had frustrated the development of stable communities; nation building had been swamped by relentless self-aggrandizement. More distressing still was the exclusion from meaningful participation in American government of the natural aristocracy on whom Cooper had based his hopes for national development. The victims of their culture's commitment to a false equality, the Effinghams had become cynical and isolated figures reduced, Cooper sadly concluded, to incestuous marriages and impotent complaint.

In *The Pathfinder*, and again in *The Deerslayer*, Cooper considers the consequences of his disillusionment. No longer does he attempt to articulate principles that might direct American development and secure republican values. Here his enquiry is personal. How, he asks, might men live a principled life in the fallen world of American democracy? What, in short, are the alternatives to flight or complicity? The search for direction, the bases of moral choice, and the temptations of hubris are Cooper's principal concerns. His intentions are explicit in the novel's title. Natty is called the Pathfinder, he tells Mabel, because 'I rather pride myself in finding my way, where there is no path, than in finding it where there is. But the regular troops be by no means particular, and half the time they do'n't know the difference atween a trail and a path, though one is a matter for the eye, while the other is little more than scent'. Where others blur distinctions and are 'by no means particular', Natty is a figure of absolute clarity. He possesses, Cooper writes, 'a beautiful and unerring sense of justice'. His 'fidelity was like the immoveable rock . . . no casuist could have made clearer decisions in matters relating to right and wrong'.

Natty's discrimination is of crucial importance because the world in which he must find his way is without demarcation. The forests that surround Ontario are vast and trackless; its fogs make direction uncertain. The Thousand Islands that dot the lake are indistinguishable and uncharted. 'Nobody knows all about them, or anything about them', a young seaman says, 'They are a puzzle to the oldest sailor on the lake, and we don't pretend to know even their names. For that matter, most of them have no more names than a child that dies before it is christened.' The French and Indian Wars have made traversing Ontario's forests a dangerous as well as a disorienting experience. The renewal of five centuries of French and British rivalry on the American frontier has generated a particularly brutal conflict. European military codes have disintegrated in the wilderness; massacres and scalpings have replaced pitched battles and the exchange of colours; traditional conceptions of honour have yielded to the exigencies of the forests. Cooper's European armies are lost on the American frontier. Their battle-lines are uncertain, their alliances with native tribes precarious. Frontier warfare is as corrosive for tribal culture. Traditional loyalties have blurred under the weight of French and British pressure; native struggles to preserve autonomy have faltered. As allies of the British and French, Cooper's Indians become the agents of their own annihilation.

Survival in this environment depends on precision. Conditions must be accurately assessed and appropriate choices made. In the two major military encounters of the novel, the failure of British soldiers to recognize Indian ambushes results in their destruction. But it is not only military circumstances which require certain vision and discriminating judgement. In the course of the perilous journey to Ontario which opens the novel, Jasper Western twice directs his canoe through harrowing passages: first, he runs his craft over the Oswego Falls; later, he drives it through a series of dangerous rapids. In both cases his extraordinary skill guides the canoe safely through the narrowest of channels. Even Natty is inadequate to these tasks. He rides as Jasper's passenger in the falls run and capsizes his canoe when he attempts to follow Jasper through the rapids. 'I can't do it myself,' he admits, 'it needs Jasper's hand, and Jasper's eye, to make sure of a dry passage.' Throughout *The Pathfinder*, recognizing limits, as Natty does here, is a crucial measure of moral precision. 'We white folk', Natty tells Mabel's uncle, Charles Cap, 'fancy we are always wiser than our fellows. I'm curing myself fast of the weakness, but it needs time, to root up the tree that has been growing more than thirty years.'

Cooper's assault on hubris is balanced by his rejection of a mindless adherence to tradition. The British soldiers at Ontario refuse to adapt to their frontier circumstance and pay for their recalcitrance with their lives. 'Experience', Natty complains, 'makes them but little wiser, and they wheel, and platoon about, here, in the forest, just as they did in their parks, at home, of which they are all so fond of talking.' Cooper's prime example of British arrogance is Serjeant Dunham's subaltern, Corporal McNab. When Mabel warns McNab of an impending ambush, he dismisses her fears and insists that 'this American mode of fighting that is getting into so much favor, will destroy the reputation of His Majesty's army, if it no destroy its spirit'. Rather than alerting his troops, he lectures Mabel on Scottish history, a lesson that is interrupted by an Indian bullet. More disturbing than McNab's rigidity is that of the colonial troops who serve with the British expeditionary force. Despite the discrimination he has experienced from his British superiors, Serjeant Dunham sees through European eyes. He accepts Major Duncan's argument that Jasper's ability to speak French compromises his honour, even though he has served with Jasper and witnessed his loyalty. Seduced by British suspicion, he relieves Jasper of his command of the *Scud* and entrusts the ship to Charles Cap. An ocean-going seaman, Cap has had no experience on Lake Ontario and nearly sinks the *Scud*. Jasper rescues the ship, but Dunham does not profit from experience.

When he returns to his camp from an expedition against the French, he again subordinates native wit to British convention and blunders into an ambush.

Cooper considers the consequences of such dependence on a wide range of narrative levels. The social hierarchy of Fort Oswego is limiting and absurd. Mabel's education and personal merit are more than sufficient to establish her as an equal of the officers' wives, but her father's rank excludes her from a full association with them. When Jasper gives Mabel a calash he has won in a shooting match, the 'ladies' of this crude frontier garrison debate 'the fitness of so handsome a thing's passing into the possession of a non-commissioned officer's child', and offer to buy it from her because 'it is an article of dress [she] can never wear'. The paternal discipline Dunham attempts to impose on his daughter is grounded on a similarly destructive rigidity. Having decided that Natty will be her husband, Dunham dismisses the scout's misgivings and assures him that 'the hussy would never dream of refusing to marry a man who was her father's friend before she was born'. He rejects Major Duncan's suggestion that Mabel be permitted to choose her own husband by telling him that 'disobedience is the next crime to mutiny'.

Dunham, Cap, and Chingachgook court disaster because they are consistently incapable of overcoming the weight of their own histories. Dunham, whose father 'was a soldier before him', is circumscribed by his military heritage and 'looks at most things in this world over the barrel of his musket'. He resists common-sense revisions of British strategies, even when they are clearly called for, and imposes a military grid on every aspect of his life, including the marriage of his daughter. He has not 'planned this marriage', he tells Natty, 'without thinking it over, as a general does his campaign'. Cap's subservience to his heritage is even more pronounced. Despite ample evidence to the contrary he refuses to believe that Lake Ontario demands particular navigational techniques and fails to adapt the maxims of ocean seamanship to his altered circumstances. When Jasper argues that he must anchor the *Scud* to avoid a wreck, Cap angrily dismisses him from the ship's deck. 'No man induces me to commit such a sin against my own bringing up', he insists. 'If I sink, I sink, but d——e, I'll go down ship-shape and with dignity.' Chingachgook too endangers his life and those of his companions by subordinating reason to tradition. Rather than avoiding a party of Iroquois, he launches a reckless one-man attack. When Natty chastises him for his foolhardy behaviour, Chingachgook cites the burden of his ancestry. 'The Great Serpent is a Mohican warrior,' he tells his friend, 'he sees only his enemies, when he is on the war-path, and his fathers have struck the Mingoes from behind, since the waters began to run.'

Cooper's assault on narrow traditionalism is paralleled by an equally strenuous rejection of unbridled originality. Each of the novel's three villains has abandoned the restraints of his heritage. The Tuscarora guide, Arrowhead, is a renegade loyal only to himself. He has freed himself from his history, but in the process has become an outcast and a moral leper. Lieutenant Muir prides himself on 'his auld blood', but he surrenders his heritage and his honour for a purse of double-louis. Confronted with evidence of Muir's treachery, Natty exclaims: 'What an awful sinner! To plot, right and left, ag'in country, friends, and the Lord!' It 'isn't so much', he tells Jasper, that Muir has disgraced his office, but that 'he had a commission from God to act right, and to deal fairly with his fellow creatur's and he has failed awfully in his duty'. Captain Sanglier's treason is more subtle than that of Arrowhead and Muir. The French liaison to the Iroquois, he never betrays the military interests of his country, but as an instigator of Indian ambushes and the paymaster of traitors he violates principles which transcend national loyalties. He observes neither Christian nor savage restraints and becomes a frightening emblem of the fragility of civilization in the wilderness.

In a world in which both submission and licence lead to destruction, Natty's role as moral pole-star acquires crucial significance. Throughout the Leatherstocking series Natty stands between civilization and the wilderness. 'His "gifts" were "white gifts" ', Cooper noted in his preface to the 1850 edition of the Tales,

> and he was not disposed to bring on them discredit. On the other hand, removed from nearly all the temptations of civilized life, placed in the best associations of that which is deemed savage, and favorably disposed by nature to improve such advantages, it appeared to the writer that his hero was a fit subject to represent the better qualities of both conditions, without pushing either to extremes.

Certainly, Natty occupies a middle ground in *The Pathfinder*, but Cooper's stress is on moral balance rather than on cultural mediation. Here Natty's relation to the parallel worlds of the civilized and the wild is framed in terms of resistance rather than incorporation. Both his autonomy and his identity are dependent on maintaining distance from the seductions of either realm rather than on internalizing 'the better qualities of both conditions'. The Pathfinder, Cooper writes,

> was a fair example of what a just-minded and pure man might be, while untempted by unruly or ambitious desire, and left to follow the bias of his feelings, amid the solitary grandeur and ennobling influences of a sublime nature; neither led aside by the inducements which influence all to do evil amid the incentives of civilization, nor forgetful of the Almighty Being whose spirit pervades the wilderness as well as the town.

Cooper's description of Natty as a tightrope walker balanced between civilized and savage vice has broad cultural resonance. Doubtless, the French and Indian Wars had historic interest for Cooper's contemporaries; his was a generation much given to creating a useable American past. The novel's Ontario setting would also have elicited memories of the naval battles fought there during the War of 1812. But *The Pathfinder*'s principal referent is more immediate. Cooper's attention to the competing demands of freedom and order locate this novel at the heart of Jacksonian political discourse. That tension—epitomized for many of Cooper's contemporaries in the conflicting emphases of the Declaration of Independence and the

Constitution—gave shape to the period's debate about cultural authority. Concern about the erosion of discipline, the blurring of boundaries, and the difficulty of forging a new political order without foundering in moral anarchy and social chaos was not unique to Fenimore Cooper. Factionalism was the hallmark of America's political day, but a nostalgic attraction to the republican era and the certain authority of the Founding Fathers cut across partisan divisions. In *Home As Found* Cooper acknowledged this cultural longing and explicitly associated it with the figure of Natty Bumppo. In that novel, 'the commodore', an eccentric survivor of an earlier age, praises Jackson as a worthy leader but concludes that: 'They may talk of their Jeffersons and Jacksons, but I set down Washington and Natty Bumppo as the two only really great men of my time.'

Cooper's quest for clarity in *The Pathfinder* unfolds against the frontier collision of Europeans, Indians, and colonials, but that conflict is secondary to the romance which drives his narrative. By involving Natty in the social ritual of courtship, Cooper clouds his moral vision and compromises the purity of his existence. Before he meets Mabel, Natty's priorities and values are certain. He finds paths where the soldiers see trackless wilderness, and unfailingly distinguishes friend from foe. He assails hubris in others and bewails the unruly desires of the weaker men who surround him. His pursuit of Mabel disrupts that life of certainty and contentment. His fear that his attraction to Mabel 'will be the spoiling of one of the best and most experienced scouts on the lines' is well founded. On Mabel's first morning at Ontario, Natty chooses to stay by her side rather than accompanying a scouting party. 'The Sarpent is in his place', he tells Mabel when she asks for Chingachgook, 'while I am not in mine.' Natty's absence is without consequence in this episode, but because he is not 'in his place' some nights later, Arrowhead and Sanglier enter the garrison and plot the betrayal of Dunham's expedition. During the course of that mission Natty leaves Dunham to return to camp where Mabel awaits their return. Without Natty's guidance Dunham fails to recognize an ambush and leads his men to their deaths. 'I do think', Natty tells Mabel, 'if I had stayed with the boats, this would not have come to pass!'

It is not only Natty's sense of duty that has been obscured. His courtship has made him a victim of what Cooper calls 'ambitious desire'. He knows he is an inappropriate candidate for Mabel's hand. As he tells Dunham, he is 'a poor hunter, and Mabel is f'it to be an officer's lady'. It is, he concludes, of 'no avail to attempt to make the dove consort with the wolf'. When Mabel rejects his initial proposal, he agrees that their marriage would be 'agin natur' ', and acknowledges that he has 'been on a false trail since we met'. Still, Natty succumbs to the Serjeant's promptings and does not abandon his suit until Mabel indicates her preference for Jasper. Many of Cooper's critics have read Natty's courtship as an elaborate and ultimately successful attempt to extricate himself from a romance entirely of Serjeant Dunham's making. Such a reading, however, does not account for Natty's persistence in the face of Mabel's obvious reluctance, or the over-whelming sorrow he feels when she refuses him. Throughout his courtship Natty is incapable of abandoning his suit because of 'something pulling at my heart strings which seems hard to undo'. When Mabel rejects his initial proposal, 'tears rolled down the cheeks of the scout like rain'. He tells Jasper that 'I do think it would quite break me down, now, to lose Mabel Dunham'; and when Mabel does finally choose Jasper, Natty is 'overcome with a sense of loneliness' and becomes 'conscious of his isolated condition in the world'.

That Natty's attachment to Mabel is heartfelt is crucial to Cooper's narrative intentions. If nothing is at stake, Natty's decision to allow Mabel to choose her husband freely would be of little consequence. But Natty does desire Mabel and the domesticity she represents. 'It is time', he concludes, 'I did begin to think of a house, and furniture, and a home'. He maintains that 'we all ought to seek for wives, for the man that lives altogether in the woods, and in company with his inimies, or his prey, gets to lose some of the feelin' of kind, in the ind'. He tells Mabel that 'all other creatur's mate . . . and it was intended that man should do so, too . . . Providence makes nothing that lives, to live quite alone.' Natty dreams of a clearing in the woods where he and Mabel will live with Jasper and his wife. He will still scout and hunt; Jasper will continue to sail the *Scud*. When they return from their travels, their wives will greet them and 'none could be happier than we four'. The longing implicit in this vision redefines Natty's solitary life as an unnatural state. When he abandons the garrison for the wilderness in the novel's final passages, he embraces an incomplete existence. He does so voluntarily. The pledge to marry Natty that the dying Dunham extracts from Mabel places him in a position to realize his dream, but he refuses to exercise the paternal power Dunham has ceded to him and permits Mabel to choose Jasper. In so doing, Natty resists self-interest and turns his back on hubris. He recovers the moral authority he had begun to lose.

Mabel's position parallels Natty's. In course of *The Pathfinder* she receives four marriage proposals. Three are clearly inappropriate, but each presents a significant temptation. Her refusal to become Arrowhead's squaw is phrased in conventional rhetoric—'To me it would be a lighter evil to be killed than to become the wife of an Indian'—but her defence of racial barriers is not advanced in the comfort of a drawing-room. She is Arrowhead's prisoner and knows that the price of preserving her integrity is torture and death. Lieutenant Muir's age and his five previous marriages disqualify him as an appropriate suitor, but his social rank complicates Mabel's decision. As the daughter of a non-commissioned officer, she has been denied the position her education and talents merit. 'While I am not', she tells Jasper, 'good enough to be the wife of one of the gentlemen of the garrison, I think even you will admit . . . I am too good to be the wife of one of the common soldiers.' Marrying Muir would resolve that dilemma and allow her to claim the rank she has been prepared to occupy. Natty's proposal demands an even more troubling choice. She recognizes that a match with a man she 'reverences as a daughter' would be 'unwise—unnatural, perhaps', but her judgement is clouded both by her father's dying wish and by Natty's devotion. In each case, Mabel acts in a principled manner. She rejects inappropriate choices and marries Jasper.

The generic conventions of the romance have been satisfied. Mabel deserves, as Natty tells her, 'the best husband America can produce', and within the limits of her possibilities she achieves precisely what her merits demand. Natty resists temptation and returns to his proper 'place'. By novelistic standards *The Pathfinder*'s ending is a happy one: an appropriate marriage is effected, order is restored. But the dominant tone of Cooper's final chapters is melancholic. Natty does not win his cabin in a clearing; he retreats to the isolation of the wilderness. His encounter with Mabel has taught him to see his solitude as unnatural. For all its pleasures and clarity, his life in nature is incomplete. In the novel's final chapter, Natty, Chingachgook, and Arrowhead's widow, Dew-of-June, enter their canoes and bid farewell to Mabel and Jasper. Chingachgook is bereft of wife, son, and tribe; Dew-of-June is 'without a tribe, as well as without a husband'. Natty explicitly aligns his condition with theirs when he tells Jasper that it will not be easy for June to reconcile herself to her losses, but 'what have I to do, with other people's miseries, and marriages, as if I had n't affliction enough of my own'.

The Westerns move east. As Natty himself admits, Mabel is unsuited to life on the unsettled frontier; to remain at Ontario would require from Jasper a callous disregard of her welfare. But as fitting as their removal may be, it has the feel of geographic retreat and self-betrayal. Earlier in the novel Natty reacts to Cap's proposal that Jasper return east with him to become an ocean-going seaman with shock:

You Jasper Western, you, quit the lakes, the forest, and the lines, and this too, for the town and wasty ways of settlements, and a little difference in the taste of the water. Haven't we the salt-licks, if salt is necessary to you? And ought not a man to be satisfied with what contents the other creatur's of God?

Jasper's destiny is even more remote from his gifts than Natty imagines; it is as a merchant and not as an ocean-going seaman that he will earn his living. In the context of the Leatherstocking series, Jasper and Mabel's decision is even more dispiriting. Together they rewrite the destinies of the young lovers of the earlier Tales. Jasper's New York career is an honourable one, but it lacks the resonance of Effingham's, Heyward's, and Middleton's more culturally significant achievements. Mabel, who has been an object of devotion and bloody rivalry, becomes the wife of a merchant and the mother of several children. Their marriage does not bind a divided republic or generate 'thriving villages', but yields instead the ordinary comforts of bourgeois respectability.

By no means does Cooper characterize either the Westerns' marriage or their return to New York as a mistake. Rather, he suggests that in making their choice Jasper and Mabel confront the limitations inherent in their humanity. Mabel discovers that she cannot both submit to and rebel against her father; neither can she have both Natty and Jasper—she must choose between them. Similarly, Jasper must resign the *Scud* and his friendship with Natty if he is to marry Mabel. The price of conjugal bliss, he learns, is the resignation of wilderness pleasure. Natty too is the victim of Cooper's binary syntax. His vision of a cabin in a clearing evaporates when he chooses to grant Mabel her freedom. His dream of perfect contentment, of conjoined freedom and restraint, of male and female bonding, is dismissed as a fond but empty hope.

Natty and the Westerns become, in *The Pathfinder*'s conclusion, inverted images of each other. Mabel and Jasper are insulated from loneliness but are bound by convention; Natty is free from, but longs for, context. They have made admirable decisions, but the consequence of choice has been sorrow. Natty remains true to his gifts, but loses Mabel and embraces sterility. His pledge that 'I shall never think of you, nor anyone else, again, in that way' is perhaps the bleakest moment in the entire Leatherstocking Saga. Cooper implies that Jasper will dream of the *Scud* as he manages his affairs, and tells us that when Mabel returns to Ontario and sees Natty across the Mohawk, she experiences 'a sleepless night'. Her 'distant glimpse' of Natty, Cooper writes, 'cast a shade of melancholy over her still lovely face, that lasted many a day'. The gloom which pervades *The Pathfinder*'s final chapters is no more suggestive of Cooper's hostility toward the domestic than it is indicative of his contempt for Natty's celibate state. Rather, it marks his recognition that the plenitude we long for in our lives is ungraspable, that choice implies denial.

Cooper's insistence on the conflicted nature of desire runs counter to the American grain. In discourse ranging from explorers' narratives and the Declaration of Independence to contemporary political rhetoric, America has consistently been imagined as a realm in which irreconcilable desires might be held in productive balance. Wilderness and civilization, independence and tradition, freedom and order, self-reliance and democratic brotherhood are not antimonies in the American mind but paired constructs inexorably yoked under the banner of national identity. At the heart of this national attraction to the oxymoronic is a vision of American originality. The New World is new because it promises the transcendence of precedent, the rewriting of Old World constriction. Like Natty, who embodies 'the better qualities' of civilization and wilderness 'without pushing either to the extreme', America is *sui generis*, a culture predicated on the repudiation of conventional limitations.

The foundations of American originality have been located most frequently in the nation's peculiarly intimate attachment to nature—and in a corollary belief in that attachment's capacity to remake mankind. Cooper's engagement of this customary idealization of the American environment is apparent in his recurrent use of the word 'nature' in *The Pathfinder*. He invokes nature so frequently, and in so many contexts, that it becomes an almost self-cancelling term, emptied of meaning by its pluri-significance. But careful attention to Cooper's language identifies three principal usages of the word. Nature refers first to the

non-human environment; secondly, to the universal character of mankind; and thirdly, to the particular make-up of
individual men. American rationalism was, of course,
predicated on the alignment of these categories: non-human
nature is a realm of order and harmony; universal human
nature reflects that larger order; particular nature is
inherently unstable, but by attending to the order of the
natural world men may bring their lives into balance.

But in *The Pathfinder*, Ontario's environment is difficult to
read. In the novel's opening scene, Mabel, Cap, Arrowhead,
and Dew-of-June, mount 'a pile of trees that had been
uptorn by a tempest' to reconnoitre their position. The
forest around them is 'one broad and seemingly interminable
carpet of foliage', formed by the mingling of the branches of
elms, maples, and oaks. But 'here and there, by some
accident of the tempests or a caprice of nature, a trifling
opening among these giant members of the forest, permitted
an inferior tree to struggle upward toward the light'. The
tangled trees on which the company stands—'broken and
riven by the force of the gust . . . blended like jack-straws'—
bear further testimony to nature's destructive and arbitrary
force. 'Philosophy', Cooper concludes, 'has not yet determined the nature of the power that so often lays desolate
spots of this description, some ascribing it to the whirlwinds
that produce water-spouts on the ocean, while others again
impute it to sudden and violent passages of streams of the
electric fluid.'

This scene acquires considerable metaphoric power in
the course of Cooper's narrative. Throughout *The Pathfinder*,
nature is at once a realm of order and beauty and a locus of
chaos and caprice. Natty defends nature as a repository of
certain wisdom and a record of providential design. 'God is
unchanged', he tells Cap; 'his works are unchanged—his
holy word is unchanged and all that ought to bless and
honor his name should be unchanged too.' But however
constant nature may be in the abstract, the nature that
surrounds the characters of *The Pathfinder* is tumultuous.
Men cannot find their way through its precincts, much less
decipher its order. Lake Ontario, in particular, is

emblematic of this confusion. At tranquil times the lake is a mirror of divine benevolence. Confronted by its beauty, the eye turned, Cooper writes, 'from the endless but gentle heavings of the lake, to the holy calm, and poetical solitude of the forest, with wonder and delight'. But a shift of the wind transforms these gentle waters into a raging sea. So violent are Ontario's storms that chaos rather than order appears to be the lake's natural state: 'The raging of the tempest had a character of duration, that rendered it easy to imagine it might be a permanent feature of the spot.' Far from securing Cap's belief in an unchanging nature, Ontario confirms his distrust of the wilderness. 'Ay, ay', he complains, 'so much for your fresh water! It has always some trick that is opposed to nature.'

Human nature is as problematic a subject. Natty's recurrent generalizations about human 'natur' ' are riven by inconsistencies. To some degree his confusion is the product of America's multi-racial history. When he wonders whether Indian nature is the same as white nature, he reproduces the contentious rhetoric attendant to the dis-placement of the eastern tribes during the Jackson administration, as well as the corrosive debate that sur-rounded American slavery. Like most white Americans of Cooper's era, Natty insists on the determinant character of racial identity. 'Every skin has its own natur' ', he says, 'and every natur' has its own laws, as well as its own skin.' No 'christianizing', he concludes, 'will ever make even a Delaware a white; nor any whooping and yelling convart a pale face into a red skin'. But despite his insistence that 'colour will have its way', Natty clings to a stubborn defence of the uniformity of human nature. Late in the novel he attempts to reconcile these contradictory positions by drawing a distinction between 'nature' and 'gifts'. Racial differences, he tells Cap, are the product of 'edication and nat'ral gifts'. 'A good Delaware is a good Christian, though he never saw a Moravian, and a good Christian a good Delaware, so far as natur' is consarned.' But Natty's efforts only reset his logical dilemma. If human conduct is determined by disparate racial gifts, and those gifts are 'nat'ral', where might we locate the constant human nature that unifies good Christians and good Delawares?

On this issue Natty's confusion reproduces that of his culture, but his epistemological problems are both more general and more particular. Even within racial groups human behaviour is so varied that Natty is forced to question the existence of a transcendent nature. Men and women, Europeans and colonials, scouts and townsmen respond 'nat'rally' in radically different fashions to the same circumstances. Natty attributes these differences to the unalterable power of training. 'A king's soldier will swear', he tells Jasper, 'and he will drink, and it is of little use to try to prevent him; a gentleman likes his delicacies, and a lady her feathers, and it does not avail much to struggle ag'in either.'

Both Dunham and Cap support Natty's vision of the determinant force of context. Dunham reacts to Duncan's recurrent—and unfulfilled—promises of advancement to an officer's rank by telling him that 'I am what nature made me'. Further, he supports Duncan's irrational doubts about Jasper's loyalties by citing his youth among the French: 'Jasper did not get his French as a prisoner, he took it in, in boyhood, when the mind is easily impressed, and gets its permanent notions; when nature has a presentiment, as it were, which way the character is likely to incline.' Cap, who applauds the Serjeant's prejudice as evidence that 'he understands human nature', offers additional testimony about the variability of mankind. When Mabel asks him whether human nature is not 'the same, on shore, or at sea; on a lake like this, or on the ocean?' he reacts with ill-disguised derision: 'Is not nature the same, indeed!—Now, Mabel, do you imagine that the nature of a soldier is the same as that of a sea-faring man? You've relations in both callings, and ought to be able to answer.'

Natty, Dunham, and Cap each speak from the limitations of their humble origins; their vocabularies are inadequate to craft acceptable distinctions between nature and culture. But their doubts about human constancy are shared both by Major Duncan and by Cooper himself. Duncan forecloses

an argument with Serjeant Dunham by maintaining that
'all general rules have their exceptions'. More directly,
Cooper notes in a narrative aside that: 'In truth, while all
men act under one common law that is termed human
nature, the varieties in their dispositions, modes of judging,
feelings and selfishness are infinite.' Here Cooper reinscribes
Natty's distinction between gifts and nature but in a more
troubling manner. If the 'common law that is termed
human nature' is manifested in infinite variety, how might
we discover its tenets and thereby bring our conduct into
alignment with our nature?

Cooper provides an answer of sorts by identifying
appetite as the single human constant. The 'great concern
of human nature', he writes 'is a breakfast'. That assump-
tion is echoed throughout *The Pathfinder*. Driven from hiding
by hunger, Cap surrenders to Arrowhead and sadly notes
that: 'A man may say that grub is the foundation of human
nature.' Mabel counsels her dying father not to rely on his
'frail and sinful nature', but to seek succour in Christ. Natty
acknowledges his dereliction of duty by telling Jasper that
'we are all human and all do wrong', and reacts to Jasper's
desire to best him in a rifle match by exclaiming: 'What a
thing is mortal man! He overlooks his own gifts and craves
them of another!' Human nature, then, is not an ordering
principle which might be recovered but is itself the source of
man's weakness and folly.

Man's corrupt nature sorely complicates Natty's role as a
pathfinder. If the natural world is indecipherable and
human nature 'frail and sinful', on what foundation might a
man ground his conduct? More important, if 'gifts',
imagined as the irreversible legacies of birth, are determining, how might the new world remake men? For Natty, of
course, truth continues to reside in the natural world, but in
The Pathfinder nature speaks only to those men who live
entirely within its precincts. 'The woods are never silent . . .
to such as understand their meaning', Natty tells Mabel,
'for such as can comprehend their language, there is no
want of rational and instructive discourse.' But choosing a
life which permits such 'comprehension' requires the denial

of civilization and the embrace of unnatural sterility. Conversely, choosing civilization, as Jasper and Mabel do, implies the subordination of nature to culture. Uninformed by the American wilderness, Jasper's life as a merchant is a repetition of Old World forms and not a departure from them.

Cooper glosses the Westerns' union with an Adamic allusion. Overcome by the pain they have caused Natty, 'Mabel and Jasper sat', he writes, 'resembling Milton's picture of our first parents, when the consciousness of sin first laid its leaden weight on their souls'. Cooper's point is not that Mabel and Jasper have sinned in repudiating Natty, but rather that, like their countrymen, they have chosen to abandon a life in Eden. That decision is hardly surprising; to have done otherwise would have been 'unnatural'. But again Cooper stresses his contention that choice implies loss. Here the principal metaphoric casualty of Mabel and Jasper's decision is the newness of the New World. Americans have turned away from nature toward culture; in the terms of Cooper's Adamic paradigm, even the American Revolution—the cornerstone of national independence—is a repetitive act anticipated in Genesis. By denying American difference, Cooper leads us away from the illusion of originality. Having chosen civilization, we embrace human frailty. Pathfinding requires, then, that we acknowledge the consequences of our choice and reject the limitless demands of 'ambitious desire'.

NOTE ON THE TEXT

THIS edition reprints the text of *The Pathfinder* established by Richard Dilworth Rust for *The Writings of James Fenimore Cooper*, published by the State University of New York Press. I have included the 1839 and 1851 prefaces Cooper wrote for the novel, as well as the 1850 preface to the Leatherstocking Tales, which appears here as an appendix. I have also added an essay which discusses the historical context of *The Pathfinder*.

SELECT BIBLIOGRAPHY

James Fenimore Cooper: Letters, Biography, Criticism

Charles Hansford Adams, 'The Guardian of the Law': Authority and Identity in James Fenimore Cooper, 1990.

Allan M. Axelrad, History and Utopia: A Study of the World View of James Fenimore Cooper, 1978.

James F. Beard, ed., The Letters and Journals of James Fenimore Cooper, six volumes, 1960–8.

Robert Clark, ed., James Fenimore Cooper: New Critical Essays, 1985.

Susan F. Cooper, Pages and Pictures from the Writings of James Fenimore Cooper, 1861.

George Dekker, James Fenimore Cooper: The American Scott, 1967.

George Dekker, and John P. McWilliams, eds., Fenimore Cooper: The Critical Heritage, 1973.

Wayne Franklin, The New World of James Fenimore Cooper, 1982.

James Grossman, James Fenimore Cooper, 2nd edition, 1967.

Kay Seymour House, Cooper's Americans, 1965.

William P. Kelly, Plotting America's Past: Fenimore Cooper and the Leatherstocking Tales, 1983.

John P. McWilliams, Political Justice in a Republic: James Fenimore Cooper's America, 1972.

Blake Nevius, Cooper's Landscapes: An Essay on the Picturesque Vision, 1976.

H. Daniel Peck, A World By Itself: The Pastoral Moment in Cooper's Fiction, 1977.

Stephen Railton, Fenimore Cooper: A Study of His Life and Imagination, 1978.

Geoffrey Rans, Cooper's Leather-Stocking Novels: A Secular Reading, 1991.

Donald A. Ringe, James Fenimore Cooper, 1962.

James D. Wallace, Early Cooper and His Audience, 1986.

Cooper's Place in American Literature

Marius Bewley, The Eccentric Design: Form in the Classic American Novel, 1959.

Robert Clark, History, Ideology and Myth in American Fiction: 1823–1852, 1984.

George Dekker, *The American Historical Romance*, 1987.

Leslie Fiedler, *Love and Death in the American Novel*, 1959.

Philip Fisher, *Hard Facts: Setting and Form in the American Novel*, 1985.

Annette Kolodny, *The Lay of the Land: Metaphor as Experience in American Life and Letters*, 1975.

D. H. Lawrence, *Studies in Classic American Literature*, 1927.

R. W. B. Lewis, *The American Adam: Innocence, Tragedy, and Tradition in the Nineteenth Century*, 1965.

Marvin Meyers, *The Jacksonian Persuasion*, 1960.

Warren Motley, *The American Abraham*, 1987.

Joel Porte, *The Romance in America: Studies in Cooper, Poe, Hawthorne, Melville and James*, 1969.

Donald Ringe, *The Pictorial Mode: Space and Time in the Art of Bryant, Irving and Cooper*, 1971.

Richard Slotkin, *Regeneration through Violence: The Mythology of the American Frontier, 1600–1860*, 1973.

Henry Nash Smith, *Virgin Land: The American West as Symbol and Myth*, 1950.

Eric Sundquist, *Home as Found: Authority and Genealogy in Nineteenth-Century American Literature*, 1979.

Jane Tompkins, *Sensational Designs: The Cultural Work of American Fiction, 1790–1860*, 1985.

Historical Contexts for The Pathfinder

Harrison Bird, *Battle for a Continent*, 1965.

Guy Fregault, *Canada: The War of Conquest*, 1969.

Lawrence Henry Gipson, *The Great War for Empire*, vol. 7, 1949.

Edward P. Hamilton, *The French and Indian Wars*, 1962.

Francis Jennings, *Empire of Fortune: Crowns, Colonies, and Tribes in the Seven Years War in America*, 1988.

Francis Jennings, ed., *The History and Culture of Iroquois Diplomacy*, 1985.

Alice Beck Kehoe, *North American Indians: A Comprehensive Account*, 1981.

Samuel Eliot Morison, *The Oxford History of the American People*, 1972.

Francis Parkman, *France and England in North America*, 1897–8.

Michael Rogin, *Fathers and Children: Andrew Jackson and the Subjugation of the American Indian*, 1975.

Articles: The Pathfinder

Allan M. Axelrad, 'Wish Fulfillment in the Wilderness: D. H.
   Lawrence and the Leatherstocking Tales', *American Quarterly*
   39 (1987), 563–85.

Nina Baym, 'The Women of Cooper's Leatherstocking Tales',
   American Quarterly, 23 (1971), 696–709.

Steven Blakemore, 'Language and World in *The Pathfinder*', *Modern
   Language Studies*, 16 (1986), 237–46.

Kay Seymour House, 'Introduction' to *The Pathfinder*, Penguin
   Classics edition, 1989.

Terence Martin, 'Beginnings and Endings in the Leatherstocking
   Tales', *Nineteenth-Century Fiction*, 33 (1978), 69–87.

William Owen, 'In War as in Love: The Significance of Analogous
   Plots in Cooper's *The Pathfinder*', *English Studies in Canada*, 10
   (1984), 289–98.

Roy Harvey Pearce, 'The Leatherstocking Tales Reexamined',
   South Atlantic Quarterly, 46 (1947), 524–36.

H. Daniel Peck, 'James Fenimore Cooper and the Writers of the
   Frontier', in *Columbia Literary History of the United States*, 1987,
   240–67.

Paul Rosenzweig, 'The Pathfinder: The Wilderness Initiation of
   Mabel Dunham', *Modern Language Quarterly*, 44 (1983),
   339–58.

A CHRONOLOGY OF
JAMES FENIMORE COOPER

1786   William Cooper establishes Cooperstown at the southern
        tip of Lake Otsego in New York State.

1789   James Cooper born in Burlington, New Jersey. William
        Cooper moves his family to Cooperstown the following
        year.

1803   Cooper matriculates at Yale College; dismissed for mis-
        conduct two years later.

1806–8 Sails before the mast to England and the continent
        aboard the *Stirling*; serves as a midshipman in the United
        States Navy at Fort Oswego on Lake Ontario.

1811   Marries Susan Augusta De Lancey.

1811–19 Lives as a gentleman farmer on family lands in
        Westchester County, New York and in Cooperstown.

1820   Writes his first novel, *Precaution*, and, in the following
        year, *The Spy* (1821).

1822–6 Moves to New York City and writes *The Pioneers* (1823),
        The Pilot (1824), *Lionel Lincoln* (1825), and *The Last of the
        Mohicans* (1826).

1826–33 Resides in Europe with his family. Lives most frequently
        in Paris but takes lengthy trips to England, the Low
        Countries, Switzerland, Germany and Italy. Concern
        with, and involvement in, the European revolutionary
        movements of 1830. Writes *The Prairie* (1827), *The Red
        Rover* (1827), *Notions of the Americans* (1828), *The Wept of
        Wish-ton-Wish* (1829), and *The Water-Witch* (1830). After
        1830, turns to novels that concern European politics: *The
        Bravo* (1831), *The Heidenmauer* (1832), and *The Headsman*
        (1833).

1833–6 Returns to America and resides in New York City.
        Political correspondent for the *Evening Post*. Writes *A
        Letter to His Countrymen* (1834) and *The Monikins* (1835).

1836   Returns to Cooperstown and remodels Otsego Hall,
        William Cooper's home.

1837–8 Publishes five volumes of sketches describing his
        European travels. Much publicized land controversy

over the ownership and use of Three Mile Point on Lake Otsego. Writes *Homeward Bound* and *Home As Found* (1838). Lengthy libel suits against Whig editors begin. Writes *The American Democrat* (1838) and *History of the Navy of the United States* (1839).

1840   Resumes writing novels about the frontier and the sea: *The Pathfinder* (1840), *Mercedes of Castille* (1840), *The Deerslayer* (1841), *The Two Admirals* (1842), *The Wing-and-Wing* (1842), *Wyandotte* (1843).

1844–6   Defends the landowners' position in the Anti-Rent Wars occurring near Albany by writing a trilogy entitled *The Littlepage Manuscripts: Satanstoe* (1845), *The Chainbearer* (1846), and *The Redskins* (1846). Also writes *Afloat and Ashore* and *Miles Wallingford* (1844).

1847–9   Writes the first American utopian novel, *The Crater* (1847). Last frontier and sea novels: *Jack Tier* (1848), *The Oak Openings* (1848), and *The Sea Lions* (1849).

1850   Prepares the Putnam Author's Revised Edition of his writings. Writes the Preface to the Leatherstocking Tales and a novel about criminal law, *The Ways of the Hour*.

1851   Dies in Cooperstown, leaving *The Towns of Manhattan* (also titled *New York*) unfinished.

1852   Memorial gathering for Cooper held in New York City, Daniel Webster presiding. Letters and tributes by Bancroft, Bryant, Emerson, Hawthorne, Irving, Longfellow, Melville, Parkman, Prescott, and Simms.

THE PATHFINDER

Preface
[First edition]

THE plan of this tale suggested itself to the writer, many years since, though the details are altogether of recent invention. The idea of associating seamen and savages, in incidents that might be supposed characteristic of the Great Lakes, having been mentioned to a publisher, the latter obtained something like a pledge from the author to carry out the design, at some future day, which pledge is now tardily and imperfectly redeemed.

The reader may recognize an old friend, under new circumstances, in the principal character of this legend. If the exhibition made of this old acquaintance, in the novel circumstances in which he now appears, should be found not to lessen his favor with the public, it will be a source of extreme gratification to the writer, since he has an interest in the individual in question, that falls little short of reality. It is not an easy task, however, to reproduce the same character in four separate works, and to maintain the peculiarities that are indispensable to identity, without incurring a risk of fatiguing the reader with sameness, and the present experiment has been so long delayed, quite as much from doubts of its success, as from any other cause. In this, as in every other undertaking, it must be the "end" that will "crown the work."

The Indian character has so little variety, that it has been my object to avoid dwelling on it too much, on the present occasion. Its association with the sailor, too, it is feared, will be found to have more novelty than interest.

It may strike the novice as an anachronism, to place vessels on Ontario, in the middle of the eighteenth century, but, in this particular, facts will fully bear out all the licence of the fiction. Although the precise vessels mentioned in these pages may never have existed on that water, or anywhere else, others so nearly resembling them are known to have navigated that inland sea, even at a period much earlier than the one just mentioned, as to form a sufficient authority for their introduction into a work of fiction. It is a fact not generally remembered, however well known it may be, that there are isolated spots, along the line of the great lakes that date, as settlements, as far back, as many of the oldest American towns, and which were the seats of a species of civilization, long before the greater portion of even the original states was rescued from the wilderness.

Ontario, in our own times, has been the scene of important naval evolutions. Fleets have manœuvred on those waters, which, half a century ago, were as near desert as waters well can be, and the day is not distant, when the whole of that vast range of lakes will become the seat of empire, and fraught with all the interests of human society. A passing glimpse, even though it be in a work of fiction, of what that vast region so lately was, may help to make up*the sum of knowledge by which alone, a just appreciation can be formed of the wonderful means by which Providence is clearing the way for the advancement of civilization across the whole American continent.

DECEMBER, 1839.

Preface.

[Author's Revised Edition, 1851]

FOLLOWING the order of events, this book should be the third in the Series of the Leather-Stocking Tales. In the Deerslayer, Natty Bumppo, under the *Sobriquet* which forms the title of that work, is represented as a youth, just commencing his forest career as a warrior; having for several years been a hunter so celebrated, as already to have gained the honorable appellation he then bore. In the Last of the Mohicans he appears as Hawkeye, and is present at the death of young Uncas; while in this tale, he re-appears in the same war of '56, in company with his Mohican* friend, still in the vigor of manhood, and young enough to feel that master passion to which all conditions of men, all tempers, and we might almost say all ages, submit, under circumstances that are incited to call it into existence.

The Pathfinder did not originally appear for several years after the publication of the Prairie, the work in which the leading character of both had closed his career by death. It was, perhaps, a too hazardous experiment to recall to life, in this manner, and after so long an interval, a character that was somewhat a favorite with the reading world, and which had been regularly consigned to his grave, like any living man. It is probably owing to this severe ordeal that the work, like its successor, the Deerslayer, has been so little noticed; scarce one in ten of those who know all about the three earliest books of the series having even a knowledge of the existence of the last at all. That this caprice in taste and favor is in no way dependent on merit, the writer feels certain; for, though the world will ever maintain that an author is always the worst judge of his own productions, one who has written much, and regards all his literary progeny with more or less of a paternal eye, must have a reasonably accurate knowledge of what he has been about the greater part of his life. Such a man may form too high an estimate of his relative merits, as relates to others; but it is not easy to see why he should fall into this error, more than another, as relates to himself. His general standard may be raised too high by means of self-love; but, unless he be disposed to maintain the equal perfection of what he has done, as probably no man was ever yet fool enough to do, he may very well have shrewd conjectures as to the comparative merits and defects of his own productions.

This work, on its appearance, was rudely and maliciously assailed by certain individuals out of pure personal malignancy. It is scarcely worth the author's while, nor would it have any interest for the reader, to expose the motives and frauds of these individuals, who have pretty effectually vindicated the writer by their own subsequent conduct. But even the falsest of men pay so much homage to truth, as to strive to seem its votaries. In attacking the Pathfinder, the persons alluded to pointed out faults, that the author, for the first time, has now ascertained to be real; and much to his surprise, as of most of them he is entirely innocent. They are purely errors of the press, unless, indeed, the writer can justly be accused of having been a careless proof reader. A single instance of the mistakes he means may be given in explanation of the manner in which the book was originally got up.

The heroine of this tale was at first called "Agnes." In the fifth or sixth chapter this name was changed to "Mabel," and the manuscript was altered accordingly. Owing to inadvertency, however, the original appellation stood in several places, and the principal female character of the book, until now, has had the advantage of going by two names! Many other typographical errors exist in the earlier editions, most of which, it is believed, are corrected in this.

There are a few discrepancies in the facts of this work, as connected with the facts of the different books of the series. They are not material, and it was thought fairer to let them stand as proof of the manner in which the books were originally written, than to make any changes in the text.

In youth, when belonging to the navy, the writer of this book served for some time on the great Western lakes. He was, indeed, one of those who first carried the cockade of the republic, on those inland seas. This was pretty early in the present century, when the navigation was still confined to the employment of a few ships and schooners. Since that day, light may be said to have broken into the wilderness, and the rays of the sun have penetrated to tens of thousands of beautiful valleys and plains, that then lay in "grateful shade." Towns have been built along the whole of the extended line of coasts, and the traveller now stops at many a place of ten or fifteen, and at one of even fifty, thousand inhabitants, where a few huts then marked the natural sites of future marts. In a word, though the scenes of this book are believed to have once been as nearly accurate as is required by the laws which govern fiction, they are so no longer. Oswego is a large and thriving town; Toronto and Kingston, on the other side of the lake, compete with it; while Buffalo, Detroit, Cleveland, Milwaukie, and Chicago, on the upper lakes, to say nothing of a hundred places of lesser note, are fast advancing to the level of commercial places of great local importance. In these changes, the energy of youth and abundance is quite as much apparent as anything else; and it is ardently to be hoped that the fruits of the gifts of a most bountiful Providence may not be mistaken for any peculiar qualities in those who have been their beneficiaries. A just appreciation of the first of these facts will render us grateful and meek; while the vainglorious, who are so apt to ascribe all to themselves, will be certain to live long enough to ascertain the magnitude of their error. That great results are intended to be produced by means of these wonderful changes, we firmly believe; but that they will prove to be the precise results now so generally anticipated, in consulting the experience of the past, and taking the nature of man into the account, the reflecting and intelligent may be permitted to doubt.

It may strike the novice as an anachronism, to place vessels on Ontario in the middle of the eighteenth century; but, in this particular, facts will fully bear out all the license of the fiction. Although the precise vessels mentioned in these pages may never have existed on that water, or anywhere else, others so nearly resembling them as to form a sufficient authority for their introduction into a work of fiction, are known to have navigated that inland sea, even at a period much earlier than the one just mentioned. It is a fact not generally remembered, however well known it may be, that there are isolated spots, along the line of the great lakes, that date, as settlements, as far back as many of the oldest American towns, and which were the seats of a species of civilization, long before the greater portion of even the original states was rescued from the wilderness.

Ontario, in our own times, has been the scene of important naval evolutions. Fleets have manœuvred on those waters, which, half a century since, were desert wastes; and the day is not distant, when the whole of that vast range of lakes will become the seat of empire, and fraught with all the interests of human society. A passing glimpse, even though it be in a work of fiction, of what that vast region so lately was, may help to make up the sum of knowledge by which alone a just appreciation can be formed of the wonderful means by which Providence is clearing the way for the advancement of civilization across the whole American continent.

Chapter 1.

"The turf shall be my fragrant shrine;
My temple, Lord! that arch of thine;
My censer's breath the mountain airs,
And silent thoughts my only prayers."
Moore, "The Turf Shall Be
My Fragrant Shrine," ll. 1–4.

THE sublimity connected with vastness, is familiar to every eye. The most abstruse, the most far-reaching, perhaps the most chastened of the poet's thoughts, crowd on the imagination as he gazes into the depths of the illimitable void; the expanse of the ocean is seldom seen by the novice, with indifference, and the mind, even in the obscurity of night, finds a parallel to that grandeur, which seems inseparable from images that the senses cannot compass. With feelings akin to this admiration and awe, the offspring of sublimity, were the different characters with which the action of this tale must open, gazing on the scene before them. Four persons in all, two of each sex, they had managed to ascend a pile of trees, that had been uptorn by a tempest, to catch a view of the objects that surrounded them. It is still the practice of the country to call these spots wind-rows. By letting in the light of heaven upon the dark and damp recesses of the woods, they form a sort of oases in the solemn obscurity of the virgin forests of America. The particular wind-row of which we are writing lay on the brow of a gentle acclivity, and it had opened the way for an extended view, to those who might occupy its upper margins, a rare occurrence to the traveller in the woods. As usual, the spot was small, but owing to the circumstance of its lying on the low acclivity mentioned, and that of the opening's extending downward, it offered more than common advantages to the eye. Philosophy has not yet determined the nature of the power that so often lays desolate spots of this description, some ascribing it to the whirlwinds that produce water-spouts on the ocean, while others again impute it to sudden and violent passages of streams of the electric fluid; but the effects in the woods are familiar to all. On the upper margin of the opening, to which there is allusion, the viewless influence had piled tree on tree, in such a manner as had not only enabled the two males of the party to ascend to an elevation of some thirty feet above the level of the earth, but, with a little care and encouragement, to induce their more timid companions to accompany them. The vast trunks, that had been broken and riven by the force of the gust, lay blended like jack-straws, while their branches, still exhaling the fragrance of wilted leaves, were interlaced in a manner to afford sufficient support to the hands. One tree had been completely uprooted, and its lower end, filled with earth, had been cast uppermost, in a way to supply a sort of staging for the four adventurers, when they had gained the desired distance from the ground.

The reader is to anticipate none of the appliances of people of refinement, in the description of the personal appearances of the group in question. They were all way-farers in the wilderness, and had they not been, neither their previous habits, nor their actual social positions would have accustomed them to many of the luxuries of rank. Two of the party, indeed, a male and a female, belonged to the native owners of the soil, being Indians of the well known tribe of the Tuscaroras,* while their companions were a man, who bore about him the peculiarities of one who had passed his days on the ocean, and that, too, in a station little if any above that of a common mariner, while his female associate was a maiden of a class, in no great degree superior to his own, though her youth, sweetness of countenance, and a modest but spirited mien, lent that character of intellect and refinement, which adds so much to the charm of beauty, in the sex. On the present occasion, her full blue eye reflected the feeling of sublimity that the scene excited, and her pleasant face was beaming with the pensive expression, with which all deep emotions, even though they bring the most grateful pleasure, shadow the countenances of the ingenuous and thoughtful.

And, truly, the scene was of a nature, deeply to impress the imagination of the beholder. Towards the west, in which direction the faces of the party were turned, and in which alone could much be seen, the eye ranged over an ocean of leaves.

glorious and rich in the varied but lively verdure of a generous vegetation, and shaded by the luxuriant tints that belong to the forty second degree of latitude. The elm, with its graceful and weeping top, the rich varieties of the maple, most of the noble oaks of the American forest, with the broad leafed linden, known in the parlance of the country as the bass-wood, mingled their uppermost branches, forming one broad and seemingly interminable carpet of foliage, that stretched away towards the setting sun, until it bounded the horizon, by blending with the clouds, as the waves and sky meet at the base of the vault of Heaven. Here and there, by some accident of the tempests, or by a caprice of nature, a trifling opening among these giant members of the forest, permitted an inferior tree to struggle upward toward the light, and to lift its modest head nearly to a level with the surrounding surface of verdure. Of this class were the birch, a tree of some account, in regions less favored, the quivering aspen, various generous nut-woods, and divers others, that resembled the ignoble and vulgar, thrown by circumstances, into the presence of the stately and great. Here and there, too, the tall, straight trunk of the pine, pierced the vast field, rising high above it, like some grand monument reared by art on the plain of leaves.

It was the vastness of the view, the nearly unbroken surface of verdure, that contained the principle of grandeur. The beauty was to be traced in the delicate tints, relieved by gradations of light and shadow, while the solemn repose, induced a feeling allied to awe.

"Uncle," said the wondering but pleased girl, addressing her male companion, whose arm she rather touched than leaned on, to steady her own light but firm footing—"this is like a view of the ocean you so much love!"

"So much for ignorance, and a girl's fancy, Magnet"—a term of affection, the sailor often used in allusion to his niece's personal attractions—"No one but a child would think of likening this handful of leaves, to a look at the real Atlantic. You might stop all these tree-tops to Neptune's jacket, and they would make no more than a nosegay in his bosom."

"More fanciful than true, I think, uncle. Look, thither; it must be miles on miles, and yet we see nothing but leaves! What more could one behold, if looking at the ocean?"

"More!" returned the uncle, giving an impatient gesture with the elbow the other touched, for his arms were crossed, and the hands were thrust into the bosom of a vest of red cloth, a fashion of the times, "More, Magnet; say, rather, what less. Where are your combing-seas, your blue-water, your rollers, your breakers, your whales, or your water-spouts and your endless motion, in this bit of a forest, child?"

"And where are your tree-tops, your solemn silence, your fragrant leaves and your beautiful green, uncle, on the ocean?"

"Tut, Magnet; if you understood the thing, you would know that green water is a sailor's bane. He scarcely relishes a green horn, less."

"But green trees are a different thing. Hist! that sound is the air breathing among the leaves!"

"You should hear a nor-wester breathe, girl, if you fancy noise aloft. Now where are your gales, and hurricanes, and trades, and Levanters* and such like incidents in this bit of a forest, and what fishes have you swimming beneath yonder tame surface?"

"That there have been tempests here, these signs around us plainly show, and beasts, if not fishes, are beneath these leaves."

"I do not know that—" returned the uncle, with a sailor's dogmatism. "They told us many stories, at Albany, of the wild animals we should fall in with, and yet we have seen nothing to frighten a seal. I doubt any of your inland animals, will compare with a low latitude shark."

"See!" exclaimed the niece, who was more occupied with the sublimity and beauty of the "boundless wood," than with her uncle's arguments, "yonder is a smoke curling over the tops of the trees—can it come from a house?"

"Ay—ay—there is a look of humanity in that smoke," returned the old seaman, "which is worth a thousand trees. I must show it to Arrowhead, who may be running past a port without knowing it. It is a probable there is a camboose,* where there is a smoke."

As he concluded, the uncle drew a hand from his bosom, touched the male Indian, who was standing near him, lightly on the shoulder, and pointed out a thin line of vapor, that was stealing slowly out of the wilderness of leaves, at a distance of about a mile, and was diffusing itself in almost imperceptible threads of humidity, in the quivering atmosphere. The Tusca-rora was one of those noble-looking warriors that were oftener met with among the aborigines of this continent a century since, than to day, and, while he had mingled sufficiently with the colonists to be familiar with their habits, and even with their language, he had lost little, if any, of the wild grandeur, and simple dignity of a chief. Between him and the old seaman the intercourse had been friendly, but distant, for the Indian had been too much accustomed to mingle with the officers of the different military posts he had frequented, not to understand that his present companion was only a subordinate. So impos-ing indeed, had been the quiet superiority of the Tuscarora's reserve, that Charles Cap, for so was the seaman named, in his most dogmatical or facetious moments had not ventured on familiarity, in an intercourse that had now lasted more than a week. The sight of the curling smoke, however, had struck the latter like the sudden appearance of a sail at sea, and, for the first time since they met, he ventured to touch the warrior, as has been related.

The quick eye of the Tuscarora instantly caught a sight of the smoke, and for quite a minute, he stood, slightly raised on tip-toe, with distended nostrils, like the buck that scents a taint in the air, and a gaze as riveted as that of the trained pointer, while he waits his master's aim. Then falling back on his feet, a low exclamation, in the soft tones that form so singular a con-trast to its harsher cries, in the Indian warrior's voice, was barely audible. Otherwise he was undisturbed. His countenance was calm, and his quick, dark, eagle eye moved over the leafy panorama, as if to take in at a glance every circumstance that might enlighten his mind.

That the long journey they had attempted to make through a broad belt of wilderness, was necessarily attended with danger, both uncle and niece well knew, though neither could at once determine whether the sign that others were in their vicinity, was the harbinger of good, or evil.

"There must be Oneidas,* or Tuscaroras, near us, Arrow-head," said Cap, addressing his Indian companion by his con-ventional English name; "will it not be well to join company with them, and get a comfortable berth for the night in their wigwam?"

"No wigwam there," Arrowhead answered in his unmoved manner—"too much tree."

"But Indians must be there; perhaps some old mess-mates of your own, Master Arrowhead."

"No Tuscarora—no Oneida—no Mohawk—pale-face fire."

"The devil it is! Well, Magnet, this surpasses a seaman's philosophy—we old sea-dogs can tell a soldier's from a sailor's quid,* or a lubber's nest from a mate's hammock, but I do not think the oldest admiral in His Majesty's Fleet can tell a King's smoke from a collier's!"

The idea that human beings were in their vicinity in that ocean of wilderness, had deepened the flush on the blooming cheek, and brightened the eye of the fair creature at his side, but she now turned with a look of surprise to her relative, and said hesitatingly,—for both had often admired the Tuscarora's knowledge, or we might almost say, instinct—

"A pale face's fire! Surely, uncle, he cannot know *that*!"

"Ten days since, child, I would have sworn to it; but, now, I hardly know what to believe. May I take the liberty of asking, Arrowhead, why you fancy that smoke, now, a pale face's smoke, and not a red skin's?"

"Wet wood—" returned the warrior, with the calmness with which the pedagogue might point out an arithmetical demonstration to his puzzled pupil. "Much wet—much smoke—much water, black smoke."

"But, begging your pardon, Master Arrowhead, the smoke is not black, nor is there much of it. To my eye, now, it is as light and fanciful a smoke as ever rose from a captain's tea kettle, when nothing was left to make the fire, but a few chips from the dunnage."*

"Too much water—" returned Arrowhead, with a slight nod of the head. "Tuscarora too cunning to make fire with water; pale face too much book and burn anything. Much book, little know."

"Well, that's reasonable, I allow," said Cap, who was no devotee of learning. "He means that as a hit at your reading, Magnet, for the chief has sensible notions of things, in his own way. How far, now, Arrowhead, do you make us by your calculation, from the bit of a pond, that you call the Great Lake, and towards which we have been so many days shaping our course?"

The Tuscarora looked at the seaman with quiet superiority, as he answered.

"Ontario like heaven; one sun, and the great traveller know it."

"Well, I have been a great traveller, I cannot deny, but of all my v'y'ges this has been the longest, the least profitable, and the farthest inland. If this body of fresh water is so nigh, Arrowhead, and at the same time so large, one might think a pair of good eyes would find it out, for apparently, every thing within thirty miles, is to be seen from this look out."

"Look," said Arrowhead, stretching an arm before him, with quiet grace; "Ontario!"

"Uncle, you are accustomed to cry 'land ho,' but not 'water ho,' and you do not see it," cried the niece, laughing as girls will laugh at their own idle conceits.

"How now, Magnet, dost suppose that I shouldn't know my native element, if it were in sight?"

"But Ontario is not your native element, dear uncle, for you come from the salt water, while this is fresh."

"That might make some difference to your young mariner, but none in the world to the old ones. I should know water, child, were I to see it in China."

"Ontario—" repeated the Arrowhead, with emphasis, again stretching his hand towards the North West.

Cap looked at the Tuscarora, for the first time since their acquaintance, with something like an air of contempt, though he did not fail to follow the direction of the chief's eye and arm, both of which were pointing, to all appearance, toward a vacant spot in the heavens, a short distance above the plain of leaves.

"Ay, ay; this is much as I expected, when I left the coast to come in search of a fresh-water pond," resumed Cap, shrugging his shoulders like one whose mind was made up, and who thought no more need be said. "Ontario may be there, or, for that matter, it may be in my pocket. Well I suppose there will be room enough, when we reach it, to work our canoe. But, Arrowhead, if there be pale faces in our neighborhood, I confess I should like to get within hail of them."

The Tuscarora now gave a quiet inclination of his head, and the whole party descended from the roots of the uptorn tree, in silence. When they had reached the ground, Arrowhead intimated his intention to go towards the fire, and ascertain who had lighted it, while he advised his wife, and the two others to proceed to a canoe, which they had left in the adjacent stream, and await his return.

"Why, chief, this might do on soundings,* and in an offing* where one knew the channel," returned old Cap, "but in an unknown region like this, I think it unsafe to trust the pilot alone too far from the ship, so, with your leave, we will not part company."

"What my brother want?" asked the Indian gravely, though without taking offence at a distrust that was sufficiently plain.

"Your company, Master Arrowhead, and no more. I will go with you, and speak these strangers."

The Tuscarora assented without difficulty, and again he directed his patient and submissive little wife, who seldom turned her full rich black eye on him, but to express equally her respect, her dread, and her love, to proceed to the boat. But, here, Magnet raised a difficulty. Although spirited, and of unusual energy under circumstances of trial, she was but woman, and the idea of being entirely deserted by her two male protectors, in the midst of a wilderness, that her senses had just told her was seemingly illimitable, became so keenly painful that she expressed a wish to accompany her uncle.

"The exercise will be a relief, dear sir, after sitting so long in the canoe," she added, as the rich blood slowly returned to a cheek that had paled, in spite of her effort to be calm, "and there may be females, with the strangers."

"Come, then, child—it is but a cable's length, and we shall return an hour before the sun sets."

With this permission, the girl, whose real name was Mabel Dunham, prepared to be of the party, while the Dew-of-June, as the wife of Arrowhead was called, passively went her way towards the canoe, too much accustomed to obedience, solitude, and the gloom of the forest, to feel apprehension.

The three who remained in the wind-row, now picked their way around its tangled maze, and gained the margin of the woods, in the necessary direction. A few glances of the eye sufficed for Arrowhead, but old Cap, deliberately set the smoke by a pocket compass, before he trusted himself within the shadows of the trees.

"This steering by the nose, Magnet, may do well enough for an Indian, but your thorough-bred knows the virtue of the needle," said the uncle, as he trudged at the heels of the light stepping Tuscarora. "America would never have been discovered, take my word for it, if Columbus had been nothing but nostrils. Friend Arrowhead, didst ever see a machine like this?"

The Indian turned, cast a glance at the compass, which Cap held in a way to direct his course, and gravely answered—

"A pale face eye. The Tuscarora see in his head. The salt water (for so the Indian styled his companion) all eye—now; no tongue."

"He means, uncle, that we had needs be silent; perhaps he distrusts the persons we are about to meet."

"Ay—'tis an Indian's fashion of going to quarters. You perceive he has examined the priming of his rifle, and it may be as well, if I look to that of my own pistols."

Without betraying alarm at these preparations, to which she had become accustomed by her long journey in the wilderness, Mabel followed with a step as light and elastic as that of the Indian, keeping close in the rear of her companions. For the first half mile, no other caution, beyond a rigid silence was observed, but as the party drew nearer to the spot, where the fire was known to be, much greater care became necessary.

The forest, as usual, had little to intercept the view, below the branches, but the tall straight trunks of trees. Every thing, belonging to vegetation, had struggled towards the light, and beneath the leafy canopy one walked, as it might be, through a vast natural vault, that was upheld by myriads of rustic columns. These columns, or trees, however, often served to conceal the adventurer, the hunter, or the foe, and as Arrowhead swiftly approached the spot where his practised and unerring senses told him the strangers ought to be, his footstep gradually became lighter, his eye more vigilant, and his person was more carefully concealed.

"See, Salt-Water," he said exultingly, pointing at the same time through the vista of trees, "pale-face fire!"

"By the Lord, the fellow is right!" muttered Cap. "There they are, sure enough, and eating their grub as quietly as if they were in the cabin of a three decker."

"Arrowhead is but half right," whispered Mabel, "for there are two Indians and only one white man."

"Pale face," said the Tuscarora, holding up two fingers; "red man" holding up one.

"Well," rejoined Cap, "it is hard to say, which is right and which is wrong. One is certainly white; and a comely, fine lad he is, with an air of life and respectability about him; one is a red skin as plain as paint and nature can make him; but the third chap is half-rigged; being neither brig, nor schooner."

"Pale-face," repeated Arrowhead, again raising two fingers; "red-man," showing but one.

"He must be right, uncle, for his eye seems never to fail. But it is now urgent to know whether we meet as friends, or foes. They may be French."

"One hail will soon satisfy us, on that head," returned Cap. "Stand you, behind this tree, Magnet, lest the knaves take it into their heads to fire a broadside, without a parley, and I will soon learn what colours they sail under."

The uncle had placed his two hands to his mouth, to form a trumpet, and was about to give the promised hail, when a rapid movement from Arrowhead defeated the intention, by deranging the instrument.

"Red man, Mohican," said the Tuscarora; "good; pale-face, Yengeese."

"These are heavenly tidings," murmured Mabel, who little relished the prospect of a deadly fray in that remote wilderness. "Let us approach at once, dear uncle, and proclaim ourselves friends."

"Good—" said the Tuscarora—"red man cool, and know; pale-face hurried, and fire. Let squaw go."

"What," said Cap, in astonishment; "send little Magnet ahead, as a look out, while two lubbers like you and me, lie-to, to see what sort of a land-fall she will make! If I do, I——"

"It is wisest, uncle," interrupted the generous girl, "and I have no fear. No christian, seeing a woman approach alone, would fire upon her, and my presence will be a pledge of peace. Let me go forward, as Arrowhead wishes, and all will be well.

We are, as yet, unseen and the surprise of the strangers will not partake of alarm."

"Good—" returned Arrowhead, who did not conceal his approbation of Mabel's spirit.

"It has an unseaman like look," answered Cap, "but, being in the woods, no one will know it. If you think, Mabel—"

"Uncle, I know. There is no cause to fear for me, and you are always nigh to protect me."

"Well, take one of the pistols, then—"

"Nay, I had better rely on my youth and feebleness," said the girl, smiling while her colour heightened under her feelings—"Among christian men, a woman's best guard is her claim to their protection. I know nothing of arms, and wish to live in ignorance of them."

The uncle desisted, and, after receiving a few cautious instructions from the Tuscarora, Mabel rallied all her spirit, and advanced alone towards the group seated near the fire. Although the heart of the girl beat quick, her step was firm and her movements, seemingly, were without reluctance. A death-like silence reigned in the forest, for they towards whom she approached, were too much occupied in appeasing that great natural appetite, hunger, to avert their looks, for an instant, from the important business in which they were all engaged. When Mabel, however, had got within a hundred feet of the fire, she trod upon a dried stick, and the trifling noise that was produced by her light footstep caused the Mohican, as Arrowhead had pronounced the Indian to be, and his companion whose character had been thought so equivocal, to rise to their feet, as quick as thought. Both glanced at the rifles that leaned against a tree, and then each stood without stretching out an arm, as his eyes fell on the form of the girl. The Indian uttered a few words to his companion, and resumed his seat and his meal, as calmly as if no interruption had occurred. On the contrary, the white man, left the fire, and came forward to meet Mabel.

The latter saw, as the stranger approached, that she was about to be addressed by one of her own colour, though his dress was so strange a mixture of the habits of the two races, that it required a near look to be certain of the fact. He was of middle age, but there was an open honesty, a total absence of guile, in his face, which otherwise would not have been thought handsome, that at once assured Magnet she was in no danger. Still she paused, in obedience to a law of her habits, if not of nature, which rendered her averse to the appearance of advancing too freely to meet one of the other sex, under the circumstances in which she was placed.

"Fear nothing, young woman," said the hunter, for such his attire would indicate him to be, "you have met christian men, in the wilderness, and such as know how to treat all kindly that are disposed to peace and justice. I'm a man well known in all these parts, and perhaps one of my names may have reached your ears. By the Frenchers, and the red-skins on the other side of the Big Lakes, I am called la Longue Carabine; by the Mohicans, a just-minded and upright tribe, what is left of them, Hawk Eye; while the troops and rangers along this side of the water call me Pathfinder, inasmuch as I have never been known to miss one end of the trail, when there was a Mingo, or a friend, who stood in need of me, at the other."

This was not uttered boastfully, but with the honest confidence of one, who well knew that by whatever name others might have heard of him, he had no reason to blush at the reports. The effect on Mabel was instantaneous. The moment she heard the last *soubriquet* she clasped her hands eagerly and repeated the word.

"Pathfinder!"

"So they call me, young woman, and many a great lord has got a title that he did not half so well merit, though, if truth be said, I rather pride myself in finding my way, where where there is no path, than in finding it where there is. But the regular troops be by no means particular, and half the time they do'n't know the difference atween a trail and a path, though one is a matter for the eye, while the other is little more than scent."

"Then you are the friend, my father promised to send to meet us!"

"If you are Sarjeant Dunham's daughter, the Great Prophet of the Delawares never uttered a plainer truth."

"I am Mabel, and yonder, hid by the trees, are my uncle, whose name is Cap, and a Tuscarora called Arrowhead. We did not hope to meet you until we had nearly reached the shores of the Lake."

"I wish a juster-minded Indian had been your guide," said Pathfinder, "for I am no lover of the Tuscaroras, who have travelled too far from the graves of their fathers always to remember the Great Spirit, and Arrowhead is an ambitious chief. Is the Dew of June with him?"

"His wife accompanies us, and a humble and mild creature she is."

"Ay, and true-hearted, which is more than any who know him will say of Arrowhead. Well, we must take the fare that Providence bestows, while we follow the trail of life. I suppose worse guides might have been found than the Tuscarora, though he has too much Mingo blood, for one who consorts altogether with the Delawares."

"It is then, perhaps, fortunate we have met—" said Mabel.

"It is not misfortinate, at any rate, for I promised the Sarjeant I would see his child safe to the garrison, though I died for it. We expected to meet you before you reached the falls; where we have left our own canoe, while we thought it might do no harm to come up, a few miles, in order to be of sarvice if wanted. It's lucky we did, for I doubt if Arrowhead be the man to shoot the current."

"Here come my uncle and the Tuscarora, and our parties can now join."

As Mabel concluded Cap and Arrowhead, who saw that the conference was amicable, drew nigh, and a few words sufficed to let them know as much, as the girl herself had learned from the stranger. As soon as this was done, the party proceeded towards the two who still remained near the fire.

Chapter II.

"Yea! long as Nature's humblest Child
Hath kept her temple undefiled
By sinful sacrifice,
Earth's fairest scenes are all his own,
He is a Monarch, and his Throne
Is built amid the skies!"

> Wilson, "Lines Written in a
> Highland Glen," ll. 31–36.

THE Mohican continued to eat, though the second white man rose, and courteously took off his cap to Mabel Dunham. He was young, healthful and manly in appearance, and wore a dress, which, while it was less rigidly professional than that of the uncle, also denoted one accustomed to the water. In that age, real seamen were a class entirely apart from the rest of mankind, their ideas, ordinary language, and attire being as strongly indicative of their calling, as the opinions, speech and dress of a Turk denote a Mussulman. Although the Pathfinder was scarcely in the prime of life, Mabel had met him with a steadiness that may have been the consequence of having braced her nerves for the interview, but when her eyes encountered those of the young man at the fire, they fell before the gaze of admiration, with which she saw, or fancied she saw, he greeted her. Each, in truth, felt that interest in the other, which similarity of age, condition, mutual comeliness and their novel situation would be likely to inspire in the young and ingenuous.

"Here," said Pathfinder, with an honest smile bestowed on Mabel–"are the friends your worthy father has sent to meet you. This is a great Delaware; and one that has had honors as well as trouble, in his day. He has an Injin name fit for a chief, but as the language is not always easy for the inexperienced to pronounce, we nat'rally turn it into English, and call him the Big Sarpent. You are not to suppose, howsever, that by this name we wish to say that he is treacherous, beyond what is lawful in a red skin, but that he is wise, and has the cunning that becomes a warrior. Arrowhead, there, knows what I mean."

While the Pathfinder was delivering this address, the two Indians gazed on each other steadily, and then the Tuscarora advanced and spoke to the other, in an apparently friendly manner.

"I like to see this," continued Pathfinder; "the salutes of two red-skins, in the woods, Master Cap, are like the hailing of friendly vessels on the ocean. But, speaking of water, it reminds me of my young friend Jasper Western, here, who can claim to know something of these matters, seeing that he has passed his days on Ontario."

"I am glad to see you, friend," said Cap, giving the young fresh-water sailor, a cordial gripe, "though you must have something still to learn, considering the school to which you have been sent. This is my niece Mabel—I call her Magnet, for a reason she never dreams of, though you may possibly have education enough to guess at it, having some pretensions to understand the compass, I suppose."

"The reason is easily comprehended," said the young man, involuntarily fastening his keen dark eye, at the same time, on the suffused face of the girl; "and I feel sure that the sailor who steers by your Magnet, will never make a bad land-fall."

"Ha—you do make use of some of the terms, I find, and that with propriety and understanding. Though, on the whole, I fear you have seen more green than blue water!"

"It is not surprising that we should get some of the phrases that belong to the land, for we are seldom out of sight of it, twenty four hours at a time."

"More's the pity, boy; more's the pity. A very little land ought to go a great way, with a seafaring man. Now, if the truth were known, Master Western, I suppose there is more or less land all round your lake."

"And, uncle, is there not more or less land all round the ocean—" said Magnet quickly, for she dreaded a premature display of the old seaman's peculiar dogmatism, not to say pedantry.

"No, child, there is more or less ocean all round the land. That's what I tell the people ashore, youngster; they are living, as it might be, in the midst of the sea, without knowing it; by sufferance, as it were; the water being so much the more powerful, and the largest. But there is no end to conceit in this world, for a fellow who never saw salt water often fancies he knows more than one who has gone round the Horn. No—no—this earth is pretty much an island, and all that can be truly said not to be so, is water."

Young Western had a profound deference for a mariner of the ocean, on which he had often pined to sail, but he had, also, a natural regard for the broad sheet on which he had passed his life and which was not without its beauties, in his eyes.

"What you say, sir," he answered modestly, "may be true, as to the Atlantic, but we have a respect for the land, up here on Ontario."

"That is because you are always land-locked," returned Cap, laughing heartily: "but yonder is the Pathfinder, as they call him, with some smoking platters, inviting us to share in his mess, and I will confess that one gets no venison at sea. Master Western, civility to girls at your time of life, comes as easy as taking in the slack of the ensign halyards,* and if you will just keep an eye to her kid and can,* while I join the mess of the Pathfinder and our Indian friends, I make no doubt she will remember it."

Master Cap uttered more than he was aware of, at the time. Jasper Western did look to the wants of Mabel, and she long remembered the kind manly attentions of the young sailor, at this their first interview. He placed the end of a log for a seat, obtained for her a delicious morsel of the venison, gave her a draught of pure water from the spring, and as he sat near, and opposite to her, fast won his way to her esteem, by his gentle, but frank, manner of manifesting his care; a homage that woman always wishes to receive, but which is never so flattering or so agreeable, as when it comes from the young to those of their own age; from the manly to the gentle. Like most of those who pass their time excluded from the society of the softer sex, young Western was earnest, sincere and kind in his attentions, which, though they wanted a conventional refinement that perhaps Mabel never missed, had those winning qualities that prove more efficient as substitutes. Leaving these two inexperienced and unsophisticated young people, to become acquainted through their feelings rather than their expressed thoughts, we will turn to the group, in which the uncle, with a facility of taking care of himself that never deserted him, had already become a principal actor.

The party had taken their places around a platter of venison steaks, which served for the common use, and the discourse naturally partook of the characters of the different individuals that composed it. The Indians were silent and industrious, the appetite of the Aboriginal American for venison, being seemingly inappeasable, while the two white men, were communicative and discursive, each of the latter being garrulous and opinionated in his way. But as the dialogue will serve to put the reader in possession of certain facts that may render the succeeding narrative more clear, it will be well to record it.

"There must be satisfaction in this life of yours, no doubt, Master Pathfinder," continued Cap, when the hunger of the travellers was so far appeased that they began to pick and choose, among the savory morsels; "it has some of the chances and luck that we seamen love, and if ours is all water, yours is all land."

"Nay, we have water too, in our journeyings and marches," returned his white companion. "We border men, handle the paddle and the spear, almost as much as the rifle and the hunting knife."

"Ay, but do you handle the brace and the bow line; the wheel and the lead-line; the reef-point and the top-rope? The paddle is a good thing, out of doubt, in a canoe, but of what use is it in the ship?"

"Nay, I respect all men in their callings, and I can believe the things you mention have their uses. One, who has lived, like myself, in company with many tribes, understands the differences in usages. The paint of a Mingo,* is not the paint of a Delaware;* and he who should expect to see a warrior in the dress of a squaw, might be disapp'inted. I'm not very old, but I have lived in the woods, and have some acquaintance with human natur'. I never believed much in the larning of them that dwell in towns, for I never yet met with one that had an eye for a rifle, or a trail."

"That's my manner of reasoning, Master Pathfinder, to a yarn. Walking about streets, going to church of Sundays, and hearing rumours never yet made a man of a human being. Send the boy out upon the broad ocean, if you wish to open his eyes, and let him look upon foreign nations, or, what I call the face of natur', if you wish him to understand his own character. Now, there is my brother-in-law, the Serjeant, he is as good a fellow as ever broke a biscuit, in his own way; but what is he, after all; why nothing but a soger. A serjeant, to be sure, but that is a sort of a soger, you know. When he wished to marry poor Bridget, my sister, I told the girl what he was, as in duty bound, and what she might expect from such a husband, but you know how it is with girls when their minds are jammed by an inclination. It is true, the Serjeant has risen in his calling, and they say he is an important man at the fort, but his poor wife has not lived to see it all, for she has now been dead these fourteen years."

"A soldier's calling is an honorable calling, provided he has fit only on the side of right," returned the Pathfinder; "and as the Frenchers are always wrong, and His Sacred Majesty and these colonies are always right, I take it the sarjeant has a quiet conscience, as well as a good character. I have never slept more sweetly than when I have fit the Mingos, though it is a law with me to fight always like a white man, and never like an Injin. The Sarpent, here, has his fashions and I have mine; and yet have we fou't, side by side, these many years, without either's thinking a hard thought consarning the other's ways. I tell him there is but one heaven and one hell, notwithstanding his traditions, though there are many paths to both."

"That is rational, and he is bound to believe you, though I fancy most of the roads to the last, are on dry land. The sea is what my poor sister Bridget used to call a 'purifying place,' and one is out of the way of temptation when out of sight of land. I doubt if as much can be said in favor of your lakes, up hereaway."

"That towns and settlements lead to sin, I will allow, but our lakes are bordered by the forests, and one is every day called upon to worship God, in such a temple. That men are not always the same, even in the wilderness, I must admit, for the difference atween a Mingo and a Delaware, is as plain to be seen as the difference atween the sun and the moon. I am glad, friend Cap, that we have met, howsever, if it be only that you may tell the Big Sarpent, here, that there be lakes in which the water is salt. We have been pretty much of one mind, since our acquaintance began, and if the Mohican has only half the faith in me that I have in him, he believes all that I have told him, touching the white men's ways and natur's laws; but, it has always seemed to me that none of the red skins have given as free a belief, as an honest man likes, to the accounts of the Big Salt Lakes, and to that of there being rivers that flow up stream."

"This comes of getting things wrong end foremost," answered Cap, with a condescending nod. "You have thought of your lakes and rifts, as the ship, and of the ocean and the tides, as the boat. Neither Arrowhead nor the Serpent need doubt what you have said concerning both, though I confess myself, to some difficulty in swallowing the tale about there being inland seas, at all, and still more that there is any sea of fresh water. I have come this long journey, as much to satisfy my own eyes and palate concerning these facts, as to oblige the Serjeant and Magnet, though the first was my sister's husband, and I love the last like a child."

"You are wrong—you are wrong, friend Cap, very wrong to distrust the power of God, in any thing," returned Pathfinder, earnestly. "Them that live in the settlements and the towns get to have confined and unjust opinions consarning the might of His hand, but we who pass our time, in his very presence, as it might be, see things differently—I mean such of us as have white natur's. A red skin has his notions, and it is right that it should be so, and if they are not exactly the same as a Christian white man's, there is no harm in it. Still there are matters that belong altogether to the ordering of God's Providence, and these salt and fresh water lakes are some of them. I do not pretend to account for these things, but I think it the duty of all to believe in them. For my part, I am one of them who think that the same hand which made the sweet water, can make the salt."

"Hold on there, Master Pathfinder—" interrupted Cap, not without some heat; "in the way of a proper and manly faith, I will turn my back on no one, ashore or afloat. Although more accustomed to make all snug aloft, and to show the proper canvass than to pray, when the hurricane comes, I know that we are but helpless mortals, at times, and I hope I pay reverence where reverence is due. All I mean to say, and that is rather insiniated than said, is this; which is, as you all know, simply an intimation that being accustomed to see waters in large bodies salt, I should like to taste it, before I can believe it to be fresh."

"God has given the salt licks to the deer, and he has given to man, red skin and white, the delicious spring at which to slake his thirst. It is onreasonable to think that he may not have given lakes of pure water to the west, and lakes of impure water to the east."

Cap was awed, in spite of his overweening dogmatism, by the earnest simplicity of the Pathfinder, though he did not relish the idea of believing a fact which, for many years, he had pertinaciously insisted could not be true. Unwilling to give up the point, and, at the same time, unable to maintain it against a reasoning to which he was unaccustomed, and which possessed equally the force of truth, faith and probability, he was glad to get rid of the subject by evasion.

"Well, well, friend Pathfinder," he said, "we will nipper the argument where it is, and, as the serjeant has sent you to give us pilotage to this same lake, we can only try the water when we reach it—only mark my words, I do not say that it may not be fresh on the surface; the Atlantic is sometimes fresh on the surface, near the mouths of great rivers; but, rely on it, I shall show you a way of tasting the water many fathoms deep, of which you never dreamed; and then we shall know more about it."

The guide seemed content to let the matter rest, and the conversation changed.

"We are not over-consated consarning our gifts," observed the Pathfinder after a short pause, "and well know that such as live in the towns, and near the sea—"

"On the sea," interrupted Cap.

"On the sea, if you wish it, friend, have opportunities that do not befall us of the wilderness. Still, we know our own callings, and they are what I consider nat'ral callings, and are not parvarted by vanity and wantonness. Now, my gifts are with the rifle, and on a trail, and in the way of game and scoutin', for, though I can use the spear and the paddle, I pride not myself on either. The youth, Jasper there, who is discoursing with the sarjeant's daughter, is a different creatur', for he may be said to breathe the water, as it might be, like a fish. The Indians and Frenchers of the north shore, call him Eau douce, on account of his gifts, in this particular. He is better at the oar and the rope-tie, than in making fires on a trail."

"There must be something about these gifts of which you speak after all," said Cap. "Now this fire, I will acknowledge, has overlaid all my seamanship. Arrowhead, there, said the smoke came from a pale-face's fire, and that is a piece of philosophy that I hold to be equal to steering in a dark night by the edges of the scud."*

"It's no great secret—it's no great secret," returned Pathfinder, laughing with great inward glee, though habitual caution prevented the emission of any noise. "Nothing is easier to us who pass our time in the great school of Providence than to l'arn its lessons. We should be as useless on a trail, or in carrying tidings through the wilderness, as so many woodchucks, did we not soon come to a knowledge of these niceties. Eau douce, as we call him, is so fond of the water that he gathered a damp stick or two for our fire, and there be plenty of them, as well as those that are thoroughly dried, lying scattered about, and wet will bring dark smoke, as I suppose even you followers of the sea must know. It's no great secret—it's no great secret—though all is mystery to such as does'n't study the Lord and his mighty ways, with humility and thankfulness."

"That must be a keen eye of Arrowhead's, to see so slight a difference."

"He would be but a poor Injin if he did'n't! No—no—it is war-time, and no red-skin is outlying without using his senses. Every skin has its own natur', and every natur' has its own laws, as well as its own skin. It was many years afore I could master all them higher branches of a forest edication, for red-skin knowledge does'n't come as easy to white skin natur', as what I suppose is intended to be white skin knowledge; though I have but little of the latter, having passed most of my time in the wilderness."

"You have been a ready scholar, Master Pathfinder, as is seen by your understanding these things so well. I suppose it would be no great matter, for a man regularly brought up to the sea, to catch these trifles, if he could only bring his mind fairly to bear upon them."

"I don't know that—The white man has his difficulties in getting red skin habits, quite as much as the Injin in getting white skin ways. As for the raal natur', it is my opinion that neither can actually get that of the other."

"And yet we sailors, who run about the world so much, say there is but one nature, whether it be in the Chinaman, or a Dutchman. For my own part, I am much of that way of thinking, too, for I have generally found that all nations like gold and silver, and most men relish tobacco."

"Then you sea-faring men know little of the red-skins. Have you ever known any of your China-men who could sing their death songs, with their flesh torn with splinters, and cut with knives, the fire raging around their naked bodies, and death staring them in the face? Until you can find me a China-man, or a Christian-man that can do all this, you cannot find a man with a red-skin natur', let him look ever so valiant, or know how to read all the books that were ever printed."

"It is the Savages, only, that play each other such hellish tricks," said Master Cap, glancing his eyes about him, uneasily, at the apparently endless arches of the forest; "no white man is ever condemned to undergo these trials."

"Nay, therein, you are ag'in mistaken," returned the Pathfinder, coolly selecting a delicate morsel of the venison, as his *bonne bouche*; "for though these torments belong only to the red-skin natur', in the way of bearing them like braves, white-skin natur', may be, and often has been agonized by them."

"Happily," said Cap, with an effort to clear his throat, "none of His Majesty's allies, will be likely to attempt such damnable cruelties, on any of His Majesty's loyal subjects. I have not served much in the royal navy, it is true, but I have served—and that is something; and, in the way of privateering and worrying the enemy in his ships and cargoes, I've done my full share. But I trust there are no French savages on this side of the lake, and I think you said that Ontario is a broad sheet of water?"

"Nay, it is broad in our eyes," returned Pathfinder, not caring to conceal the smile which lighted a face, that had been burnt by exposure to a bright red, "though I mistrust that some may think it narrow; and narrow it is, if you wish it to keep off the foe. Ontario has two inds, and the inimy that is afraid to cross it, will be sartain to come round it."

"Ah! that comes of your d——d fresh water ponds!" growled

Cap, hemming so loud, as to cause him instantly to repent the indiscretion. "No man, now, ever heard of a pirate's, or a thief's getting round an end of the Atlantic!"

"Mayhap the ocean has no inds?"

"That it has'n't; nor sides, nor bottom. The nation that is snugly moored on one of its coasts need fear nothing from the one anchored abeam, let it be ever so savage, unless it possesses the art of ship-building. No–no–the people who live on the shores of the Atlantic need fear but little for their skins, or their scalps. A man may lie down at night, in those regions, in the hope of finding the hair on his head in the morning, unless he wears a wig."

"It is'n't so here. I don't wish to flurry the young woman, and therefore I will be no way particular–though she seems pretty much listening to Eau douce, as we call him–but without the edication I have received, I should think it, at this very moment, a risky journey to go over the very ground that lies atween us and the garrison, in the present state of this frontier. There are about as many Iroquois* on this side of Ontario, as there be on the other. It is for this very reason, friend Cap, that the sarjeant has engaged us to come out and show you the path."

"What!–do the knaves dare to cruise so near the guns of one of His Majesty's works?"

"Do not the ravens resort near the carcase of the deer, though the fowler is at hand? They come this-a-way, as it might be nat'rally. There are more or less whites passing atween the forts and the settlements, and they are sure to be on their trails. The Sarpent has come up one side of the river, and I have come up the other, in order to scout for the outlying rascals, while Jasper brought up the canoe, like a bold-hearted sailor, as he is. The Sarjeant told him, with tears in his eyes, all about his child, and how his heart yearned for her, and how gentle and obedient she was, until I think the lad would have dashed into a Mingo camp, single handed, rather than not acome."

"We thank him–we thank him; and shall think the better of him for his readiness, though I suppose the boy has run no great risk, after all."

"Only the risk of being shot from a cover, as he forced the canoe up a swift rift, or turned an elbow in the stream, with his eyes fastened on the eddies. Of all risky journeys, that on an ambushed river, is the most risky, in my judgment, and that risk has Jasper run."

"And why the devil, has the serjeant sent for me to travel a hundred and fifty miles, in this outlandish manner! Give me an offing, and the enemy in sight, and I'll play with him in his own fashion, as long as he pleases, long bows, or close quarters; but to be shot like a turtle asleep, is not to my humour. If it were not for little Magnet, there, I would tack*ship this instant, make the best of my way back to York, and let Ontario take care of itself, salt water or fresh water."

"That would'n't mend the matter much, friend mariner, as the road to return is much longer, and almost as bad as the road to go on. Trust to us, and we will carry you through safe, or lose our scalps."

Cap wore a tight solid cue, done up in eel-skin, while the top of his head was nearly bald; and he mechanically passed his hand over both, as if to make certain that each was in its right place. He was at the bottom, however, a brave man, and had often faced death with coolness, though never in the frightful forms in which it presented itself, under the brief but graphic pictures of his companion. It was too late to retreat, and he determined to put the best face on the matter, though he could not avoid muttering inwardly a few curses on the indifference and indiscretion with which his brother-in-law, the serjeant, had led him into his present dilemma.

"I make no doubt, Master Pathfinder," he answered, when these thoughts had found time to glance through his mind, "that we shall reach port in safety. What distance may we now be from the fort?"

"Little more than fifteen miles; and swift miles too, as the river runs, if the Mingos let us go clear."

"And I suppose the woods will stretch along, starboard and larboard, as heretofore?"

"Anan?"*

"I mean that we shall have to pick our way, through these damned trees!"

"Nay, nay, you will go in the canoe, and the Oswego has been cleared of its flood-wood by the troops. It will be floating down stream, and that, too, with a swift current."

"And what the devil is to prevent these Minks, of which you speak, from shooting us as we double a head-land, or are busy in steering clear of the rocks."

"The Lord!—He who has so often helped others, in greater difficulties. Many and many is the time that my head would have been stripped of hair, skin and all, had'n't the Lord fit of my side. I never go into a skrimmage, friend mariner, without thinking of this great ally, who can do more in battle, than all the battalions of the 60th, were they brought into a single line."

"Ay—ay—this may do well enough for a scouter, but we seamen like our offing, and to go into action with nothing on our minds, but the business before us—plain broadside and broadside work, and no trees, or rocks, to thicken the water."

"And no Lord, too, I dare to say, if the truth were known! Take my word for it, Master Cap, that no battle is the worse fou't, for having the Lord on your side. Look at the head of the Big Sarpent, there; you can see the mark of a knife, all along there by his left ear; now, nothing but a bullet from this long rifle of mine, saved his scalp that day, for it had fairly started, and half a minute more would have left him without the warlock. When the Mohican squeezes my hand, and intermates that I befriended him in that matter, I tell him, no; it was the Lord, who led me to the only spot where execution could be done, or his necessity be made known, on account of the smoke. Sartain when I got the right position, I finished the affair of my own accord, for a friend under the tomahawk is apt to make a man think quick and act at once, as was my case, or the Sarpent's spirit would be hunting in the happy land of his people, at this very moment."

"Come, come, Pathfinder, this palaver is worse than being skinned from stem to stern; we have but a few hours of sun, and had better be drifting down this said current of yours, while we may. Magnet, dear, are you not ready to get under way?"

Magnet started, blushed brightly, and made her preparations, for an immediate departure. Not a syllable of the discourse just related, had she heard, for Eau douce, as young Jasper was oftener called than any thing else, had been filling her ears with a description of the yet distant post towards which she was journeying, with accounts of her father, whom she had not seen since a child, and with the manner of life of those who lived in the frontier garrisons. Unconsciously, she had become deeply interested, and her thoughts had been too intently directed to these interesting matters, to allow any of the less agreeable subject, discussed by those so near to reach her ears. The bustle of departure put an end to the conversation entirely, and the baggage of the scouts, or guides, being trifling, in a few minutes, the whole party was ready to proceed. As they were about to quit the spot, however, to the surprise of even his fellow guides, Pathfinder collected a quantity of branches, and threw them upon the embers of the fire, taking care even to see that some of the wood was damp, in order to raise as dark and dense a smoke as possible.

"When you can hide your trail, Jasper," he said, "a smoke at leaving an encampment may do good, instead of harm. If there are a dozen Mingos within ten miles of us, some of 'em, are on the heights, or in the trees, looking out for smokes; let them see this, and much good may it do them. They are welcome to our leavings."

"But may they not strike, and follow on our trail?" asked the youth, whose interest in the hazards of his situation had much increased, since the meeting with Magnet. "We shall leave a broad path to the river."

"The broader the better; when there, it will surpass Mingo cunning, even, to say which way the canoe has gone; up stream, or down. Water is the only thing in natur' that will thoroughly wash out a trail, and even water will not always do it, when the scent is strong. Do you not see, Eau douce, that if any Mingos have seen our path below the falls, they will strike off towards this smoke, and that they will nat'rally conclude they who began by going up stream, will ind by going up stream. If they know any thing, they now know a party is out from the fort, and it will exceed even Mingo wit, to fancy that we have come up here, just for the pleasure of going back again, and that, too, the same day, and at the risk of our scalps."

"Certainly," added Jasper, who was talking apart with the Pathfinder, as they moved towards the wind-row, "they cannot know any thing, about the serjeant's daughter, for the greatest secrecy has been observed, on her account."

"And they will larn nothing, here," returned Pathfinder, causing his companion to see that he trod with the utmost care, on the impressions left on the leaves, by the little foot of Mabel, "unless this old salt-water fish, has been trotting his niece about in the wind-row, like a fa'n playing by the side of the old doe."

"Buck, you mean, Pathfinder."

"Isn't he a queerity!—Now, I can consort with such a sailor as yourself, Eau douce, and find nothing very contrary, in our gifts, though yourn belong to the lakes and mine to the woods. Harkee, Jasper—" continued the scout, laughing in his noiseless manner; "suppose we try the temper of his blade, and run him over the falls?"

"And what would be done with the pretty niece, in the mean while?"

"Nay—nay—no harm shall come to her; she must walk round the portage, at any rate, but you and I can try this Atlantic Oceaner, and then all parties will become better acquainted. We shall find out, whether his flint will strike fire, and he may come to know something of frontier tricks."

Young Jasper smiled, for he was not averse to fun, and had been a little touched by Cap's superciliousness, but Mabel's fair face, light agile form, and winning smiles, stood like a shield, between her uncle and the intended experiment.

"Perhaps the serjeant's daughter will be frightened," he said.

"Not she, if she has any of the sarjeant's spirit in her. She does'n't look like a skeary thing, at all. Leave it to me, Eau douce, and I will manage the affair alone."

"Not you, Pathfinder; you would only drown both. If the canoe goes over, I must go in it."

"Well have it so, then; shall we smoke the pipe of agreement on the bargain."

Jasper laughed, nodded his head, by way of consent, and the subject was dropped, for the party had reached the canoe, so often mentioned, and fewer words had determined much graver things between the parties.

Chapter III.

"Before these fields were shorn and tilled,
Full to the brim our rivers flowed;
The melody of waters filled
The fresh and boundless wood;
And torrents dashed, and rivulets played,
And fountains spouted in the shade."

> Bryant, "An Indian at the Burial Place
> of His Fathers," ll. 67–72.

IT is generally known, that the waters which flow into the southern side of Ontario, are, in general, narrow, sluggish and deep. There are some exceptions to this rule, for many of the rivers have rapids, or as they are termed in the language of the region, rifts, and some have falls. Among the latter was the particular stream on which our adventurers were now journeying. The Oswego is formed by the junction of the Oneida and the Onondaga, both of which flow from lakes, and it pursues its way, through a gently undulating country, a few miles, until it reaches the margin of a sort of natural terrace, down which it tumbles some ten or fifteen feet, to another level, across which it glides, or glances, or pursues its course with the silent stealthy progress of deep water, until it throws its tribute into the broad receptacle of Ontario. The canoe, in which Cap and his party had travelled from Fort Stanwix,* the last military station on the Mohawk, lay by the side of this river, and into it the whole party now entered, with the exception of the Pathfinder, who remained on the land, in order to shove the light vessel off.

"Let her starn drift down stream, Jasper," said the man of the woods, to the young mariner of the lake, who had dispossessed Arrowhead of his paddle, and taken his own station as steersman, "let it go down with the current. Should any of them infarnals, the Mingos, strike our trail, or follow it to this point, they will not fail to look for the signs in the mud, and if they discover that we have left the shore, with the nose of the canoe up stream, it is a nat'ral belief to think we went that-a-way."

This direction was followed, and giving a vigorous shove, the Pathfinder, who was in the flower of his strength and activity, made a leap, landing lightly, and without disturbing its equilibrium, in the bows of the canoe. As soon as it had reached the centre of the river, or the strength of the current, the boat was turned, and it began to glide noiselessly down the stream.

The vessel in which Cap and his niece had embarked for their long and adventurous journey, was one of the canoes of bark, which the Indians are in the habit of constructing, and which, by their exceeding lightness and the ease with which they are propelled, are admirably adapted to a navigation, in which shoals, flood-wood, and other similar obstructions so often occur. The two men who composed its original crew had several times carried it, when emptied of its luggage, many hundred yards; and it would not have exceeded the strength of a single man to lift its weight. Still it was long, and for a canoe, wide, a want of steadiness being its principal defect, in the eyes of the uninitiated. A few hours practice, however, in a great measure remedied this evil, and both Mabel and her uncle had learned so far to humour its movements, that they now maintained their places with perfect composure. Nor did the additional weight of the three guides tax its powers, in any particular degree, the breadth of the rounded bottom allowing the necessary quantity of water to be displaced, without bringing the gunwale very sensibly nearer to the surface of the stream. Its workmanship was neat, the timbers were small and secured by thongs, and the whole fabric, though it was so slight and precarious to the eye, was probably capable of conveying double the number of persons, that it now contained.

Cap was seated on a low thwart, in the centre of the canoe; the Big Serpent knelt near him; Arrowhead and his wife occupied places forward of both, the former having relinquished his post aft; Mabel was half-reclining on some of her own effects, behind her uncle, while the Pathfinder and Eau douce stood erect, the one in the bows, and the other in the stern, each using a paddle with a long, steady, noiseless sweep. The conversation was carried on in low tones, all of the party beginning to feel the necessity of prudence, as they drew nearer to the outskirts of the fort, and had no longer the cover of the woods.

The Oswego just at that place was a deep, dark stream, of no great width, its still gloomy looking current winding its way, among overhanging trees, that, in particular spots, almost shut out the light of the heavens. Here and there some half fallen giant of the forest, lay nearly across its surface, rendering care necessary to avoid the limbs, and most of the distance, the lower branches and leaves of the trees of smaller growth were laved by its waters. The picture which has been so beautifully described by our own admirable poet, and which we have placed at the head of this chapter, as an epigraph, was here realized, the earth fattened by the decayed vegetation of centuries, and black with loam, the stream that filled the banks nearly to overflowing, and the "fresh and boundless wood," being all as visible to the eye, as the pen of Bryant has elsewhere vividly presented them to the imagination. In short, the entire scene was one of a rich and benevolent nature, before it has been subjected to the uses and desires of man; luxuriant, wild, full of promise, and not without the charm of the picturesque, even in its rudest state. It will be remembered that this was in the year 175–, or long before even speculation had brought any portion of Western New-York, within the bounds of civilization, or the projects of the adventurous. At that distant day, there were two great channels of military communications, between the inhabited portions of the colony of New-York, and the frontiers that lay adjacent to the Canadas; that by Lakes Champlain and George, and that by means of the Mohawk, Wood Creek, the Oneida, and the rivers we have been describing. Along both these lines of communications military posts had been established, though there existed a blank space of a hundred miles, between the last fort at the head of the Mohawk, and the outlet of the Oswego, which embraced most of the distance that Cap and Mabel had journeyed under the protection of Arrowhead.

"I sometimes wish for peace, again," said the Pathfinder, "when one can range the forest, without s'arching for any other inimy than the beasts and fishes. Ah's! me; many is the day that the Sarpent, there, and I have passed happily among the streams, living on venison, salmon and trout, without thought of a Mingo, or a scalp! I sometimes wish that them blessed days might come back, for it is not my raal gift to slay my own kind. I'm sartain the sarjeant's daughter, don't think me a wretch that takes pleasure in preying on human natur'?"

At this remark, a sort of half interrogatory, Pathfinder looked behind him, and, though the most partial friend could scarcely term his sunburnt and hard features handsome, even Mabel thought his smile attractive, by its simple ingenuousness, and the uprightness that beamed in every lineament of his honest countenance.

"I do not think my father would have sent one like those you mention, to see his daughter through the wilderness," the young woman answered, returning the smile as frankly as it was given, and much more sweetly.

"That he would'n't, that he would'n't; the sarjeant is a man of feelin', and many is the march and the fight that we have stood shoulder to shoulder in, as *he* would call it, though I always keep my limbs free, when near a Frencher, or a Mingo."

"You are then the young friend of whom my father has spoken so often in his letters?"

"His *young* friend—the sarjeant has the advantage of me by thirty years; yes, he is thirty years my senior, and as many my better."

"Not in the eyes of the daughter, perhaps, friend Pathfinder—" put in Cap, whose spirits began to revive, when he found the water once more flowing around him. "The thirty years that you mention, are not often thought to be an advantage in the eyes of girls of nineteen."

Mabel coloured, and in turning aside her face, to avoid the looks of those in the bows of the canoe, she encountered the admiring gaze of the young man in the stern. As a last resource her spirited, but soft blue eyes, sought refuge in the water. Just at this moment, a dull heavy sound swept up the avenue formed by the trees, borne along by a light air that hardly produced a ripple on the water.

"That sounds pleasantly," said Cap, pricking up his ears like a dog that hears a distant baying; "it is the surf on the shores of your lake, I suppose?"

"Not so—not so—" answered the Pathfinder—"it is merely this river tumbling over some rocks, half a mile below us."

"Is there a fall in this stream?" demanded Mabel, a still brighter flush glowing on her face.

"The Devil! Master Pathfinder –or you, Mr. Oh! the-deuce (for so Cap began to style Jasper, by way of entering cordially into the border usages) had you not better give the canoe a sheer, and get nearer to the shore. These water-falls have generally rapids above them, and one might as well get into the Maelstrom, at once, as to run into their suction."

"Trust to us–trust to us, friend Cap," answered Pathfinder; "we are but fresh-water sailors, it is true, and I cannot boast of being much even of that, but we understand rifts and rapids and cataracts, and, in going down these, we shall do our endivours, not to disgrace our edication."

"In going down!" exclaimed Cap–"the devil, man! you do not dream of going down a water-fall, in this egg-shell of bark!"

"Sartain; the path lies over the falls, and it is much easier to shoot them, than to unload the canoe, and to carry that, and all it contains, around a portage of a mile, by hand."

Mabel turned her pallid countenance towards the young man in the stern of the canoe, for just at that moment a fresh roar of the fall, was borne to her ears, by a new current of the air, and it really sounded terrific, now that the cause was understood.

"We thought, that by landing the females, and the two Indians," Jasper quietly observed, "we three white men, all of whom are used to the water, might carry the canoe over in safety, for we often shoot these falls."

"And we counted on you, friend mariner, as a mainstay;" said Pathfinder, winking at Jasper over his shoulder, "for you are accustomed to see waves tumbling about, and without some one to steady the cargo, all the finery of the sarjeant's daughter might be washed into the river, and be lost."

Cap was puzzled. The idea of going over a water-fall was perhaps more serious, in his eyes, than it would have been in those of one totally ignorant of all that pertained to boats, for he understood the power of the element, and the total feebleness of man when exposed to its fury. Still, his pride revolted at the thought of deserting the boat, while others not only courageously, but coolly, proposed to continue in it. Notwithstanding the latter feeling, and his innate as well as acquired steadiness in danger, he would probably have deserted his post, had not the images of Indians tearing scalps from the human head taken so strong hold of his fancy, as to induce him to imagine the canoe a sort of sanctuary.

"What is to be done with Magnet," he demanded, affection for his niece raising another qualm in his conscience. "We cannot allow Magnet to land if there are enemy's Indians near?"

"Nay—no Mingo will be near the portage, for that is a spot too public for their deviltries," answered the Pathfinder, confidently. "Natur' is natur', and it is an Injin's natur' to be found where he is least expected. No fear of him, on a beaten path, for he wishes to come upon you, when unprepared to meet him, and the fiery villains make it a point to deceive you, one way or another. Sheer in, Eau douce, and we will land the sarjeant's daughter, on the end of that log, where she can reach the shore with a dry foot."

The injunction was obeyed, and in a few minutes the whole party had left the canoe, with the exception of Pathfinder and the two sailors. Notwithstanding his professional pride, Cap would have gladly followed, but he did not like to exhibit so unequivocal a weakness in the presence of a fresh-water sailor.

"I call all hands to witness," he said, as those who had landed moved away, "that I do not look on this affair, as any thing more than canoeing in the woods. There is no seamanship in tumbling over a water-fall, which is a feat the greatest lubber can perform, as well as the oldest mariner."

"Nay, nay, you need'n't despise the Oswego Falls, neither," put in Pathfinder, "for though they may not be Niagara, nor the Genessee, nor the Cahoos, nor Glenn's, nor them on the Canada, they are narvous enough, for a new beginner. Let the sarjeant's daughter stand on yonder rock, and she will see the manner in which we ignorant back-woodsmen get over a difficulty that we can't get under. Now, Eau douce, a steady hand and a true eye, for all rests on you, seeing that we can count Master Cap for no more than a passenger."

The canoe was leaving the shore, as he concluded, while Mabel went hurriedly and trembling to the rock that had been pointed out, talking to her companions of the danger her uncle so unnecessarily ran, while her eyes were riveted on the agile and vigorous form of Eau douce, as he stood erect in the stern of the light boat, governing its movements. As soon, however, as she reached a point where she got a view of the fall, she gave an involuntary but suppressed scream, and covered her eyes. At the next instant, the latter were again free, and the entranced girl stood, immovable as a statue, a scarcely breathing observer of all that passed. The two Indians seated themselves passively on a log, hardly looking towards the stream, while the wife of Arrowhead came near Mabel, and appeared to watch the motions of the canoe, with some such interest as a child regards the leaps of a tumbler.

As soon as the boat was in the stream, Pathfinder sunk on his knees, continuing to use the paddle though it was slowly, and in a manner not to interfere with the efforts of his companion. The latter still stood erect, and, as he kept his eye on some object beyond the fall, it was evident that he was carefully looking for the spot proper for their passage.

"Farther west, boy; farther west–" muttered Pathfinder; "there, where you see the water foam. Bring the top of the dead oak in a line with the stem of the blasted hemlock."

Eau douce made no answer, for the canoe was in the centre of the stream, with its head pointed towards the fall, and it had already begun to quicken its motion, by the increased force of the current. At that moment, Cap would cheerfully have renounced every claim to glory that could possibly be acquired by the feat, to have been safe again, on the shore. He heard the roar of the water, thundering as it might be behind a screen, but, becoming more and more distinct, louder and louder, and before him he saw its line cutting the forest below, along which the green and angry element seemed stretched and shining, as if the particles were about to lose their principle of cohesion.

"Down with your helm–down with your helm, man!" he exclaimed, unable any longer to suppress his anxiety, as the canoe glided towards the edge of the fall.

"Ay–ay–down it is, sure enough," answered Pathfinder, looking behind him for a single instant, with his silent joyous laugh–"down we go, of a sartainty! Heave her starn up, boy; farther up with her starn!"

The rest was like the passage of the viewless wind. Eau douce gave the required sweep with his paddle, the canoe glanced into the channel, and for a few seconds, it seemed to Cap, that he was tossing in a cauldron. He felt the bows of the canoe tip, saw the raging, foaming water, careering madly by his side, was sensible that the light fabric in which he floated was tossed about like an egg shell, and then, not less to his great joy than to his surprise, he discovered that it was gliding across the basin of still water, below the fall, under the steady impulse of Jasper's paddle.

The Pathfinder continued to laugh, but he arose from his knees, and searching for a tin pot and a horn spoon, he began deliberately to measure the water that had been taken in, in the passage.

"Fourteen spoonsfull, Eau douce; fourteen fairly measured spoonsfull. I have you must acknowledge known you go down with only ten."

"Master Cap leaned so hard up stream," returned Jasper seriously, "that I had difficulty in trimming the canoe."

"It may be so—it may be so; no doubt it *was* so, since you say it; but I have known you go over with only ten!"

Cap now gave a tremendous hem, felt for his cue, as if to ascertain its safety, and then looked back, in order to examine the danger he had gone through. His impunity is easily explained. Most of the river fell perpendicularly, ten or twelve feet, but near its centre, the force of the current had so far worn away the rock, as to permit the water to shoot through a narrow passage at an angle of about forty, or forty five degrees. Down this ticklish descent the canoe had glanced, amid fragments of broken rock, whirlpools, foam, and furious tossings of the element, which an uninstructed eye would believe menaced inevitable destruction to an object so fragile. But the very lightness of the canoe had favored its descent, for, borne on the crests of the waves, and directed by a steady eye and an arm full of muscle, it had passed like a feather, from one pile of foam to another, scarcely permitting its glossy side to be wetted. There were a few rocks to be avoided, the proper direction was to be rigidly observed, and the fierce current did the rest.*

To say that Cap was astonished, would not be expressing half his feelings. He felt awed, for the profound dread of rocks, which most seamen entertain, came in aid of his admiration of

---

*Lest the reader suppose we are dealing purely in fiction, the writer will add that he has known a long thirty two pounder carried over these same falls, in perfect safety.

the boldness of the exploit. Still he was indisposed to express all he felt, lest it might be conceding too much in favor of fresh water and inland navigation, and no sooner had he cleared his throat, with the aforesaid hem, than he loosened his tongue, in the usual strain of superiority.

"I do not gainsay your knowledge of the channel, Master Oh! the deuce, (for such he religiously believed to be Jasper's *soubriquet*) and, after all, to know the channel, in such a place is the main point. I have had cockswains with me, who could come down that shoot too, if they only knew the channel."

"It is'n't enough to know the channel, friend Mariner," said Pathfinder; "it needs narves and skill to keep the canoe straight, and to keep her clear of the rocks too. There is'n't another boatman in all this region that can shoot the Oswego, but Eau douce, there, with any sartainty, though, now and then, one has blundered through. I can't do it myself, unless by means of Providence, and it needs Jasper's hand, and Jasper's eye, to make sure of a dry passage. Fourteen spoonsfull, after all, are no great matter, though I wish it had been but ten, seeing that the Sarjeant's daughter was a looker on!"

"And yet you conned the canoe; you told him how to head, and how to sheer."

"Human frailty, Master Mariner; that was a little of white-skin natur'. Now, had the Sarpent, yonder, been in the boat, not a word would he have spoken, or thought would he have given to the public. An Injin knows how to hold his tongue, but we white folk fancy we are always wiser than our fellows. I'm curing myself fast of the weakness, but it needs time, to root up the tree that has been growing more than thirty years."

"I think little of this affair, sir; nothing at all, to speak my mind freely. It's a mere wash of spray to shooting London Bridge, which is done every day by hundreds of persons, and often by the most delicate ladies in the land. The King's Majesty has shot the bridge, in his royal person."

"Well I want no delicate ladies or king's majesties, (God bless 'em), in the canoe, in going over these falls, for a boat's breadth, either way, may make a drowning matter of it. Eau douce, we shall have to carry the sarjeant's brother over Niagara, yet, to show him what may be done on a frontier!"

"The devil! Master Pathfinder, you must be joking, now! Surely it is not possible for a bark canoe to go over that mighty cataract!"

"You never were more mistaken, Master Cap, in your life. Nothing is easier, and many is the canoe I have seen go over it, with my own eyes, and, if we both live, I hope to satisfy you that the feat can be done. For my part, I think the largest ship that ever sailed on the ocean might be carried over, could she once get into the rapids."

Cap did not perceive the wink which Pathfinder exchanged with Eau douce, and he remained silent some time; for, sooth to say, he had never suspected the possibility of going down Niagara, feasible as the thing must appear to every one, on a second thought, the real difficulty existing in going up it.

By this time, the party had reached the place, where Jasper had left his own canoe, concealed in the bushes, and they all re-embarked; Cap, Jasper and his niece, in one boat, and Pathfinder, Arrowhead and the wife of the latter, in the other. The Mohican had already passed down the banks of the river by land, looking cautiously and with the skill of his people for the signs of an enemy.

The cheek of Mabel did not recover all its bloom, until the canoe was again in the current, down which it floated swiftly, occasionally impelled by the paddle of Jasper. She witnessed the descent of the falls, with a degree of terror that had rendered her mute, but her fright had not been so great as to prevent admiration of the steadiness of the youth, who directed the movement, from blending with the passing terror. In truth, one much less quick and sensitive, might have had her feelings awakened by the cool and gallant air with which Eau douce had accomplished this clever exploit. He had stood firmly erect, notwithstanding the plunge, and to those who were on the shore, it was evident that by a timely application of his skill and strength, the canoe had received a sheer that alone carried it clear of a rock, over which the boiling water was leaping in *jets d'eau*, now leaving the brown stone visible, and now covering it with a limpid sheet, as if machinery controlled the play of the element. The tongue cannot always express what the eyes view, but Mabel saw enough, even in that moment of fear, to blend forever in her mind, the pictures presented by the plunging canoe, and the unmoved steersman. She admitted that insidious sentiment which binds woman so strongly to man, by feeling additional security in finding herself under his care, and for the first time since leaving Fort Stanwix, she was entirely at her ease in the frail bark, in which she travelled. As the other canoe kept quite near her own, however, and the Pathfinder, by floating at her side was most in view, the conversation was principally maintained with that person, Jasper seldom speaking unless addressed, and constantly exhibiting a wariness in the management of his own boat, that might have been remarked by one accustomed to his ordinary, confident, careless manner, had such an observer been present to rate what was passing.

"We know too well, a woman's gifts, to think of carrying the sarjeant's daughter over the falls," said Pathfinder, looking at Mabel, while he addressed her uncle, "though I've been acquainted with some of her sex, in these regions, that would think but little of doing the thing."

"Mabel is faint-hearted like her mother," returned Cap, "and you did well, friend, to humour her weakness. You will remember the child has never been at sea."

"No—no—it was easy to discover that, by your own fearlessness—any one might have seen how little you cared about the matter! I went over once, with a raw hand, and he jumped out of the canoe, just as it tipped, and you may judge what a time he had of it!"

"What became of the poor fellow?" asked Cap, scarce knowing how to take the other's manner, which was so dry, while it was so simple, that a less obtuse subject than the old sailor might well have suspected its sincerity. "One who has passed the place knows how to feel for him."

"He was a *poor* fellow, as you say; and a poor frontier man, too, though he came out to show his skill among us ignoranters. What became of him?—why he went down the falls, topsy turvey like, as would have happened to a court-house or a fort."

"If it should jump out of a canoe—" interrupted Jasper, smiling, though he was evidently more disposed than his friend to let the passage of the falls be forgotten.

"The boy is right—" rejoined Pathfinder laughing in Mabel's

face, the canoes being now so near that they almost touched; "he is sartainly right. But you have not told us what you think of the leap we took?"

"It was perilous and bold," said Mabel; "while looking at it, I could have wished it had not been attempted, though, now it is over, I can admire its boldness, and the steadiness with which it was made."

"Now, do not think that we did this thing, to set ourselves off in female eyes. It may be pleasant to the young to win each other's good opinions, by doing things that may seem praise-worthy and bold, but neither Eau douce, nor myself, am of that race. My natur', though perhaps the Sarpent would be a better witness, has few turns in it, and is a straight natur', nor would it be likely to lead me into a vanity of this sort, while out on duty. As for Jasper, he would sooner go over the Oswego falls, with-out a looker on, than do it before a hundred pair of eyes. I know the lad well, from use and much consorting, and I am sure he is not boastful or vain-glorious."

Mabel rewarded the scout with a smile, that served to keep the canoes together some time longer, for the sight of youth and beauty was so rare on that remote frontier, that even the rebuked and self mortified feelings of this wanderer of the forest, were sensibly touched by the blooming loveliness of the girl.

"We did it for the best," Pathfinder continued; "'twas all for the best. Had we waited to carry the canoe across the portage, time would have been lost, and nothing is so precious as time, when you are mistrustful of Mingos."

"But we can have little to fear, now! The canoes move swiftly, and two hours, you have said, will carry us down to the fort."

"It shall be a cunning Iroquois who hurts a hair of your head, pretty one, for all here are bound to the sarjeant, and most I think to yourself, to see you safe from harm. Ha! Eau douce; what is that in the river, at the lower turn—yonder beneath the bushes, I mean standing on the rock?"

"'Tis the Big Serpent, Pathfinder; he is making signs to us, in a way I don't understand."

"'Tis the Sarpent, as sure as I'm a white man, and he wishes us to drop in nearer to his shore. Mischief is brewin', or one of his deliberation and steadiness would never take this trouble. Courage, all; we are men, and must meet deviltry as becomes our colour, and our callings. Ah! I never knew good come of boastin', and here, just as I was vauntin' of our safety comes danger to give me the lie!"

Chapter IV.

"——Art, stryving to compare
With nature, did an arber greene dispred,
Framed of wanton yvie flowring fayre,
Through which the fragrant eglantine did spred–"
          Spenser, *The Faerie Queene*, II.v.29.1–4.

THE Oswego, below the falls, is a more rapid, unequal stream, than it is above them. There are places where the river flows in the quiet stillness of deep water, but many shoals and rapids occur, and, at that distant day, when every thing was in its natural state, some of the passes were not altogether without hazard. Very little exertion was required on the part of those who managed the canoes, except in those places where the swiftness of the current, and the presence of the rocks required care, when, indeed, not only vigilance, but great coolness, readiness and strength of arm became necessary, in order to avoid the dangers. Of all this the Mohican was aware, and he had judiciously selected a spot, where the river flowed tranquilly, to intercept the canoes, in order to make his communication without hazard to those he wished to speak.

The Pathfinder had no sooner recognised the form of his red friend, than, with a strong sweep of his paddle he threw the head of his own canoe towards the shore, motioning for Jasper to follow. In a minute, both boats were silently drifting down the stream, within reach of the bushes that overhung the water, all observing a profound silence; some from alarm, and others from habitual caution. As the travellers drew nearer the Indian, he made a sign for them to stop, and then he and Pathfinder had a short but earnest conference, in the language of the Delawares.

"The chief is not apt to see enemies in a dead log," observed the white man, to his red associate; "why does he tell us to stop?"

"Mingos are in the woods."

"That, we have believed these two days; does the chief know it?"

The Mohican quietly held up the head of a pipe, formed of stone.

"It lay on a fresh trail that led towards the garrison"—for so it was the usage of that frontier to term a military work whether it was occupied or not.

"That may be the bowl of a pipe belonging to a soldier. Many use the red skin pipes."

"See," said the Big Serpent, again holding the thing he had found up to the view of his friend.

The bowl of the pipe was of soap stone, and it had been carved with great care, and with a very respectable degree of skill. In its centre was a small Latin cross, made with an accuracy that permitted no doubt of its meaning.

"That does foretell deviltry and wickedness," said the Pathfinder, who had all the provincial horror of the holy symbol in question, that then pervaded the country, and which became so incorporated with its prejudices, by confounding men with things, as to have left its traces strong enough on the moral feeling of the community to be discovered even at the present hour; "no Injin who had not been parvarted by the cunning priests of the Canadas would dream of carving a thing like that on his pipe! I'll warrant ye, the knave prays to the image every time he wishes to sarcumvent the innocent, and work his fearful wickednesses. It looks fresh, too, Chingachgook?"

"The tobacco was burning when I found it."

"That is close work, chief—where was the trail?"

The Mohican pointed to a spot not a hundred yards distant from that where they stood.

The matter now began to look very serious, and the two principal guides conferred apart for several minutes, when both ascended the bank, approached the indicated spot, and examined the trail with the utmost care. After this investigation had lasted a quarter of an hour, the white man returned alone, his red friend having disappeared in the forest.

The ordinary expression of the countenance of the Pathfinder was that of simplicity, integrity and sincerity, blended in an air of self reliance, that usually gave great confidence to those who found themselves under his care, but now a look of concern cast a shade over his honest face, that struck the whole party.

"What cheer, Master Pathfinder?" demanded Cap, permitting a voice that was usually deep, loud and confident to sink into the cautious tones that better suited the dangers of the wilderness; "has the enemy got between us and our port?"

"Anan?"

"Have any of these painted scaramouches anchored off the harbor towards which we are running, with the hope of cutting us off in entering?"

"It may be all as you say, friend Cap, but I am none the wiser for your words, and in ticklish times the plainer a man makes his English, the easier he is understood. I know nothing of ports and anchors, but there is a direful Mingo trail, within a hundred yards of this very spot, and as fresh as venison without salt. If one of the fiery devils has passed, so have a dozen; and what is worse, they have gone down towards the garrison, and not a soul crosses the clearing around it, that some of their piercing eyes will not discover, when sartain bullets will follow."

"Cannot this said fort, deliver a broadside, and clear every thing within the sweep of its hawse?"*

"Nay, the forts this-a-way, are not like forts in the settlements, and two, or three light cannon are all they have down at the mouth of the river; and then broadsides fired at a dozen outlying Mingos, lying behind logs and in a forest, would be powder spent in vain. We have but one course, and that is a very nice one. We are judgematically placed here, both canoes being hid by the high bank and the bushes, from all eyes except them of any lurker directly opposite. Here, then, we may stay, without much present fear; but how to get the blood thirsty devils up the stream again?—Ha—I have it—I have it—If it does no good, it can do no harm. Do you see the wide-top chestnut, here, Jasper, at the last turn in the river? On our own side of the stream, I mean."

"That near the fallen pine?"

"The very same. Take the flint and tinder box, creep along the bank and light a fire at that spot. Maybe the smoke will draw them above us. In the mean while, we will drop the canoes carefully down beyond the point below, and find another shelter. Bushes are plenty, and covers are easily to be had, in this region, as witness the many ambushments."

"I will do it, Pathfinder," said Jasper springing to the shore. "In ten minutes the fire shall be lighted."

"And, Eau douce; use plenty of damp wood, this time," half whispered the other, laughing heartily, in his own peculiar manner. "When smoke is wanted, water helps to thicken it."

The young man, who too well understood his duty to delay unnecessarily, was soon off, making his way rapidly towards the desired point. A slight attempt of Mabel to object to the risk was disregarded, and the party immediately prepared to change its position, as it could be seen from the place where Jasper intended to light his fire. The movement did not require haste, and it was made leisurely and with care. The canoes were got clear of the bushes, then suffered to drop down with the stream, until they reached the spot, where the chestnut, at the foot of which Jasper was to light the fire, was almost shut out from view, when they stopped, and every eye was turned in the direction of the adventurer.

"There goes the smoke!" exclaimed the Pathfinder, as a current of air whirled a little column of the vapor from the land, allowing it to rise spirally above the bed of the river. "A good flint, a small bit of steel, and plenty of dry leaves make a quick fire! I hope Eau douce will have the wit to bethink him of the damp wood, now, when it may sarve us all a good turn."

"Too much smoke—too much cunning," said Arrowhead, sententiously.

"That is gospel truth, Tuscarora, if the Mingos didn't know that they are near soldiers; but soldiers commonly think more of their dinners, at a halt, than of their wisdom and danger. No—no—let the boy pile on his logs, and smother them well too; it will all be laid to the stupidity of some Scotch, or Irish blunderer, who is thinking more of his oatmeal, or his potatoes, than of Injin sarcumventions, or Injin rifles."

"And, yet, I should think, from all we have heard in the towns, that the soldiers on this frontier are used to the artifices of their enemies," said Mabel, "and have got to be almost as wily as the red men, themselves."

"Not they—not they. Exper'ence makes them but little wiser, and they wheel, and platoon, and battalion it about, here, in the forest, just as they did in their parks, at home, of which they are all so fond of talking. One red skin has more cunning in his natur', than a whole rigiment from the other side of the water—that is what I call cunning of the woods. But there is smoke enough, of all conscience, and we had better drop into another cover. The lad has thrown the river on his fire, and there is danger that the Mingos will believe a whole rigiment is out."

While speaking the Pathfinder permitted his canoe to drift away from the bush by which it had been retained, and in a couple of minutes the bend in the river concealed the smoke and the tree. Fortunately, a small indentation in the shore presented itself, within a few yards of the point they had just passed, and the two canoes glided into it, under the impulsion of the paddles.

A better spot could not have been found for the purpose of the travellers, than the one they now occupied. The bushes were thick, and they overhung the water, forming a complete canopy of leaves. There was a small gravelly strand, at the bottom of the little bay, where most of the party landed to be more at their ease, and the only position from which they could possibly be seen, was a point on the river directly opposite. There was little danger, however, of discovery from that quarter, as the thicket there was even denser than common, and the land beyond it, was so wet and marshy, as to render it difficult to be trodden.

"This is a safe cover," said the Pathfinder, after he had taken a scrutinizing survey of his position; "but it may be necessary to make it safer. Master Cap, I ask nothing of you, but silence and a quieting of such gifts as you may have got at sea, while the Tuscarora and I make provision for the evil hour."

The guide then went a short distance into the bushes, accompanied by the Indian, where the two cut off the larger stems of several alders and other bushes, using the utmost care not to make a noise. The ends of these little trees, for such in fact they were, were forced into the mud, outside of the canoes, the depth of the water being very trifling, and in the course of ten minutes a very effectual screen was interposed between them and the point of principal danger. Much ingenuity and readiness were manifested in making this simple arrangement, in which the two workmen were essentially favored by the natural formation of the bank, the indentation in the shore, the shallowness of the water and the manner in which the tangled bushes dipped into the stream. The Pathfinder had the address to look for bushes that had curved stems, things easily found in such a place, and by cutting them some distance beneath the bend, and permitting the latter to touch the water, the artificial little thicket had not the appearance of growing in the stream, which might have excited suspicion, but, one passing it, would have thought, that the bushes shot out horizontally from the bank before they inclined upwards towards the light. In short, the shelter was so cunningly devised, and so artfully prepared, that none but an unusually distrustful eye, would have been turned for an instant towards the spot, in quest of a hiding place.

"This is the best cover, I ever yet got into," said the Pathfinder, with his quiet laugh, after having been on the outside to reconnoitre; "the leaves of our new trees fairly touch the bushes over our heads, and even the painter who has been in the garrison, of late, could not tell which belong to Providence and which are ourn. Hist!—yonder comes Eau douce, wading like a sensible boy, as he is, to lose his trail, in the water, and we shall soon see, whether our cover is good for any thing or not."

Jasper had, indeed, returned from his duty above, and missing the canoes, he at once inferred that they had dropped round the next bend in the river, in order to get out of sight of the fire. His habits of caution immediately suggested the expediency of stepping into the water, in order that there might exist no visible communication between the marks left by the party, on the shore, and the place where he believed them to have taken refuge below. Should the Canadian Indians return on their own trail, and discover that made by the Pathfinder and the Serpent, in their ascent from, and descent to, the river, the clue to their movements would cease at the shore, water leaving no prints of footsteps. The young man had, therefore, waded, knee-deep, as far as the point, and was now seen making his way slowly down the margin of the stream, searching curiously for the spot, in which the canoes were hid.

It was in the power of those behind the bushes, by placing their eyes near the leaves, to find many places to look through, while one at a little distance lost this advantage, or, even, did his sight happen to fall on some small opening, the bank and the shadows beyond prevented him from detecting forms and outlines of sufficient dimensions, to expose the fugitives. It was evident to those who watched his motions, from behind their cover, and they were all in the canoes, that Jasper was totally at a loss to imagine, where the Pathfinder had secreted himself. When fairly round the curvature in the shore, and out of sight of the fire he had lighted above, the young man stopped and began examining the bank deliberately, and with great care. Occasionally, he advanced eight or ten paces, and then halted again, to renew the search. The water being much shoaler than common, he stepped aside, in order to walk with greater ease to himself, and came so near the artificial plantation that he might have touched it with his hand. Still he detected nothing, and was actually passing the spot, when Pathfinder made an opening beneath the branches, and called to him, in a low voice, to enter.

"This is pretty well," said the Pathfinder, laughing; "though pale-face eyes, and red-skin eyes are as different as human spyglasses. I would wager, with the sarjeant's daughter here, a horn of powder agin a wampum belt* for her girdle, that her father's rigiment should march by this ambushment of ourn, and never find out the fraud! But, if the Mingos actilly get down into the bed of the river, where Jasper passed, I should tremble for the plantation. It will do, for their eyes, even, across the stream, howsever, and will not be without its use."

"Don't you think, Master Pathfinder, that it would be wisest, after all," said Cap, "to get under way, at once, and carry sail hard down stream, as soon as we are satisfied these rascals are fairly astern of us. We seamen call a stern chase, a long chase."

"I would'n't move from this spot, until we hear from the Sarpent, with the sarjeant's pretty da'ter, here, in our company, for all the powder in the magazine of the fort, below! Sartain captivity, or sartain death would follow. If a tender fa'n, such as the maiden we have in charge, could thread the forest like old deer, it might, indeed, do to quit the canoes, for by making a circuit, we could reach the garrison afore morning."

"Then let it be done," said Mabel, springing to her feet, under the sudden impulse of awakened energy; "I am young, active, used to exercise, and could easily out-walk my dear uncle. Let no one think me a hindrance. I cannot bear that all your lives should be exposed on my account."

"No—no—pretty one; we think you any thing but a hindrance, or any thing that is onbecoming, and would willingly run twice this risk to do you and the honest sarjeant a sarvice. Do I not speak your mind, Eau douce?"

"To do *her* a service," said Jasper, with emphasis. "Nothing shall tempt me to desert Mabel Dunham, until she is safe in her father's arms."

"Well said, lad; bravely and honestly said, too; and I join in it, heart and hand. No—no, you are not the first of your sex I have led through the wilderness, and never but once did any harm befal any of them. That was a sad day, sartainly; but its like may never come again."

Mabel looked from one of her protectors to the other, and her fine eyes swam in tears. Frankly placing a hand in that of each, she answered them, though at first her voice was choked,

"I have no right to expose you, on my account. My dear father will thank you—I thank you. God will reward you—but let there be no unnecessary risk. I can walk far, and have often gone miles, on some girlish fancy; why not now exert myself, for my life—nay, for your precious lives."

"She is a true dove, Jasper," said the Pathfinder, neither relinquishing the hand he held until the girl herself, in native modesty, saw fit to withdraw it, "and wonderfully winning! We get to be rough, and sometimes even hard hearted in the woods, Mabel, but the sight of one like you, brings us back agin to our young feelin's, and does us good for the remainder of our days. I dare say, Jasper, here, will tell you the same; for, like me in the forest, the lad sees but few such as yourself, on Ontario, to soften his heart, and remind him of love for his kind. Speak out, now, Jasper, and say if it is not so."

"I question if many like Mabel Dunham are to be found any-where," returned the young man gallantly, an honest sincerity glowing in his face, that spoke more eloquently than his tongue; "you need not mention woods and lakes, to challenge her equals, but I would go into the settlements and towns."

"We had better leave the canoes," Mabel hurriedly rejoined, "for I feel it is no longer safe to be here."

"You can never do it; you can never do it. It would be a march of more than twenty miles, and that, too, of tramping over brush and roots, and through swamps, in the dark; the trail of such a party would be wide, and we might have to fight our way into the garrison, a'ter all. We will wait for the Mohican."

Such appearing to be the decision of him to whom all, in their present strait, looked up for counsel, no more was said on the subject. The whole party now broke up into groups, Arrowhead and his wife, sitting apart under the bushes, conversing in a low tone, though the man spoke sternly and the woman answered with the subdued mildness that marks the degraded condition of a savage's wife. Pathfinder and Cap occupied one canoe, chatting of their different adventures, by sea and land, while Jasper and Mabel sat in the other, making greater progress in intimacy in a single hour than might have been effected under other circumstances, in a twelvemonth. Notwithstanding their situation, as regards the enemy, the time flew by swiftly, and the young people, in particular, were astonished when Cap informed them how long they had been thus occupied.

"If one could smoke, Master Pathfinder," observed the old sailor, "this berth would be snug enough, for, to give the devil his due, you have got the canoes handsomely landlocked, and into moorings that would defy a monsoon. The only hardship is the denial of the pipe."

"The scent of the tobacco would betray us, and where is the use of taking all these precautions against the Mingos' eyes, if we are to tell them where the cover is to be found through the nose. No—no—deny your appetites; deny your appetites, and l'arn one virtue from a red skin, who will pass a week without eating even, to get a single scalp.—Did you hear nothing, Jasper?"

"The Serpent is coming."

"Then let us see if Mohican eyes are better than them of a lad who follows the water."

The Mohican made his appearance in the same direction as that by which Jasper had rejoined his friends. Instead of coming directly on, however, no sooner did he pass the bend, where he was concealed from any who might be higher up stream, than he moved close under the bank, and, using the utmost caution, got a position where he could look back, with his person sufficiently concealed by the bushes, to prevent its being seen by any in that quarter.

"The Sarpent sees the knaves!" whispered Pathfinder—"as I'm a christian white man they have bit at the bait, and have ambushed the smoke!"

Here a hearty, but silent, laugh, interrupted his words, and nudging Cap with his elbow, they all continued to watch the movements of Chingachgook, in profound stillness. The Mohican remained stationary as the rock on which he stood, fully ten minutes, and then it was apparent that something of interest had occurred within his view, for he drew back with a hurried manner, looked anxiously and keenly along the margin of the stream, and moved quickly down it, taking care to lose his trail in the shallow water. He was evidently in a hurry and concerned, now looking behind him, and then casting eager glances towards every spot on the shore, where he thought a canoe might be concealed.

"Call him in," whispered Jasper, scarce able to restrain his impatience—"call him in, or it will be too late. See, he is actually passing us."

"Not so—not so, lad; nothing presses, depend on it—" returned his companion, "nothing presses, or the Sarpent would begin to creep. The Lord help us, and teach us wisdom! I *do* believe even Chingachgook, whose sight is as faithful as the hound's scent, overlooks us, and will not find out the ambushment we have made!"

This exultation was untimely, for the words were no sooner spoken, than the Indian, who had actually got several feet lower down the stream than the artificial cover, suddenly stopped, fastened a keen riveted glance, among the transplanted bushes, made a few hasty steps backward, and, bending his body and carefully separating the branches, he appeared among them.

"The accursed Mingos!" said Pathfinder, as soon as his friend was near enough to be addressed with prudence.

"Iroquois;" returned the sententious Indian.

"No matter—no matter—Iroquois—devil—Mingo, Mengwe, or furies—all are pretty much the same. I call all rascals, Mingos. Come hither, chief, and let us convarse rationally."

The two then stepped aside and conversed earnestly in the dialect of the Delawares. When their private communication was over, Pathfinder rejoined the rest, and made them acquainted with all he had learned.

The Mohican had followed the trail of their enemies, some distance towards the fort, until the latter caught a sight of the smoke of Jasper's fire, when they instantly retraced their steps. It now became necessary for Chingachgook, who ran the greatest risk of detection, to find a cover where he could secrete himself, until the party might pass. It was perhaps fortunate for him, that the savages were so intent on their recent discovery that they did not bestow the ordinary attention on the signs of the forest. At all events, they passed him swiftly, fifteen in number, treading lightly in each other's footsteps, and he was enabled again to get into their rear. After proceeding to the place where the footsteps of Pathfinder and the Mohican joined the principal trail, the Iroquois had struck off to the river, which they reached just as Jasper disappeared behind the bend below. The smoke being now in plain view, the savages plunged into the woods, and endeavored to approach the fire unseen. Chingachgook profited by this occasion to descend to the water, and to gain the bend in the river also, which he thought had been effected undiscovered. Here he paused, as has been stated, until he saw his enemies at the fire, where their stay, however, was very short.

Of the motives of the Iroquois the Mohican could judge only by their acts. He thought they had detected the artifice of the fire, and were aware that it had been kindled with a view to mislead them; for, after a hasty examination of the spot, they separated, some plunging again into the woods, while six or eight followed the footsteps of Jasper along the shore, and came down the stream towards the place where the canoes had landed. What course they might take on reaching that spot, was only to be conjectured, for the Serpent had felt the emergency to be too pressing to delay looking for his friends any longer. From some indications that were to be gathered from their gestures, however, he thought it probable that their enemies might follow down on the margin of the stream, but could not be certain.

As the Pathfinder related these facts to his companions, the professional feelings of the two other white men came uppermost, and both naturally reverted to their habits, in quest of the means of escape.

"Let us run out the canoes, at once," said Jasper, eagerly; "the current is strong, and by using the paddles vigorously we shall soon be beyond the reach of these scoundrels!"

"And this poor flower, that first blossomed in the clearin's; shall it wither in this forest?" objected his friend, with a poetry that he had unconsciously imbibed by his long association with the Delawares.

"We must all die first," answered the youth, a generous colour mounting to his temples; "Mabel, and Arrowhead's wife may lie down in the canoes, while we do our duty, like men, on our feet."

"Ay, you are actyve at the paddle and the oar, Eau douce, I will allow, but an accursed Mingo is more actyve, at his mischief; the canoes are swift, but a rifle bullet is swifter."

"It is the business of men, engaged by a confiding father as we have been, to run this risk—"

"But it is not their business to overlook prudence."

"Prudence! A man may carry his prudence so far as to forget his courage."

The group was standing on the narrow strand, the Pathfinder leaning on his rifle, the butt of which rested on the gravelly beach, while both his hands clasped the barrel, at the height of his own shoulders. As Jasper threw out this severe and unmerited imputation, the deep red of his comrade's face, maintained its hue unchanged, though the young man perceived that the fingers grasped the iron of the gun with the tenacity of a vice. Here all betrayal of emotion ceased.

"You are young, and hot-headed," returned Pathfinder, with a dignity that impressed his listeners with a keen sense of his moral superiority; "but my life has been passed among dangers of this sort, and my exper'ence and gifts are not to be mastered by the impatience of a boy. As for courage, Jasper, I will not send back an angry and unmeaning word, to meet an angry and an unmeaning word, for I know that you are true, in your station and according to your knowledge, but take the advice of one who faced the Mingos when you were a child, and know that their cunning is easier sarcumvented by prudence, than outwitted by foolishness."

"I ask your pardon, Pathfinder," said the repentant Jasper, eagerly grasping the hands that the other permitted him to seize. "I ask your pardon, humbly and sincerely. 'Twas a foolish, as well as wicked thing to hint of a man whose heart, in a good cause, is as firm as the rocks on the lake shore."

For the first time, the colour deepened on the cheek of the Pathfinder, and the solemn dignity that he had assumed, under a purely natural impulse, disappeared in the expression of the earnest simplicity that was inherent in all his feelings. He met the grasp of his young friend, with a squeeze as cordial, as if no chord had jarred between them, and a slight sternness that had gathered about his eye disappeared in a look of natural kindness.

"'Tis well, Jasper, 'tis well," he answered, laughing. "I bear no ill will, nor shall any one in my behalf. My natur' is that of a white man, and that is to bear no malice. It might have been ticklish work to have said half as much to the Sarpent here, though he is a Delaware, for colour will have its way—"

A touch on his shoulder caused the speaker to cease. Mabel was standing erect in the canoe, her light, but swelling form, bent forward in an attitude of graceful earnestness, her finger on her lips, her head averted, the spirited eyes riveted on an opening in the bushes, and one arm extended with a fishing-rod, the end of which had touched the Pathfinder. The latter bowed his head to a level with a look-out, near which he had intentionally kept himself, and then whispered to Jasper—

"The accursed Mingos! Stand to your arms, my men, but lay quiet as the corpses of dead trees!"

Jasper advanced rapidly, but noiselessly, to the canoe, and with a gentle violence induced Mabel to place herself in such an attitude as concealed her entire body, though it would have probably exceeded his means to induce the girl so far to lower her head that she could not keep her gaze fastened on their enemies. He then took his own post near her, with his rifle cocked and poised, in readiness to fire. Arrowhead and Chingachgook crawled to the cover, and lay in wait like snakes, with their arms prepared for service, while the wife of the former bowed her head between her knees, covered it with her calicoe robe, and remained passive and immovable. Cap loosened both his pistols, in their belt, but seemed quite at a loss what course to pursue. The Pathfinder did not stir. He had originally got a position where he might aim with deadly effect through the leaves, and whence he could watch the movements of his enemies, and he was far too steady to be disconcerted at a moment so critical.

It was truly an alarming instant. Just as Mabel touched the shoulder of her guide, three of the Iroquois appeared in the water, at the bend of the river, within a hundred yards of the cover, and halted to examine the stream below. They were all naked to the waist, armed for an expedition against their foes, and in their war paint. It was apparent, that they were undecided as to the course they ought to pursue, in order to find the fugitives. One pointed down the river, a second up the stream, and the third towards the opposite bank.

Chapter V.

"Death is here, and death is there,
Death is busy every where."
                    Shelley, "Death," ll. 1–2.

IT was a breathless moment. The only clue the fugitives possessed to the intentions of their pursuers, was in their gestures, and the indications that escaped them in the fury of disappointment. That a party had returned, already, on their own footsteps, by land, was pretty certain, and all the benefit expected from the artifice of the fire was necessarily lost. But that consideration became of little moment, just then, for the secreted were menaced with an immediate discovery, by those who had kept on a level with the river. All the facts presented themselves clearly, and as it might be by intuition, to the mind of Pathfinder, who perceived the necessity of immediate decision, and of being in readiness to act in concert. Without making any noise therefore, he managed to get the two Indians and Jasper near him, when he opened his communications in a whisper.

"We must be ready—we must be ready," he said. "There are but three of the scalping devils, and we are five, four of whom may be set down as manful warriors for such a skrimmage. Eau douce, do you take the fellow that is painted like death; Chingachgook, I give you the chief, and Arrowhead must keep his eye on the young one. There must be no mistake; for two bullets in the same body would be a sinful waste, with one like the sarjeant's daughter in danger. I shall hold myself in resarve ag'in accidents, lest a fourth riptyle appear, for one of your hands may prove unsteady. By no means fire until I give the word; we must not let the crack of the rifle be heard except in the last resort, since all the rest of the miscreants are still within its hearing. Jasper, boy, in case of any movement behind us, on the bank, I trust to you to run out the canoe, with the sarjeant's daughter, and to pull for the garrison, by God's leave."

The Pathfinder had no sooner given these directions than the near approach of their enemies, rendered profound silence necessary. The Iroquois in the river were slowly descending the stream, keeping of necessity near the bushes that overhung the water, while the rustling of leaves, and the snapping of twigs soon gave fearful evidence that another party was moving along the bank at an equally graduated pace, and directly abreast of them. In consequence of the distance between the bushes planted by the fugitives and the true shore, the two parties became visible to each other, when opposite that precise point. Both stopped, and a conversation ensued, that may be said to have passed directly over the heads of those who were concealed. Indeed nothing sheltered the travellers, but the branches and leaves of plants so pliant, that they yielded to every current of air, and which a puff of wind, a little stronger than common, would have blown away. Fortunately the line of sight, carried the eyes of the two parties of savages, whether they stood in the water, or on the land, above the bushes, and the leaves appeared blended in a way to excite no suspicion. Perhaps the very boldness of the expedient prevented an exposure. The conversation that took place, was conducted earnestly, but in guarded tones, as if those who spoke wished to defeat the intentions of any listeners. It was in a dialect that both the Indian warriors beneath, as well as the Pathfinder, understood. Even Jasper comprehended a portion of what was said.

"The trail is washed away by the water!" said one from below, who stood so near the artificial cover of the fugitives, that he might have been struck by the salmon spear that lay in the bottom of Jasper's canoe. "Water has washed it so clean, that a Yengeese hound could not follow."

"The pale faces have left the shore, in their canoes," answered the speaker on the bank.

"It cannot be. The rifles of our warriors below, are certain."

The Pathfinder gave a significant glance at Jasper, and he clenched his teeth in order to suppress the sound of his own breathing.

"Let my young men look as if their eyes were eagles'," said the eldest warrior among those who were wading in the river. "We have been a whole moon on the war-path, and have found but one scalp. There is a maiden among them, and some of our braves want wives."

Happily these words were lost on Mabel, but Jasper's frown became deeper, and his face fiercely flushed.

The savages now ceased speaking, and the party that was concealed, heard the slow and guarded movements of those who were on the bank, as they pushed the bushes aside in their wary progress. It was soon evident that the latter had passed the cover, but the group in the water still remained, scanning the shore, with eyes that glared through their war-paint, like coals of living fire. After a pause of two or three minutes, these three began, also, to descend the stream, though it was step by step, as men move who look for an object that has been lost. In this manner, they passed the artificial screen, and Pathfinder opened his mouth, in that hearty but noiseless laugh, that nature and habit had contributed to render a peculiarity of the man. His triumph, however, was premature; for the last of the retiring party, just at this moment casting a look behind him, suddenly stopped, and his fixed attitude and steady gaze, at once betrayed the appalling fact that some neglected bush had awakened his suspicions.

It was perhaps fortunate for the concealed that the warrior who manifested these fearful signs of distrust was young, and had still a reputation to acquire. He knew the importance of discretion and modesty in one of his years, and most of all did he dread the ridicule and contempt that would certainly follow a false alarm. Without recalling any of his companions, therefore, he turned on his own footsteps, and while the others continued to descend the river, he cautiously approached the bushes, on which his looks were still fastened, as by a charm. Some of the leaves, which were exposed to the sun, had drooped a little, and this slight departure from the usual natural laws, had caught the quick eyes of the Indian, for so practised and acute do the senses of the savage become, more especially when he is on the war-path, that trifles apparently of the most insignificant sort, often prove to be clues to lead him to his object.

The trifling nature of the change which had aroused the suspicion of this youth, was an additional motive for not acquainting his companions with his discovery. Should he really detect any thing, his glory would be the greater for being unshared, and should he not, he might hope to escape that derision which the young Indian so much dreads. Then there were the dangers of an ambush and a surprise, to which every warrior of the woods is ever keenly alive, to render his approach slow and cautious. In consequence of the delay that proceeded from these combined causes, the two parties had descended some fifty, or sixty yards before the young savage was again near enough to the bushes of the Pathfinder to touch them with his hand.

Notwithstanding their critical situation, the whole party behind the cover, had their eyes fastened on the working countenance of the young Iroquois, who was agitated by conflicting feelings. First came the eager hope of obtaining success where some of the most experienced of his tribe had failed, and with it a degree of glory that had seldom fallen to the share of one of his years, or a brave on his first war-path; then followed doubts, as the drooping leaves seemed to rise again, and to revive in the currents of air; and distrust of hidden danger lent its exciting feeling to keep the eloquent features in play. So very slight, however, had been the alteration produced by the heat on bushes, of which the stems were in the water, that when the Iroquois actually laid his hand on the leaves, he fancied that he had been deceived. As no man ever distrusts strongly, without using all convenient means of satisfying his doubts, however, the young warrior cautiously pushed aside the branches, and advanced a step within the hiding place, when the forms of the concealed party met his gaze, resembling so many breathing statues. The low exclamation, the slight start, and the glaring eye, were hardly seen and heard, before the arm of Chingachgook was raised, and the tomahawk of the Delaware descended on the shaven head of his foe. The Iroquois raised his hands, frantically bounded backward, and fell into the water, at a spot where the current swept the body away, the struggling limbs still tossing and writhing in the agony of death. The Delaware made a vigorous but unsuccessful attempt to seize an arm, with the hope of securing the scalp, but the blood-stained waters whirled down their current, carrying with them their quivering burthen.

All this passed in less than a minute, and the events were so sudden and unexpected, that men less accustomed to forest warfare than the Pathfinder and his associates, would have been at a loss how to act.

"There is not a moment to lose," said Jasper, tearing aside the bushes, as he spoke earnestly, but in a suppressed voice. "Do as I do, Master Cap, if you would save your niece, and you, Mabel, lie at your length in the canoe."

The words were scarcely uttered, when seizing the bow of the light bark, he dragged it along the shore, wading himself while Cap aided behind, keeping so near the bank as to avoid being seen by the savages below, and striving to gain the turn in the river above him, which would effectually conceal the party from the enemy. The Pathfinder's canoe lay nearest to the bank, and it was necessarily the last to quit the shore. The Delaware leaped on the narrow strand, and plunged into the forest, it being his assigned duty to watch the foe, in that quarter, while Arrowhead motioned to his white companion to seize the bow of the boat, and to follow Jasper. All this was the work of an instant. But when the Pathfinder reached the current, that was sweeping round the turn, he felt a sudden change in the weight he was dragging, and looking back he found that both the Tuscarora and his wife had deserted him. The thought of treachery flashed upon his mind, but there was no time to pause, for the wailing shout that arose from the party below, proclaimed that the body of the young Iroquois had floated as low as the spot reached by his friends. The report of a rifle followed, and then the guide saw that Jasper, having doubled the bend in the river, was crossing the stream, standing erect, in the stern of the canoe, while Cap was seated forward, both propelling the light boat with vigorous strokes of the paddles. A glance, a thought, and an expedient followed each other quickly, in one so trained in the vicissitudes of the frontier warfare. Springing into the stern of his own canoe, he urged it by a vigorous shove into the current, and commenced crossing the stream himself, at a point so much lower than that of his companions, as to offer his own person for a target to the enemy, well knowing that their keen desire to secure a scalp would control all other feelings.

"Keep well up the current, Jasper," shouted the gallant

guide, as he swept the water with long, steady, vigorous strokes of the paddle—"keep well up the current, and push for the alder bushes opposite. Presarve the sarjeant's daughter, before all things, and leave these Mingo knaves to the Sarpent and me."

Jasper flourished his paddle, as a signal of understanding, while shot succeeded shot in quick succession, all now being aimed at the solitary man in the nearest canoe.

"Ay, empty your rifles, like simpletons as you be," said the Pathfinder, who had acquired a habit of speaking when alone, from passing so much of his time in the solitude of the forest; "empty your rifles, with an onsteady aim, and give me time to put yard upon yard of river atween us. I will not revile you, like a Delaware, or a Mohican, for my gifts are a white man's gifts, and not an Injin's; and boasting in battle is no part of a christian warrior; but I may say, here, all alone by myself, that you are little better than so many men from the town, shooting at robins in the orchards! That was well meant—" throwing back his head, as a rifle bullet cut a lock of hair from his temple—"but the lead that misses by an inch, is as useless as the lead that never quits the barrel. Bravely done, Jasper! The Sarjeant's sweet child must be saved, even if we go in without our own scalps."

By this time the Pathfinder was in the centre of the river, and almost abreast of his enemies, while the other canoe, impelled by the vigorous arms of Cap and Jasper, had nearly gained the opposite shore, at the precise spot that had been pointed out to them. The old mariner now played his part manfully, for he was on his proper element, loved his niece sincerely, had a proper regard for his own person, and was not unused to fire, though his experience certainly lay in a very different species of warfare. A few strokes of the paddles were given, and the canoe shot into the bushes, Mabel was hurried to the land by Jasper, and, for the present, all three of the fugitives were safe.

Not so with the Pathfinder. His hardy self-devotion had brought him into a situation of unusual exposure, the hazards of which were much increased, by the fact that just as he drifted nearest to the enemy, the party on the shore rushed down the bank, and joined their friends who still stood in the water. The

Oswego was about a cable's length in width at this point, and the canoe being in the centre, the object was only a hundred yards from the rifles, that were constantly discharged at it; or, at the usual target distance for that weapon.

In this extremity the steadiness and skill of the Pathfinder did him good service. He knew that his safety depended altogether on keeping in motion, for a stationary object, at that distance, would have been hit nearly every shot. Nor was motion of itself sufficient, for accustomed to kill the bounding deer, his enemies probably knew how to vary the line of aim, so as to strike him, should he continue to move in any one direction. He was consequently compelled to change the course of the canoe, at one moment shooting down with the current, with the swiftness of an arrow, and at the next checking its progress in that direction, to glance athwart the stream. Luckily the Iroquois could not reload their pieces in the water, and the bushes that everywhere fringed the shore, rendered it difficult to keep the fugitive in view, when on the land. Aided by these circumstances, and having received the fire of all his foes, the Pathfinder was gaining fast in distance, both downwards and across the current, when a new danger suddenly, if not unexpectedly presented itself, by the appearance of the party that had been left in ambush below, with a view to watch the river.

These were the savages alluded to in the short dialogue that has been already related. They were no less than ten in number, and understanding all the advantages of their bloody occupation, they had posted themselves at a spot, where the water dashed among rocks and over shallows, in a way to form a rapid, which in the language of the country, is called a rift. The Pathfinder saw that if he entered this rift, he should be compelled to approach a point where the Iroquois had posted themselves, for the current was irresistible, and the rocks allowed no other safe passage, while death or captivity would be the probable result of the attempt. All his efforts, therefore, were turned towards reaching the western shore, the foe being all on the eastern side of the river. But the exploit surpassed human power, and to attempt to stem the stream, would at once have so far diminished the motion of the canoe, as to render aim certain. In this exigency the guide came to a decision with his usual, cool, promptitude, making his preparations accordingly. Instead of endeavouring to gain the channel, he steered towards the shallowest part of the stream, on reaching which, he seized his rifle and pack, leaped into the water, and began to wade from rock to rock, taking the direction of the western shore. The canoe whirled about in the furious current, now rolling over some slippery stone, now filling, and then emptying itself, until it lodged on the strand, within a few yards of the spot where the Iroquois had posted themselves.

In the meanwhile the Pathfinder was far from being out of danger. For the first minute, admiration of his promptitude and daring, which are high virtues in the mind of an Indian, kept his enemies motionless, but the desire of revenge, and the cravings for the much prized trophy, soon overcame this transient feeling, and aroused them from their stupor. Rifle flashed after rifle, and the bullets whistled around the head of the fugitive, amid the roar of the waters. Still he proceeded like one who bore a charmed life, for while his rude, frontier garments were more than once cut, his skin was not razed.

As the Pathfinder, in several instances, was compelled to wade in water that rose nearly to his arms, while he kept his rifle and ammunition elevated above the raging current, the toil soon fatigued him, and he was glad to stop at a large stone, or small rock, which rose so high above the river, that its upper surface was dry. On this stone he placed his powder-horn, getting behind it himself, so as to have the advantage of a partial cover for his body. The western shore was only fifty feet distant, but the quiet, swift, dark current that glanced through the interval, sufficiently showed that here he would be compelled to swim.

A short cessation in the firing now took place on the part of the Indians, who gathered about the canoe, and, having found the paddles, were preparing to cross the river.

"Pathfinder," called a voice from among the bushes, at the point nearest to the person addressed, on the western shore.

"What would you have, Jasper?"

"Be of good heart—Friends are at hand, and not a single Mingo shall cross without suffering for his boldness. Had you not better leave the rifle on the rock, and swim to us before the rascals can get afloat?"

"A true woodsman never quits his piece, while he has any powder in his horn, or a bullet in his pouch. I have not drawn a trigger this day, Eau douce, and should'n't relish the idea of parting with them riptyles, without causing them to remember my name. A little water will not harm my legs, and I see that blackguard, Arrowhead, among the scamps, and wish to send him the wages he has so faithfully earned. You have not brought the Sarjeant's daughter down here in a range with their bullets, I hope, Jasper!"

"She is safe, for the present at least, though all depends on our keeping the river between us and the enemy. They must know our weakness, now, and should they cross, no doubt some of their party will be left on the other side."

"This canoeing touches your gifts rather than mine, boy, though I will handle a paddle with the best Mingo that ever struck a salmon. If they cross below the rift, why can't we cross in the still water above, and keep playing at dodge and turn with the wolves?"

"Because, as I have said, they will leave a party on the other shore—and, then, Pathfinder, would you expose Mabel, to the rifles of the Iroquois!"

"The Sarjeant's daughter must be saved," returned the guide with calm energy. "You are right, Jasper, she has no gift to authorize her in offering her sweet face and tender body, to a Mingo rifle. What can be done then? They must be kept from crossing for an hour or two, if possible, when we must do our best in the darkness."

"I agree with you, Pathfinder, if it can be effected; but are we strong enough for such a purpose?"

"The Lord is with us, boy; the Lord is with us; and it is onreasonable to suppose that one like the Sarjeant's daughter will be altogether abandoned by Providence, in such a strait. There is not a boat between the falls and the garrison, except these two canoes, to my sartain knowledge, and I think it will go beyond red-skin gifts to cross in the face of two rifles, like these of yourn' and mine. I will not vaunt, Jasper, but it is well known on all this frontier that Killdeer seldom fails!"

"Your skill is admitted by all, far and near, Pathfinder, but a rifle takes time to be loaded; nor are you on the land, aided by a good cover, where you can work to the advantage you are used to. If you had our canoe, might you not pass to the shore, with a dry rifle?"

"Can an eagle fly, Jasper?" returned the other laughing, in his usual manner, and looking back as he spoke. "But it would be onwise to expose yourself on the water, for them miscreants are beginning to bethink them again of powder and bullets."

"It can be done without any such chances. Master Cap has gone up to the canoe, and will cast the branch of a tree into the river to try the current, which sets from the point above in the direction of your rock. See, there it comes already; if it float fairly, you must raise your arm, when the canoe will follow. At all events, if the boat should pass you, the eddy below will bring it up, and I can recover it."

While Jasper was still speaking the floating branch came in sight, and quickening its progress with the increasing velocity of the current, it swept swiftly down towards the Pathfinder, who seized it as it was passing, and held it in the air, as a sign of success. Cap understood the signal, and presently the canoe was launched into the stream, with a caution and an intelligence that the habits of the mariner fitted him to observe. It floated in the same direction as the branch, and in a minute was arrested by the Pathfinder.

"This has been done with a frontier man's judgment, Jasper," said the guide laughing; "but you have your gifts, which incline most to the water, as mine incline to the woods. Now, let them Mingo knaves cock their rifles and get rests, for this is the last chance they are likely to have at a man without a cover."

"Nay, shove the canoe towards the shore, quartering the current, and throw yourself into it, as it goes off," said Jasper eagerly; "there is little use in running any risk."

"I like to stand up face to face, with my inimies like a man, while they set me the example," returned the Pathfinder, proudly. "I am not a red skin born, and it is more a white man's gifts to fight openly, than to lie in ambushment."

"And Mabel?"

"True, boy, true—the Sarjeant's daughter must be saved; and, as you say, foolish risks only become boys. Think you, that you can catch the canoe, where you stand?"

"There can be no doubt, if you give a vigorous push."

Pathfinder made the necessary effort, the light bark shot

across the intervening space, and Jasper seized it, as it came to land. To secure the canoe, and to take proper positions in the cover, occupied the friends but a moment, when they shook hands cordially, like those who had met after a long separation.

"Now, Jasper, we shall see if a Mingo of them all dare cross the Oswego in the teeth of Killdeer. You are handier with the oar and the paddle and the sail, than with the rifle, perhaps, but you have a stout heart and a steady hand, and them are things that count, in a fight."

"Mabel will find me between her and her enemies," said Jasper, calmly.

"Yes, yes, the Sarjeant's daughter must be protected. I like you, boy, on your own account, but I like you all the better that you think of one so feeble, at a moment when there is need for all our manhood. See, Jasper; three of the knaves are actually getting into the canoe! They must believe we have fled, or they would not surely ventur' so much, directly in the very face of Killdeer!"

Sure enough, the Iroquois did appear bent on venturing across the stream, for, as the Pathfinder and his friends, now kept their persons strictly concealed, their enemies began to think that the latter had taken to flight. The course was that which most white men would have followed, but Mabel was under the care of those who were much too well skilled in forest warfare, to neglect to defend the only pass, that, in truth, now offered even a probable chance for protection.

As the Pathfinder had said, three warriors were in the canoe, two holding their rifles at a poise, kneeling in readiness to aim the deadly weapons; the other standing erect in the stern to wield the paddle. In this manner they left the shore, having had the precaution to haul the canoe, previously to entering it, so far up stream, as to get into the comparatively still water above the rift. It was apparent, at a glance, that the savage who guided the boat was skilled in the art, for the long steady sweep of his paddle sent the light bark over the glassy surface of the tranquil river, as if it were a feather floating in air.

"Shall I fire?" demanded Jasper in a whisper, trembling with eagerness to engage.

"Not yet, boy; not yet. There are but three of them, and if Master Cap, yonder, knows how to use the pop-guns he carries in his belt, we may even let them land, and then we shall recover the canoe."

"But Mabel?—"

"No fear for the Sarjeant's daughter. She is safe, in the hollow stump you say, with the opening judgematically hid by brambles. If what you tell me of the manner in which you concealed the trail be true, the sweet-one might lie there a month, and laugh at the Mingos."

"We are never certain—I wish we had brought her nearer to our own cover!"

"What for, Eau douce?—To place her pretty little head and leaping heart among flying bullets. No—no—she is better where she is, because she is safer."

"We are never certain—we thought ourselves safe, behind the bushes, and yet you saw that we were discovered."

"And the Mingo imp paid for his cur'osity, as them knaves are about to do—"

At that instant, the sharp report of a rifle was heard, when the Indian in the stern of the canoe leaped high into the air, and fell into the water holding the paddle in his hand. A small wreath of smoke floated out from among the bushes of the eastern shore, and was soon absorbed by the atmosphere.

"That is the Sarpent hissing!" exclaimed the Pathfinder, exultingly. "A bolder or a truer heart never beat in the breast of a Delaware. I am sorry that he interfered, but he could not have known our condition—he could not have known our condition."

The canoe no sooner lost its guide, than it floated with the stream, and was soon sucked into the rapids of the rift. Perfectly helpless, the two remaining savages gazed wildly about them, but could offer no resistance to the power of the element. It was perhaps fortunate for Chingachgook that the attention of most of the Iroquois was intently given to the situation of those in the boat, else would his escape have been to the last degree difficult, if not totally impracticable. But not a foe moved, except to conceal his person behind some cover, and every eye was riveted on the two remaining adventurers. In less time than has been necessary to record these occurrences, the canoe was whirling and tossing in the rift, while both the savages had stretched themselves in its bottom, as the only means of preserving the equilibrium. This natural expedient soon failed them, for striking a rock the light craft rolled over, and the two warriors were thrown into the river. The water is seldom deep on a rift, except in particular places where it may have worn channels, and there was little to be apprehended from drowning, though their arms were lost, and the two savages were fain to make the best of their way to the friendly shore, swimming and wading as circumstances required. The canoe itself lodged on a rock, in the centre of the stream, where, for the moment, it became useless to both parties.

"Now is our time, Pathfinder," cried Jasper, as the two Iroquois exposed most of their persons, while wading in the shallowest part of the rapids—"The fellow up stream is mine, and you can take the lower."

So excited had the young man become, by all the incidents of the stirring scene, that the bullet sped from his rifle as he spoke, but uselessly as it would seem, for both the fugitives tossed their arms in disdain. The Pathfinder did not fire.

"No—no—Eau douce," he answered—"I do not seek blood without a cause, and my bullet is well leathered and carefully driven down, for the time of need. I love no Mingo, as is just, seeing how much I have consorted with the Delawares, who are their mortal and nat'ral inimies, but I pull no trigger on one of the miscreants, unless it be plain that his death will lead to some good ind. The deer never leaped, that fell by my hand wantonly. By living much alone with God in the wilderness, a man gets to feel the justice of such opinions. One life is sufficient for our present wants, and there may yet be occasion to use Killdeer in behalf of the Sarpent, who has done an untimorsome thing to let them rampant devils so plainly know that he is in their neighborhood. As I'm a wicked sinner, there is one of them prowling along the bank, this very moment, like one of the boys of the garrison skulking behind a fallen tree to get a shot at a squirrel!"

As the Pathfinder pointed with his finger, while speaking, the quick eye of Jasper soon caught the object towards which it was directed. One of the young warriors of the enemy, burning with a desire to distinguish himself, had stolen from his party towards the cover in which Chingachgook had concealed himself, and as the latter was deceived by the apparent apathy of his foes, as well as engaged in some further preparations of his own, he had evidently obtained a position where he got a sight of the Delaware. This circumstance was apparent by the arrangements the Iroquois was making to fire, for Chingachgook himself was not visible from the western side of the river. The rift was at a bend in the Oswego, and, the sweep of the eastern shore formed a curve so wide that Chingachgook was quite near to his enemies in a straight direction, though separated by several hundred feet on the land, owing to which fact, air lines brought both parties nearly equidistant from the Pathfinder and Jasper. The general width of the river being a little less than two hundred yards, such necessarily was about the distance between his two observers and the skulking Iroquois.

"The Sarpent must be thereabouts," observed Pathfinder, who never turned his eye for an instant from the young warrior, "and yet he must be strangely off his guard to allow a Mingo devil to get his stand so near, with manifest signs of bloodshed in his heart."

"See," interrupted Jasper—"there is the body of the Indian, the Delaware shot! It has drifted on a rock, and the current has forced the head and face above the water."

"Quite likely, boy; quite likely. Human natur' is little better than a log of drift wood, when the life that was breathed into its nostrils has departed. That Iroquois will never harm any one more, but yonder skulking savage is bent on taking the scalp of my best and most tried friend——"

The Pathfinder suddenly interrupted himself, by raising his rifle, a weapon of unusual length, with admirable precision, and firing the instant it had got its level. The Iroquois, on the opposite shore, was in the act of aiming when the fatal messenger from Killdeer arrived. His rifle was discharged it is true, but it was with the muzzle in the air, while the man himself plunged into the bushes, quite evidently hurt, if not slain.

"The skulking reptyle brought it on himself," muttered Pathfinder, sternly, as dropping the breech of his rifle, he carefully commenced re-loading it. "Chingachgook and I have consorted togither since we were boys, and have fou't in company, on the Horican,* the Mohawk, the Ontario, and all the other bloody passes between the country of the Frenchers and our own; and did the foolish knave believe that I would stand by and see my best friend cut off in an ambushment!"

"We have served the Serpent as good a turn, as he served us. Those rascals are troubled, Pathfinder, and are falling back into their covers, since they find we can reach them across the river!"

"The shot is no great matter, Jasper; no great matter. Ask any of the 60th, and they can tell you, what Killdeer can do, and has done, and that too when the bullets were flying about our heads like hail-stones. No—no—this is no great matter, and the onthoughtful vagabond drew it down on himself."

"Is that a dog or a deer, swimming towards this shore?"

Pathfinder started, for, sure enough, an object was crossing the stream, above the rift, towards which, however, it was gradually setting by the force of the current. A second look satisfied both the observers that it was a man and an Indian, though so concealed as, at first, to render it doubtful. Some stratagem was apprehended, and the closest attention was given to the movements of the stranger.

"He is pushing something before him, as he swims, and his head resembles a drifting bush!" said Jasper.

"'Tis Injin deviltry, boy; but christian honesty shall sarcumvent their arts."

As the man slowly approached, the observers began to doubt the accuracy of their first impressions, and it was only when two thirds of the stream was passed, that the truth was really known.

"The Big Sarpent, as I live!" exclaimed Pathfinder, looking at his companion, and laughing until the tears came into his eyes, with pure delight at the success of the artifice. "He has tied bushes to his head, so as to hide it, put the horn on top, lashed the rifle to that bit of log he is pushing afore him, and has come over to join his friends. Ah's! me. The times, and times, that he and I have cut such pranks, right in the teeth of Mingos raging for our blood, in the great thoroughfare round and about Ty!"

"It may not be the Serpent, after all, Pathfinder—I can see no feature that I remember."

"Featur'! Who looks for featur's in an Injin?—No—no—boy; 'tis the paint that speaks, and none but a Delaware would wear that paint. Them are his colours, Jasper, just as your craft on the lake wears St. George's Cross, and the Frenchers set their table cloths to fluttering in the wind, with all the stains of fish bones and venison steaks upon them. Now, you see the eye, lad, and it is the eye of a chief. But, Eau douce, fierce as it is, in battle, and glaring as it looks from among the leaves—" here the Pathfinder laid his finger lightly but impressively on his companion's arm—"I have seen it shed tears like rain. There is a soul and a heart, under that red skin, rely on it, although they are a soul and a heart with gifts different from our own."

"No one, who is acquainted with the chief, ever doubted that."

"I *know* it," returned the other proudly, "for I have consorted with him in sorrow and in joy; in one I have found him a man, however stricken; in the other a chief who knows that the women of his tribe are the most seemly in light merriment. But, hist! It is too much like the people of the settlements to pour soft speeches into another's ear, and the Sarpent has keen senses. He knows I love him, and that I speak well of him behind his back, but a Delaware has modesty in his inmost natur', though he will brag like a sinner when tied to a stake."

The Serpent now reached the shore, directly in the front of his two comrades, with whose precise position he must have been acquainted before leaving the eastern side of the river, and rising from the water he shook himself like a dog, and made the usual exclamation—

"Hugh!"

Chapter VI.

"These, as they change, Almighty Father, these
Are but the varied God."
Thomson, "A Hymn on the Seasons," ll. 1–2.

As the Chief landed he was met by the Pathfinder, who addressed him in the language of the warrior's people.

"Was it well done, Chingachgook," he said reproachfully, "to ambush a dozen Mingos, alone! Killdeer seldom fails me, it is true, but the Oswego makes a distant mark, and that miscreant showed little more than his head and shoulders above the bushes, and an onpractysed hand and eye might have failed. You should have thought of this, chief; you should have thought of this!"

"The Great Serpent is a Mohican warrior—he sees only his enemies, when he is on the war-path, and his fathers have struck the Mingos from behind, since the waters began to run!"

"I know your gifts—I know your gifts, and respect them, too. No man shall hear me complain that a red skin obsarved red skin natur', but prudence as much becomes a warriour as valour; and had not the Iroquois devils been looking after their friends who were in the water, a hot trail they would have made of yourn!"

"What is the Delaware about to do?" exclaimed Jasper, who observed, at that moment, that the chief suddenly left the Pathfinder, and advanced to the water's edge, apparently with an intention of again entering the river. "He will not be so mad as to return to the other shore, for any trifle he may have forgotten!"

"Not he—not he; he is as prudent as he is brave, in the main, though so forgetful of himself in the late ambushment. Harkee, Jasper," leading the other a little aside, just as they heard the Indian's plunge into the water—"Harkee, lad; Chingachgook is not a christian white man like ourselves, but a Mohican chief, who has his gifts and traditions to tell him what he ought to do; and he who consorts with them that are not strictly and altogether of his own kind, had better leave natur' and use to govern his comrades. A king's soldier will swear, and he will drink, and it is of little use to try to prevent him; a gentleman likes his delicacies, and a lady her feathers, and it does not avail much to struggle ag'in either; whereas an Indian's natur' and gifts are much stronger than these, and no doubt were bestowed by the Lord for wise inds, though neither you, nor me, can follow them in all their windings."

"What does this mean?—See, the Delaware is swimming towards the body that is lodged on the rock. Why does he risk this?"

"For honor, and glory, and renown, as great gentlemen quit their quiet homes, beyond seas, where as they tell me, heart has nothing left to wish for, that is such hearts as can be satisfied in a clearin', to come hither to live on game and fight the Frenchers."

"I understand you—your friend has gone to secure the scalp."

"'Tis his gift, and let him enjoy it. We are white men, and cannot mangle a dead enemy, but it is honor in the eyes of a red skin to do so. It may seem singular to you, Eau douce, but I've known white men of great name and character manifest as remarkable idees consarning their honor, I have."

"A savage will be a savage, Pathfinder, let him keep what company he may."

"It is well for us to say so, lad, but, as I tell you, white honor will not always conform to reason, or to the will of God. I have passed days thinking of them matters, out in the silent woods, and I have come to the opinion, boy, that, as Providence rules all things, no gift is bestowed without some wise and reasonable ind. If Injins are of no use, Injins would not have been created, and I do suppose, could one dive to the bottom of things, it would be found that even the Mingo tribes were produced for some rational and proper purpose, though I confess it surpasses my means to say what it is."

"The Serpent greatly exposes himself to the enemy, in order to get his scalp!—This may lose us the day."

"Not in his mind, Jasper. That one scalp has more honor in it, according to the Sarpent's notions of warfare, than a field covered with slain, that kept the hair on their heads. Now, there was the fine young captain of the 6oth that threw away his life, in trying to bring off a three-pounder from among the Frenchers, in the last skrimmage we had; he thought he was sarving honor; and I have known a young ensign wrap himself up in his colours, and go to sleep in his blood, fancying that he was lying on something softer even than buffaloe skins!"

"Yes, yes; one can understand the merit of not hauling down an ensign–."

"And these are Chingachgook's colours–he will keep them to show his children's children–" here the Pathfinder interrupted himself, shook his head in melancholy, and slowly added– "Ah's! me! no shoot of the old Mohican stem remains! He has no children to delight with his trophies; no tribe to honor by his deeds; he is a lone man in this world, and yet he stands true to his training and his gifts! There is something honest and respectable in that, you must allow, Jasper; yes, there is something decent in that."

Here a great outcry from among the Iroquois, was succeeded by the quick reports of their rifles, and so eager did the enemy become, in the desire to drive the Delaware back from his victim, that a dozen rushed into the river, several of whom even advanced near a hundred feet into the foaming current, as if they actually meditated a serious sortie. But Chingachgook continued as unmoved, as he remained unhurt by the missiles, accomplishing his task with the dexterity of long habit. Flourishing his reeking trophy, he gave the war-whoop in its most frightful intonations, and for a minute the arches of the silent woods, and the deep vista formed by the course of the river, echoed with cries so terrific that Mabel bowed her head, in irrepressible fear, while her uncle, for a single instant, actually meditated flight.

"This surpasses all I have heard from the wretches," Jasper exclaimed, stopping his ears, equally in horror and disgust.

"'Tis their music, boy; their drum and fife; their trumpets and clarions. No doubt they love them sounds, for they stir up in them, fierce feelings, and a desire for blood," returned the Pathfinder, totally unmoved. "I thought them rather frightful when a mere youngster, but they have got to be like the whistle of the whip-poor-will, or the song of the cat-bird in my ear,

now. All the screeching riptyles that could stand atween the
Falls and the garrison, would have no effect on my narves, at
this time of day. I say it not in boasting, Jasper, for the man that
lets in cowardice through the ears, must have but a weak heart,
at the best; sounds and outcries being more intended to alarm
women and children, than such as scout the forest, and face the
foe. I hope the Sarpent is now satisfied, for here he comes with
the scalp at his belt."

Jasper turned away his head as the Delaware rose from the
water, in pure disgust at his late errand, but the Pathfinder regarded his friend with the philosophical coolness of one who
had made up his mind to be indifferent to things he deemed
immaterial. As the Delaware passed deeper into the bushes,
with a view to wring his trifling calicoe dress, and to prepare his
rifle for service, he gave one glance of triumph at his companions, and then all emotion connected with the recent exploit
seemed to cease.

"Jasper," resumed the guide—"step down to the station of
Master Cap, and ask him to join us. We have little time for a
council, and yet our plans must be laid quickly, for it will not be
long before them Mingos will be plotting our ruin."

The young man complied, and in a few minutes, the four
were assembled near the shore, completely concealed from the
view of their enemies, while they kept a vigilant watch over the
proceedings of the latter, in order to consult on their own future movements. By this time, the day had so far advanced, as
to leave but a few minutes between the passing light, and an
obscurity that promised to be even deeper than common. The
sun had already set, and the twilight of a low latitude would
soon pass into the darkness of deep night. Most of the hopes of
the party rested on this favorable circumstance, though it was
not without its dangers, also, as the very obscurity which would
favor their escape would be as likely to conceal the movements
of their wily enemies.

"The moment has come, men," Pathfinder commenced,
"when our plans must be coolly laid, in order that we may act
together, and with a right understanding of our errand and
gifts. In an hour's time, these woods will be as dark as midnight,
and if we are ever to gain the garrison, it must be done under
favor of this advantage. What say you, Master Cap; for though

none of the most exper'enced in combats and retreats in the woods, your years entitle you to speak first, in a matter like this, and in a council."

"And my near relationship to Mabel, Pathfinder, ought to count for something—"

"I do'n't know that—I do'n't know that. Regard is regard, and liking, liking, whether it be a gift of natur', or come from one's own judgment and inclinations. I will say nothing for the Sarpent, who is past placing his mind on the women, but as for Jasper and myself, we are as ready to stand atween the Sarjeant's daughter and the Mingos, as her own brave father, himself, could be. Do I say more than the truth, lad?"

"Mabel may count on me, to the last drop of my blood," said Jasper, speaking low, but with intense feeling.

"Well, well," rejoined the uncle, "we will not discuss this matter, as all seem willing to serve the girl, and deeds are better than words. In my judgment, all we have to do, is to go on board the canoe, when it gets to be so dark the enemy's look-outs ca'n't see us, and run for the haven, as wind and tide will allow."

"That is easily said, but not so easily done," returned the guide. "We shall be more exposed in the river than by following the woods, and then there is the Oswego rift below us, and I am far from sartain that Jasper, himself, can carry a boat safely through it, in the dark. What say you, lad, as to your own skill and judgment?"

"I am of Master Cap's opinion about using the canoe. Mabel is too tender to walk through swamps, and among roots of trees, on such a night as this promises to be, and then I always feel myself stouter of heart, and truer of eye, when afloat, than when ashore."

"Stout of heart, you always be, lad, and I think tolerably true of eye, for one who has lived so much in broad sunshine, and so little in the woods. Ah's! me, the Ontario has no trees, or it would be a plain to delight a hunter's heart! As to your opinion, friends, there is much for, and much ag'inst it. For it, it may be said water leaves no trail—"

"What do you call the wake?" interrupted the pertinacious and dogmatical Cap.

"Anan!"

"Go on," said Jasper. "Master Cap thinks he is on the Ocean—Water leaves no trail—"

"It leaves none, Eau douce, hereaway, though I do not pretend to say what it may leave on the sea. Then a canoe is both swift and easy, when it floats with the current, and the tender limbs of the Sarjeant's daughter will be favored by its motion. But, on the other hand, the river will have no cover but the clouds in the heavens, the rift is a ticklish spot for a bark to venture into even by day-light, and it is six fairly measured miles by water, from this spot to the garrison. Then a trail on land, is not easy to be found in the dark. I am troubled, Jasper, to say which way we ought to counsel and advise."

"If the Serpent and myself could swim into the river, and bring off the other canoe," the young sailor replied, "it would seem to me, that our safest course would be the water."

"If, indeed! and yet it might easily be done, as soon as it is a little darker. Well, well, considering the Sarjeant's daughter, and her gifts, I am not sartain it will not be the best. Though were we only a party of men, it would be like a hunt to the lusty and brave, to play at hide and seek with yonder miscreants, on the other shore. Jasper," continued the guide, into whose character there entered no ingredient that belonged to vain display, or theatrical effect, "will you undertake to bring in the canoe?"

"I will undertake any thing that will serve and protect Mabel, Pathfinder."

"That is an upright feeling, and I suppose it is natur'. The Sarpent, who is nearly naked already, can help you, and that will be cutting off, one of the means of them devils, to work their harm."

This material point being settled, the different members of the party, prepared themselves to put the project into execution. The shades of evening fell fast upon the forest, and by the time all was ready for the attempt, it was found impossible to discern objects on the opposite shore. Time now pressed, for Indian cunning could devise so many expedients for passing so narrow a stream, that the Pathfinder was getting impatient to quit the spot. While Jasper and his companion entered the river, armed with nothing but their knives and the Delaware's tomahawk, observing the greatest caution not to betray their movements, the guide brought Mabel from her place of concealment, and bidding her and Cap proceed along the shore to the foot of the rapids, he got into the canoe that remained in his possession, in order to carry it to the same place.

This was easily effected. The canoe was laid against the bank, and Mabel and her uncle entered it, taking their seats as usual, while the Pathfinder, erect in the stern, held by a bush, in order to prevent the swift stream from sweeping them down its current. Several minutes of intense and breathless expectation followed, while they awaited the result of the bold attempt of their comrades.

It will be understood that the two adventurers were compelled to swim, across a deep and rapid channel, ere they could reach a part of the rift that admitted of wading. This portion of the enterprize was soon effected, and Jasper and the Serpent struck the bottom, side by side, at the same instant. Having secured firm footing, they took hold of each other's hands, and waded slowly and with extreme caution, in the supposed direction of the canoe. But the darkness was already so deep, that they soon ascertained they were to be but little aided by the sense of sight, and that their search must be conducted on that species of instinct which enables the woodsman to find his way, when the sun is hid, no stars appear, and all would seem chaos to one less accustomed to the mazes of the forest. Under these circumstances Jasper submitted to be guided by the Delaware, whose habits best fitted him to take the lead. Still it was no easy matter to wade amid the roaring element, at that hour, and retain a clear recollection of the localities. By the time they believed themselves to be in the centre of the stream, the two shores were discernible merely by masses of obscurity denser than common, the outlines against the clouds being barely distinguishable by the ragged tops of the trees. Once or twice the wanderers altered their course in consequence of unexpectedly stepping into deep water, for they knew that the boat had lodged on the shallowest part of the rift. In short, with this fact for their compass, Jasper and his companion wandered about in the water, for near a quarter of an hour, and at the end of that period, which began to appear interminable to the young man, they found themselves apparently no nearer the object of their search than they had been at its commencement. Just as the Delaware was about to stop, in order to inform his associate that they woiuld do well to return to the land, in order to take a fresh departure, he saw the form of a man, moving about in the water, almost within reach of his arm. Jasper was at his side, and he at once understood that the Iroquois were engaged in the same errand as he was himself.

"Mingo!" he uttered in Jasper's ear—"The Serpent will show his brother how to be cunning."

The young sailor caught a glimpse of the figure, at that instant, and the startling truth also flashed on his mind. Understanding the necessity of trusting all to the Delaware chief, he kept back, while his friend moved cautiously in the direction in which the strange form had vanished. In another moment, it was seen again evidently moving towards themselves. The waters made such an uproar, that little was to be apprehended from ordinary sounds, and the Indian, turning his head, hastily said—

"Leave it to the cunning of the Great Serpent."

"Hugh!" exclaimed the strange savage, adding in the language of his people—"The canoe is found, but there were none to help me. Come; let us raise it from the rock."

"Willingly," answered Chingachgook, who understood the dialect—"Lead; we will follow."

The stranger, unable to distinguish between voices and accents, amid the raging of the rapid, led the way in the necessary direction, and, the two others keeping close at his heels, all three speedily reached the canoe. The Iroquois laid hold of one end, Chingachgook placed himself in the centre, and Jasper went to the opposite extremity, as it was important that the stranger should not detect the presence of a pale-face, a discovery that might be made, by the parts of the dress the young man still wore, as well as by the general appearance of his head.

"Lift—" said the Iroquois in the sententious manner of his race; and by a trifling effort, the canoe was raised from the rock, held a moment in the air to empty it, and then placed carefully on the water, in its proper position. All three held it firmly, lest it should escape from their hands, under the pressure of the violent current, while the Iroquois who led of course, being at the upper end of the boat, took the direction of the eastern shore, or towards the spot where his friends waited his return.

As the Delaware and Jasper well knew there must be several more of the Iroquois on the rift, from the circumstance that their own appearance had occasioned no surprise in the individual they had met, both felt the necessity of extreme caution. Men less bold and determined would have thought that they were incurring too great a risk, by thus venturing into the midst of their enemies, but these hardy borderers were unacquainted with fear, were accustomed to hazards, and so well understood the necessity of at least preventing their foes from getting the boat, that they would have cheerfully encountered even greater risks to secure their object. So all-important to the safety of Mabel, indeed, did Jasper deem the possession, or the destruction of this canoe, that he had drawn his knife and stood ready to rip up the bark, in order to render the boat temporarily unserviceable, should any thing occur to compel the Delaware and himself to abandon their prize.

In the mean time, the Iroquois who led the way proceeded slowly, through the water, in the direction of his own party, still grasping the canoe, and dragging his reluctant followers in his train. Once, Chingachgook raised his tomahawk, and was about to bury it in the brain of his confiding and unsuspicious neighbor, but the probability that the death-cry, or the floating body might give the alarm, induced that wary chief to change his purpose. At the next moment, he regretted this indecision, for the three who clung to the canoe, suddenly found themselves in the centre of a party of no less than four others who were in quest of it.

After the usual, brief, characteristic, exclamations of satisfaction, the savages eagerly laid hold of the canoe, for all seemed impressed with the necessity of securing this important boat, the one side in order to assail their foes, and the other to secure their retreat. The addition to the party, however, was so unlooked for, and so completely gave the enemy the superiority, that, for a few moments, the ingenuity and address of even the Delaware were at fault. The five Iroquois, who seemed perfectly to understand their errand, pressed forward towards their own shore, without pausing to converse, their object being

in truth to obtain the paddles, which they had previously secured, and to embark three or four warriors, with all the rifles
and powder-horns, the want of which had alone prevented
their crossing the river, by swimming, as soon as it was dark.

In this manner, the body of friends and foes united reached
the margin of the eastern channel, where, as in the case of the
western, the river was too deep to be waded. Here a short pause
succeeded, it being necessary to determine the manner in which
the canoe was to be carried across. One of the four who had just
reached the boat, was a chief, and the habitual deference which
the American Indian pays to merit, experience and station,
kept the others silent, until this individual had spoken.

The halt greatly added to the danger of discovering the presence of Jasper, in particular, who however had the precaution
to throw the cap he wore, into the bottom of the canoe. Being
without his jacket and shirt, the outline of his figure, in the
obscurity, would now be less likely to attract observation. His
position, too, at the stern of the canoe, a little favored his concealment, the Iroquois naturally keeping their looks directed
the other way. Not so, with Chingachgook. This warrior was
literally in the midst of his most deadly foes, and he could
scarcely stir without touching one of them. Yet he was apparently unmoved, though he kept all his senses on the alert, in
readiness to escape, or to strike a blow, at the proper moment.
By carefully abstaining from looking towards those behind him,
he lessened the chances of discovery, and waited with the indomitable patience of an Indian for the instant when he should
be required to act.

"Let all my young men, but two, one at each end of the canoe,
cross and get their arms," said the Iroquois chief−, "let the two
push over the boat."

The Indians quietly obeyed, leaving Jasper at the stern, and
the Iroquois who had found the canoe, at the bows of the light
craft, Chingachgook burying himself so deep in the river, as to
be passed by the others without detection. The splashing in the
water, the tossing arms and the calls of one to another, soon
announced that the four who had last joined the party, were
already swimming. As soon as this fact was certain, the Delaware rose, resumed his former station, and began to think the
moment for action was come.

One less habitually under self-restraint, than this warrior, would probably have now aimed his meditated blow, but Chingachgook knew there were more Iroquois behind him on the rift, and he was a warrior much too trained and experienced to risk any thing unnecessarily. He suffered the Indian at the bow of the canoe to push off into the deep water, and then all three were swimming in the direction of the eastern shore. Instead, however, of helping the canoe across the swift current, no sooner did the Delaware and Jasper find themselves within the influence of its greatest force, than both began to swim in a way to check their further progress across the stream. Nor was this done suddenly, or in the incautious manner in which a civilized man would have been apt to attempt the artifice, but warily, and so gradually that the Iroquois at the bow, fancied at first he was merely struggling against the strength of the current. Of course, while acted on by these opposing efforts, the canoe drifted down stream, and in about a minute it was floating in still deeper water at the foot of the rift. Here, however, the Iroquois was not slow in finding that something unusual retarded their advance, and looking back he first learned that he was resisted by the efforts of his companions.

That second nature, which grows up through habit, instantly told the young Iroquois that he was alone with enemies. Dashing the water aside, he sprang at the throat of Chingachgook, and the two Indians relinquishing their hold of the canoe, seized each other, like tigers. In the midst of the darkness of that gloomy night, and floating in an element so dangerous to man, when engaged in deadly strife, they appeared to forget every thing but their fell animosity, and their mutual desire to conquer.

Jasper had now complete command of the canoe, which flew off, like a feather impelled by the breath, under the violent reaction of the struggles of the two combatants. The first impulse of the youth was to swim to the aid of the Delaware, but the importance of securing the boat presented itself with ten fold force, while he listened to the heavy breathings of the warriors as they throttled each other, and he proceeded as fast as possible towards the western shore. This he soon reached, and, after a short search, he succeeded in discovering the remainder of the party, and in procuring his clothes. A few words sufficed to explain the situation in which he had left the Delaware, and the manner in which the canoe had been obtained.

When those who had been left behind had heard the explanations of Jasper, a profound stillness reigned among them, each listening intently, in the vain hope of catching some clue to the result of the fearful struggle that had just taken place, if it were not still going on in the water. Nothing was audible, beyond the steady roar of the rushing river, it being a part of the policy of their enemies on the opposite shore, to observe the most death-like stillness.

"Take this paddle, Jasper," said Pathfinder, calmly, though the listeners thought his voice sounded more melancholy than usual; "and follow with your own canoe. It is unsafe for us to remain here longer."

"But the Serpent?"

"The Great Sarpent is in the hands of his own Deity, and will live, or die, according to the intentions of Providence. We can do him no good, and may risk too much by remaining here, in idleness, like women talking over their distresses. This darkness is very precious—"

A loud, long, piercing yell arose from the other shore, and cut short the words of the guide.

"What is the meaning of that uproar, Master Pathfinder?—" demanded Cap. "It sounds more like the outcries of devils, than any thing that can come from the throats of christians and men."

"Christians they are not, and do not pretend to be, and do not wish to be, and in calling them devils, you have scarcely misnamed them. That yell is one of rejoicing, and it is, as conquerors they have given it. The body of the Sarpent, no doubt, dead or alive, is in their power!"

"And we!—" exclaimed Jasper, who felt a pang of generous regret, as the idea that he might have averted the calamity presented itself to his mind, had he not deserted his comrade.

"We can do the chief no good, lad, and must quit this spot as fast as possible."

"Without one attempt to rescue him!—Without even knowing whether he be dead or living."

"Jasper is right—" said Mabel, who could speak, though her

voice sounded husky and smothered. "I have no fears, uncle, and will stay here until we know what has become of our friend."

"This seems reasonable, Pathfinder," put in Cap. "Your true seaman cannot well desert a messmate, and I am glad to find that notions so correct exist among these fresh-water people."

"Tut–tut–" returned the impatient guide, forcing the canoe into the stream as he spoke, "ye know nothing, and ye fear nothing. If ye value your lives, think of reaching the garrison, and leave the Delaware in the hands of Providence. Ah's! me. The deer that goes too often to the lick meets the hunter at last!"

Chapter VII.

"And is this—Yarrow?—this the stream
Of which my fancy cherished,
So faithfully a waking dream?
An image that hath perished?
O that some minstrel's harp were near,
To utter notes of gladness,
And chase this silence from the air,
That fills my heart with sadness."

                    Wordsworth, "Yarrow Visited," ll. 1–8.

THE scene was not without its sublimity, and the ardent, generous-minded Mabel felt her blood thrill in her veins, and her cheeks flush, as the canoe shot into the strength of the stream to quit the spot. The darkness of the night had lessened, by the dispersion of the clouds, but the overhanging woods rendered the shores so obscure, that the boats floated down the current in a belt of gloom that effectually secured them from detection. Still, there was necessarily a strong feeling of insecurity in all on board them, and even Jasper, who by this time began to tremble in behalf of the girl, at every unusual sound that arose from the forest, kept casting uneasy glances around him, as he drifted on, in company. The paddle was used lightly, and only with exceeding care, for the slightest sound in the breathing stillness of that hour and place, might apprise the watchful ears of the Iroquois of their position.

All these accessaries added to the impressive grandeur of her situation, and contributed to render the moment much the most exciting that had ever occurred in the brief existence of Mabel Dunham. Spirited, accustomed to self-reliance, and sustained by the pride of considering herself a soldier's daughter, she could hardly be said to be under the influence of fear, yet her heart often beat quicker than common, her fine blue eye lighted with an exhibition of resolution that was wasted in the darkness, and her quickened feelings came in aid of the real sublimity that belonged to the scene, and to the incidents of the night.

"Mabel!" said the suppressed voice of Jasper, as the two canoes floated so near each other that the hand of the young man held them together, "you have no dread. You trust freely to our care, and willingness to protect you?"

"I am a soldier's daughter, as you know, Jasper Western, and ought to be ashamed to confess fear."

"Rely on me—on us all. Your uncle, Pathfinder, the Delaware, were the poor fellow here, I myself, will risk every thing rather than harm should reach you."

"I believe you, Jasper," returned the girl, her hand unconsciously playing in the water. "I know that my uncle loves me, and will never think of himself until he has first thought of me; and I believe you are all my father's friends and would willingly assist his child. But I am not so feeble and weak-minded as you may think, for though only a girl from the towns, and like most of that class, a little disposed to see danger where there is none, I promise you, Jasper, no foolish fears of mine shall stand in the way of your doing your duty."

"The Sarjeant's daughter is right, and she is worthy of being honest Thomas Dunham's child," put in the Pathfinder. "Ah's! me! pretty one, many is the time that your father and I, have scouted and marched together on the flanks and rear of the inimy, in nights darker than this, and that too, when we did not know, but the next moment would lead us into a bloody ambushment. I was at his side, when he got the wound in his shoulder, and the honest fellow will tell you, when you meet, the manner in which we contrived to cross the river that lay in our rear, in order to save his scalp."

"He *has* told me," said Mabel, with more energy perhaps than her situation rendered prudent. "I have his letters, in which he has mentioned all that, and, I thank you from the bottom of my heart, for the service. God will remember it, Pathfinder, and there is no gratitude that you can ask of the daughter, which she will not cheerfully pay for her father's life."

"Ay, that is the way, with all you gentle and pure hearted creatur's! I have seen some of you afore, and have heard of others! The Sarjeant, himself, has talked to me of his own young days; and of your mother; and of the manner in which he courted her, and of all the crossings and disapp'intments, until he succeeded at last."

"My mother did not live long to repay him for what he did to win her," said Mabel with a trembling lip.

"So he tells me. The honest Sarjeant has kept nothing back, for being so many years my senior, he has looked on me, in our many scoutings together, as a sort of son."

"Perhaps, Pathfinder," observed Jasper, with a huskiness in his voice that defeated the attempt at pleasantry, "he would be glad to have you for one, in reality."

"And if he did, Eau douce, where would be the sin of it? He knows what I am on a trail, or a scout, and he has seen me often, face to face, with the Frenchers. I have sometimes thought, lad, that we all ought to seek for wives, for the man that lives altogether in the woods, and in company with his in-imies, or his prey, gets to lose some of the feelin' of kind, in the ind."

"From the specimens I have seen," observed Mabel, "I should say that they who live much in the forest, forget to learn many of the deceits and vices of the towns."

"It is not easy, Mabel, to dwell always in the presence of God, and not feel the power of his goodness. I have attended church-sarvice in the garrisons, and tried hard, as becomes a true soldier, to join in the prayers; for though no enlisted sar-vant of the King, I fight his battles and sarve his cause, and so I have endivoured to worship garrison-fashion, but never could raise within me, the solemn feelings and true affection, that I feel when alone with God, in the forest. There I seem to stand face to face, with my master; all around me is fresh and beauti-ful, as it came from his hand, and there is no nicety, or doctrine, to chill the feelin's. No—no—the woods are the true temple a'ter all, for there the thoughts are free to mount higher even than the clouds."

"You speak the truth, Master Pathfinder," said Cap, "and a truth that all who live much in solitude know. What, for in-stance, is the reason that sea-faring men, in general, are so reli-gious and conscientious in all they do, but the fact that they are so often alone with Providence, and have so little to do with the wickedness of the land. Many, and many is the time, that I have stood my watch, under the equator perhaps, or in the Southern Ocean, when the nights are lighted up with the fires of heaven, and that is the time, I can tell you, my hearties, to bring a man to his bearings, in the way of his sins. I have rattled down mine, again and again, under such circumstances, until the shrouds and lanyards of conscience have fairly creaked with the strain. I agree with you, Master Pathfinder, therefore, in saying if you want a truly religious man, go to sea, or go into the woods."

"Uncle, I thought seamen had little credit, generally, for their respect for religion."

"All d——d slander, girl. Ask your sea-faring man what his real, private opinion is of your landsmen, parsons and all, and you will hear the other side of the question. I know no class of men, who have been so belied as sea-faring men, in this particular, and it is all because they do not stay at home to defend themselves, and pay the clergy. They have'n't as much doctrine, perhaps, as some ashore, but as for all the essentials of christianity, the seaman beats the landsman, hand over hand.

"I will not answer for all this, Master Cap," returned Pathfinder, "but, I dare say, some of it may be true. I want no thunder and lightening to remind me of my God, nor am I as apt to bethink me most of all his goodness, in trouble and tribulations, as on a calm, solemn, quiet day, in the forest, when his voice is heard in the creaking of a dead branch, or in the song of a bird, as much in my ears at least, as it is ever heard in uproar and gales. How is it with you, Eau douce; you face the tempests as well as Master Cap, and ought to know something of the feelin's of storms?"

"I fear that I am too young, and too inexperienced to be able to say much on such a subject," modestly answered Jasper.

"But you have your feelings!" said Mabel quickly. "You cannot—no one can live among such scenes without feeling how much they ought to trust in God!"

"I shall not belie my training so much as to say I do not sometimes think of these things, but I fear it is not as often, or as much, as I ought."

"Fresh water!" resumed Cap pithily; "you are not to expect too much of the young man, Mabel. I think they call you, sometimes, by a name which would insinuate all this. Eau-de-vie, is it not?"

"Eau douce," quietly replied Jasper, who from sailing on the lake had acquired a knowledge of French, as well as of several of the Indian dialects. "It is a name the Iroquois have given me to distinguish me, from some of my companions who once sailed upon the sea, and are fond of filling the ears of the natives, with stories of their great salt-water lakes."

"And why should'n't they! I dare say they do the savages no harm. They may not civilize them, but they will not make them greater barbarians than they are. Ay—ay—Oh! the deuce, that must mean the white brandy, which is no great matter after all, and may well enough be called the deuce, for deuced stuff it is!"

"The signification of Eau douce is sweet-water, or water that can be drunk, and it is the manner in which the French express fresh-water," rejoined Jasper, a little nettled at the distinctions made by Cap; although the latter was the uncle of Mabel.

"And how the devil do they make water out of Oh! the deuce, when it means brandy in Eau-de-vie? This may be the French used, hereaway, but it is not that they use in Burdux, and other French ports; besides, among seamen Eau always means brandy, and Eau-de-vie, brandy of a high proof. I think nothing of your ignorance, young man, for it is natural to your situation, and cannot be helped. If you will return with me, and make a v'y'ge or two, on the Atlantic, it will serve you a good turn the remainder of your days, and, Mabel there, and all the other young women, near the coast, will think all the better of you, should you live to be as old as one of the trees in this forest."

"Nay, nay," interrupted the single hearted and generous guide, "Jasper wants not for friends, in this region, I can assure you; and though seeing the world, according to his habits, may do him good, as well as another, we shall think none the worse of him, if he never quits us. Eau douce, or Eau-de-vie, he is a brave, true-hearted youth, and I always sleep as sound, when he is on the watch as if I was up and stirring myself; ay, and for that matter, sounder too. The Sarjeant's daughter, here, does'n't believe it necessary for the lad to go to sea, in order to make a man of him, or one, who is worthy to be respected and esteemed."

Mabel made no reply to this appeal, and she even looked towards the eastern shore, although the darkness rendered the natural movement unnecessary to conceal her face. But, Jasper felt that there was a necessity for his saying something, the pride of youth and manhood revolting at the idea of his being in a condition not to command the respect of his fellows, or the smiles of his equals of the other sex. Still he was unwilling to utter aught that might be considered harsh, to the uncle of Mabel, and his self command was, perhaps, more creditable than his modesty and spirit.

"I pretend not to things I do'n't possess," he said, "and lay no claim to any knowledge of the ocean, or of navigation. We steer by the stars, and the compass on these lakes, running from head-land to head-land,* and, having little need of figures and calculations make no use of them. But, we have our claims, notwithstanding, as I have often heard from those who have passed years on the ocean. In the first place we have always the land aboard, and much of the time on a lee-shore,* and that I have frequently heard makes hardy sailors. Our gales are sudden and severe, and we are compelled to run for our ports at all hours—"

"You have your leads—"*interrupted Cap.

"They are of little use, and are seldom cast."

"The deep-seas—"*

"I have heard of such things, but confess I never saw one."

"Oh! the deuce, with a vengeance. A trader and no deep sea! Why, boy, you cannot pretend to be any thing of a mariner. Who the devil ever heard of a seaman without his deep-sea!"

"I do not pretend to any particular skill, Master Cap—"

"Except in shooting falls, Jasper; except in shooting falls and rifts," said Pathfinder, coming to the rescue; "in which business, even you, Master Cap, must allow he has some handiness. In my judgment, every man is to be esteemed or condemned according to his gifts, and if Master Cap is useless in running the Oswego falls, I try to remember that he is useful when out of sight of land; and if Jasper be useless when out of sight of land, I do not forget that he has a true eye and steady hand when running the falls."

"But Jasper is not useless—would not be useless when out of sight of land," said Mabel with a spirit and energy that caused her clear sweet voice to be startling amid the solemn stillness of that extraordinary scene. "No one can be useless there, who can do so much here, is what I mean; though I dare say, he is not as well acquainted with ships as my uncle."

"Ay, bolster each other up in your ignorance," returned Cap, with a sneer. "We seamen are so much outnumbered when ashore, that it is seldom we get our dues, but when your coast is to be defended, or trade is to be carried on, there is outcry enough for us."

"But, uncle, landsmen do not come to attack our coasts, so that seamen only meet seamen."

"So much for ignorance!—Where are all the armies that have landed in this country, French and English, let me inquire, miss?"

"Sure enough, where are they!" ejaculated Pathfinder. "None can tell better than we who dwell in the woods, Master Cap. I have often followed their line of march by bones bleaching in the rain, and have found their trail by graves, years after they and their pride had vanished together. Generals and privates, they lay scattered throughout the land, so many proofs of what men are when led on by their love of great names, and the wish to be more than their fellows."

"I must say, Master Pathfinder, that you sometimes utter opinions that are a little remarkable, for a man who lives by the rifle; seldom snuffing the air but he smells gunpowder, or turning out of his berth, but to bear down on an enemy."

"If you think I pass my days in warfare against my kind, you know neither me, nor my history. The man that lives in the woods, and on the frontiers, must take the chances of the things among which he dwells. For this I am not accountable, being but a humble and powerless hunter and scout and guide. My real calling is to hunt for the army, on its marches, and in times of peace, although I am more especially engaged in the sarvice of one officer, who is now absent in the settlements, where I never follow him. No—no—bloodshed and warfare are not my real gifts, but peace and marcy. Still, I must face the inimy as well as another, and as for a Mingo, I look upon him, as man looks on a snake, a creatur' to be put beneath the heel, whenever a fitting occasion offers."

"Well—well—I have mistaken your calling, which I had thought as regularly warlike as that of the ship's gunner. There is my brother-in-law, now; he has been a soldier since he was sixteen, and he looks upon his trade as every way as respectable as that of a sea-faring man, which is a point I hardly think it worth while to dispute with him."

"My father has been taught to believe that it is honorable to carry arms," said Mabel, "for his father was a soldier before him."

"Yes, yes—" resumed the guide—"Most of the Sarjeant's gifts are martial, and he looks at most things in this world, over the barrel of his musket. One of his notions now, is to prefar a King's piece to a regular double-sighted long-barreled rifle! Such consaits will come over men, from long habit, and prejudyce is perhaps the commonest failing of human natur'."

"Ashore, I grant you," said Cap. "I never return from a v'y'ge, but I make the very same remark. Now, the last time I came in, I found scarcely a man in all York, who would think of matters and things in general, as I thought about them myself. Every man I met, appeared to have bowsed all his idees up into the wind's eye, and when he did fall off a little from his one-sided notions, it was commonly to ware short round on his heel, and to lay up as close as ever, on the other tack."

"Do you understand this, Jasper?—" the smiling Mabel half whispered to the young man who still kept his own canoe so near, as to be close at her side.

"There is not so much difference between salt and fresh water, that we who pass our time on them cannot comprehend each other. It is no great merit, Mabel, to understand the language of our trade."

"Even religion," continued Cap, "isn't moored in exactly the same place it was, in my young days. They veer and haul upon it, ashore, as they do on all other things, and it is no wonder if, now and then, they get jammed. Every thing seems to change but the compass, and even that has its variations."

"Well," returned the Pathfinder, "I thought Christianity and the compass both pretty stationary."

"So they are, afloat, bating the variations. Religion at sea, is just the same thing to day, that it was when I first put my hand into the tar-bucket. No one will dispute it, who has the fear of God before his eyes. I can see no difference between the state of religion on board ship, now, and what it was when I was a younker. But it is not so ashore, by any means. Take my word for it, Master Pathfinder, it is a difficult thing to find a man—I mean a landsman—who views these matters, to-day exactly as he looked at them, forty years ago."

"And yet God is unchanged—his works are unchanged—his holy word is unchanged—and all that ought to bless and honor his name should be unchanged too!"

"Not ashore. That is the worst of the land, it is all the while in motion, I tell you, though it looks so solid. If you plant a tree, and leave it, on your return from a three years' v'y'ge you do'n't find it, at all, the sort of thing you left it. The towns grow, and new streets spring up, the wharves are altered, and the whole face of the earth undergoes change. Now a ship comes back from an India v'y'ge just the thing she sailed, bating the want of paint, wear and tear, and the accidents of the sea."

"That is too true, Master Cap, and more's the pity. Ah's! me—the things they call improvements and betterments are undermining and defacing the land! The glorious works of God are daily cut down and destroyed, and the hand of man seems to be upraised in contempt of his mighty will. They tell me there are fearful signs of what we may all come to, to be met with, west and south of the great lakes, though I have never yet visited that region."

"What do you mean, Pathfinder?" modestly enquired Jasper.

"I mean the spots marked by the vengeance of Heaven, or which perhaps have been raised up as solemn warnings to the thoughtless and wasteful, hereaways. They call them Prairies, and I have heard as honest Delawares as I ever knew, declare that the finger of God has been laid so heavily on them, that they are altogether without trees. This is an awful visitation to befal innocent 'arth, and can only mean to show to what frightful consequences a heedless desire to destroy may lead."

"And yet I have seen settlers, who have much fancied those open spots, because they saved them the toil of clearing. You relish your bread, Pathfinder, and yet wheat will not ripen in the shade."

"But honesty will, and simple wishes, and a love of God, Jasper. Even Master Cap will tell you a treeless plain must resemble a desert island."

"Why that as it may be," put in Cap. "Desert islands, too, have their uses, for they serve to correct the reckonings by. If my taste is consulted, I shall never quarrel with a plain for wanting trees. As nature has given a man eyes to look about with, and a sun to shine, were it not for ship-building, and now and then a house, I can see no great use in a tree; especially one that do'n't bear monkeys or fruit."

To this remark the guide made no answer, beyond a low sound, intended to enjoin silence on his companions. While the desultory conversation just related had been carried on in sub-dued voices, the canoes were dropping slowly down with the current, within the deep shadows of the western shore, the paddles being used merely to preserve the desired direction, and proper positions. The strength of the stream varied mate-rially, the water being seemingly still in places, while in other reaches it flowed at a rate exceeding two, or even three miles, in the hour. On the rifts it even dashed forward with a velocity that was appalling to the unpractised eye. Jasper was of opinion that they might drift down with the current to the mouth of the river, in two hours from the time they left the shore, and he and the Pathfinder had agreed on the expediency of suffering the canoes to float of themselves, for a time, or, at least, until they had passed the first dangers of their new movement. The dialogue had been carried on in voices guardedly low, for though the quiet of deep solitude reigned in that vast and nearly boundless forest, nature was speaking with her thousand tongues, in the eloquent language of night in a wilderness. The air sighed through ten thousand trees, the water rippled, and at places, even roared along the shores, and now and then was heard the creaking of a branch, or a trunk, as it rubbed against some object similar to itself, under the vibrations of a nicely balanced body. All living sounds had ceased. Once, it is true, the Pathfinder fancied he heard the howl of a distant wolf, of which a few prowled through those woods, but it was a transient and doubtful cry, that might possibly have been attributed to the imagination. When he desired his companions, however, to cease talking in the manner just mentioned, his vigilant ear had caught the peculiar sound that is made by the parting of a dried branch of a tree, and which, if his senses did not deceive him, came from the western shore. All who are accustomed to that particular sound will understand how readily the ear receives it, and how easy it is to distinguish the tread which breaks the branch, from every other noise of the forest.

"There is the footstep of a man on the bank," said Pathfinder to Jasper, speaking in neither a whisper, nor yet in a voice loud enough to be heard at any distance. "Can the accursed Iroquois have crossed the river, already, with their arms, and without a boat!"

"It may be the Delaware! He would follow us of course down this bank, and would know where to look for us. Let me draw closer in to the shore, and reconnoitre."

"Go, boy, but be light with the paddle, and, on no account, venture ashore on an onsartainty."

"Is this prudent?" demanded Mabel, with an impetuosity that rendered her incautious in modulating her sweet voice.

"Very imprudent, if you speak so loud, fair one. I like your voice, which is soft and pleasing, after listening so long to the tones of men, but it must not be heard too much, or too freely, just now. Your father, the honest Sarjeant, will tell you, when you meet him, that silence is a double virtue on a trail. Go, Jasper, and do justice to your own character for prudence."

Ten anxious minutes succeeded the disappearance of the canoe of Jasper, which glided away from that of the Pathfinder, so noiselessly that it had been swallowed up in the gloom, before Mabel allowed herself to believe the young man would really venture alone, on a service that struck her imagination as singularly dangerous. During this time, the party continued to float with the current, no one speaking, and it might almost be said no one breathing, so strong was the general desire to catch the minutest sound that should come from the shore. But the same solemn, we might indeed say sublime quiet, reigned as before, the washing of the water, as it piled up against some slight obstruction, and the sighing of the trees alone interrupting the slumbers of the forest. At the end of the period mentioned, the snapping of dried branches was again faintly heard, and the Pathfinder fancied that the sound of smothered voices reached him.

"I may be mistaken," he said, "for the thoughts often fancy what the heart wishes, but them were notes like the low tones of the Delawares."

"Do the dead of the savages ever walk?" demanded Cap.

"Ay, and run, too, in their happy hunting grounds, but nowhere else. A red skin finishes with the 'arth, after the breath quits the body. It is not one of his gifts to linger around his wigwam, when his hour has passed."

"I see some object on the water—" whispered Mabel, whose eye had not ceased to dwell on the body of gloom, with close intensity, since the disappearance of Jasper.

"It is the canoe!" returned the guide, greatly relieved. "All must be safe, or we should have heard from the lad."

In another minute the two canoes, which became visible to those they carried, only as they drew near each other, again floated side by side, and the form of Jasper was recognised at the stern of his own boat. The figure of a second man was seated in the bow, and as the young sailor so wielded his paddle, as to bring the face of his companion near the eyes of the Pathfinder and Mabel, they both recognised the person of the Delaware.

"Chingachgook—my brother!" said the guide in the dialect of the other's people, a tremor shaking his voice that betrayed the strength of his feelings—"Chief of the Mohicans! my heart is very glad. Often have we passed through blood and strife together, but I was afraid it was never to be so again."

"Hugh! Mingos—Squaws! Three of their scalps hang at my girdle. They do not know how to strike the Great Serpent of the Delawares. Their hearts have no blood, and their thoughts are on their return path, across the waters of the Great Lake."

"Have you been among them, chief?—and what has become of the warrior who was in the river?"

"He has turned into a fish, and lies at the bottom with the eels! Let his brothers bait their hooks for him. Pathfinder, I have counted the enemy, and have touched their rifles."

"Ah! I thought he would be venturesome," exclaimed the guide in English. "The risky fellow has been in the midst of them, and has brought us back their whole history. Speak, Chingachgook, and I will make our friends as knowing as ourselves."

The Delaware now related in a low earnest manner, the substance of all his discoveries since he was last seen struggling with his foe, in the river. Of the fate of his antagonist he said no more, it not being usual for a warrior to boast in his more direct, and useful narratives. As soon as he had conquered in that fearful strife, however, he swam to the eastern shore, landed with caution, and wound his way in amongst the Iroquois, concealed by the darkness, undetected and, in the main, even unsuspected. Once, indeed, he had been questioned, but answering that he was Arrowhead, no further inquiries were made. By the passing remarks, he soon ascertained that the party was out expressly to intercept Mabel and her uncle, concerning whose rank, however, they had evidently been deceived. He also ascertained enough to justify the suspicion that Arrowhead had betrayed them to their enemies, from some motive that it was not now easy to reach, as he had not yet received the reward of his services.

Pathfinder communicated no more of this intelligence to his companions, than he thought might relieve their apprehensions, intimating, at the same time, that now was the moment for exertion, the Iroquois not having yet entirely recovered from the confusion created by their losses.

"We shall find them at the rift, I make no manner of doubt," he continued, "and there it will be our fate, to pass them, or to fall into their hands. The distance to the garrison will then be so short, that I have been thinking of the plan of landing with Mabel, myself, that I may take her in, by some of the by-ways, and leave the canoes to their chances in the rapids."

"It will never succeed, Pathfinder," eagerly interrupted Jasper; "Mabel is not strong enough to tramp the woods, in a night like this. Put her in my skiff, and I will lose my life or carry her through the rift safely, dark as it is."

"No doubt you will, lad; no one doubts your willingness to do any thing to sarve the Sarjeant's daughter, but it must be the eye of Providence and not your own, that will take you safely through the Oswego rift, in a night like this."

"And who will lead her safely to the garrison if she land? Is not the night as dark on shore, as on the water, or, do you think I know less of my calling, than you know of yours?"

"Spiritedly said, lad, but if I should lose my way in the dark, and I believe no man can say truly that such a thing ever yet happened to me—but, if I *should* lose my way, no other harm would come of it, than to pass a night in the forest, whereas a false turn of the paddle, or a broad sheer of the canoe, would put you and the young woman into the river, out of which it is more than probable the Sarjeant's daughter would never come alive."

"I will leave it to Mabel, herself; I am certain that she will feel more secure in the canoe."

"I have great confidence in you both," answered the girl, "and have no doubts that either will do all he can to prove to my father how much he values him, but, I confess I should not like to quit the canoe, with the certainty we have of there being enemies like those we have seen, in the forest. But, my uncle can decide for me, in this matter."

"I have no liking for the woods," said Cap, "while one has a clear drift like this on the river. Besides, Master Pathfinder, to say nothing of the savages, you overlook the sharks."

"Sharks! Who ever heard of sharks in the wilderness?"

"Ay sharks, or bears, or wolves—no matter what you call a thing so it has the mind and the power to bite."

"Lord, lord, man; do you dread any creatur' that is to be found in the American forest! A catamount is a skeary animal, I will allow, but then it is nothing in the hands of a practysed hunter. Talk of the Mingos, and their deviltries, if you will; but do not raise a false alarm, about bears and wolves."

"Ay, ay, Master Pathfinder, this is all well enough for you, who probably know the name of every creature you would meet. Use is every thing, and it makes a man bold, when he might otherwise be bashful. I have known seamen in the low latitudes, swim for hours at a time, among sharks fifteen, or twenty feet long, and think no more of what they were doing, than a countryman thinks of whom he' is amongst, when he comes out of a church door of a Sunday afternoon."

"This is extraordinary!" exclaimed Jasper, who, in good sooth, had not yet acquired that material part of his trade, the ability to spin a yarn—"I have always heard that it was certain death to venture in the water, among sharks!"

"I forgot to say, that the lads always took capstan-bars,* or gunners' handspikes,* or crows with them, to rap the beasts over the noses if they got to be troublesome. No—no—I have no liking for bears and wolves, though a whale, in my eye, is very much the same sort of fish as a red-herring, after it is dried and salted. Mabel and I, had better stick to the canoe."

"Mabel would do well to change canoes," added Jasper. "This of mine is empty, and even Pathfinder will allow that my eye is surer than his own, on the water."

"That I will cheerfully, boy. The water belongs to your gifts, and no one will deny that you have improved them to the utmost. You are right enough in believing that the Sarjeant's daughter will be safer in your canoe than in this, and, though I would gladly keep her near myself, I have her welfare too much at heart, not to give her honest advice. Bring your canoe close alongside, Jasper, and I will give you what you must consider as a very precious treasure."

"I do so consider it—" returned the youth, not losing a moment in complying with the request, when Mabel passed from one canoe to the other, taking her seat on the effects which had hitherto composed its sole cargo.

As soon as this arrangement was made, the canoes separated a short distance, and the paddles were used, though with great care to avoid making any noise. The conversation gradually ceased, and as the dreaded rift was approached, all became impressed with the gravity of the moment. That their enemies would endeavor to reach this point before them, was almost certain, and it seemed so little probable any one should attempt to pass it, in the profound obscurity which reigned, that Pathfinder was confident parties were on both sides of the river, in the hope of intercepting them when they might land. He would not have made the proposal he did, had he not felt sure of his own ability to convert this very anticipation of success, into a means of defeating the plans of the Iroquois. As the arrangement now stood, however, every thing depended on the skill of those who guided the canoes, for should either hit a rock, if not split asunder, it would almost certainly be upset, and then would come not only all the hazards of the river itself but, for Mabel, the certainty of falling into the hands of her pursuers. The utmost circumspection consequently became necessary, and each one was too much engrossed with his own thoughts, to feel a disposition to utter more than was called for, by the exigencies of the case.

As the canoes stole silently along, the roar of the rift became audible, and it required all the fortitude of Cap, to keep his seat, while these boding sounds were approached, amid a darkness that scarcely permitted a view of the outlines of the wooded shore, and of the gloomy vault above his head. He retained a vivid impression of the Falls, and his imagination was not now idle, in swelling the dangers of the rift to a level with those of the headlong descent he had that day made, and even to increase them, under the influence of doubt and uncertainty. In this, however, the old mariner was mistaken, for the Oswego rift, and the Oswego Falls are very different in their characters and violence, the former being no more than a rapid, that glances among shallows and rocks, while the latter really deserved the name it bore, as has been already shown.

Mabel certainly felt distrust and apprehension, but her entire situation was so novel, and her reliance on her guides so great, that she retained a self-command that might not have existed had she clearer perceptions of the truth, or been better acquainted with the helplessness of man, when placed in opposition to the power and majesty of nature.

"That is the spot you have mentioned?" she said to Jasper, when the roar of the rift first came fresh and distinct on her ear.

"It is; and I beg you to have confidence in me. We are not old acquaintances, Mabel, but we live many days in one, in this wilderness. I think, already, that I have known you years."

"And I do not feel as if you were a stranger to me, Jasper. I have every reliance on your skill, as well as on your disposition to serve me."

"We shall see—we shall see. Pathfinder is striking the rapids too near the centre of the river. The best of the water is closer to the eastern shore; but I cannot make him hear me, now. Hold firmly to the canoe, Mabel, and fear nothing."

At the next moment, the swift current sucked them into the rift, and for three or four minutes, the awe-struck, rather than the alarmed, girl, saw nothing around her but sheets of glancing foam; heard nothing but the roar of waters. Twenty times did the canoe appear about to dash against some curling and bright wave, that showed itself even amid that obscurity, and as often did it glide away, again, unharmed; impelled by the vigorous arm of him who governed its movements. Once, and once only, did Jasper seem to lose command of his frail bark, during which brief space it fairly whirled entirely round, but, by a desperate effort, he brought it again under control, recovered the lost channel, and was soon rewarded for all his anxiety by finding himself floating quietly in the deep water below the rapids, secure from every danger, and without having taken in enough of the element to serve for a draught.

"All is over, Mabel," the young man cheerfully cried. "The danger is past, and you may now, indeed, hope to meet your father, this very night."

"God be praised! Jasper, we shall owe this great happiness to you!"

"The Pathfinder may claim a full share in the merit—but what has become of the other canoe?"

"I see something near us on the water—Is it not the boat of our friends?"

A few strokes of the paddle brought Jasper to the side of the object in question. It was the other canoe, empty and bottom upwards. No sooner did the young man ascertain this fact, than he began to search for the swimmers, and to his great joy, Cap was soon discovered drifting down with the current, the old seaman preferring the chances of drowning, to those of landing among savages. He was hauled into the canoe, though not without difficulty, and then the search ended; for Jasper was persuaded that the Pathfinder would wade to the shore, the water being shallow, in preference to abandoning his beloved rifle.

The remainder of the passage was short, though made amid darkness and doubt. After a short pause, a dull roaring sound was heard, which at times resembled the mutterings of distant thunder, and then again brought with it the washing of waters. Jasper announced to his companions that they now heard the surf of the lake. Low, curved spits of land lay before them, into the bay formed by one of which the canoe glided, and then it shot up noiselessly upon a gravelly beach. The transition that followed was so hurried and great, that Mabel scarce knew what passed. In the course of a few minutes, however, sentinels had been passed, a gate was opened, and the agitated girl found herself in the arms of a parent who was almost a stranger to her.

Chapter VIII.

"A land of love, and a land of light,
Withouten sun; or moon, or night:
Where the river swa'd a living stream,
And the light a pure celestial beam:
The land of vision it would seem,
A still, an everlasting dream."

Hogg, *The Queen's Wake*, "Kilmeny," ll. 46–51.

T HE rest that succeeds fatigue, and which attends a newly awakened sense of security, is generally sweet and deep. Such was the fact with Mabel, who did not rise from her humble pallet, such a bed as a serjeant's daughter might claim in a remote frontier post, until long after the garrison had obeyed the usual summons of the drum, and had assembled at the early parade. Serjeant Dunham, on whose shoulders fell the task of attending to these ordinary and daily duties, had got through all his morning avocations, and was beginning to think of his breakfast, ere his child left her room and came into the fresh air, equally bewildered, delighted, and grateful, at the novelty and security of her new situation.

At the time of which we are writing, Oswego was one of the extreme frontier posts of the British possessions on this continent. It had not been long occupied, and was garrisoned by a battalion of a regiment that had been originally Scotch, but into which many Americans had been received, since its arrival in this country, an innovation that had led the way to Mabel's father filling the humble but responsible situation of the oldest serjeant. A few young officers also, who were natives of the Colonies, were to be found in this corps. The fort, itself, like most works of that character, was better adapted to resist an attack of savages, than to withstand a regular siege, but the great difficulty of transporting heavy artillery and other necessaries, rendered the occurrence of the latter a probability so remote, as scarcely to enter into the estimate of the engineers who had planned the defences. These were bastions of earth and logs, a dry ditch, a stockade, a parade of considerable extent, and barracks of logs, that answered the double purpose of dwellings and fortifications. A few light field-pieces stood in the area of the fort, ready to be conveyed to any point where they might be wanted, and one or two heavy iron guns looked out from the summits of the advanced angles, so many admonitions to the audacious to respect their power.

When Mabel, quitting the convenient, but comparatively retired hut where her father had been permitted to place her, issued into the pure air of the morning, she found herself at the foot of a bastion, that lay invitingly before her, with a promise of giving a coup d'œil of all that had been concealed in the darkness of the preceding night. Tripping up the grassy ascent, the light-hearted as well as light-footed girl found herself, at once, on a point where the sight, at a few changing glances, could take in all the external novelties of her new situation.

To the southward lay the forest through which she had been journeying so many weary days, and which had proved so full of danger. It was separated from the stockade, by a belt of open land, that had been principally cleared of its wood, to form the massive constructions around her. This glacis, for such in fact was its military uses, might have covered a hundred acres, but with it every sign of civilization ceased. All beyond was forest, that dense, interminable forest that Mabel could now picture to herself, through her recollections, with its hidden, glassy lakes, its dark, rolling streams, and its world of nature!

Turning from this view, our heroine felt her cheek fanned by a fresh and grateful breeze such as she had not experienced since quitting the far-distant coast. Here a new scene presented itself. Although expected, it was not without a start, and a low exclamation indicative of pleasure, that the eager eyes of the girl drank in its beauties. To the north and east, and west, in every direction, in short, over one entire half of the novel panorama lay a field of rolling waters. The element was neither of that glassy green which distinguishes the American waters in general, nor yet of the deep blue of the ocean; the colour being of a slightly amber hue, that scarcely affected its limpidity. No land was to be seen, with the exception of the adjacent coast, which stretched to the right and left, in an unbroken outline of forest, with wide bays, and low head-lands, or points. Still, much of the shore was rocky, and into its caverns the sluggish waters occasionally rolled, producing a hollow sound, that resembled the concussions of a distant gun. No sail whitened the surface, no whale, or other fish gambolled on its bosom, no sign of use, or service, rewarded the longest and most minute gaze, at its boundless expanse. It was a scene, on one side, of apparently endless forest while a waste of seemingly interminable water spread itself on the other. Nature had appeared to delight in producing grand effects, by setting two of her principal agents in bold relief to each other, neglecting details; the eye turning from the broad carpet of leaves, to the still broader field of fluid, from the endless but gentle heavings of the lake, to the holy calm, and poetical solitude of the forest, with wonder and delight.

Mabel Dunham, though unsophisticated, like most of her countrywomen of that period, and ingenuous and frank as any warm-hearted and sincere-minded girl well could be, was not altogether without a feeling for the poetry of this beautiful earth of ours. Though she could scarcely be said to be educated at all, for few of her sex at that day, and in this country, received much more than the rudiments of plain English instruction, still she had been taught much more than was usual for young women in her own station in life, and, in one sense certainly, she did credit to her teaching. The widow of a Field Officer, who formerly belonged to the same regiment as her father, had taken the child in charge, at the death of its mother, and under the care of this lady, Mabel had acquired some tastes, and many ideas, which otherwise might always have remained strangers to her. Her situation in the family had been less that of a domestic, than of a humble companion, and the results were quite apparent, in her attire, her language, her sentiments, and even in her feelings; though neither perhaps rose to the level of those which would properly characterize a lady. She had lost the coarser and less refined habits and manners of one in her original position, without having quite reached a point that disqualified her for the situation in life that the accidents of birth and fortune would probably compel her to fill. All else that was distinctive and peculiar in her, belonged to natural character.

With such antecedents, it will occasion the reader no wonder, if he learns that Mabel viewed the novel scene before her, with a pleasure far superior to that produced by vulgar surprise. She felt its ordinary beauties, as most would have felt them, but she had also a feeling for its sublimity; for that softened solitude, that calm grandeur, and eloquent repose that ever pervades broad views of natural objects which are yet undisturbed by the labors and uneasy struggles of man.

"How beautiful!" she exclaimed, unconscious of speaking, as she stood on the solitary bastion, facing the air from the lake, and experiencing the genial influence of its freshness pervading both her body and her mind. "How very beautiful; and yet how singular!"

The words, and the train of her ideas, were interrupted by a touch of a finger on her shoulder, and turning, in the expectation of seeing her father, Mabel found Pathfinder at her side. He was leaning quietly on his long rifle, and laughing in his quiet manner, while with an outstretched arm, he swept over the whole panorama of land and water.

"Here you have both our domains," he said, "Jasper's and mine. The lake is for him, and the woods are for me. The lad sometimes boasts of the breadth of his dominions, but I tell him my trees make as broad a plain on the face of this 'arth, as all his water. Well, Mabel, you are fit for either, for I do not see that fear of the Mingos, or night marches can destroy your pretty looks."

"It is a new character for the Pathfinder to appear in, to compliment a silly girl."

"Not silly, Mabel; no, not in the least silly. The Sarjeant's daughter would do discredit to her worthy father were she to do, or say, any thing that, in common honesty, could be called silly."

"Then she must take care and not put too much faith, in treacherous, flattering words. But, Pathfinder, I rejoice to see you among us again, for, though Jasper did not seem to feel much uneasiness, I was afraid some accident might have happened to you, and your friend, on that frightful rift."

"The lad knows us both, and was sartain that we should not drown, which is scarcely one of my gifts. It would have been hard swimming, of a sartainty, with a long-barrelled rifle in the hands, and what between the game, and the savages, and the French, Killdeer and I have gone through too much in company, to part very easily. No—no—we waded ashore, the rift being shallow enough for that, with small exceptions, and we landed with our arms in our hands. We had to take our time for it, on account of the Iroquois, I will own, but, as soon as the skulking vagabonds saw the lights, that the sarjeant sent down to your canoe, we well understood they would decamp, since a visit might have been expected from some of the garrison. So it was only sitting patiently on the stones, for an hour, and all the danger was over. Patience is the greatest of virtues in a woodsman."

"I rejoice to hear this, for fatigue itself could scarcely make me sleep, for thinking of what might befal you."

"Lord bless your tender little heart, Mabel! But this is the way, with all you gentle ones. I must say, on my part, howsever, that I was right glad to see the lanterns come down to the water side, which I knew to be a sure sign of *your* safety. We hunters and guides are rude beings, but we have our feelin's, and our idees, as well as any giniral in the army. Both Jasper and I would have died, before you should have come to harm, we would!"

"I thank you for all you did for me, Pathfinder; from the bottom of my heart, I thank you, and depend on it my father shall know it. I have already told him much, but have still a duty to perform, on this subject."

"Tush, Mabel, the Sarjeant knows what the woods be, and what men—true, real men be, too. There is little need to tell him any thing about it. Well, now you have met your father, do you find the honest old soldier, the sort of person you expected to find?"

"He is my own dear father, and received me as a soldier and a father should receive a child. Have you known him long, Pathfinder?"

"That is as people count time. I was just twelve when the sarjeant took me on my first scouting, and that is now more than twenty years ago. We had a tramping time of it, and as it was before your day, you would have had no father, had not the rifle been one of my nat'ral gifts."

"Explain yourself."

"It is too simple for many words. We were ambushed, and the sarjeant got a bad hurt, and would have lost his scalp, but for a sort of inbred turn I took to the weapon. We brought him off, howsever, and a handsomer head of hair, for his time of life, is not to be found in the rigiment, than the Sarjeant carries about with him, this blessed day."

"You saved my father's life, Pathfinder!" exclaimed Mabel, unconsciously, though warmly, taking one of his hard sinewy hands into both her own. "God bless you for this, too, among your other good acts."

"Nay, I did not say that much, though I believe I did save his scalp. A man might live without a scalp, and so I cannot say I saved his life. Jasper may say that much consarning you, for without his eye and arm the canoe would never have passed the rift in safety, on a night like the last. The gifts of the lad are for the water, while mine are for the hunt and the trail. He is yonder in the cove, there, looking after the canoes, and keeping an eye on his beloved little craft. To my eye, there is no likelier youth, in these parts, than Jasper Western."

For the first time since she had left her room, Mabel now turned her eyes beneath her, and got a view of what might be called the fore-ground of the remarkable picture she had been studying with so much pleasure. The Oswego threw its dark waters into the lake, between banks of some height; that on its eastern side, being bolder and projecting farther north, than that on its western. The fort was on the latter, and immediately beneath it, were a few huts of logs, which, as they could not interfere with the defence of the place, had been erected along the strand for the purpose of receiving and containing such stores, as were landed, or were intended to be embarked, in the communications between the different posts on the shores of Ontario. There were two low, curved gravelly points, that had been formed with surprising regularity by the counteracting forces of the northerly winds and the swift current, and which, inclining from the storms of the lake, formed two coves within the river. That on the western side was the most deeply indented, and as it also had the most water, it formed a sort of picturesque little port, for the post. It was along the narrow strand that lay between the low height of the fort and the water of this cove, that the rude buildings just mentioned, had been erected.

Several skiffs, batteaux and canoes were hauled upon the shore, and in the cove itself lay the little craft, from which Jasper obtained his claim to be considered a sailor. She was cutter-rigged,* might have been of forty tons burthen, was so neatly constructed and painted as to have something of the air of a vessel of war, though entirely without quarters, and rigged and sparred with so scrupulous a regard to proportions and beauty, as well as fitness and judgment, as to give her an appearance that even Mabel at once distinguished to be gallant and trim. Her mould was admirable, for a wright of great skill had sent her drafts from England at the express request of the officer who had caused her to be constructed; her paint dark, warlike and neat, and the long coach-whip pennant that she wore, at once proclaimed her to be the property of the king. Her name was the Scud.

"That, then, is the vessel of Jasper!" said Mabel, who associated the master of the little craft quite naturally with the cutter itself. "Are there many others on this lake?"

"The Frenchers have three; one of which they tell me is a real ship, such as are used on the ocean, another a brig, and a third is a cutter, like the Scud, here, which they call the Squirrel, in their own tongue howsever, and which seems to have a nat'ral hatred of our own pretty boat, for Jasper seldom goes out that the Squirrel is not at his heels."

"And is Jasper one to run from a Frenchman though he appear in the shape of a squirrel, and that, too, on the water!"

"Of what use would valor be without the means of turning it to account? Jasper is a brave boy, as all on this frontier know, but he has no gun except a little howitzer, and then his crew consists only of two men besides himself and a boy. I was with him in one of his trampooses,* and the youngster was risky enough, for he brought us so near the inimy that rifles began to talk, but the Frenchers carry cannon, and ports, and never show their faces outside of Frontenac,* without having some twenty men, besides their Squirrel, in their cutter. No—no—this Scud was built for flying, and the Major says he will not put her in a fighting humour, by giving her men and arms lest she should take him at his word, and get her wings clipped. I know little of these things, for my gifts are not at all, in that way, but I see the reason of the thing—I see its reason, though Jasper does not."

"Ah! here is my uncle, none the worse for his swim, coming to look at this inland sea."

Sure enough Cap, who had announced his approach by a couple of lusty hems, now made his appearance on the bastion, where, after nodding to his niece and her companion, he made a deliberate survey of the expanse of water before him. In order to effect this at his ease, the mariner mounted on one of the old iron guns, folded his arms across his breast, and balanced his body, as if he felt the motion of a vessel. To complete the picture he had a short pipe in his mouth.

"Well, Master Cap," asked the Pathfinder innocently, for he did not detect the expression of contempt that was gradually settling on the features of the other—"is it not a beautiful sheet, and fit to be named a sea?"

"This, then, is what you call your lake?" demanded Cap, sweeping the northern horizon with his pipe. "I say, is this, really, your lake."

"Sartain; and if the judgment of one who has lived on the shores of many others can be taken, a very good lake it is."

"Just as I expected! A pond in dimensions, and a scuttlebutt* in taste. It is all in vain to travel inland, in the hope of seeing any thing either full-grown, or useful. I knew it would turn out just in this way."

"What is the matter with Ontario, Master Cap? It is large, and fair to look at, and pleasant enough to drink, for those who ca'n't get at the waters of the spring."

"Do you call this large?" asked Cap, again sweeping the air with the pipe. "I will just ask you what there is large about it? Did'n't Jasper himself confess that it was only some twenty leagues from shore to shore, hereaway?"

"But, uncle," interposed Mabel, "no land is to be seen, except here on our own coast. To me it looks exactly like the ocean."

"This bit of a pool look like the ocean! Well, Magnet, that from a girl who has had real seamen in her family is downright nonsense. What is there about it pray, that has even the outline of a sea on it?"

"Why, there is water–water–water–nothing but water, for miles on miles–far as the eye can see."

"And is'n't there water–water–water–nothing but water for miles on miles, in your rivers, that you have been canoeing through, too; ay, and 'as far as the eye can see,' in the bargain?"

"Yes, uncle, but the rivers have their banks, and there are trees along them, and they are narrow."

"And is'n't this a bank where we stand–don't these soldiers call this the bank of the lake, and ar'n't there trees in thousands, and ar'n't twenty leagues narrow enough of all conscience? Who the devil ever heard of the banks of the ocean, unless it might be the banks that are under water?"

"But, uncle, we cannot see across this lake, as we can see across a river."

"There you are out, Magnet. Ar'n't the Amazon, and Oronoco, and La Plata rivers, and can you see across them? Harkee, Pathfinder, I very much doubt if this stripe of water here, be even a lake; for to me it appears to be only a river. You are by no means particular about your geography, I find, up here in the woods."

"There *you* are out, Master Cap. There is a river, and a noble one too, at each end of it, but this is old Ontario before you, and, though it is not my gift to live on a lake, to my judgment there are few better than this."

"And, uncle, if we stood on the beach at Rockaway, what more should we see, than we now behold? There is a shore on one side, or banks there, and trees, too, as well as those which are here."

"This is perverseness, Magnet, and young girls should steer clear of any thing like obstinacy. In the first place, the ocean has coasts, but no banks, except the Grand Banks, as I tell you, which are out of sight of land; and you will not pretend that this bank is out of sight of land, or even under water?"

As Mabel could not very plausibly set up this extravagant opinion, Cap pursued the subject, his countenance beginning to discover the triumph of a successful disputant.

"And then the trees bear no comparison to these trees. The

coasts of the ocean have farms, and cities, and country seats, and, in some parts of the world, castles and monasteries, and light-houses—ay—ay—light-houses in particular on them; not one of all which things is to be seen here. No—no—Master Pathfinder, I never heard of an ocean that had'n't more or less light-houses on it, whereas, hereaway, there is not even a beacon."

"There is what is better—there's what is better, a forest and noble trees, a fit temple of God."

"Ay, your forest may do for a lake, but of what use would an ocean be, if the earth all around it were forest. Ships would be unnecessary, as timber might be floated in rafts, and there would be an end of trade, and what would a world be without trade. I am of that philosopher's opinion, who says human nature was invented for the purposes of trade. Magnet, I am astonished that you should think this water even looks like sea-water! Now, I dare say, that there is'n't such a thing as a whale, in all your lake, Master Pathfinder?"

"I never heard of one, I will confess, but I am no judge of animals that live in the water, unless it be the fishes of the rivers and the brooks."

"Nor a grampus, nor a porpoise even; not so much as a poor devil of a shark?"

"I will not take it on myself to say there is either. My gifts are not in that way, I tell you, Master Cap."

"Nor herring, nor albatross, nor flying-fish—" continued Cap, who kept his eye fastened on the guide, in order to see how far he might venture. "No such thing as a fish that can fly, I dare say?"

"A fish that can fly! Master Cap—Master Cap do not think, because we are mere borderers, that we have no idees of natur', and what she has been pleased to do. I know there are squirrels that can fly—"

"A squirrel fly!—the d——l, Master Pathfinder. Do you suppose that you have got a boy on his first v'y'ge, up here among you?"

"I know nothing of your v'y'ges, Master Cap, though I suppose them to have been many; but, as for what belongs to natur' in the woods, what I have seen I may tell, and not fear the face of man."

"And do you wish me to understand that you have seen a squirrel fly?"

"If you wish to understand the power of God, Master Cap, you will do well to believe that, and many other things of a like natur', for you may be quite sartain it is true."

"And yet, Pathfinder—" said Mabel, looking so pretty and sweet even while she played with the guide's infirmity, that he forgave her in his heart—"you, who speak so reverently of the power of the Deity, appear to doubt that a fish can fly?"

"I have not said it—I have not said it, and if Master Cap is ready to testify to the fact, unlikely as it seems, I am willing to try to think it true. I think it every man's duty to believe in the power of God, however difficult it may be."

"And why is'n't my fish as likely to have wings, as your squirrel?" demanded Cap, with more logic than was his wont. "That fishes do and can fly is as true as it is reasonable—"

"Nay, that is the only difficulty in believing the story," rejoined the guide. "It seems onreasonable to give an animal that lives in the water wings, which seemingly can be of no use to them."

"And do you suppose that the fishes are such asses as to fly about under water, when they are once fairly fitted out with wings?"

"Nay, I know nothing of the matter, but that fish should fly in the air seems more contrary to natur' still, than that they should fly in their own quarters; that, in which they were born and brought up, as one might say."

"So much for contracted ideas, Magnet. The fish fly out of water, to run away from their enemies under water, and there you see not only the fact, but the reason for it."

"Then I suppose it must be true," said the guide, quietly. "How long are their flights?"

"Not quite as far as those of pigeons, perhaps, but far enough to make an offing. As for those squirrels of yours, we'll say no more about them, friend Pathfinder, as I suppose they were mentioned just as a make-weight to the fish, in favor of the woods—But what is this thing, anchored here under the hill."

"That is the cutter of Jasper, uncle," said Mabel, hurriedly—"and a very pretty vessel, I think it is. Its name, too, is the Scud."

"Ay, it will do well enough for a lake, perhaps, but it's no great affair. The lad has got a standing bowsprit, and who ever saw a cutter with a standing bowsprit, before!"

"But may there not be some good reason for it, on a lake like this, uncle?"

"Sure enough—I must remember this is not the ocean, though it does look so much like it."

"Ah! uncle, then Ontario *does* look like the ocean, after all!"

"In your eyes, I mean, and those of Pathfinder; not, in the least, in mine, Magnet. Now you might set me down, out yonder, in the middle of this bit of a pond, and that, too, in the darkest night that ever fell from the heavens, and in the smallest canoe, and I could tell you it was only a lake. For that matter, the Dorothy (the name of his vessel) would find it out as quick as I could myself. I do not believe that brig would make more than a couple of short stretches at the most, before she would perceive the difference between Ontario and the old Atlantic. I once took her down into one of the large South American bays, and she behaved herself as awkwardly as a booby would in a church, with the congregation in a hurry. And Jasper sails that boat? I must have a cruise with the lad, Magnet, before I quit you, just for the name of the thing. It would never do to say I got in sight of this pond, and went away without taking a trip it."

"Well, well, you need'n't wait long for that," returned Pathfinder—"for the serjeant is about to embark with a party, to relieve a post among the Thousand Islands, and, as I heard him say, he intended that Mabel should go along, you can join company too."

"Is this true, Magnet?"

"I believe it is," returned the girl, a flush so imperceptible as to escape the observation of her companions, glowing on her cheeks, "though I have had so little opportunity to talk with my dear father, that I am not quite certain. Here he comes, however, and you can inquire of himself."

Notwithstanding his humble rank, there was something in the mien and character of Serjeant Dunham that commanded respect. Of a tall imposing figure, grave and saturnine disposition, and accurate and precise in his acts and manner of thinking, even Cap, dogmatical and supercilious as he usually was with landsmen, did not presume to take the same liberties with the old soldier, as he did with his other friends. It was often remarked that Serjeant Dunham received more true respect from Duncan of Lundie, the Scotch Laird who commanded the post, than most of the subalterns, for experience and tried services were of quite as much value in the eyes of the veteran Major, as birth and money. While the serjeant never even hoped to rise any higher, he so far respected himself and his present station, as always to act in a way to command attention, and the habit of mixing so much with inferiors, whose passions and dispositions he felt it necessary to restrain by distance and dignity, had so far coloured his whole deportment, that few were altogether free from its influence. While the captains treated him kindly, and as an old comrade, the lieutenants seldom ventured to dissent from his military opinions, and the ensigns, it was remarked, actually manifested a species of respect, that amounted to something very like deference. It is no wonder then, that the announcement of Mabel put a sudden termination to the singular dialogue we have just related, though it had been often observed that the Pathfinder was the only man, on that frontier, beneath the condition of a gentleman, who presumed to treat the Serjeant at all as an equal, or even with the cordial familiarity of a friend.

"Good morrow, Brother Cap," said the Serjeant, giving the military salute, as he walked, in a grave, stately manner on the bastion. "My morning duty has made me seem forgetful of you and Mabel, but we have now an hour or two to spare, and to get acquainted. Do you not perceive, brother, a strong likeness in the girl, to her we have so long lost?"

"Mabel is the image of her mother, serjeant, as I have always said, with a little of your firmer figure; though, for that matter, the Caps were never wanting in spring and activity."

Mabel cast a timid glance at the stern, rigid countenance of her father, of whom she had ever thought as the warm-hearted dwell on the affection of their absent parents, and, as she saw that the muscles of his face were working, notwithstanding the stiffness and method of his manner, her very heart yearned to throw herself on his bosom, and to weep at will. But he was so much colder in externals, so much more formal and distant than she had expected to find him, that she would not have dared to hazard the freedom, even had they been alone.

"You have taken a long and troublesome journey, brother, on my account, and we will try to make you comfortable, while you stay among us."

"I hear you are likely to receive orders to lift your anchor, serjeant, and to shift your berth into a part of the world where they say there are a thousand islands?"

"Pathfinder, this is some of your forgetfulness?—"

"Nay, nay, sarjeant; I forgot nothing, but it did not seem to me necessary to hide your intentions so very closely from your own flesh and blood."

"All military movements ought to be made with as little conversation as possible," returned the Serjeant, tapping the guide's shoulder, in a friendly but reproachful manner. "You have passed too much of your life in front of the French, not to know the value of silence. But, no matter. The thing must soon be known, and there is no great use in trying, now, to conceal it. We shall embark a relief party, shortly, for a post on the lake, though I do not say it is for the Thousand Islands, and I may have to go with it; in which case, I intend to take Mabel, to make my broth for me, and I hope, brother, you will not despise a soldier's fare, for a month or so."

"That will depend on the manner of marching. I have no love for woods and swamps."

"We shall sail in the Scud, and, indeed, the whole service, which is no stranger to us, is likely enough to please one accustomed to the water."

"Ay, to salt-water, if you will, but not to lake-water. If you have no person to handle that bit of a cutter for you, I have no objection to ship for the v'y'ge, notwithstanding, though I shall look on the whole affair as so much time thrown away, for I consider it an imposition to call sailing about this pond, going to sea."

"Jasper is every way able to manage the Scud, Brother Cap, and in that light I cannot say that we have need of your services, though we shall be glad of your company. You cannot return to the settlements until a party is sent in, and that is not likely to happen until after my return. Well, Pathfinder, this is the first time I ever knew men on the trail of the Mingos, and you not at their head!"

"To be honest with you, Sarjeant," returned the guide, not without a little awkwardness of manner, and a perceptible difference in the hue of a face that had become so uniformly red by exposure, "I have not felt that it was my gift, this morning. In the first place, I very well know that the soldiers of the fifty fifth are not the lads to overtake Iroquois in the woods, and the knaves did not wait to be surrounded, when they knew that Jasper had reached the garrison. Then, a man may take a little rest, after a summer of hard work, and no impeachment of his good will. Besides, the Sarpent is out with them, and if the miscreants are to be found at all, you may trust to his inmity and sight; the first being stronger, and the last nearly if not quite as good as my own. He loves the skulking vagabonds as little as myself, and, for that matter, I may say that my own feelin's towards a Mingo, are not much more than the gifts of a Delaware grafted on a christian stock. No–no–I thought I would leave the honor, this time, if honor there is to be, to the young ensign that commands, who, if he do'n't lose his scalp, may boast of his campaign in his letters to his mother, when he gets in. I thought I would play idler once in my life."

"And no one has a better right, if long and faithful service entitles a man to a furlough," returned the Serjeant, kindly. "Mabel will think none the worse of you, for preferring her company to the trail of the savages, and I dare say will be happy to give you a part of her breakfast, if you are inclined to eat. You must not think, however, girl, that the Pathfinder is in the habit of letting prowlers around the fort, beat a retreat without hearing the crack of his rifle."

"If I thought she did, Sarjeant, though not much given to showy and parade evolutions, I would shoulder Killdeer, and quit the garrison before her pretty eyes had time to frown. No–no–Mabel, knows me better, though we are but new acquaintances, for there has been no want of Mingos to enliven the short march we have already made in company."

"It would need a great deal of testimony, Pathfinder, to make me think ill of you, in any way, and more than all in the way you mention;" returned Mabel, colouring with the sincere earnestness with which she endeavored to remove any suspicions to the contrary, from his mind. "Both father and daughter, I believe, even owe you their lives, and believe me that neither will ever forget it."

"Thank you, Mabel, thank you with all my heart. But I will not take advantage of your ignorance neither, girl, and therefore shall say I do not think the Mingos would have hurt a hair of your head, had they succeeded by their deviltries and contrivances, in getting you into their hands. My scalp, and Jasper's, and Master Cap's, there, and the Sarpent's, too, would sartainly have been smoked, but as for the Sarjeant's daughter, I do not think they would have hurt a hair of her head!"

"And why should I suppose that enemies known to spare neither women nor children would have shown more mercy to me than to another. I feel, Pathfinder, that I owe you my life."

"I say nay, Mabel, they would'n't have had the heart to hurt you. No, not even a fiery Mingo devil, would have had the heart to hurt a hair of your head! Bad as I suspect the vampires to be, I do not suspect them of anything so wicked as that. They might have wished you—nay forced you to become the wife of one of their chiefs, and that would be torment enough to a christian young woman, but beyond that I do not think even the Mingos themselves would have gone."

"Well, then, I shall owe my escape from this great misfortune to you," said Mabel, taking his hard hand into her own, frankly and cordially, and certainly in a way to delight the honest guide. "To me it would be a lighter evil to be killed, than to become the wife of an Indian."

"That is her gift, sarjeant," exclaimed Pathfinder, turning to his old comrade with gratification written on every lineament of his honest countenance, "and it will have its way. I tell the Sarpent, that no christianizing will ever make even a Delaware a white man; nor any whooping and yelling convart a pale face into a red skin. That is the gift of a young woman born of christian parents, and it ought to be maintained."

"You are right, Pathfinder, and so far as Mabel Dunham is concerned, it *shall* be maintained. But, it is time to break your fasts, and if you will follow me, Brother Cap, I will show you how we poor soldiers live, here on a distant frontier."

Chapter IX.

"Now my co-mates and partners in exile,
Hath not old custom made this life more sweet
Than that of painted pomp? Are not these woods
More free from peril than the envious court?
Here feel we but the penalty of Adam—"
　　　As You Like It, II.i.1–5.

SERJEANT Dunham made no empty vaunt, when he gave the promise, conveyed in the closing words of the last chapter. Notwithstanding the remote frontier position of the post, they who lived at it, enjoyed a table that, in many respects, kings and princes might have envied. At the period of our tale, and, indeed, for half a century later, the whole of that vast region, which has been called the west, or the new countries, since the war of the revolution, lay a comparatively unpeopled desert, teeming with all the living productions of nature, that properly belonged to the climate, man and the domestic animals excepted. The few Indians that roamed its forests then could produce no visible effects on the abundance of the game, and the scattered garrisons, or occasional hunters, that here and there were to be met with on that vast surface, had no other influence, than the bee on the buckwheat field, or the humming-bird on the flower.

The marvels that have descended to our own times, in the way of tradition, concerning the quantities of beasts, birds and fishes that were then to be met with, on the shores of the great lakes in particular, are known to be sustained by the experience of living men, else might we hesitate about relating them, but having been eye-witnesses of some of these prodigies, our office shall be discharged with the confidence that certainty can impart. Oswego was particularly well placed to keep the larder of an epicure amply supplied. Fish, of various sorts, abounded in its river, and the sportsman had only to cast his line to haul in a bass, or some other member of the finny tribe, which then peopled the waters, as the air above the swamps of this fruitful latitude is known to be filled with insects. Among others, was the salmon of the lakes, a variety of that well-known species, that is scarcely inferior to the delicious salmon of Northern Europe. Of the different migratory birds that frequent forests and waters, there was the same affluence, hundreds of acres of geese and ducks being often seen, at a time, in the great bays that indented the shores of the lake. Deer, bears, rabbits and squirrels, with divers other quadrupeds, among which was sometimes included the elk, or moose, helped to complete the sum of the natural supplies, on which all the posts depended more or less, to relieve the unavoidable privations of their remote frontier positions.

In a place where viands, that would elsewhere be deemed great luxuries, were so abundant, no one was excluded from their enjoyment. The meanest individual at Oswego habitually feasted on game that would have formed the boast of a Parisian table, and it was no more than a healthful commentary on the caprices of taste, and of the waywardness of human desires, that the very diet, which in other scenes would have been deemed the subject of envy and repinings, got to pall on the appetites. The coarse and regular food of the army, which it became necessary to husband on account of the difficulty of transportation, rose in the estimation of the common soldier, and, at any time, he would cheerfully desert his venison, and ducks, and pigeons, and salmon, to banquet on the sweets of pickled pork, stringy turnips and half-cooked cabbage.

The table of Serjeant Dunham, as a matter of course, partook of the abundance and luxuries of the frontier, as well as of its privations. A delicious broiled salmon smoked on a homely platter, hot venison steaks sent up their appetizing odours and several dishes of cold meats, all of which were composed of game, had been set before the guests, in honor of the newly-arrived visiters, and in vindication of the old soldier's hospitality.

"You do not seem to be on short allowance, in this quarter of the world, serjeant," said Cap, after he had got fairly initiated into the mysteries of the different dishes: "your salmon might satisfy a Scotsman."

"It fails to do it, notwithstanding, brother Cap, for, among two or three hundred of the fellows, that we have in this garrison, there are not half a dozen, who will not swear that fish is unfit to be eaten. Even some of the lads, who never tasted venison except as poachers at home, turn up their noses at the fattest haunches that we get here."

"Ay, that is christian natur'," put in the Pathfinder, "and I must say it is none to its credit. Now, a redskin never repines, but is always thankful for the food he gets, whether it be fat, or lean; venison, or bear; wild turkey's breast, or wild goose's wing. To the shame of us white men be it said, that we look upon blessings without satisfaction, and consider trifling evils as matters of great account."

"It is so with the 55th, as I can answer, though I cannot say as much for their christianity;" returned the Serjeant. "Even the Major, himself, old Duncan of Lundie, will sometimes swear an oat-meal cake is better fare than the Oswego bass, and sigh for a swallow of Highland water, when, if so minded, he has the whole of Ontario to quench his thirst in."

"Has Major Duncan a wife and children?" asked Mabel, whose thoughts naturally turned towards her own sex, in her new situation.

"Not he, girl, though they do say that he has a betrothed, at home. The lady, it seems, is willing to wait, rather than suffer the hardships of service, in this wild region, all of which, brother Cap, is not according to my notions of a woman's duties. Your sister thought differently, and had it pleased God to spare her, would have been sitting, at this moment, on the very camp stool that her daughter so well becomes."

"I hope, Serjeant, you do not think of Mabel, for a soldier's wife," returned Cap, gravely. "Our family has done its share, in that way already, and it's high time that the sea was again remembered."

"I do not think of finding a husband for the girl in the 55th, or any other regiment, I can promise you, brother, though I do think it getting to be time that the child were respectably married."

"Father!"

"'Tis not their gifts, Sarjeant, to talk of these matters in so open a manner," said the guide, "for I've seen it verified by exper'ence, that he who would follow the trail of a virgin's good-will, must not go shouting out his thoughts behind her. So; if you please we will talk of something else."

"Well, then, brother Cap, I hope that bit of cold roasted pig is to your mind; you seem to fancy the food."

"Ay, ay, give me civilized grub, if I must eat," returned the pertinacious seaman. "Venison is well enough for your inland sailors, but we of the ocean like a little of that which we understand."

Here Pathfinder laid down his knife and fork, and indulged in a hearty laugh, though always in his silent manner. Then he asked, with a little curiosity in his manner—

"Do'n't you miss the skin, Master Cap; do'n't you miss the skin?"

"It would have been better for its jacket, I think myself, Pathfinder, but I suppose it is a fashion of the woods to serve up shoats, in this style."

"Well, well, a man may go round the 'arth and not know every thing! If you had had the skinning of that pig, Master Cap, it would have left you sore hands. The creatur' is a hedge-hog!"

"Blast me, if I thought it wholesome natural pork, either;" returned Cap. "But then I believed even a pig might lose some of its good qualities, up, hereaway, in the woods. It seemed no more than reason that a fresh-water hog, should not be altogether as good as a salt-water hog. I suppose, serjeant, by this time, it is all the same to you?"

"If the skinning of it, brother, does not fall to my duty. Pathfinder, I hope you did'n't find Mabel disobedient on the march?"

"Not she—not she. If Mabel is only half as well satisfied with Jasper and the Pathfinder, as the Pathfinder and Jasper are satisfied with her, sarjeant, we shall be friends for the remainder of our days."

As the guide spoke, he turned his eyes towards the blushing girl, with a sort of innocent desire to know her opinion, and then with an inborn delicacy that proved he was far superior to the vulgar desire to invade the sanctity of feminine feeling, he looked at his plate, and seemed to regret his own boldness.

"Well, well, we must remember that women are not men, my

friend," resumed the serjeant, "and make proper allowances for nature and education. A recruit is not a veteran. Any man knows that it takes longer to make a good soldier, than it takes to make any thing else, and it ought to require unusual time to make a good soldier's daughter."

"This is new doctrine, serjeant," said Cap, with some spirit. "We old seamen are apt to think that six soldiers, ay, and capital soldiers too, might be made, while one sailor is getting his education."

"Ay, brother Cap, I've seen something of the opinions which sea-faring men have of themselves," returned the brother-in-law, with a smile as bland as comported with his saturnine features; "for I was many years one of the garrison in a sea-port. You and I have conversed on the subject before, and I'm afraid we shall never agree. But if you wish to know what the difference is, between a real soldier, and man in what I should call a state of nature, you have only to look at a battalion of the 55th, on parade this afternoon, and then, when you get back to York, to examine one of the militia regiments making its greatest efforts."

"Well, to my eye, serjeant, there is very little difference–not more than you'll find between a brig and a snow.* To me they seem alike; all scarlet, and feathers, and powder, and pipe clay."

"So much, sir, for the judgment of a sailor," returned the serjeant with dignity; "but perhaps you are not aware that it requires a year to teach a true soldier how to eat."

"So much the worse for him! The militia know how to eat at starting, for I have often heard, that, on their marches, they commonly eat all before them, even if they do nothing else."

"They have their gifts, I suppose, like other men," observed Pathfinder, with a view to preserve the peace, which was evidently in some danger of being broken, by the obstinate predilection of each of the disputants in favor of his own calling; "and when a man has his gift from Providence it is commonly idle to endivor to bear up ag'in it. The 55th, sarjeant, is a judicious rigiment, in the way of eating, as I know from having been so long in its Company, though I dare say militia corps could be found that would outdo them in feats of that natur', too."

"Uncle," said Mabel, "if you have breakfasted, I will thank

you to go out upon the bastion with me, again. We have neither of us, half seen the lake, and it would be hardly seemly for a young woman to be walking about the fort, the first day of her arrival, quite alone."

Cap understood the motive of Mabel, and having, at the bottom, a hearty friendship for his brother-in-law, he was willing enough to defer the argument until they had been longer together, for the idea of abandoning it altogether, never crossed the mind of one so dogmatical and obstinate. He accordingly accompanied his niece, leaving Serjeant Dunham and his friend the Pathfinder, alone, together. As soon as his adversary had beaten a retreat, the serjeant, who did not quite so well understand the manœuvre of his daughter, turned to his companion, and with a smile that was not without triumph, he remarked—

"The army, Pathfinder, has never yet done itself justice; and, though modesty becomes a man, whether he is in a red coat or a black one, or for that matter, in his shirt-sleeves, I don't like to let a good opportunity slip of saying a word in its behalf. Well, my friend," laying his own hand, on one of the Pathfinder's, and giving it a hearty squeeze—"how do you like the girl?"

"You have reason to be proud of her, sarjeant; you have great reason to be proud at finding yourself the father of so handsome and well mannered a young woman. I have seen many of her sex, and some that were great and beautiful, but never before did I meet with one, in whom I thought Providence had so well balanced the different gifts."

"And the good opinion, I can tell you, Pathfinder, is mutual. She told me last night all about your coolness, and spirit, and kindness—particularly the last; for kindness counts for more than half with females, my friend—and the first inspection seems to give satisfaction on both sides. Brush up the uniform, and pay a little more attention to the outside, Pathfinder, and you will have the girl, heart and hand."

"Nay, nay, sarjeant, I've forgotten nothing that you have told me, and grudge no reasonable pains to make myself as pleasant in the eyes of Mabel, as she is getting to be in mine. I cleaned and brightened up Killdeer, this morning, as soon as the sun rose, and, in my judgment, the piece never looked better than it does at this very moment."

"That is according to your hunting notions, Pathfinder, but firearms should sparkle and glitter in the sun, and I never yet could see any beauty in a clouded barrel."

"Lord Howe thought otherwise, sarjeant, and he was accounted a good soldier!"

"Very true—his Lordship had all the barrels of his regiment darkened, and what good came of it? You can see his 'scutcheon hanging in the English Church at Albany! No—no, my worthy friend, a soldier should be a soldier, and at no time ought he to be ashamed, or afraid, to carry about him the signs and symbols of his honorable trade. Had you much discourse with Mabel, Pathfinder, as you came along in the canoe?"

"There was not much opportunity, sarjeant, and then I found myself so much beneath her in idees, that I was afraid to speak of much beyond what belonged to my own gifts."

"Therein, you are partly right, and partly wrong, my friend. Women love trifling discourse, though they like to have most of it to themselves. Now, you know, I'm a man that do not loosen my tongue at every giddy thought, and yet there were days when I could see that Mabel's mother thought none the worse of me, because I descended a little from my manhood. It is true, I was twenty two years younger then, than I am to day, and, moreover, instead of being the oldest serjeant in the regiment, I was the youngest. Dignity is commanding and useful, and there is no getting on without it, as respects the men, but if you would be thoroughly esteemed by a woman, it is necessary to condescend a little, on occasions."

"Ah's! me, sarjeant; I sometimes fear it will never do!"

"Why do you think so discouragingly of a matter on which I thought both our minds were made up?"

"We did agree that if Mabel should prove what you told me she was, and if the girl could fancy a rude hunter and guide, that I would quit some of my wandering ways, and try to humanize my mind down to a wife and children. But since I have seen the girl, I will own that many misgivin's have come over me!"

"How's this!" interrupted the serjeant, sternly—"Did I not understand you to say that you were pleased?—And is Mabel a young woman to disappoint expectation?"

"Ah! sarjeant, it is not Mabel that I distrust, but myself. I am but a poor ignorant woodsman, after all, and perhaps I'm not, in truth, as good as even you and I may think me!"

"If you doubt your own judgment of yourself, Pathfinder, I beg you will not doubt mine. Am I not accustomed to judge men's characters?—Is it not my especial duty, and am I often deceived. Ask Major Duncan, sir, if you desire any assurances in this particular."

"But, sarjeant, we have long been friends; have fou't side by side, a dozen times, and have done each other many sarvices. When this is the case, men are apt to think overkindly of each other, and I fear me that the daughter may not be so likely to view a plain, ignorant hunter as favorably as the father does."

"Tut—tut—Pathfinder—you do'n't know yourself, man, and may put all faith in my judgment. In the first place, you have experience, and as all girls must want that, no prudent young woman would overlook such a qualification. Then you are not one of the coxcombs that strut about when they first join a regiment, but a man who has seen service, and who carries the marks of it on his person and countenance. I dare say you have been under fire, some thirty or forty times, counting all the skirmishes and ambushes that you've seen."

"All of that, sarjeant, all of that, but what will it avail, in gaining the good will of a tender-hearted young female?"

"It will gain the day. Experience in the field is as good in love, as in war. But you are as honest-hearted, and as loyal a subject, as the King can boast of, God bless him!"

"That may be too—that may be too; but I'm afeard I'm too rude, and too old, and too wild like, to suit the fancy of such a young and delicate girl, as Mabel, who has been unused to our wilderness ways, and may think the settlements better suited to her gifts and inclinations."

"These are new misgivings for you, my friend, and I wonder they were never paraded before."

"Because I never knew my own worthlessness, perhaps, until I saw Mabel. I have travelled with some as fair, and have guided them through the forest, and seen them in their perils and in their gladness, but they were always too much above me, to make me think of them, as more than so many feeble ones I was bound to protect and defend. The case is now different. Mabel and I are so nearly alike, that I feel weighed down with a load that is hard to bear, at finding us so unlike. I do wish, sarjeant, that I was ten years younger, more comely to look at, and better suited to please a handsome young woman's fancy!"

"Cheer up, my brave friend, and trust to a father's knowledge of womankind. Mabel half loves you already, and a fortnight's intercourse and kindnesses, down among the islands yonder, will close ranks with the other half. The girl as much as told me this herself, last night."

"Can this be so, sarjeant!" said the guide, whose meek and modest nature shrunk from viewing himself in colours so favorable. "Can this be truly so! I am but a poor hunter, and Mabel, I see, is fit to be an officer's lady. Do you think the gal will consent to quit all her beloved settlement usages, and her visitin's, and church-goin's to dwell with a plain guide and hunter, up, hereaway, in the woods? Will she not in the ind crave her old ways, and a better man?"

"A better man, Pathfinder, would be hard to find," returned the father. "As for town usages, they are soon forgotten in the freedom of the forest, and Mabel has just spirit enough to dwell on a frontier. I've not planned this marriage, my friend, without thinking it over, as a general does his campaign. At first I thought of bringing you into the regiment, that you might succeed me when I retire, which must be sooner, or later, but on reflection, Pathfinder, I think you are scarcely fitted for the office. Still if not a soldier, in all the meanings of the word, you are a soldier in its best meaning, and I know that you have the good will of every officer in the corps. As long as I live, Mabel can dwell with me, and you will always have a home, when you return from your scoutings and marches."

"This is very pleasant to think of, sarjeant, if the girl can only come into our wishes with good will. But, Ah's! me, it does not seem that one like myself, can ever be agreeable in her handsome eyes! If I were younger, and more comely, now, as Jasper Western is, for instance, there might be a chance—yes, then, indeed, there might be some chance."

"That, for Jasper Eau douce, and every younker of them in, or about the fort!" returned the Serjeant snapping his fingers— "If not actually a younger, you are a younger looking, ay and a better looking man than the Scud's master——"

"Anan!" said Pathfinder, looking up at his companion, with an expression of doubt, as if he did not understand his meaning.

"I say, if not actually younger in days and years, you look more hardy and like whip-cord, than Jasper, or any of them, and there will be more of you, thirty years hence, than of all of them put together. A good conscience will keep one like you a mere boy, all his life."

"Jasper has as clear a conscience as any youth, I know, Sarjeant!—And is as likely to wear, on that account, as any young man in the colony."

"Then you are my friend," squeezing the other's hand—"my tried, sworn and constant friend."

"Yes, we have been friends, sarjeant, near twenty years. Before Mabel was born."

"True enough; before Mabel was born, we were well-tried friends, and the hussy would never dream of refusing to marry a man who was her father's friend before she was born!"

"We do'n't know, sarjeant, we do'n't know. Like loves like. The young prefar the young for companions, and the old the old."

"Not for wives, Pathfinder; I never knew an old man, now, who had an objection to a young wife. Then you are respected and esteemed by every officer in the fort, as I have said already, and it will please her fancy to like a man that every one else likes."

"I hope I have no inimies but the Mingos," returned the guide, stroking down his hair meekly, and speaking thoughtfully. "I've *tried* to do right, and that ought to make friends, though it sometimes fails."

"And you may be said to keep the best company, for even old Duncan of Lundie is glad to see you, and you pass hours in his society. Of all the guides, he confides most in you."

"Ay, even greater than he is, have marched by my side for days, and have convarsed with me as if I were their brother; but, sarjeant, I have never been puffed up by their company, for I know that the woods often bring men to a level, who would not be so in the settlements."

"And you are known to be the greatest rifle shot that ever pulled trigger in all this region."

"If Mabel could fancy a man for that, I might have no great reason to despair; and, yet, sarjeant, I sometimes think that it is all as much owing to Killdeer, as to any skill of my own. It is sartainly a wonderful piece, and might do as much in the hands of another!"

"That is your own humble opinion of yourself, Pathfinder, but we have seen too many fail with the same weapon, and you succeed too often with the rifles of other men, to allow me to agree with you. We will get up a shooting match, in a day or two, when you can show your skill, and then Mabel will form some judgment concerning your true character."

"Will that be fair, sarjeant? Every body knows that Killdeer seldom misses, and ought we to make a trial of this sort, when we all know what must be the result?"

"Tut—tut, man; I foresee I must do half this courting for you. For one who is always inside of the smoke, in a skirmish, you are the faintest-hearted suitor I ever met with. Remember Mabel comes of a bold stock, and the girl will be as likely to admire a man, as her mother was before her."

Here the serjeant arose, and proceeded to attend to his never ceasing duties, without apology, the terms on which the guide stood with all in the garrison, rendering this freedom quite a matter of course.

The reader will have gathered from the conversation just related one of the plans that Serjeant Dunham had in view, in causing his daughter to be brought to the frontier. Although necessarily much weaned from the caresses and blandishments that had rendered his child so dear to him, during the first year or two of his widower-hood, he had still a strong, but somewhat latent, love for her. Accustomed to command and to obey, without being questioned himself, or questioning others concerning the reasonableness of the mandates, he was perhaps too much disposed to believe that his daughter would marry the man he might select, while he was far from being disposed to do violence to her wishes. The fact was, few knew the Pathfinder intimately, without secretly coming to believe him to be one of extraordinary qualities. Ever the same, simple-minded, faithful, utterly without fear and yet prudent, foremost in all warrantable enterprises, or what the opinion of the day considered as such, and never engaged in any thing to call a blush to his

cheek, or censure on his acts, it was not possible to live much
with this being, who in his peculiar way, was a sort of type of
what Adam might have been supposed to be before the fall,
though certainly not without sin, and not feel a respect and
admiration for him, that had no reference to his position in life.
It was remarked that no officer passed him, without saluting
him as if he had been his equal, no common man without addressing him with the confidence and freedom of a comrade.
The most surprising peculiarity about the man himself, was the
entire indifference with which he regarded all distinctions that
did not depend on personal merit. He was respectful to his
superiors from habit, but had often been known to correct their
mistakes and to reprove their vices, with a fearlessness that
proved how essentially he regarded the more material points,
and with a natural discrimination that appeared to set education
at defiance. In short, a disbeliever in the ability of man to distinguish between good and evil, without the aid of instruction,
would have been staggered by the character of this extraordinary inhabitant of the frontier. His feelings appeared to possess
the freshness and nature of the forests in which he passed so
much of his time, and no casuist could have made clearer decisions in matters relating to right and wrong; and, yet, he was
not without his prejudices, which, though few and coloured by
the character and usages of the individual, were deep-rooted,
and had almost got to form a part of his nature. But the most
striking feature about the moral organization of Pathfinder was
his beautiful and unerring sense of justice. This noble trait,
and without it no man can be truly great, with it no man other
than respectable, probably had its unseen influence on all who
associated with him, for the common, rude and unprincipled
brawler of the camp had been known to return from an expedition made in his company, rebuked by his sentiments, softened
by his language and improved by his example. As might have
been expected with so elevated a quality, his fidelity was like the
immoveable rock. Treachery in him was classed among the
things that are impossible, and as he seldom retired before his
enemies, so was he never known, under any circumstances that
admitted of an alternative, to abandon a friend. The affinities
of such a character were, as a matter of course, those of like for

like. His associates and intimates, though more or less determined by chance, were generally of the higher order as to moral propensities, for he appeared to possess a species of instinctive discrimination that led him, insensibly to himself most probably, to cling closest to those, whose characters would best reward his friendship. In short, it was said of the Pathfinder, by one accustomed to study his fellows, that he was a fair example of what a just-minded and pure man might be, while untempted by unruly or ambitious desires, and left to follow the bias of his feelings, amid the solitary grandeur and ennobling influences of a sublime nature; neither led aside by the inducements which influence all to do evil amid the incentives of civilization, nor forgetful of the Almighty Being whose spirit pervades the wilderness as well as the town.

Such was the man whom Serjeant Dunham had selected as the husband of Mabel. In making this choice he had not been as much governed by a clear and judicious view of the merits of the individual, perhaps, as by his own likings; still no one knew the Pathfinder as intimately as himself, without always conceding to the honest guide a high place in his esteem, on account of these very virtues. That his daughter could find any serious objections to the match, the old soldier did not apprehend, while, on the other hand, he saw many advantages to himself, in dim perspective, that were connected with the decline of his days, and an evening of life passed among descendants, who were equally dear to him through both parents. He first made the proposition to his friend, who had listened to it kindly, but who, the serjeant was now pleased to find, already betrayed a willingness to come into his own views, that was proportioned to the doubts and misgivings proceeding from his humble distrust of himself.

Chapter X.

"Think not I love him, though I ask for him;
'Tis but a peevish boy:—yet he talks well;—
But what care I for words?—"
As You Like It, III.v.109–11.

A week passed in the usual routine of a garrison. Mabel was becoming used to a situation that, at first, she had found not only novel, but a little irksome, and the officers and men, in their turn, gradually familiarized to the presence of a young and blooming girl, whose attire and carriage had that air of modest gentility about them, which she had obtained in the family of her patroness, annoyed her less by their ill concealed admiration, while they gratified her by the respect which, she was fain to think, they paid her on account of her father; but which, in truth, was more to be attributed to her own modest, but spirited deportment, than to any deference for the worthy serjeant.

Acquaintances made in a forest, or in any circumstances of unusual excitement, soon attain their limits. Mabel found one week's residence at Oswego, sufficient to determine her, as to those with whom she might be intimate, and those whom she ought to avoid. The sort of neutral position occupied by her father, who was not an officer while he was so much more than a common soldier, by keeping her aloof from the two great classes of military life, lessened the number of those whom she was compelled to know, and made the duty of decision comparatively easy. Still she soon discovered that there were a few, even among those that could aspire to a seat at the commandant's table, who were disposed to overlook the halbert,* for the novelty of a well turned figure and of a pretty, winning face, and by the end of the first two or three days, she had admirers even among the gentlemen. The quarter-master, in particular, a middle aged soldier, who had more than once tried the blessings of matrimony, but was now a widower, was evidently disposed to increase his intimacy with the Serjeant, though their duties often brought them together, and the youngsters among his messmates did not fail to note that this man of method, who was a Scotchman of the name of Muir, was much more frequent in his visits to the quarters of his subordinate than had formerly been his wont. A laugh, or a joke, in honor of the "Serjeant's daughter," however, limited their strictures, though "Mabel Dunham" was soon a toast that even the ensign or the lieutenant did not disdain to give.

At the end of a week, Duncan of Lundie sent for Serjeant Dunham, after evening roll call, on business of a nature that, it was understood, required a personal conference. The old veteran dwelt in a moveable hut, which being placed on trucks, he could order to be wheeled about at pleasure, sometimes living in one part of the area within the fort, and sometimes in another.* On the present occasion, he had made a halt near the centre, and there he was found by his subordinate, who was admitted to his presence without any delay, or dancing attendance in an ante-chamber. In point of fact, there was very little difference in the quality of the accommodations given to the officers and those allowed to the men, the former being merely granted the most room, and Mabel and her father were lodged nearly, if not quite as well, as the commandant of the place, himself.

"Walk in, serjeant, walk in, my good friend," said old Lundie, heartily, as his inferior, stood in a respectful attitude at the door of a sort of library and bed-room into which he had been ushered; "walk in, and take a seat on that stool. I have sent for you, man, to discuss any thing but rosters and pay-rolls, this evening. It is now many years since we have been comrades, and 'auld lang syne' should count for something, even between a Major and his orderly, a Scot and a Yankee. Sit ye down, man, and just put yourself at your ease. It has been a fine day, serjeant?"

"It has indeed, Major Duncan," returned the other, who, though he complied so far as to take the seat, was much too practised not to understand the degree of respect it was neces-

This circumstance is a real incident, taken from the "American Lady" of Mrs. Grant, of Laggan.

sary to maintain in his manner; "a very fine day, sir, it has been, and we may look for more of them, at this season."

"I hope so, with all my heart. The crops look well, as it is, man, and you'll be finding that the 55th make almost as good farmers as soldiers. I never saw better potatoes in Scotland, than we are likely to have, in that new patch, of ours."

"They promise a good yield, Major Duncan, and, in that light, a more comfortable winter than the last."

"Life is progressive, serjeant, in its comforts, as well as in its need of them. We grow old, and I begin to think it time to retire and settle in life. I feel that my working days are nearly over."

"The King, God bless him, sir, has much good service, in your honor, yet."

"It may be so, Serjeant Dunham, especially if he should happen to have a spare Lt-Colonelcy left."

"The 55th will be honored the day that commission is given to Duncan of Lundie, sir."

"And Duncan of Lundie will be honored the day he receives it. But, serjeant, if you have never had a Lt-Colonelcy you have had a good wife, and that is the next thing to rank, in making a man happy."

"I have been married, Major Duncan, but it is now a long time since I have had no drawback on the love I bear His Majesty and my duty."

"What, man, not even the love you bear that active, little, round-limbed, rosy-cheeked daughter, that I have seen in the fort, these last few days! Out upon you, serjeant! old fellow as I am, I could almost love that little lassie, myself, and send the Lt-Colonelcy to the devil."

"We all know where Major Duncan's heart is, and that is in Scotland, where a beautiful lady is ready and willing to make him happy, as soon as his own sense of duty shall permit."

"Ay, hope is ever a far off thing, serjeant," returned the superior, a shade of melancholy passing over his hard Scottish features as he spoke; "and bonny Scotland is a far off country. Well, if we have no heather, and oat-meal in this region, we have venison for the killing it, and salmon as plenty as at Berwick upon Tweed. Is it true, serjeant, that the men complain of having been over-venisoned, and over-pigeoned of late?"

"Not for some weeks, Major Duncan, for neither deer nor birds are so plenty at this season as they have been. They begin to throw their remarks about concerning the salmon, but I trust we shall get through the summer without any serious disturbance on the score of food. The Scotch in the battalion do, indeed, talk more than is prudent of their want of oat-meal, grumbling occasionally of our wheaten bread."

"Ah! that is human nature, serjeant, pure unadulterated Scotch human nature. A cake, man, to say the truth is an agreeable morsel, and I often see the time, when I pine for a bite, myself."

"If the feeling gets to be troublesome, Major Duncan—in the men I mean, sir; for I would not think of saying so disrespectful a thing to your honor—but if the men ever pine seriously for their natural food, I would humbly recommend that some oat-meal be imported, or prepared in this country for them, and I think we shall hear no more of it. A very little would answer for a cure, sir."

"You are a wag, serjeant, but hang me if I am sure you are not right. There may be sweeter things in this world, after all, than oat-meal. You have a sweet daughter, Dunham, for one."

"The girl is like her mother, Major Duncan, and will pass inspection," said the serjeant proudly. "Neither was brought up on any thing better than good American flour. The girl will pass inspection, sir!"

"That would she, I'll answer for it. Well, I may as well come to the point at once, man, and bring up my reserve into the front of the battle. Here is Davy Muir, the quarter-master, disposed to make your daughter his wife, and he has just got me to open the matter to you, being fearful of compromitting his own dignity—and I may as well add, that half the youngsters in the fort toast her, and talk of her from morning till night."

"She is much honored, sir," returned the father, stiffly, "but I trust the gentlemen will find something more worthy of them to talk about, ere long. I hope to see her the wife of an honest man before many weeks, sir."

"Yes, Davy is an honest man, and that is more than can be said for all in the Quarter-Master's department, I'm thinking, serjeant," returned Lundie, with a slight smile. "Well, then, may

I tell the Cupid-stricken youth, that the matter is as good as settled?"

"I thank your honor, but Mabel is betrothed to another."

"The devil she is! That will produce a stir in the fort, though I'm not sorry to hear it, either, for to be frank with you, serjeant, I'm no great admirer of unequal matches."

"I think, with your honor, and have no desire to see my daughter an officer's lady. If she can get as high as her mother was before her, it ought to satisfy any reasonable woman."

"And may I ask, serjeant, who is the lucky man that you intend to call son-in-law?"

"The Pathfinder, your honor."

"Pathfinder!"

"The same, Major Duncan, and in naming him to you, I give you his whole history. No one is better known on this frontier, than my honest, brave, true-hearted friend."

"All that is true enough, but is he, after all, the sort of person to make a girl of twenty happy."

"Why not, your honor; the man is at the head of his calling. There is no other guide, or scout, connected with the army that has half the reputation of Pathfinder, or who deserves to have it, half as well."

"Very true, serjeant, but is the reputation of a scout, exactly the sort of renown to captivate a girl's fancy."

"Talking of girls' fancies, sir, is, in my humble opinion, much like talking of a recruit's judgment. If we were to take the notions of the awkward squad, sir, as a guide, we should never form a decent line, in battalion, Major Duncan."

"But your daughter has nothing awkward about her, for a genteeler girl of her class, could not be found in old Albin itself. Is she of your way of thinking, in this matter, though, I suppose she must be, as you say she is betrothed."

"We have not yet conversed on the subject, your honor, but I consider her mind as good as made up, from several little circumstances that might be named."

"And what are these circumstances, Serjeant?" asked the Major, who began to take more interest than he had at first felt, in the subject. "I confess a little curiosity to learn something about a woman's mind, being, as you know, a bachelor myself."

"Why, your honor, when I speak of the Pathfinder to the girl, she always looks me full in the face; chimes in with every thing I say in his favor, and has a frank open way with her, which says as much as if she half considered him, already, as a husband."

"Hum—and these signs you think, Dunham, are faithful tokens of your daughter's feelings?"

"I do, your honor, for they strike me as natural. When I find a man, sir, who looks me full in the face, while he praises an officer—for, begging your honor's pardon, the men will sometimes pass their strictures on their betters—and when I find a man looking me in the eyes, as he praises his captain, I always set it down that the fellow is honest, and means what he says."

"Is there not some material difference in the age of the intended bridegroom, and that of his pretty bride, serjeant?"

"You are quite right, sir; Pathfinder is well advanced towards forty, and Mabel has every prospect of happiness that a young woman can derive from the certainty of possessing an experienced husband. I was quite forty myself, your honor, when I married her mother."

"But, will your daughter be as likely to admire a green hunting shirt, such as that our worthy guide wears, with a fox-skin cap, as the smart uniform of the 55th?"

"Perhaps not, sir, and therefore she will have the merit of self-denial, which always makes a young woman wiser and better."

"And are you not afraid that she may be left a widow while still a young woman?—What between wild beasts, and wilder savages, Pathfinder may be said to carry his life in his hand."

"'Every bullet has its billet,' Lundie," for so the Major was fond of being called, in his moments of condescension, and when not engaged in military affairs, "and no man in the 55th can call himself beyond, or above, the chances of sudden death. In that particular, Mabel would gain nothing by a change. Besides, sir, if I may speak freely on such a subject, I much doubt if ever Pathfinder dies in battle, or by any of the sudden chances of the wilderness."

"And why so, Serjeant?" asked the Major, looking at his inferior, with the sort of reverence which a Scot of his day, was more apt than at present to entertain for mysterious agencies.

"He is a soldier, so far as danger is concerned, and one that is much more than usually exposed, and, being free of his person, why should he expect to escape, when others do not?"

"I do not believe, your honor, that the Pathfinder considers his own chances, better than any one's else, but the man will never die by a bullet. I have seen him so often, handling his rifle with as much composure as if it were a shepherd's crook, in the midst of the heaviest showers of bullets, and under so many extraordinary circumstances, that I do not think Providence means he should ever fall in that manner. And, yet, if there be a man in His Majesty's dominions who really deserves such a death, it is Pathfinder!"

"We never know, serjeant," returned Lundie, with a countenance that was grave with thought, "and the less we say about it, perhaps, the better. But, will your daughter–Mabel, I think, you call her–will Mabel be as willing to accept one, who, after all, is a mere hanger-on of the army, as to take one from the service itself. There is no hope of promotion for the guide, serjeant!"

"He is at the head of his corps, already, your honor. In short, Mabel has made up her mind on this subject, and as your honor has had the condescension to speak to me about Mr. Muir, I trust you will be kind enough to say that the girl is as good as billeted for life."

"Well, well, this is your own matter, and, now,–Serjeant Dunham!"

"Your honor," said the other rising, and giving the customary salute.

"You have been told it is my intention to send you down among the Thousand Islands, for the next month. All the old subalterns have had their tours of duty in that quarter–all that I like to trust, at least, and it has, at length, come to your turn. Lt. Muir, it is true, claims his right, but being the Quarter Master, I do not like to break up well established arrangements. Are the men drafted?"

"Every thing is ready, your honor. The draft is made, and I understood that the canoe, which got in, last night, brought a message to say that the party already below, is looking out for the relief."

"It did, and you must sail the day after to-morrow, if not to-morrow night. It will be wise, perhaps, to sail in the dark."

"So Jasper thinks, Major Duncan, and I know no one more to be depended on, in such an affair, than young Jasper Western."

"Young Jasper Eau douce!" said Lundie, a slight smile gathering around his usually stern mouth. "Will that lad be of your party, Serjeant?"

"Your honor will remember that the Scud never quits port without him."

"True, but all general rules have their exceptions. Have I not seen a seafaring person about the fort within the last few days?"

"No doubt, your honor; it is Master Cap, a brother-in-law of mine, who brought my daughter from below."

"Why not put him in the Scud for this cruise, serjeant, and leave Jasper behind. Your brother-in-law would like the variety of a fresh water cruise, and you would enjoy more of his company."

"I intended to ask your honor's permission to take him along, but he must go as a volunteer. Jasper is too brave a lad to be turned out of his command without a reason, Major Duncan, and I'm afraid Brother Cap despises fresh water too much to do duty on it."

"Quite right, serjeant, and I leave all this to your own discretion. Eau douce must retain his command, on second thoughts—You intend that Pathfinder shall also be of the party?"

"If your honor approves of it. There will be service for both the guides, the Indian as well as the white man."

"I think you are right. Well, serjeant, I wish you good luck in the enterprise, and remember the post is to be destroyed and abandoned when your command is withdrawn. It will have done its work by that time or we shall have failed entirely, and it is too ticklish a position to be maintained unnecessarily. You can retire."

Serjeant Dunham gave the customary salute, turned on his heels, as if they had been pivots, and had got the door nearly drawn-to after him, when he was suddenly recalled.

"I had forgotten, serjeant, the younger officers have begged for a shooting match, and to-morrow has been named for the day. All competitors will be admitted, and the prizes will be a silver mounted powder horn, a leathern flask, ditto," reading from a piece of paper, "as I see by the professional jargon of this bill, and a silk calash,* for a lady. The latter is to enable the victor to show his gallantry, by making an offering of it to her he best loves."

"All very agreeable, your honor, at least to him that succeeds. Is the Pathfinder to be permitted to enter?"

"I do not well see how he can be excluded, if he choose to come forward. Latterly, I have observed that he takes no share in these sports, probably from a conviction of his own unequalled skill."

"That's it, Major Duncan; the honest fellow knows there is not a man on the frontier who can equal him, and he does not wish to spoil the pleasure of others. I think we may trust to his delicacy, in any thing, sir. Perhaps it may be as well, to let him have his own way."

"In this instance, we must, serjeant. Whether he will be as successful in all others, remains to be seen. I wish you good evening, Dunham."

The serjeant now withdrew, leaving Duncan of Lundie to his own thoughts. That they were not altogether disagreeable was to be inferred from the smiles which occasionally crossed a countenance that was hard and martial in its usual expression, though there were moments in which all its severe sobriety prevailed. Half an hour might have passed when a tap at the door, was answered by a direction to enter. A middle-aged man, in the dress of an officer but whose uniform wanted the usual smartness of the profession, made his appearance, and was saluted as "Mr. Muir."

"I have come, sir, at your bidding to know my fortune," said the Quarter Master, in a strong Scotch accent, as soon as he had taken the seat which was proffered to him. "To say the truth to you, Major Duncan, this girl is making as much havoc in the garrison, as the French did before Ty;*I never witnessed so general a rout, in so short a time!"

"Surely, Davy, you do'n't mean to persuade me that your young and unsophisticated heart, is in such a flame, after one week's ignition! Why, man, this is worse than the affair in Scotland, where it was said the heat within was so intense that it just burnt a hole through your own precious body, and left a place for all the lassies to peer in at, to see what the combustible material was worth."

"Ye'll have your own way, Major Duncan, and your father and mother would have theirs before ye even if the enemy were in the camp. I see nothing so extraordinar' in young people's following the bent of their inclinations and wishes."

"But you've followed yours so often, Davy, that I should think, by this time, it had lost the edge of novelty. Including that informal affair in Scotland, when you were a lad, you've been married four times, already."

"Only three, Major, as I hope to get another wife! I've not yet had my number; no—no—only three."

"I'm thinking, Davy, you don't include the first affair, I mentioned; that, in which there was no parson."

"And why should I, Major? The courts decided that it was no marriage, and what more could a man want! The woman took advantage of a slight amorous propensity, that may be a weakness in my disposition, perhaps, and inveigled me into a contract that was found to be illegal."

"If I remember right, Muir, there were thought to be two sides to that question, in the time of it!"

"It would be but an indifferent question, my dear Major, that had'n't two sides to it; and I've know many that had three. But the poor woman's dead, and there was no issue, so nothing came of it, after all. Then I was particularly unfortunate with my second wife—I say second, Major, out of deference to you, and on the mere supposition that the first was a marriage at all—but first, or second, I was particularly unfortunate with Jeannie Graham, who died in the first lustrum, leaving neither chick nor chiel behind her. I do think if Jeannie had survived I never should have turned my thoughts towards another wife."

"But as she did not, you married twice after her death, and are desirous of doing so a third time."

"The truth can never justly be gainsayed, Major Duncan, and I am always ready to avow it. I'm thinking, Lundie, you are melancholar', this fine evening?"

"No, Muir, not melancholy absolutely, but a little thoughtful, I confess. I was looking back to our boyish days, when I, the Laird's son, and you the parson's, roamed about our native hills, happy and careless boys, taking little heed to the future, and then have followed some thoughts, that may be a little painful, concerning that future, as it has turned out to be."

"Surely, Lundie, ye do not complain of your portion of it. You've risen to be a Major, and will soon be a Lt.-Colonel, if letters tell the truth, while I am just one step higher than when your honored father gave me my first commission, and a poor deevil of a Quarter Master!"

"And, the four wives."

"Three, Lundie; three only that were legal, even under our own liberal and sanctified laws."

"Well, then, let it be three. Ye know, Davy," said Major Duncan, insensibly dropping into the pronunciation and dialect of his youth, as is much the practice with educated Scotchmen, as they warm with a subject that comes near the heart,—"Ye know, Davy, that my own choice has long been made, and in how anxious and hope-wearied a manner, I've waited for that happy hour when I can call the woman I've so long loved a wife; and, here, have you, without fortune, name, birth, or merit—I mean particular merit—"

"Na—na—dinna say that, Lundie—the Muirs are of gude bluid."

"Well then, without aught but bluid, ye've wived four times—"

"I tall ye, but thrice, Lundie. Ye'll weaken auld frindship, if ye call it four."

'Put it at ye'r own number, Davy, and its far more than ye'r share. Our lives have been very different on the score of matrimony, at least; you must allow that, my old friend.'

"And which do you think has been the gainer, Major, speaking as frankly the'gither, as we did when lads."

"Nay, I've nothing to conceal. My days have passed, in hope deferred, while yours have passed in—"

"Not in hope realized, I give you my honor, Major Duncan," interrupted the Quarter Master. "Each new experiment I have thought might prove an advantage, but disappointment seems the lot of man. Ah! this is a vain world of ours, Lundie, it must be owned, and in nothing vainer than in matrimony."

"And yet you are ready to put your neck into the noose for the fifth time!"

"I desire to say, it will be but the fourth, Major Duncan," said the Quarter Master, positively; then instantly changing the expression of his face to one of boyish rapture, he added—"But this Mabel Dunham, is a rara avis! Our Scotch lassies are fair and pleasant, but it must be owned these colonials are of surpassing comeliness."

"You will do well to recollect your commission and blood, Davy; I believe all four of your wives—"

"I wish my dear Lundie, ye'd be more accurate in your arithmetick—three times one, make three."

"All three, then, were what might be termed gentlewomen."

"That's just it, Major. Three were gentlewomen, as you say, and the connections were suitable."

"And the fourth being the daughter of my father's gardener, the connection was unsuitable. But have you no fear that marrying the child of a non-commissioned officer, who is in the same corps with yourself, will have the effect to lessen your consequence in the regiment?"

"That's just been my weakness through life, Major Duncan; for I've always married without regard to consequences. Every man has his besetting sin, and matrimony, I fear is mine. And, now, that we have discussed what may be called the principles of the connection, I will just ask, if you did me the favor to speak to the Serjeant on the trifling affair?"

"I did, David, and am sorry to say for your hopes, that I see no great chances of your succeeding."

"Not succeeding!—An officer, and a Quarter Master, in the bargain, and not succeed with a serjeant's daughter."

"It's just that, Davy."

"And why not, Lundie?—Will you have the goodness to answer, just that?"

"The girl is betrothed. Hand plighted, word passed, love pledged—no, hang me if I believe that either, but she is betrothed."

"Well that's an obstacle, it must be avowed, Major, though it counts for little, if the heart is free."

"Quite true, and I think it probable the heart is free, in this case, for the intended husband appears to the choice of the father, rather than of the daughter."

"And who may it be, Major," asked the Quarter Master, who viewed the whole matter, with the philosophy and coolness that are acquired by use. "I do not recollect any plausible suitor, that is likely to stand in my way."

"No, *you* are the only *plausible* suitor on the frontier, Davy. The happy man is Pathfinder."

"Pathfinder, Major Duncan!"

"No more, nor any less, David Muir. Pathfinder is the man, but it may relieve your jealousy a little, to know that, in my judgment at least, it is a match of the father's, rather than of the daughter's seeking."

"I thought as much!" exclaimed the Quarter Master, drawing a long breath, like one who felt relieved; "it's quite impossible, that with my experience in human nature,–"

"Particularly hu-woman's nature, David!"

"Ye will have yer joke, Lundie, lat who will suffer! But I did not think it possible I could be deceived as to the young woman's inclinations, which I think I may boldly pronounce to be altogether above the condition of Pathfinder. As for the individual himself, why time will show."

"Now, tell me frankly, Davy Muir," said Lundie, stopping short in his walk, and looking the other earnestly in the face, with a comical expression of surprise, that rendered the veteran's countenance ludicrously earnest–"do you really suppose, a girl like the daughter of Serjeant Dunham, can take a serious fancy to a man of your years, and appearance, and experience, I might add?"

"Hout, awa', Lundie, ye dinna know the sax, and that's the reason yer unmarried in yer forty fifth year. It's a fearfu' time ye've been a bachelor, Major!"

"And what may be *your* age, Lt. Muir, if I may presume to ask so delicate a question?"

"Forty seven, I'll no deny it, Lundie, and if I get Mabel, there'll be just a wife for every twa lustrums! But I did'na think Serjeant Dunham would be so humble-minded, as to dream of giving that sweet lass of his to one like the Pathfinder!"

"There's no dream about it, Davy; the man is as serious as a soldier about to be flogged."

"Well, well, Major, we are auld friends–" both ran into the

Scotch, or avoided it, as they approached or drew away from their younger days, in the dialogue, "and ought to know how to take and give a joke off duty. It is possible the worthy man has not understood my hints, or he never would have thought of such a thing. The difference between an officer's consort, and a guide's woman is as vast, as that between the antiquity of Scotland and the antiquity of America. I'm auld bluid, too, Lundie."

"Take my word for it, Davy, your antiquity will do you no good, in this affair, and as for your blood it is not older than your bones. Well, well, man, ye know the Serjeant's answer, and so you perceive that my influence, on which you counted so much, can do nought for ye.—Let us take a glass the'gither Davy, for auld acquaintance sake, and then ye'll be doing well to remember the party that marches the morrow, and to forget Mabel Dunham as fast as ever you can."

"Ah! Major, I have always found it easier to forget a wife, than to forget a sweetheart! When a couple are fairly married, all is settled but the death, as one may say, which must finally part us all, and it seems to me awfu' irreverent to disturb the departed; whereas, there is so much anxiety, and hope, and felicity in expectation, like, with the lassie, that it keeps thought alive."

"That is just my idea of your situation, Davy, for I never supposed you expected any more felicity with either of your wives. Now, I've heard of fellows who were so stupid as to look forward to happiness with their wives, even beyond the grave. I drink to your success, or to your speedy recovery from this attack, Lieutenant, and admonish you to be more cautious in the future, as some of these violent cases may yet carry you off."

"Many thanks, my dear Major, and a speedy termination to an old courtship, of which I know something. This is real Mountain Dew, Lundie, and it warms the heart, like a gleam of bonny Scotland. As for the men you've just mentioned, they could have had but one wife apiece, for where there are several, the deeds of the women, themselves, may carry them different ways. I think a reasonable husband ought to be satisfied with passing his allotted time with any particular wife, in this world, and not to go about moping for things unattainable. I'm infinitely obliged to you, Major Duncan, for this and all your other acts of friendship, and if you could but add another, I should think you had not altogether forgotten the play-fellow of your boyhood."

"Well, Davy, if the request be reasonable, and such as a superior ought to grant, out with it, man."

"If ye could only contrive a little service for me, down among the Thousand Isles, for a fortnight, or so, I think this matter might be settled to the satisfaction of all parties. Just remember, Lundie, the lassie is the only marriageable white female on this frontier!"

"There is always duty for one in your line at a post however small, but this below can be done by the Serjeant as well as by the Quarter Master General, and better too."

"But not better than by a regimental officer. There is great waste, in common, among the orderlies."

"I'll think of it, Muir," said the Major laughing, "and you shall have my answer in the morning. Here will be a fine occasion, man, the morrow, to show yourself off before the lady; you are expert with the rifle, and prizes are to be won. Make up your mind to display your skill, and who knows what may yet happen before the Scud sails."

"I'm thinking most of the young men will try their hands in this sport, Major."

"That will they, and some of the old ones, too, if you appear. To keep you in countenance, I'll try a shot or two myself, Davy, and you know I have some name that way."

"It might, indeed, do good! The female heart, Major Duncan, is susceptible in many different modes, and sometimes in a way that the rules of philosophy might reject. Some require a suitor to sit down before them, as it might be in a regular siege, and only capitulate when the place can hold out no longer; others again like to be carried by storm, while there are hussies who can only be caught by leading them into an ambush. The former is the most creditable and officer-like process, perhaps, but I must say I think the last the most pleasing."

"An opinion formed from experience, out of all question. And what of the storming parties?"

"They may do for younger men, Lundie," returned the Quarter Master, rising and winking, a liberty that he often took with his commanding officer, on the score of a long intimacy; "every period of life has its necessities, and at forty seven it's just as well to trust a little to the head. I wish you a verry good even, Major Duncan, and freedom from gout, with a sweet and refreshing sleep."

"The same to yourself, Mr. Muir, with many thanks. Remember the passage of arms for the morrow."

The Quarter Master withdrew, leaving Lundie in his library to reflect on what had just passed. Use had so accustomed Major Duncan to Lt. Muir, and all his traits and humours, that the conduct of the latter did not strike the former with the same force, as it will probably strike the reader. In truth, while all men act under one common law that is termed human nature, the varieties in their dispositions, modes of judging, feelings and selfishness are infinite.

Chapter XI.

"Compel the hawke, to sit that is unmann'd,
Or make the hound, untaught to draw the deere,
Or bring the free, against his will in band,
Or move the sad, a pleasant tale to heere,
Your time is lost, and you no whit the neere!
So love ne learnes, of force the heart to knit:
She serves but those, that feel sweet fancies fit."
        Churchyard, *A Mirror for Magistrates*,
        "Shore's Wife," ll. 127-33.

Iᴛ is not often that hope is rewarded by fruition, as completely as the wishes of the young men of the garrison were met by the state of the weather, on the succeeding day. It may be no more than the ordinary waywardness of man, but the Amerians are a little accustomed to taking pride in things, that the means of intelligent comparisons would probably show, were in reality of a very inferior quality, while they overlook, or undervalue advantages that place them certainly on a level with, if not above most of their fellow creatures. Among the latter is the climate, which, as a whole, though far from perfect, is infinitely more agreeable, and quite as healthy, as those of most of the countries which are loudest in their denunciations of it. The heats of summer were little felt at Oswego, at the period of which we are writing, for the shade of the forest added to the refreshing breezes from the lake, so far reduced the influence of the sun, as to render the nights always cool, and the days seldom oppressive.

It was now September, a month in which the strong gales of the coast often appear to force themselves across the country as far as the great lakes, where the inland sailor sometimes feels that genial influence which characterizes the winds of the ocean, invigorating his frame, cheering his spirits, and arousing his moral force. Such a day was that on which the garrison of Oswego assembled, to witness what its commander had jocularly called a "passage of arms." Lundie was a scholar, in military matters at least, and it was one of his sources of honest pride to direct the reading and thoughts of the young men under his orders, to the more intellectual parts of their profession. For one in his situation, his library was both good and extensive, and its books were freely lent to all who desired to use them. Among other whims that had found their way into the garrison, through these means, was a relish for the sort of amusement in which it was now about to indulge, and around which, some chronicles of the days of chivalry had induced them to throw a parade and romance, that were not unsuited to the characters and habits of soldiers, or to the insulated and wild post, occupied by this particular garrison. While so earnestly bent on pleasure, however, they on whom that duty devolved, did not neglect the safety of the garrison. One standing on the ramparts of the fort, and gazing on the waste of glittering water that bounded the view all along the northern horizon, and on the slumbering and seemingly boundless forest, that filled the other half of the panorama, would have fancied the spot the very abode of peacefulness and security; but Duncan of Lundie too well knew that the woods might at any moment give up their hundreds bent on the destruction of the fort and all it contained, and that even the treacherous lake offered a highway of easy approach, by which his more civilized, and scarcely less wily foes, the French, could come upon him, at an unwelcome and unguarded moment. Parties were sent out, under old and vigilant officers, men who cared little for the sports of the day, to scour the forest, and one entire company held the fort, under arms, with orders to maintain a vigilance as strict as if an enemy of superior force was known to be near. With these precautions, the remainder of the officers and men abandoned themselves, without apprehension, to the business of the morning.

The spot selected for the sports, was a sort of esplanade a little west of the fort, and on the immediate bank of the lake. It had been cleared of its trees and stumps, that it might answer the purpose of a parade ground, as it possessed the advantage of having its rear protected by the water, and one of its flanks by the works. Men drilling on it, could be attacked, consequently, on two sides only, and as the cleared space beyond it, in the direction of the west and south, was large, any assailants would be compelled to quit the cover of the woods, before they could make an approach sufficiently near to render them dangerous.

Although the regular arms of the regiment were muskets, some fifty rifles were produced on the present occasion. Every officer had one, as a part of his private provision for amusement, many belonged to the scouts and friendly Indians, of whom more or less were always hanging about the post, and there was a public provision of them, for the use of those who followed the game with the express object of obtaining supplies. Among those who carried the weapon were some five or six, who had reputations for knowing how to use it particularly well—so well indeed as to have given them a celebrity on the frontier—twice that number who were believed to be much better than common, and many who would have been thought expert, in almost any situation, but the precise one in which they now happened to be placed.

The distance was a hundred yards, and the weapon was to be used without a rest. The target a board, with the customary circular lines in white paint, having the bull's eye in the centre. The first trials in skill commenced with challenges among the more ignoble of the competitors, to display their steadiness and dexterity in idle competition. None but the common men, engaged in this strife, which had little to interest the spectators, among whom no officer had yet appeared.

Most of the soldiers were Scotch, the regiment having been raised at Stirling and its vicinity, not many years before, though, as in the case of Serjeant Dunham, many Americans had joined it since its arrival in the colonies. As a matter of course, the provincials were generally the most expert marksmen, and after a desultory trial of half an hour, it was necessarily conceded that a youth, who had been born in the colony of New York, and who, coming of Dutch extraction, bore the euphonious name of Van Valtenburg, but was familiarly called Follock, was the most expert of all who had yet tried their skill. It was just as this opinion prevailed, that the oldest captain, accompanied by most of the gentlemen and ladies of the fort, appeared on the parade. A train of some twenty females of humbler condition followed, among whom was seen the well turned form, intelligent, blooming, animated countenance, and neat, becoming attire of Mabel Dunham.

Of females who were officially recognised as belonging to the class of ladies, there were but three in the fort, all of whom were officers' wives; staid matronly women, with the simplicity of the habits of middle life, singularly mixed in their deportment, with their notions of professional superiority, the rights and duties of caste, and the etiquette of rank. The other women were the wives of non-commissioned officers and privates, Mabel being strictly, as had been stated by the Quarter Master, the only real candidate for matrimony among her sex. There were a dozen other girls it is true, but they were still classed among the children, none of them being yet of an age to elevate them into objects of legitimate admiration.

Some little preparation had been made for the proper reception of the females, who were placed on a low staging of planks, near the immediate bank of the lake. In their vicinity the prizes were suspended from a post. Great care was taken to reserve the front seat of the stage, for the three ladies and their children, while Mabel, and those who belonged to the non-commissioned officers of the regiment, occupied the second. The wives and daughters of the privates, were huddled together in the rear, some standing and some sitting as they could find room. Mabel, who had already been admitted to the society of the officers' wives, on the footing of a humble companion, was a good deal noticed by the ladies in front, who had a proper appreciation of modest self-respect and gentle refinement, though they were all fully aware of the value of rank, more particularly in a garrison.

As soon as this important portion of the spectators had got into their places, Lundie gave orders for the trial of skill to proceed, in the manner that had been prescribed in his previous orders. Some eight or ten of the best marksmen of the garrison now took possession of the stand, and began to fire in succession. Among them were officers and men, indiscriminately placed, nor were the casual visiters in the fort excluded from the competition. As might have been expected, of men, whose amusements and comfortable subsistence equally depended on skill in the use of their weapons, it was soon found that they were all sufficiently expert to hit the bull's eye, or the white spot in the centre of the target. Others, who succeeded them, it is true were less sure, their bullets striking in the different circles that surrounded the centre of the target, without touching it.

According to the rules of the day, none could proceed to the second trial who had failed in the first, and the adjutant of the place, who acted as master of the ceremonies or marshal of the day, called upon the successful adventurers by name, to get ready for the next effort, while he gave notice that those who failed to present themselves for the shot at the bull's eye, would necessarily be excluded from all the higher trials. Just at this moment, Lundie, the Quarter Master, and Jasper Eau douce appeared in the group at the stand, while the Pathfinder walked leisurely on the ground, without his beloved rifle, for him a measure so unusual as to be understood by all present, as a proof that he did not consider himself a competitor for the honors of the day. All made way as he approached the stand, for Major Duncan, who, in a good-humoured way took his station, levelled his rifle carelessly and fired. The bullet missed the required mark by several inches.

"Major Duncan is excluded from the other trials!" proclaimed the adjutant, in a voice so strong and confident, that all the elder officers and the serjeants, well understood that this failure was preconcerted, while all the younger gentlemen and the privates felt new encouragement to proceed, on account of the evident impartiality with which the laws of the sports were administered, nothing being so attractive to the unsophisticated as the appearance of rigorous justice; and nothing so rare as its actual administration.

"Now, Master Eau douce, comes your turn," said Muir, "and if you do no beat the Major, I shall say that your hand is better skilled with the oar, than with the rifle."

Jasper's handsome face flushed, he stepped upon the stand, cast a hasty glance at Mabel, whose pretty form he ascertained was bending eagerly forward, as if to note the result, dropped the barrel of his rifle, with but little apparent care into the palm of his left hand, raised the muzzle for a single instant with exceeding steadiness, and fired. The bullet passed directly through the centre of the bull's eye, much the best shot of the morning, since the others had merely touched the paint.

"Wall performed, Master Jasper," said Muir, as soon as the result was declared; "and a shot that might have done credit to an older head and a more experienced eye. I'm thinking, notwithstanding, there was some of a youngster's luck in it, for ye were no partic'lar in the aim ye took. Ye may be quick, Eau douce, in the movement, but ye'r not philosophic, nor scientifick in ye'r management of the weepon. Now, Serjeant Dunham, I'll thank you to request the ladies to give a closer attention than common, for I'm about to make that use of the rifle which may be called the intellectual. Jasper's would have killed, I allow, but then there would not have been half the satisfaction in receiving such a shot, as in receiving one that is discharged scientifically."

All this time, the Quarter Master was preparing himself for the scientifick trial, but he delayed his aim until he saw that the eye of Mabel, in common with those of her companions, was fastened on him in curiosity. As the others left him room, out of respect to his rank, no one stood near the competitor but his commanding officer, to whom he now said, in his familiar manner—

"Ye see, Lundie, that something is to be gained by exciting a female's curiosity. It's an active sentiment, is curiosity, and properly improved may lead to gentler inclinations in the end."

"Very true, Davy, but ye keep us all waiting while ye make your preparations, and here is Pathfinder drawing near to catch a lesson, from your greater experience."

"Wall, Pathfinder, and so *you* have come to get an idea, too, concerning the philosophy of shooting! I do not wish to hide my light under a bushel, and ye'r welcome to all ye'll learn. Do ye no mean to try a shot, yersel', man?"

"Why should I, Quarter Master—why should I? I want none of the prizes, and as for honor, I have had enough of that, if it's any honor to shoot better than yourself. I'm not a woman to wear a calash."

"Very true, but ye might find a woman that is precious in your eyes to wear it for ye as—"

"Come, Davy—" interrupted the Major—"your shot, or a retreat. The adjutant is getting to be impatient."

"The quarter-master's department, and the adjutant's department, are seldom compliable, Lundie, but I'm ready—stand a little aside, Pathfinder, and give the ladies an opportunity—"

Lt. Muir now took his attitude with a great deal of studied elegance, raised his rifle slowly, lowered it, raised it again, repeated the manœuvres, and fired.

"Missed the target altogether!" shouted the man whose duty it was to mark the bullets, and who had little relish for the Quarter Master's tedious science—"Missed the target!"

"It cannot be," cried Muir, his face flushing equally with indignation and shame; "it cannot be, adjutant, for I never did so awkward a thing in my life. I appeal to the ladies for a juster judgment."

"The ladies shut their eyes when you fired," exclaimed the regimental wag—"Your preparations alarmed them."

"I will na believe such a calumny of the leddies, nor sic' a reproach on my own skill," returned the Quarter Master, growing more and more Scotch, as he warmed with his feelings; "it's a conspiracy to rob a meritorious man of his dues."

"It's a dead miss, Muir," said the laughing Lundie, "and ye'll just sit down quietly with the disgrace."

"No—no—Major," Pathfinder at length observed—"the Quarter Master *is* a good shot, for a slow one, and a measured distance, though nothing extr'ornary, for raal sarvice. He has covered Jasper's bullet, as will be seen, if any one will take the trouble to examine the target."

The respect for Pathfinder's skill, and for his quickness and accuracy of sight, was so profound and general, that the instant he made this declaration, the spectators began to distrust their own opinions, and a dozen rushed to the target, in order to ascertain the fact. There, sure enough, it was found that the Quarter Master's bullet had gone through the hole made by Jasper's, and that, too, so accurately as to require a minute examination to be certain of the circumstance; which, however, was soon clearly established by discovering one bullet over the other, in the stump against which the target was placed.

"I told ye, ladies, ye were about to witness the influence of science on gunnery," said the Quarter Master, advancing towards the staging occupied by the females. "Major Duncan derides the idea of mathematics entering into target shooting, but I tell him, philosophy colours, and enlarges, and improves, and dilates, and explains every thing that belongs to human life,

whather it be a shooting match or a sermon. In a word philosophy is philosophy, and that is saying all that the subject requires."

"I trust you exclude love from the catalogue," observed the
wife of a captain, who knew the history of the Quarter Master's
marriages, and who had a woman's malice against the
monopolizer of her sex—"it seems that philosophy has little in
common with love."

"You would'n't say that, madam, if your heart had experienced many trials. It's the man, or the woman that has had
many occasions to improve the affections, that can best speak of
such matters, and, believe me, of all love, philosophical is the
most lasting, as it is the most rational."

"You would then recommend experience as an improvement
on the passion?"

"Your quick mind has conceived the idea at a glance. The
happiest marriages are those in which youth, and beauty, and
confidence, on one side, rely on the sagacity, moderation and
prudence of years—middle age, I mean, madam, for I'll no
deny that there is such a thing as a husband's being too old for a
wife. Here is Serjeant Dunham's charming daughter, now, to
approve of such sentiments, I'm certain, her character for discretion being already well established in the garrison, short as
has been her residence among us."

"Serjeant Dunham's daughter, is scarcely a fitting interlocutor in a discourse between you and me, Lt. Muir," rejoined
the captain's lady, with a careful respect for her own dignity,
"and yonder is the Pathfinder about to take his chance, by way
of changing the subject."

"I protest. Major Duncan, I protest—" cried Muir, hurrying
back towards the stand, with both arms elevated by way of enforcing his words—"I protest in the strongest terms, gentlemen,
against Pathfinder's being admitted into these sports with
Killdeer, which is a piece, to say nothing of long habit, that is
altogether out of proportion, for a trial of skill against government rifles."

"Killdeer is taking its rest, Quarter Master," returned Pathfinder, calmly, "and no one here thinks of disturbing it. I did
not think, myself, of pulling a trigger to day, but Sarjeant Dunham has been persuading me that I shall not do proper honor

to his handsome daughter, who came in under my care, if I am backward on such an occasion. I'm using Jasper's rifle, Quarter Master, as you may see, and that is no better than your own."

Lt. Muir was now obliged to acquiesce, and every eye turned towards the Pathfinder, as he took the required station. The air and attitude of this celebrated guide and hunter were extremely fine, as he raised his tall form, and levelled the piece, showing perfect self-command, and a thorough knowledge of the power of the human frame, as well as of the weapon. Pathfinder was not what is usually termed a handsome man, though his appearance excited so much confidence and commanded respect. Tall, and even muscular, his frame might have been esteemed nearly perfect, were it not for the total absence of every thing like flesh. Whip-cord was scarcely more rigid than his arms and legs, or, at need, more pliable; but the outlines of his person were rather too angular for the proportions that the eye most approves. Still, his motions being natural were graceful, and being calm and regulated, they gave him an air of dignity that associated well with the idea that was so prevalent, of his services and peculiar merits. His honest, open features were burnt to a bright red, that comported well with the notion of exposure and hardships, while his sinewy hands denoted force and a species of use that was removed from the stiffening and deforming effects of labor. Although no one perceived any of those gentler, or more insinuating qualities, which are apt to win upon a woman's affections, as he poised his rifle, not a female eye was fastened on him, without a silent approbation of the freedom of his movements, and the manliness of his air. Thought was scarcely quicker than his aim, and, as the smoke floated above his head, the breech of the rifle was seen on the ground, the hand of the Pathfinder was leaning on the barrel, and his honest countenance was illuminated by his usual silent, hearty laugh.

"If one dared to hint at such a thing," cried Major Duncan, "I should say that the Pathfinder had also missed the target!"

"No–no–Major," returned the guide, confidently. "That *would* be a risky declaration. I did'n't load the piece, and can't say what was in it; but if it was lead, you will find the bullet driving down those of the Quarter Master's and Jasper's; else is not my name, Pathfinder."

A shout from the target announced the truth of this assertion.

"That's not all – that's not all, boys," called out the guide, who was now slowly advancing towards the stage occupied by the females – "if you find the target touched at all, I'll own to a miss. The Quarter Master cut the wood, but you'll find no wood cut, by that last messenger."

"Very true, Pathfinder, very true," answered Muir, who was lingering near Mabel, though ashamed to address her particularly, in the presence of the officers' wives. "The Quarter Master did cut the wood, and by that means he opened a passage for your bullet, which went through the hole he had made."

"Well, Quarter Master, there goes the nail, and we'll see who can drive it closest, you or I; for, though I did not think of showing what a rifle can do to day, now my hand is in, I'll turn my back to no man that carries King George's commission. Chingachgook is outlying, or he might force me into some of the niceties of the art, but as for you, Quarter Master, if the nail don't stop you, the potatoe will."

"You're over boastful this morning, Pathfinder, but you'll find you've no green boy, fresh from the settlements and the towns, to deal with, I will assure ye!"

"I know that well, Quarter Master; I know that well, and shall not deny your experience. You've lived many years on the frontiers, and I've heard of you, in the colonies, and among the Injins, too, quite a human life ago."

"Na–na–" interrupted Muir, in his broadest Scotch, "this is injustice, man. I've no lived so very long, neither."

"I'll do you justice, lieutenant, even if you get the best in the potatoe trial. I say you've passed a good human life, for a soldier, in places where the rifle is daily used, and I know you are a creditable and ingenious marksman; but then you are not a true rifle shooter. As for boasting, I hope I'm not a vain talker about my own exploits, but a man's gifts are his gifts, and it's flying in the face of Providence to deny them. The sarjeant's daughter, here, shall judge atween us, if you have the stomach to submit to so pretty a judge."

The Pathfinder had named Mabel as the arbiter, because he admired her, and because, in his eyes, rank had little or no value, but Lt. Muir shrunk at such a reference in the presence of the wives of officers. He would gladly keep himself constantly before the eyes and the imagination of the object of his wishes, but he was still too much under the influence of old prejudices, and perhaps too wary, to appear openly as her suitor, unless he saw something very like a certainty of success. On the discretion of Major Duncan he had a full reliance; and he apprehended no betrayal from that quarter; but he was quite aware, should it ever get abroad that he had been refused by the child of a non-commissioned officer, he would find great difficulty in making his approaches to any other woman of a condition to which he might reasonably aspire. Notwithstanding these doubts and misgivings, Mabel looked so prettily, blushed so charmingly, smiled so sweetly, and altogether presented so winning a picture of youth, spirit, modesty and beauty, that he found it exceedingly tempting to be kept so prominently before her imagination, and to be able to address her freely.

"You shall have it your own way, Pathfinder," he answered as soon as his doubts had settled down into determination—"Let the Serjeant's daughter—his charming daughter, I should have termed her—be the umpire then, and to her we will both dedicate the prize, that one or the other must certainly win. Pathfinder must be humored, ladies, as you perceive, else, no doubt, we should have had the honor to submit ourselves to one of your charming society."

A call for the competitors, now drew the Quarter Master and his adversary away, and in a few moments the second trial of skill commenced. A common wrought nail was driven lightly into the target, its head having been first touched with paint, and the marksman was required to hit it, or he lost his chances in the succeeding trials. No one was permitted to enter, on this occasion, who had already failed in the essay against the bull's eye.

There might have been half a dozen aspirants for the honors of this trial, one or two who had barely succeeded in touching the spot of paint, in the previous strife, preferring to rest their reputations there, feeling certain that they could not succeed, in the greater effort that was now exacted of them. The three first adventurers failed, all coming quite near the mark, but neither touching it. The fourth person who presented himself was the Quarter Master, who, after going through his usual attitudes, so far succeeded as to carry away a small portion of the head of the nail, planting his bullet by the side of its point. This was not considered an extraordinary shot, though it brought the adventurer within the category.

"You've saved your bacon, Quarter Master, as they say in the settlements of their creatur's," cried Pathfinder laughing, "but it would take a long time to build a house with a hammer no better than yourn. Jasper, here, will show you how a nail is to be started, or the lad has lost some of his steadiness of hand, and sartainty of eye. You would have done better yourself, Lieutenant, had you not been so much bent on so'gerizing your figure. Shooting is a nat'ral gift, and is to be exercised in a nat'ral way."

"We shall see, Pathfinder; I call that a pretty attempt at a nail, and I doubt if the 55th has another hammer, as you call it, that can do just the same thing, over again."

"Jasper is not in the 55th, but there goes his rap!"

As the Pathfinder spoke, the bullet of Eau douce hit the nail square, and drove it into the target, within an inch of the head.

"Be all ready to clench it, boys," cried out Pathfinder, stepping into his friend's tracks the instant they were vacant. "Never mind a new nail; I can see that, though the paint is gone, and what I can see, I can hit at a hundred yards, though it were only a mosquitoe's eye. Be ready to clench!"

The rifle cracked, the bullet sped its way, and the head of the nail was buried in the wood, covered by the piece of flattened lead.

"Well, Jasper, lad," continued Pathfinder, dropping the breech of his rifle to the ground, and resuming the discourse, as if he thought nothing of his own exploit, "you improve daily. A few more tramps on land, in my company, and the best marksman on the frontiers will have occasion to look keenly, when he takes his stand ag'in you. The Quarter Master is respectable, but he will never get any farther, whereas you, Jasper, have the gift, and may one day defy any who pull trigger."

"Hoot—hoot!" exclaimed Muir, "do you call hitting the head of a nail respectable only, when it's the perfection of the art! Any one, in the least refined and elevated in sentiment, knows that the delicate touches denote the master, whereas your sledge-hammer blows come from the rude and uninstructed. If 'a miss is as good as a mile,' a hit ought to be better, Pathfinder, whether it wound or kill."

"The surest way of settling this rivalry, will be to make another trial," observed Lundie; "and that will be of the potatoe. You're Scotch, Mr. Muir, and might fare better were it a cake or a thistle, but frontier law has declared for the American fruit, and the potatoe, it shall be."

As Major Duncan manifested some impatience of manner, Muir had too much tact to delay the sports any longer, with his discursive remarks, but judiciously prepared himself for the next appeal. To say the truth, the Quarter Master had little, or no faith in his own success in the trial of skill that was to follow, nor would he have been so free in presenting himself as a competitor, at all, had he anticipated it would have been made, but Major Duncan, who was somewhat of a humorist, in his own quiet Scotch way, had secretly ordered it to be introduced, expressly to mortify him; for, a Laird himself, Lundie did not relish the notion that one who might claim to be a gentleman, should bring discredit on his caste by forming an unequal alliance. As soon as every thing was prepared, Muir was summoned to the stand, and the potatoe was held in readiness to be thrown. As the sort of feat we are about to offer to the reader, however, may be new to him, a word in explanation will render the matter more clear. A potatoe of large size was selected, and given to one, who stood at the distance of twenty yards from the stand. At the word "heave," which was given by the marksman, the vegetable was thrown, with a gentle toss, into the air, and it was the business of the adventurer to cause a ball to pass through it, before it reached the ground.

The Quarter Master, in a hundred experiments, had once succeeded in accomplishing this difficult feat, but he now essayed to perform it again, with a sort of blind hope, that was fated to be disappointed. The potatoe was thrown in the usual manner, the rifle was discharged, but the flying target was untouched.

"To the right-about, and fall out, Quarter Master," said Lundie, smiling at the success of his own artifice—"The honor of the silken calash will lie between Jasper Eau douce and Pathfinder."

"And how is the trial to end, Major?" enquired the latter.

"Are we to have the two potatoe trial, or is it to be settled by centre and skin?"

"By centre and skin, if there is any perceptible difference; otherwise the double shot must follow."

"This is an awful moment to me, Pathfinder," observed Jasper, as he moved towards the stand, his face actually losing its colour in intensity of feeling.

Pathfinder gazed earnestly at the young man, and then begging Major Duncan to have patience for a moment he led his friend out of the hearing of all near him, before he spoke.

"You seem to take this matter to heart, Jasper?" the hunter remarked keeping his eyes fastened on those of the youth.

"I must own, Pathfinder, that my feelings were never before so much bound up in success."

"And do you so much crave to outdo me, an old and tried friend, and, that, as it might be, in my own way? Shooting is my gift, boy, and no common hand can equal mine!"

"I know it—I know it, Pathfinder—but—yet—"

"But what, Jasper, boy;—speak freely; you talk to a friend."

The young man compressed his lips, dashed a hand across his eye, and flushed and paled, alternately like a girl, confessing her love. Then squeezing the other's hand he said calmly, like one whose manhood has overcome all other sensations—

"I would lose an arm, Pathfinder, to be able to make an offering of that calash to Mabel Dunham."

The hunter dropped his eyes to the ground, and as he walked slowly back towards the stand, he seemed to ponder deeply on what he had just heard.

"You never could succeed in the double trial, Jasper?" he suddenly remarked.

"Of that I am certain, and it troubles me."

"What a creatur' is mortal man! He pines for things which are not of his gift, and treats the bounties of Providence lightly. No matter—no matter. Take your station, Jasper, for the Major is waiting—and, harkee, lad—I must touch the skin, for I could not show my face in the garrison with less than that."

"I suppose I must submit to my fate," returned Jasper, flushing and losing his colour, as before, "but I will make the effort, if I die."

"What a thing is mortal man!" repeated Pathfinder, falling

back to allow his friend room to take his aim—"he overlooks his own gifts, and craves them of another!"

The potatoe was thrown, Jasper fired, and the shout that followed preceded the announcement of the fact, that he had driven his bullet through its centre, or so nearly so, as to merit that award.

"Here is a competitor worthy of you, Pathfinder," cried Major Duncan with delight, as the former took his station, "and we may look to some fine shooting, in the double trial."

"What a thing is mortal man!" repeated the hunter, scarce seeming to notice what was passing around him, so much were his thoughts absorbed in his own reflections—"Toss."

The potatoe was tossed, the rifle cracked, it was remarked just as the little black ball seemed stationary in the air, for the marksman evidently took unusual heed to his aim, and then a look of disappointment and wonder succeeded among those who caught the falling target.

"Two holes in one?" called out the Major.

"The skin—the skin—" was the answer—"only the skin!"

"How's this, Pathfinder! Is Jasper Eau douce to carry off the honors of the day!"

"The calash is hisn," returned the other, shaking his head, and walking quietly away from the stand. "What a creatur' is a mortal man! Never satisfied with his own gifts, but forever craving that which Providence denies!"

As Pathfinder had not buried his bullet in the potatoe, but had cut through the skin, the prize was immediately adjudged to Jasper. The calash was in the hands of the latter, when the Quarter Master approached, and with a politic air of cordiality, he wished his successful rival, joy for his victory.

"But now you've got the calash, lad, it's of no use to you," he added; "it will never make a sail, nor even an ensign. I'm thinking, Eau douce, you'd no be sorry to see its value in good siller of the King?"

"Money cannot buy it, Lieutenant," returned Jasper, whose eye lighted up with all the fire of success and joy. "I would rather have won this calash, than have obtained fifty new suits of sails for the Scud!"

"Hoot—hoot—lad; you are going mad, like all the rest of

them. I'd even venture to offer half a guinea for the trifle, rather than it should lie kicking about in the cabin of your cutter, and, in the end, become an ornament for the head of a squaw."

Although Jasper did not know that the wary Quarter Master had not offered half the actual cost of the prize, he heard the proposition with indifference. Shaking his head in the negative, he advanced towards the stage, where his approach excited a little commotion, the officers' ladies, one and all, having determined to accept the present should the gallantry of the young sailor induce him to offer it. But Jasper's diffidence, no less than admiration for another, would have prevented him from aspiring to the honor of complimenting any whom he thought so much his superiors.

"Mabel," he said, "this prize is for you, unless—"

"Unless, what, Jasper—" answered the girl, losing her own bashfulness, in the natural and generous wish to relieve his embarrassment, though both reddened in a way to betray strong feeling.

"Unless you may think too indifferently of it, because it is offered by one who may have no right to believe his gift will be accepted."

"I do accept it, Jasper, and it shall be a sign of the danger I have passed in your company, and of the gratitude I feel for your care of me—your care and that of the Pathfinder."

"Never mind me, never mind me," exclaimed the latter; "this is Jasper's luck and Jasper's gift, give him full credit for both. My turn may come another day; mine and the Quarter Master's, who seems to grudge the boy the calash, though what *he* can want of it, I cannot understand, for he has no wife."

"And has Jasper Eau douce a wife? Or have you a wife, yoursel', Pathfinder? I may want it to help get a wife, or as a memorial that I have had a wife, or as a proof how much I admire the sex, or because it is a female garment, or for some other equally respectable motive. It's not the unreflecting that are the most prized by the thoughtful, and there is no surer sign that a man made a good husband to his first consort, let me tell ye all, than to see him speedily looking round for a competent successor. The affections are good gifts from Providence, and they that have loved one faithfully, prove how much of this bounty has been lavished upon them, by loving another as soon as possible."

"It may be so—it may be so. I am no practitioner in such things, and cannot gainsay it. But Mabel, here, the sarjeant's daughter, will give you full credit for the words. Come, Jasper, although our hands are out, let us see what the other lads can do with the rifle."

Pathfinder and his companions retired, for the sports were about to proceed. The ladies, however, were not so much engrossed with rifle shooting as to neglect the calash. It passed from hand to hand; the silk was felt, the fashion criticised and the work examined, and divers opinions were privately ventured concerning the fitness of so handsome a thing's passing into the possession of a non-commissioned officer's child.

"Perhaps you will be disposed to sell that calash, Mabel, when it has been a short time in your possession?" inquired the captain's lady—"Wear it, I should think, you never can."

"I may not wear it, madam," returned our heroine modestly, "but I should not like to part with it, either."

"I dare say Serjeant Dunham keeps you above the necessity of selling your clothes, child, but, at the same time, it is money thrown away to keep an article of dress you can never wear."

"I should be unwilling to part with the gift of a friend."

"But the young man himself, will think all the better of you, for your prudence, after the triumph of the day is forgotten. It is a pretty and a becoming calash, and ought not to be thrown away."

"I've no intention to throw it away, ma'am, and, if you please, would rather keep it."

"As you will child; girls of your age often overlook their real advantages. Remember, however, if you do determine to dispose of the thing, that it is bespoke, and that I will not take it, if you ever even put it on your own head."

"Yes, ma'am," said Mabel, in the meekest voice imaginable, though her eyes looked like diamonds and her cheeks reddened to the tints of two roses, as she placed the forbidden garment over her well turned shoulders, where she kept it a minute, as if to try its fitness, and then quietly removed it, again.

The remainder of the sports offered nothing of interest. The shooting was reasonably good, but the trials were all of a scale lower than those related, and the competitors were soon left to themselves. The ladies, and most of the officers withdrew, and the remainder of the females soon followed their example. Mabel was returning along the low flat rocks that line the shore of the lake, dangling her pretty calash from a prettier finger, when Pathfinder met her. He carried the rifle which he had used that day, but his manner had less of the frank ease of the hunter about it, than usual, while his eye seemed roving and uneasy. After a few unmeaning words concerning the noble sheet of water before them, he turned towards his companion with strong interest in his countenance, and said—

"Jasper earned that calash for you, Mabel, without much trial of his gifts."

"It was fairly done, Pathfinder."

"No doubt—no doubt. The bullet passed neatly through the potatoe, and no man could have done more; though others might have done as much."

"But no one did as much!" exclaimed Mabel with an animation that she instantly regretted, for she saw by the pained look of the guide that he was mortified equally by the remark, and by the feeling with which it was uttered.

"It is true—it is true, Mabel, no one did as much there, but—yes, there is no reason I should deny my gifts which come from Providence—yes, yes; no one did as much there, but you shall know what *can* be done here. Do you observe the gulls that are flying over our heads?"

"Certainly, Pathfinder—there are too many to escape notice."

"Here, where they cross each other, in sailing about—" he added, cocking and raising his rifle—"the two—the two—now look!"

The piece was presented quick as thought, as two of the birds came in a line, though distant from each other many yards, the report followed, and the bullet passed through the bodies of both the victims. No sooner had the gulls fallen into the lake, than Pathfinder dropped the breech of the rifle, and laughed in his own peculiar manner, every shade of dissatisfaction and mortified pride having left his honest face.

"That is something, Mabel, that is something; although I've

no calash to give you! But ask Jasper, himself; I'll leave it all to Jasper, for a truer tongue and heart, are not in America."

"Then it was not Jasper's fault that he gained the prize!"

"Not it. He did his best, and he did well. For one that has water gifts, rather than land gifts, Jasper is oncommonly expart, and a better backer no one need wish, ashore or afloat. But it was my fault, Mabel, that he got the calash; though it makes no difference—it makes no difference, for the thing has gone to the right person."

"I believe I understand you, Pathfinder," said Mabel, blushing in spite of herself, "and I look upon the calash as the joint gift of yourself and Jasper."

"That would not be doing justice to the lad, neither. He won the garment, and had a right to give it away. The most you may think, Mabel, is to believe that had I won it, it would have gone to the same person."

"I will remember that, Pathfinder, and take care that others know your skill, as it has been proved upon the poor gulls, in my presence."

"Lord bless you, Mabel, there is no more need of your talking in favor of my shooting, on this frontier, than of your talking about the water in the lake, or the sun in the heavens. Every body knows what I can do in that way, and your words would be thrown away, as much as French would be thrown away on an American bear."

"Then you think that Jasper knew you were giving him this advantage, of which he has so unhandsomely availed himself?" said Mabel, the colour which had imparted so much lustre to her eyes gradually leaving her face, which became grave and thoughtful.

"I do not say that, but very far from it. We all forget things that we have known, when eager after our wishes. Jasper is satisfied that I can pass one bullet through two potatoes, as I sent my bullet through the gulls, and he knows no other man on the frontier can do the same thing. But with the calash before his eyes, and the hope of giving it to you, the lad was inclined to think better of himself, just at that moment, perhaps, than he ought. No—no—there's nothing mean or distrustful about Jasper Eau douce, though it is a gift nat'ral to all young men to wish to appear well in the eyes of handsome young women."

"I'll try to forget all, but the kindness you've both shown to a poor motherless girl," said Mabel, struggling to keep down emotions that she scarcely knew how to account for, herself. "Believe me, Pathfinder, I can never forget all you have already done for me—you and Jasper—and this new proof of your regard is not thrown away. Here—here is a brooch that is of silver, and I offer it as a token that I owe you life, or liberty."

"What shall I do with this, Mabel?" asked the bewildered hunter, holding the simple trinket in his hand. "I have neither buckle nor button about me, for I wear nothing but leathern strings and them of good deer-skins. It's pretty to the eye, but it is prettier far on the spot it came from, than it can be about me."

"Nay put it in your hunting shirt; it will become it well. Remember, Pathfinder, that it is a token of friendship between us, and a sign that I can never forget you or your services."

Mabel then smiled an adieu, and bounding up the bank, she was soon lost to view behind the mounds of the fort.

Chapter XII.

"Lo! dusky masses steal in dubious sight,
Along the leaguer'd wall, and bristling bank
Of the arm'd river; while with straggling light,
The stars peep through the vapour, dim and dank."
Byron, *Don Juan*, VII.LXXXVI.683–86.

A few hours later, Mabel Dunham was on the bastion that overlooked the river and the lake, seemingly in deep thought. The evening was calm and soft, and the question had arisen whether the party for the Thousand Islands would be able to get out that night, or not, on account of the total absence of wind. The stores, arms and ammunition were already shipped, and even Mabel's effects were on board, but the small draft of men that was to go was still ashore, there being no apparent prospect of the cutter's getting under way. Jasper had warped the Scud out of the cove, and so far up the stream as to enable him to pass through the outlet of the river whenever he chose, but there he still lay, riding at single anchor. The drafted men were lounging about the shore of the cove, undecided whether or not to pull off.

The sports of the morning had left a quiet in the garrison that was in harmony with the whole of the beautiful scene, and Mabel felt its influence on her feelings, though probably too little accustomed to speculate on such sensations, to be aware of the cause. Every thing near appeared lovely and soothing, while the solemn grandeur of the silent forest and placid expanse of the lake, lent a sublimity that other scenes might have wanted. For the first time, Mabel felt the hold that the towns and civilization had gained on her habits sensibly weakened, and the warm-hearted girl began to think that a life passed amid objects such as these around her, might be happy. How far the experience of the last ten days came in aid of that calm and holy eventide, and contributed towards producing that young conviction, may be suspected, rather than affirmed, in this early portion of our legend.

"A charming sunset, Mabel," said the hearty voice of her uncle, so close to the ear of our heroine as to cause her to start—"a charming sunset, girl, for a fresh water concern, though we should think but little of it at sea."

"And is not nature the same, on shore, or at sea; on a lake like this, or on the ocean? Does not the sun shine on all alike, dear uncle, and can we not feel gratitude for the blessings of Providence as strongly on this remote frontier, as in our own Manhattan?"

"The girl has fallen in with some of her mother's books!—Though I should think the serjeant would scarcely make a second march with such trumpery among his baggage. Is not nature the same, indeed!—Now, Mabel, do you imagine that the nature of a soldier is the same as that of a sea-faring man?—You've relations in both callings, and ought to be able to answer."

"But, uncle, I mean human nature—"

"So do I, girl; the human nature of a seaman, and the human nature of one of these fellows of the 55th, not even excepting your own father. Here have they had a shooting match—target firing I should call it—this day, and what a different thing has it been from a target firing afloat. There we should have sprung our broadside, sported with round shot, at an object half a mile off, at the very nearest, and the potatoes, if there happened to be any on board, as quite likely would not have been the case, would have been left in the cook's coppers. It may be an honorable calling, that of a soldier, Mabel, but an experienced hand sees many follies and weaknesses in one of these forts. As for that bit of a lake, you know my opinion of it, already, and I wish to disparage nothing. No real sea-farer disparages any thing; but d——e, if I regard this here Ontario, as they call it, as more than so much water in a ship's scuttle-butt. Now, look you here, Mabel, if you wish to understand the difference between the ocean and a lake, I can make you comprehend it, with a single look. This is what one may call a calm, seeing that there is no wind, though, to own the truth, I do not think the calms are as calm as them we get outside—"

"Uncle, there is not a breath of air! I do not think it possible for the leaves to be more immoveably still than those of the entire forest are, at this very moment."

"Leaves! what are leaves, child; there are no leaves at sea. If you wish to know whether it is a dead calm, or not, try a mould candle—your dips flaring too much—and then you may be certain whether there is, or is not, any wind. If you were in a latitude where the air was so still that you found a difficulty in stirring it to draw it in, in breathing, you might fancy it a calm. People are often on a short allowance of air, in the calm latitudes. Here, again, look at that water!—It is like milk in a pan, with no more motion than there is in a full hogshead before the bung is started. Now, on the ocean the water is never still, let the air be as quiet as it may."

"The water of the ocean never still, uncle Cap!—Not even in a calm!"

"Bless your heart, no, child. The ocean breathes like a living being, and its bosom is always heaving, as the poetizers call it, though there be no more air than is to be found in a syphon. No man ever saw the ocean still, like this lake, but it heaves and sets, as if it had lungs."

"And this lake is not absolutely still, for you perceive there is a little ripple on the shore, and you may even hear the surf, plunging, at moments, against the rocks."

"All d——d poetry! One may call a bubble a ripple, if he will, and washing decks a surf, but Lake Ontario is no more the Atlantic, than a Powles Hook periagua is a first rate.* That Jasper, notwithstanding, is a fine lad, and wants instruction only to make a man of him!"

"Do you think him ignorant, uncle," answered Mabel, prettily adjusting her hair, in order to do which she was obliged, or fancied she was obliged, to turn away her face—"To me, Jasper Eau douce appears to know more than most of the young men of his class. He has read but little, for books are not plenty in this part of the world, but he has thought much; at least, so it seems to me, for one so young."

"He is ignorant, he is ignorant, as all must be who navigate an inland water, like this. He can make a flat knot and a timber hitch, it is true, but he has no more notion of crowning a cable,* now, or of a carrick bend,* than you have of catting an anchor.* No—no—Mabel; we both owe something to Jasper and the Pathfinder, and I have been thinking how I can best serve them, for I hold ingratitude to be the vice of a hog. Some people say it is the vice of a king; but I say it is the failing of a hog, for treat the animal to your own dinner, and he would eat you for the dessert."

"Very true, dear uncle, and we ought indeed, to do all we can to express our proper sense of the services of both these brave men."

"Spoken like your mother's daughter, girl, and in a way to do credit to the Cap family. Now, I've hit upon a traverse, that will just suit all parties, and as soon as we get back from this little expedition down the lake, among them there thousand islands, and I am ready to return, it is my intention to propose it."

"Dearest uncle! this is so considerate in you, and will be so just! May I ask what your intentions are?"

"I see no reason for keeping them a secret from you, Mabel, though nothing need be said to your father about them, for the serjeant has his prejudices, and might throw difficulties in the way. Neither Jasper, nor his friend, Pathfinder, can ever make any thing hereabouts, and I propose to take both with me, down to the coast, and get them fairly afloat. Jasper would find his sea legs in a fortnight, and a twelvemonth's v'y'ge would make him a man. Although Pathfinder might take more time, or never get to be rated able, yet one could make something of him, too, particularly as a look-out, for he has unusually good eyes."

"Uncle, do you think either would consent to this!" said Mabel smiling.

"Do I suppose them simpletons! What rational being would neglect his own advancement. Let Jasper alone to push his way, and the lad may yet die the master of some square rigged craft."

"And would he be any the happier for it, dear uncle? How much better is it to be the master of a square rigged craft, than to be master of a round rigged craft?"

"Pooh—Pooh, Magnet, you do'n't know what you are talking about; you are just fit to read lectures about ships before some hysterical society. Leave these things to me, and they'll be properly managed. Ah! here is the Pathfinder himself, and I may just as well drop him a hint of my benevolent intentions, as regards himself. Hope is a great encourager of our exertions."

Cap nodded his head, and then ceased to speak, while the hunter approached, not with his usual frank and easy manner, but in a way to show that he was slightly embarrassed, if not distrustful of his reception.

"Uncle and niece make a family party," said Pathfinder, when near the two—"and a stranger may not prove a welcome companion?"

"You are no stranger, Master Pathfinder," returned Cap, "and no one can be more welcome than yourself. We were talking of you, but a moment ago, and when friends speak of an absent man, he can guess what they have said."

"I ask no secrets—I ask no secrets. Every man has his inimies, and I have mine, though I count neither you, Master Cap, nor pretty Mabel, here, among the number. As for the Mingos, I will say nothing, though they have no just cause to hate me."

"That I'll answer for, Pathfinder, for, you strike my fancy as being well disposed and upright. There is a method, however, of getting away from the enmity of even these Mingos, and if you choose to take it, no one will more willingly point it out, than myself, without a charge for my advice either."

"I wish no inimies, Saltwater," for so the Pathfinder had begun to call Cap, having insensibly to himself adopted the term by translating the name given him by the Indians, in and about the fort, "I wish no inimies. I'm as ready to bury the hatchet with the Mingos as with the French, though you know that it depends on one greater than either of us, so to turn the heart, as to leave a man without inimies."

"By lifting your anchor, and accompanying me down to the coast, friend Pathfinder, when we get back from this short cruise on which we are bound, you will find yourself beyond the sound of the war-whoop, and safe enough from any Indian bullet."

"And what should I do on the salt-water? Hunt in your towns!—Follow the trails of people going and coming from market, and ambush dogs and poultry. You are no friend to my happiness, Master Cap, if you would lead me out of the shade of the woods, to put me in the sun of the clearin's!"

"I did not propose to leave you in the settlements, Pathfinder, but to carry you out to sea, where only a man can be said to breathe freely. Mabel will tell you that such was my intention, before a word was said on the subject."

"And what does Mabel think would come of such a change? She knows that a man has his gifts, and that it is as useless to pretend to others, as to withstand them that come from Providence. I am a hunter, and a scout, or a guide, Saltwater, and it is not in me to fly so much in the face of Heaven, as to try to become any thing else. Am I right Mabel, or are you so much a woman as to wish to see a natur' altered?"

"I would wish to see no change in you, Pathfinder," Mabel answered with a cordial sincerity and frankness that went directly to the hunter's heart; "and much as my uncle admires the sea, and great as is all the good that he thinks may come of it, I could not wish to see the best and noblest hunter of the woods transformed into an admiral. Remain what you are, my brave friend, and you need fear nothing, short of the anger of God."

"Do you hear this, Saltwater?—Do you hear what the Sarjeant's daughter is saying, and she is much too upright and fair-minded, and pretty, not to think what she says. So long as she is satisfied with me as I am, I shall not fly in the face of the gifts of Providence, by striving to become any thing else. I may seem useless, here, in a garrison, but when we get down among the Thousand Islands, there may be an opportunity to prove that a sure rifle is sometimes a God-send."

"You are then to be of our party?" said Mabel, smiling so frankly and so sweetly on the guide, that he would have followed her to the end of the earth. "I shall be the only female, with the exception of one soldier's wife, and shall feel none the less secure, Pathfinder, because you will be among our protectors."

"The sarjeant would do that, Mabel; the sarjeant would do that, though you were not of his kin. No one will overlook you. I should think your uncle, here, would like an expedition of this sort, where we shall go with sails, and have a look at our inland sea?"

"Your inland sea is no great matter, Master Pathfinder, and I expect nothing from it. I confess, however, I should like to know the object of the cruise, for one does not wish to be idle, and my brother-in-law, the serjeant, is as close-mouthed as a free mason. Do you know, Mabel, what all this means?"

"Not in the least, uncle. I dare not ask my father any questions about his duty, for he thinks it is not a woman's business, and all I can say is that we are to sail as soon as the wind will permit, and that we are to be absent a month."

"Perhaps, Master Pathfinder can give me a useful hint, for a v'y'ge without an object is never pleasant to an old sailor."

"There is no great secret, Saltwater, consarning our post and object, though it is forbidden to talk much about either in the garrison. I am no soldier, howsever, and can use my tongue as I please, though as little given as another to idle conversation I hope; still, as we sail so soon, and you are both to be of the party, you may as well be told where you are to be carried. You know that there are such things as the Thousand Islands, I suppose, Master Cap?"

"Ay, what are so called, hereaway, though I take it for granted that they are not real islands, such as we fall in with on the ocean, and that the Thousand means some such matter as two or three, like the killed and wounded of a great battle."

"My eyes are good, and yet have I often been foiled in trying to count them very islands."

"Ay—ay—I've known people who could'n't count beyond a certain number. Your real land birds never know their own roosts, even, in a land fall at sea. They are what I call 'all things to all men.' How many times have I seen the beach, and houses and churches, when the passengers have not been able to see any thing but water. I have no idea that a man can get fairly out of sight of land, on fresh water. The thing appears to me to be irrational and impossible."

"You don't know the lakes, Master Cap, or you would not say that. Before we get to the Thousand Islands, you will have other notions of what natur' has done in this wilderness."

"I have my doubts whether you have such a thing as a real island in all this region. To my notion, fresh water can't make a bony fidy island; not what *I* call an island."

"We'll show you hundreds of them—not exactly a thousand, perhaps, but so many that eye cannot see them all, or tongue count them."

"And what sort of things may they be?"

"Land with water entirely around them."

"Ay, but what sort of land, and what sort of water? I'll en-gage, when the truth comes to be known, they'll turn out to be nothing but peninsulas, or promontories, or continents, though these are matters, I dare say, of which you know little or nothing. But islands, or no islands, what is the object of the cruise, Master Pathfinder?"

"Why as you are the sarjeant's brother, and pretty Mabel here, is his da'hter, and we are all to be of the party, there can be no harm in giving you some idea of what we are going to do. Being so old a sailor, Master Cap, you've heard, no doubt, of such a port as Frontenac?"

"Who has'n't? I will not say I've ever been inside the harbor, but I've frequently been off the place."

"Then you are about to go upon ground with which you are acquainted, though how you could ever have got there, from the ocean, I do not understand. These great lakes, you must know, make a chain, the water passing out of one into the other, until it reaches Erie, which is a sheet off here to the westward, as large as Ontario itself. Well, out of Erie the water comes, until it reaches a low mountain like, over the edge of which it passes—"

"I should like to know how the devil it can do that?"

"Why easy enough, Master Cap," returned Pathfinder laughing, "seeing that it has only to fall down hill. Had I said the water went *up* the mountain, there would have been natur' ag'in it; but we hold it no great matter for water to run down hill—that is *fresh* water."

"Ay ay—but you speak of the water of a lake's coming down the side of a mountain; it's in the teeth of reason, if reason has any teeth."

"Well—well—we will not dispute the point, but what I've seen, I've seen: as for reason's having any teeth, I'll say nothing, but conscience has, and sharp ones too. After getting into Ontario, all the water of *all* the lakes passes down into the sea, by a river, and in the narrow part of the sheet where it is neither river nor lake, lie the islands spoken of. Now, Frontenac is a post of the Frenchers above these same islands, and as they hold the garrisons below, their stores and ammunition are sent up the river to Frontenac, to be forwarded along the shores of this and the other lakes, in order to enable the inimy to play his deviltries among the savages, and to take christian scalps."

"And will our presence prevent these horrible acts?" demanded Mabel with interest.

"It may, or it may not, as Providence wills. Lundie, as they call him, he who commands this garrison, sent a party down to take a station among the islands, to cut off some of the French boats, and this expedition of ours will be the second relief. As yet they've not done much, though two batteaux loaded with Indian goods have been taken; but a runner came in, last week, and brought such tidings that the Major is about to make a last effort to sarcumvent the knaves, Jasper knows the way, and we shall be in good hands, for the Sarjeant is prudent, and of the first quality at an ambushment—yes, he is both prudent, and alert."

"Is this all!" said Cap, contemptuously—"by the preparations and equipments, I had thought there was a forced trade in the wind, and that an honest penny might be turned, by taking an adventure. I suppose there are no shares in your fresh water prize money?"

"Anan?"

"I take it for granted the King gets all, in these so'gering parties and ambushments, as you call them?"

"I know nothing about that, Master Cap. I take my share of the lead and powder, if any falls into our hands, and say nothing to the King about it. If any one fares better, it is not I—though it is time I did begin to think of a house, and furniture, and a home."

Although the Pathfinder did not dare to look at Mabel, while he made this direct allusion to his change of life, he would have given the world to know whether she were listening, and what was the expression of her countenance. Mabel little suspected the nature of the allusion, however, and her countenance was perfectly unembarrassed, as she turned her eyes towards the river, where the appearance of some movement on board the Scud, began to be visible.

"Jasper is bringing the cutter out," observed the guide, whose look was drawn in the same direction, by the fall of some heavy article on the deck. "The lad sees the signs of wind no doubt and wishes to be ready for it."

"Ay, now we shall have an opportunity of learning seamanship—" returned Cap, with a sneer. "There is a nicety in getting a craft under her canvass, that shows the thorough-bred mariner as much as any thing else. It's like a so'ger buttoning his coat, and one can see whether he begins at the top, or the bottom."

"I will not say that Jasper is equal to your seafarers below," observed Pathfinder, across whose upright mind an unworthy feeling of envy, or of jealousy never passed, "but he is a bold boy, and manages his cutter as skilfully as any man can desire, on this lake at least. You did'n't find him backward at the Oswego Falls, Master Cap, where fresh water contrives to tumble down hill, with little difficulty."

Cap made no other answer than a dissatisfied ejaculation, and then a general silence followed, all on the bastion studying the movements of the cutter, with the interest that was natural to their own future connection with the vessel. It was still a dead calm, the surface of the lake literally glittering with the last rays of the sun. The Scud had been warped up to a kedge, that lay a hundred yards above the points of the outlet, where she had room to manœuvre in the river, which then formed the harbor of Oswego. But the total want of air prevented any such attempt, and it was soon evident that the light vessel was to be taken through the passage, under her sweeps. Not a sail was loosened, but as soon as the kedge was tripped, the heavy fall of the sweeps was heard, when the cutter, with her head up stream, began to sheer towards the centre of the current, on reaching which the efforts of the men ceased, and she drifted towards the outlet. In the narrow pass itself her movement was rapid, and in less than five minutes, the Scud was floating outside of the two low gravelly points that intercepted the waves of the lake. No anchor was let go, but the vessel continued to set off from the land, until her dark hull was seen resting on the glassy surface of the lake, fully a quarter of a mile beyond the low bluff, which formed the eastern extremity of what might be called the outer harbor, or roadstead. Here the influence of the river current ceased, and she became, virtually, stationary.

"She seems very beautiful to me, uncle," said Mabel, whose gaze had not been averted from the cutter, for a single moment, while it had thus been changing its position; "I dare say you can find faults in her appearance, and in the way she is managed, but to my ignorance both are perfect!"

"Ay—ay—she drops down with the current well enough, girl, and so would a chip. But when you come to niceties, an old tar, like myself, has no need of spectacles to find fault."

"Well, Master Cap," put in the guide, who seldom heard any thing to Jasper's prejudice, without manifesting a disposition to interfere, "I've heard old and experienced salt-water mariners confess, that the Scud is as pretty a craft as floats. I know nothing of such matters, myself, but one may have his own notions about a ship, even though they be wrong notions; and it would take more than one witness to persuade me Jasper does not keep his boat in good order."

"I do not say that the cutter is downright lubberly, Master Pathfinder, but she has faults, and great faults."

"And what are they, uncle; if he knew them, Jasper would be glad to mend them."

"What are they?—Why fifty; ay, for that matter a hundred. Very material and manifest faults."

"Do name them, sir, and Pathfinder will mention them to his friend."

"Name them? it is no easy matter to call off the stars, for the simple reason that they are so numerous. Name them, indeed!—Why, my pretty niece, Miss Magnet, what do you think of that main boom* now? To my ignorant eyes, it is topped at least a foot too high; and then the pennant is foul; and—and—ay, d——e, if there is'n't a topsail gasket*adrift—and, it would'n't surprise me at all, if there should prove to be a round turn in that hawser, if the kedge*were to be let go, this instant! Faults, indeed. No seaman could look at her a moment without seeing that she is as full of faults, as a servant that has asked for his discharge."

"This may be very true, uncle, though I much question if Jasper knows of them. I do not think he would suffer these things, Pathfinder, if they were pointed out to him."

"Let Jasper manage his own cutter, Mabel; let him manage his own cutter. His gifts lie that-a-way, and I'll answer for it, no one can teach him how to keep the Scud out of the hands of the Frontenackers, or their devilish Mingo friends. Who cares for round turns in kedges, and for hawsers that are topped too high, Master Cap, so long as the craft sails well, and keeps clear of the Frenchers. I will trust Jasper, against all the sea-farers of the coast, up here on the lakes—but I do not say he has any gift for the ocean, for there he has never been tried."

Cap smiled condescendingly, but he did not think it necessary to push his criticisms any farther just at that moment. His air and manner gradually became more supercilious and lofty, though he now wished to seem indifferent to any discussions on points of which one of the parties was entirely ignorant. By this time the cutter had begun to drift at the mercy of the currents of the lake, her head turning in all directions, though slowly and not in a way to attract particular attention. Just at this moment the jib was loosened and hoisted, and presently the canvass swelled towards the land, though no evidences of air were yet to be seen on the surface of the water. Slight, however, as was the impulsion, the light hull yielded, and, in another minute, the Scud was seen standing across the current of the river, with a movement so easy and moderate as to be scarcely perceptible. When out of the stream, she struck an eddy, and shot up towards the land, under the eminence where the fort stood, when Jasper dropped his kedge.

"Not lubberly done—" muttered Cap, in a sort of soliloquy— "not over-lubberly, though he should have put his helm a starboard instead of a port, for a vessel ought always to come to with her head off shore, whether she is a league from the land, or only a cable's length, since it has a careful look; and looks are something in this world."

"Jasper is a handy lad—" suddenly observed Serjeant Dunham, at his brother-in-law's elbow, "and we place great reliance on his skill in our expeditions. But come, one and all, we have but half an hour more of day-light to embark in, and the boats will be ready for us, by the time we are ready for them."

On this intimation the whole party separated, each to find those trifles which had not been shipped already. A few taps of the drum gave the necessary signal to the soldiers, and in a minute all were in motion.

Chapter XIII.

"The goblin now the fool alarms,
Hags meet to mumble o'er their charms,
The night-mare rides the dreaming ass,
And fairies trip it on the grass."
Cotton, "Night Quatrains," XVII.65–68.

THE embarkation of so small a party was a matter of no great delay, or embarrassment. The whole force confided to the care of Serjeant Dunham consisted of but ten privates and two non-commissioned officers, though it was now positively known that Mr. Muir was to accompany the expedition. The Quarter Master, however, went as a volunteer, while some duty connected with his own department, as had been arranged between him and his commander, was the avowed object. To these must be added the Pathfinder and Cap, with Jasper and his subordinates, one of whom was a boy. The males of the entire party consequently consisted of less than twenty men, and a lad of fourteen. Mabel, and the wife of a common soldier, were the only females.

Serjeant Dunham carried off his command in a large batteau, and then returned for his final orders, and to see that his brother-in-law and daughter were properly attended to. Having pointed out to Cap the boat that he and Mabel were to use, he ascended the hill to seek his last interview with Lundie. The Major was met on the bastion so often mentioned. Leaving him and the serjeant together, for a short time, we will return to the beach.

It was nearly dark, when Mabel found herself in the boat that was to carry her off to the cutter. So very smooth was the surface of the lake, that it was not found necessary to bring the batteaux into the river to receive their freights, but the beach outside being totally without surf, and the water as tranquil as that of a pond, every body embarked there. As Cap had said, there was no heaving and setting, no working of vast lungs, nor any respiration of an ocean; for, on Ontario, unlike the Atlantic, gales were not agitating the element at one point, while calms prevailed at another. This the distances did not permit, and it is the usual remark of mariners, that the seas get up faster and go down sooner, on all the great lakes of the west, than on the different seas of their acquaintance. When the boat left the land, therefore, Mabel would not have known that she was afloat, on so broad a sheet of water, by any movement that is usual to such circumstances. The oars had barely time to give a dozen strokes, when the boat lay at the cutter's side.

Jasper was in readiness to receive his passengers, and, as the deck of the Scud was but two or three feet above the water, no difficulty was experienced in getting on board her. As soon as this was effected, the young man pointed out to Mabel and her companion, the accommodations prepared for their reception, and they took possession of them. The little vessel contained four apartments below, all between decks having been expressly constructed with a view to the transportation of officers and men, with their wives and families. First in rank, was what was called the after cabin, a small apartment that contained four berths, and which enjoyed the advantage of possessing small windows, for the admission of air and light. This was uniformly devoted to females, whenever any were on board, and as Mabel and her companion were alone, they had ample space and accommodations. The main cabin was larger, and lighted from above. It was now appropriated to the uses of the Quarter Master, the Serjeant, Cap, and Jasper, the Pathfinder roaming through any part of the cutter he pleased; the female apartment excepted. The corporals and common soldiers occupied the space beneath the main hatch, which had a deck for such a purpose, while the crew were berthed, as usual, in the forecastle. Although the cutter did not measure quite fifty tons, the draft of officers and men was so light, that there was ample room for all on board, there being space enough to accommodate treble the number, if necessary.

As soon as Mabel had taken possession of her own really comfortable and pretty cabin, in doing which she could not abstain from indulging in the pleasant reflection that some of Jasper's favor had been especially manifested in her behalf, she went on deck again. Here all was momentarily in motion; the men were roving to and fro, in quest of their knapsacks and other effects, but method and habit soon reduced things to order, when the stillness on board became even imposing, for it was connected with the idea of future adventure, and ominous preparation.

Darkness was now beginning to render objects on shore indistinct, the whole of the land forming one shapeless black outline, of even, forest, summits, that was to be distinguished from the impending heavens only by the greater light of the sky. The stars, however, soon began to appear in the latter, one after another, in their usual mild, placid lustre, bringing with them that sense of quiet which ordinarily accompanies night. There was something soothing, as well as exciting in such a scene, and Mabel, who was seated on the quarter-deck sensibly felt both influences. The Pathfinder was standing near her, leaning as usual on his long rifle, and she fancied that, through the growing darkness of the hour, she could trace even stronger lines of thought than usual, in his rugged countenance.

"To you, Pathfinder, expeditions like this, can be no great novelty," she said, "though I am surprised to find how silent and thoughtful the men appear to be."

"We l'arn this, by making war ag'in Injins. Your militia are great talkers, and little doers, in gin'ral, but the soger who has often met the Mingos, l'arns to know the valu of a prudent tongue. A silent army, in the woods, is doubly strong; and a noisy one, doubly weak. If tongues made soldiers, the women of a camp would generally carry the day."

"But we are neither an army, nor in the woods. There can be no danger of Mingos, in the Scud."

"Ask Jasper, how he got to be master of this cutter, and you will find yourself answered, as to that opinion! No one is safe from a Mingo, who does not understand his very natur'; and, even then, he must act up to his own knowledge, and that closely. Ask Jasper how he got command of this very cutter!"

"And how *did* he get the command?" inquired Mabel, with an earnestness and interest that delighted her simple-minded and true-hearted companion, who was never better pleased than when he had an opportunity of saying aught in favor of a friend. "It is honorable to him, that he has reached this station, while yet so young."

"That is it—but he deserved it all, and more. A frigate would'n't have been too much to pay for so much spirit and coolness, had there been such a thing on Ontario, as there is not, howsever, or likely to be."

"But Jasper—you have not yet told me how he got the command of this schooner?"

"It is a long story, Mabel, and one your father, the sarjeant, can tell much better than I, for he was present, while I was off on a distant scoutin'. Jasper is not good at a story, I will own that; I've heard him questioned about this affair, and he never made a good tale of it, although every body knows it was a good thing. No—no—Jasper is not good at a story, as his best friends must own. The Scud had near fallen into the hands of the French and the Mingos, when Jasper saved her, in a way, that none but a quick-witted mind and a bold heart would have attempted. The Sarjeant will tell the tale better than I can, and I wish you to question him, some day, when nothing better offers. As for Jasper, himself, there will be no use in worrying the lad, since he will make a bungling matter of it, for he don't know how to give a history, at all."

Mabel determined to ask her father to repeat the incidents of the affair that very night, for it struck her young fancy that nothing better could well offer than to listen to the praises of one who was a bad historian of his own exploits.

"Will the Scud remain with us, when we reach the islands?" she asked, after a little hesitation about the propriety of the question, "or shall we be left to ourselves?"

"That's as may be. Jasper does not often keep the cutter idle, when any thing is to be done, and we may expect activity on his part. My gifts, howsever, run so little towards the water, and vessels, gin'rally, unless it be among rapids and falls, and in canoes, that I pretend to know nothing about it. We shall have all right, under Jasper, I make no doubt, who can find a trail on Ontario as well as a Delaware, can find one, on the land."

"And our own Delaware, Pathfinder—the Big Serpent—why is he not with us, to-night?"

"Your question would have been more nat'ral, had you said, 'why are *you* here, Pathfinder?'—The Sarpent is in his place, while I am not in mine. He is out, with two or three more, scouting the lake shore, and will join us down among the islands, with the tidings he may gather. The sarjeant is too good a soldier, to forget his rear, while he is facing the inimy in front. It's a thousand pities, Mabel, your father was'n't born a gin'ral, as some of the English are who come among us, for I feel sartain he would'n't leave a Frencher in the Canadas a week, could he have his own way with them."

"Shall we have enemies to face in front?" asked Mabel, smiling, and for the first time, feeling a slight apprehension about the dangers of the expedition. "Are we likely to have an engagement?"

"If we have, Mabel, there will be men enough ready and willing to stand atween you and harm. But you are a soldier's daughter, and we all know, have the spirit of one. Don't let the fear of a battle, keep your pretty eyes from sleeping."

"I do feel braver, out here in the woods, Pathfinder, than I ever felt before, amid the weaknesses of the towns, although I have always tried to remember what I owe to my dear father."

"Ay, your mother was so before you!–'You will find Mabel like her mother, no screamer, or a fainthearted girl, to trouble a man in his need, but one who would encourage her mate, and help to keep his heart up, when sorest pressed by danger'–said the sarjeant to me, before I ever laid eyes on that sweet countenance of yours, he did!"

"And why should my father have told you this, Pathfinder?" the girl demanded a little earnestly. "Perhaps he fancied you would think the better of me, if you did not believe me a silly coward, as so many of my sex love to make themselves appear."

Deception, unless it were at the expense of his enemies in the field, nay, concealment of even a thought, was so little in accordance with the Pathfinder's very nature, that he was not a little embarrassed by this simple question. To own the truth openly, he felt, by a sort of instinct for which it would have puzzled him to account, would not be proper, and to hide it agreed with neither his sense of right, nor his habits. In such a strait he involuntarily took refuge in a middle course, not revealing that which he fancied ought not to be told, nor yet absolutely concealing it.

"You must know, Mabel," he said, "that the sarjeant and I, are old friends, and have stood, side by side, or if not actually side by side, I a little in advance as became a scout, and your father with his own men, as better suited a soldier of the King, on many a hard fou't and bloody day. It's the way of us skirmishers to think little of the fight, when the rifle has done cracking; and at night around our fires, or on our marches, we talk of the things we love, just as you young women converse about your fancies and opinions when you get together to laugh over your idees. Now it was nat'ral that the sarjeant, having such a daughter as you, should love her better than any thing else, and that he should talk of her oftener than of any thing else, while I, having neither daughter, nor sister, nor mother, nor kith nor kin, nor any thing but the Delawares to love, I nat'rally chimed in, as it were, and got to love you, Mabel, afore I ever saw you—yes I did—just by talking about you so much."

"And now you *have* seen me," returned the smiling girl, whose unmoved and natural manner proved how little she was thinking of any thing more than parental or fraternal regard, "you are beginning to see the folly of forming friendships for people before you know any thing about them, except by hearsay."

"It wasn't friendship—it isn't friendship, Mabel, that I feel for you. I am the friend of the Delawares, and have been so from boyhood; but my feelings for them, or for the best of them, are not the same as them I got from the sarjeant for you; and, especially, now that I begin to know you better. I'm sometimes afear'd it is'n't wholesome for one who is much occupied in a very manly calling, like that of a guide, or a scout, or a soldier even, to form friendships for women—young women in particular—as they seem to me to lessen the love of enterprize, and to turn the feelings away from their gifts and nat'ral occupations."

"You, surely, do not mean, Pathfinder, that a friendship for a girl like me, would make you less bold, and more unwilling to meet the French, than you were before?"

"Not so—not so. With you in danger, for instance, I fear I might become fool hardy, but afore we became so intimate, as I may say, I loved to think of my scoutin's, and of my marches, and outlyings, and fights, and other adventures; but now my mind cares less about them; I think more of the barracks and of evenings passed in discourse, of feelings in which there are no wranglings and bloodshed, and of young women, and of their laughs, and their cheerful soft voices, their pleasant looks, and their winning ways! I sometimes tell the sarjeant, that he and his daughter will be the spoiling of one of the best and most experienced scouts on the lines!"

"Not they, Pathfinder; they will try to make that which is already so excellent, perfect. You do not know us, if you think that either wishes to see you, in the least, changed. Remain as at present, the same honest, upright, conscientious, fearless, intelligent, trustworthy guide that you are, and neither my dear father, nor myself, can ever think of you differently from what we now do."

It was too dark for Mabel to note the workings of the countenance of her listener, but her own sweet face was turned towards him, as she spoke with an energy equal to her frankness, in a way to show how little embarrassed were her thoughts, and how sincere were her words. Her countenance was a little flushed, it is true, but it was with earnestness and truth of feeling, though no nerve thrilled, no limb trembled, no pulsation quickened. In short her manner and appearance were those of a sincere-minded and frank girl, making such a declaration of good will and regard for one of the other sex, as she felt that his services and good qualities merited, without any of the emotion that invariably accompanies the consciousness of an inclination, which might lead to softer disclosures. The Pathfinder was too unpractised, however, to enter into distinctions of this kind, and his humble nature was encouraged by the directness and strength of the words he had just heard. Unwilling, if not unable to say any more, he walked away, and stood leaning on his rifle, and looking up at the stars, for quite ten minutes, in profound silence.

In the mean while, the interview on the bastion, to which we have already alluded, took place, between Lundie and the Serjeant.

"Have the men's knapsacks been examined?" demanded Major Duncan, after he had cast his eye at a written report handed to him by the serjeant, but which it was too dark to read.

"All, your honor; and all are right."

"The ammunition—arms—?"

"All in order, Major Duncan, and fit for any service."

"You have the men named in my own draft, Dunham?"

"Without an exception, sir. Better men could not be found in the regiment."

"You have need of the best of our men, serjeant. This experiment has now been tried three times; always under one of the ensigns, who have flattered me with success, but have as often failed. After so much preparation and expense, I do not like to abandon the project entirely, but this will be the last effort, and the result will mainly depend on you, and on the Pathfinder."

"You may count on us both, Major Duncan. The duty you have given us, is not above our habits and experience, and I think it will be well done—I know that the Pathfinder will not be wanting."

"On that, indeed, it will be safe to rely. He is a most extraordinary man, Dunham; one who long puzzled me, but, who, now that I understand him, commands as much of my respect as any general in His Majesty's service."

"I was in hopes, sir, that you would come to look at the proposed marriage with Mabel, as a thing I ought to wish, and forward."

"As for that, serjeant, time will show," returned Lundie, smiling; though here too, the obscurity concealed the nicer shades of expression,—"one woman is sometimes more difficult to manage than a whole regiment of men. By the way, you know that your would-be son-in-law, the Quarter Master, will be of the party, and I trust you will, at least, give him an equal chance, in the trial for your daughter's smiles."

"If respect for his rank, sir, did not cause me to do this, your honor's wish would be sufficient."

"I thank you, serjeant—we have served much together, and ought to value each other, in our several stations—Understand me, however; I ask no more for Davy Muir than 'a clear field and no favor.' In love, as in war, each man must gain his own victories. Are you certain that the rations have been properly calculated?"

"I'll answer for it, Major Duncan; but, if they were not, we cannot suffer with two such hunters as Pathfinder and the Serpent, in company."

"That will never do, Dunham," interrupted Lundie, sharply, "and it comes of your American birth, and American training!

No thorough soldier ever relies on any thing but his commissary for supplies, and I beg no part of my regiment may be the first to set an example to the contrary."

"You have only to command, Major Duncan, to be obeyed; and, yet, if I might presume, sir—"

"Speak freely, serjeant; you are talking with a friend."

"I was merely about to say, that I find even the Scotch soldiers, like venison and birds, quite as well as pork, when they are difficult to be had."

"That may be very true, but likes and dislikes have nothing to do with system. An army can rely on nothing but its commissaries. The irregularity of the provincials has played the devil with the King's service, too often, to be winked at any longer."

"Gen. Braddock,* your honor, might have been advised by Col. Washington—"

"Out upon your Washington!—You're all provincials together, man, and uphold each other, as if you were of a sworn confederacy."

"I believe His Majesty has no more loyal subjects than the Americans, your honor."

"In that, Dunham, I'm thinking you're right, and I have been a little too warm, perhaps. I do not consider *you* a provincial, however, serjeant, for, though born in America, a better soldier never shouldered a musket."

"And Col. Washington, your honor—"

"Well, and Col. Washington may be a useful subject too. He is the American prodigy, and I suppose I may as well give him all the credit you ask. You have no doubt of the skill of this Jasper Eau douce?"

"The boy has been tried, sir, and found equal to all that can be required of him."

"He has a French name, and has passed much of his boyhood in the French colonies—has he French blood, in his veins, serjeant?"

"Not a drop, your honor. Jasper's father was an old comrade of my own, and his mother came of an honest and loyal family, in this very province."

"How came he then so much among the French, and whence his name?—He speaks the language of the Canadas, too, I find!"

"That is easily explained, Major Duncan. The boy was left

under the care of one of our mariners in the old war, and he took to the water, like a duck. Your honor knows that we have no ports on Ontario, that can be named as such, and he naturally passed most of his time on the other side of the lake, where the French have had a few vessels, these fifty years. He learned to speak their language, as a matter of course, and got his name from the Indians and Canadians, who are fond of calling men by their qualities as it might be."

"A French master, is but a poor instructor for a British sailor, notwithstanding!"

"I beg your pardon, sir; Jasper Eau douce was brought up under a real English seaman; one that had sailed under the King's Pennant, and may be called a thorough bred: that is to say, a subject born in the colonies, but none the worse at his trade, I hope, Major Duncan, for that."

"Perhaps not, serjeant; perhaps not; nor any better. This Jasper behaved well, too, when I gave him the command of the Scud; no lad could have conducted himself more loyally, or better."

"Or more bravely, Major Duncan. I am sorry to see, sir, that you have doubts as to the fidelity of Jasper."

"It is the duty of the soldier, who is entrusted with the care of a distant and important post like this, Dunham, never to relax in his vigilance. We have two of the most artful enemies, that the world has ever produced, in their several ways, to contend with; the Indians and the French; and nothing should be overlooked that can lead to injury."

"I hope your honor considers me fit to be intrusted with any particular reason that may exist for doubting Jasper, since you have seen fit to intrust me with this command."

"It is not that I doubt you, Dunham, that I hesitate to reveal all I may happen to know, but from a strong reluctance to circulate an evil report concerning one of whom I have hitherto thought well. You must think well of the Pathfinder, or you would not wish to give him your daughter?"

"For the Pathfinder's honesty I will answer with my life, sir—" returned the serjeant firmly, and not without a dignity of manner that struck his superior. "Such a man does'n't know how to be false."

"I believe you are right, Dunham, and yet this last information has unsettled all my old opinions. I have received an anonymous communication, serjeant, advising me to be on my guard against Jasper Western, or Jasper Eau douce, as he is called; who it alleges has been bought by the enemy, and giving me reason to expect that further and more precise information will soon be sent."

"Letters without signatures to them, sir, are scarcely to be regarded in war."

"Or in peace, Dunham. No one can entertain a lower opinion of the writer of an anonymous letter, in ordinary matters, than myself. The very act denotes cowardice, meanness, and baseness, and it usually is a token of falsehood, as well as of other vices. But, in matters of war, it is not exactly the same thing. Besides, several suspicious circumstances have been pointed out to me—"

"Such as is fit for an orderly to know, your honor?"

"Certainly, one in whom I confide as much, as in yourself, Dunham. It is said for instance, that your daughter and her party were permitted to escape the Iroquois, when they came in, merely to gain Jasper credit with me. I am told that the gentry at Frontenac will care more for the capture of the Scud, with Serjeant Dunham and a party of men, together with the defeat of our favorite plan, than for the capture of a girl, and the scalp of her uncle."

"I understand the hint, sir, but I do not give it credit. Jasper can hardly be true, and Pathfinder false; and, as for the last, I would as soon distrust your honor, as distrust him!"

"It would seem so, serjeant; it would indeed seem so. But Jasper is not the Pathfinder after all, and I will own, Dunham, I should put more faith in the lad, if he did'nt speak French!"

"It's no recommendation in my eyes, I assure your honor, but the boy learned it by compulsion, as it were, and ought not to be condemned too hastily, for the circumstance, by your honor's leave. If he does speak French, it's because he can't well help it."

"It's a d——d lingo, and never did any one good—at least no British subject; for I suppose the French themselves must talk together, in some language or other. I should have much more faith in this Jasper, did he know nothing of their language. This letter has made me uneasy, and were there another, to whom I could trust the cutter, I would devise some means to detain him here. I have spoken to you already of a brother-in-law, who goes with you, serjeant, and who is a sailor?"

"A real sea-faring man, your honor, and somewhat prejudiced against fresh-water. I doubt if he could be induced to risk his character on a lake, and I'm certain he never could find the station."

"The last is probably true, and, then, the man cannot know enough of this treacherous lake to be fit for the employment! You will have to be doubly vigilant, Dunham. I give you full powers, and should you detect this Jasper in any treachery, make him a sacrifice at once to offended justice."

"Being in the service of the crown, your honor, he is amenable to martial law—"

"Very true—then iron him, from his head to his heels, and send him up here, in his own cutter. That brother-in-law of yours must be able to find the way back, after he has once travelled the road."

"I make no doubt, Major Duncan, we shall be able to do all that will be necessary, should Jasper turn out as you seem to anticipate; though, I think I would risk my life on his truth."

"I like your confidence; it speaks well for the fellow, but that infernal letter!—There is such an air of truth about it—nay there is so much truth in it, touching other matters—"

"I think your honor said it wanted the name at the bottom; a great omission for an honest man to make."

"Quite right, Dunham, and no one but a rascal, and a cowardly rascal in the bargain, would write an anonymous letter, on private affairs. It *is* different, however, in war. Despatches are feigned, and artifice is generally allowed to be justifiable."

"Military, manly artifices, sir, if you will; such as ambushes, surprises, feints, false attacks, and even spies; but I never heard of a true soldier who could wish to undermine the character of an honest young man, by such means as these!"

"I have met with many strange events, and some stranger people, in the course of my experience. But fare you well, serjeant; I must detain you no longer. You are now on your guard, and I recommend to you, untiring vigilance. I think Muir means shortly to retire, and should you fully succeed in this enterprize, my influence will not be wanting, in endeavoring to put you in the vacancy, to which you have many claims."

"I humbly thank your honor," coolly returned the serjeant who had been encouraged in this manner, any time for the preceding twenty years, "and hope I shall never disgrace my station, whatever it may be. I am what nature, and Providence have made me, and I hope I'm satisfied."

"You have not forgotten the howitzer?"

"Jasper took it on board this morning, sir."

"Be wary, and do not trust that man unnecessarily. Make a confidant of Pathfinder at once; he may be of service in detecting any villainy that may be stirring. His simple honesty will favor his observation, by concealing it. *He must* be true."

"For him, sir, my own head shall answer, or even my rank in the regiment. I have seen him too often tried to doubt him."

"Of all wretched sensations, Dunham, distrust, where one is compelled to confide, is the most painful. You have bethought you of the spare flints?"

"A serjeant is a safe commander, for all such details, your honor."

"Well then, give me your hand, Dunham. God bless you, and may you be successful. Muir means to retire—by the way, let the man have an equal chance with your daughter, for it may facilitate future operations, about the promotion. One would retire more cheerfully, with such a companion as Mabel, than in cheerless widowerhood, and with nothing but oneself to love, and such a self, too, as Davy's!"

"I hope, sir, my child will make a prudent choice, and I think her mind is already pretty much made up in favor of Pathfinder. Still she shall have fair play, though disobedience is the next crime to mutiny."

"Have all the ammunition carefully examined and dried, as soon as you arrive; the damp of the lake may affect it. And now, once more farewell, serjeant. Beware of that Jasper, and consult with Muir, in any difficulty. I shall expect you to return triumphant, this day month."

"God bless, your honor—if any thing should happen to me, I trust to you, Major Duncan, to care for an old soldier's character."

"Rely on me, Dunham; you will rely on a friend. Be vigilant; remember you will be in the very jaws of the lion—pshaw of no lion, neither; but of treacherous tigers—in their very jaws and beyond support. Have the flints counted, and examined in the morning—and—farewell, Dunham, farewell."

The serjeant took the extended hand of his superior, with proper respect, and they finally parted; Lundie hastening into his own moveable abode, while the other left the fort, descended to the beach, and got into a boat.

Duncan of Lundie had said no more than the truth, when he spoke of the painful nature of distrust. Of all the feelings of the human mind, it is that which is the most treacherous in its workings, the most insidious in its approaches, and the least at the command of a generous temperament. While doubt exists, every thing may be suspected, the thoughts having no definite facts to set bounds to their wanderings, and distrust once admitted it is impossible to say to what extent conjecture may lead, or whither credulity may follow. That which had previously seemed innocent, assumes the hue of guilt, as soon as this uneasy tenant has taken possession of the thoughts, and nothing is said, or done, without being subjected to the colourings and disfigurations of jealousy and apprehension. If this is true, in ordinary affairs, it is doubly true, when any heavy responsibility, involving life or death, weighs on the unsettled mind of its subject, as in the case of the military commander, or the agent in the management of any grave political interest. It is not to be supposed, then, that Serjeant Dunham, after he had parted from his commanding officer, was likely to forget the injunctions he had received. He thought highly of Jasper, in general, but distrust had been insinuated between his former confidence and the obligations of duty, and, as he now felt that every thing depended on his own vigilance, by the time the boat reached the side of the Scud, he was in a proper humour to let no suspicious circumstance go unheeded, or any unusual movement in the young sailor, pass without its comment. As a matter of course, he viewed things in the light suited to his peculiar mood, and his precautions, as well as his distrust, partook of the habits, opinions and education of the man.

The Scud's kedge was lifted, as soon as the boat with the serjeant, who was the last person expected, was seen to quit the shore, and the head of the cutter was cast to the eastward, by means of the sweeps. A few vigorous strokes of the latter, in which the soldiers aided, sent the light craft into the line of the current that flowed from the river, when she was suffered to drift into the offing again. As yet, there was no wind, the light and almost imperceptible air from the lake, that had existed previously to the setting of the sun having entirely failed.

All this time, an unusual quiet prevailed in the cutter. It appeared as if those on board of her felt that they were entering upon an uncertain enterprize, in the obscurity of night, and that their duty, the hour, and the manner of their departure lent a solemnity to their movements. Discipline also came in aid of these feelings. Most were silent, and those who said anything, spoke seldom and in low voices. In this manner, the cutter set slowly out into the lake, until she had got as far as the river-current would carry her, when she became stationary, waiting for the usual land breeze. An interval of half an hour followed, during the whole of which time, the Scud lay as motionless as a log, floating on the water. While the little changes just mentioned were occurring in the situation of the vessel, notwithstanding the general quiet that prevailed, all conversation had not been repressed, for Serjeant Dunham, having first ascertained that both his daughter and her female companion were on the quarter-deck, led the Pathfinder to the after-cabin, where, closing the door with great caution, and otherwise making certain he was beyond the reach of eaves-droppers, he commenced as follows.

"It is now many years, my friend, since you began to experience the hardships and dangers of the woods in my company."

"It is, sarjeant, yes it is. I sometimes fear I am too old for Mabel, who was not born until you and I had fou't the French-ers as comrades."

"No fear on that account, Pathfinder. I was near your age, before I prevailed on the mind of her mother, and Mabel is a steady, thoughtful girl; one that will regard character, more than any thing else. A lad like Jasper Eau douce, for instance, will have no chance with her, though he is both young and comely."

"Does Jasper think of marrying?" inquired the guide, simply, but earnestly.

"I should hope not—at least not until he has satisfied every one of his fitness to possess a wife."

"Jasper is a gallant boy, and one of great gifts in his way; he may claim a wife, as well as another."

"To be frank with you, Pathfinder, I brought you here to talk about this very youngster. Major Duncan has received some information which has led him to suspect that Eau douce is false, and in the pay of the enemy; I wish to hear your opinion on the subject."

"Anan!"

"I say the Major suspects Jasper of being a traitor—a French spy—or what is worse, of being bought to betray us. He has received a letter to this effect, and has been charging me to keep an eye on the boy's movements, for he fears we shall meet with enemies when we least suspect it, and by his means."

"Duncan of Lundie has told you this, Sarjeant Dunham?"

"He has, indeed, Pathfinder; and though I have been loth to believe any thing to the injury of Jasper, I have a feeling, which tells me I ought to distrust him. Do you believe in presentiments, my friend?"

"In what, Sarjeant?"

"Presentiments—a sort of secret foreknowledge of events that are about to happen. The Scotch of our regiment are great sticklers for such things, and my opinion of Jasper is changing so fast, that I begin to fear there must be some truth in their doctrines."

"But you've been talking with Duncan of Lundie, consarning Jasper, and his words have raised misgivin's."

"Not it—not so, in the least. For, while conversing with the Major, my feelings were altogether the other way; and I endeavored to convince him, all I could, that he did the boy injustice. But there is no use in holding out against a presentiment, I find, and I fear there is something in the suspicion after all."

"I know nothing of presentiments, Sarjeant, but I have known Jasper Eau douce since he was a boy, and I have as much faith in his honesty, as I have in my own, or that of the Sarpent, himself."

"But the Serpent, Pathfinder, has his tricks and ambushes in war, as well as another!"

"Ay, them are his nat'ral gifts, and are such as belong to his people. Neither red skin nor pale face can deny natur'; but Chingachgook is not a man to feel a presentiment ag'in."

"That I believe, nor should I have thought ill of Jasper, this very morning. It seems to me, Pathfinder, since I've taken up this presentiment, that the lad does not bustle about his deck, naturally, as he used to do, but that he is silent, and moody, and thoughtful, like a man who has a load on his conscience."

"Jasper is never noisy, and he tells me noisy ships are generally ill worked ships. Master Cap agrees in this too. No—no—I will believe naught against Jasper, until I see it. Send for your brother, sarjeant, and let us question him in this matter, for to sleep with distrust of one's fri'nd in the heart, is like sleeping with lead there. I have no faith in your presentiments!"

The serjeant, although he scarce knew himself, with what object, complied, and Cap was summoned to join in the consultation. As Pathfinder was more collected than his companion, and felt so strong a conviction of the good faith of the party accused, he assumed the office of spokesman.

"We have asked you to come down, Master Cap," he commenced, "in order to inquire if you have remarked any thing out of the common way, in the movements of Eau douce, this evening."

"His movements are common enough I dare say, for fresh water, Master Pathfinder, though we should think most of his proceedings irregular, down on the coast."

"Yes, yes—we know you will never agree with the lad about the manner the cutter ought to be managed, but it is on another p'int we wish your opinion."

The Pathfinder then explained to Cap the nature of the suspicions which the Serjeant entertained, and the reasons why they had been excited, so far as the latter had been communicated by Major Duncan.

"The youngster talks French, does he?"

"They say he speaks it better than common," returned the Serjeant, gravely. "Pathfinder knows this to be true."

"I'll not gainsay it—I'll not gainsay it," answered the guide: "at least they tell me such is the fact. But this would prove nothing ag'in' a Mississagua,* and least of all ag'in' one like Jasper. I speak the Mingo dialect myself, having l'arnt it while a prisoner among the reptyles, but who will say I am their fri'nd?—Not that I am an inimy, either, according to Injin notions, though I am their inimy, I will admit, agreeable to christianity."

"Ay, Pathfinder, but Jasper did not get his French as a prisoner; he took it in, in boyhood, when the mind is easily impressed, and gets its permanent notions; when nature has a presentiment, as it were, which way the character is likely to incline."

"A very just remark," added Cap, "for that is the time of life, when we all learn the catechism, and other moral improvements. The Serjeant's observation shows that he understands human nature, and I agree with him perfectly; it *is* a damnable thing for a youngster, up here, on this bit of fresh water, to talk French. If it were down on the Atlantic now, where a sea-faring man has occasion sometimes to converse with a pilot, or a linguister, in that language, I should not think so much of it, though we always look with suspicion, even there, at a shipmate who knows too much of the tongue, but up here on Ontario, I hold it to be a most suspicious circumstance."

"But Jasper must talk in French to the people on the other shore," said Pathfinder, "or hold his tongue, as there are none but French to speak to."

"You do'n't mean to tell me, Pathfinder, that France lies hereaway, on the opposite coast?" cried Cap, jerking a thumb over his shoulder, in the direction of the Canadas; "that one side of this bit of fresh water, is York, and the other France!"

"I mean to tell you this is York, and that is Upper Canada, and that English and Dutch and Indian are spoken in the first, and French and Indian in the last. Even the Mingos have got many of the French words in their dialect, and it is no improvement, neither."

"Very true, and what sort of people are the Mingos, my friend?" inquired the serjeant, touching the other on a shoulder, by way of enforcing a remark, the inherent truth of which sensibly increased its value in the eyes of the speaker—"No one knows them better than yourself, and I ask you what sort of a tribe are they?"

"Jasper is no Mingo, Sarjeant."

"He speaks French, and he might as well be, in that particular. Brother Cap, can you recollect no movement of this unfortunate young man, in the way of his calling, that would seem to denote treachery?"

"Not distinctly, serjeant, though he has gone to work wrong end fore most, half his time. It is true, that one of his hands coiled a rope against the sun, and he called it *querling* a rope, too, when I asked him what 'he was about,' but I am not certain that any thing was meant by it; though I dare say the French coil half their running rigging the wrong way, and may call it 'querling it down,' too, for that matter. Then Jasper, himself, belayed the end of the jib halyards to a stretcher in the rigging, instead of bringing them into the mast, where they belong, at least among British sailors."

"I dare say Jasper may have got some Canada notions, about working his craft, from being so much on the other side—" Pathfinder interposed—, "but catching an idee, or a word, is'n't treachery and bad faith. I sometimes get an idee from the Mingos themselves, but my heart has always been with the Delawares. No—no—Jasper is true, and the King might trust him with his crown, just as he would trust his own eldest son, who, as he is to wear it one day, ought to be the last man to wish to steal it."

"Fine talking—fine talking—" said Cap, rising to spit out of the cabin window, as is customary with men when they most feel their own great moral strength, and happen to chew tobacco—"all fine talking, Master Pathfinder, but d——d little logic. In the first place, the King's Majesty cannot lend his crown, it being contrary to the Laws of the Realm, which require him to wear it, at all times, in order that his sacred person may be known, just as the 'Silver Oar' is necessary to a sheriff's officer afloat. In the next place, it's high treason by law, for the eldest son of His Majesty ever to covet the crown, or to have a child, except in lawful wedlock, as either would derange the succession. Thus you see, friend Pathfinder, that in order to reason truly, one must get under way, as it might be, on the right tack. Law is reason, and reason is philosophy, and philosophy is a steady drag, whence it follows that crowns are regulated by law, reason and philosophy."

"I know little of all this, Master Cap, but nothing short of seeing and feeling will make me think Jasper Western a traitor."

"There you are wrong again, Pathfinder, for there is a way of proving a thing much more conclusively than by either seeing or feeling, or by both together, and that is by a circumstance."

"It may be so, in the settlements, but it is not so, here, on the lines."

"It is so in nature, which is monarch over all. Now, according to our senses, young Eau douce is this moment on deck, and by going up there, either of us might see and feel him; but, should it afterwards appear that a fact was communicated to the French at this precise moment, which fact no one but Jasper *could* communicate, why we should be bound to believe that the circumstance was true, and that our eyes and fingers deceived us. Any lawyer will tell you that."

"This is hardly right," said Pathfinder; "nor is it possible, seein' that it is ag'in fact."

"It is much more than possible, my worthy guide, it is law; absolute, King's law of the realm, and, as such to be respected and obeyed. I'd hang my own brother on such testimony; no reflections on the family, being meant, serjeant."

"God knows how far all this applies to Jasper, though I do believe Mr. Cap is right, as to the law, Pathfinder, circumstances being much stronger than the senses, on such occasions. We must all of us be watchful, and nothing suspicious should be overlooked."

"Now I, I recollect me," continued Cap, again using the window. "There was a circumstance, just after we came on board this evening, that is extremely suspicious, and which may be set down at once, as a make-weight against this lad. Jasper bent on the King's ensign with his own hands, and while he pretended to be looking at Mabel, and the soldier's wife, giving directions about showing them below, here, and all that, he got the flag Union down!"

"That might have been accident," returned the Serjeant, "for such a thing has happened to myself; besides the halyards lead to a pulley, and the flag would have come right, or not, according to the manner in which the lad hoisted it."

"A pulley!" exclaimed Cap, with strong disgust—"I wish, Serjeant Dunham, I could prevail on you to use proper terms: An ensign halyard-block is no more a pulley, than your halbert is a boarding pike. It is true that by hoisting on one part, another part would go uppermost; but I look upon that affair of the ensign, now you have mentioned your suspicions, as a circumstance, and shall bear it in mind. I trust supper is not to be overlooked, however, even if we have a hold full of traitors."

"It will be duly attended to, Brother Cap, but I shall count on you, for aid in managing the Scud, should any thing occur to induce me to arrest Jasper."

"I'll not fail you, serjeant, and in such an event you'll probably learn what this cutter can really perform, for, as yet, I fancy it is pretty much matter of guess work."

"Well, for my part," said Pathfinder, drawing a heavy sigh—"I shall cling to the hope of Jasper's innocence, and recommend plain dealing, by asking the lad, himself, without further delay, whether he is, or is not a traitor. I'll put Jasper Western ag'in all the presentiments and circumstances in the Colony."

"That will never do," rejoined the Serjeant. "The responsibility of this affair rests with me, and I request and enjoin, that nothing be said to any one, without my knowledge. We will all keep watchful eyes about us, and take proper note of circumstances."

"Ay—ay—circumstances are the things after all," returned Cap—"One circumstance is worth fifty facts. That I know to be the law of the realm. Many a man has been hanged on circumstances."

The conversation now ceased, and after a short delay, the whole party returned to the deck, each individual disposed to view the conduct of the suspected Jasper, in the manner most suited to his own habits and character.

Chapter XIV.

"Even such a man, so faint, so spiritless,
So dull, so dead in look, so woe-begone,
Drew Priam's curtain in the dead of night,
And would have told him, half his Troy was burned–"
    2 Henry IV, I.i.70–73.

ALL this time, matters were elsewhere passing in their usual train. Jasper, like the weather, and his vessel seemed to be waiting for the land breeze, while the soldiers accustomed to early rising had, to a man, sought their pallets, in the main hold. None remained on deck but the people of the cutter, Mr. Muir and the two females. The Quarter Master was endeavoring to render himself agreeable to Mabel, while, our heroine herself, little affected by his assiduities, which she ascribed partly to the habitual gallantry of a soldier, and partly, perhaps, to her own pretty face, was enjoying the peculiarities of a scene and situation, that, to her, were full of the charms of novelty.

The sails had been hoisted, but as yet not a breath of air was in motion, and so still and placid was the lake that not the smallest motion was perceptible in the cutter. She had drifted in the river-current to a distance a little exceeding a quarter of a mile from the land, and there she lay, beautiful in her symmetry and form, but like a fixture. Young Jasper was on the quarterdeck, near enough to hear occasionally the conversation which passed, but too diffident of his own claim, and too intent on his duties, to attempt to mingle in it. The fine blue eyes of Mabel followed his motions in curious expectation, and more than once the Quarter Master had to repeat his compliments ere she heard them, so intent was she on the little occurrences of the vessel, and, we might add, so indifferent to the eloquence of her companion. At length, even Lt. Muir became silent, and there was a deep stillness on the water. Presently an oar blade fell in a boat, beneath the fort, and the sound reached the cutter as distinctly as if it had been produced on her deck. Then came a murmur, like a sigh of the night, a fluttering of the canvass, the creaking of the boom, and the flap of the jib. These well known sounds were followed by a slight heel in the cutter, and by the bellying of all the sails.

"Here's the wind, Anderson—" called out Jasper to the oldest of his sailors—"take the helm."

This brief order was obeyed, the helm was put up, the cutter's bows fell off, and, in a few minutes, the water was heard murmuring under her head, as the Scud glanced through the lake at the rate of five miles in the hour. All this passed in profound silence, when Jasper again gave the order—"ease off the sheets a little, and keep her along the land."

It was at this instant that the party from the after cabin reappeared on the quarter-deck.

"You've no inclination, Jasper, lad, to trust yourself too near our neighbours the French," observed Muir, who took that occasion to recommence the discourse. "Well, well, your prudence will never be questioned by me, for I like the Canadas, as little as you can possibly like them yoursel'."

"I hug this shore, Mr. Muir, on account of the wind. The land breeze is always freshest close in, provided you are not so near as to make a lee of the trees. We have Mexico Bay to cross, and that, on the present course, will give us quite offing enough."

"I'm right glad it's not the Bay of Mexico," put in Cap, "which is a part of the world I would rather not visit in one of your inland craft. Does your cutter bear a weather helm, Master Oh! the deuce?"

"She is easy on her rudder, Master Cap, but likes looking up at the breeze as well as another, when in lively motion."

"I suppose you have such things as reefs, though you can hardly have occasion to use them?"

Mabel's bright eye detected the smile that gleamed, for an instant, on Jasper's handsome face, but no one else saw that momentary exhibition of surprise and contempt.

"We have reefs, and often have occasion to use them;" quietly returned the young man. "Before we get in, Master Cap, an opportunity may offer to show you the manner in which we do so, for there is easterly weather brewing, and the wind cannot chop, even on the ocean itself, more readily than it flies round on Lake Ontario."

"So much for knowing no better! I have seen the wind, on the Atlantic, fly round like a coach wheel, in a way to keep your sails shaking for an hour, and the ship would become perfectly motionless from not knowing which way to turn."

"We have no such sudden changes here, certainly," Jasper mildly answered—"though we think ourselves liable to unexpected shifts of wind. I hope, however, to carry this land breeze as far as the first islands; after which there will be less danger of our being seen and followed, by any of the look-out boats from Frontenac."

"Do you thik the French keep spics out on the broad lake, Jasper?" inquired the Pathfinder.

"We know they do; one was off Oswego, during the night of Monday, last. A bark canoe came close in with the eastern point, and landed an Indian and an officer. Had you been outlying that night, as usual, we should have secured one, if not both of them."

It was too dark to betray the colour that deepened on the weather burned features of the guide, for he felt the consciousness of having lingered in the fort that night, listening to the sweet tones of Mabel's voice, as she sang ballads to her father, and gazing at a countenance that, to him, was radiant with charms. Probity, in thought and deed, being the distinguishing quality of this extraordinary man's mind, while he felt that a sort of disgrace ought to attach to his idleness, on the occasion mentioned, the last thought that could occur would be to attempt to palliate, or deny, his negligence.

"I confess it, Jasper, I confess it," he said humbly. "Had I been out that night and I now remember no sufficient reason why I was not—it might, indeed, have turned out as you say."

"It was the evening you passed with us, Pathfinder," Mabel innocently remarked; "surely one who lives so much of his time in the forest, in front of the enemy, may be excused for giving a few hours of his time to an old friend, and his daughter."

"Nay, nay, I've done little else but idle, since we reached the garrison," returned the other, sighing, "and it is well that the lad should tell me of it. The idler needs a scoldin': yes, he needs a scoldin'."

"Scolding, Pathfinder! I never dreamed of saying any thing

disagreeable, and least of all would I think of rebuking you, because a solitary spy, and an Indian, or two, have escaped us! Now I know where you were, I think your absence the most natural thing in the world."

"I think nothing of it, Jasper, I think nothing of what you said, since it was desarved. We are all human, and all do wrong."

"This is unkind, Pathfinder."

"Give me your hand, lad, give me your hand. It was'n't you that gave the lesson; it was conscience."

"Well, well," interrupted Cap, "now this latter matter is settled to the satisfaction of all parties, perhaps you will tell us how it happened to be known that there were spies near us, so lately. This looks amazingly like a circumstance!"

As the mariner uttered the last sentence, he pressed a foot slyly on that of the Serjeant, and nudged the guide with his elbow, winking, at the same time, though this sign was lost in the obscurity.

"It is known, because their trail was found next day, by the Serpent, and it was that of a military boot and a moccasin. One of our hunters, moreover, saw the canoe crossing towards Frontenac next morning."

"Did the trail lead near the garrison, Jasper," Pathfinder asked in a manner so meek and subdued that it resembled the tone of a rebuked school boy. "Did the trail lead near the garrison, lad?"

"We thought not—though, of course, it did not cross the river. It was followed down to the eastern point, at the river's mouth, where what was doing in port might be seen; but it did not cross, as we could discover."

"And why did'n't you get under way, Master Jasper," Cap demanded, "and give chase. On Tuesday morning it blew a good breeze; one in which this cutter might have run nine knots."

"That may do on the ocean, Master Cap," put in Pathfinder, "but it would not do here. Water leaves no trail, and a Mingo and a Frenchman are a match for the devil, in a pursuit."

"Who wants a trail, when the chase can be seen from the deck, as Jasper, here, said was the case with this canoe, and it mattered nothing if there were twenty of your Mingos and

Frenchmen, with a good British-built bottom in their wake. I'll engage, Master Oh-the-deuce, had you given me a call, that said Tuesday morning, that we should have overhauled the blackguards."

"I dare say, Master Cap, that the advice of as old a seaman as you, might have done no harm to as young a sailor as myself, but it is a long and a hopeless chase that has a bark canoe in it."

"You would have had only to press it hard, to drive it ashore."

"Ashore, Master Cap! You do not understand our lake navigation, at all, if you suppose it an easy matter to force a bark canoe ashore. As soon as they find themselves pressed, these bubbles paddle right into the wind's eye, and before you know it, you find yourself a mile or two, dead under their lee."

"You do'n't wish me to believe, Master Jasper, that any one is so heedless of drowning, as to put off into this lake, in one of them egg shells, when there is any wind?"

"I have often crossed Ontario in a bark canoe, even when there has been a good deal of sea on. Well managed, they are the driest boats of which we have any knowledge."

Cap now led his brother-in-law and Pathfinder aside, when he assured him, that the admission of Jasper concerning the spies was "a circumstance," and "a strong circumstance," and as such, it deserved his deliberate investigation, while his account of the canoes was so improbable, as to wear the appearance of browbeating the listeners. Jasper spoke confidently of the character of the two individuals who had landed, and this Cap deemed pretty strong proof that he knew more about them, than was to be gathered from a mere trail. As for moccasins, he said that they were worn, in that part of the world, by white men, as well as by Indians, he had purchased a pair himself, and boots, it was notorious, did not particularly make a soldier. Although much of this logic was thrown away on the Serjeant, still it produced some effect. He thought it a little singular himself, that there should have been spies detected so near the fort, and he know nothing of it; nor did he believe that this was a branch of knowledge that fell particularly within the sphere of Jasper. It was true, that the Scud had, once or twice, been sent across the lake to land men of this character, or to bring them off; but then the part played by Jasper, to his own certain knowledge, was very secondary, the master of the cutter remaining as ignorant as any one else, of the purport of the visits of those whom he had carried to and fro, nor did he see why he, alone, of all present, should know any thing of the late visit. Pathfinder viewed the matter differently. With his habitual diffidence, he reproached himself with a neglect of duty, and that knowledge, of which the want struck him as a fault in one whose business it was to possess it, appeared a merit in the young man. He saw nothing extraordinary in Jasper's knowing the facts he had related, while he did feel it was unusual, not to say disgraceful, that he himself now heard of them for the first time.

"As for moccasins, Master Cap," he said, when a short pause invited him to speak, "they may be worn by pale faces, as well as by red skins, it is true, though they never leave the same trail on the foot of one, as on the foot of the other. Any one who is used to the woods, can tell the footstep of an Injin, from the footstep of a white man, whether it be made by a boot, or a moccasin. It will need better evidence than this, to make me believe that Jasper is false."

"You will allow, Pathfinder, that there are such things in the world, as traitors," put in Cap logically.

"I never knew an honest-minded Mingo; one that you could put faith in, if he had a temptation to deceive you. Cheatin' seems to be their gift, and I sometimes think they ought to be pitied for it, rather than parsecuted."

"Then why not believe that this Jasper may have the same weakness? A man is a man, and human nature is sometimes but a poor concern, as I know by experience; I may say we all know by experience; at least I speak for my own human nature."

This was the opening of another long and desultory conversation, in which the probability of Jasper's guilt or innocence was argued, pro and con, until both the serjeant and his brother-in-law, had nearly reasoned themselves into settled convictions, in favor of the first, while their companion grew sturdier and sturdier in his defence of the accused, and still more fixed in his opinions of his being unjustly charged with treachery. In this there was nothing out of the common course of things, for there is no more certain way of arriving at any particular notion, than by undertaking to defend it, and among the most obstinate of our opinions, may be classed those which are derived from discussions in which we affect to search for truth, while in reality we are only fortifying prejudice. By this time, the serjeant had reached a state of mind that disposed him to view every act of the young sailor with distrust, and he soon got to coincide with his relative in deeming the peculiar knowledge of Jasper, in reference to the spies, a branch of information that certainly did not come within the circle of his regular duties, as "a circumstance."

While this matter was thus discussed near the taffrail, Mabel sat silent by the companion-way. Mr. Muir having gone below, to look after his personal comforts, and Jasper standing a little aloof, with his arms crossed and his eyes wandering from the sails to the clouds, from the clouds to the dusky outline of the shore, from the shore to the lake, and from the lake back again to the sails. Our heroine, too, began to commune with her own thoughts. The excitement of the late journey, the incidents which marked the day of her arrival at the fort, the meeting with a father who was virtually a stranger to her, the novelty of her late situation in the garrison, and her present voyage, formed a vista for the mind's eye to look back through, that seemed lengthened into months. She could with difficulty believe that she had so recently left the town, with all its usages of civilized life, and she wondered, in particular, that the incidents which had occurred during the descent of the Oswego, had made so little impression on her mind. Too inexperienced to know that events, when crowded, have the effect of time, or that the quick succession of novelties that pass before us in travelling, elevate objects, in a measure, to the dignity of events, she drew upon her memory for days and dates, in order to make certain that she had known Jasper, and the Pathfinder, and her own father but little more than a fortnight. Mabel was a girl of heart, rather than of imagination, though by no means deficient in the last, and she could not easily account for the strength of her feelings in connection with those who were so lately strangers to her, for she was not sufficiently accustomed to analyze her sensations to understand the nature of the influences that have just been mentioned. As yet, however, her pure mind was free from the blight of distrust, and she had no suspicion of the views of either of her suitors, and one of the last thoughts that could have voluntarily disturbed her confidence, would have been to suppose it possible either of her companions was a traitor to his King and Country.

America, at the time of which we are writing, was remarkable for its attachment to the German family that then sat on the British throne, for, as is the fact with all provinces, the virtues and qualities that are proclaimed near the centre of power, as incense and policy, get to be a part of political faith, with the credulous and ignorant at a distance. This truth is just as apparent to-day, in connection with the prodigies of the republic, as it then was in connection with those distant rulers, whose merits it was always safe to applaud, and whose demerits it was treason to reveal. It is a consequence of this mental dependence, that public opinion is so much placed at the mercy of the designing, and the world, in the midst of its idle boasts of knowledge and improvement, is left to receive its truth, on all such points as touch the interests of the powerful and managing, through such a medium, and such a medium only, as may serve the particular views of those who pull the wires. Pressed upon by the subjects of France, who were then encircling the British colonies, with a belt of forts and settlements, that completely secured the savages for allies, it would have been difficult to say, whether the Americans loved the English more than they hated the French, and those who then lived probably would have considered the alliance which took place between the cis-Atlantic subjects, and the ancient rivals of the British crown, some twenty years later, as an event entirely without the circle of probabilities. In a word, as fashions are exaggerated in a province, so are opinions; and the loyalty, that, at London, merely formed a part of a political scheme, at New York was magnified into a faith that might almost have moved mountains. Disaffection was consequently a rare offence, and most of all, would treason that should favor France, or Frenchmen, have been odious in the eyes of the provincials. The last thing that Mabel would suspect of Jasper, was the very crime with which he now stood secretly charged, and, if others near her endured the pain of distrust, she at least was filled with the generous confidence of a woman. As yet, no whisper had reached her ear to disturb the feeling of reliance with which she had early regarded the young sailor, and her own mind would have been the last to suggest such a thought, of itself. The pictures of the past and of the present, therefore, that exhibited themselves so rapidly to her active imagination, were unclouded with a shade that might affect any in whom she felt an interest, and ere she had mused, in the manner related, a quarter of an hour, the whole scene around her was filled with unalloyed satisfaction.

The season and the night, to represent them truly, were of a nature to stimulate the sensations which youth, health and happiness are wont to associate with novelty. The weather was warm, as is not always the case in that region even in summer, while the air that came off the land, in breathing currents, brought with it the coolness and fragrance of the forest. The wind was far from being fresh, though there was enough of it to drive the Scud merrily ahead, and perhaps to keep attention alive, in the uncertainty that, more or less, accompanies darkness. Jasper, however, appeared to regard it with complacency, as was apparent by what he said in a short dialogue that now occurred between him and Mabel.

"At this rate, Eau douce," for so Mabel had also learned to style the young sailor, "we cannot be long in reaching our place of destination."

"Has your father then told you where that is, Mabel?"

"He has told me nothing; my father is too much of a soldier, and too little used to have a family around him, to talk of such matters. Is it forbidden to say whither we are bound?"

"It cannot be far, while we steer in this direction, for sixty or seventy miles will take us into the St. Lawrence, which the French might make too hot for us; and no voyage on this lake can be very long."

"So says my uncle Cap; but, to me, Jasper, Ontario and the ocean appear very much the same."

"You have then been on the ocean, while I, who pretend to be a sailor, have never yet seen salt water! You must have a great contempt for such a mariner as myself, in your heart, Mabel Dunham!"

"Then I have no such thing, in my heart, Jasper Eau douce. What right have I, a girl without experience or knowledge, to despise any; much less one like you, who are trusted by the

Major and who command a vessel like this! I have never been on the ocean, though I have seen it; and, I repeat, I see no difference between this lake and the Atlantic."

"Nor, in them that sail on both? I was afraid, Mabel, your uncle has said so much against us fresh-water sailors, that you had begun to look upon us as little better than pretenders."

"Give yourself no uneasiness on that account, Jasper, for I know my uncle, and he says as many things against those who live ashore, when at York, as he now says against those who sail on fresh water. No–no–; neither my father, nor myself think any thing of such opinions! My uncle Cap, if he spoke openly, would be found to have even a worse notion of a soldier, than of a sailor who never saw the sea."

"But your father, Mabel, has a better opinion of soldiers, than of any one else; he wishes you to be the wife of a soldier."

"Jasper Eau douce!–I, the wife of a soldier!–My father wishes it?–Why should he wish any such thing–what soldier is there in the garrison that I could marry–that he could *wish me* to marry."

"One may love a calling so well, as to fancy it will cover a thousand imperfections."

"But one is not likely to love his own calling so well, as to cause him to overlook every thing else. You say my father wishes me to marry a soldier, and yet there is no soldier at Oswego, that he would be likely to give me to. I am in an awkward position, for while I am not good enough to be the wife of one of the gentlemen of the garrison, I think, even you will admit, Jasper, I am too good to be the wife of one of the common soldiers?"

As Mabel spoke thus frankly, she blushed, she knew not why, though the obscurity concealed the fact from her companion, and she laughed faintly, like one who felt that the subject, however embarrassing it might be, deserved to be treated fairly. Jasper, it would seem, viewed her position differently from herself.

"It is true, Mabel," he said, "you are not what is called a lady, in the common meaning of the word–"

"Not in any meaning, Jasper," the generous girl eagerly interrupted; "on that head, I have no vanities, I hope. Providence has made me the daughter of a serjeant, and I am content to remain in the station in which I was born."

"But all do not remain in the stations in which they were born, Mabel, for some rise above them, and some fall below them. Many serjeants have become officers; even generals; and why may not serjeants' daughters become officers' ladies?"

"In the case of Serjeant Dunham's daughter, I know no better reason than the fact that no officer is likely to wish to make her his wife," returned Mabel, laughing.

"*You* may think so, but there are some in the 55th, that know better. There is certainly one officer in that regiment, Mabel, who *does* wish to make you his wife."

Quick as the flashing lightning, the rapid thoughts of Mabel Dunham glanced over the five or six subalterns of the corps, who by age and inclinations, would be the most likely to form such a wish, and we should do injustice to her habits, perhaps, were we not to say that a lively sensation of pleasure rose momentarily in her bosom, at the thought of being raised above a station, which, whatever might be her professions of contentment, she felt that she had been too well educated to fill with perfect satisfaction. But this emotion was as transient as it was sudden, for Mabel Dunham was a girl of too much pure and womanly feeling, to view the marriage tie, through any thing so worldly as the mere advantages of station. The passing emotion, was a thrill produced by habit, while the more settled opinion which remained, was the offspring of nature and principles.

"I know no officer in the 55th, or any other regiment, who would be likely to do so foolish a thing; nor do I think I, myself, would do so foolish a thing, as to marry an officer."

"Foolish, Mabel!"

"Yes, foolish, Jasper. You know, as well as I can know, what the world would think of such matters, and I should be sorry, very sorry, to find that my husband ever regretted that he had so far yielded to a fancy for a face, or a figure, as to have married the daughter of one so much his inferior as a serjeant."

"*Your* husband, Mabel, will not be so likely to think of the father, as to think of the daughter."

The girl was talking with spirit, though feeling evidently entered into her part of the discourse, but she paused for near a minute after Jasper had made the last observation, before she uttered another word. Then she continued, in a manner less playful, and one critically attentive might have fancied in a manner that was slightly melancholy:

"Parent and child ought so to live, as not to have two hearts, or two modes of feeling and thinking. A common interest in all things, I should think as necessary to happiness, in man and wife, as between the other members of the same family. Most of all, ought neither the man nor the woman to have any unusual cause for unhappiness, the world furnishing so many of itself."

"Am I to understand, then, Mabel, you would refuse to marry an officer, merely because he was an officer?"

"Have you a right to ask such a question, Jasper?" said Mabel, smiling.

"No other right, than what a strong desire to see you happy can give, which, after all, may be very little. My anxiety has been increased, from happening to know that it is your father's intention to persuade you to marry Lt. Muir."

"My dear, dear father, can entertain no notion so ridiculous; no notion so cruel!"

"Would it then be cruel to wish you the wife of a quarter master?"

"I have told you what I think on that subject, and cannot make my words stronger. Having answered you so frankly, Jasper, I have a right to ask how you know that my father thinks of any such thing."

"That he has chosen a husband for you, I know from his own mouth; for he has told me this much, during our frequent conversations, while he has been superintending the shipment of the stores; and that Mr. Muir is to offer for you, I know from the officer himself, who has told me as much. By putting the two things together, I have come to the opinion, mentioned."

"May not, my dear father, Jasper—" Mabel's face glowed like fire, while she spoke, though her words escaped her slowly and by a sort of involuntary impulse—"May not my dear father, have been thinking of another?—It does not follow from what you say, that Mr. Muir was in his mind."

"Is it not probable, Mabel, from all that has passed? What brings the Quarter Master here? He has never found it necessary, before, to accompany the parties that have gone below; he thinks of you for his wife, and your father has made up his own mind that you shall be so. You must see, Mabel, that Mr. Muir follows *you*."

Mabel made no answer. Her feminine instinct had indeed told her that she was an object of admiration with the Quarter Master, though she had hardly supposed to the extent that Jasper believed, and she, too, had even gathered from the discourse of her father, that he thought seriously of having her disposed of, in marriage; but, by no process of reasoning, could she ever have arrived at the inference that Lt. Muir was to be the man. She did not believe it now, though she was far from suspecting the truth. Indeed, it was her opinion that those casual remarks of her father which had struck her, had proceeded from a general wish to have her settled, rather than from any desire to see her united to any particular individual. These thoughts, however, she kept secret, for self respect and feminine reserve showed her the impropriety of making them the subject of discussion with her present companion. By way of changing the conversation, therefore, after the pause had lasted long enough to be embarrassing to both parties, she said—

"Of one thing you may be certain, Jasper, and that is all I wish to say on the subject—Lt. Muir, though he were a colonel, will never be the husband of Mabel Dunham. And now, tell me of our voyage—when will it end?"

"That is uncertain. Once afloat, we are at the mercy of the winds and waves. Pathfinder will tell you that he who begins to chase the deer in the morning, cannot tell where he will sleep at night."

"But we are not chasing a deer, nor is it morning; so Pathfinder's moral is thrown away."

"Although we are not chasing a deer, we are after that which may be as hard to catch. I can tell you no more than I have said already, for it is our duty to be close-mouthed, whether any thing depends on it, or not. I am afraid, however, I shall not keep you long enough in the Scud, to show you what she can do in fair and foul."

"I think a woman unwise who ever marries a sailor," said Mabel abruptly, and almost involuntarily.

"This is a strange opinion; why do you hold it?"

"Because a sailor's wife is certain to have a rival in his vessel. My uncle Cap, too, says, that a sailor should never marry."

"He means salt-water sailors," returned Jasper laughing. "If he thinks wives not good enough for those who sail on the ocean, he will fancy them just suited to those who sail on the lakes. I hope, Mabel, you do not take your opinions of us fresh-water mariners from all that Master Cap says?"

"Sail ho!" exclaimed the very individual of whom they were conversing–"or, boat ho! would be nearer the truth."

Jasper ran forward, and, sure enough, a small object was discernible about a hundred yards ahead of the cutter, and nearly on her lee bow. At the first glance, he saw it was a bark canoe, for though the darkness prevented hues from being distinguished, the eye that had got to be accustomed to the night, might discern forms, at some little distance; and the eye, which, like Jasper's, had long been familiar with things aquatic, could not be at a loss in discovering the outlines necessary to come to the conclusion he did.

"This may be an enemy," the young man coolly remarked, "and it may be well to overhaul him."

"He is paddling with all his might, lad," observed the Pathfinder, "and means to cross your bows and get to windward, when you might as well chase a full-grown buck on snow shoes!"

"Let her luff!–" cried Jasper, to the man at the helm–"Luff up, 'till she shakes.–There, steady and hold all that."

The helmsman complied, and, as the Scud was now dashing the water aside, merrily, a minute, or two, put the canoe so far to leeward as to render escape impracticable. Jasper now sprang to the helm, himself, and by judicious and careful handling, he got so near his chase that it was secured by a boat hook. On receiving an order, the two persons who were in the canoe, left it, and no sooner had they reached the deck of the cutter, than they were found to be Arrowhead and his wife.

Chapter XV.

"What pearl is it that rich men cannot buy,
That learning is too proud to gather up;
But which the poor and the despised of all
Seek and obtain, and often find unsought?
Tell me—and I will tell thee what is truth."
Cowper, *The Task*, III.285–89.

THE meeting with the Indian and his wife excited no surprise in the majority of those who witnessed the occurrence, but
Mabel, and all who knew of the manner in which this chief had
been separated from the party of Cap, simultaneously entertained suspicions, which it was far easier to feel, than to follow
out, by any plausible clue, to certainty. Pathfinder, who, alone,
could converse freely with the prisoners, for such they might
now be considered, took Arrowhead aside, and held a long
conversation with him, concerning the reasons of the latter for
having deserted his charge, and the manner in which he had
been since employed.

The Tuscarora met these inquiries, and he gave his answers,
with the stoicism of an Indian. As respects the separation, his
excuses were very simply made, and they seemed to be
sufficiently plausible. When he found that the party was discovered in its place of concealment, he naturally sought his own
safety, which he secured by plunging into the woods, for he
made no doubt that all who could not effect this much, would
be massacred on the spot. In a word, he had run away, in order
to save his life.

"This is well," returned Pathfinder, affecting to believe the
other's apologies; "my brother did very wisely; but his woman
followed?"

"Do not the Pale Faces' women follow their husbands? Would
not Pathfinder have looked back to see if one he loved was coming?"

This appeal was made to the guide, while he was in a most
fortunate frame of mind to admit its force, for Mabel, and her

blandishments and constancy, were getting to be images familiar to his thoughts. The Tuscarora, though he could not trace the reason, saw that his excuse was admitted, and he stood, with quiet dignity, awaiting the next inquiry.

"This is reasonable and nat'ral," returned Pathfinder in English, passing from one language to the other, insensibly to himself, as his feelings, or habit dictated, "this is nat'ral, and may be so. A woman would be likely to follow the man to whom she had plighted faith, and husband and wife are one flesh. Mabel, herself, would have been likely to follow the sarjeant, had he been present, and retreated in this manner, and no doubt, no doubt, the warm-hearted girl would have followed her husband! Your words are honest, Tuscarora," changing the language to the dialect of the other, "your words are honest, and very pleasant, and just. But, why has my brother been so long from the fort; his friends have thought of him often, but have never seen him!"

"If the doe follows the buck, ought not the buck to follow the doe!" answered the Tuscarora smiling, and laying a finger significantly on the shoulder of his interrogator. "Arrowhead's wife followed Arrowhead; it was right in Arrowhead to follow his wife. She lost her way, and they made her cook in a strange wigwam."

"I understand you, Tuscarora. The woman fell into the hands of the Mingos, and you kept upon their trail."

"Pathfinder can see a reason, as easily as he can see the moss on the trees. It is so."

"And how long have you got the woman back, and in what manner has it been done?"

"Two suns. The Dew of June was not long in coming, when her husband whispered to her the path."

"Well, well, all this seems nat'ral, and according to materimony—But, Tuscarora, how did you get that canoe, and why are you paddling towards the St. Lawrence, instead of the garrison?"

"Arrowhead can tell his own from that of another. This canoe is mine; I found it on the shore, near the fort."

"That sounds reasonable, too, for the canoe does belong to the man, and an Injin would make few words about taking it. Still, it is extr'ord'nary that we saw nothing of the fellow and his wife, for the canoe must have left the river before we did ourselves."

This idea, which passed rapidly through the mind of the guide, was now put to the Indian in the shape of a question.

"Pathfinder knows that a warrior can have shame. The father would have asked me for his daughter, and I could not give her to him. I sent the Dew of June for the canoe, and none spoke to the woman. A Tuscarora woman would not be free in speaking to strange men."

All this, too, was plausible, and in conformity with Indian character, and Indian customs. As was usual, Arrowhead had received one half of his compensation, previously to quitting the Mohawk, and his refraining to demand the residue was a proof of that conscientious consideration of mutual rights that quite as often distinguishes the morality of a savage as that of a christian. To one as upright as Pathfinder, Arrowhead had conducted himself with delicacy and propriety, though it would have been more in accordance with his own frank nature, to have met the father, and abided by the simple truth. Still, accustomed to the ways of Indians, he saw nothing out of the ordinary track of things, in the course the other had taken.

"This runs like water flowing down hill, Arrowhead," he answered, after a little reflection, "and truth obliges me to own it. It was the gift of a red skin to act in this way, though I do not think it was the gift of a Pale Face. You would not look upon the grief of the girl's father."

Arrowhead made a quiet inclination of the body, as if to assent.

"One thing more my brother will tell me," continued Pathfinder, "and there will be no cloud between his wigwam and the strong house of the Yengeese. If he can blow away this bit of fog, his friends will look at him, as he sits by his own fire, and he can look at them, as they lay aside their arms, and forget that they are warriors. Why was the head of Arrowhead's canoe, looking towards the St. Lawrence, where there are none but inimies to be found?"

"Why were the Pathfinder and his friends looking the same way?" asked the Tuscarora calmly. "A Tuscarora may look in the same direction as a Yengeese."

"Why, to own the truth, Arrowhead, we are out scouting,

like;—that is sailing—in other words, we are on the King's business, and we have a right to be here, though we may not have a right to say *why* we are here."

"Arrowhead saw the big canoe, and he loves to look on the face of Eau douce. He was going towards the sun at evening, in order to seek his wigwam, but finding that the young sailor was going the other way, he turned that he might look in the same direction. Eau douce and Arrowhead were together, on the last trail."

"This may all be true, Tuscarora, and you are welcome. You shall eat of our venison, and then we must separate. The setting sun is behind us, and both of us move quick, my brother will get too far from that which he seeks, unless he turns round."

Pathfinder now returned to the others, and reported the result of his examination. He appeared himself to believe that the account of Arrowhead might be true, though he admitted that caution would be prudent with one he disliked; but his auditors, Jasper excepted, seemed less disposed to put faith in the explanations.

"This chap must be ironed at once, Brother Dunham," said Cap, as soon as Pathfinder finished his narration; "he must be turned over to the Master at Arms, if there is any such officer on fresh water, and a court martial ought to be ordered, as soon as we reach port."

"I think it wisest to detain the fellow," the serjeant answered, "but irons are unnecessary so long as he remains in the cutter. In the morning, the matter shall be inquired into."

Arrowhead was now summoned, and told the decision. The Indian listened gravely and made no objections. On the contrary, he submitted with the calm and reserved dignity with which the American Aborigines are known to yield to fate, and he stood apart, an attentive but calm observer of what was passing. Jasper caused the cutter's sails to be filled, and the Scud resumed her course.

It was now getting towards the hour to set the watch, and when it was usual to retire for the night. Most of the party went below, leaving no one on deck but Cap, the Serjeant, Jasper, and two of the crew. Arrowhead and his wife also remained, the former standing aloof in proud reserve, and the latter exhibiting, by her attitude and passiveness, the meek humility that characterizes an Indian woman.

"You will find a place for your wife below, Arrowhead, where my daughter will attend to her wants," said the Serjeant kindly, who was himself on the point of quitting the deck; "yonder is a sail, where you may sleep, yourself."

"I thank my father. The Tuscaroras are not poor. The woman will look for my blankets in the canoe."

"As you wish, my friend. We think it necessary to detain you, but not necessary to confine, or to maltreat you. Send your squaw into the canoe for the blankets, and you may follow her yourself and hand us up the paddles. As there may be some sleepy heads in the Scud, Eau douce," added the serjeant, in a lower tone, "it may be well to secure the paddles."

Jasper assented, and Arrowhead and his wife, with whom resistance appeared to be out of the question, silently complied with the directions. A few expressions of sharp rebuke passed from the Indian to his wife, while both were employed in the canoe, which the latter received with submissive quiet, immediately repairing an error she had made, by laying aside the blanket she had taken, and searching another that was more to her tyrant's mind.

"Come, bear a hand, Arrowhead," said the Serjeant, who stood at the gunwale, overlooking the movements of the two, which were proceeding too slowly for the impatience of a drowsy man, "it is getting late, and we soldiers have such a thing as reveillé. Early to bed, and early to rise."

"Arrowhead is coming—" was the answer, as the Tuscarora stepped towards the head of his canoe.

One blow of his keen knife severed the rope which held the boat, when the cutter glanced ahead, leaving the light bubble of bark, which instantly lost its way, almost stationary. So suddenly and dexterously was this manœuvre performed, that the canoe was on the lee quarter of the Scud, before the serjeant was aware of the artifice, and quite in her wake, ere he had time to announce it to his companions.

"Hard a-lee!" shouted Jasper, letting fly the jib sheet with his own hands, when the cutter came swiftly up to the breeze, with all her canvass flapping, or was running into the wind's eye, as

seamen term it, until the light craft was a hundred feet to
windward of her former position. Quick and dexterous as was
this movement, and ready as had been the expedient, it was not
quicker, or more ready, than that of the Tuscarora. With an
intelligence that denoted some familiarity with vessels, he had
seized his paddle, and was already skimming the water, aided
by the efforts of his wife. The direction he took was south-
westerly, or on a line that led him equally towards the wind and
the shore, while it also kept him so far aloof from the cutter, as
to avoid the danger of the latter's falling on board of him, when
she filled on the other tack.

Swiftly as the Scud had shot into the wind, and far as she had
forged ahead, Jasper knew it was necessary to cast her, ere she
lost her way, and it was not two minutes from the time the helm
had been put down, before the lively little craft was aback forward, and rapidly falling off, in order to allow her sails to fill on
the opposite tack.

"He will escape!" said Jasper, the instant he caught a glimpse
of the relative bearings of the cutter and the canoe. "The cunning knave is paddling dead to windward, and the Scud can
never overtake him!"

"You have a canoe!" exclaimed the serjeant, manifesting the
eagerness of a boy to join in the pursuit—"Let us launch it, and
give chase!"

"'Twill be useless. If Pathfinder had been on deck, there
might have been a chance; but there is none now. To launch the
canoe would have taken three or four minutes, and the time
lost would have been sufficient for the purposes of Arrowhead."

Both Cap and the serjeant saw the truth of this, which would
have been nearly self evident even to one unaccustomed to vessels. The shore was distant less than half a mile, and the canoe
was already glancing into its shadows, at a rate to show that it
would reach the land, ere its pursuers could probably get half
the distance. The canoe itself, might have been seized, but it
would have been a useless prize, for Arrowhead in the woods,
would be more likely to reach the other shore without detection
than if he still possessed the means to venture on the lake again,
though it might be, and probably would be at greater bodily

labor to himself. The helm of the Scud, was reluctantly put up again, and the cutter wore short round on her heel, coming up to her course on the other tack, as if acting on instinct. All this was done by Jasper in profound silence, his assistants understanding what was necessary, and lending their aid in a sort of mechanical imitation. While these manœuvres were in the course of execution, Cap took the Serjeant by a button and led him towards the cabin door, where he was out of ear-shot, and began to unlock his stores of thought.

"Harkee, Brother Dunham," he said with an ominous face, "this is a matter that requires mature thought, and much circumspection."

"The life of a soldier, Brother Cap, is one of constant thought and circumspection. On this frontier, were we to overlook either, our scalps might be taken from our heads in the first nap."

"But I consider this capture of Arrowhead as a circumstance —and I might add his escape as another. This Jasper Freshwater must look to it!"

"They are both circumstances truly, brother, but they tell different ways. If it is a circumstance against the lad, that the Indian has escaped, it is a circumstance in his favor, that he was first taken."

"Ay, ay, but two circumstances do not contradict each other, like two negatives. If you will follow the advice of an old seaman, serjeant, not a moment is to be lost, in taking the steps necessary, for the security of the vessel, and all on board of her. The cutter is now slipping through the water at the rate of six knots, and as the distances are so short on this bit of a pond, we may all find ourselves in a French port before morning, and in a French prison before night."

"This may be true enough; what would you advise me to do, brother?"

"In my opinion you should put this Master Freshwater under arrest, on the spot; send him below, under the charge of a sentinel, and transfer the command of the cutter to me. All this you have power to perform, the craft belonging to the army, and you being the commanding officer of the troops present."

Serjeant Dunham deliberated more than an hour on the propriety of this proposal, for, though sufficiently prompt when his mind was really made up, he was habitually thoughtful and wary. The habit of superintending the personal police of the garrison had made him acquainted with character, and he had long been disposed to think well of Jasper. Still that subtle poison, suspicion, had entered his soul, and so much were the artifices and intrigues of the French dreaded, that, especially warned as he had been by his commander, it is not to be wondered the recollection of years of good conduct, should vanish under the influence of a distrust so keen, and seemingly so plausible. In this embarrassment, the Serjeant consulted the Quarter Master, whose opinion, as his superior, he felt bound to respect, though, at the moment, independent of his control. It is an unfortunate occurrence, for one who is in a dilemma, to ask advice of another who is desirous of standing well in his favor, the party consulted being almost certain to try to think in the manner which will be the most agreeable to the party consulting. In the present instance, it was equally unfortunate, as respects a candid consideration of the subject, that Cap, instead of the Serjeant himself, made the statement of the case, for the earnest old sailor was not backward in letting his listener perceive to which side he was desirous that the Quarter Master should lean. Lt. Muir was much too politic to offend the uncle and father of the woman he hoped and expected to win, had he really thought the case admitted of doubt, but, in the manner in which the facts were submitted to him, he was seriously inclined to think that it would be well to put the control of the Scud temporarily into the management of Cap, as a precaution against treachery. This opinion, then, decided the serjeant, who, forthwith, set about the execution of the necessary measures.

Without entering into any explanations, Serjeant Dunham simply informed Jasper that he felt it to be his duty to deprive him, temporarily, of the command of the cutter, and to confer it on his own brother-in-law. A natural and involuntary burst of surprise, which escaped the young man, was met by a quiet remark, reminding him that military service was often of a nature that required concealment, and a declaration that the present duty was of such a character that this particular arrangement had become indispensable. Although Jasper's astonishment remained undiminished—the serjeant cautiously abstaining from making any allusions to his suspicions—the young man was accustomed to obey with military submission; and he quietly acquiesced—with his own mouth directing the little crew to receive their future orders from Cap, until another change should be effected. When, however, he was told the case required that not only he, himself, but his principal assistant, who, on account of his long acquaintance with the lake, usually was termed the pilot, were to remain below, there was an alteration in his countenance and manner that denoted deep mortification, though it was so well mastered as to leave even the distrustful Cap in doubt as to its meaning. As a matter of course, however, when distrust existed, it was not long before the worst construction was put upon it.

As soon as Jasper and the pilot were below, the sentinel at the hatch received private orders to pay particular attention to both; to allow neither to come on deck again, without giving instant notice to the person who might then be in charge of the cutter, and to insist on his return below, as soon as possible. This precaution, however, was uncalled for, Jasper and his assistant, both throwing themselves silently on their pallets, which neither quitted again that night.

"And, now, Serjeant," said Cap, as soon as he found himself master of the deck, "you will just have the goodness to give me the courses and distance, that I may see the boat keeps her head the right way."

"I know nothing of either, Brother Cap," returned Dunham, not a little embarrassed at the question. "We must make the best of our way to the station among the Thousand Islands, where 'we shall land, relieve the party that is already out and get information for our future government.' That's it, nearly word for word, as it stands in the written orders."

"But you can muster a chart—something in the way of bearings and distances, that I may see the road?"

"I do not think Jasper ever had any thing of the sort to go by."

"No chart, Serjeant Dunham!"

"Not a scrap of a pen, even. Our sailors navigate this lake without any aid from maps."

"The devil they do!—They must be regular Yahoos. And do you suppose, Serjeant Dunham, that I can find one island out of a thousand, without knowing its name, or its position—without even a course, or a distance?"

"As for the *name*, Brother Cap, you need not be particular, for not one of the whole thousand *has* a name, and so a mistake can never be made on that score. As for the position, never having been there, myself, I can tell you nothing about it, nor do I think its position of any particular consequence, provided we find the spot. Perhaps one of the hands on deck can tell us the way."

"Hold on, Serjeant—hold on, a moment, if you please, Serjeant Dunham. If I am to command this craft, it must be done, if you please, without holding any councils of war with the cook and cabin boy. A ship-master is a ship-master, and he must have an opinion of his own, even if it be a wrong one. I suppose you know service well enough to understand that it is better in a commander to go wrong, than to go nowhere. At all events, the Lord High Admiral could'n't command a yawl with dignity, if he consulted the cockswain every time he wished to go ashore. No—no—if I sink, I sink; but d——e, I'll go down ship-shape and with dignity."

"But, Brother Cap, I have no wish to go down any where, unless it be to the station among the Thousand Islands, whither we are bound."

"Well, well, serjeant, rather than ask advice, that is direct, bare-faced advice, of a foremast hand, or any other than a quarter-deck officer, I would go round to the whole thousand, and examine them one by one, until we got the right haven. But, there is such a thing, as coming at an opinion, without manifesting ignorance, and I will manage to rowse all there is, out of these hands, and make them think, all the while, that I am cramming them, with my own experience. We are sometimes obliged to use the glass at sea, when there is nothing in sight, or to heave the lead, long before we strike soundings. I suppose you know in the army, serjeant, that the next thing to knowing that which is desirable, is to seem to know all about it.

When a youngster, I sailed two v'y'ges with a man who navigated his ship pretty much by the latter sort of information, which sometimes answers."

"I know we are steering in the right direction, at present," returned the serjeant; "but in the course of a few hours we shall be up with a head-land, where we must feel our way, with more caution."

"Leave me to pump the man at the wheel, brother, and you shall see that I will make him suck, in a very few minutes."

Cap and the serjeant now walked aft, until they stood by the sailor who was at the helm, Cap maintaining an air of security and tranquillity, like one who was entirely confident of his own powers.

"This is a wholesome air, my lad," Cap observed, as it might be incidentally, and in the manner that a superior on board a vessel sometimes condescends to use to a favored inferior. "Of course, you have it, in this fashion, off the land, every night?"

"At this season of the year, sir," the man returned, touching his hat, out of respect to his new commander and Serjeant Dunham's connection.

"The same thing, I take it, among the Thousand Islands?– The wind will stand of course, though we shall then have land on every side of us."

"When we get further east, sir, the wind will probably shift, for there can then be no particular land breeze."

"Ay, ay–so much for your fresh water! It has always some trick that is opposed to nature. Now, down among the West-India islands, one is just as certain of having a land breeze, as he is of having a sea breeze. In that respect there is no difference, though it's quite in rule, it should be different up here, on this bit of fresh water. Of course, my lad, you know all about these said Thousand Islands?"

"Lord bless you, Master Cap, nobody knows all about them, or any thing about them. They are a puzzle to the oldest sailor on the lake, and we don't pretend to know even their names. For that matter, most of them have no more names than a child that dies before it is christened."

"Are you a Roman Catholic?–" demanded the serjeant, sharply.

"No sir, nor any thing else. I'm a generalizer about religion, never troubling that which don't trouble me."

"Hum! a generalizer; that is, no doubt, one of the new sects that afflict the country!" muttered Mr. Dunham, whose grandfather had been a New-Jersey quaker, his father a presbyterian, and who had joined the church of England, himself, after he entered the army.

"I take it, John," resumed Cap—"Your name is Jack, I believe?"

"No sir; I am called Robert."

"Ay, Robert—it's very much the same thing—Jack, or Bob—we use the two indifferently. I say, Bob, it's good holding ground, is it, down at this same station for which we are bound?"

"Bless you sir, I know no more about it, than one of the Mohawks, or a soldier of the 55th."

"Did you never anchor there?"

"Never, sir. Master Eau douce always makes fast to the shore."

"But in running in for the town, you kept the lead going, out of question, and must have tallowed*as usual?"

"Tallow! and town, too! Bless you heart, Master Cap, there is no more town, than there is on your chin, and not half as much tallow."

The serjeant smiled grimly, but his brother-in-law did not detect this proof of facetiousness.

"No church tower, nor light, nor fort, ha! There is a garrison, as you call it hereaway, at least."

"Ask Serjeant Dunham, sir, if you wish to know that! All the garrison is on board the Scud."

"But, in running in, Bob, which of the channels do you think the best, the one you went last, or—or—or—ay, or the other?"

"I can't say, sir. I know nothing of either."

"You did'n't go to sleep, fellow, at the wheel did you?"

"Not at the wheel, sir, but down in the fore peak, in my berth. Eau douce sent us below, so'gers and all, with the exception of the pilot, and we know no more of the road than if we had never been over it. This he has always done, in going in and coming out, and, for the life of me, I could tell you nothing of the channel, or of the course, after we are once fairly up with the islands. No one knows any thing of either, but Jasper and the pilot."

"Here's a circumstance for you, serjeant," said Cap, leading his brother-in-law, a little aside. "There is no one on board to pump, for they all suck from ignorance, at the first stroke of the brake. How the devil am I to find the way to this station."

"Sure enough, Brother Cap; your question is more easily put than answered. Is there no such thing as figuring it out, by navigation? I thought you salt-water mariners were able to do as small a thing as that! I have often read of their discovering islands, surely."

"That you have, brother; that you have; and this discovery would be the greatest of them all, for it would not only be dis-covering one island, but one island out of a thousand. I might make out to pick up a single needle on this deck, old as I am, but I much doubt if I could pick one out of a haystack."

"Still, the sailors of the lake, have a method of finding the places they wish to go to."

"If I have understood you, serjeant, this station, or block house, is particularly private?"

"It is indeed; the utmost care having been taken to prevent a knowledge of its position, from reaching the enemy."

"And you expect me, a stranger on your lake, to find this place without chart, course, distance, latitude, longitude, or soundings—ay, d——e, or tallow! Allow me to ask if you think a mariner runs by his nose, like one of Pathfinder's hounds?"

"Well, brother, you may yet learn something by questioning the young man at the helm; I can hardly think that he is as ignorant as he pretends to be."

"Hum—this looks like another circumstance! For that matter, the case is getting to be so full of circumstances, that one hardly knows how to foot up the evidence. But we will soon see how much the lad knows."

Cap and the serjeant now returned to their station near the helm, and the former renewed his inquiries.

"Do you happen to know what may be the latitude and lon-gitude of this said island, my lad?" he asked.

"The what, sir?"

"Why the latitude or the longitude; one or both; I'm not particular which, as I merely inquire in order to see how they bring up young men on this bit of fresh water."

"I'm not particular about either, myself, sir, and so I do not happen to know what you mean."

"Not what I mean!—You know what latitude is?"

"Not I, sir," returned the man, hesitating, "though I believe it is French, for the Upper Lakes."

"Whe-e-e-w," whistled Cap, drawing out his breath, like the broken stop of an organ—"Latitude, French for upper lakes! Harkee, young man; do you know what longitude means?"

"I believe I do, sir—that is five feet six, the regulation height for soldiers in the King's service."

"There's the longitude found out for you, serjeant, in the rattling of a brace block! You have some notion about a degree, and minutes, and seconds, I hope?"

"Yes sir, degree means my betters, and minutes and seconds, are for the short or long log-lines. We all know these things, as well as the salt-water people."

"D——e, Brother Dunham, if I think even Faith can get along on this lake, much as they say it can do with mountains. I'm sure character is in no security. Well, my lad, you understand the azimuth, and measuring distances, and how to box the compass."*

"As for the first, sir, I can't say I do. The distances we all know, as we measure them from point to point, and as for boxing the compass, I will turn my back to no admiral in His Majesty's fleet. Nothe-nothe and by east, nothe-nothe east, nothe east and by nothe, nothe east; nothe east and by east, east nothe east, east and by nothe, east;—"

"That will do—that will do. You'll bring about a shift of wind, if you go on in this manner. I see very plainly, serjeant," walking away again, and dropping his voice, "we've nothing to hope for, from that chap. I'll stand on two hours longer, on this tack, when we'll heave-to and get the soundings; after which we will be governed by circumstances."

To this the serjeant, who, to coin a word, was very much of an idiosyncratist, made no objections, and, as the wind grew lighter, as usual with the advance of night, and there were no immediate obstacles to the navigation, he made a bed of a sail, on deck, and was soon lost in the sound sleep of a soldier. Cap continued to walk the deck, for he was one whose iron frame set fatigue at defiance, and not once that night did he close his eyes.

It was broad day-light when Serjeant Dunham awoke, and the exclamation of surprise that escaped him, as he rose to his feet, and began to look about him, was stronger than it was usual for one so drilled to suffer to be heard. He found the weather entirely changed, the view bounded by driving mist, that limited the visible horizon to a circle of about a mile in diameter, the lake raging and covered with foam, and the Scud lying to. A brief conversation with his brother-in-law, let him into the secrets of all these sudden changes.

According to the account of Master Cap, the wind had died away to a calm, about midnight, or just as he was thinking of heaving to, to sound, for islands ahead were beginning to be seen. At one A.M. it began to blow from the north east, accompanied by a drizzle, and he stood off to the northward and westward, knowing that the coast of New York lay in the opposite direction. At half past one, he stowed the staysail, reefed the mainsail, and took the bonnet off the jib.* At two, he was compelled to get a second reef aft, and by half past two, he had put a balance reef in the sail, and was lying to.

"I can't say but the boat behaves well, Serjeant," the old sailor added, "but it blows forty two pounders! I had no idea there were any such currents of air, up here on this bit of fresh water, though I care not the knotting of a yarn for it, as your lake has now somewhat of a natural look, and–" spitting from his mouth, with distaste, a dash of the spray that had just wetted his face, "and if this d——d water, had a savor of salt about it, one might be comfortable."

"How long have you been heading in this direction, Brother Cap?" enquired the prudent soldier. "And at what rate may we be going through the water?"

"Why two or three hours, mayhap, and she went like a horse for the first pair of them. Oh! we've a fine offing, now, for, to own the truth, little relishing the neighborhood of them said islands, although they are to windward, I took the helm myself, and run her off free, for some league or two. We are well to leeward of them, I'll engage. I say to leeward, for, though one might wish to be well to windward of one island, or even half a dozen, when it comes to a thousand, the better way is to give it up at once, and to slide down under their lee, as fast as possible. No—no—there they are, up yonder in the drizzle, and there they may stay, for any thing Charles Cap cares!"

"As the north shore lies only some five or six leagues from us, Brother, and I know there is a large bay, in that quarter, might it not be well to consult some of the crew concerning our position, if indeed we do not call up, Jasper Eau douce, and tell him to carry us back to Oswego? It is quite impossible we should ever reach the station with this wind directly in our teeth."

"There are several serious professional reasons, serjeant, against all your propositions. In the first place, an admission of ignorance on the part of a commander, would destroy discipline—No matter, brother, I understand your shake of the head, but nothing capsizes discipline so much, as to confess ignorance. I once knew a master of a vessel who went a week on a wrong course, rather than allow he had made a mistake, and it was surprising how much he rose in the opinions of his people, just because they could not understand him."

"That may do on salt water, Brother Cap, but it will hardly do on fresh. Rather than wreck my command on the Canada shore, I shall feel it a duty to take Jasper out of arrest."

"And make a haven in Frontenac! No, serjeant, the Scud is in good hands, and will now learn something of seamanship. We have a fine offing, and no one but a madman would think of going upon a coast in a gale like this. I shall ware every watch, and then we shall be safe against all dangers, but those of the drift, which in a light low craft like this, without top hamper, will be next to nothing. Leave it all to me, serjeant, and I pledge you the character of Charles Cap, that all will go well."

Serjeant Dunham was fain to yield. He had great confidence in his connection's professional skill, and hoped that he would take such care of the cutter as would amply justify his good opinion. On the other hand, as distrust like love, "grows by what it feeds on," he entertained so much apprehension of treachery, that he was quite willing any one but Jasper should, just then, have the control of the fate of the whole party. Truth, moreover, compels us to admit another motive. The particular duty on which he was now sent, should have been confided to a commissioned officer, of right, and Major Duncan had excited a good deal of discontent among the subalterns of the garrison, by having confided it to one of the Serjeant's humble station. To return, without having even reached the point of destination, therefore, the latter felt would be a failure from which he was not likely soon to recover, and the measure would at once be the means of placing a superior in his shoes.

Chapter XVI.

"Thou glorious mirror, where the Almighty's form
Glasses itself in tempests; in all time,
Calm or convulsed—in breeze, or gale, or storm,
Icing the pole, or in the torrid clime
Dark heaving;—boundless, endless and sublime—
The image of Eternity; the throne
Of the Invisible; even from out thy slime
The monsters of the deep are made; each zone
Obeys thee; thou goest forth, dread, fathomless, alone."
     Byron, *Childe Harold's Pilgrimage*, IV.CLXXXIII.

As the day advanced, the portion of the inmates of the vessel that had the liberty of doing so, appeared on deck. As yet the sea was not very high, from which it was inferred that the cutter was still under the lee of the islands, but it was apparent to all who understood the lake, that they were about to experience one of the heavy autumnal gales of that region. Land was nowhere visible, and the horizon, on every side, exhibited that gloomy void, which lends to all views on vast bodies of water, the sublimity of mystery. The swells, or as landsmen term them, the waves, were short and curling, breaking of necessity sooner than the longer seas of the ocean, while the element itself, instead of presenting that beautiful hue, which rivals the deep tint of the southern sky, looked green and angry, though wanting in the lustre that is derived from the rays of the sun.

The soldiers were soon satisfied with the prospect, and, one by one, they disappeared, until none were left on deck but the crew, the Serjeant, Cap, Pathfinder, the Quarter Master, and Mabel. There was a shade on the brow of the latter, who had been made acquainted with the real state of things, and who had fruitlessly ventured an appeal in favor of Jasper's restoration to the command. A night's rest and a night's reflection appeared also to have confirmed the Pathfinder in his opinion of the young man's innocence, and he, too, had made a warm appeal in behalf of his friend, though with the same want of success.

Several hours passed away, the wind gradually getting to be heavier, and the sea rising, until the motion of the cutter compelled Mabel and the Quarter Master to retreat, also. Cap wore several times, and it was now evident that the Scud was drifting into the broader and deeper parts of the lake, the seas raging down upon her in a way that none but a vessel of superior mould and build could have long ridden, and withstood. All this, however, gave Cap no uneasiness, but like the hunter that pricks his ears at the sound of the horn, or the war horse that paws and snorts with pleasure at the roll of the drum, the whole scene awakened all that was man within him, and instead of the captious, supercilious and dogmatic critic, quarrelling with trifles and exaggerating immaterial things, he began to exhibit the qualities of the hardy and experienced seaman, that he truly was. The hands soon imbibed a respect for his skill, and, though they wondered at the disappearance of their old commander and the pilot, for which no reason had been publicly given, they soon yielded an implicit and cheerful obedience to the new one.

"This bit of fresh water, after all, Brother Dunham, has some spirit, I find," cried Cap, about noon, rubbing his hands in pure satisfaction at finding himself once more wrestling with the elements. "The wind seems to be an honest old-fashioned gale, and the seas have a fanciful resemblance to those of the Gulph Stream. I like this, serjeant, I like this; and shall get to respect your lake, if it hold out twenty four hours, longer, in the fashion, in which it has begun."

"Land ho!" shouted the man who was stationed on the forecastle.

Cap hurried forward, and there, sure enough, the land was visible through the drizzle, at the distance of about half a mile, the cutter heading directly towards it. The first impulse of the old seaman was to give an order to, "stand by to ware off shore," but the cool headed soldier, restrained him.

"By going a little nearer," said the serjeant, "some of us may recognize the place. Most of us know the American shore, in this part of the lake, and it will be something gained to learn our position."

"Very true—very true; if, indeed, there is any chance of that, we will hold on. What is this, off here, a little on our weather bow?—It looks like a low head-land."

"The garrison, by Jove!" exclaimed the other, whose trained eye sooner recognized the military outlines, than the less instructed senses of his connection.

The Serjeant was not mistaken. There was the fort sure enough, though it looked dim and indistinct through the fine rain, as if it were seen in the dusk of evening, or the haze of morning. The low, sodded and verdant ramparts, the sombre palisades, now darker than ever with water, the roof of a house or two, the tall, solitary flag-staff, with its halyards blown steadily out, into a curve that appeared traced in immovable lines in the air, were all soon to be seen, though no sign of animated life could be discovered. Even the sentinel was housed, and, at first, it was believed that no eye would detect the presence of their own vessel. But the unceasing vigilance of a border garrison did not slumber. One of the look outs probably made the interesting discovery, a man or two were seen on some elevated stands, and then the entire ramparts, next the lake, were dotted with human beings.

The whole scene was one in which sublimity was singularly relieved by the picturesque. The raging of the tempest had a character of duration, that rendered it easy to imagine it might be a permanent feature of the spot. The roar of the wind was without intermission, and the raging water answered to its dull but grand strains, with hissing spray, a menacing wash, and sullen surges. The drizzle made a medium for the eye which closely resembled that of a thin mist, softening and rendering mysterious the images it revealed, while the genial feeling that is apt to accompany a gale of wind on water, contributed to aid the milder influences of the moment. The dark, interminable forest hove up out of the obscurity, grand, sombre and impressive, while the solitary, peculiar and picturesque glimpses of life that were caught in and about the fort, formed a refuge for the eye to retreat to, when oppressed with the more imposing objects of nature.

"They see us," said the Serjeant, "and think we have returned on account of the gale, and have fallen to leeward of the port. Yes, there is Major Duncan himself, on the north eastern bastion; I know him by his height, and by the officers around him!"

"Serjeant, it would be worth standing a little jeering, if we could fetch into the river, and come safely to an anchor! In that case, too, we might land this Master Oh! the deuce, and purify the boat."

"It would indeed, but poor sailor as I am, I well know it cannot be done. Nothing that sails the lake can turn to windward against this gale, and there is no anchorage outside, in weather like this."

"I know it–I see it–serjeant, and pleasant as is that sight to you landsmen, we must leave it. For myself, I am never so happy, in heavy weather, as when I am certain that the land is behind me."

The Scud had now forged so near in, that it became indispensable to lay her head off shore, again, and the necessary orders were given. The storm stay-sail was set forward, the gaff lowered, the helm put up, and the light craft, that seemed to sport with the elements like a duck, fell off a little, drew ahead swiftly, obeyed her rudder, and was soon flying away on the top of the surges, dead before the gale. While making this rapid flight, though the land still remained in view, on her larboard beam, the fort, and the groups of anxious spectators on its ramparts were swallowed up in the mist. Then followed the evolutions necessary to bring the head of the cutter up to the wind, when she again began to wallow her weary way towards the north shore.

Hours now passed, before any further change was made, the wind increasing in force, until even the dogmatical Cap fairly admitted it was blowing a thorough gale of wind. About sunset the Scud wore again, to keep her off the north shore, during the hours of darkness; and at midnight her temporary master, who by questioning the crew in an indirect manner had obtained some general knowledge of the size and shape of the lake, believed himself to be about midway between the two shores. The height and length of the seas, aided this impression, and it must be added that Cap, by this time, began to feel a respect for fresh water, that twenty four hours earlier he would have derided as impossible. Just as the night turned, the fury of the wind became so great, that he found it impossible to bear up against it, the water falling on the deck of the little craft in such masses as to cause her to shake to the centre, and, though a vessel of singularly lively qualities, to threaten to bury her beneath its weight. The people of the Scud averred that never before had they been out in such a tempest, which was true, for possessing a perfect knowledge of all the rivers and head-lands and havens, Jasper would have carried the cutter in shore, long ere this, and placed her in safety, in some secure anchorage. But, Cap still disdained to consult the young master, who continued below, determining to act like a mariner of the broad ocean.

It was one in the morning, when the storm staysail was again got on the Scud, the head of the mainsail lowered, and the cutter put before the wind. Although the canvass now exposed was merely a rag in surface, the little craft nobly justified the use of the name she bore. For eight hours did she scud, in truth, and it was almost with the velocity of the gulls that wheeled wildly over her in the tempest, apparently afraid to alight in the boiling caldron of the lake. The dawn of day brought little change, for no other horizon became visible, than the narrow circle of drizzling sky and water, already described, in which it seemed as if the elements were rioting in chaotic confusion. During this time the crew and passengers of the cutter were of necessity passive. Jasper and the pilot remained below, but, the motion of the vessel having become easier, nearly all the rest were on deck. The morning meal had been taken in silence, and eye met eye, as if their owners asked each other, in dumb show, what was to be the end of this strife in the elements. Cap, however, was perfectly composed, and his face brightened, his step grew firmer, and his whole air more assured, as the storm increased, making larger demands on his professional skill, and personal spirit. He stood on the forecastle, his arms crossed, balancing his body with a seaman's instinct, while his eyes watched the caps of the seas, as they broke and glanced past the reeling cutter, itself in such swift motion, as if they were the scud flying athwart the sky. At this sublime instant one of the hands gave the unexpected cry of "a sail!"

There was so much of the wild and solitary character of the wilderness about Ontario, that one scarcely expected to meet with a vessel on its waters. The Scud herself, to those who were in her, resembled a man threading the forest alone, and the meeting was like that of two solitary hunters beneath the broad canopy of leaves, that then covered so many millions of acres, on the continent of America. The peculiar state of the weather served to increase the romantic, almost supernatural appearance of the passage. Cap alone regarded it with practised eyes, and even he felt his iron nerves thrill under the sensations that were awakened by the wild features of the scene.

The strange vessel was about two cables' length ahead of the Scud, standing by the wind athwart her bows, and steering a course to render it probable that the latter would pass within a few yards of her. She was a full-rigged ship, and seen through the misty medium of the tempest, the most experienced eye could detect no imperfection in her gear or construction. The only canvass she had set, was a close reefed main-top-sail, and two small storm staysails, one forward and the other aft. Still the power of the wind pressed so hard upon her, as to bear her down nearly to her beam-ends, whenever the hull was not righted by the buoyancy of some wave under her lee. Her spars were all in their places, and by her motion through the water, which might have equalled four knots in the hour, it was apparent that she steered a little free.

"The fellow must know his position well," said Cap, as the cutter flew down towards the ship, with a velocity almost equalling that of the gale, "for he is standing boldly to the southward, where he expects to find anchorage or a haven. No man in his senses would run off free in that fashion, that was not driven to scudding, like ourselves, who did not perfectly understand where he was going."

"We have made an awful run, captain," returned the man to whom this remark had been addressed. "That is the French King's ship, Lee My Calm (le Montcalm)*and she is standing in for the Niagara, where her owner has a garrison and a port. We've made an awful run of it!"

"Ay, bad luck to him! Frenchman like, he skulks into port, the moment he sees an English bottom."

"It might be well for us, if we could follow him," returned the man shaking his head despondingly, "for we are getting into the end of a bay, up here at the head of the lake, and it is uncertain whether we ever get out of it again!"

"Poh! man, poh!—We have plenty of sea room, and a good English hull beneath us. We are no Johnny Crapauds*to hide ourselves behind a point, or a fort, on account of a puff of wind. Mind your helm, sir!"

The order was given on account of the menacing appearance of the approaching passage. The Scud was now heading directly for the forefoot of the Frenchman, and, the distance between the two vessels having diminished to a hundred yards, it was momentarily questionable if there was room to pass.

"Port, sir—port!" shouted Cap. "Port your helm and pass astern!"

The crew of the Frenchman were seen assembling to windward, and a few muskets were pointed, as if to order the people of the Scud to keep off. Gesticulations were observed, but the scene was too wild and menacing to admit of the ordinary expedients of war. The water was dripping from the muzzles of two or three light guns, on board the ship, but no one thought of loosening them for service, in such a tempest. Her black sides, as they emerged from a wave, glistened and seemed to frown, but the wind howled through her rigging, whistling the thousand notes of a ship, and the hails and cries, that escape a Frenchman with so much readiness, were inaudible.

"Let him hollow himself hoarse!" growled Cap—"This is no weather to whisper secrets in. Port, sir, port!"

The man at the helm obeyed, and the next send of the sea drove the Scud down upon the quarter of the ship, so near her that the old mariner, himself, recoiled a step, in a vague expectation that, at the next surge ahead, she would drive bows foremost into the planks of the other vessel. But this was not to be. Rising from the crouching posture she had taken, like a panther about to leap, the cutter dashed onward, and, at the next instant, she was glancing past the stern of her enemy, just clearing the end of his spanker boom, with her own lower yard.

The young Frenchman who commanded the Montcalm, leaped on the taffrail, and with that high toned courtesy which relieves even the worst acts of his countrymen, he raised his cap, and smiled a salutation as the Scud shot past. There were *bonhommie* and good taste in this act of courtesy, when circumstances allowed of no other communications, but they were lost on Cap, who, with an instinct quite as true to his race, shook his fist menacingly and muttered to himself—

"Ay—ay—it's d——d lucky for you, I've no armament on board here, or I'd send you in to get new cabin windows fitted. Serjeant, he's a humbug."

"'T was civil, Brother Cap," returned the other, lowering his hand from the military salute, which his pride as a soldier had induced him to return—"'t was civil, and that's as much as you can expect from a Frenchman. What he really meant by it, no one can say."

"He is not heading up to this sea without an object, neither! Well, let him run in, if he can get there; we will keep the lake, like hearty English mariners."

This sounded gloriously, but Cap eyed with envy, the glittering black mass of the Montcalm's hull, her waving top-sail, and the misty tracery of her spars, as she grew less and less distinct, and finally disappeared in the drizzle, in a form as shadowy as that of some unreal image. Gladly would he have followed in her wake, had he dared, for, to own the truth, the prospect of another stormy night in the midst of the wild waters that were raging around him, brought little consolation. Still he had too much professional pride to betray his uneasiness, and those under his care relied on his knowledge and resources, with the implicit and blind confidence, that the ignorant are apt to feel.

A few hours succeeded, and darkness came again to increase the perils of the Scud. A lull in the gale, however, had induced Cap to come by the wind once more, and throughout the night the cutter was lying-to, as before, head reaching as a matter of course, and occasionally waring to keep off the land. It is unnecessary to dwell on the incidents of this night, which resembled those of any other gale of wind. There were the pitching of the vessel, the hissing of the waters, the dashing of spray, the shocks that menaced annihilation to the little craft as she plunged into the seas, the undying howlings of the wind, and the fearful drift. The last was the most serious danger, for, though exceedingly weatherly under her canvass, and totally without top-hamper, the Scud was so light that the combing of the swells would seem, at times, to wash her down to leeward, with a velocity as great as that of the surges themselves.

During this night Cap slept soundly and for several hours. The day was just dawning, when he felt himself shaken by the shoulder, and on rousing himself he found the Pathfinder standing at his side. During the gale, the guide had appeared little on deck, for his natural modesty told him that seamen alone should interfere with the management of the vessel, and he was willing to show the same reliance on those who had charge of the Scud, as he expected those who followed through the forest, ought to manifest in his own skill. But he now thought himself justified in interfering, which he did in his own unsophisticated and peculiar manner.

"Sleep is sweet, Master Cap," he said, as soon as the eyes of the latter were fairly open, and his consciousness had sufficiently returned—"Sleep is sweet, as I know from experience, but life is sweeter still. Look about you, and say if this is exactly the moment for a commander to be off his feet."

"How now—how now—Master Pathfinder!" growled Cap, in the first moments of his awakened faculties—"Are you, too, getting on the side of the grumblers? When ashore, I admired your sagacity in running through the worst shoals, without a compass, and since we have been afloat, your meekness and submission have been as pleasant, as your confidence on your own ground; I little expected such a summons from you."

"As for myself, Master Cap, I feel I have my gifts, and I believe they'll interfere with those of no other man, but the case may be different with Mabel Dunham. She has her gifts, too, it is true, but they are not rude like ourn, but gentle, and womanish, as they ought to be. It's on her account that I speak, and not on my own."

"Ay—ay—I begin to understand. The girl is a good girl, my worthy friend, but she is a soldier's daughter and a sailor's niece, and ought not to be too taut, or too tender, in a gale. Does she show any fear?"

"Not she—not she. Mabel is a woman, but she is reasonable and silent. Not a word have I heard from her, consarning our doings, though I do think, Master Cap, she would like it better, if Jasper Eau douce were put into his proper place, and things were restored to their old situation, like. This is human natur'."

"I'll warrant it!—Girl like, and Dunham like, too. Any thing is better than an old uncle, and every body knows more than an old seaman! *This* is human natur', Master Pathfinder, and, d——e, if I'm the man to sheer a fathom, starboard or port, for all the human natur' that can be found in a minx of twenty—ay,—or—" lowering his voice a little—"for all that can be paraded in His Majesty's 55th regiment of Foot. I've not been at sea forty years, to come up on this bit of fresh water to be taught human natur'.—How this gale holds out! It blows as hard, at this moment, as if Boreas had just clapped his hand upon the bellows. And what is all this to leeward?" rubbing his eyes—"Land as sure as my name is Cap; and high land, too!"

The Pathfinder made no immediate answer, but shaking his head, he watched the expression of his companion's face, with a look of strong anxiety, in his own.

"Land, as certain as this is the Scud!—" repeated Cap—"A lee shore, and that, too, within a league of us, with as pretty a line of breakers, as one could find on the beach of all Long Island!"

"And is that encouraging, or is it disheartening?" demanded the Pathfinder.

"Ha! Encouraging—disheartening?—Why, neither. No—no—there is nothing encouraging about it; and, as for disheartening, nothing ought to dishearten a seaman. You never get disheartened, or afraid in the woods, my friend."

"I'll not say that—I'll not say that. When the danger is great, it is my gift to see it, and know it, and to try to avoid it; else would my scalp, long since, have been drying in a Mingo wigwam. On this lake, howsever, I can see no trail, and I feel it my duty to submit; though I think we ought to remember there is such a person as Mabel Dunham, on board. But here comes her father, and he will nat'rally feel for his own child."

"We are seriously situated, I believe, Brother Cap," said the serjeant, when he had reached the spot, "by what I can gather from the two hands on the forecastle. They tell me the cutter cannot carry any more sail, and her drift is so great we shall go ashore in an hour or two. I hope their fears have deceived them?"

Cap made no reply, but he gazed at the land with a rueful face, and then looked to windward, with an expression of ferocity, as if he would have gladly quarrelled with the weather.

"It may be well, brother," the serjeant continued, "to send for Jasper and consult him, as to what is to be done. There are no

French here to dread, and, under all circumstances, the boy will save us from drowning if possible."

"Ay–ay–'Tis these cursed circumstances that have done all the mischief! But let the fellow come; let him come; a few well-managed questions will bring the truth out of him, I'll warrant you."

This acquiescence on the part of the dogmatical Cap was no sooner obtained, than Jasper was sent for. The young man instantly made his appearance, his whole air, countenance and mien, expressive of mortification, humility, and, as his observers fancied, rebuked deception. When he first stepped on deck, Jasper cast one hurried anxious glance around, as if curious to know the situation of the cutter, and that glance sufficed, it would seem, to let him into the secret of all her peril. At first he looked to windward, as is usual with every seaman, then he turned round the horizon, until his eye caught a view of the highlands to leeward, when the whole truth burst upon him, at once.

"I've sent for you, Master Jasper," said Cap, folding his arms, and balancing his body with the dignity of the forecastle, "in order to learn something about the haven to leeward. We take it for granted, you do not bear malice so hard, as to wish to drown us all; especially the women; and I suppose you will be man enough to help us to run the cutter into some safe berth, until this bit of a gale has done blowing?"

"I would die myself, rather than harm should come to Mabel Dunham," the young man earnestly answered.

"I knew it!–I knew it!" cried Pathfinder, clapping his hand kindly on Jasper's shoulder. "The lad is as true as the best compass that ever run a boundary, or brought a man off from a blind trail! It is a moral sin to believe otherwise."

"Humph!" ejaculated Cap, "Especially the women!–As if *they* were in any particular danger. Never mind, young man; we shall understand each other, by talking like two plain seamen. Do you know of any port under our lee?"

"None. There is a large bay, at this end of the lake, but it is unknown to us all, and not easy of entrance."

"And this coast to leeward–it has nothing particular to recommend it, I suppose?"

"It is a wilderness until you reach the mouth of the Niagara, in one direction, and Frontenac in the other. North and west, they tell me there is nothing but forest and prairies, for a thousand miles."

"Thank God, then, there can be no French. Are there many savages, hereaway, on the land?"

"The Indians are to be found, in all directions, though they are nowhere very numerous. By accident, we might find a party, at any point on the shore; or, we might pass months there, without seeing one."

"We must take our chance, then, as to the blackguards—but, to be frank with you, Master Western, if this little unpleasant matter about the French had not come to pass, what would you now do with the cutter?"

"I am a much younger sailor than yourself, Master Cap," said Jasper, modestly, "and am hardly fitted to advise you."

"Ay—ay—we all know that. In a common case, perhaps not. But this is an uncommon case and a circumstance, and on this bit of fresh water it has what may be called its peculiarities, and, so, every thing considered, you may be fitted to advise even your own father. At all events, you can speak, and I can judge of your opinion, agreeably to my own experience."

"I think, sir, before two hours are over, the cutter will have to anchor."

"Anchor!—not out here in the lake?"

"No, sir; but in yonder, near the land."

"You do not mean to say, Master Oh! the deuce, you would anchor on a lee shore, in a gale of wind!"

"If I would save my vessel, that is exactly what I would do, Master Cap."

"Whe—e—e—w!—This is fresh water, with a vengeance. Harkee, young man, I've been a seafaring animal, boy and man, forty one years, and I never yet heard of such a thing. I'd throw my ground tackle overboard, before I would be guilty of so lubberly an act!"

"That is what we do, on this lake," modestly replied Jasper, "when we are hard pressed. I dare say we might do better, had we been better taught."

"That you might indeed! No; no man induces me to commit

such a sin against my own bringing up. I should never dare show my face inside of Sandy Hook,* again, had I committed so know-nothing an exploit. Why, Pathfinder, here, has more seamanship in him, than that comes to. You can go below, again, Master Oh! the-deuce."

Jasper quietly bowed and withdrew. Still, as he passed down the ladder, the spectators observed that he cast a lingering, anxious look at the horizon to windward, and the land to leeward, and then disappeared with concern strongly expressed in every lineament of his face.

Chapter XVII.

"His still refuted quirks he still repeats;
New raised objections with new quibbles meets;
Till sinking in the quicksand he defends,
He dies disputing, and the contest ends."
Cowper, *The Progress of Error*, ll. 550–53.

As the soldier's wife was sick in her berth, Mabel Dunham was the only person in the outer cabin, when Jasper returned to it; for, by an act of grace in the serjeant, he had been permitted to resume his proper place, in this part of the vessel. We should be ascribing too much simplicity of character to our heroine, if we said that she had felt no distrust of the young man, in consequence of his arrest, but we should also be doing injustice to her warmth of feelings and generosity of disposition, if we did not add that this distrust was insignificant and transient. As he now took his seat near her, his whole countenance clouded with the uneasiness he felt concerning the situation of the cutter, every thing like suspicion was banished from her mind, and she saw in him only an injured man.

"You let this affair weigh too heavily on your mind, Jasper," she said eagerly, or with that forgetfulness of self with which the youthful of her sex are wont to betray their feelings, when a strong and generous interest has obtained the ascendency—"no one, who knows you, can or does believe you guilty. Pathfinder says he will pledge his life for you."

"Then you, Mabel," returned the youth, his eyes flashing fire, "do not look upon me, as the traitor that your father seems to believe me to be?"

"My dear father is a soldier, and is obliged to act as one. My father's daughter is not, and will think of you, as she ought to think of a man who has done so much to serve her already."

"Mabel—I'm not used to talking with one like you—or, saying all I think and feel with any. I never had a sister, and my mother died when I was a child, so that I know little what your sex most likes to hear—"

Mabel would have given the world to know what lay behind the teeming word, at which Jasper hesitated, but the indefinable and controlling sense of womanly diffidence, made her suppress her womanly curiosity. She waited in silence for him to explain his own meaning.

"I wish to say, Mabel," the young man continued, after a pause which he found sufficiently embarrassing—"that I am unused to the ways and opinions of one like you, and that you must imagine all I would add."

Mabel had imagination enough to fancy any thing, but there are ideas and feelings that her sex prefer to have expressed, before they yield them all their own sympathies, and she had a vague consciousness that these of Jasper's might properly be enumerated in the class. With a readiness that belonged to her sex, therefore, she preferred changing the discourse to permitting it to proceed any further, in a manner so awkward, and so unsatisfactory.

"Tell me one thing, Jasper, and I shall be content," she said, speaking now with a firmness that denoted confidence not only in herself, but in her companion—"you do not deserve this cruel suspicion which rests upon you?"

"I do not, Mabel," answered Jasper, looking into her full blue eyes, with an openness and simplicity that might have shaken strong distrust. "As I hope for mercy, hereafter, I do not."

"I knew it—I could have sworn it—" returned the girl, warmly. "And yet my father means well—but do not let this matter disturb you, Jasper."

"There is so much more to apprehend from another quarter, just now, that I scarce think of it."

"Jasper!"

"I do not wish to alarm you, Mabel, but if your uncle could be persuaded to change his notions about handling the Scud—and, yet, he is so much older, and more experienced than I am, that he ought, perhaps, to place more reliance on his own judgment than on mine."

"Do you think the cutter is in any danger?" demanded Mabel, as quick as thought.

"I fear so—at least she would have been thought in great danger, by us of the lake; perhaps an old seaman of the ocean may have means of his own, to take care of her."

"Jasper, all agree in giving you credit for skill in managing the Scud!—You know the lake, you know the cutter—you *must* be the best judge of our real situation!"

"My concern for you, Mabel, may make me more cowardly than common; but, to be frank, I see but one method of keeping the cutter from being wrecked in the course of the next two or three hours, and that your uncle refuses to take. After all, this may be my ignorance, for, as he says, Ontario is merely fresh water."

"You cannot believe this will make any difference. Think of my dear father, Jasper!—Think of yourself, of all the lives that depend on a timely word from you to save them!"

"I think of you, Mabel, and that is more, much more, than all the rest put together—" returned the young man, with a strength of expression and an earnestness of look, that uttered infinitely more than the words themselves.

Mabel's heart beat quick, and a gleam of grateful satisfaction shot across her blushing features, but the alarm was too vivid and too serious to admit of much relief from happier thoughts. She did not attempt to repress a look of gratitude, and then she returned to the feeling that was naturally uppermost.

"My uncle's obstinacy must not be permitted to occasion this disaster. Go once more on deck, Jasper, and ask my father to come into the cabin."

While the young man was complying with this request, Mabel sat listening to the howling of the storm, and the dashing of the water against the cutter, in a dread to which she had hitherto been a stranger. Constitutionally an excellent sailor, as the term is used among passengers, she had not, hitherto, bethought her of any danger, and had passed her time since the commencement of the gale, in such womanly employments, as her situation allowed; but now alarm was seriously awakened, she did not fail to perceive, that never before had she been on the water in such a tempest. The minute or two that elapsed ere the serjeant came appeared an hour, and she scarcely breathed before she saw him and Jasper descending the ladder in company. Quick as language could express her meaning, she acquainted her father with Jasper's opinion of their situation, and intreated him, if he loved her, or had any regard for his own life, or for those of his men, to interpose with her uncle, and to induce him

to yield the control of the cutter, again, to its proper commander.

"Jasper is true, father," she added earnestly, "and if false, he
could have no motive in wrecking us in this distant part of the
lake, at the risk of all our lives, his own included. I will pledge
my own life, for his truth."

"Ay, this is well enough, for a young woman who is frightened," answered the more phlegmatick parent; "but it might
not be so prudent, or excusable in one in command of an expedition. Jasper may think the chance of drowning in getting
ashore, fully repaid by the chance of escaping as soon as he
reaches the land."

"Serjeant Dunham!"

"Father!"

These exclamations were made simultaneously, but they
were uttered in tones expressive of different feelings. In Jasper
surprise was the emotion uppermost; in Mabel, reproach. The
old soldier, however, was too much accustomed to deal frankly
with subordinates, to heed either, and, after a moment's
thought, he continued, as if neither had spoken.

"Nor is Brother Cap a man likely to submit to be taught his
duty, on board a vessel."

"But, father, when all our lives are in the utmost jeopardy!"

"So much the worse. The fair weather commander is no great
matter; it is when things go wrong, that the best officer shows
himself in his true colours. Charley Cap will not be likely to quit
the helm because the ship is in danger. Besides, Jasper Eau
douce, he says your proposal, in itself, has a suspicious air about
it, and sounds more like treachery than reason."

"He may think so, but let him send for the pilot, and hear his
opinion. It is well known, I have not seen the man since yester-
day evening."

"This does sound reasonably, and the experiment shall be
tried. Follow me on deck, then, that all may be honest and
above board."

Jasper obeyed, and so keen was the interest of Mabel, that
she, too, ventured as far as the companion way, where her garments were sufficiently protected against the violence of the
wind and her person from the spray. Here maiden modesty

induced her to remain, though an absorbed witness of what was passing.

The pilot soon appeared, and there was no mistaking the look of concern that he cast around at the scene, as soon as he was in the open air. Some rumours of the situation of the Scud had found their way below, it is true, but, in this instance rumour had lessened, instead of magnifying the dangers. He was allowed a few minutes to look about him, and then the question was put as to the course that he thought it prudent to follow.

"I see no means of saving the cutter but to anchor," he answered simply, and without hesitation.

"What, out here, in the lake?" enquired Cap, as he had previously done of Jasper.

"No—but closer in; just at the outer line of the breakers."

The effect of this communication, was to leave no doubt in the mind of Cap, that there was a secret arrangement between her commander and the pilot, to cast away the Scud; most probably with the hope of effecting their escape. He consequently treated the opinion of the latter with the indifference he had manifested towards that of the former.

"I tell you, Brother Dunham," he said, in answer to the remonstrances of the serjeant against his turning a deaf ear to this double representation, "that no seaman would give such an opinion honestly. To anchor on a lee shore, in a gale of wind, would be an act of madness that I could never excuse to the underwriters, under any circumstances, as long as a rag can be set, but to anchor close to breakers would be insanity."

"His Majesty underwrites the Scud, Brother, and I am responsible for the lives of my command. These men are better acquainted with Lake Ontario than we can possibly be, and I do think their telling the same tale, entitles them to some credit."

"Uncle!" said Mabel, earnestly, but a gesture from Jasper induced the girl to restrain her feelings.

"We are drifting down upon the breakers so rapidly," said the young man, "that little need be said on the subject. Half an hour must settle the matter, one way or the other, but I warn Master Cap that the surest footed man among us, will not be able to keep his feet an instant on the deck of this low craft, should she fairly get within them. Indeed, I make little doubt that we shall fill and founder before the second line of rollers is passed!"

"And how would anchoring help the matter?" demanded Cap furiously, as if he felt that Jasper was responsible for the effects of the gale, as well as for the opinion he had just given.

"It would at least do no harm," Eau douce mildly replied. "By bringing the cutter head to sea we should lessen her drift, and even if we dragged through the breakers, it would be with the least possible danger. I hope, Master Cap, you will allow the pilot and myself to *prepare* for anchoring, since the precaution may do good, and can do no harm."

"Overhaul your ranges if you will, and get your anchors clear, with all my heart. We are now in a situation that cannot be much affected by any thing of that sort. Serjeant a word with you, aft here, if you please."

Cap led his brother-in-law out of ear-shot, and then, with more of human feeling in his voice and manner than he was apt to exhibit, he opened his heart on the subject of their real situation.

"This is a melancholy affair for poor Mabel," he said, blowing his nose, and speaking with a slight tremor–"You and I, Serjeant, are old fellows, and used to being near death, if not to actually dying. Our trades fit us for such scenes, but poor Mabel, she is an affectionate and kind-hearted girl, and I had hoped to see her comfortably settled and a mother, before my time came. Well, well; we must take the bad with the good, in every v'y'ge, and the only serious objection that an old sea-faring man can with propriety make to such an event, is that it should happen on this bit of d——d fresh water."

Serjeant Dunham was a brave man, and had shown his spirit in scenes that looked much more appalling than this. But, on all such occasions, he had been able to act his part against his foes, while here he was pressed upon by an enemy whom he had no means of resisting. For himself, he cared far less, than for his daughter; feeling some of that self-reliance which seldom deserts a man of firmness, who is in vigorous health, and who has been accustomed to personal exertions, in moments of jeopardy. But, as respects Mabel, he saw no means of escape, and with a father's fondness he at once determined that, if either was doomed to perish, he and his daughter must perish together.

"Do you think this must come to pass?" he asked of Cap firmly, but with strong feeling.

"Twenty minutes will carry us into the breakers, and, look for yourself, serjeant, what chance will even the stoutest man among us have in that cauldron to leeward!"

The prospect was, indeed, little calculated to encourage hope. By this time the Scud was within a mile of the shore, on which the gale was blowing at right angles, with a violence that forbade the idea of showing any additional canvass, with a view to claw off. The small portion of the mainsail that was actually set, and which merely served to keep the head of the Scud so near the wind as to prevent the waves from breaking over her, quivered under the gusts, as if, at each moment, the stout threads which held the complicated fabric together, were about to be torn asunder. The drizzle had ceased, but the air, for a hundred feet above the surface of the lake, was filled with dazzling spray, which had an appearance not unlike that of a brilliant mist, while above all, the sun was shining gloriously, in a cloudless sky. Jasper had noted the omen, and had foretold that it announced a speedy termination to the gale, though the next hour, or two, must decide their fate. Between the cutter and the shore, the view was still more wild and appalling. The breakers extended near half a mile; while the water within their line was white with foam, the air above them was so far filled with vapor and spray, as to render the land beyond hazy and indistinct. Still it could be seen that the latter was high, not a usual thing for the shores of Ontario, and that it was covered with the verdant mantle of the interminable forest.

While the serjeant and Cap were gazing at this scene, in silence, Jasper and his people were actively engaged on the forecastle. No sooner had the young man received permission to resume his old employment, than appealing to some of the soldiers for aid, he mustered five or six assistants, and set about in earnest, the performance of a duty that had been too long delayed. On these narrow waters, anchors are never stowed in board, or cables that are intended for service unbent, and

Jasper was saved much of the labor that would have been necessary in a vessel at sea. The two bowers were soon ready to be let
go, ranges of the cables were overhauled, and then the party
paused to look about them. No change for the better had occurred, but the cutter was falling slowly in, and each instant
rendered it more certain that she could not gain an inch to
windward.

One long earnest survey of the lake ended, Jasper gave new
orders in a manner to prove how much he thought that the
time pressed. Two kedges were got on deck, and hawsers were
bent to them. The inner ends of the hawsers were bent, in their
turns, to the crowns of the anchors, and every thing was got
ready to throw them overboard, at the proper moment. These
preparations completed, Jasper's manner changed from the
excitement of exertion, to a look of calm but settled concern.
He quitted the forecastle, where the seas were dashing inboard,
at every plunge of the vessel, the duty just mentioned having
been executed with the bodies of the crew frequently buried in
the water, and walked to a drier part of the deck, aft. Here he
was met by the Pathfinder, who was standing near Mabel and
the Quarter Master. Most of those on board, with the exception
of the individuals who have already been particularly mentioned, were below, some seeking relief from physical suffering
on their pallets, and others tardily bethinking them of their
sins. For the first time, most probably since her keel had dipped
into the limpid waters of Ontario, the voice of prayer was heard
on board the Scud.

"Jasper," commenced his friend, the guide, "I have been of
no use this morning, for my gifts are of little account, as you
know, in a vessel like this; but should it please God to let the
sarjeant's daughter reach the shore alive, my acquaintance with
the forest, may still carry her through in safety to the garrison."

"'Tis a fearful distance thither, Pathfinder!" Mabel rejoined,
the party being so near together that all which was said by one,
was overheard by the others. "I am afraid none of us could live
to reach the fort."

"It would be a risky path, Mabel, and a crooked one; though
some of your sex have undergone even more than that, in this
wilderness. But, Jasper, either you or I, or both of us must man

this bark canoe; Mabel's only chance will lie in getting through the breakers in that."

"I would willingly man any thing to save Mabel," answered Jasper, with a melancholy smile, "but no human hand, Pathfinder, could carry that canoe through yonder breakers, in a gale like this. I have hopes from anchoring, after all, for once before, have we saved the Scud in an extremity nearly as great as this."

"If we are to anchor, Jasper," the serjeant enquired, "why not do it at once? Every foot we lose in drifting now, would come into the distance we shall probably drag, when the anchors are let go."

Jasper drew nearer to the Serjeant, and took his hand, pressing it earnestly, and in a way, to denote strong, almost uncontrollable feelings.

"Serjeant Dunham," he said solemnly, "you are a good man, though you have treated me harshly in this business. You love your daughter."

"That you cannot doubt, Eau douce," returned the serjeant huskily.

"Will you give her—give us all, the only chance for life, that is left."

"What would you have me do, boy; what would you have me do? I have acted according to my judgment hitherto—what would you have me do?"

"Support me against Master Cap, for five minutes, and all that man can now do, towards saving the Scud, shall be done."

The serjeant hesitated, for he was too much of a disciplinarian to fly in the face of regular orders. He disliked the appearance of vacillation too, and then he had a profound respect for his kinsman's seamanship. While he was deliberating Cap came from the post he had some time occupied, which was at the side of the man at the helm, and drew near the group.

"Master Eau-deuce," he said, as soon as near enough to be heard, "I have come to enquire if you know any spot near-by, where this cutter can be beached? The moment has arrived when we are driven to this hard alternative."

That instant of indecision on the part of Cap, secured the triumph of Jasper. Looking at the Serjeant, the young man received a nod that assured him of all he asked, and he lost not one of those moments that were getting to be so very precious.

"Shall I take the helm," he inquired of Cap, "and see if we can reach a creek that lies to leeward?"

"Do so—do so—" said the other, hemming to clear his throat, for he felt oppressed by a responsibility that weighed all the heavier on his shoulders, on account of his ignorance. "Do so, Oh-the-deuce, since, to be frank with you, I can see nothing better to be done. We must beach, or swamp."

Jasper required no more; springing aft, he soon had the tiller in his own hands. The pilot was prepared for what was to follow, and, at a sign from his young commander, the rag of sail that had so long been set was taken in. At that moment, Jasper, watching his time, put the helm up, the head of a staysail was loosened forward, and the light cutter, as if conscious she was now under the control of familiar hands, fell off, and was soon in the trough of the sea. This perilous instant was passed in safety, and, at the next moment, the little vessel appeared flying down toward the breakers, at a rate that threatened instant destruction. The distance had got to be so short, that five or six minutes sufficed for all that Jasper wished, and he put the helm down again, when the bows of the Scud came up to the wind, notwithstanding the turbulence of the waters, as gracefully as the duck varies its line of direction on the glassy pond. A sign from Jasper set all in motion on the forecastle, and a kedge was thrown from each bow. The fearful nature of the drift was now apparent even to Mabel's eyes, for the two hawsers ran out like tow-lines. As soon as they straightened to a slight strain, both anchors were let go, and cable was given to each, nearly to the better ends. It was not a difficult task to snub so light a craft, with ground tackle of a quality better than common, and in less than ten minutes from the moment when Jasper went to the helm, the Scud was riding, head to sea, with the two cables stretched ahead in lines that resembled bars of iron.

"This is not well done, Master Jasper!" angrily exclaimed Cap, as soon as he perceived the trick that had been played him—"This is not well done, sir; I order you to cut, and to beach the cutter, without a moment's delay."

No one, however, seemed disposed to comply with this order,

for so long as Eau douce saw fit to command, his own people were disposed to obey. Finding that the men remained passive, Cap, who believed they were in the utmost peril, turned fiercely to Jasper, and renewed his remonstrances.

"You did not head for your pretended creek," he added, after dealing in some objurgatory remarks that we do not deem it necessary to record, "but steered for that bluff, where every soul on board would have been drowned, had we gone ashore!"

"And you wish to cut, and put every soul ashore, at that very spot!" Jasper retorted a little drily.

"Throw a lead line over board, and ascertain the drift—" Cap now roared to the people forward. A sign from Jasper sustaining this order, it was instantly obeyed. All on deck gathered around the spot, and watched, with nearly breathless interest, the result of the experiment. The lead was no sooner on the bottom, than the line tended forward, and in about two minutes it was seen that the cutter had drifted her length, dead in towards the bluff. Jasper looked grave, for he well knew nothing would hold the vessel did she get within the vortex of the breakers, the first line of which, was appearing and disappearing about a cable's length directly under their stern.

"Traitor!" exclaimed Cap, shaking a finger at the young commander, though passion choked the rest. "You must answer for this with your life," he added after a short pause, "If I were at the head of this expedition, Serjeant, I would hang him at the end of the main-boom, lest he escape drowning."

"Moderate your feelings, brother—be more moderate, I beseech you; Jasper appears to have done all for the best, and matters may not be as bad as you believe them."

"Why did he not run for the creek, he mentioned—why has he brought us here, dead to windward of that bluff, and to a spot where even the breakers are only of half the ordinary width, as if in a hurry to drown all on board!"

"I headed for the bluff, for the precise reason that the breakers are so narrow at this spot," answered Jasper mildly, though his gorge had risen at the language the other held.

"Do you mean to tell an old seaman like me, that this cutter could live in those breakers?"

"I do not, sir. I think she would fill and swamp, if driven into the first line of them—I am certain she would never reach the shore on her bottom, if fairly entered. I hope to keep her clear of them, altogether."

"With a drift of her length in a minute!"

"The backing of the anchors does not yet fairly tell, nor do I even hope that *they* will entirely bring her up."

"On what then do you rely? To moor a craft head and stern, by faith, hope and charity!"

"No, sir—I trust to the under-tow. I headed for the bluff, because I knew that it was stronger at that point than at any other, and because we could get nearer in with the land, without entering the breakers."

This was said with spirit, though without any particular show of resentment. Its effect on Cap was marked, the feeling that was uppermost being evidently that of surprise.

"Under-tow!" he repeated—"Who the devil ever heard of saving a vessel from going ashore by the under-tow!"

"This may never happen on the ocean, sir," Jasper answered modestly, "but we have known it to happen here."

"The lad is right, brother," put in the serjeant, "for though I do not well understand it, I have often heard the sailors of the lake speak of such a thing. We shall do well to trust to Jasper, in this strait."

Cap grumbled and swore, but as there was no remedy, he was compelled to acquiesce, Jasper being now called on to explain what he meant by the under-tow, gave this account of the matter. The water that was driven up on the shore by the gale, was necessarily compelled to find its level, by returning to the lake, by some secret channels. This could not be done on the surface, where both wind and waves were constantly urging it towards the land, and it necessarily formed a sort of lower eddy, by means of which it flowed back again, to its ancient and proper bed. This inferior current had received the name of the under-tow, and as it would necessarily act on the bottom of a vessel that drew as much water as the Scud, Jasper trusted to the aid of this reaction to keep his cables from parting. In short, the upper and lower currents, would, in a manner, counteract each other.

Simple and ingenious as was this theory, however, as yet there was little evidence of its being reduced to practice. The drift continued, though, as the kedges and hawsers, with which the anchors were backed, took the strains, it became sensibly less. At length the man at the lead announced the joyful intelligence, that the anchors had ceased to drag, and that the vessel had brought up! At this precise moment, the first line of breakers was about a hundred feet astern of the Scud, even appearing to approach much nearer, as the foam vanished and returned on the raging surges. Jasper sprang forward, and casting a glance over the bows, he smiled in triumph, as he pointed exultingly to the cables. Instead of resembling bars of iron in rigidity, as before, they were curving downwards, and to a seaman's senses, it was evident that the cutter rose and fell on the seas as they came in, with the ease of a ship in a tides-way, when the power of the wind is relieved by the counteracting pressure of the water.

"'Tis the undertow!" he exclaimed with delight, fairly bounding along the deck to steady the helm, in order that the cutter might ride still easier—"Providence has placed us directly in its current, and there is no longer any danger!"

"Ay—ay, Providence is a good seaman—" growled Cap, "and often helps lubbers out of difficulty. Under tow, or upper tow, the gale has abated, and fortunately for us all, the anchors have met with good holding ground. Then this d——d fresh water has an unnatural way with it."

Men are seldom inclined to quarrel with good fortune, but it is in distress that they grow clamorous and critical. Most on board were disposed to believe that they had been saved from shipwreck by the skill and knowledge of Jasper, without regarding the opinions of Cap, whose remarks were now little heeded.

There was half an hour of uncertainty and doubt, it is true, during which period the lead was anxiously watched, and then a feeling of security came over all, and the weary slept without dreaming of instant death.

Chapter XVIII

"It is to be all made of sighs and tears;—
It is to be all made of faith and service:—
It is to be all made of fantasy,
All made of passion, and all made of wishes:
All adoration, duty, and observance,
All humbleness, all patience, and impatience,
All purity, all trial, all observance."
         As You Like It, V.ii.84, 89, 94–98.

Iᴛ was near noon when the gale broke, and then its force abated as suddenly as its violence had arisen. In less than two hours after the wind fell, the surface of the lake, though still agitated, was no longer glittering with foam, and in double that time, the entire sheet presented the ordinary scene of disturbed water, that was unbroken by the violence of a tempest. Still the waves came rolling incessantly towards the shore, and the lines of breakers remained, though the spray had ceased to fly, the combing of the swells was more moderate, and all that there was of violence proceeded from the impulsion of wind that had abated.

As it was impossible to make head against the sea that was still up, with the light opposing air that blew from the eastward, all thoughts of getting under way that afternoon, were abandoned. Jasper, who had now quietly resumed the command of the Scud, busied himself, however, in heaving up to the anchors, which were lifted in succession. The kedges that backed them were weighed, and every thing was got in readiness for a prompt departure, as soon as the state of the weather would allow. In the mean time, they who had no concern with these duties, sought such means of amusement, as their peculiar circumstances allowed.

As is common with those who are unused to the confinement of a vessel, Mabel cast wistful eyes towards the shore, nor was it long before she expressed a wish that it were possible to land.

The Pathfinder was near her at the time, and he assured her that nothing would be easier, as they had a bark canoe on deck, which was the best possible mode of conveyance to go through a surf in. After the usual doubts and misgivings, the Serjeant was appealed to. His opinion proved to be favorable, and preparations to carry the whim into effect, were immediately made.

The party that was to land, consisted of Serjeant Dunham, his daughter and the Pathfinder. Accustomed to the canoe, Mabel took her seat in the centre with great steadiness, her father was placed in the bows, while the guide assumed the office of conductor, by steering in the stern. There was little need of impelling the canoe by means of the paddle, for the rollers sent it forward, at moments, with a violence that put every effort to govern its movements at defiance. More than once, ere the shore was reached, Mabel repented of her temerity, but Pathfinder encouraged her, and really manifested so much self-possession, coolness and strength of arm, himself, that even a female might have hesitated about owning all her apprehensions. Our heroine was no coward, and while she felt the novelty of her situation, she also experienced a fair proportion of its wild delight. At moments, indeed, her heart was in her mouth, as the bubble of a boat floated on the very crest of a foaming breaker, appearing to skim the water like a swallow, and then she flushed and laughed, as, left by the glancing element, they appeared to linger behind, ashamed at having been out-done in the headlong race. A few minutes sufficed for this excitement, for, though the distance between the cutter and the land considerably exceeded a quarter of a mile, the intermediate space was passed in a very few minutes.

On landing, the Serjeant kissed his daughter kindly, for he was so much of a soldier as always to feel more at home, on terra firma, then when afloat, and taking his gun, he announced his intention to pass an hour, in quest of game.

"Pathfinder will remain near you, girl, and no doubt he will tell you some of the traditions of this part of the world, or some of his own experiences with the Mingos."

The guide laughed, promised to have a care of Mabel, and in a few minutes the father had ascended a steep acclivity, and disappeared in the forest. The others took another direction which, after a few minutes of a sharp ascent also, brought them to a small naked point on the promontory, where the eye over-looked an extensive and very peculiar panorama. Here Mabel seated herself on a fragment of fallen rock, to recover her breath and strength, while her companion, on whose sinews no personal exertion seemed to make any impression, stood at her side, leaning in his own, and not ungraceful manner on his long rifle. Several minutes passed, and neither spoke; Mabel, in par-ticular, being lost in admiration of the view.

The position the two had obtained was sufficiently elevated, to command a wide reach of the lake, which stretched away towards the north east, in a boundless sheet, glittering beneath the rays of an afternoon's sun, and yet betraying the remains of that agitation which it had endured while tossed by the late tempest. The land set bounds to its limits, in a huge crescent, disappearing in distance towards the south-east and the north. Far as the eye could reach, nothing but forest was visible, not even a solitary sign of civilization breaking in upon the uniform and grand magnificence of nature. The gale had driven the Scud beyond the line of those posts, with which the French were then endeavoring to gird the English North American possessions, for following the channels of communications be-tween the great lakes, their posts were on the banks of the Niag-ara, while our adventurers had reached a point many leagues westward of that celebrated streight. The cutter rode at single anchor, without the breakers, resembling some well imagined and accurately executed toy, that was intended rather for a glass case, than for the struggles with the elements which she had so lately gone through, while the canoe lay on the narrow beach, just out of reach of the waves that came booming upon the land, a speck upon the shingle.

"We are very far, here, from human habitations!" exclaimed Mabel, when, after a long and musing survey of the scene, its principal peculiarities forced themselves on her active and even brilliant imagination; "this is indeed being on a frontier!"

"Have they more sightly scenes than this, nearer the sea, and around their large towns?" demanded Pathfinder, with an interest he was apt to discover in such a subject.

"I will not say that; there is more to remind one of his fellow beings, there than here; less, perhaps, to remind one of God."

"Ay, Mabel, that is what my own feelings say. I am but a poor hunter I know; untaught and unlarned; but God is as near me, in this my home, as he is near the king in his royal palace."

"Who can doubt it—" returned Mabel, looking from the view up into the hard-featured but honest face of her companion, though not without surprise at the energy of his manner—"One feels nearer to God, in such a spot, I think, than when the mind is distracted by the objects of the towns."

"You say all I wish to say myself, Mabel, but in so much plainer speech, that you make me ashamed of wishing to let others know what I feel on such matters. I have coasted this lake, in s'arch of skins, afore the war, and have been here already; not at this very spot, for we landed yonder where you may see the blasted oak that stands above the cluster of hemlocks—"

"How, Pathfinder, can you remember all these trifles so accurately!"

"These are our streets and houses; our churches and palaces. Remember them, indeed! I once made an appointment with the Big Sarpent, to meet at twelve o'clock at noon, near the foot of a certain pine, at the end of six months, when neither of us was within three hundred miles of the spot. The tree stood, and stands still unless the judgment of Providence has lighted on that too, in the midst of the forest, fifty miles from any settlement, but in a most extraordinary neighborhood for beaver."

"And did you meet at that very spot and hour!"

"Does the sun rise and set? When I reached the tree, I found the Sarpent leaning against its trunk, with torn leggings and muddied moccasins. The Delaware had got into a swamp, and it worried him not a little to find his way out of it, but as the sun which comes over the eastern hills in the morning goes down behind the western at night, so was he true to time and place. No fear of Chingachgook when there is either a friend or an enemy in the case. He is equally sartain with each."

"And where is the Delaware now—why is he not with us to-day?"

"He is scouting on the Mingo trail, where I ought to have been too, but for a great human infirmity."

"You seem above, beyond, superior to all infirmity, Path-finder–I never yet met with a man, who appeared to be so little liable to the weaknesses of nature."

"If you mean in the way of health and strength, Mabel, Providence has been kind to me; though I fancy, the open air, long hunts, or actyve scoutings, forest fare, and the sleep of a good conscience may always keep the doctors at a distance. But I'm human after all; yes, I find I'm very human in some of my feelin's!"

Mabel looked surprised, and it would be no more than delineating the character of her sex, if we added that her sweet countenance expressed a good deal of curiosity, too, though her tongue was more discreet.

"There is something bewitching in this wild life of yours, Pathfinder!" she exclaimed, the tinge of enthusiasm mantling her cheeks. "I find I'm fast getting to be a frontier girl, and am coming to love all this grand silence of the woods. The towns seem tame to me, and, as my father will probably pass the remainder of his days, here, where he has already lived so long, I begin to feel that I should be happy to continue with him, and not return to the sea-shore."

"The woods are never silent, Mabel, to such as understand their meaning. Days at a time, have I travelled them alone, without feeling the want of company, and, as for conversation, for such as can comprehend their language, there is no want of rational and instructive discourse."

"I believe you are happier when alone, Pathfinder, than when mingling with your fellow creatures."

"I will not say that–I will not say exactly that. I have seen the time, when I have thought that God was sufficient for me in the forest, and that I craved no more than his bounty and his care. But other feelin's have got uppermost, and I suppose natur' will have its way. All other creatur's mate, Mabel, and it was intended man should do so, too."

"And have you never bethought you of seeking a wife, Pathfinder, to share your fortunes," enquired the girl, with the directness and simplicity that the pure of heart and undesigning are the most apt to manifest and with that feeling of affection which is inbred in her sex. "To me, it seems, you only want a home to return to, from your wanderings, to render your life completely happy. Were I a man, it would be my delight to roam through these forests at will, or to sail over this beautiful lake!"

"I understand you, Mabel, and God bless you, for thinking of the welfare of men as humble as we are. We have our pleasures, it is true, as well as our gifts, but we might be happier; yes, I do think, we might be happier!"

"Happier!—In what way, Pathfinder?—In this pure air, with these cool and shaded forests to wander through, this lovely lake to gaze at, and sail upon, with clear consciences and abundance for all the real wants, men ought to be nothing less than as perfectly happy, as their infirmities will allow."

"Every creatur' has its gifts, Mabel, and men have theirn," answered the guide looking stealthily at his beautiful companion, whose cheeks had flushed and eyes brightened under the ardor of feelings excited by the novelty of a striking situation, "and all must obey them. Do you see yonder pigeon, that is just alightin' on the beech, here in a line with the fallen chestnut?"

"Certainly; it is the only thing stirring with life in it, besides ourselves, that is to be seen in this vast solitude."

"Not so, Mabel, not so: Providence makes nothing that lives, to live quite alone. Here is its mate, just rising on the wing; it has been feedin' near the other beech, but it will not long be separated from its companion."

"I understand you, Pathfinder," returned Mabel smiling sweetly, though as calmly as if the discourse was with her father—"But a hunter may find a mate, even in this wild region. The Indian girls are affectionate and true, I know, for such was the wife of Arrowhead to a husband who oftener frowned than smiled."

"That would never do, Mabel, and good would never come of it. Kind must cling to kind, and country to country, if one would find happiness. If, indeed, I could meet with one like you, who would consent to be a hunter's wife, and who would not scorn my ignorance and rudeness, then, indeed, would all the toil of the past appear like the sporting of the young deer, and all the future like sunshine!"

"One like me!—A girl of my years and indiscretion would

hardly make a fit companion for the boldest scout and surest hunter on the lines!"

"Ah! Mabel, I fear me, that I have been improving a red skin's gifts, with a Pale face's natur'! Such a character would insure a wife, in an Injin village."

"Surely, surely, Pathfinder, you would not think of choosing one as ignorant, as frivolous, as vain, and as inexperienced as I, for your wife!" Mabel would have added, "and as young," but an instinctive feeling of delicacy repressed the words.

"And why not, Mabel? If you are ignorant of frontier usages, you know more than all of us, of pleasant anecdotes and town customs; as for frivolous, I know not what it means, but if it signifies beauty, Ah's! me; I fear it is no fault in my eyes. Vain you are not, as is seen by the kind manner in which you listen to all my idle tales about scoutings and trails, and, as for experience, that will come with years. Besides, Mabel, I fear men think little of these matters, when they are about to take wives, I do."

"Pathfinder—your words—your looks—surely all this is meant in trifling—you speak in pleasantry!"

"To me it is always agreeable to be near you, Mabel, and I should sleep sounder this blessed night, than I have done for a week past, could I think that you find such discourse as pleasant as I do."

We shall not say that Mabel Dunham had not believed herself a favorite with the guide. This her quick, feminine, sagacity had early discovered, and perhaps she had occasionally thought there had mingled with his regard and friendship, some of that manly tenderness which the ruder sex must be coarse indeed not to show, on occasions, to the gentler; but, the idea that he seriously sought her for his wife had never before crossed the mind of the spirited and ingenuous girl. Now, however, a gleam of something like the truth broke in upon her imagination, less induced by the words of her companion, perhaps, than by his manner. Looking earnestly into the rugged, honest countenance of the scout, Mabel's own features became concerned and grave, and when she spoke again, it was with a gentleness of manner that attracted him to her, even more powerfully than the words themselves were calculated to repel.

"You and I should understand each other, Pathfinder," she said, with an earnest sincerity, "nor should there be any cloud between us. You are too upright and frank to meet with any thing but sincerity and frankness in return. Surely—surely, all this means nothing—has no other connection with your feelings, than such a friendship as one of your wisdom and character would naturally feel for a girl like me?"

"I believe it's all nat'ral, Mabel; yes, I do; the Sarjeant tells me he had such feelings towards your own mother, and I think I've seen something like it, in the young people I have, from time to time, guided through the wilderness. Yes, yes—I dare say it's all nat'ral enough, and that makes it come so easy, and is a great comfort to me."

"Pathfinder, your words make me uneasy! Speak plainer, or change the subject forever. You do not—cannot mean that—you—cannot wish me to understand—" even the tongue of the spirited Mabel faultered, and she shrunk with maiden shame, from adding what she wished so earnestly to say. Rallying her courage, however, and determined to know all as soon and as plainly as possible, after a moment's hesitation she continued—"I mean, Pathfinder, that you do not wish me to understand that you seriously think of me as a wife?"

"I do, Mabel; that's it—that's just it, and you have put the matter in a much better point of view than I, with my forest gifts and frontier ways, would ever be able to do. The Sarjeant and I have concluded on the matter, if it is agreeable to you, as he thinks is likely will be the case, though I doubt my own power to please one who deserves the best husband America can produce."

Mabel's countenance changed from uneasiness to surprise, and, then by a transition still quicker, from surprise to pain.

"My father!" she exclaimed. "My dear father has thought of my becoming your wife, Pathfinder!"

"Yes, he has, Mabel; he has indeed. He has even thought such a thing might be agreeable to you, and has almost encouraged me to fancy it might be true."

"But, you, yourself—you, certainly can care nothing, whether this singular expectation shall ever be realized or not?"

"Anan?"

"I mean, Pathfinder, that you have talked of this match more to oblige my father than any thing else; that your feelings are no way concerned, let my answer be what it may?"

The scout looked earnestly into the beautiful face of Mabel, which had flushed with the ardor and novelty of her sensations, and it was impossible to mistake the intense admiration that betrayed itself in every lineament of his ingenuous countenance.

"I have often thought myself happy, Mabel, when ranging the woods, on a successful hunt, breathing the pure air of the hills, and filled with vigor and health, but, I now feel that it has all been idleness and vanity compared with the delight it would give me to know that you thought better of me than you think of most others."

Better of you!—I do indeed think better of you, Pathfinder, than of most others—I am not certain that I do not think better of you, than of any other; for your truth, honesty, simplicity, justice and courage are scarcely equalled by any of earth."

"Ah! Mabel!—These are sweet and encouraging words from you, and the serjeant, a'ter all, was not as near wrong as I feared."

"Nay, Pathfinder—in the name of all that is sacred and just, do not let us misunderstand each other, in a matter of so much importance. While I esteem, respect—nay reverence you, almost as much as I reverence my own dear father, it is impossible that I should ever become your wife—that I——"

The change is her companion's countenance was so sudden and so great that the moment the effect of what she had uttered became visible in the face of the Pathfinder, Mabel arrested her own words, notwithstanding her strong desire to be explicit, the reluctance with which she could at any time cause pain being sufficient of itself to induce the pause. Neither spoke for some time, the shade of disappointment that crossed the rugged lineaments of the hunter, amounting so nearly to anguish as to frighten his companion, while the sensation of choking became so strong in the Pathfinder, that he fairly griped his throat, like one who sought physical relief for physical suffering. The convulsive manner in which his fingers worked actually struck the alarmed girl with a feeling of awe.

"Nay, Pathfinder," Mabel eagerly added, the instant she

could command her voice—"I may have said more than I mean, for all things of this nature are possible, and women they say are never sure of their own minds. What I wish you to understand is, that it is not likely that you and I should ever think of each other, as man and wife ought to think of each other."

"I do not—I shall never think in that way, again, Mabel—" gasped forth the Pathfinder, who appeared to utter his words, like one just raised above the pressure of some suffocating substance. "No—no—I shall never think of you, or any one else, again, in that way."

"Pathfinder—dear Pathfinder—understand me—do not attach more meaning to my words, than I do myself. A match like that would be unwise—unnatural, perhaps—"

"Yes, unnat'ral—ag'in natur', and so I told the sarjeant, but he *would* have it otherwise."

"Pathfinder!—Oh! this is worse than I could have imagined—take my hand, excellent Pathfinder, and let me see that you do not hate me. For God's sake smile upon me again!"

"Hate you, Mabel!—Smile upon you! Ah's! me."

"Nay, give you your hand; you hardy, true and manly hand—both, both, Pathfinder, for I shall not be easy until I feel certain that we are friends again, and that all this has been a mistake."

"Mabel," said the guide, looking wistfully into the face of the generous and impetuous girl, as she held his two hard and sunburnt hands in her own pretty and delicate fingers, and laughing in his own silent and peculiar manner, while anguish gleamed over lineaments which seemed incapable of deception, even while agitated with emotions so conflicting, "Mabel, the sarjeant was wrong!"

The pent-up feelings would endure no more, and the tears rolled down the cheeks of the scout, like rain. His fingers again worked convulsively at his throat, and his breast heaved, as if it possessed a tenant of which it would be rid, by any effort, however desperate.

"Pathfinder!—Pathfinder!" Mabel almost shrieked—"any thing but this—any thing but this—Speak to me, Pathfinder—smile, again—say one kind word—any thing to prove you can forgive me."

"The sarjeant was wrong—" exclaimed the guide, laughing,

amid his agony, in a way to terrify his companion by the unnatural mixture of anguish and light-heartedness. "I knowed it—I knowed it, and said it; yes, the sarjeant was wrong, a'ter all."

"We can be friends, though we cannot be man and wife," continued Mabel, almost as much disturbed as her companion, scarce knowing what she said; "we can always be friends, and always will."

"I thought the sarjeant was mistaken," resumed the Pathfinder, when a great effort had enabled him to command himself, "for I did not think my gifts were such as would please the fancy of a town bred gal. It would have been better, Mabel, had he not overpersuaded me into a different notion, and it might have been better, too, had you not been so pleasant and friendly, like; yes, it would."

"If I thought any error of mine had raised false expectations in you, Pathfinder, however unintentionally on my part, I should never forgive myself; for, believe me, I would rather endure pain in my own feelings than you should suffer."

"That's just it, Mabel; that's just it. These speeches and opinions, spoken in so soft a voice, and in a way I'm so unused to in the woods, have done the mischief. But I now see plainly, and begin to understand the difference between us better, and will strive to keep down thought, and to go abroad ag'in, as I used to do, looking for the game and the inimy. Ah's! me; Mabel, I have indeed, been on a false trail, since we met!"

"But you will now travel on the true one. In a little while you will forget all this, and think of me as a friend, who owes you her life."

"This may be the way in the towns, but I doubt if it's nat'ral to the woods. With us, when the eye sees a lovely sight, it is apt to keep it long in view, or when the mind takes in an upright and proper feeling, it is loath to part with it."

"But it is not a proper feeling that you should love me, nor am I a lovely sight. You will forget it all, when you come seriously to recollect that I am altogether unsuited to be your wife."

"So I told the sarjeant, but he would have it otherwise. I knowed you were too young and beautiful, for one of middle age like myself, and who never was comely to look at, even in youth; and then your ways have not been my ways, nor would a hunter's cabin be a fitting place for one who was edicated among chiefs, as it were. If I were younger and comelier, though, like Jasper Eau douce—"

"Never mind Jasper Eau douce—" interrupted Mabel, impatiently—". e can talk of something else."

"Jasper is a worthy lad, Mabel; ay, and a comely," returned the guileless guide, looking earnestly at the girl, as if he distrusted her judgment in speaking slightingly of his friend—"Were I only half as comely as Jasper Western, my misgivings in this affair, would not have been so great, and they might not have been so true."

"We will not talk of Jasper Western," repeated Mabel, the colour mounting to her temples—" he may be good enough in a gale, or on the lake, but he is not good enough to talk of, here."

"I fear me, Mabel, he is better than the man who is likely to be your husband, though the sarjeant says that never can take place. But the sarjeant was wrong once, and he may be wrong twice."

"And who is likely to be my husband, Pathfinder?—This is scarcely less strange, than what has just passed between us!"

"I know it is nat'ral for like to seek like, and for them that have consorted much with officers' ladies, to wish to be officers' ladies themselves. But, Mabel, I may speak plainly to you, I know, and I hope my words will not give you pain, for, now, I understand what it is to be disappointed in such feelings, I would'n't wish to cause even a Mingo sorrow, on this head. But, happiness is not always to be found in a marquee, any more than in a tent, and though the officers' quarters may look more tempting than the rest of the barracks, there is often great misery, between husband and wife, inside of their doors."

"I do not doubt it, in the least, Pathfinder, and did it rest with me to decide, I would sooner follow you to some cabin in the woods, and share your fortune, whether it might be better or worse, than go inside the door of any officer I know, with an intention of remaining there as its master's wife."

"Mabel, this is not what Lundie hopes, or Lundie thinks!"

"And what care I for Lundie?—He is Major of the 55th and may command his men to wheel and march about, as he pleases, but he cannot compel me to wed the greatest or the meanest of his mess. Besides, what can you know of Lundie's wishes on such a subject?"

"From Lundie's own mouth. The sarjeant had told him that he wished me for a son-in-law, and the Major being an old and a true friend conversed with me on the subject: He put it to me, plainly, whether it would not be more ginerous in me to let an officer succeed, than to strive to make you share a hunter's fortune. I owned the truth, I did; and that was, that I thought it might; but when he told me that the Quarter Master would be his choice, I would not abide by the conditions. No—no—Mabel; I know Davy Muir well, and though he may make you a lady, he can never make you a happy woman, or himself a gentleman. I say this honestly, I do; for I now plainly see, that the sarjeant has been wrong."

"My father has been very wrong, if he has said or done aught to cause you sorrow, Pathfinder; and so great is my respect for you, so sincere my friendship, that were it not for one—I mean that no person need fear Lt. Muir's influence with me. I would rather remain as I am, to my dying day, than become a lady at the cost of being his wife."

"I do not think you would say that which you do not feel, Mabel," returned Pathfinder, earnestly.

"Not at such a moment, on such a subject, and least of all to you. No; Lt. Muir may find wives where he can, my name shall never be on his catalogue."

"Thank you—thank you, for that, Mabel; for though there is no longer any hope for me, I could never be happy were you to take to the Quarter Master. I feared the commission might count for something, I did, and I know the man. It is not jealousy that makes me speak in this manner, but truth, for I know the man. Now, were you to fancy a desarving youth, one like Jasper Western for instance—"

"Why always mention Jasper Eau douce, Pathfinder; he can have no concern with our friendship. Let us talk of yourself, and of the manner in which you intend to pass the winter."

"Ah's! me. I'm little worth at the best, Mabel, unless it may be on a trail, or with the rifle, and less worth now that I've discovered the sarjeant's mistake. There is no need, therefore, of talking of me. It has been very pleasant to me, to be near you so long, and even to fancy that the sarjeant was right; but that is all over now. I shall go down the lake with Jasper, and then there will be business to occupy us, and that will keep useless thoughts out of the mind."

"And you will forget this—forget me—no, not forget me either, Pathfinder; but you will resume your old pursuits, and cease to think a girl of sufficient importance to disturb your peace?"

"I never know'd it afore, Mabel, but girls—as you call them, though gals is the name I've been taught to use—are of more account in this life, than I could have believed. Now, afore I knowd you, the new-born babe did not sleep more sweetly than I used to could; my head was no sooner on the root, or the stone, or mayhap on the skin, than all was lost to the senses unless it might be to go over in the night, the business of the day, in a dream, like; and there I lay till the moment came to be stirring, and the swallows were not more certain to be on the wing, with the light, than I to be afoot, at the moment I wished to be. All this seemed a gift, and might be calculated on, even in the midst of a Mingo camp; for I've been outlying, in my time, in the very villages of the vagabonds."

"And all this will return to you, Pathfinder, for one so upright and sincere will never waste his happiness on a mere fancy. You will dream again, of your hunts, of the deer you have slain, and of the beaver you have taken."

"Ah's! me, Mabel; I wish never to dream again! Before we met, I had a sort of pleasure, in following up the hounds, in fancy as it might be; and even in striking a trail of the Iroquois—nay, I've been in skrimmages, and ambushments, in thought like, and found satisfaction in it, according to my gifts; but all those things have lost their charms since I've made acquaintance with you. Now, I think no longer of any thing rude in my dreams, but the very last night we staid in the garrison, I imagined I had a cabin in a grove of sugar maples, and at the root of every tree was a Mabel Dunham, while the birds that were among the branches, sung ballads, instead of the notes that natur' gave, and even the deer stopped to listen. I tried to shoot a fa'an, but Killdeer missed fire, and the creatur' laughed in my face, as pleasantly as a young girl laughs in her merriment, and then it bounded away, looking back, as if expecting me to follow."

"No more of this, Pathfinder—we'll talk no more of these things—" said Mabel, dashing the tears from her eyes, for the simple, earnest manner in which this hardy woodsman betrayed the deep hold she had taken of his feelings, nearly proved too much for her own generous heart. "Now, let us look for my father; he cannot be distant, as I heard his gun, quite near."

"The sarjeant was wrong—yes, he was wrong, and it's of no use to attempt to make the doe consort with the wolf!"

"Here comes my dear father," interrupted Mabel; "let us look cheerful and happy, Pathfinder, as such good friends ought to look, and keep each other's secrets."

A pause succeeded; the serjeant's foot was heard crushing the dried twigs hard by, and then his form appeared shoving aside the bushes of a copse, quite near. As he issued into the open ground, the old soldier scrutinised his daughter and her companion, and speaking good-naturedly, he said—

"Mabel, child; you are young and light of foot—look for a bird I've shot, that fell just beyond the thicket of young hemlocks, on the shore; and, as Jasper is showing signs of an intention of getting under way, you need not take the trouble to clamber up this hill again, but we will meet you, on the beach, in a few minutes."

Mabel obeyed, bounding down the hill with the elastic step of youth and health. But, notwithstanding the lightness of her steps, the heart of the girl was heavy, and no sooner was she hid from observation, by the thicket, than she threw herself on the root of a tree, and wept as if her heart would break. The serjeant watched her until she disappeared, with a father's pride, and then turned to his companion, with a smile as kind and as familiar as his habits would allow him to use towards any.

"She has her mother's lightness and activity, my friend, with somewhat of her father's force," he said. "Her mother was not quite as handsome, I think myself; but the Dunhams were always thought comely, whether men or women. Well, Pathfinder, I take it for granted you've not overlooked the opportunity, but have spoken plainly to the girl? Women like frankness, in matters of this sort."

"I believe Mabel and I understand each other, at last, sarjeant," returned the other, looking another way to avoid the soldier's face.

"So much the better. Some people fancy that a little doubt and uncertainty make love all the livelier, but I am one of those who think the plainer the tongue speaks, the easier the mind will comprehend. Was Mabel surprised?"

"I fear she was, sarjeant; I fear she was taken quite by surprise—yes, I do."

"Well, well, surprises in love, are like an ambush in war, and quite as lawful; though it is not as easy to tell when a woman is surprised, as to tell when it happens to an enemy. Mabel did not run away, my worthy friend, did she?"

"No, sarjeant, Mabel did not try to escape; *that* I can say with a clear conscience."

"I hope the girl was not too willing, neither! Her mother was shy and coy for a month, at least, but frankness, after all, is a recommendation, in man or woman."

"That it is—that it is—and judgment, too."

"You are not to look for too much judgment in a young creature of twenty, Pathfinder, but let it come with experience. A mistake in you, or in me, for instance, might not be so easily overlooked, but in a girl of Mabel's years, one is not to strain at a gnat, lest they swallow a camel."

The muscles of the listener's face twitched, as the serjeant was thus delivering his sentiments, though the former had now recovered a portion of that stoicism which formed so large a part of his character, and which he had probably imbibed from long association with the Indians. His eyes rose and fell, and once a gleam shot athwart his hard features, as if he were about to indulge in his peculiar laugh, but the joyous feeling, if it really existed, was as quickly lost in a look allied to anguish. It was this unusual mixture of wild and keen mental agony, with native, simple, joyousness, that had most struck Mabel, who, in the interview just related, had a dozen times been on the point of believing that her suitor's heart was only lightly touched, as images of happiness and humour gleamed over a mind that was almost infantine in its simplicity and nature, an impression, however, that was soon driven away, by the discovery of emotions so painful and so deep, that they seemed to harrow the very soul. Indeed, in this respect, the Pathfinder was a mere child. Unpractised in the ways of the world, he had no idea of concealing a thought of any kind, and his mind received and reflected each emotion, with the pliability and readiness of that period of life. The infant scarcely yielded its wayward imagination to the passing impression, with greater facility, than this man, so simple in all his personal feelings, so stern, stoical, masculine and severe in all that touched his ordinary pursuits.

"You say true, sarjeant," Pathfinder answered—"a mistake in one like you is indeed a more serious matter."

"You will find Mabel sincere and honest in the end, give her but a little time."

"Ah's! me, Sarjeant!"

"A man of your merits, would make an impression on a rock, give him time, Pathfinder."

"Sarjeant Dunham, we are old fellow campaigners—that is, as campaigns are carried on here in the wilderness; and we have done so many kind acts to each other, that we can afford to be candid—what has caused you to believe that a girl like Mabel could ever fancy one as rude as I am?"

"What?—Why a variety of reasons, and good reasons, too, my friend. Those same acts of kindness, perhaps, and the campaigns you mention; moreover, you are my sworn and tried comrade."

"All this sounds well, so far as you and I be consarned, but they do not touch the case of your pretty da'ghter. She may think these very campaigns have destroyed the little comeliness I may once have had, and I am not quite sartain that being an old friend of her father would lead any young maiden's mind into a particular affection for a suitor. Like loves like, I tell you, sarjeant, and my gifts are not altogether the gifts of Mabel Dunham."

"These are some of your old modest qualms, Pathfinder, and will do you no credit with the girl. Women distrust men who distrust themselves, and take to men who distrust nothing. Modesty is a capital thing in a recruit, I grant you; or in a young subaltern who has just joined, for it prevents his railing at the non-commissioned officers, before he knows what to rail at; I'm not sure it is out of place in a commissary, or a parson, but it's the devil and all when it gets possession of either a real soldier, or a lover. Have as little to do with it as possible, if you would win a woman's heart. As for your doctrine that like loves like, it is as wrong as possible, in matters of this sort. If like loved like, women would love one another, and men also. No–no–like loves dislike,–" the serjeant was merely a scholar of the camp, "and you have nothing to fear from Mabel on that score. Look at Lt. Muir; the man has had five wives, already, they tell me, and there is no more modesty in him, than there is in a cat-o'-nine-tails."

"Lt. Muir will never be the husband of Mabel Dunham, let him ruffle his feathers as much as he may."

"That is a sensible remark of yours, Pathfinder, for my mind is made up that you shall be my son-in-law. If I were an officer myself, Mr. Muir might have some chance; but time has placed one door between my child and myself, and I do'n't intend there shall be that of a marquee, also."

"Sarjeant, we must let Mabel follow her own fancy; she is young and light of heart, and God forbid! that any wish of mine should lay the weight of a feather on a mind that is all gaiety, now, or take one note of happiness from her laughter."

"Have you conversed freely with the girl?" the serjeant demanded quickly, and with some asperity of manner.

Pathfinder was too honest to deny a truth plain as that which the answer required, and yet too honorable to betray Mabel, and expose her to the resentment of one, whom he well knew to be stern in his anger.

"We have laid open our minds," he said, "and though Mabel's is one that any man might love to look at, I find little there, sarjeant, to make me think any better of myself."

"The girl has not dared to refuse you–to refuse her father's best friend?"

Pathfinder turned his face away to conceal the look of anguish, that consciousness told him was passing athwart it, but he continued the discourse in his own quiet manly tones.

"Mabel is too kind to refuse any thing, or to utter harsh words to a dog. I have not put the question in a way to be downright refused, sarjeant."

"And did you expect my daughter to jump into your arms, before you asked her? She would not have been her mother's child had she done any such thing, nor do I think she would have been mine. The Dunhams like plain dealing, as well as the King's Majesty, but they are no jumpers. Leave me to manage this matter for you, Pathfinder, and there shall be no unnecessary delay. I'll speak to Mabel myself, this very evening, using your name as principal in the affair."

"I'd rather not–I'd rather not, sarjeant. Leave the matter to Mabel and me, and I think all will come right in the ind. Young gals be like timorsome birds; they do not over relish being hurried or spoken harshly to, nither. Leave the matter to Mabel and me."

"On one condition, I will, my friend; and that is, that you promise me, on the honor of a scout, that you will put the matter plainly to Mabel, the first suitable opportunity, and no mincing of words."

"I will ask her, sarjeant–yes I will ask her, on condition that you promise not to meddle in the affair–yes, I will promise to ask Mabel the question whether she will marry me, even though she laugh in my face, at my doing so, on that condition."

Serjeant Dunham gave the desired promise, very cheerfully, for he had completely wrought himself up into the belief that the man he so much esteemed and respected himself, must be acceptable to his daughter. He had married a woman much younger than himself, and he saw no unfitness in the respective years of the intended couple. Mabel was educated so much above him, too, that he was not aware of the difference which actually existed between the parent and child, in this respect, for it is one of the most unpleasant features in the intercourse between knowledge and ignorance, taste and unsophistication, refinement and vulgarity, that the higher qualities are often necessarily subjected to the judgments of those who have absolutely no perceptions of their existence. It followed that Serjeant Dunham was not altogether qualified to appreciate his daughter's tastes, or to form a very probable conjecture of the direction taken by those feelings which oftener depend on impulses and passion, than on reason. Still, the worthy soldier was not so wrong in his estimate of the Pathfinder's chances, as might at first, appear. Knowing, as he well did, all the sterling qualities of the man, his truth, integrity of purpose, courage, self devotion, disinterestedness, it was far from unreasonable to suppose that qualities like these, would produce a deep impression on any female heart, where there was an opportunity to acquire a knowledge of their existence, and the father erred principally in fancying that the daughter might know, as it might be, by intuition, what he himself had acquired by years of intercourse and adventure.

As Pathfinder and his military friend descended the hill to the shore of the lake, the discourse did not flag. The latter continued to endeavor to persuade the former, that his diffidence, alone, prevented complete success with Mabel, and that he had only to persevere, in order to prevail. Pathfinder was much too modest by nature, and had been too plainly, though so delicately, discouraged, in the recent interview, to believe all he heard; still, the father used so many arguments that seemed plausible, and it was so grateful to fancy that the daughter might yet be his, the reader is not to be surprised, when he is told that this unsophisticated being did not view Mabel's recent conduct in precisely the light in which he may be inclined to view it, himself. He did not credit all that the Serjeant told him, it is true, but he began to think virgin coyness, and ignorance of her own feelings might have induced Mabel to use the language she had.

"The Quarter Master is no favorite," said Pathfinder, in answer to one of his companion's remarks. "Mabel will never look on him as more than one who has had four or five wives already."

"Which is more than his share. A man may marry twice, without offence to good morals and decency, I allow, but four times is an aggravation."

"I should think even marrying once, what Master Cap calls a circumstance!" put in Pathfinder, laughing, in his quiet way, for, by this time, his spirits had recovered some of their buoyancy.

"It is, indeed, my friend, and a most solemn circumstance, too. If it were not that Mabel is to be your wife, I would advise you to remain single. But here is the girl, herself, and discretion is the word."

"Ah's! me, sarjeant, I fear you are mistaken!"

Chapter XIX

"Thus was this place,
A happy rural seat of various view:"
Paradise Lost, IV.246–47.

MABEL was in waiting on the beach, and the canoe was soon launched. Pathfinder carried the party out through the surf, in the same skilful manner he had brought it in, and, though Mabel's colour heightened with excitement, and her heart seemed often ready to leap out of her mouth again, they reached the side of the Scud, without having received even a drop of spray.

Ontario is like a quick-tempered man, sudden to be angered, and as soon appeased. The sea had already fallen, and though the breakers bounded the shore, far as the eye could reach, it was merely in lines of brightness, that appeared and vanished, like the returning waves produced by the stone that has been dropped into a pool. The cable of the Scud was scarce seen above the water, and Jasper had already hoisted his sails, in readiness to depart, as soon as the expected breeze from the shore should fill the canvass.

It was just sunset, as the cutter's mainsail flapped, and its stem began to sever the water. The air was light and southerly, and the head of the vessel was kept looking up along the south shore, it being the intention to get to the eastward, again, as fast as possible. The night that succeeded was quiet, and the rest of those who slept, deep and tranquil.

Some difficulty occurred concerning the command of the vessel, but the matter had been finally settled by an amicable compromise. As the distrust of Jasper was far from being appeased, Cap retained a supervisory power, while the young man was allowed to work the craft, subject, at all times, to the control and interference of the old seaman. To this Jasper consented, in preference to exposing Mabel any longer to the dangers of their present situation, for, now that the violence of the elements had ceased, he well knew, that the Montcalm would be in search of them. He had the discretion, however, not to reveal his apprehensions on this head, for it happened that the very means he deemed the best to escape the enemy where those which would be most likely to awaken new suspicions of his honesty, in the minds of those who held the power to defeat his intentions. In other words, Jasper believed that the gallant young Frenchman who commanded the ship of the enemy, would quit his anchorage under the fort at Niagara, and stand up the lake, as soon as wind abated, in order to ascertain the fate of the Scud, keeping mid-way between the two shores, as the best means of commanding a broad view, and that, on his part, it would be expedient to hug one coast or the other, not only to avoid a meeting, but as affording a chance of passing without detection, by blending his sails and spars with objects on the land. He preferred the south, because it was the weather shore, and because he thought it was that which the enemy would the least expect him to take, though it necessarily led near his settlements, and in front of one of the strongest posts he held in that part of the world.

Of all this, however, Cap was happily ignorant, and the serjeant's mind was too much occupied with the details of his military trust, to enter into these niceties, which so properly belonged to another profession. No opposition was made, therefore, and, ere morning, Jasper had apparently dropped quietly into all his former authority, issuing his orders freely, and meeting with obedience without hesitation, or cavil.

The appearance of day brought all on board, on deck again, and, as is usual with adventurers on the water, the opening horizon was curiously examined, as objects started out of the obscurity, and the panorama brightened under the growing light. East, west and north, nothing was visible, but water, glittering in the rising sun, but southward stretched the endless belt of woods, that then held Ontario in a setting of forest verdure. Suddenly an opening appeared ahead, and then the massive walls of a château-looking house, with outworks, bastions, block-houses and palisadoes, frowned on a head-land, that bordered the outlet of a broad stream. Just as the post became visible, a little cloud rose over it, and the white ensign of France was seen fluttering from a lofty flag-staff.

Cap gave an ejaculation as he witnessed this ungrateful exhibition, and he cast a quick suspicious glance at his brother-in-law.

"The dirty table-cloth hung up to air, as my name is Charles Cap!" he muttered, "and we hugging this d——d shore, as if it were our wife and children, met on the return from an India v'y'ge! Harkee, Jasper, are you in search of a cargo of frogs, that you keep so near in to this New France?"

"I hug the land, sir, in hope of passing the enemy's ship without being seen, for I think she must be somewhere down here to leeward."

"Ay, ay; this sounds well, and I hope it may turn out as you say. I trust there is no under-tow, here."

"We are on a weather shore, now," said Jasper smiling; "and, I think you will admit, Master Cap, that a strong under-tow makes an easy cable. We owe all our lives to the under-tow of this very lake."

"French flummery!" growled Cap, though he did not care to be heard by Jasper. "Give me a fair, honest, English-Yankee-American tow, above board and above water, too, if I must have a tow, at all, and none of your sneaking drift that is below the surface, where one can neither see nor feel. I dare say, if the truth could be come at, that this late escape of ours was all a contrived affair."

"We have now a good opportunity, at least, to reconnoitre the enemy's post at Niagara, Brother, for such I take this fort to be," put in the Serjeant. "Let us be all eyes in passing, and remember that we are almost in face of the enemy."

This advice of the serjeant's needed nothing to enforce it, for the interest and novelty of passing a spot occupied by human beings were of themselves sufficient to attract deep attention in that scene of a vast but deserted nature. The wind was now fresh enough to urge the Scud through the water with considerable velocity, and Jasper eased her helm as she opened the river, and luffed nearly into the mouth of that noble strait, or river as it is termed. A dull, distant, heavy roar came down through the opening in the banks, swelling on the currents of the air like the deeper notes of some immense organ, and occasionally seeming to cause the earth itself to tremble.

"That sounds like surf on some long unbroken coast!"

exclaimed Cap, as a swell deeper than common came to his ears.

"Ay, that is such surf as we have in this quarter of the world," Pathfinder answered. "There is no under-tow there, Master Cap, but all the water that strikes the rocks stays there, so far as going back, ag'in, is consarned. That is old Niagara that you hear, or this noble stream tumbling down a mountain!"

"No one will have the impudence to pretend that this fine broad river falls over yonder hills."

"It does, Master Cap; it does; and all for the want of stairs, or a road to come down by. This is natur' as we have it up here-away, though I dare say you beat us down on the ocean. Ah's! me; Mabel, a pleasant hour it would be if we could walk on the shore some ten or fifteen miles up this stream, and gaze on all that God has done there!"

"You have then seen these renowned falls, Pathfinder?" the girl eagerly enquired.

"I have—yes I have, and an awful sight I witnessed at that same time. The Sarpent and I were out, scouting about the garrison there, when he told me that the traditions of his people gave an account of a mighty cataract in this neighborhood, and he asked me to vary from the line of march a little to look at the wonder. I had heard some marvels consarning the spot from the soldiers of the 60th, which is my nat'ral corps like, and not the 55th, with which I have sojourned so much of late, but there are so many terrible liars in all rigiments, that I hardly believed half they told me. Well, we went; and though we expected to be led by our ears, and to hear some of that awful roaring that we hear to-day, we were disapp'inted, for natur' was not then speaking in thunder, as she is this morning. Thus it is, in the forest, Master Cap, there being moments when God seems to be walking abroad in power, and then ag'in there is a calm over all, as if his spirit lay in quiet along the 'arth. Well, we came suddenly upon the stream, a short distance above the fall, and a young Delaware who was in our company, found a bark canoe, and he would push into the current, to reach an island that lies in the very centre of the confusion and strife. We told him of his folly, we did, and we reasoned with him on the wickedness of tempting Providence by seeking danger that led to no ind, but the youth among the Delawares are very much the same as the youth among the soldiers, risky and vain. All we could say did not change his mind, and the lad had his way. To me it seems, Mabel, that whenever a thing is really grand and potent, it has a quiet majesty about it, that is altogether unlike the frothy and flustering manner of smaller matters, and so it was with them rapids. The canoe was no sooner fairly in them, than down it went, as it might be as one sails through the air on the 'arth, and no skill of the young Delaware could resist the stream. And yet he struggled manfully for life, using the paddle to the last, like the deer that is swimming to cast the hounds. At first, he shot across the current so swiftly that we thought he would prevail, but he had miscalculated his distance, and when the truth really struck him, he turned the head up stream, and struggled in a way that was fearful to look at. I could have pitied him, even had he been a Mingo! For a few moments his efforts were so frantic that he actually prevailed over the power of the cataract; but natur' has its limits, and one faltering stroke of the paddle set him back, and then he lost ground, foot by foot, inch by inch, until he got near the spot where the river looked even and green and as if it were made of millions of threads of water, all bent over some huge rock, when he shot backward like an arrow and disappeared, the bows of the canoe tipping just enough to let us see what had become of him. I met a Mohawk, some years later, who had witnessed the whole affair, from the bed of the stream below, and he told me that the Delaware continued to paddle, in the air, until he was lost in the mists of the falls!"

"And what became of the poor wretch?" demanded Mabel, who had been strongly interested by the natural eloquence of the speaker.

"He went to the happy hunting grounds of his people, no doubt, for though he was risky and vain, he was also just and brave. Yes, he died foolishly, but the Manitou of the red skin has compassion on his creatur's as well as the God of a christian!"

A gun, at this moment, was discharged from a block-house, near the fort, and the shot, one of light weight, came whistling over the cutter's mast, an admonition to approach no nearer.

Jasper was at the helm, and he kept away, smiling at the same time, as if he felt no anger at the rudeness of the salutation. The Scud was now in the current, and her outward set soon carried her far enough to leeward to avoid the danger of a repetition of the shot, and then she quietly continued her course along the land. As soon as the river was fairly opened, Jasper ascertained that the Montcalm was not at anchor in it, and a man sent aloft, came down with the report that the horizon showed no sail. The hope was now strong, that the artifice of Jasper had succeeded, and that the French commander had missed them by keeping the middle of the lake, as he steered towards its head.

All that day the wind hung to the southward, and the cutter continued her course about a league from the land, running six or eight knots an hour, in perfectly smooth water. Although the scene had one feature of monotony, the outline of unbroken forest, it was not without its interest and pleasure. Various head-lands presented themselves, and the cutter, in running from one to another, stretched across bays so deep, as almost to deserve the names of gulphs, but nowhere did the eye meet with the evidences of civilization. Rivers occasionally poured their tribute into the great reservoir of the lake, but their banks could be traced inland for miles, by the same outlines of trees, and even large bays, that lay embosomed in woods, communicating with Ontario, only by narrow outlets, appeared and disappeared, without bringing with them a single trace of a human habitation.

Of all on board, the Pathfinder viewed the scene with the most unmingled delight. His eyes feasted on the endless line of forest, and, more than once that day, notwithstanding he found it so grateful to be near Mabel, listening to her pleasant voice, and echoing, in feelings at least, her joyous laugh, did his soul pine to be wandering beneath the high arches of the maples, oaks and lindens, where his habits had induced him to fancy lasting and true joys were only to be found. Cap viewed the prospect differently. More than once, he expressed his disgust at there being no light-houses, church-towers, beacons, or roadsteds with their shipping. Such another coast, he protested, the world did not contain, and taking the serjeant aside, he gravely assured him that the region could never come to any thing, as the havens were neglected, the rivers had a deserted and useless look, and that even the breeze had a smell of the forest about it, which spoke ill of its properties.

But the humours of the different individuals in her, did not stay the speed of the Scud. When the sun was setting, she was already a hundred miles on her route towards Oswego, into which river Serjeant Dunham now thought it his duty to go, in order to receive any communications that Major Duncan might please to make. With a view to effect this purpose, Jasper continued to hug the shore all night, and though the wind began to fail him towards morning, it lasted long enough to carry the cutter up to a point that was known to be but a league or two from the fort. Here the breeze came out light at the northward, and the cutter hauled a little from the land in order to obtain a safe offing should it come on to blow, or should the weather again get to be easterly.

When the day dawned the cutter had the mouth of the Oswego well under her lee, distant about two miles, and just as the morning gun from the fort was fired, Jasper gave the order to ease off the sheets, and to bear up for his port. At that moment a cry from the forecastle drew all eyes towards the point on the eastern side of the outlet, and there, just without the range of shot from the light guns of the works, with her canvass reduced to barely enough to keep her stationary, lay the Montcalm, evidently in waiting for their appearance. To pass her was impossible, for, by filling her sails, the French ship could have intercepted them in a few minutes, and the circumstances called for a prompt decision. After a short consultation, the serjeant again changed his plan, determining to make the best of his way towards the station for which he had been originally destined, trusting to the speed of the Scud to throw the enemy so far astern, as to leave no clue to her movements.

The cutter, accordingly, hauled upon a wind, with the least possible delay, with every thing set that would draw. Guns were fired from the fort, ensigns shown, and the ramparts were again crowded. But sympathy was all the aid that Lundie could lend to his party, and the Montcalm, also firing four or five guns of defiance, and throwing abroad several of the banners of France, was soon in chase, under a cloud of canvass.

For several hours the two vessels were pressing through the

water, as fast as possible, making short stretches to windward, apparently with a view to keep the port under their lee, the one to enter it, if possible, and the other to intercept it in the attempt.

At meridian, the French ship was hull down, dead to leeward, the disparity of sailing, on a wind, being very great, and some islands were near by, behind which Jasper said it would be possible for the cutter to conceal her future movements. Although Cap and the serjeant, and particularly Lt. Muir, to judge by his language, still felt a good deal of distrust of the young man, and Frontenac was not distant, this advice was followed, for time pressed, and the Quarter Master discreetly observed that Jasper could not well betray them, without running openly into the enemy's harbor, a step they could at any time prevent, since the only cruiser of force the French possessed, at the moment, was under their lee, and not in a situation to do them any immediate injury.

Left to himself, Jasper Western soon proved how much was really in him. He weathered upon the islands, passed them, and, on coming out to the eastward, kept broad away, with nothing in sight, in his wake, or to leeward. By sunset, again, the cutter was up with the first of the islands that lie in the outlet of the lake, and ere it was dark she was running through the narrow channels, on her way to the long sought station. At nine o'clock, however, Cap insisted that they should anchor, for the maze of islands became so complicated and obscure, that he feared, at every opening, the party would find themselves under the guns of a French fort. Jasper consented cheerfully, it being a part of his standing instructions to approach the station, under such circumstances as would prevent the men from obtaining any very accurate notion of its position, lest a deserter might betray the little garrison to the enemy.

The Scud was brought-to in a small retired bay, where it would have been difficult to find her by day-light and where she was perfectly concealed at night, when all but a solitary sentinel on deck sought their rest. Cap had been so harassed during the previous eight and forty hours, that his slumbers were long and deep, nor did he awake from his first nap, until the day was just beginning to dawn. His eyes were scarcely open, however, when his nautical instinct told him, that the cutter was under way.

Springing up, he found the Scud threading the islands again, with no one on deck but Jasper and the pilot, unless the sentinel be excepted, who had not in the least interfered with movements that he had every reason to believe were as regular as they were necessary.

"How's this, Master Western!" demanded Cap, with sufficient fierceness for the occasion—"Are you running us into Frontenac, at last, and we all asleep below, like so many mariners waiting for the 'sentry go.'"

"This is according to orders, Master Cap, Major Duncan having commanded me never to approach the station, unless at a moment when the people were below, for he does not wish there should be more pilots in these waters, than the King has need of."

"Whe-e-e-w! A pretty job I should have made of running down among these bushes and rocks with no one on deck! Why a regular York branch could make nothing of such a channel."

"I always thought, sir," said Jasper smiling, "you would have done better, had you left the cutter in my hands, until she had safely reached her place of destination."

"We should have done it, Jasper, we should have done it, had it not been for a circumstance—these circumstances are serious matters, and no prudent man will overlook them."

"Well, sir, I hope there is now an end of them. We shall arrive in less than an hour, if the wind holds, and then you'll be safe from any circumstances that I can control."

"Humph!"

Cap was obliged to acquiesce, and as every thing around him had the appearance of Jasper's being sincere, there was not much difficulty in making up his mind to submit. It would not have been easy, indeed, for a person the most sensitive on the subject of circumstances, to fancy that the Scud was anywhere in the vicinity of a port as long established, and as well known on the frontiers, as Frontenac. The islands might not have been literally a thousand in number, but they were so numerous and small as to baffle calculation, though occasionally one of larger size than common was passed. Jasper had quitted what might have been termed the main channel, and was winding his way, with a good stiff breeze, and a favorable current, through passes that were sometimes so narrow that there appeared to be barely room sufficient for the Scud's spars to clear the trees, while at other moments, he shot across little bays, and buried the cutter again, amid rocks, forests and bushes. The water was so transparent, that there was no occasion for the lead, and being of equal depth, little risk was actually run, though Cap, with his maritime habits, was in a constant fever lest they should strike.

"I give it up!—I give it up, Pathfinder!—" the old seaman at length exclaimed, when the little vessel emerged in safety from the twentieth of these narrow inlets, through which she had been so boldly carried—"this is defying the very nature of seamanship, and sending all its laws and rules to the d——l!"

"Nay, nay, Salt-water, 'tis the parfection of the art. You perceive that Jasper never falters, but, like a hound with a true nose, he runs with his head high, as if he had a strong scent. My life on it, the lad brings us out right in the ind, as he would have done in the beginning had we given him leave."

"No pilot, no lead, no beacons, buoys or light-houses, no—"

"Trail!" interrupted Pathfinder, "for that to me, is the most mysterious part of the business. Water leaves no trail, as every one knows, and yet here is Jasper moving ahead as boldly as if he had before his eyes, the prints of moccasins on leaves, as plainly as we can see the sun in the heavens."

"D——e, if I believe there is even any compass!"

"Stand by, to haul down the jib—" called out Jasper, who merely smiled at the remarks of his companion. "Haul down—starboard your helm—starboard hard—so—melt her—gently there with the helm—touch her lightly—now jump ashore with the fast, lad—No; heave—there are some of our people ready to take it."

All this passed so quickly, as barely to allow the spectators time to note the different evolutions, ere the Scud had been thrown into the wind until her mainsail shivered, next cast a little by the use of the rudder only, and then she set bodily along side of a natural rocky quay, where she was immediately secured, by good fasts run to the shore. In a word, the station was reached, and the men of the 55th were greeted by their expecting comrades, with the satisfaction that a relief usually brings.

Mabel sprang upon the shore with a delight which she did

not care to express, and her father led his men after her, with an alacrity which proved how wearied he had become of the cutter. The station, as the place was familiarly termed by the soldiers of the 55th, was indeed a spot to raise expectations of enjoyment, among those who had been cooped up so long in a vessel of the dimensions of the Scud. None of the islands were high, though all lay at a sufficient elevation above the water, to render them perfectly healthy and secure. Each had more or less of wood, and the greater number, at that distant day, were clothed with the virgin forest. The one selected by the troops for their purpose was small, containing about twenty acres of land, and by some of the accidents of the wilderness it had been partly stripped of its trees, probably centuries before the period of which we are writing, and a little grassy glade covered nearly half its surface. It was the opinion of the officer who had made the selection of this spot for a military post, that a sparkling spring near by, had early caught the attention of the Indians, and that they had long frequented this particular place, in their hunts, or when fishing for salmon, a circumstance that had kept down the second growth, and given time for the natural grasses to take root, and to gain dominion over the soil. Let the cause be what it might, the effect was to render this island far more beautiful than most of those around it, and to lend it an air of civilization that was then wanting in so much of that vast region of country.

The shores of Station Island were completely fringed with bushes, and great care had been taken to preserve them, as they answered as a screen to conceal the persons and things collected within their circle. Favored by this shelter, as well as by that of several thickets of trees, and different copses, some six or eight low huts had been erected, to be used as quarters for the officer and his men, to contain stores, and to serve the purposes of kitchen, hospital &c. These huts were built of logs, in the usual manner, had been roofed by bark brought from a distance, lest the signs of labour should attract attention, and as they had now been inhabited some months, were as comfortable as dwellings of that description usually ever get to be.

At the eastern extremity of the island, however, was a small densely wooded peninsula, with thickets of under-brush so closely matted, as nearly to prevent the possibility of seeing across it, so long as the leaves remained on the branches. Near the narrow neck that connected this acre with the rest of the island, a small block-house had been erected, with some attention to its means of resistance. The logs were bullet-proof, squared and jointed with a care to leave no defenceless points; the windows were loop-holes, the door massive and small, and the roof, like the rest of the structure was framed of hewn timber, covered properly with bark to exclude the rain. The lower apartment, as usual, contained stores and provisions; here indeed the party kept all their supplies; the second story was intended for a dwelling, as well as for the citadel, and a low garret was subdivided into two or three rooms, and could hold the pallets of some ten or fifteen persons. All the arrangements were exceedingly simple and cheap, but they were sufficient to protect the soldiers against the effects of a surprise. As the whole building was considerably less than forty feet high, its summit was concealed by the tops of the trees, except from the eyes of those who had reached the interior of the island. On that side the view was open from the upper loops, though bushes even there, more or less concealed the base of the wooden tower.

The object being purely defence, care had been taken to place the block house so near an opening in the lime-stone rock, that formed the base of the island, as to admit of a bucket's being dropped into the water, in order to obtain that great essential, in the event of a siege. In order to facilitate this operation, and to enfilade the base of the building, the upper stories projected several feet beyond the lower, in the manner usual to block houses, and pieces of wood filled the apertures cut in the log flooring which were intended as loops and traps. The communications between the different stories were by means of ladders. If we add, that these blockhouses were intended as citadels for garrisons or settlements to retreat to, in cases of attack, the general reader will obtain a sufficiently correct idea of the arrangements it is our wish to explain.

But the situation of the island itself, formed its principal merit as a military position. Lying in the midst of twenty others, it was not an easy matter to find it, since boats might pass quite near it, and, by the glimpses caught through the openings, this particular island would be taken for a part of some other. Indeed, the channels between the islands, that lay around the one we have been describing, were so narrow that it was even difficult to say which portions of the land were connected, or which separated, even as one stood in their centre, with the express desire of ascertaining the truth. The little bay in particular, that Jasper used as a harbor, was so embowered with bushes, and shut in with islands, that, the sails of the cutter being lowered, her own people, on one occasion, had searched for hours, before they could find the Scud, in their return, from an excursion among the adjacent channels, in quest of fish. In short, the place was admirably adapted, to its present uses, and its natural advantages had been as ingeniously improved as economy and the limited means of a frontier post would very well allow.

The hour that succeeded the arrival of the Scud was one of hurried excitement. The party in possession had done nothing worthy of being mentioned, and wearied with their seclusion, they were all eager to return to Oswego. The Serjeant and the officer he came to relieve, had no sooner gone through the little ceremonial of transferring the command, than the latter hurried on board the Scud, with his whole party, and Jasper, who would gladly have passed the day on the island, was required to get under way, forthwith, the wind promising a quick passage up the river, and across the lake. Before separating, however, Lt. Muir, Cap, and the Serjeant had a private conference with the ensign, who had been relieved, in which the latter was made acquainted with the suspicions that existed against the fidelity of the young sailor. Promising due caution, the officer embarked, and in less than three hours from the time when she had arrived, the cutter was again in motion.

Mabel had taken possession of a hut, and, with female readiness and skill, she made all the simple little domestic arrangements, of which the circumstances would admit, not only for her own comfort, but for that of her father. To save labor, a mess table was prepared in a hut set apart for that purpose, where all the heads of the detachment were to eat, the soldier's wife performing the necessary labor. The hut of the Serjeant, which was the best on the island, being thus freed from any of the vulgar offices of a household, admitted of such a display of womanly taste, that for the first time since her arrival on the frontier, the girl felt proud of her home. As soon as these important duties were discharged, she strolled out on the island, taking a path that led through the pretty glade, and which conducted to the only point that was not covered with bushes. Here she stood gazing at the limpid water, which lay with scarcely a ruffle on it, at her feet, musing on the novel situation in which she was placed, and permitting a pleasing and deep excitement to steal over her feelings, as she remembered the scenes through which she had so lately passed, and conjectured those which still lay veiled in the future.

"You're a beautiful fixture, in a beautiful spot, Mistress Mabel," said David Muir, suddenly appearing at her elbow, "and I'll no engage you're not just the handsomest of the two."

"I will not say, Mr. Muir, that compliments on my person are altogether unwelcome, for I should not gain credit for speaking the truth, perhaps," answered Mabel with spirit, "but I will say that if you would condescend to address to me some remarks of a different nature, I may be led to believe you think I have sufficient faculties to understand them."

"Hoot! your mind, beautiful Mabel, is polished just like the barrel of a soldier's musket, and your conversation is only too discreet and wise for a poor d——l, who has been chewing birch these four years, up here on the lines, instead of receiving it in an application that has the virtue of imparting knowledge. But you are no sorry, I take it, young lady, that you've got your pretty foot on *terra firma*, once more."

"I thought so, two hours since, Mr. Muir, but the Scud looks so beautiful, as she sails through these vistas of trees, that I almost regret I am no longer one of her passengers."

As Mabel ceased speaking, she waved her handkerchief in return to a salutation from Jasper, who kept his eyes fastened on her form, until the white sails of the cutter had swept round a point, and were nearly lost behind its green fringe of leaves.

"There they go, and I'll no say 'joy go with them,' but may they have the luck to return safely, for without them we shall be in danger of passing the winter on this island; unless indeed we have the alternative of the castle at Quebec. Yon Jasper Eau douce is a vagrant sort of a lad, and they have reports of him in the garrison, that it pains my very heart to hear. Your worthy father, and almost-as-worthy uncle, have none of the best opinion of him."

"I am sorry to hear it, Mr. Muir; I doubt not that time will remove all their distrust."

"If time would only remove mine, pretty Mabel," rejoined the Quarter Master, in a wheedling tone, "I should feel no envy of the commander in chief. I think if I were in a condition to retire, the serjeant would just step into my shoes."

"If my dear father is worthy to step into your shoes, Mr. Muir," returned the girl, with malicious pleasure, "I'm sure that the qualification is mutual, and that you are every way worthy to step into his."

"The deuce is in the child! You would not reduce me to the rank of a non-commissioned officer, Mabel!"

"No indeed, sir, I was not thinking of the army at all, as you spoke of retiring. My thoughts were more egotistical, and I was thinking how much you reminded me of my dear father, by your experience, wisdom, and suitableness to take his place, as the head of a family."

"As its bridegroom, pretty Mabel, but not as its parent, or natural chief. I see how it is with you, loving your repartee, and brilliant with wit! Well, I like spirit in a young woman, so it be not the spirit of a scold. This Pathfinder is an extraordinair, Mabel, if truth may be said of the man."

"Truth should be said of him, or nothing. Pathfinder is my friend—my very particular friend, Mr. Muir, and no evil can be said of him, in my presence, that I shall not deny."

"I shall say nothing evil of him, I can assure you, Mabel; but, at the same time, I doubt if much good can be said in his favor."

"He is at least expert with the rifle," returned Mabel, smiling. "That *you* cannot deny."

"Let him have all the credit of his exploits in that way, if you please; but he is as illiterate as a Mohawk."

"He may not understand Latin, but his knowledge of Iroquois is greater than that of most men, and it is the more useful language of the two, in this part of the world."

"If Lundie, himself, were to call on me for an opinion which I admired most, your person, or your wit, beautiful and caustic Mabel, I should be at a loss to answer. My admiration is so nearly divided between them, that I often fancy this is the one that bears off the palm, and then the other! Ah! The late Mrs. Muir was a paragon, in that way, also!"

"The latest Mrs. Muir, did you say, sir?" asked Mabel, looking up innocently at her companion.

"Hoot–hoot!–That is some of Pathfinder's scandal. Now, I dare say, that the fellow has been trying to persuade you, Mabel, that I have had more than one wife, already."

"In that case, his time would have been thrown away, sir, as every body knows that you have been so unfortunate as to have had four."

"Only three, as sure as my name is David Muir. The fourth is pure scandal–or, rather, pretty Mabel, she is yet *in petto*, as they say at Rome, and that means, in matters of love, in the heart, my dear."

"Well, I'm glad, I'm not that fourth person, *in petto*, or in any thing else, as I should not like to be a scandal!"

"No fear of that, charming Mabel, for were you the fourth, all the others would be forgotten, and your wonderful beauty and merit would, at once, elevate you to be the first. No fear of your being the fourth in any thing."

"There is consolation in that assurance, Mr. Muir," said Mabel laughing, "whatever there may be in your other assurance, for I confess I should prefer being even a fourth-rate beauty, to being a fourth wife."

So saying she tripped away, leaving the Quarter Master to meditate on his want of success. Mabel had been induced to use her female means of defence thus freely, partly because her suitor had of late been so pointed as to stand in need of a pretty strong repulse, and partly on account of his innuendoes against Jasper and the Pathfinder. Though full of spirit and quick of intellect, she was not naturally pert, but, on the present occasion, she thought circumstances called for more than usual decision. When she left her companion, therefore, she believed she was now finally released from attentions that she thought as ill bestowed as they were certainly disagreeable. Not so, however, with David Muir. Accustomed to rebuffs, and familiar with the virtue of perseverance, he saw no reason to despair, though the half menacing, half self-satisfied manner in which he shook his head towards the retreating girl, might have betrayed designs as sinister, as they were determined. While he was thus occupied, the Pathfinder approached and got within a few feet of him, unseen.

"'T'will never do, Quarter Master, 't'will never do," commenced the latter laughing in his noiseless way, "she is young and actyve, and none but a quick foot can overtake her. They tell me you are her suitor, if you're not her follower."

"And I hear the same of yourself, man, though the presumption would be so great, that I scarce can think it true."

"I fear you're right, I do; yes, I fear you're right!–When I consider myself; what I am; how little I know, and how rude my life has been, I altogether distrust my claim even to think a moment, of one so tutored, and gay, and light of heart, and delicate–"

"You forget handsome–" coarsely interrupted Muir.

"And handsome too, I fear," returned the meek and self-abased guide, "I might have said handsome, at once, among her other qualities, for the young fa'an just as it learns to bound, is not more pleasant to the eye of the hunter, than Mabel is lovely in mine. I do indeed fear, that all the thoughts I have harbored about her, are vain and presumptuous."

"If you think this, my friend, of your own accord, and natural modesty, as it might be, my duty to you as an old fellow campaigner compels me to say–"

"Quarter Master–" interrupted the other, regarding his companion keenly, "you and I have lived together much behind the ramparts of forts, but very little in the open woods, or in front of the inimy."

"Garrison or tent, it all passes for part of the same campaign, you know, Pathfinder, and then my duty keeps me much within sight of the store-houses, greatly contrary to my inclinations, as ye may well suppose, having yourself the ardor of battle in your temperament. But had ye heard what Mabel has just been saying of you, ye'd no think another minute of making yourself agreeable to the saucy and uncompromising hussy."

Pathfinder looked earnestly at the lieutenant, for it was impossible he should not feel an interest in what might be Mabel's opinion, but he had too much of the innate and true feeling of a gentleman, to ask to hear what another had said of him. Muir, however, was not to be foiled by this self denial and self respect, for, believing he had a man of great truth and simplicity to deal with, he determined to practise on his credulity, as one means of getting rid of his rivalry. He therefore pursued the subject, as soon as he perceived that his companion's self denial was stronger than his curiosity.

"You ought to know her opinion, Pathfinder," he continued, "and I think every man ought to hear what his friends and acquaintances say of him, and, so, by way of proving my own regard for your character and feelings, I'll just tell you, in as few words as possible. You know that Mabel has a wicked malicious way with those eyes of hers or when she has a mind to be hard upon one's feelings?"

"To me her eyes, Lieutenant Muir, have always seemed winning and soft—though I will acknowledge that they sometimes laugh—yes, I have known them to laugh; and that right heartily, and with down-right good will."

"Well, it was just that, there. Her eyes were laughing with all their might, as it were, and in the midst of all her fun, she broke out with an exclamation to this effect—I hope 't'will no hurt your sensibility, Pathfinder?"

"I will not say, Quarter Master, I will not say—Mabel's opinion of me is of more account than that of most others."

"Then I'll no tell ye, but just keep discretion on the subject. And why should a man be telling another what his friends say of him, especially when they happen to say that which may not be pleasant to hear. I'll not add another word to this present communication."

"I cannot make you speak, Quarter Master, if you are not so minded, and perhaps it is better for me not to know Mabel's opinion, as you seem to think it is not in my favor. Ah's! me—if we could be what we wish to be, instead of being only what we are, there would be a great difference in our characters, and knowledge and appearance. One may be rude, and coarse and ignorant, and yet happy, if he does not know it, but it is hard to see our own failings, in the strongest light, just as we wish to hear the least about them."

"That's just the *rationale*, as the French say, of the matter; and so I was telling Mabel, when she ran away, and left me. You noticed the manner in which she skipped off, as you approached?"

"It was very observable—" answered Pathfinder, drawing a long breath, and clenching the barrel of his rifle, as if the fingers would bury themselves in the iron.

"It was more than observable—it was flagrant—that's just the word, and the dictionary would'n't supply a better, after an hour's search. Well, you must know, Pathfinder—for I cannot reasonably deny you the gratification of hearing this—so you must know, the minx bounded off in that manner, in preference to hearing what I had to say in your justification."

"And what could you find to say, in my behalf, Quarter Master?"

"Why, d'ye understand, my friend, I was ruled by circumstances, and no ventured indiscreetly into generalities, but was preparing to meet particulars, as it might be, with particulars. If you were thought wild, half-savage, or of a frontier formation, I could tell her, ye know, that it came of the frontier, wild and half-savage life ye'd led; and all her objections must cease at once, or there would be a sort of misunderstanding with Providence."

"And did you tell her this, Quarter Master?"

"I'll no swear to the exact words, but the idea was prevalent in my mind, ye'll understand. The girl was impatient, and would not hear the half I had to say; but away she skipped, as ye saw with your own eyes, Pathfinder, as if her opinion were fully made up, and she cared to listen no longer. I fear her mind may be said to have come to its conclusion!"

"I fear it has, indeed, Quarter Master, and her father, after all, is mistaken. Yes, yes; the sarjeant has fallen into a grievous error."

"Well, man, why need ye lament, and undo all the grand reputation ye've been so many years making? Shoulder the rifle that ye use so well, and off into the woods with ye, for there's not the female breathing that is worth a heavy heart for a minute, as I know from experience. Tak' the word of one who knows the sax, and has had two wives, that women, after all, are very much the sort of creatures we do not imagine them to be. Now, if you would really mortify Mabel, here is as glorious an occasion, as any rejected lover could desire."

"The last wish I have, Lieutenant, would be to mortify Mabel."

"Well, ye'll come to that in the end, notwithstanding; for it's human nature to desire to give unpleasant feelings to them, that give unpleasant feelings to us. But a better occasion never offered to make your friends love you, than is to be had at this very moment, and that is the certain means of causing one's enemies to envy us."

"Quarter Master, Mabel is not my inimy; and if she was, the last thing I could desire, would be to give her an uneasy moment."

"Ye say so, Pathfinder—ye say so, and I dare say, ye think so; but reason and nature are both against you, as ye'll find in the end. Ye've heard the saying of 'love me, love my dog:' well, now, that means, read backwards, 'do'n't love me, do'n't love my dog.' Now, listen to what is in your power to do. You know we occupy an exceedingly precarious and uncertain position, here, almost in the jaws of the lion, as it were?"

"Do you mean the Frenchers, by the lion, and this island as his jaws, lieutenant?"

"Metaphorically only, my friend, for the French are no lions, and this island is not a jaw—unless, indeed, it may prove to be, what I greatly fear may come true, the jaw-bone of an ass!"

Here the Quarter Master indulged in a sneering laugh, that proclaimed any thing but respect and admiration for his friend Lundie's sagacity in selecting that particular spot for his operations.

"The post is as well chosen, as any I ever put foot in," said Pathfinder, looking around him, as one surveys a position.

"I'll no deny it—I'll no deny it. Lundie is a great soldier, in a small way, and his father was a great laird, with the same qualifications. I was born on the estate, and have followed the Major so long that I've got to reverence all he says and does. That's just my weakness, ye'll know, Pathfinder. Well, this post may be the post of an ass, or of a Solomon, as men fancy, but it's most critically placed, as is apparent by all Lundie's precautions and injunctions. There are savages out, scouting through these thousand islands, and over the forest, searching for this very spot, as is known to Lundie himself, on certain information, and the greatest service you can render the 55th, is to discover their trails, and lead them off, on a false scent. Unhappily, Serjeant Dunham has taken up the notion, that the danger is to be apprehended from up stream, because Frontenac lies above us, whereas all experience tells us, that Indians come on the side that is most contrary to reason, and, consequently, are to be expected from below. Take your canoe, therefore, and go down stream, among the islands, that we may have notice if any danger approaches from that quarter. If ye should look a few miles on the main, especially on the York side, the information you'd bring in would be all the more accurate, and consequently the more valuable.

"The Big Sarpent is on the look out, in that quarter, and as he knows the station well, no doubt he will give us timely notice, should any wish to sarcumvent us, in that direction."

"He is but an Indian, after all, Pathfinder, and this is an affair that calls for the knowledge of a white man. Lundie will be eternally grateful to the man that shall help this little enterprise to come off with flying colours. To tell you the truth, my friend, he is conscious it should never have been attempted, but he has too much of the old laird's obstinacy about him, to own an error, though it be as manifest as the morning star."

The Quarter Master then continued to reason with his companion, in order to induce him to quit the island, without delay, using such arguments as first suggested themselves, sometimes contradicting himself, and not unfrequently urging at one moment a motive that at the next was directly opposed by another. The Pathfinder, simple as he was, detected these flaws in the Lieutenant's philosophy, though he was far from suspecting that they proceeded from a desire to clear the coast, of Mabel's suitor. He met bad reasons by good ones, resisted every inducement that was not legitimate, by his intimate acquaintance with his peculiar duties, and was blind, as usual, to the influence of every incentive that could not stand the test of integrity. He did not exactly suspect the secret objects of Muir, but he was far from being blind to his sophistry. The result was that the two parted, after a long dialogue, unconvinced and distrustful of each other's motives, though the distrust of the guide, like all that was connected with the man, partook of his own upright, disinterested and ingenuous nature.

A conference that took place, soon after, between Serjeant Dunham and the Lieutenant led to more consequences. When it was ended, secret orders were issued to the men, the block-house was taken possession of, the huts were occupied, and one accustomed to the movements of soldiers, might have detected that an expedition was in the wind. In fact, just as the sun was setting, the Serjeant who had been much occupied at what was called the harbor, came into his own hut, followed by Pathfind-er and Cap, and, as he took his seat at the neat table that Mabel had prepared for him, he opened the budget of his intelligence.

"You are likely to be of some use, here, my child," the old soldier commenced, "as this tidy and well ordered supper can testify, and, I trust, when the proper moment arrives, you will show yourself to be the descendant of those who know how to face their enemies."

"You do not expect me, dear father, to play Joan of Arc, and to lead the men to battle?"

"Play whom, child—Did you ever hear of the person Mabel mentions, Pathfinder?"

"Not I, sarjeant, but what of that? I am ignorant and onedi-cated, and it is too great a pleasure to me to listen to her voice, and take in her words, to be particular about persons."

"I know her," said Cap, decidedly. "She sailed a privateer out of Morlaix, in the last war; and good cruises she made of them."

Mabel blushed at having inadvertently made an allusion that went beyond her father's reading, to say nothing of her uncle's dogmatism; and perhaps a little at the Pathfinder's simple in-genuous earnestness, but she did not forbear the less to smile.

"Why, father, I am not expected to fall in with the men, and help defend the island."

"And, yet, women have often done such things, in this quar-ter of the world, girl, as our friend, the Pathfinder, here, will tell you. But lest you should be surprised at not seeing us, when you awake in the morning, it is proper that I now tell you we intend to march in the course of this very night."

"*We*, father—and leave me and Jennie on this island alone!"

"No, my daughter, not quite as unmilitary as that. We shall leave Lt. Muir, brother Cap, Corporal McNab, and three men, to compose the garrison during our absence. Jennie will remain with you, in this hut, and brother Cap will occupy my place."

"And Mr. Muir?" said Mabel, half unconscious of what she uttered, though she foresaw a great deal of unpleasant persecution in the arrangement.

"Why, he can make love to you, if you like it, girl, for he is an amorous youth, and having already disposed of four wives, is impatient to show how much he honors their memories, by taking a fifth."

"The Quarter Master tells me," said Pathfinder, innocently, "that when a man's feelings have been harrowed by so many losses, there is no wiser way to soothe them, than by ploughing up the soil anew, in such a manner as to leave no traces of what have gone over it afore."

"Ay, that is just the difference between ploughing and harrowing," returned the Serjeant with a grim smile. "But let him tell Mabel his mind, and there will be an end of his suit. I very well know that *my* daughter will never be the wife of Lieutenant Muir."

This was said in a way that was tantamount to declaring that no daughter of his, ever *should* become the wife of the person in question. Mabel had coloured, trembled, half laughed, and looked uneasy, but rallying her spirit, she said in a voice so cheerful as completely to conceal her agitation—

"But, father, we might better wait until Mr. Muir manifests a wish that your daughter would have him—or rather a wish to have your daughter, lest we get the fable of sour grapes thrown into our faces."

"And what is that fable, Mabel," eagerly demanded Pathfinder, who was any thing but learned in the ordinary lore of white men—"tell it to us, in your own pretty way; I dare say the sarjeant never heard it."

Mabel repeated the well known fable, and as her suitor had desired, in her own pretty way, which was a way to keep his eyes rivetted on her face, and the whole of his honest countenance covered with a smile.

"That was like a fox!" cried Pathfinder, when she had ceased, "ay, and like a Mingo, too. Cunning and cruel; that is the way with both the riptyles. As to grapes, they are sour enough in this part of the country, even to them that can get at them, though I dare say there are seasons, and times, and places, where they are sourer to them that can't. I should judge, now, my scalp is very sour in Mingo eyes."

"The sour grapes will be the other way, child, and it is Mr. Muir who will make the complaint. You would never marry that man, Mabel?"

"Not she," put in Cap, "a fellow who is only half a soldier, after all! The story of them there grapes, is quite a circumstance."

"I think little of marrying any one, dear father, and dear uncle, and would rather talk about it less, if you please. But, did I think of marrying at all, I do believe a man whose affections have already been tried by three or four wives would scarcely be my choice."

The serjeant nodded at the guide, as much as to say, you see how the land lies, and then he had sufficient consideration for his daughter's feelings to change the subject.

"Neither you, nor Mabel, brother Cap," he resumed, "can have any legal authority with the garrison I leave behind, on the island, but you may counsel and influence. Strictly speaking Corporal McNab will be the commanding officer, and I have endeavored to impress him with a sense of his dignity, lest he might give way too much to the superior rank of Lieutenant Muir, who, being a volunteer, can have no right to interfere with the duty. I wish you to sustain the corporal, brother Cap, for should the Quarter Master once break through the regulations of the expedition, he may pretend to command me, as well as McNab."

"More particularly, should Mabel really cut him adrift, while you are absent. Of course, Serjeant, you'll leave every thing that is afloat, under my care? The most d——le confusion has grown out of misunderstandings between commanders in chief, ashore and afloat."

"In one sense, brother, though, in a general way, the corporal is commander in chief. History does indeed tell us that a division of command leads to difficulties, and I shall avoid that danger. The corporal must command, but you can counsel freely, particularly in all matters relating to the boats, of which I shall leave one behind, to secure your retreat should there be occasion. I know the corporal well; he is a brave man, and a good soldier; and one that may be relied on, if the Santa Cruz can be kept from him. But then he is a Scotchman, and will be liable to the Quarter Master's influence, against which I desire both you and Mabel to be on your guard."

"But why leave us behind, dear father?–I have come thus far to be a comfort to you, and why not go farther?"

"You are a good girl, Mabel, and very like the Dunhams! But you must halt here. We shall leave the island to-morrow, before the day dawns, in order not to be seen by any prying eyes, coming from our cover, and we shall take the two largest boats, leaving you the other, and one bark canoe. We are about to go into the channel used by the French, where we shall lie in wait, perhaps a week, to intercept their supply boats that are about to pass up, on their way to Frontenac, loaded, in particular, with a heavy amount of Indian goods."

"Have you looked well to your papers, brother?" Cap anxiously demanded. "Of course, you know a capture on the high seas is piracy, unless your boat is regularly commissioned, either as a public, or a private armed cruiser."

"I have the honor to hold the colonel's appointment as Serjeant Major of the 55th," returned the other, drawing himself up with dignity, "and that will be sufficient even for the French King. If not, I have Major Duncan's written orders."

"No papers them, for a warlike cruiser."

"They must suffice, brother, as I have no other. It is of vast importance to His Majesty's interests, in this part of the world, that the boats in question should be captured and carried into Oswego. They contain the blankets, trinkets, rifles, ammunition,–in short, all the stores with which the French bribe their accursed savage allies to commit their unholy acts, setting at naught our holy religion and its precepts, the laws of humanity, and all that is sacred and dear among men. By cutting off these supplies, we shall derange their plans, and gain time on them, for the articles cannot be sent across the ocean again, this autumn."

"But, father, does not His Majesty employ Indians also?" asked Mabel, with some curiosity.

"Certainly, girl, and he has a right to employ them–God bless him! It's a very different thing, whether an Englishman or a Frenchman employs a savage, as every body can understand."

"That is plain enough, brother Dunham;—but I do not see my way so clear, in the matter of the ship's papers."

"An *English* colonel's appointment ought to satisfy any *Frenchman* of my authority; and what is more, brother, it shall."

"But I do not see the difference, father, between an Englishman's and a Frenchman's employing savages in war?"

"All the odds in the world, child, though you may not be able to see it. In the first place, an Englishman is naturally humane and considerate, while a Frenchman is naturally ferocious and timid."

"And you may add, brother, that he will dance from morning 'till night, if you'll let him."

"Very true," gravely returned the Serjeant.

"But, father, I cannot see that all this alters the case. If it be wrong in a Frenchman to hire savages to fight his enemies, it would seem to be equally wrong in an Englishman. *You* will admit this, Pathfinder."

"It's reasonable—it's reasonable, and I have never been one of them that has raised a cry ag'in the Frenchers for doing the very thing we do ourselves. Still, it is worse to consort with a Mingo, than to consort with a Delaware. If any of that just tribe were left, I should think it no sin to send them out ag'in the foe."

"And yet they scalp, and slay young and old—women and children!"

"They have their gifts, Mabel, and are not to be blamed for following them. Natur' is natur', though the different tribes have different ways of showing it. For my part, I am white, and endivor to maintain white feelings."

"This is all unintelligible to me," answered Mabel. "What is right in King George, it would seem ought to be right in King Lewis."

"The King of France's real name is Caput," observed Cap, with his mouth full of venison. "I once carried a great scholar, as a passenger, and he told me that these Lewises thirteenth, fourteenth and fifteenth were all humbugs, and that the men's real name was Caput, which is French for 'foot,' meaning that they ought to be put at the *foot* of the ladder, until ready to go up to be hanged."

"Well this does look like being given to scalping, as a nat'ral gift," Pathfinder remarked, with the air of surprise with which one receives a novel idea, "and I shall have less compunction than ever in sarving ag'in the miscreants, though I can't say I ever yet felt any worth naming."

As all parties, Mabel excepted, seemed satisfied with the course the discussion had taken, no one appeared to think it necessary to pursue the subject. The trio of men, indeed, in this particular, so much resembled the great mass of their fellow creatures, who usually judge of character equally without knowledge and without justice, that we might not have thought it necessary to record the discourse, had it not some bearing in its facts, on the incidents of the legend, and in its opinions on the motives of the characters.

Supper was no sooner ended, than the Serjeant dismissed his guests, and then held a long and confidential dialogue with his daughter. He was little addicted to giving way to the gentler emotions, but the novelty of his present situation awakened feelings that he was unused to experience. The soldier, or the sailor, so long as he acts under the immediate supervision of a superior, thinks little of the risks he runs, but the moment he feels the responsibility of command, all the hazards of his undertaking begin to associate themselves in his mind, with the chances of success or failure. While he dwells less on his own personal danger, perhaps, than when that is the principal consideration, he has more lively general perceptions of all the risks, and submits more to the influence of the feelings which doubt creates. Such was now the case with Serjeant Dunham, who, instead of looking forward to victory as certain, according to his usual habits, began to feel the possibility that he might be parting with his child, forever.

Never before had Mabel struck him as so beautiful, as she appeared that night. Possibly she never had displayed so many engaging qualities to her father, for concern on his account had begun to be active in her breast, and then her sympathies met with unusual encouragement, through those which had been stirred up in the sterner bosom of the veteran. She had never been entirely at her ease with her parent, the great superiority of her education, creating a sort of chasm which had been widened by the military severity of manner he had acquired, by dealing so long and intimately with beings who could only be kept in subjection, by an unremitted discipline. On the present occasion, however, or after they were left alone, the conversation between the father and daughter became more confidential than usual, until Mabel rejoiced to find that it was gradually becoming endearing; a state of feeling that the warm-hearted girl had silently pined for in vain, ever since her arrival.

"Then mother was about my height?" Mabel said, as she held one of her father's hands in both her own—looking up into his face with humid eyes. "I had thought her taller."

"That is the way with most children, who get a habit of thinking of their parents with respect, until they fancy them larger and more commanding than they actually are. Your mother, Mabel, was as near your height, as one woman could be to another."

"And her eyes, father?"

"Her eyes were like thine, child, too—blue, and soft, and inviting like; though hardly so laughing."

"Mine will never laugh again, dearest father, if you do not take care of yourself in this expedition."

"Thank you, Mabel—hem—thank you, child, but I must do my duty. I wish I had seen you comfortably married before we left Oswego! My mind would be easier."

"Married!—To whom, father?"

"You know the man I wish you to love. You may meet with many gayer, and many dressed in finer clothes, but with none with so true a heart, and just a mind."

"None, father?"

"I know of none; in these particulars, Pathfinder has few equals, at least."

"But I need not marry at all. You are single, and I can remain to take care of you."

"God bless you, Mabel!—I know you would, and I do not say that the feeling is not right, for I suppose it is; and yet I believe there is another, that is more so."

"What can be more right than to honor one's parents?"

"It is just as right to honor one's husband, my dear child."

"But I have no husband, father."

"Then take one, as soon as possible, that you may have a husband to honor. I cannot live forever, Mabel, but must drop off in the course of nature, ere long, if I am not carried off in the course of war. You are young, and may yet live long; and it is proper that you should have a male protector, who can see you safe through life, and take care of you in age, as you now wish to take care of me."

"And do you think, father—" said Mabel, playing with his sinewy fingers, with her own little hands, and looking down at them, as if they were subjects of intense interest, though her lips curled in a slight smile, as the words came from them— "And do you think, father, that Pathfinder is just the man to do this?—Is he not within ten or twelve years, as old as yourself?"

"What of that?—His life has been one of moderation and exercise, and years are less to be counted, girl, than constitution. Do you know another more likely to be your protector?"

Mabel did not; at least another who had expressed a desire to that effect, whatever might have been her hopes and her wishes.

"Nay, father, we are not talking of another, but of the Pathfinder," she answered evasively. "If he were younger, I think it would be more natural for me to think of him for a husband."

"'Tis all in the constitution, I tell you, child. Pathfinder is a younger man than half our subalterns."

"He is certainly younger than one, sir—Lieutenant Muir."

Mabel's laugh was joyous and light-hearted, as if just then, she felt no care.

"That he is—young enough to be his grandson—he is younger in years too. God forbid, Mabel! that you should ever become an officer's lady, at least until you are an officer's daughter."

"There will be little fear of that, father, if I marry Pathfinder!" returned the girl, looking up archly in the serjeant's face, again.

"Not by the King's commission, perhaps, though the man is even now the friend and companion of generals. I think I could die happy, Mabel, if you were his wife."

"Father!"

"'Tis a sad thing to go into battle, with the weight of an unprotected daughter laid upon the heart."

"I would give the world to lighten yours of its load, my dear sir!"

"It might be done—" said the serjeant, looking fondly at his child, "though I could not wish to put a burthen on yours, in order to do so."

The voice was deep and tremulous, and never before had Mabel witnessed such a show of affection in her parent. The habitual sternness of the man, lent an interest to his emotions, that they might otherwise have wanted, and the daughter's heart yearned to relieve the father's mind.

"Father, speak plainly," she cried, almost convulsively.

"Nay, Mabel, it might not be right—your wishes and mine may be very different."

"I have no wishes—know nothing of what you mean—would you speak of my future marriage?"

"If I could see you promised to Pathfinder—know that you were pledged to become his wife, let my own fate be what it might, I think I could die happy. But I will ask no pledge of you my child—I will not force you to do what you might repent. Kiss me, Mabel, and go to your bed."

Had Serjeant Dunham exacted of Mabel the pledge that he really so much desired, he would have encountered a resistance that he might have found difficult to overcome, but, by letting nature have its course, he enlisted a powerful ally on his side, and the warm-hearted, generous-minded Mabel was ready to concede to her affections, much more than she would ever have yielded to menace. At that touching moment she thought only of her parent, who was about to quit her perhaps forever, and all of that ardent love for him, which had possibly been as much fed by the imagination as by any thing else, but which had received a little check by the restrained intercourse of the last fortnight, now returned with a force that was increased by pure and intense feeling. Her father seemed all in all to her, and to render him happy, there was no proper sacrifice that she was not ready to make. One painful, rapid, almost wild gleam of thought shot across the brain of the girl, and her resolution wavered; but endeavoring to trace the foundation of the pleasing hope on which it was based, she found nothing positive to support it. Trained like a woman, to subdue her most ardent feelings, her thoughts reverted to her father, and to the blessings that awaited the child who yielded to a parent's wishes.

"Father," she said quietly, almost with a holy calm–"God blesses the dutiful daughter!"

"He will, Mabel; we have the good book for that."

"I will marry whomever you desire."

"Nay–nay, Mabel–you may have a choice of your own–"

"I have no choice–that is–none have asked me to have a choice, but Pathfinder and Mr. Muir, and between *them*, neither of us would hesitate. No, father; I will marry whomever you may choose."

"Thou knowest my choice, beloved girl; none other can make thee as happy, as the noble-hearted guide."

"Well, then, if he wish it–if he ask me again–for, father, you would not have me offer myself, or that any one should do that office for me–" and the blood stole across the pallid cheeks of Mabel, as she spoke, for high and generous resolution had driven back the stream of life to her heart,–"no one must speak to him of it, but if he seek me again, and, knowing all that a true girl ought to tell the man she marries, and he then wishes to make me his wife, I will be his."

"Bless you, my Mabel–God in Heaven bless you, and reward you as a pious daughter deserves to be rewarded."

"Yes, father–put your mind at peace–go on this expedition with a light heart, and trust in God. For me, you will have, now, no care. In the spring–I must have a little time, father–but, in the spring, I will marry Pathfinder, if that noble hearted hunter shall then desire it."

"Mabel, he loves you, as I loved your mother. I have seen him weep like a child, when speaking of his feelings towards you."

"Yes, I believe it–I've seen enough to satisfy me, that he thinks better of me than I deserve, and, certainly the man is not living for whom I have more respect, than for Pathfinder; not even for you, dear father."

"That is as it should be, child, and the union will be blessed. May I not tell Pathfinder this?"

"I would rather you would not, father. Let it come of itself– come naturally–the man should seek the woman, and not the woman the man–" The smile that illuminated Mabel's hand-some face, was angelic, as even her parent thought, though one better practised in detecting the passing emotions, as they betray themselves in the countenance, might have traced something wild and unnatural in it—"No—no—*we* must let things take their course; but, father, you have my solemn promise."

"That will do—that will do, Mabel; now kiss me—God bless and protect you, girl—you are a good daughter."

Mabel threw herself into her father's arms, it was the first time in her life, and sobbed on his bosom like an infant. The stern old soldier's heart was melted, and the tears of the two mingled. But Serjeant Dunham soon started, as if ashamed of himself, and gently forcing his daughter from him, he bade her good night, and sought his pallet. Mabel went sobbing to the rude corner that had been prepared for her reception, and in a few minutes the hut was undisturbed by any sound, save the heavy breathing of the veteran.

Chapter XX.

"Wandering, I found on my ruinous walk,
By the dial stone aged and green,
One rose of the wilderness left on its stalk
To mark where a garden had been."
           Campbell, "Lines Written on Visiting a
           Scene in Argyleshire," ll. 10–13.

IT was not only broad day-light, when Mabel awoke, but the sun had actually been up some time. Her sleep had been tranquil, for she rested on an approving conscience, and fatigue contributed to render it sweet, and no sound of those who had been so early in motion, had interfered with her rest. Springing to her feet, and rapidly dressing herself, the girl was soon breathing the fragrance of the morning, in the open air. For the first time, she was sensibly struck with the singular beauties, as well as with the profound retirement of her present situation. The day proved to be one of those of the autumnal glory so common to a climate that is more abused than appreciated, and its influence was in every way inspiriting and genial. Mabel was benefitted by this circumstance, for, as she fancied, her heart was heavy on account of the dangers to which a father, whom she now began to love, as women love when confidence is created, was about to be exposed.

But the island seemed absolutely deserted. The previous night the bustle of the arrival, had given the spot an appearance of life that was now entirely gone, and our heroine had turned her eyes nearly around on every object in sight, before she caught a view of a single human being to remove the sense of utter solitude. Then, indeed, she beheld all who were left behind, collected in a group, around a fire which might be said to belong to the camp. The person of her uncle, to whom she was so much accustomed, reassured the girl, and she examined the remainder, with a curiosity natural to her situation. Besides Cap, and the Quarter Master, there were the corporal, the three soldiers, and the woman who was cooking. The huts were silent and empty, and the low, but tower-like summit of the block-house rose above the bushes, by which it was half concealed, in picturesque beauty. The sun was just casting its brightness into the open places of the glade, and the vault, over her head, was impending in the soft sublimity of the blue void. Not a cloud was visible, and she secretly fancied the circumstance might be taken as a harbinger of peace and security.

Perceiving that all the others were occupied with that great concern of human nature, a breakfast, Mabel walked, unobserved, towards an end of the island, where she was completely shut out of view, by the trees and bushes. Here she got a stand on the very verge of the water, by forcing aside the low branches, and stood watching the barely perceptible flow and reflow of the miniature waves that laved the shore; a sort of physical echo to the agitation that prevailed on the lake, fifty miles above her. The glimpses of natural scenery, that offered, were very soft and pleasing, and, our heroine, who had a quick and true eye for all that was lovely in nature, was not slow in selecting the more striking bits of landscape. She gazed through the different vistas formed by the openings between the islands, and thought she had never looked on aught more lovely.

While thus occupied, Mabel was suddenly alarmed by fancying that she caught a glimpse of a human form among the bushes that lined the shore of the island that lay directly before her. The distance across the water was not a hundred yards, and though she might be mistaken, and her fancy was wandering when the form passed before her sight, still she did not think she could be deceived. Aware that her sex would be no protection against a rifle bullet, should an Iroquois get a view of her, the girl instinctively drew back, taking care to conceal her person, as much as possible by the leaves, while she kept her own look rivetted on the opposite shore, vainly waiting for some time, in the expectation of the stranger. She was about to quit her post in the bushes, and hasten to her uncle in order to acquaint him of her suspicions, when she saw the branch of an alder, thrust beyond the bushes, on the other island, and waved towards her significantly, and, as she fancied, in a token of amity. This was a breathless and a trying moment, to one as inexperienced in frontier warfare as our heroine, and yet she felt the great necessity that existed for preserving her recollections, and of acting with steadiness and discretion.

It was one of the peculiarities of the exposure, to which those who dwelt on the frontiers of America were liable, to bring out the moral qualities of the women to a degree, that they must themselves, under other circumstances, have believed they were incapable of manifesting, and Mabel well knew that the borderers loved to dwell, in their legends, on the presence of mind, fortitude and spirit that their wives and sisters had displayed, under circumstances the most trying. Her emulation had been awakened by what she had heard on such subjects, and it at once struck her, that now was the moment for her to show that she was truly Serjeant Dunham's child. The motion of the branch was such as, she believed, indicated amity, and, after a moment's hesitation, she broke off a twig, fastened it to a stick, and thrusting it through an opening, waved it in return, imitating as closely as possible the manner of the other.

This dumb show lasted two or three minutes on both sides, when Mabel perceived that the bushes opposite, were cautiously pushed aside, and a human face appeared at an opening. A glance sufficed to let Mabel see that it was the countenance of a red skin, as well as of a woman. A second and a better look satisfied her, that it was the face of the Dew of June, the wife of Arrowhead. During the time she had travelled in company with this woman, Mabel had been won by the gentleness of manner, the meek simplicity and the mingled awe and affection with which she regarded her husband. Once or twice, in the course of the journey she fancied the Tuscarora had manifested towards herself an unpleasant degree of attention, and on those occasions it had struck her that his wife exhibited sorrow and mortification. As Mabel, however, had more than compensated for any pain she might, in this way, unintentionally have caused her companion, by her own kindness of manner and attentions, the woman had shown much attachment to her, and they had parted, with a deep conviction on the mind of our heroine, that, in the Dew of June, she had lost a friend.

It is useless to attempt to analyze all the ways by which the human heart is led into confidence. Such a feeling, however, had the young Tuscarora woman awakened in the breast of our heroine, and the latter, under the impression that this extraordinary visit was intended for her own good, felt every disposition to have a closer communication. She no longer hesitated about showing herself, clear of the bushes, and, was not sorry to see the Dew of June imitate her confidence, by stepping fearlessly out of her own cover. The two girls, for the Tuscarora, though married, was even younger than Mabel, now openly exchanged signs of friendship, and the latter beckoned to her friend to approach, though she knew not the manner, herself, in which this object could be effected. But, the Dew of June was not slow in letting it be seen that it was in her power, for disappearing a moment, she soon showed herself again in the end of a bark canoe, the bows of which she had drawn to the edge of the bushes, and of which the body still lay in a sort of covered creek. Mabel was about to invite her to cross, when her own name was called aloud, in the stentorian voice of her uncle. Making a hurried gesture for the Tuscarora girl to conceal herself, Mabel sprang from the bushes, and tripped up the glade towards the sound, and perceived that the whole party had just seated themselves at breakfast, Cap having barely put his appetite under sufficient restraint to summon her to join them. That this was the most favorable instant for the interview flashed on the mind of Mabel, and excusing herself on the plea of not being prepared for the meal, she bounded back to the thicket, and soon renewed her communications with the young Indian woman.

Dew of June was quick of comprehension, and with half a dozen noiseless strokes of the paddle, her canoe was concealed in the bushes of Station Island. In another minute, Mabel had her hand, and was leading her through the grove towards her own hut. Fortunately, the latter was so placed, as to be completely hidden from the sight of those at the fire, and they both entered it unseen. Hastily explaining to her guest, in the best manner she could, the necessity of quitting her for a short time, Mabel, first placing the Dew of June in her own room, with a full certainty that she would not quit it until told to do so, went to the fire, and took her seat among the rest, with all the composure it was in her power to command.

"Late come, late served, Mabel," said her uncle, between two mouthfuls of broiled salmon, for though the cookery might be very unsophisticated on that remote frontier, the viands were generally delicious; "late come, late served: it is a good rule, and keeps laggards up to their work."

"I am no laggard, uncle, for I have been stirring near an hour, and exploring our island."

"It's little you'll make o' that, Mistress Mabel," put in Muir, "that's little, by nature. Lundie, or it might be better to style him Major Duncan in this presence–" this was said in consideration of the corporal and the common men, though they were taking their meal a little apart–"it might be better to style him Major Duncan in this presence, has not added an empire to His Majesty's dominions, in getting possession of this island, which is likely to equal that of the celebrated Sancho, in revenues and profits–Sancho of whom, doubtless, Master Cap, you'll often have been reading in your leisure hours, more especially in calms, and moments of inactivity."

"I know the spot you mean, Quarter Master; Sancho's Island–coral rock, of new formation, and as bad a land fall, in a dark night and blowing weather, as a sinner could wish to keep clear of. It's a famous place for cocoa nuts and bitter water, that Sancho's Island!"

"It's no very famous for dinners," returned Muir, repressing the smile that was struggling to his lips, out of respect to Mabel, "nor do I think there'll be much to choose between its revenue, and that of this spot. In my judgment, Master Cap, this is a very unmilitary position, and I look to some calamity's befalling it, sooner or later."

"It is to be hoped not until our turn of duty is over," observed Mabel. "I have no wish to study the French language."

"We might think ourselves happy, did it not prove to be the Iroquois. I have reasoned with Major Duncan on the occupation of this position, but 'a wilfu' man maun ha' his way.' My first object, in accompanying this party, was to endeavour to make myself acceptable and useful to your beautiful niece, Master Cap; and the second was to take such an account of the stores that belong to my particular department, as shall leave no question open to controversy, concerning the manner of expenditure, when they shall have disappeared by means of the enemy."

"Do you look upon matters as so serious?" demanded Cap, actually suspending his mastication of a bit of venison, for he passed alternately, like a modern *élégant*, from fish to flesh and back again, in the interest he took in the answer. "Is the danger pressing?"

"I'll no say just that; and I'll no say, just the contrary. There is always danger in war, and there is more of it, at the advanced posts, than at the main encampment. It ought, therefore, to occasion no surprise were we to be visited by the French, at any moment."

"And what the devil, is to be done, in that case?—Six men and two women would make but a poor job, in defending such a place as this, should the enemy invade us, as no doubt Frenchmen like, they would take very good care, to come strong handed."

"That we may depend on. Some very formidable force, at the very lowest. A military disposition might be made, in defence of the island, out of all question, and according to the art of war, though we would probably fail in the force necessary to carry out the design, in any very creditable manner. In the first place, a detachment should be sent off, to the shore, with orders to annoy the enemy in landing. A strong party ought instantly to be thrown into the block-house, as the citadel, for on that all the different detachments would naturally fall back for support, as the French advanced, and an entrenched camp might be laid out around the strong-hold, as it would be very unmilitary, indeed, to let the foe get near enough to the foot of the walls to mine them. Chevaux de frise*would keep the cavalry in check, and as for the artillery, redoubts should be thrown up, under cover of yon woods. Strong skirmishing parties, moreover, would be exceedingly serviceable in retarding the march of the enemy, and these different huts, if properly picketted and ditched, could be converted into very eligible positions for that object."

"Whe-e-e-w! Quarter Master. And who the d——l, is to find all the men to carry out such a plan?"

"The King, out of all question, Master Cap. It is his quarrel, and it's just he should bear the burthen o' it."

"And we are only six! This is fine talking, with a vengeance. You could be sent down to the shore, to oppose the landing, Mabel might skirmish with her tongue at least, the soldier's wife might act chevaux de frise, to entangle the cavalry, the corporal should command the entrenched camp, his three men could occupy the five huts, and I would take the block-house. Whe-e-e-w, you describe well, Lieutenant, and should have been a limner, instead of a soldier!"

"Na—I've been very literal and upright in my exposition of matters. That there is no greater force here, to carry out the plan, is a fault of His Majesty's ministers, and none of mine."

"But, should an enemy really appear," asked Mabel, with more interest than she might have shown, had she not remembered the guest in the hut; "what course ought we to pursue?"

"My advice would be to attempt to achieve that, Pretty Mabel, which rendered Xenophon so justly celebrated."*

"I think you mean a retreat, though I half guess at your allusion."

"You've imagined my meaning from the possession of a strong native sense, young lady. I am aware that your worthy father has pointed out to the corporal, certain modes and methods by which he fancies this island could be held, in case the French should discover its position; but the excellent serjeant, though your father, and as good a man in his duties as ever wielded a 'spontoon,* is not the great Lord Stair,* or even the Duke of Marlborough.* I'll no deny the serjeant's merits, in his particular sphere, though I cannot exaggerate qualities, however excellent, into those of men who may be in some trifling degree his superiors. Serjeant Dunham has taken counsel of his heart, instead of his head, in resolving to issue such orders; but, if the post fall, the blame will lie on him that ordered it to be occupied, and not on him whose duty it was to defend it. Whatever may be the determination of the latter, should the French and their allies land, a good commander never neglects the precautions necessary to effect a retreat, and I would advise Master Cap, who is the admiral of our navy, to have a boat in readiness to evacuate the island, if need comes to need. The largest boat that we have left, carries a very ample sail, and by hauling it round, here, and mooring it under those bushes, there will be a convenient place for a hurried embarkation, and then you'll perceive, Pretty Mabel, that it is scarce fifty yards before we shall be in a channel between two other islands, and hid from the sight of those who may happen to be on this."

"All that you say, is very true, Mr. Muir; but may not the French come from that quarter themselves? If it is so good for a retreat, it is equally good for an advance."

"They'll no have the sense to do so discreet a thing," returned Muir, looking furtively and a little uneasily, around him, "they'll no have sufficient discretion. Your French are a head-over-heels nation, and usually come forward in a random way; so, we may look for them, if they come at all, on the other side of the island—"

The discourse now became exceedingly desultory, touching principally, however, on the probabilities of an invasion, and the best means of meeting it.

To most of this, Mabel paid but little attention, though she felt some surprise that Lt. Muir, an officer whose character for courage stood well, should openly recommend an abandonment of what appeared to her to be doubly a duty, her father's character being connected with the defence of the island. Her mind, however, was so much occupied with her guest, that seizing the first favorable moment she left the table, and was soon in her own hut again. Carefully fastening the door, and seeing that the simple curtain was drawn before the single little window, Mabel next led the Dew of June, or June, as she was familiarly termed by those who spoke to her in English, into the outer room, making signs of affection and confidence.

"I am glad to see you, June," said Mabel, with one of her sweetest smiles, and in her own winning voice, "very glad to see you—but what has brought you, hither, and how did you discover the island?"

"Talk slow," said June, returning smile for smile, and pressing the little hand she held, with one of her own that was scarcely larger, though it had been hardened by labor—"more slow—too quick."

Mabel repeated her questions, endeavoring to repress the impetuosity of her feelings, and she succeeded in speaking so distinctly as to be understood.

"June friend—" returned the Indian woman.

"I believe you, June; from my soul, I believe you. What has this to do with your visit?"

"Friend come to see friend," answered June, again smiling openly in the other's face.

"There is some other reason, June; else would you never run this risk, and alone. You are alone, June?"

"June wid you—no one else. June come alone—paddle canoe."

"I hope so—I think so—nay, I *know* so. You would not be treacherous with me, June?"

"What treacherous?"

"You would not betray me—would not give me to the French—to the Iroquois—to Arrowhead—" June shook her head earnestly, "—you would not sell my scalp."

Here, June passed her arm fondly around the slender waist of Mabel, and pressed her to her heart, with a tenderness and affection, that brought tears into the eyes of our heroine. It was done, in the fond caressing manner of a woman, and it was scarcely possible that it should not obtain credit for sincerity, with a young and ingenuous person of the same sex. Mabel returned the pressure, and then held the other off, at the length of her arm, looked her steadily in the face, and continued her inquiries.

"If June has something to tell her friend, let her speak plainly," she said. "My ears are open."

"June 'fraid Arrowhead kill her."

"But Arrowhead will never know it—" Mabel's blood mounted to her temples, as she said this; for she felt that she was urging a wife to be treacherous to her husband—"That is, Mabel will not tell him."

"He bury tomahawk in June's head."

"That must never be, dear June; I would rather you should say no more, than run this risk."

"Block house good place to sleep—good place to stay."

"Do you mean that I may save my life by keeping in the block-house, June? Surely, surely, Arrowhead will not hurt you for telling me that—He cannot wish me any great harm, for I never injured him."

"Arrowhead wish no harm to handsome Pale face," returned June, averting her face, and, though she always spoke in the soft, gentle, voice of an Indian girl, permitting its notes to fall so low, as to cause them to sound melancholy and timid—"Arrowhead love pale face girls."

Mabel blushed, she knew not why, and for a moment, her questions were repressed by a feeling of inherent delicacy. But it was necessary to know more, for her apprehensions had been keenly awakened, and she resumed her inquiries.

"Arrowhead can have no reason to love, or to hate *me*," she said. "Is he near you?"

"Husband always near wife, here," said June, laying her hand on her heart.

"Excellent creature!—But, tell me, June, ought I to keep in the block-house to-day—this morning—now?"

"Block-house very good—good for squaw. Block-house got no scalp."

"I fear I understand you only too well, June—Do you wish to see my father?"

"No here; gone away."

"You cannot know that, June; you see the island is full of his soldiers."

"No full; gone away—" here June held up four of her fingers—"so many red coat."

"And Pathfinder; would you not like to see the Pathfinder?—he can talk to you in the Iroquois tongue."

"Tongue gone wid him—" said June laughing—"keep tongue in his mout'."

There was something so sweet and contagious in the infantile laugh of an Indian girl, that Mabel could not refrain from joining in it, much as her fears were aroused by all that had passed.

"You appear to know, or to think you know all about us, June. But, if Pathfinder be gone, Eau-douce can speak French, too. You know Eau douce; shall I run and bring *him* to talk with you?"

"Eau douce gone, too, all but heart; that there." As June said this, she laughed again, looked in different directions, as if unwilling to confuse the other, and laid her hand on Mabel's bosom.

Our heroine had often heard of the wonderful sagacity of the Indians, and of the surprising manner in which they noted all things, while they appeared to regard none, but she was scarce prepared for the direction the discourse had so singularly taken. Willing to change it, and, at the same time, truly anxious to learn how great the danger that impended over them might really be, she rose from the camp-stool, on which she had been seated, and, by assuming an attitude of less affectionate confidence, she hoped to hear more of that she really desired to learn, and to avoid allusions to that which she found so embarrassing.

"You know how much, or how little you ought to tell me, June," she said, "and I hope you love me well enough to give me the information I ought to hear. My dear uncle, too, is on the island, and you are, or ought to be, his friend, as well as mine, and both of us will remember your conduct, when we get back to Oswego."

"Maybe never get back; who know?" This was said doubtingly, or as one lays down an uncertain proposition, and not with a taunt, or a desire to alarm.

"No one knows what will happen, but God. Our lives are in his hands. Still, I think, you are to be his instrument in saving us."

This passed June's comprehension, and she only looked her ignorance, for it was evident she wished to be of use.

"Block-house very good," she repeated as soon as her countenance ceased to express uncertainty, laying strong emphasis on the two last words.

"Well, I understand this, June, and will sleep in it to-night. Of course, I am to tell my uncle, what you have said."

The Dew of June started, and she discovered a very manifest uneasiness, at the interrogatory.

"No–no–no–no–" she answered with a volubility and vehemence that was imitated from the French of the Canadas–"no good to tell Salt-water. He much talk, and long tongue. Think woods all water; understand not'ing. Tell Arrowhead, and June die."

"You do my dear uncle injustice, for he would be as little likely to betray you, as any one."

"No understand. Salt-water got tongue, but no eye, no ear, no nose–not'ing but tongue, tongue, tongue."

Although Mabel did not exactly coincide in this opinion, she saw that Cap had not the confidence of the young Indian woman, and that it was idle to expect she would consent to his being admitted to their interview.

"You appear to think you know our situation pretty well, June," Mabel continued, "have you been on the island before this visit?"

"Just come."

"How then do you know that what you say is true; my father, the Pathfinder and Eau douce may all be here within sound of my voice, if I choose to call them."

"All gone," said June positively, smiling good-humouredly at the same time.

"Nay, this is more than you *can* say certainly, not having been over the island to examine it."

"Got good eyes; see boat with men go away—see ship with Eau douce."

"Then you have been some time watching us—I think, however, you have not counted them that remain."

June laughed, held up her four fingers again, and then pointed to her two thumbs—passing a finger over the first, she repeated the words "red-coat," and touching the last, she added—"Salt-water," "Quarter Master." All this was being very accurate, and Mabel began to entertain serious doubts of the propriety of her permitting her visiter to depart without her becoming more explicit. Still it was so repugnant to her feelings to abuse the confidence this gentle and affectionate creature had evidently reposed in her, that Mabel had no sooner admitted the thought of summoning her uncle, than she rejected it, as unworthy of herself, and unjust to her friend. To aid this good resolution, too, there was the certainty that June would reveal nothing, but take refuge in a stubborn silence, if any attempt was made to coerce her.

"You think, then, June," Mabel continued, as soon as these thoughts had passed through her mind, "that I had better live in the block-house?"

"Good place for squaw. Block-house got no scalp. Logs t'ick."

"You speak confidently, June, as if you had been in it, and had measured its walls."

June laughed, and she looked knowing, though she said nothing.

"Does any one but yourself know how to find this island—have any of the Iroquois seen it?"

June looked sad, and she cast her eyes warily about her, as if distrusting a listener.

"Tuscarora everywhere—Oswego, here, Frontenac, Mohawk—everywhere. If he see June, kill her."

"But we thought that no one knew of this island, and that we had no reason to fear our enemies while on it."

"Much eye, Iroquois."

"Eyes will not always do, June—This spot is hid from ordinary sight, and few of even our own people know how to find it."

"One man can tell—Some Yengeese talk French."

Mabel felt a chill at her heart. All the suspicions against Jasper, which she had hitherto disdained entertaining crowded in a body on her thoughts, and the sensation that they brought was so sickening, that for an instant, she imagined she was about to faint. Arousing herself, and remembering her promise to her father, she arose and walked up and down the hut, for a minute, fancying that Jasper's delinquencies were naught to her, though her inmost heart yearned with the desire to think him innocent.

"I understand your meaning, June," she then said—"You wish me to know that some one has treacherously told your people where and how to find the island."

June laughed, for in her eyes artifice in war, was oftener a merit than a crime, but she was too true to her tribe, herself, to say more than the occasion required. Her object was to save Mabel, and Mabel only, and she saw no sufficient reason for "travelling out of the record," as the lawyers express it, in order to do any thing else.

"Pale face know now—" she added—"Block-house good for girls—no matter for men and warriors."

"But it is much matter with me, June, for one of these men is my uncle, whom I love, and the others are my countrymen and friends. I must tell them what has passed."

"Then June be kill—" returned the young Indian quietly, though she spoke with concern.

"No—they shall not know that you have been here. Still, they must be on their guard, and we can all go into the block-house."

"Arrowhead know—see every thing, and June be kill. June come to tell young pale face friend, not to tell men. Every warrior watch his own scalp. June squaw, and tell squaw; no tell men."

Mabel was greatly distressed at this declaration of her wild friend, for it was now evident the young creature understood that her communication was to go no farther. She was ignorant how far these people considered the point of honor interested in her keeping the secret, and most of all, was she unable to say how far any indiscretion of her own might actually commit June, and endanger her life. All these considerations flashed on her mind, and reflection only rendered their influence more painful. June, too, manifestly viewed the matter gravely, for she began to gather up the different little articles she had dropped, in taking Mabel's hand, and was preparing to depart. To attempt detaining her, was out of the question, and to part from her, after all she had hazarded to serve her, was repugnant to all the just and kind feelings of our heroine's nature.

"June," she said eagerly, folding her arms around the gentle but uneducated being, "we are friends. From me you have nothing to fear, for no one shall know of your visit. If you could give me some signal just before the danger comes, some sign by which to know when to go into the block-house—how to take care of myself."

June paused, for she had been in earnest in her intention to depart, and then she said quietly—

"Bring June pigeon."

"A pigeon! Where shall I find a pigeon to bring you?"

"Next hut—bring old one—June go to canoe."

"I think I understand you, June—but had I not better lead you back to the bushes, lest you meet some of the men?"

"Go out first—count men—one—two—tree—four—five—six"—here June held up her fingers and laughed—"All out of way, good—all but one, call him one side. Then sing, and fetch pigeon."

Mabel smiled at the readiness and ingenuity of the girl, and prepared to execute her requests. At the door, however, she stopped, and looked back entreatingly at the Indian woman.

"Is there no hope of your telling me more, June?" she said.

"Know all now—Block-house good—pigeon tell—Arrowhead kill."

The last words sufficed, for Mabel could not urge further communications when her companion herself told her, that the penalty of her revelations might be death by the hand of her husband. Throwing open the door, she made a sign of adieu to June, and went out of the hut. Mabel resorted to the simple expedient of the young Indian girl, to ascertain the situation of the different individuals on the island. Instead of looking about her, with the intention of recognizing faces and dresses, she merely counted them, and found that three still remained at the fire, while two had gone to the boat, one of whom was Mr. Muir. The sixth man was her uncle, and he was coolly arranging some fishing tackle, at no great distance from the fire. The woman was just entering her own hut, and this accounted for the whole party. Mabel now, affecting to have dropped something, returned nearly to the hut she had left, warbling an air, stooped as if to pick up some object from the ground, and hurried towards the hut June had mentioned. This was a dilapidated structure, and it had been converted by the soldiers of the last detachment, into a sort of store house for their live stock. Among other things, it contained a few dozen pigeons, which were regaling on a pile of wheat, that had been brought off from one of the farms plundered on the Canada shore. Mabel had not much difficulty in catching one of these pigeons, although they fluttered and flew about the hut, with a noise like that of drums, and concealing it in her dress, she stole back towards her own hut with the prize. It was empty; and without doing more than cast a glance in at the door, the eager girl hurried down to the shore. She had no difficulty in escaping observation, for the trees and bushes made a complete cover to her person. At the canoe, she found June, who took the pigeon, placed it in a basket of her own manufacturing, and repeating the words "Block-house good," she glided out of the bushes and across the narrow passage, as noiselessly as she had come. Mabel waited some time to catch a signal of leave taking or amity, after her friend had landed, but none was given. The adjacent islands, without exception, were as quiet as if no one had ever disturbed the sublime repose of nature, and nowhere could any sign or symptom be discovered, as Mabel then thought, that might denote the proximity of the sort of danger of which June had given notice.

On returning, however, from the shore, Mabel was struck with a little circumstance, that, in an ordinary situation, would have attracted no attention, but which, now that her suspicions had been aroused, did not pass before her uneasy eye, unnoticed. A small piece of red bunting, such as is used in the ensigns of ships, was fluttering at the lower branch of a small tree, fastened in a way to permit it to blow out, or to droop like a vessel's pennant.

Now that Mabel's fears were awakened, June herself could not have manifested greater quickness in analyzing facts that she believed might affect the safety of the party. She saw at a glance, that this bit of cloth could be observed from an adjacent island, that it lay so near the line between her own hut and the canoe, as to leave no doubt that June had passed near it, if not directly under it, and that it might be a signal to communicate some important fact connected with the mode of attack, to those who were probably lying in ambush near them. Tearing the little strip of bunting from the tree, Mabel hastened on, scarce knowing what duty next required. June might be false to her; but her manner, her looks, her affection, and her disposition as Mabel had known it in the journey, forbade the idea. Then came the allusion to Arrowhead's admiration of the Pale face beauties, some dim recollections of the looks of the Tuscarora, and a painful consciousness that few wives could view with kindness one who had estranged a husband's affections. None of these images were distinct and clear, but they rather gleamed over the mind of our heroine than rested in it, and they quickened her pulses, as they did her step, without bringing with them the prompt and clear decisions that usually followed her reflections. She had hurried onwards towards the hut occupied by the soldier's wife, intending to remove at once to the block-house, with the woman, though she could persuade no other to follow, when her impatient walk was interrupted by the voice of Muir.

"Whither so fast, Pretty Mabel," he cried, "and why so given to solitude?–The worthy serjeant will deride my breeding, if he hear that his daughter passes the mornings alone and unattended to, though he well knows that it is my ardent wish to be her slave and companion, from the beginning of the year to its end."

"Surely, Mr. Muir, you must have some authority here," Mabel suddenly arrested her steps to say. "One of your rank would be listened to, at least, by a corporal!"

"I do'n't know that—I do'n't know that—" interrupted Muir, with an impatience and appearance of alarm that might have excited Mabel's attention at another moment. "Command is command, discipline, discipline, and authority, authority. Your good father would be sore grieved did he find me interfering to sully, or carry off the laurels he is about to win, and I cannot command the corporal, without equally commanding the serjeant. The wisest way will be for me to remain in the obscurity of a private individual in this enterprize, and it is so that all parties, from Lundie down, understand the transaction."

"This I know, and it may be well; nor would I give my dear father any cause of complaint, but you may influence the corporal to his own good."

"I'll no say that," returned Muir, in his sly Scotch way;—"it would be far safer to promise to influence him to his injury—Mankind, pretty Mabel, have their peculiarities, and to influence a fellow being to his own good, is one of the most difficult tasks of human nature, while the opposite is just the easiest. You'll no forget this, my dear, but bear it in mind for your edification and government—but, what is that you're twisting round your slender finger, as you may be said to twist hearts?"

"It is nothing but a bit of cloth—a sort of flag—a trifle that is hardly worth our attention at this grave moment—If—"

"A trifle! it's no so trifling as ye may imagine, Mistress Mabel," taking the bit of bunting from her, and stretching it at full length with both his arms extended, while his face grew grave, and his eye watchful. "Ye'll no ha' been finding this, Mabel Dunham, in the breakfast?"

Mabel simply acquainted him with the spot where, and the manner in which she had found the bit of cloth. While she was speaking, the eye of the Quarter Master was not quiet for a moment, glancing from the rag to the face of our heroine, then back again to the rag. That his suspicions were awakened was easy to be seen, nor was he long in letting it be known what direction they had taken.

"We are not in a part of the world, where our ensigns and

gauds ought to be spread abroad to the winds, Mabel Dunham!" he said, with an ominous shake of his head.

"I thought as much myself, Mr. Muir, and brought away the little flag, lest it might be the means of betraying our presence here, to the enemy, even though nothing is intended by its display. Ought not my uncle to be made acquainted with the circumstance?"

"I no see the necessity for that, pretty Mabel, for as you justly say it is a circumstance, and circumstances sometimes worry the worthy mariner. But this flag, if flag it can be called, belongs to a seaman's craft. You may perceive that it is made of what is called bunting, and that is a description of cloth used only by vessels for such purposes, *our* colours being of silk, as you may understand, or painted canvass. It's surprisingly like the fly of the Scud's ensign! And now I recollect me, to have observed that a piece had been cut from that very flag!"

Mabel felt her heart sink, but she had sufficient self command not to attempt an answer.

"It must be looked to," Muir continued, "and, after all, I think it may be well to hold a short consultation with Master Cap, than whom a more loyal subject does not exist in the British Empire."

"I have thought the warning so serious," Mabel rejoined, "that I am about to remove to the block-house, and to take the woman with me."

"I do not see the prudence of that, Mabel. The block-house will be the first spot assailed, should there really be an attack, and it's no well provided for a siege, that must be allowed. If I might advise in so delicate a contingency, I would recommend your taking refuge in the boat, which, as you may now perceive, is most favorably placed to retreat by that channel opposite, where all in it would be hid by the islands, in one or two minutes. Water leaves no trail, as Pathfinder well expresses it, and there appear to be so many different passages, in that quarter, that escape would be more than probable. I've always been of opinion that Lundie hazarded too much, in occupying a post as far advanced, and as much exposed as this."

"It's too late to regret it now, Mr. Muir, and we have only to consult our own security."

"And the King's honor, pretty Mabel. Yes, His Majesty's

arms, and his glorious name, are not to be overlooked on any occasion."

"Then I think it might be better, if we all turned our eyes towards the place that has been built to maintain them, instead of the boat," said Mabel, smiling, "and so, Mr. Muir, I am for the block-house, with a disposition to await there the return of my father, and his party. He would be sadly grieved, at finding we had fled, when he got back, successful himself, and filled with the confidence of our having been as faithful to our duties, as he has been to his own."

"Nay, nay, for Heaven's sake, do not misunderstand me, Mabel," Muir interrupted with some alarm of manner, "I am far from intimating that any but you females ought to take refuge in the boat. The duty of us men is sufficiently plain no doubt, and my resolution has been formed from the first, to stand or fall by the block-house."

"And did you imagine, Mr. Muir, that two females could row that heavy boat, in a way to escape the bark canoe of an Indian?"

"Ah! my pretty Mabel, love is seldom logical, and its fears and misgivings are apt to warp the faculties. I only saw your sweet person in possession of the means of safety, and overlooked the want of ability to use them. But you'll no be so cruel, lovely creature, as to impute to me as a fault, my intense anxiety on your own account!"

Mabel had heard enough. Her mind was too much occupied with what had passed that morning, and with her fears, to wish to linger further to listen to love speeches, that, in her most joyous and buoyant moments, she would have found unpleasant. She took a hasty leave of her companion, and was about to trip away towards the hut of the other woman, when Muir arrested the movement, by laying a hand on her arm.

"One word, Mabel," he said, "before you leave me. This little flag may, or it may not have a particular meaning; if it has, now that we are aware of its being shown, may it not be better to put it back again, while we watch vigilantly for some answer, that may betray the conspiracy; and if it mean nothing, why nothing will follow."

"This may be all right, Mr. Muir, though if the whole is accidental, the flag might be the occasion of the post's being discovered."

Mabel stayed to utter no more, but she was soon out of sight, running into the hut towards which she had been first proceeding. The Quarter Master remained on the very spot, and in the precise attitude, in which she had left him, for quite a minute, first looking at the bounding figure of the girl, and then at the bit of bunting, which he still held before him, in a way to denote indecision. His irresolution lasted but for this minute, however, for he was soon beneath the tree, where he fastened the mimic flag to a branch, again, though, from his ignorance of the precise spot from whence it had been taken by Mabel, he left it fluttering from a part of the oak, where it was still more exposed than before, to the eyes of any passengers on the river, though less in view from the island itself.

Chapter XXI.

"Each one has had his supping mess,
The cheese is put into the press,
The pans and bowls clean scalded all,
Reared up against the milk house wall."
Cotton, "Evening Quatrains," ll. 33–36.

I<small>T</small> seemed strange to Mabel Dunham, as she passed along, on her way to find her female companion, that others should be so composed, while she herself felt as if the responsibilities of life and death rested on her shoulders. It is true, that distrust of June's motives, mingled with her forebodings, but when she came to recall the affectionate and natural manner of the young Indian girl, and all the evidences of good faith and sincerity that she had seen in her conduct, during the familiar intercourse of their journey, she rejected the idea, with the willingness of a generous disposition, to believe the best of others. She saw, however, that she could not put her companions properly on their guard, without letting them into the secret of her conference with June, and she found herself, compelled to act cautiously and with a forethought to which she was unaccustomed, more especially in a matter of so much moment.

The soldier's wife was told to transport the necessaries into the block-house, and admonished not to be far from it, at any time, during the day. Mabel did not explain her reasons. She merely stated that she had detected some signs, in walking about the island, that induced her to apprehend that the enemy had more knowledge of its position, than had been previously believed, and that they two, at least, would do well to be in readiness to seek a refuge at the shortest notice. It was not difficult to arouse the apprehension of this person, who, though a stout-hearted Scotch woman, was ready enough to listen to any thing that confirmed her dread of Indian cruelties. As soon as Mabel believed that her companion was sufficiently frightened to render her wary, she threw out some hints touching the inexpediency of letting the soldiers know the extent of their own fears. This was done, with a view to prevent discussions and inquiries that might embarrass our heroine, she determining to render her uncle, the corporal and his men more cautious by adopting a different course. Unfortunately, the British army could not have furnished a worse person, for the particular duty that he was now required to discharge, than Corporal McNab, the individual who had been left in command, during the absence of Serjeant Dunham. On the one hand he was resolute, prompt, familiar with all the details of a soldier's life, and used to war; on the other, he was supercilious as regards the provincials, opinionated on every subject connected with the narrow limits of his professional practice, and much disposed to fancy the British empire the centre of all that is excellent in the world, and Scotland the focus of at least all moral excellence in that empire. In short, he was an epitome, though on a scale suited to his rank, of those very qualities, which were so peculiar to the servants of the crown, that were sent into the colonies, as these servants estimated themselves in comparison with the natives of the country, or, in other words he considered the American as an animal inferior to the parent stock, and viewed all his notions of military service in particular as undigested and absurd. Braddock, himself, was not less disposed to take advice from a provincial, than his humble imitator, and he had been known, on more than one occasion, to demur to the directions and orders of two or three commissioned officers of the corps, who happened to be born in America, simply for that reason; taking care, at the same time, with true Scotch wariness, to protect himself from the pains and penalties of positive disobedience. A more impracticable subject, therefore, could not well have offered for the purposes of Mabel, and yet she felt obliged to lose no time in putting her plan in execution.

"My father has left you a responsible command, corporal," she said, as soon as she could catch McNab, a little apart from the rest of the soldiers, "for should the island fall into the hands of the enemy, not only would we be captured, but the party that is now out, would in all probability, become their prisoners also."

"It needs no journey from Scotland to this place, to learn the facts needful to be o' that way of thinking," returned McNab, drily.

"I do not doubt your understanding it, as well as myself, Mr. McNab, but I'm fearful that you veterans, accustomed as you are to dangers and battles, are a little apt to overlook some of the precautions that may be necessary in a situation, as peculiar as ours."

"They say Scotland is no conquered country, young woman, but I'm thinking there must be some mistak' in the matter, as we her children, are so drowsy headed and apt to be o'ertaken when we least expect it."

"Nay, my good friend, you mistake my meaning. In the first place, I'm not thinking of Scotland at all, but of this island; and then I am far from doubting your vigilance when you think it necessary to practise it, but my great fear is that there may be danger to which your courage will make you indifferent."

"My courage, Mistress Dunham, is doubtless of a very poor quality, being nothing but Scottish courage; your father's is yankee, and were he here amang us, we should see different preparations beyond a doubt. Well, times are getting wrang, when foreigners hold commissions and carry halberds in Scottish corps; and I no wonder that battles are lost, and campaigns go wrang end foremost."

Mabel was almost in despair, but the quiet warning of June was still too vividly impressed on her mind, to allow her to yield the matter. She changed her mode of operating, therefore, still clinging to the hope of getting the whole party within the block-house, without being compelled to betray the source whence she obtained her notices of the necessity of vigilance.

"I dare say you are right, Corporal McNab," she resumed, "for I've often heard of the heroes of your country, who have been among the first of the civilized world, if what they tell me of them is true."

"Have you read the history of Scotland, Mistress Dunham?" demanded the corporal, looking up at his pretty companion, for the first time, with something like a smile, on his hard, repulsive countenance.

"I have read a little of it, corporal, but I've heard much more. The lady who brought me up had Scottish blood in her veins, and was fond of the subject."

"I'll warrant ye, the serjeant no troubled himself to expatiate on the renown of the country, where his regiment was raised?"

"My father has other things to think of, and the little I know, was got from the lady I have mentioned."

"She'll no be forgetting to tall ye o' Wallace?"

"Of him, I've even read a good deal."

"And o' Bruce—and the affair o' Bannockburn?"

"Of that too, as well as of Culloden Muir."

The last of these battles was then a recent event, it having actually been fought within the recollection of our heroine, whose notions of it, however, were so confused that she scarcely appreciated the effect her allusion might produce on her companion. She knew it had been a victory, and had often heard the guests of her patroness mention it with triumph; and she fancied their feelings would find a sympathetic chord in those of every British soldier. Unfortunately, McNab had fought throughout that luckless day, on the side of the Pretender, and a deep scar that garnished his face, had been left there, by the sabre of a German soldier, in the service of the House of Hanover. He fancied that his wound bled afresh, at Mabel's allusion, and it is certain that the blood rushed to his face in a torrent, as if it would pour out of his skin, at the cicatrix.

"Hoot! Hoot awa'!" he fairly shouted, "with your Cullodens and Sherrif Muirs, young woman, ye'll no be understanding the subject, at all, and will manifast not only wisdom, but modesty, in speaking o' your ain country and its many failings. King George has some loyal subjects in the colonies, na doubt, but 't will be a lang time bafore he sees or knows any guid of them."

Mabel was surprised at the corporal's heat, for she had not the smallest idea where the shoe pinched, but she was determined not to give up the point.

"I've always heard that the Scotch had two of the great qualities of soldiers," she said, "courage and circumspection, and I feel persuaded that Corporal McNab will sustain the national renown."

"Ask yer own father, Mistress Dunham; he is acquaint' with Corporal McNab, and will no be backward to point out his demerits. We have been in battle th'gither, and he is my superior officer, and has a sort o' official right to give the characters of his subordinates."

"My father thinks well of you, McNab, or he would not have left you in charge of this island, and all it contains, his own daughter included. Among other things I well know that he calculates largely on your prudence. He expects the block-house, in particular, to be strictly attended to."

"If he wishes to defend the honor of the 55th, behind logs, he ought to have remained in command himsal', for to speak frankly, it goes against a Scotsman's bluid and opinions, to be beaten out of the field, even before he is attacked. We are broad-sword men, and love to stand foot to foot with the foe. This American mode of fighting, that is getting into so much favor, will destroy the reputation of His Majesty's army, if it no destroy its spirit."

"No true soldier despises caution; even Major Duncan himself, than whom there is none braver, is celebrated for his care of his men."

"Lundie ha' his weaknesses, and is fast forgetting the broad-sword and open heaths, in his tree and rifle practice; but, Mistress Mabel, tak' the word of an old soldier, who has seen his fifty-fifth year, when he talls ye, that there is no surer method to encourage your enemy, than to seem to fear him, and, that there is no danger in this Indian warfare, that the fancies and imaginations of your Americans have not augmented and enlarged upon, until they see a savage in every bush. We Scots come from a naked region, and have no need, and less relish for covers, and so, ye'll be seeing, Mistress Dunham—"

The corporal gave a spring into the air, fell forward on his face, and rolled over on his back; the whole passing so suddenly that Mabel had scarcely heard the sharp crack of the rifle, that sent a bullet through his body. Our heroine did not shriek; did not even tremble; for the occurrence was too sudden, too awful, and too unexpected for that exhibition of weakness. On the contrary, she stepped hastily forward, with a natural impulse to aid her companion. There was just enough of life left in McNab, to betray his entire consciousness of all that had passed. His countenance had the wild look of one who had been over-taken by death, by surprise, and Mabel, in her calmer moments, fancied that it showed the tardy repentance of a wilful and obstinate sinner.

"Ye'll be getting into the block-house, as fast as possible," McNab whispered, as Mabel leaned over him to catch his dying words.

Then came over our heroine, the full consciousness of her situation, and of the necessity of exertion. She cast a rapid glance at the body at her feet, saw that it had ceased to breathe, and fled. It was but a few minutes' run to the block-house, the door of which Mabel had barely gained, when it was closed violently in her face, by Jennie, the soldier's wife, who, in blind terror, thought only of her own safety. The reports of five or six rifles were heard, while Mabel was calling out for admittance, and the additional terror they produced, prevented the woman within from undoing quickly the very fastenings she had been so expert, in applying. After a minute's delay, however, Mabel found the door reluctantly yielding to her constant pressure, and she forced her slender body through the opening, the instant it was large enough to allow of its passage. By this time, Mabel's heart ceased to beat tumultuously, and she gained sufficient self-command to act collectedly. Instead of yielding to the almost convulsive efforts of her companion, to close the door, again, she held it open long enough to ascertain that none of her own party was in sight, or likely, on the instant, to endeavor to gain admission; then she allowed the opening to be shut. Her orders and proceedings, now, became more calm and rational. But a single bar was crossed, and Jennie was directed to stand in readiness to remove even that, at an application from a friend. She then ascended the first ladder to the room above, where by means of loop-holes, she was enabled to get as good a view of the island as the surrounding bushes would allow. Admonishing her associate below to be firm and steady, she made as careful an examination of the environs as her situation permitted.

To her great surprise, Mabel could not, at first, see a living soul on the island, friend or enemy. Neither Frenchman, nor Indian was visible, though a small straggling white cloud that was floating before the wind, told her in which quarter, she ought to look for them. The rifles had been discharged from the direction of the island whence June had come, though whether the enemy were on that island, or had actually landed on her own, Mabel could not say. Going to the loop that commanded a view of the spot, where McNab lay, her blood curdled at perceiving all three of his soldiers lying apparently lifeless at his side. These men had rushed to a common centre, at the first alarm, and had been shot down almost simultaneously, by the invisible foe, whom the corporal had affected to despise.

Neither Cap, nor Lieutenant Muir was to be seen. With a beating heart, Mabel examined every opening through the trees, and ascended even to the upper story, or garret of the block-house, where she got a full view of the whole island, so far as its covers would allow; but with no better success. She had expected to see the body of her uncle, lying on the grass, like those of the soldiers, but it was nowhere visible. Turning towards the spot where the boat lay, Mabel saw that it was still fastened to the shore, and then she supposed that, by some accident Muir had been prevented from effecting his retreat, in that quarter. In short, the island lay in the quiet of the grave, the bodies of the soldiers rendering the scene as fearful as it was extraordinary.

"For God's holy sake, Mistress Mabel," called out the woman from below, for, though her fear had got to be too ungovernable to allow her to keep silence, our heroine's superior refinement, more than the regimental station of her father, still controlled her mode of address, "For His Holy Sake! Mistress Mabel, tell me if any of our friends are living? I think I hear groans that grow fainter and fainter, and fear that they will all be tomahawked."

Mabel now remembered that one of the soldiers was this woman's husband, and she trembled at what might be the immediate effect of her sorrow, should his death become suddenly known to her. The groans, too, gave a little hope, though she feared they might come from her uncle, who lay out of view.

"We are in his holy keeping, Jennie," she answered. "We must trust in Providence, while we neglect none of its benevolent means of protecting ourselves. Be careful with the door; on no account open it, without my directions."

"Oh! Tell me, Mistress Mabel, if you can anywhere see Sandy?—If I could only lat him know that I'm in safety, the guid man would be easier in his mind, whather free or a prisoner!"

Sandy was Jennie's husband, and he lay dead in plain view of the loop, from which our heroine was then looking.

"You no tall me if you're seeing of Sandy," the woman repeated from below, impatient at Mabel's silence.

"There are some of our people gathered about the body of McNab," was the answer, for it seemed sacrilegious in her eyes to tell a direct untruth, under the awful circumstances in which she was placed.

"Is Sandy amang them?" demanded the woman, in a voice that sounded appalling by its hoarseness and energy.

"He may be certainly—for I see, one, two, three, four, and all in the scarlet coats of the regiment."

"Sandy!" called out the woman frantically—"Why d'ye no care for yoursal', Sandy? Come hither the instant, man, and share your wife's fortunes, in weal or woe. It's no a moment for your silly discipline, and vainglorious notions of honor! Sandy!—Sandy!"

Mabel heard the bar turn, and then the door creaked on its hinges. Expectation, not to say terror, held her in suspense at the loop, and she soon beheld Jennie rushing through the bushes, in the direction of the cluster of the dead. It took the woman but an instant to reach the fatal spot. So sudden and unexpected had been the blow, that she, in her terror, did not appear to comprehend its weight. Some wild and half frantic notion of a deception troubled her fancy, and she imagined that the men were trifling with her fears. She took her husband's hand, and it was still warm, while she thought a covert smile was struggling on his lip.

"Why will ye fool life away, Sandy?" she cried, pulling at the arm. "Ye'll all be murdered by these accursed Indians, and you no takin' to the block like trusty soldiers! Awa'!—awa', and no be losing the precious moments."

In her desperate efforts, the woman pulled the body of her husband in a way to cause the head to turn completely over, when the small hole in the temple, caused by the entrance of a rifle bullet, and a few drops of blood trickling over the skin, revealed the meaning of her husband's silence. As the horrid truth flashed, in its full extent, on her mind, the woman clasped her hands, gave a shriek that pierced the glades of every island near, and fell at length on the dead body of the soldier. Thrilling, heart-reaching, appalling as was that shriek, it was melody to the cry that followed it so quickly as to blend the sounds. The terrific war-whoop arose out of the covers of the island, and some twenty savages, horrible in their paint, and the other devices of Indian ingenuity, rushed forward, eager to secure the covetted scalps. Arrowhead was foremost, and it was his tomahawk that brained the insensible Jennie, and her reeking hair was hanging at his girdle, as a trophy, in less than two minutes after she had quitted the block-house. His companions were equally active, and McNab and his soldiers, no longer presented the quiet aspects of men who slumbered. They were left in their gore, unequivocally butchered corpses.

All this passed in much less time, than has been required to relate it, and all this did Mabel witness. She had stood riveted to the spot, gazing on the whole horrible scene, as if enchained by some charm, nor did the idea of self, or of her own danger, once obtrude itself on her thoughts. But, no sooner did she perceive the place where the men had fallen, covered with savages, exulting in the success of their surprise, than it occurred to her, that Jennie had left the block-house door unbarred. Her heart beat violently, for that defence alone stood between her and immediate death, and she sprang towards the ladder, with the intention of descending to make sure of it. Her foot had not yet reached the floor of the second story, however, when she heard the door grating on its hinges, and she gave herself up for lost. Sinking on her knees, the terrified but courageous girl endeavored to prepare herself for death, and to raise her thoughts to God. The instinct of life, however, was too strong for prayer, and while her lips moved, the jealous senses watched every sound beneath. When her ears heard the bars, which went on pivots secured to the centre of the door, turning into their fastenings, not one as she herself had directed with a view to admit her uncle should he apply, but all three, she started again to her feet, all spiritual contemplations vanishing in her actual temporal condition, and it seemed as if all her faculties were absorbed in the sense of hearing.

The thoughts are active, in a moment so fearful. At first Mabel fancied that her uncle had entered the block-house and she was about to descend the ladder and throw herself into his arms; then the idea that it might be an Indian, who had barred the door to shut out intruders, while he plundered at leisure, arrested the movement. The profound stillness below, was unlike the bold, restless movements of Cap, and it seemed to savor more of the artifices of an enemy. If a friend, at all, it could only be her uncle, or the Quarter Master, for the horrible conviction now presented itself to our heroine, that to these two and herself were the whole party suddenly reduced, if, indeed, the two first survived. This consideration held Mabel in check, and for quite two minutes more, a breathless silence reigned in the building. During this time, the girl stood at the foot of the upper ladder, the trap which led to the lower opening on the opposite side of the floor. The eyes of Mabel were riveted on this spot, for she now began to expect to see, at each instant, the horrible sight of a savage face at the hole. This apprehension soon became so intense, that she looked about her, for a place of concealment. The procrastination of the catastrophe she now fully expected, though it were only for a moment, afforded a relief. The room contained several barrels, and behind two of these, Mabel crouched, placing her eyes at an opening by which she could still watch the trap. She made another effort to pray, but the moment was too horrible for that relief. She thought, too, that she heard a low rustling, as if one was ascending the lower ladder, with an effort at caution so great, as to betray itself by its own excess. Then followed a creaking, that she was certain came from one of the steps of the ladder, which had made the same noise, under her own light weight as she ascended. This was one of those instants, into which are compressed the sensations of years of ordinary existence. Life, death, eternity and extreme bodily pain, were all standing out in bold relief, from the plane of every-day occurrences, and she might have been taken, at that moment, for a beautiful, pallid, representation of herself, equally without motion and without vitality. But, while such was the outward appearance of the form, never had there been a time, in her brief career, when Mabel heard more acutely, saw more clearly, or felt more vividly. As yet nothing was visible at the trap, but her ears, rendered exquisitely sensitive by intense feeling, distinctly acquainted her that some one was within a few inches of the opening in the

floor. Next followed the evidence of her eyes, which beheld the
dark hair of an Indian rising so slowly through the passage that
the movement of the head might be likened to that of the minute hand of a clock. Then came the dark skin and wild features,
until the whole of the swarthy face had risen above the floor.
The human countenance seldom appears to advantage when
partially concealed, and Mabel imagined many additional horrors, as she first saw the black, roving eyes, and the expression
of wildness, as the savage countenance was revealed, as it might
be inch by inch. But, when the entire head was raised above the
floor, a second and better look assured our heroine that she saw
the gentle, anxious and even handsome, face of June.

Chapter XXII.

> "–Spectre though I be,
> I am not sent to scare thee or deceive;
> But in reward of thy fidelity."
>
> Wordsworth, *Laodamia*, ll. 38–40.

Iᴛ would be difficult to say which evinced the most satisfaction, when Mabel sprang to her feet, and appeared in the centre of the room, our heroine on finding that her visiter was the wife of Arrowhead, and not Arrowhead himself, or June, at discovering that her advice had been followed, and that the block-house contained the person she had so anxiously and almost hopelessly sought. They embraced each other, and the unsophisticated Tuscarora woman laughed in her sweet accents, as she held her friend at arm's length, and made certain of her presence.

"Block-house good," said the young Indian–"got no scalp."

"It is indeed good, June," Mabel answered with a shudder, veiling her eyes at the same time, as if to shut out a view of the horrors she had so lately witnessed. "Tell me, for God's sake! if you know what has become of my dear uncle?–I have looked in all directions, without being able to see him."

"No here, in block-house?" June asked, with some curiosity.

"Indeed he is not–I am quite alone in this place, Jennie, the woman, who was with me, having rushed out to join her husband, and perishing for her imprudence."

"June know–June see. Very bad. Arrowhead no feel for any wife–no feel for his own."

"Ah! June; your life, at least, is safe!"

"Don't know. Arrowhead kill me, if he knows all."

"God bless and protect you, June–he *will* bless and protect you for your humanity. Tell me what is to be done, and if my poor uncle is still living?"

"Don't know. Salt-water has boat, maybe he go on river."

"The boat is still on the shore, but neither my uncle, nor the Quarter Master is anywhere to be seen."

"No kill, or June would see. Hide away. Red man hide; no shame for pale-face."

"It is not the shame that I fear for them, but the opportunity. Your attack was awfully sudden, June!"

"Tuscarora—" returned the other, smiling with exultation at the dexterity of her husband. "Arrowhead great warrior."

"You are too good and gentle for his sort of life, June. You *cannot* be happy in such scenes!"

June's countenance grew clouded, and Mabel fancied there was some of the savage fire of a chief in her frown as she answered.

"Yengeese too greedy—take away all hunting grounds—chase Six Nation from morning to night; wicked king—wicked people. Pale Face very bad."

Mabel knew that, even in that distant day, there was much truth in this opinion, though she was too well instructed not to understand that the monarch, in this as in a thousand other cases, was blamed for acts of which he was most probably ignorant. She felt the justice of the rebuke, therefore, too much to attempt an answer, and her thoughts naturally reverted to her own situation.

"And what am I to do, June," she demanded. "It cannot be long before your people will assault this building."

"Block-house good—got no scalp."

"But they will soon discover that it has got no garrison, too, if they do not know it already. You, yourself, told me the number of people that were on the island, and doubtless you learned it from Arrowhead."

"Arrowhead know," answered June, holding up six fingers to indicate the number of the men. "All red men know. Four lose scalp already—two got 'em, yet!"

"Do not speak of it, June; the horrid thought curdles my blood. Your people cannot know that I am alone in the block-house, but may fancy my uncle and the Quarter Master with me, and may set fire to the building, in order to dislodge them. They tell me that fire is the great danger to such places."

"No burn block-house," said June, quietly.

"You cannot know that, my good June, and I have no means to keep them off."

"No burn block-house. Block-house good; got no scalp."

"But tell me why, June—I fear they will burn it!"

"Block-house wet—much rain—logs green—no burn easy—Red man know it—first t'ing—then no burn it, to tell Yengeese that Iroquois been here. Fader come back, miss block-house, no land. No—no—Injin too cunning—no touch any thing."

"I understand you, June, and hope your prediction may be true; for as regards my dear father, should he escape—perhaps he is already dead, or captured, June!"

"No touch fader—don't know where he gone. Water got no trail—red-man can't follow. No burn block-house—block-house good—got no scalp."

"Do you think it possible for me to remain here, safely, until my father returns?"

"Don't know—daughter tell best, when fader come back."

Mabel felt uneasy at the glance of June's dark eye, as she uttered this, for the unpleasant surmise arose, that her companion was endeavoring to discover a fact that might be useful to her own people, while it would lead to the destruction of her parent and his party. She was about to make an evasive answer, when a heavy push at the outer door, suddenly drew all her thoughts to the immediate danger.

"They come!" she exclaimed—"Perhaps, June, it is my uncle or the Quarter Master—I cannot keep out even Mr. Muir, at a moment like this."

"Why no look—plenty loop-hole—made purpose."

Mabel took the hint, and going to one of the downward loops, that had been cut through the logs, in the part that overhung the basement, she cautiously raised the little block that ordinarily filled the small hole, and caught a glance at what was passing at the door. The start and changing countenance told her companion that some of her own people were below.

"Red men," said June, lifting a finger in admonition to be prudent.

"Four, and horrible in their paint and bloody trophies. Arrowhead is among them."

June had moved to a corner, where several spare rifles were deposited, and had already taken one into her hand, when the name of her husband appeared to arrest her movements. It was but for an instant, however, for she immediately went to the loop, and was about to thrust the muzzle of the piece through it, when a feeling of natural aversion, induced Mabel to seize her arm.

"No–no–no–June," said the latter–"not against your own husband, though my life be the penalty."

"No hurt Arrowhead–" returned June, with a slight shudder–"no hurt red man at all. No fire at 'em;–only scare."

Mabel now comprehended the intention of June, and no longer opposed it. The latter thrust the muzzle of the rifle through the loop-hole, and taking care to make noise enough to attract attention, she pulled the trigger. The piece had no sooner been discharged than Mabel reproached her friend, for the very act that was intended to serve her.

"You declared it was not your intention to fire," she said, "and you may have destroyed your own husband."

"All run away, before I fire–" returned June laughing, and going to another loop to watch the movements of her friends, laughing still heartier.–"See–get cover–every warrior. Think Salt-water and Quarter Master here. Take good care, now."

"Heaven be praised! And now, June, I may hope for a little time to compose my thoughts to prayer, that I may not die like Jennie, thinking only of life and the things of the world!"

June laid aside the rifle, and came and seated herself near the box on which Mabel had sunk, under that physical reaction which accompanies joy as well as sorrow. She looked steadily in our heroine's face, and the latter thought that her countenance had an expression of severity mingled with its concern.

"Arrowhead great warrior–" said the Tuscarora's wife–"All the gals of tribe, look at him much. The pale face beauty has eyes, too."

"June!–What do these words–that look imply–what would you say?"

"Why you so 'fraid June shoot Arrowhead?"

"Would it not have been horrible, to see a wife destroy her own husband! No, June; rather would I have died myself."

"Very sure, dat all?"

"That was all, June, as God is my judge–and surely that was enough. No–no–there have been sufficient horrors to-day, without increasing them by an act like this. What other motive can you suspect?"

"Don't know. Poor Tuscarora gal, very foolish. Arrowhead great chief, and look all round him. Talk of pale face beauty in his sleep–Great chief like many wives."

"Can a chief possess more than one wife, June, among your people?"

"Have as many as he can keep–Great hunter marry often. Arrowhead got only June now, but he look too much, see too much–talk too much of Pale Face gal!"

Mabel was conscious of this fact, which had distressed her not a little, in the course of their journey; but it shocked her to hear this allusion, coming, as it did, from the mouth of the wife herself. She knew that habit and opinions made great differences in such matters, but, in addition to the pain and mortification she experienced at being the unwilling rival of a wife, she felt an apprehension that jealousy would be but an equivocal guarantee for her personal safety, in her present situation. A closer look at June, however, reassured her, for while it was easy to trace in the unpractised features of this unsophisticated being, the pain of blighted affections, no distrust could have tortured the earnest expression of her honest countenance, into that of treachery or hate.

"You will not betray me, June," Mabel said, pressing the other's hand, and yielding to an impulse of generous confidence. "You will not give up one of your own sex, to the tomahawk?"

"No tomahawk touch you. Arrowhead no let 'em. If June must have sister-wife–love to have you."

"No, June; my religion, my feelings, both forbid it; and, if I could be the wife of an Indian, at all, I would never take the place that is yours, in a wigwam."

June made no answer, but she looked gratified, and even grateful. She knew that few, perhaps no Indian girl, within the circle of Arrowhead's acquaintance, could compare with herself, in personal attractions, and though it might suit her husband to marry a dozen wives, she knew of no one, beside Mabel, whose influence she could really dread. So keen an interest, however, had she taken in the beauty, winning manners, kindness, and feminine gentleness of our heroine, that when jealousy came to chill these feelings, it had rather lent strength to that interest, and, under its wayward influence, had actually been one of the strongest of the incentives that had induced her to risk so much, in order to save her imaginary rival from the consequences of the attack that she so well knew was about to take place. In a word, June, with a wife's keenness of perception, had detected Arrowhead's admiration of Mabel, and instead of feeling that harrowing jealousy, that might have rendered her rival hateful, as would have been apt to be the case with a woman unaccustomed to defer to the superior rights of the lordly sex, she had studied the looks and character of the pale face beauty, until, meeting with nothing to repel her own feelings, but every thing to encourage them, she had got to entertain an admiration and love for her, which, though certainly very different, was scarcely less strong than that of her husband. Arrowhead himself had sent her to warn Mabel of the coming danger, though he was ignorant that she had stolen upon the island, in the rear of the assailants, and was now entrenched in the citadel along with the object of their joint care. On the contrary, he supposed, as his wife had said, that Cap and Muir were in the block-house with Mabel, and that the attempt to repel him and his companions had been made by the men.

"June sorry, the 'Lily,'" for so the Indian, in her poetical language had named our heroine, "June sorry, the Lily no marry Arrowhead. His wigwam big, and a great chief must get wives enough to fill it."

"I thank you, June, for this preference, which is not according to the notions of us white women," returned Mabel, smiling in spite of the fearful situation in which she was placed; "but I may not, probably never shall marry at all."

"Must have good husband—" said June; "marry Eau douce, if do'n't like Arrowhead."

"June!—this is not a fit subject for a girl who scarce knows if she is to live another hour, or not. I would obtain some signs of my dear uncle's being alive and safe, if possible."

"June go see."

"Can you?—will you?—would it be safe for you to be seen on

the island—Is your presence known to the warriors, and would they be pleased to find a woman on the war-path, with them?"

All this Mabel asked in rapid connection, fearing that the answer might not be as she wished. She had thought it extraordinary that June should be of the party, and, improbable as it seemed, she had fancied that the woman had covertly followed the Iroquois in her own canoe, and had got in their advance merely to give her the notice which had probably saved her life. But in all this she was mistaken, as June, in her imperfect manner, now found means to let her know.

Arrowhead, though a chief, was in disgrace with his own people, and was acting with the Iroquois, temporarily, though with a perfect understanding. He had a wigwam it is true, but was seldom in it; feigning friendship for the English, he had passed the summer ostensibly in their service, while he was in truth acting for the French, and his wife journeyed with him in his many migrations, most of the distances being passed over in canoes. In a word her presence was no secret, her husband seldom moving without her. Enough of this to embolden Mabel to wish that her friend might go out, to ascertain the fate of her uncle, did June succeed in letting the other know, and it was soon settled between them, that the Indian woman should quit the block house with that object, the moment a favorable opportunity offered.

They first examined the island, as thoroughly as their position would allow, from the different loops, and found that its conquerors were preparing for a feast, having seized upon the provisions of the English, and rifled the huts. Most of the stores were in the block-house, but enough were found outside to reward the Indians for an attack attended by so little risk. A party had already removed the dead bodies, and Mabel saw that their arms were collected in a pile, near the spot chosen for the banquet. June suggested that, by some signs she understood, the dead themselves were carried into a thicket, and either buried, or concealed from view. None of the more prominent objects on the island, however, were disturbed, it being the desire of the conquerors to lure the party of the Serjeant into an ambush, on its return. June made her companion observe a man in a tree, a look-out, as she said, to give timely notice of the approach of any boat, although the departure of the expedition being so recent, nothing but some unexpected event would be likely to bring it back so soon. There did not appear to be any design to attack the block-house immediately, but every indication, as understood by June, rather showed that it was the intention of the Indians to keep it besieged until the return of the Serjeant's party, lest the signs of an assault should give a warning to eyes as practised as those of Pathfinder. The boat, however, had been secured, and was removed to the spot where the canoes of the Indians were hid in the bushes.

June now announced her intention of joining her friends, the moment being particularly favorable for her to quit the block-house. Mabel felt some distrust as they descended the ladder, but, at the next instant, she was ashamed of the feeling as unjust to her companion, and unworthy of herself, and by the time they both stood on the ground, her confidence was restored. The process of unbarring the door was conducted with the utmost caution, and when the last bar was ready to be turned, June took her station near the spot where the opening must necessarily be. The bar was just turned free of the brackets, the door was opened merely wide enough to allow her body to pass, and June glided through the space. Mabel closed the door again, with a convulsive movement, and as the bar turned into its place, her heart beat audibly. She then felt secure, and the two other bars were turned down in a more deliberate manner. When all were fast again, she ascended to the first floor, where, alone, she could get a glimpse of what was going on without.

Long and painfully melancholy hours passed, during which Mabel had no intelligence from June. She heard the yells of the savages, for liquor had carried them beyond the bounds of precaution, occasionally caught glimpses of their mad orgies through the loops, and at all times was conscious of their fearful presence, by sounds and sights that would have chilled the blood of one who had not so lately witnessed scenes so much more terrible. Towards the middle of the day, she fancied she saw a white man on the island, though his dress and wild appearance at first made her take him for a newly arrived savage. A view of his face, although it was swarthy naturally, and much darkened by exposure, left no doubt that her conjecture was true, and she felt as if there was now one of a species more like her own present, and one to whom she might appeal for succor, in the last emergency. Mabel little knew, alas! how small was the influence exercised by the whites over their savage allies, when the latter had begun to taste of blood, or how slight, indeed, was the disposition to divert them from their cruelties.

The day seemed a month by Mabel's computation, and the only part of it that did not drag, were the minutes spent in prayer. She had recourse to this relief, from time to time, and at each effort she found her spirit firmer, her mind more tranquil, and her tendency to resignation more confirmed. She understood the reasoning of June, and believed it highly probable, that the block-house would be left unmolested, until the return of her father, in order to entice him into an ambuscade, and she felt much less apprehension of immediate danger in consequence; but the future offered little grounds of hope, and her thoughts had already begun to calculate the chances of her captivity. At such moments, Arrowhead and his offensive admiration, filled a prominent part in the back-ground, for our heroine well knew that the Indians usually carried off to their villages, for the purposes of adoption, such captives as they did not slay, and that many instances had occurred, in which individuals of her sex had passed the remainder of their lives in the wigwams of their conquerors. Such thoughts as these, invariably drove her to her knees, and to her prayers.

While the light lasted, the situation of our heroine was sufficiently alarming, but as the shades of evening gradually gathered over the island, it became fearfully appalling. By this time, the savages had wrought themselves up to the point of fury, for they had possessed themselves of all the liquor of the English, and their outcries and gesticulations were those of men truly possessed of evil spirits. All the efforts of their French leader to restrain them, were entirely fruitless, and he had wisely withdrawn to an adjacent island, where he had a sort of bivouac, that he might keep at a safe distance from friends so apt to run into excesses. Before quitting the spot, however, this officer, at great risk to his own life, succeeded in extinguishing the fire, and in securing the ordinary means to relight it. This precaution he took, lest the Indians should burn the block-house, the preservation of which was necessary to the success of his future plans. He would gladly have removed all the arms, also, but this he found impracticable, the warriors clinging to their knives and tomahawks with the tenacity of men who regarded a point of honor, as long as a faculty was left, and to carry off the rifles, and leave behind him the very weapons that were generally used on such occasions, would have been an idle expedient. The extinguishing of the fire, proved to be the most prudent measure, for no sooner was the officer's back turned, than one of the warriors, in fact, proposed to fire the block-house. Arrowhead had also withdrawn from the group of drunkards, as soon as he found that they were losing their senses, and had taken possession of a hut, where he had thrown himself on the straw, and sought the rest that two wakeful and watchful nights rendered necessary. It followed that no one was left among the Indians to care for Mabel, if indeed any knew of her existence at all, and the proposal of the drunkard was received with yells of delight by eight or ten more, as much intoxicated and habitually as brutal as himself.

This was the fearful moment for Mabel. The Indians, in their present condition, were reckless of any rifles that the block-house might hold, though they did retain dim recollections of its containing living beings, an additional incentive to their enterprise, and they approached its base whooping and leaping like demons. As yet they were excited, not overcome by the liquor they had drunk. The first attempt was made at the door, against which they ran in a body, but the solid structure, which was built entirely of logs, defied their efforts. The rush of a hundred men, with the same object, would have been useless. This Mabel, however, did not know, and her heart seemed to leap into her mouth, as she heard the heavy shock, at each renewed effort. At length, when she found that the door resisted these assaults as if it were of stone, neither trembling, nor yielding, and only betraying its not being a part of the wall, by rattling a little on its heavy hinges, her courage revived, and she seized the first moment of a cessation, to look down through the loop, in order, if possible, to learn the extent of her danger. A silence, for which it was not easy to account, stimulated her curiosity, for nothing is so alarming to those who are conscious of the presence of imminent danger, as to be unable to trace its approach.

Mabel found that two or three of the Iroquois had been raking the embers, where they had found a few small coals, and with these they were endeavoring to light a fire. The interest with which they labored, the hope of destroying, and the force of habit enabled them to act intelligently and in unison, so long as their fell object was kept in view. A white man would have abandoned the attempt to light a fire in despair, with coals that came out of the ashes resembling sparks, but these children of the forests had many expedients that were unknown to civilization. By the aid of a few dry leaves, which they alone knew where to seek, a blaze was finally kindled, and then the addition of a few light sticks made sure of the advantage that had been obtained. When Mabel stooped down over the loop, the Indians were making a pile of brush against the door, and as she remained gazing at their proceedings, she saw the twigs ignite, the flame dart from branch to branch, until the whole pile was cracking and snapping under a bright blaze. The Indians now gave a yell of triumph and returned to their companions, well assured that the work of destruction was commenced. Mabel remained looking down, scarcely able to tear herself away from the spot, so intense and engrossing was the interest she felt in the progress of the fire. As the pile kindled throughout, however, the flames mounted, until they flashed so near her eyes, as to compel her to retreat. Just as she reached the opposite side of the room, to which she had retired in her alarm, a forked stream shot up through the loop-hole, the lid of which she had left open, and illuminated the rude apartment, with Mabel and her desolation. Our heroine now naturally enough supposed that her hour was come, for the door, the only means of retreat, had been blocked up by the brush and fire, with hellish ingenuity, and she addressed herself, as she believed for the last time, to her maker, in prayer. Her eyes were closed, and for more than a minute her spirit was abstracted, but the interests of the world too strongly divided her feelings, to be altogether suppressed, and when they involuntarily opened again, she perceived that the streak of flame was no longer flaring in the room, though the wood around the little aperture had kindled, and the blaze was slowly mounting under the impulsion of a current of air that sucked inward. A barrel of water stood in a corner, and Mabel, acting more by instinct than by reason, caught up a vessel, filled it, and pouring it on the wood, with a trembling hand, succeeded in extinguishing the fire, at that particular spot. The smoke prevented her from looking down again, for a couple of minutes, but when she did, her heart beat high with delight and hope, at finding that the pile of blazing brush had been overturned and scattered, and that water had been thrown on the logs of the door, which were still smoking, though no longer burning.

"Who is there?" said Mabel, with her mouth at the loop— "What friendly hand has a merciful Providence sent to my succour?"

A light footstep was audible below, and one of those gentle pushes at the door was heard, which just moved the massive beams on the hinges.

"Who wishes to enter?—Is it you, dear, dear, uncle?"

"Salt-water no here—St. Lawrence sweet water—" was the answer. "Open quick—want to come in."

The step of Mabel was never lighter, or her movements more quick and natural, than while she was descending the ladder and turning the bars, for all her motions were earnest and active. This time she thought only of her escape, and she opened the door with a rapidity that did not admit of caution. Her first impulse was to rush into the open air, in the blind hope of quitting the block-house, but June repulsed the attempt, and, entering, she coolly barred the door, again, before she would notice Mabel's eager efforts to embrace her.

"Bless you—bless you, June," cried our heroine, most fervently—"you are sent by Providence to be my guardian angel!"

"No hug so tight—" answered the Tuscarora woman—"Pale face women all cry, or all laugh. Let June fasten door."

Mabel became more rational, and in a few minutes the two were again in the upper room, seated as before, hand in hand, all feeling of distrust, or rivalry between them, being banished on the one side by the consciousness of favors received, and on the other by the consciousness of favors conferred.

"Now tell me, June," Mabel commenced, as soon as she had given and received one warm embrace, "have you seen or heard aught of my poor uncle?"

"Do'n't know. No one see him; no one hear him; no one know any t'ing. Salt-water run into river, I t'ink, for I no find him. Quarter Master gone, too. I look, and look, and look; but no see 'em, one t'other no where."

"Blessed be God! They must have escaped, though the means are not known to us. I thought I saw a Frenchman on the island, June?"

"Yes—French captain come, but he go away, too. Plenty of Injin, on island."

"Oh! June. June, are there no means to prevent my beloved father from falling into the hands of his enemies!"

"Do'n't no t'ink dat.—Warriors wait in ambush, and Yengeese must lose scalps."

"Surely, surely, June, you, who have done so much for the daughter, will not refuse to help the father!"

"Do'n't know fader—do'n't love fader. June help her own people, help Arrowhead—husband love scalps."

"June, this is not yourself! I cannot, will not believe that you wish to see our men murdered!"

June turned her dark eyes quietly on Mabel, and, for a moment, her look was stern, though it soon changed into one of melancholy compassion.

"Lily, Yengeese gal?" she said, as one asks a question.

"Certainly, and as a Yengeese girl, I would save my countrymen from slaughter."

"Very good—if can. June no Yengeese; June, Tuscarora—got Tuscarora husband—Tuscarora heart—Tuscarora feelings—all over Tuscarora. Lily would'n't run and tell French dat her fader was coming to gain victory?"

"Perhaps not," returned Mabel, pressing a hand on a brain that felt bewildered,—"perhaps not; but you serve me, aid me—have saved me, June! Why have you done this, if you only feel as a Tuscarora?"

"Do'n't only feel as Tuscarora—feel as gal—feel as squaw. Love pretty Lily, and put it in my bosom."

Mabel melted into tears, and she pressed the affectionate

creature to her heart. It was near a minute before she could re-new the discourse, but then she succeeded in speaking more calmly and with greater coherence.

"Let me know the worst, June;" she said—"To-night, your people are feasting; what do they intend to do tomorrow?"

"Do'n't know—afraid to see Arrowhead—afraid to ask questions—t'ink hide away, till Yengeese come back."

"Will they not attempt any thing against the block-house?—You have seen what they can threaten if they will?"

"Too much rum. Arrowhead sleep, or no dare; French captain gone away, or no dare. All go to sleep, now."

"And you think I am safe for this night, at least?"

"Too much rum—If Lily was like June, might do much for her people."

"I am like you, June, if a wish to serve my countryman, can make a resemblance with one as courageous as yourself."

"No—no—no—" muttered June, in a low voice—"no got heart, and June no let you, if had. June's moder prisoner once, and warriors got drunk; moder tomahawked 'em all. Such the way red skin women do, when people in danger, and want scalps."

"You say what is true," returned Mabel shuddering, and un-consciously dropping June's hand—"I cannot do that. I have neither the strength, the courage, nor the will to dip my hands in blood."

"T'ink that too; then stay where you be—block-house good—got no scalp."

"You believe, then, that I am safe, here, at least, until my father and his people return?"

"Know so. No one dare touch block-house in morning. Hark! All still, now—drink rum 'till head falls down, and sleep like log."

"Might I not escape?—Are there not several canoes on the island?—might I not get one, and go and give my father notice of what has happened?"

"Know how to paddle?" demanded June, glancing her eye furtively, at her companion.

"Not as well as yourself, perhaps, but enough to get out of sight before morning."

"What do then?—could'n't paddle six—ten—eight mile!"

"I do not know! I would do much to warn my father, and the excellent Pathfinder, and all the rest, of the danger they are in."

"Like Pathfinder?"

"All like him who know him—you would like him, nay love him, if you only knew his heart!"

"No like him, at all. Too good rifle—too good eye—too much shoot Iroquois, and June's people. Must get his scalp, if can."

"And I must save it, if I can, June. In this respect, then, we are opposed to each other. I will go and find a canoe the instant they are all asleep, and quit the island."

"No can—June won't let you. Call Arrowhead."

"June! You could not betray me—you would not give me up, after all you have done for me!"

"Just so—" returned June, making a backward gesture with her hand, and speaking with a warmth and earnestness Mabel had never witnessed in her before. "Call Arrowhead in loud voice. One call from wife, wake a warrior up. June no let Lily help enemy—no let Injin hurt Lily."

"I understand you, June, and feel the nature and justice of your sentiments; and, after all, it were better that I should remain here, for I have most probably overrated my strength. But, tell me one thing; if my uncle comes, in the night, and asks to be admitted, you will let me open the door of the block house that he may enter?"

"Sartain—He prisoner here, and June like prisoner, better than scalp. Scalp good for honor; prisoner good for feeling. But, Salt-Water hide so close, he do'n't know where he be himself."

Here June laughed, in her girlish mirthful way, for to her, scenes of violence were too familiar to leave impressions sufficiently deep, to change her natural character. A long and discursive dialogue now followed, in which Mabel endeavored to obtain clearer notions of her actual situation, under a faint hope that she might possibly be enabled to turn some of the facts she thus learned, to advantage. June answered all her interrogatories simply, but with a caution which showed she fully distinguished between that which was immaterial and that which might endanger the safety, or embarrass the future operations of her friends. Our heroine was incapable of making

an attempt to entrap her companion, though she plainly perceived, that, could she have been guilty of the meanness, she
would have found the undertaking one of extreme difficulty.
June however was not required to exercise more than a discreet
discrimination about what she revealed, and the substance of
the information she gave, may be summed up as follows.

Arrowhead had long been in communication with the
French, though this was the first occasion on which he had ever
entirely thrown aside the mask. He no longer intended to trust
himself among the English, for he had discovered traces of distrust, particularly in Pathfinder, and with Indian bravado, he
now rather wished to blazon, than to conceal his treachery. He
had led the party of warriors, in the attack on the island, subject
however to the supervision of the Frenchman who has been
mentioned, though June declined saying whether he had been
the means of discovering the position of a place that had been
thought to be so concealed from the eyes of the enemy, or not.
On this point, she would say nothing, but she admitted that she
and her husband had been watching the departure of the Scud,
at the time they were overtaken and captured by the cutter.
The French had obtained their information of the precise position of the station, but very recently, and Mabel felt a pang like
that of some sharp instrument piercing her heart, when she
thought that there was covert allusion of the Indian woman,
which would convey the meaning that the intelligence had
come from a pale face, in the employment of Duncan of Lundie. This was intimated, however, rather than said, and when
Mabel had time to reflect on her companion's words, and to
remember how sententious and brief her periods were, she
found room to hope that she had misunderstood her, and that
Jasper Western would yet come out of the affair freed from
every injurious imputation.

June did not hesitate to confess that she had been sent to the
island to ascertain the precise number, and the occupations of
those who had been left on it, though she also betrayed in her
naïve way, that the wish to serve Mabel, had induced her principally to consent to come. In consequence of her report, and
information otherwise obtained, the enemy was aware of precisely the force that could be brought against them. They also
knew the number of men that had gone with Serjeant Dunham,

and were acquainted with the object he had in view, though they were ignorant of the spot where he expected to meet the French boats. It would have been a pleasant sight to witness the eager desire of each of these two sincere females to ascertain all that might be of consequence to their respective friends, and yet the native delicacy, with which each refrained from pressing the other to make revelations that would have been improper, as well as the sensitive, almost intuitive feeling with which each avoided saying aught that might prove injurious to her own nation. As respects each other, there was perfect confidence; as regarded their respective people, entire fidelity. June was quite as anxious, as Mabel could be on any other point, to know where the Serjeant had gone, and when he was expected to return, but she abstained from putting the question, with a delicacy that would have done honor to the highest civilization. nor did she once frame any other inquiry in a way to lead indirectly to a betrayal of the much desired information, on that particular point; though, when Mabel of her own accord touched on any matter that might, by possibility throw light on the subject, she listened with an intentness that almost suspended respiration.

In this manner the hours passed away, unheeded, for both were too much interested to think of rest. Nature asserted her rights, however, towards morning, and Mabel was persuaded to lie down on one of the straw beds provided for the soldiers, where she soon fell into a deep sleep. June lay near her, and a quiet reigned on the whole island, as profound as if the dominion of the forest had never been invaded by man.

When Mabel awoke, the light of the sun was streaming in through the loop-holes, and she found that the day was considerably advanced. June still lay near her, sleeping as tranquilly as if she reposed on–we will not saý down, for the superior civilization of our own times repudiates the simile, but on a French mattress, and as profoundly, as if she had never experienced concern. The movements of Mabel, notwithstanding, soon awakened one so accustomed to vigilance, and then the two took a survey of what was passing around them, by means of the friendly apertures.

Chapter XXIII.

"What had th' Eternal Maker need of thee
The world in his continuall course to keepe,
That dost all things deface, ne lettest see
The beautie of his worke? Indeede in sleepe
The slouthfull body that doth love to steepe
His lustless limbs, and drowne his baser mind,
Doth praise thee oft, and oft from Stygian deepe
Calles thee his goddesse, in his errour blind,
And great dame Nature's handmaide chearing every kind."
The Faerie Queene, III.iv.56.1–9.

THE tranquillity of the previous night, was not contradicted by the movements of the day. Although Mabel and June went to every loop-hole, not a sign of the presence of a living being on the island was at first to be seen, themselves excepted. There was a smothered fire on the spot where McNab and his comrades had cooked, as if the smoke that curled upwards from it, was intended as a lure to the absent, and all around the huts had been restored to former order and arrangement. Mabel started involuntarily, when her eye at length fell on a group of three men, dressed in the scarlet of the 55th, seated on the grass in lounging attitudes, as if they chatted in listless security, and her blood curdled, as on a second look she traced the bloodless faces, and glassy eyes of the dead. They were quite near the block-house, so near indeed as to have been overlooked at the first eager inquiry, and there was a mocking levity in their postures and gestures, for their limbs were stiffening in different attitudes intended to resemble life, at which the soul revolted. Still, horrible as these objects were to those near enough to discover the frightful discrepancy between their assumed and their real characters, the arrangement had been made, with an art that would have deceived a negligent observer, at the distance of a hundred yards. After carefully examining the shores of the island, June pointed out to her companion, the fourth soldier seated with his feet hanging over the water, his back fastened to a sapling, and holding a fishing-rod in his hands. The scalpless heads were covered with their caps, and all appearance of blood had been carefully washed from each countenance.

Mabel sickened at this sight, which not only did so much violence to all her notions of propriety, but which was, in itself, so revolting and so opposed to natural feeling. She withdrew to a seat, and hid her face in her apron, for several minutes, until a low call from June, again drew her to a loop-hole. The latter then pointed out the body of Jennie, seemingly standing in the door of a hut, leaning forward, as if to look at the group of men, her cap fluttering in the wind, and her hand grasping a broom. The distance was too great to distinguish the features, very accurately, but Mabel fancied that the jaw had been depressed, as if to distort the mouth into a sort of horrible laugh.

"June! June!" she exclaimed; "this exceeds all I have ever even heard, or imagined as possible, in the treachery and artifices of your people!"

"Tuscarora very cunning—" said June, in a way to show that she rather approved of, than condemned the uses to which the dead bodies had been applied—"Do soldier no harm now; do Iroquois, good. Got the scalps, first; now make bodies work. By and by, burn 'em."

This speech told Mabel how far she was separated from her friend, in character, and it was several minutes before she could again address her. But this temporary aversion was lost on June, who set about preparing their simple breakfast, in a way to show how insensible she was to feelings in others, that her own habits taught her to discard. Mabel ate sparingly, and her companion as if nothing had happened. Then they had leisure again for their thoughts, and for further surveys of the island. Our heroine, though devoured with a feverish desire to be always at the loops, seldom went that she did not immediately quit them in disgust, though compelled by her apprehensions to return again, in a few minutes, called by the rustling of leaves, or the sighing of the wind. It was, indeed, a solemn thing, to look out upon that deserted spot, peopled by the dead in the panoply of the living, and thrown into the attitudes and acts of careless merriment and rude enjoyment. The effect on our heroine, was much as if she had found herself an observer of the revelries of demons.

Throughout the live-long day, not an Indian, nor a Frenchman was to be seen, and night closed over the frightful but silent masquerade, with the steady and unalterable progress with which the earth obeys her laws, indifferent to the petty actors, and petty scenes, that are in daily bustle and daily occurrence on her bosom. The night was far more quiet than that which had preceded it, and Mabel slept with an increasing confidence, for she now felt satisfied that her own fate would not be decided, until the return of her father. The following day he was expected, however, and when our heroine awoke, she ran eagerly to the loops in order to ascertain the state of the weather and the aspect of the skies, as well as the condition of the island. There lounged the fearful group on the grass, the fisherman still hung over the water, seemingly intent on his sport, and the distorted countenance of Jennie glared from out the hut, in horrible contortions. But the weather had changed. The wind blew fresh from the southward, and though the air was bland, it was filled with the elements of storm.

"This grows more and more difficult to bear, June," Mabel said, when she left the window. "I could even prefer to see the enemy, than to look any longer on this fearful array of the dead."

"Hush;—here they come. June thought hear a cry, like a warrior's shout, when he take scalp."

"What mean you!—There is no more butchery! There *can* be no more."

"Salt-water!" exclaimed June laughing, as she stood peeping through a loop-hole.

"My dear uncle!—Thank God, he then lives—Oh! June—June, *you* will not let them harm *him*!"

"June poor squaw—What warrior t'ink of what she say? Arrowhead bring him, here."

By this time Mabel was at a loop, and, sure enough, there were Cap and the Quarter Master in the hands of the Indians, eight or ten of whom were conducting them to the foot of the block, for, by this capture, the enemy now well knew that there could be no man in the building. Mabel scarcely breathed until the whole party stood ranged, directly before the door, when she was rejoiced to see that the French officer was among them. A low conversation followed, in which both the white leader and Arrowhead spoke earnestly to their captives, when the Quarter Master called out to her, in a voice loud enough to be heard.

"Pretty Mabel!—Pretty Mabel!" he said—"look out of one of the loop-holes, and pity our condition. We are threatened with instant death, unless you open the door to the conquerors. Relent then, or we'll no be wearing our scalps, half an hour from this blessed moment!"

Mabel thought there were mockery and levity in this appeal, and its manner rather fortified than weakened her resolution to hold the place as long as possible.

"Speak to me, uncle," she said, with her mouth at a loop, "and tell me what I ought to do."

"Thank God!—thank God!" ejaculated Cap, "the sound of your sweet voice, Magnet, lightens my heart of a heavy load, for I feared you had shared the fate of poor Jennie. My breast has felt the last four and twenty hours, as if a ton of kentledge had been stowed in it. You ask me what you ought to do, child, and I do not know how to advise you, though you are my own sister's daughter! The most I can say, just now, my poor girl, is most heartily to curse the day you or I ever saw this bit of fresh water—"

"But, uncle, is your life in danger—do *you* think I ought to open the door?"

"A round turn and two half-hitches make a fast belay, and I would counsel no one who is out of the hands of these devils, to unbar, or unfasten any thing, in order to fall into them. As to the Quarter Master and myself, we are both elderly men, and not of much account to mankind in general, as honest Pathfinder would say, and it can make no great odds to him, whether he balances the purser's books this year or the next; and as for myself, why, if I were on the sea-board, I should know what to do, but up here in this watery wilderness, I can only say that if I were behind that bit of a bulwark, it would take a great deal of Indian logic to rowse me out of it."

"You'll no be minding all your uncle says, Pretty Mabel," put in Muir, "for distress is obviously fast unsettling his faculties, and he is far from calculating all the necessities of the emergency. We are in the hands, here, of very considerate and gentlemanly pairsons, it must be acknowledged, and one has little occasion to apprehend disagreeable violence. The casualties that have occurred, are the common incidents of war, and can no change our sentiments of the enemy, for they are far from indicating that any injustice will be done the prisoners. I'm sure that neither Master Cap, nor myself, has any cause of complaint since we have given ourselves up to Master Arrowhead, here, who reminds me of a Roman, or a Spartan, by his virtues and moderation, but, ye'll be remembering that usages differ, and that our scalps may be lawful sacrifices to appease the manes of fallen foes, unless you save them by capitulation."

"I shall do wiser to keep within the block-house, until the fate of the island is settled," returned Mabel. "Our enemies can feel no concern on account of one like me, knowing that I can do them no harm, and I greatly prefer to remain here, as more befitting my sex and years."

"If nothing but your convenience were concerned, Mabel, we should all cheerfully acquiesce in your wishes, but these gentlemen fancy that the work will aid their operations, and they have a strong desire to possess it. To be frank with you, finding myself and your uncle in a very peculiar situation, I acknowledge that, to avert consequences, I have assumed the power that belongs to His Majesty's commission, and entered into a verbal capitulation, by which I have engaged to give up the block-house and the whole island. It is the fortune of war, and must be submitted to; so open the door, Pretty Mabel, forthwith, and confide yourself to the care of those who know how to treat beauty and virtue in distress. There's no courtier in Scotland more complaisant than this chief, or who is more familiar with the laws of decorum."

"No leave block-house," muttered June, who stood at Mabel's side, attentive to all that passed. "Block-house good; got no scalp."

Our heroine might have yielded, but for this appeal, for it began to appear to her that the wisest course would be to conciliate the enemy by concessions, instead of exasperating him by resistance. They must know, she thought, now that Muir and her uncle were in their power, that there was no man in the building, and she feared they might proceed to batter down the door, or to cut their way through the logs with axes, if she obstinately refused to give them peaceable admission, since there was no longer any reason to dread the rifle. But the words of June induced her to hesitate, and the earnest pressure of the hand, and entreating looks of her companion, strengthened a resolution that was faltering.

"No prisoner yet—" whispered June—"Let 'em make prisoner, before 'ey take prisoner. Talk big; June manage 'em."

Mabel now began to parley more resolutely with Muir, for her uncle seemed disposed to quiet his conscience by holding his tongue, and she plainly intimated that it was not her intention to yield the building.

"You forget the capitulation, Mistress Mabel," said Muir—"the honor of one of His Majesty's servants is concerned, and the honor of His Majesty through his servant. You will remember the finesse and delicacy that belong to military honor?"

"I know enough, Mr. Muir, to understand that you have no command in this expedition, and therefore can have no right to yield the block-house, and, I remember, moreover, to have heard my father say, that a prisoner loses all his authority, for the time being."

"Rank sophistry, Pretty Mabel, and treason to the king, as well as dishonoring his commission, and discrediting his name. You'll no be persevering in your intentions, when your better judgment has had leisure to reflect, and to make conclusions, on matters and circumstances."

"Ay," put in Cap—"this *is* a circumstance, and be d——d to it!"

"No mind what 'e uncle say," ejaculated June, who was occupied in a far corner of the room. "Block-house good; got no scalp."

"I shall remain as I am, Mr. Muir, until I get some tidings of my father. He will return in the course of the next ten days."

"Ah! Mabel, this artifice will no deceive the enemy, who, by means that would be unintelligible, did not our suspicions rest on an unhappy young man with too much plausibility, are familiar with all our doings and plans, and well know that the sun will not set before the worthy serjeant and his companions will be in their power. Aweel! Submission to Providence is truly a christian virtue!"

"Mr. Muir, you appear to be deceived in the strength of this work, and to fancy it weaker than it is. Do you desire to see what I can do, in the way of defence, if so disposed?"

"I dinna' mind if I do," answered the Quarter Master, who always grew Scotch, as he grew interested.

"What do you think of that, then?—Look at the loop of the upper story."

As soon as Mabel had spoken, all eyes were turned upward, and beheld the muzzle of a rifle cautiously thrust through a hole, June having resorted again to a *ruse* that had already proved so successful. The result did not disappoint expectation. No sooner did the Indians catch a sight of the fatal weapon, than they leaped aside, and, in less than a minute every man among them had sought a cover. The French officer, kept his eye on the barrel of the piece, in order to ascertain that it was not pointed in his particular direction, and he coolly took a pinch of snuff. As neither Muir, nor Cap, had any thing to apprehend from the quarter in which the others were menaced, they kept their ground.

"Be wise, my pretty Mabel, be wise," exclaimed the former, "and no be provoking a useless contention. In the name of all the Kings of Albin, who have ye closeted with you in that wooden tower, that seemeth so bloody-minded?—There is necromancy about this matter, and all our characters may be involved in the explanation!"

"What do ye think of the Pathfinder, Master Muir, for a garrison to so strong a post!" cried Mabel, resorting to an equivocation that the circumstances rendered very excusable. "What will your French and Indian companions think of the aim of Pathfinder's rifle."

"Bear gently on the unfortunate, Pretty Mabel, and do not confound the King's servants, may Heaven bless him and all his royal lineage, with the King's enemies. If Pathfinder be indeed in the block-house, let him speak, and we will hold our negotiations directly with him. He knows us as friends, and we fear no evil at his hands, and least of all to myself; for a generous mind is apt to render rivalry in a certain interest a sure ground of respect and amity; since admiration of the same woman proves a community of feeling and tastes."

The reliance on Pathfinder's friendship did not extend beyond the Quarter Master and Cap, however, for even the French officer, who had hitherto stood his ground so well, shrunk back at the sound of the terrible name. So unwilling, indeed, did this individual, a man of iron nerves, and one long accustomed to the dangers of the peculiar warfare in which he was engaged, appear to be to remain exposed to the assaults of Killdeer, whose reputation throughout all that frontier was as well established, as that of Marlborough in Europe, that he did not disdain to seek a cover, insisting that his two prisoners should follow him. Mabel was too glad to be rid of her enemies to lament the departure of her friends, though she kissed her hand to Cap, through the loop, and called out to him in the terms of affection as he moved slowly and unwillingly away.

The enemy now seemed disposed to abandon all attempts on the block-house for the present, and June, who had ascended to a trap in the roof, whence the best view was to be obtained, reported that the whole party, had assembled to eat, on a distant and sheltered part of the island, where Muir and Cap were quietly sharing in the good things that were going, as if they had no concern on their minds. This information greatly relieved Mabel, and she began to turn her thoughts, again, to the means of effecting her own escape, or at least of letting her father know of the danger that awaited him. The Serjeant was expected to return that afternoon, and she knew that a moment, gained or lost, might decide his fate.

Three or four hours flew by. The island was again buried in a profound quiet, the day was wearing away and yet Mabel had decided on nothing. June was in the basement preparing their frugal meal, and Mabel herself, had ascended to the roof, which was provided with a trap that allowed her to go out on the top of the building, whence she commanded the best view of surrounding objects that the island possessed. Still it was limited, and much obstructed by the tops of trees. The anxious girl did not dare to trust her person in sight, knowing well that the unrestrained passions of some savage, might induce him to send a bullet through her brain. She merely kept her head out of the trap, therefore, whence in the course of the afternoon she made as many surveys of the different channels about the island, as "Anne, sister Anne"*took of the environs of the castle of Blue Beard.

The sun had actually set, no intelligence had been received from the boats, and Mabel ascended to the roof, to take a last look, hoping that the party would arrive in the darkness, which would at least prevent the Indians from rendering their ambuscade as fatal as it might otherwise prove, and which possibly might enable her to give some more intelligible signal, by means of fire, than it would otherwise be in her power to do. Her eye had turned carefully round the whole horizon, and she was just on the point of drawing in her person, when an object that struck her as new, caught her attention. The islands lay grouped so closely, that six or eight different channels, or passages between them were in view, and in one of the most covered, concealed in a great measure by the bushes of the shore, lay, what a second look assured her, was a bark canoe. It contained a human being beyond a question. Confident that, if an enemy, her signal could do no harm, and, if a friend, that it might do good, the eager girl waved a little flag towards the stranger, which she had prepared for her father, taking care that it should not be seen from the island.

Mabel had repeated her signal eight or ten times in vain, and she began to despair of its being noticed, when a sign was given in return, by the wave of a paddle, and the man so far discovered himself, as to let her see it was Chingachgook. Here, then, at last, was a friend; one, too, who was able, and she doubted not would be willing, to aid her! From that instant her courage and her spirits revived. The Mohican had seen her; must have recognised her, as he knew that she was of the party, and no doubt, as soon as it was sufficiently dark, he would take the steps necessary to release her. That he was aware of the presence of the enemy was apparent by the great caution he observed, and she had every reliance on his prudence and address. The principal difficulty now existed with June, for Mabel had seen too much of her fidelity to her own people, relieved as it was by sympathy for herself, to believe she would consent to a hostile

Indian's entering the block-house, or indeed to her leaving it, with a view to defeat Arrowhead's plans. The half hour that succeeded the discovery of the presence of the Great Serpent, was the most painful of Mabel Dunham's life. She saw the means of effecting all she wished, as it might be within reach of her hand, and yet it eluded her grasp. She knew June's decision and coolness, notwithstanding all her gentleness and womanly feeling, and at last she came reluctantly to the conclusion that there was no other way of attaining her end, than by deceiving her tried companion and protector. It was revolting to one as sincere and natural, as pure of heart and as much disposed to ingenuousness as Mabel Dunham, to practice deception on a friend like June, but her own father's life was at stake, her companion would receive no positive injury, and she had feelings and interests directly touching herself, that would have removed greater scruples.

As soon as it was dark, Mabel's heart began to beat with violence, and she adopted and changed her plan of proceedings, at least a dozen times, in the course of a single hour. June was always the source of her greatest embarrassment, for she did not well see firstly how she was to ascertain when Chingachgook was at the door, where she doubted not he would soon appear, and, secondly, how she was to admit him, without giving the alarm to her watchful companion. Time pressed, however, for the Mohican might come and go away again, unless she was ready to receive him. It would be too hazardous to the Delaware to remain long on the island, and it became absolutely necessary to determine on some course, even at the risk of choosing one that was indiscreet. After running over various projects, in her mind, therefore, Mabel came to her companion and said with as much calmness as she could assume——

"Are you not afraid, June, now your people believe Pathfinder is in the block-house, that they will come and try to set it on fire?"

"No t'ink such t'ing. No burn block-house. Block-house good; got no scalp."

"June, we cannot know. They hid, because they believed what I told them of Pathfinder's being with us."

"Believe fear. Fear come quick; go quick. Fear make run

away; wit make come back. Fear make warrior fool, as well as young girl."

Here June laughed, as her sex is apt to laugh when any thing particularly ludicrous crosses their youthful fancies.

"I feel uneasy, June, and wish you yourself would go up again to the roof, and look out upon the island, to make certain that nothing is plotting against us; you know the signs of what your people intend to do, better than I."

"June go, Lily wish; but very well know, that Injin asleep; wait for 'e fader. Warrior eat, drink, sleep all time, when don't fight, and go on war trail. Den *never* sleep, eat, drink—never feel. Warrior sleep now."

"God send it may be so—but go up, dear June, and look well about you; danger may come when we least expect it."

June arose and prepared to ascend to the roof, but she paused with her foot on the first round of the ladder. Mabel's heart beat so violently, that she was fearful its throbs would be heard, and she fancied that some gleamings of her real intentions had crossed the mind of her friend. She was right in part; the Indian woman having actually stopped to consider whether there was any indiscretion in what she was about to do. At first, the suspicion that Mabel intended to escape flashed across her mind; then she rejected it, on the ground that the pale face had no means of getting off the island, and that the block-house was much the most secure place she could find. The next thought was, that Mabel had detected some sign of the near approach of her father. This idea lasted but an instant, for June entertained some such opinion of her companion's ability to understand symptoms of this sort, symptoms that had escaped her own sagacity, as a woman of high fashion entertains of the accomplishments of her maid. Nothing else in the same way offering, she began slowly to mount the ladder. Just as she reached the upper floor, a lucky thought suggested itself to our heroine, and by expressing it in a hurried but natural manner she gained a great advantage in executing her projected scheme.

"I will go down," she said, "and listen by the door, June, while you are on the roof, and we will thus be on our guard at the same time, above and below."

Though June thought this savored of unnecessary caution, well knowing no one could enter the building unless aided from within, nor any serious danger menace them from the exterior, without giving sufficient warning, she attributed the proposition to Mabel's ignorance and alarm; and, as it was apparently made with frankness, it was received without distrust. By these means our heroine was enabled to descend to the door, as her friend ascended to the roof, and June felt no unusual inducement to watch her. The distance between the two, was now too great to admit of conversation, and for three or four minutes one was occupied in looking about her, as well as the darkness would allow, and the other in listening at the door, with as much intentness, as if all her senses were absorbed in the single faculty of hearing.

June discovered nothing from her elevated stand. The obscurity indeed almost forbade the hope of such a result; but it would not be easy to describe the sensation with which Mabel thought she perceived a slight and guarded push against the door. Fearful that all might not be as she wished, and anxious to let Chingachgook know that she was near, she began, though in tremulous and low notes to sing. So profound was the stillness at the moment, that the sound of the unsteady warbling ascended to the roof, and in a minute June began to descend. A slight tap at the door was heard immediately after. Mabel was bewildered, for there was no time to lose. Hope proved stronger than fear, and with unsteady hands, she commenced unbarring the door. The moccasin of June was heard on the floor above her, when only a single bar was turned. The second was released as her form reached half-way down the lower ladder.

"What you do!" exclaimed June angrily.—"Run away—mad—leave block-house? Block-house good."—The hands of both were on the last bar, and it would have been cleared from the fastenings, but for a vigorous shove from without, which jammed the wood. A short struggle ensued, though both were disinclined to violence. June would probably have prevailed, had not another and more vigorous push from without forced the bar past the trifling impediment that held it, when the door opened. The form of a man was seen to enter, and both the females rushed up the ladder, as if equally afraid of the consequences. The stranger secured the door, and, first examining the lower room with great care, he cautiously ascended the ladder. June, as soon as it became dark, had closed the loops of the principal floor, and lighted a candle. By means of this dim taper then, the two females stood in expectation, waiting to ascertain the person of their visiter, whose wary ascent of the ladder was distinctly audible though sufficiently deliberate. It would not be easy to say which was the most astonished on finding, when the stranger had got through the trap, that Pathfinder stood before them!

"God be Praised!" Mabel exclaimed, for the idea that the block-house would be impregnable with such a garrison, at once crossed her mind. "Oh! Pathfinder, what has become of my father?"

"The sarjeant is safe, as yet, and victorious, though it is not in the gift of man to say what will be the ind of it. Is not that the wife of Arrowhead, skulking in the corner, there?"

"Speak not of her reproachfully, Pathfinder; I owe her my life—my present security. Tell me what has happened to my father's party, why you are here, and I will relate all the horrible events that have passed upon this island."

"Few words will do the last, Mabel, for one used to Indian deviltries needs but little explanations on such a subject. Every thing turned out as we had hoped with the expedition, for the Sarpent was on the look out, and he met us with all the information heart could desire. We ambushed three boats, druv' the Frenchers out of them, got possession and sunk them, according to orders, in the deepest part of the channel, and the Savages of Upper Canada will fare badly for Indian goods this winter. Both powder and ball, too, will be scarcer among them, than keen hunters and actyve warriors may relish. We did not lose a man, or have even a skin barked, nor do I think the inimy suffered to speak of. In short, Mabel, it has been just such an expedition as Lundie likes; much harm to the foe, and little harm to ourselves."

"Ah! Pathfinder, I fear when Major Duncan comes to hear the whole of the sad tale, he will find reason to regret he ever undertook the affair!"

"I know what you mean—I know what you mean, but, by telling my story straight, you will understand it better. As soon as the sarjeant found himself successful, he sent me and the Sarpent off in canoes, to tell you how matters had turned out, and he is following with the two boats; which being so much heavier, cannot arrive afore morning. I parted from Chingachgook this forenoon, it being agreed that he should come up one set of channels, and I another, to see that the path was clear. I've not seen the chief since."

Mabel now explained the manner in which she had discovered the Mohican, and her expectation that he would yet come to the bloc:.-house.

"Not he—not he—A regular scout will never get behind walls, or logs, so long as he can keep the open air, and find useful employment. I should not have come myself, Mabel, but I promised the sarjeant to comfort you, and to look a'ter your safety. Ah's! me. I reconnoitred the island with a heavy heart, this forenoon, and there was a bitter hour, when I fancied you might be among the slain!"

"By what lucky accident were you prevented from paddling up boldly to the island, and from falling into the hands of the enemy?"

"By such an accident, Mabel, as Providence employs to tell the hound where to find the deer, and the deer how to throw off the hound. No—no—these artifices and deviltries with dead bodies, may deceive the soldiers of the 55th, and King's officers, but they are all lost upon men who have passed their days in the forest. I came down the channel in face of the pretended fisherman, and, though the riptyles have set up the poor wretch with art, it was not ingenious enough to take in a practysed eye. The rod was held too high, for the 55th have learned to fish at Oswego, if they never knew how afore, and then the man was too quiet for one who got neither prey nor bite. But we never come in upon a post blindly, and I have lain outside a garrison a whole night, because they had changed their sentries and their mode of standing guard. Neither the Sarpent, nor myself, would be likely to be taken in, by these contrivances, which were most probably intended for the Scotch, who are cunning enough in some particulars, though any thing but witches, when Indian sarcumventions are in the wind."

"Do you think my father and his men may yet be deceived?" said Mabel, quickly.

"Not if I can prevent it, Mabel. You say the Sarpent is on the look-out, too; so there is a double chance of our succeeding in letting him know his danger; though it is by no means sartain by which channel the party may come."

"Pathfinder—" said our heroine solemnly, for the frightful scenes she had witnessed had clothed death with unusual horrors—"Pathfinder, you have professed love for me—a wish to make me your wife?"

"I did ventur' to speak on that subject, Mabel, and the sarjeant has even lately said that you are kindly disposed; but I am not a man to parsecute the thing I love."

"Hear me, Pathfinder—I respect you—honor you—revere you—save my father from this dreadful death, and I can worship you. Here is my hand, as a solemn pledge for my faith, when you come to claim it."

"Bless you—bless you, Mabel; this is more than I desarve—more, I fear, than I shall know how to profit by, as I ought. It was not wanting, howsever, to make me sarve the sarjeant. We are old comrades, and owe each other a life—though I fear me, Mabel, being a father's comrade is not always the best recommendation with the daughter!"

"You want no other recommendation than your own acts—your courage—your fidelity—all that you do and say, Pathfinder, my reason approves, and the heart will, nay, it *shall* follow."

"This is a happiness I little expected this night, but we are in God's hands, and he will protect us, in his own way. These are sweet words, Mabel, but they were not wanting to make me do all that man can do, in the present sarcumstances; they will not lessen my endivors, neither."

"Now we understand each other, Pathfinder—" Mabel added, hoarsely, "let us not lose one of the precious moments, which may be of incalculable value. Can we not get into your canoe, and go and meet my father?"

"That is not the course I advise. I do'n't know by which channel the sarjeant will come, and there are twenty; rely on it, the Sarpent will be winding his way through them all. No—no—my advice is to remain, here. The logs of this block-house are still green, and it will not be easy to set them on fire, and I can make good the place, bating a burning, ag'in a tribe. The Iroquois nation cannot dislodge me from this fortress, so long as we can keep the flames from it. The Sarjeant is now 'camped on some island, and will not come in, until morning. If we hold the block, we can give him timely warning, by firing rifles for instance; and should he determine to attack the savages, as a man of his temper will be very likely to do, the possession of this building will be of great account in the affair. No—no—my judgment says remain, if the object be to sarve the sarjeant; though escape for our two selves, will be no very difficult matter."

"Stay—" murmured Mabel—"Stay, for God's sake, Pathfinder. Any thing, every thing, to save my father."

"Yes, that is natur'. I am glad to hear you say this, Mabel, for I own a wish to see the sarjeant fairly supported. As the matter now stands he has gained himself credit, and could he once drive off these miscreants, and make an honorable retreat, laying the huts and block in ashes, no doubt, no doubt, Lundie would remember it, and sarve him accordingly—Yes, yes, Mabel, we must not only save the sarjeant's life, but we must save his ripitation."

"No blame can rest on my father, on account of the surprise of this island?"

"There's no tellin'—there's no tellin'. Military glory is a most unsartain thing. I've seen the Delawares routed when they desarved more credit, than, at other times, when they've carried the day. A man is wrong to set his heart on success of any sort, and worst of all, on success in war. I know little of the settlements or of the notions that men hold in them, but, up hereaway, even the Indians rate a warrior's character according to his luck. The principal thing with a soldier is never to be whipt; nor do I think mankind stops long to consider how the day was won, or lost. For my part, Mabel, I make it a rule when facing the inimy, to give him as good as I can send, and to try to be moderate as I can, when we get the better; as for feeling moderate, after a defeat, little need be said on that score, as a flogging is one of the most humbling things in natur'. The parsons preach about humility in the garrisons; but if humility would make christians, the King's troops ought to be saints, for they've done little, as yet, this war, but take lessons from the French, beginning at Fort du Quesne,* and ending at Ty!"

"My father could not have suspected that the position of the island was known to the enemy!" resumed Mabel, whose thoughts were running on the probable effect of the recent events on the Serjeant.

"That is true; nor do I well see how the Frenchers found it out. The spot is well chosen, and it is not an easy matter even for one who has travelled the road to and from it, to find it again. There has been treachery I fear; yes, yes there must have been treachery!"

"Oh! Pathfinder, can this be!"

"Nothing is easier, Mabel, for treachery comes as nat'ral to some men as eating. Now, when I find a man all fair words, I look close to his deeds; for when the heart is right and raally intends to do good, it is generally satisfied to let the conduct speak, instead of the tongue."

"Jasper Western is not one of these," said Mabel impetuously. "No youth can be more sincere in his manner, or less apt to make the tongue act for the heart!"

"Jasper Western!—Tongue and heart are both right with that lad, depend on it, Mabel, and the notion taken up by Lundie, and the Quarter Master, and the Sarjeant, and your uncle too, is as wrong as it would be to think that the sun shone by night, and the stars shone by day. No—no—I'll answer for Eau douce's honesty, with my own scalp, or, at need, with my own rifle."

"Bless you—bless you, Pathfinder!" exclaimed Mabel extending her own hand, and pressing the iron fingers of her companion, under a state of feeling that far surpassed her own consciousness of its strength. "You are all that is generous—all that is noble; God will reward you for it."

"Ah! Mabel; I fear me if this be true, I should not covet such a wife as yourself, but would leave you to be sued for, by some gentleman of the garrison, as your desarts require!"

"We will not talk of this any more, to night—" Mabel answered in a voice so smothered, as to sound nearly choked— "We must think less of ourselves, just now, Pathfinder, and more of our friends. But I rejoice from my soul, that you believe Jasper innocent. Now, let us talk of other things—ought we not to release June?"

"I've been thinking about the woman, for it will not be safe to shut our eyes, and leave hers open, on this side of the block-house door. If we put her in the upper room, and take away the ladder, she'll be a prisoner, at least."

"I cannot treat one thus, who has saved my life. It would be better to let her depart; I think she is too much my friend to do any thing to harm me."

"You do not know the race, Mabel; you do not know the race. It's true she's not full-blooded Mingo, but she consorts with the vagabonds, and must have l'arned some of their tricks. What is that?"

"It sounds like oars—some boat is passing through the channel."

Pathfinder closed the trap that led to the lower room, to prevent June from escaping, extinguished the candle, and went hastily to a loop; Mabel looking over his shoulder, in breathless curiosity. These several movements consumed a minute or two, and by the time the eye of the scout had got a dim view of things without, two boats had swept past, and shot up to the shore, at a spot some fifty yards beyond the block, where there was a regular landing. The obscurity prevented more from being seen, and Pathfinder whispered to Mabel, that the new comers were as likely to be foes as friends, for he did not think her father could possibly have arrived so soon. A number of men were now seen to quit the boats, and then followed three hearty English cheers, leaving no further doubts of the character of the party. Pathfinder sprang to the trap, raised it, glided down the ladder, and began to unbar the door, with an earnestness that proved how critical he deemed the moment. Mabel had followed, but she rather impeded than aided his exertions, and but a single bar was turned when a heavy discharge of rifles was heard. They were still standing in breathless suspense when the war-whoop rang in all the surrounding thickets. The door now opened, and both Pathfinder and Mabel rushed into the open air. All human sounds had ceased. After listening half a minute, however, Pathfinder thought he heard a few stifled groans near the boats, but the wind blew so fresh, and the rustling of the leaves mingled so much with the murmurs of the passing air, that he was far from certain. But, Mabel was borne away by her feelings, and she rushed by him, taking the way towards the boats.

"This will not do, Mabel—" said the Scout, in an earnest but low voice, seizing her by an arm. "This will not do. Sartain death would follow, and that without sarving any one. We must return to the block."

"Father!—My poor, dear, murdered father!" said the girl wildly, though habitual caution, even at that trying moment, induced her to speak low. "Pathfinder, if you love me, let me go to my dear father!"

"This will not do, Mabel—" said the Scout, in an earnest but low voice, seizing her by an arm. —"This will not do. Sartain in the block!—But of what use would a rifle be, when no one is to be seen!"

At that moment, the quick eye of Pathfinder, which, while he held Mabel firmly in his grasp, had never ceased to roam over the dim scene, caught an indistinct view of five or six dark, crouching forms, endeavoring to steal past him, doubtless with the intention of intercepting their retreat to the block-house. Catching up Mabel, and putting her under an arm, as if she were an infant, the sinewy frame of the woodsman was exerted to the utmost, and he succeeded in entering the building. The tramp of his pursuers seemed immediately at his heels. Dropping his burthen, he turned, closed the door, and had fastened one bar, as a rush against the solid mass threatened to force it from the hinges. To secure the other bars, was the work of an instant.

Mabel now ascended to the first floor, while Pathfinder remained as a sentinel below. Our heroine was in that state in which the body exerts itself, apparently without the control of the mind. She relighted the candle mechanically, as her companion had desired, and returned with it below, where he was waiting her reappearance. No sooner was Pathfinder in possession of the light, than he examined the place carefully, to make certain no one was concealed in the fortress, ascending to each floor, in succession, after assuring himself that he left no enemy in his rear. The result was the conviction that the block-house now contained no one but Mabel and himself, June having escaped. When perfectly convinced on this material point, Pathfinder rejoined our heroine in the principal apartment, setting down the light, and examining the priming of Killdeer, before he seated himself.

"Our worst fears are realized!" said Mabel, to whom the hurry and excitement of the last five minutes, appeared to contain the emotions of a life. "My beloved father, and all his party, are slain or captured!"

"We do'n't know that—morning will tell us all. I do not think the affair as settled as that, or we should hear the vagabond Mingos yelling out their triumph, around the block-house. Of one thing we may be sartain; if the inimy has really got the better, he will not be long in calling upon us to surrender. The squaw will let him into the secret of our situation, and, as they well know the place cannot be fired by day-light, so long as Killdeer continues to desarve his ripitation, you may depend on it, that they will not be backward in making their attempt, while darkness helps them."

"Surely, I hear a groan!"

"'Tis fancy, Mabel—When the mind gets to be skeary, especially a woman's mind, she often concaits things that have no reality. I've known them that imagined there was truth in dreams—"

"Nay, I am *not* deceived—there is surely one below, and in pain!"

Pathfinder was compelled to own that the quick senses of Mabel had not deceived her. He cautioned her, however, to repress her feelings, and reminded her that the savages were in the practice of resorting to every artifice, to attain their ends, and that nothing was more likely than that the groans were feigned with a view to lure them from the block-house, or, at least, to induce them to open the door.

"No—no—no—" said Mabel hurriedly—"there is no artifice in those sounds, and they come from anguish of body, if not of spirit. They are fearfully natural."

"Well, we shall soon know whether a friend is there, or not. Hide the light again, Mabel, and I will speak the person from a loop."

Not a little precaution was necessary, according to Pathfinder's judgment and experience, in performing even this simple act, for he had known the careless slain by their want of a proper attention to what might have seemed to the ignorant, supererogatory means of safety. He did not place his mouth to the loop itself, but so near it that he could be heard without raising his voice, and the same precaution was observed as regards his ear.

"Who is below?" Pathfinder demanded when his arrangements were made to his mind—"Is any one in suffering? If a friend, speak boldly, and depend on our aid!"

"Pathfinder!" answered a voice that both Mabel and the person addressed, at once knew to be the Serjeant's—"Pathfinder, in the name of God, tell me what has become of my daughter?"

"Father!—I am here—unhurt—safe—and oh! that I could think the same of you!"

The ejaculation of thanksgiving that followed was distinctly audible to the two, but it was clearly mingled with a groan of pain.

"My worst forebodings are realized!" said Mabel, with a sort of desperate calmness. "Pathfinder, my father must be brought within the block, though we hazard every thing to do it."

"This is natur', and it is the law of God. But, Mabel, be calm, and endivor to be cool. All that can be effected for the sarjeant by human inventions, shall be done. I only ask you to be cool."

"I am—I am—Pathfinder. Never in my life was I more calm; more collected than at this moment. But remember how precious may be every instant; for Heaven's sake! what we do, let us do without delay."

Pathfinder was struck with the firmness of Mabel's tones, and perhaps he was a little deceived by the forced tranquillity and self-possession she had assumed. At all events, he did not deem any farther exhortations necessary, but descended forthwith, and began to unbar the door. This delicate process was conducted with the usual caution, but as he warily permitted the mass of timber to swing back on the hinges, he felt a pressure against it, that had nearly induced him to close it again. But catching a glimpse of the cause through the crack, the door was permitted to swing back, when the body of Serjeant Dunham, which was propped against it, fell partly within the block. To draw in the legs and secure the fastenings, occupied the Pathfinder but a moment. Then there existed no obstacle to their giving their undivided care to the wounded man.

Mabel, in this trying scene, conducted herself with the sort of unnatural energy that her sex, when aroused, is apt to manifest.

She got the light, administered water to the parched lips of her father, and assisted Pathfinder in forming a bed of straw, for his body, and a pillow of clothes for his head. All this was done earnestly, and almost without speaking, nor did Mabel shed a tear, until she heard the blessings of her father murmured on her head, for this tenderness and care. All this time, Mabel had merely conjectured the condition of her parent. Pathfinder, however, showed greater attention to the physical danger of the serjeant. He ascertained that a rifle ball had passed through the body of the wounded man, and he was sufficiently familiar with injuries of this nature, to be certain that the chances of his surviving the hurt, were very trifling, if any.

Chapter XXIV.

"There—drink my tears, while yet they fall—
Would that my bosom's blood were balm,
And—well thou knowest—I'd shed it all
To give thy brow one minute's calm."
            Moore, *Lalla Rookh*,
            "Paradise and the Peri," ll. 274–77.

THE eyes of Serjeant Dunham had not ceased to follow the form of his beautiful daughter, from the moment that the light appeared. He next examined the door of the block, to ascertain its security, for he was left on the ground below, there being no available means of raising him to the upper floor. Then he sought the face of Mabel, for as life wanes fast, the affections resume their force, and we begin to value that most which we feel we are about to lose forever.

"God be praised, my child, you, at least, have escaped their murderous rifles!" he said, for he spoke with strength, and, seemingly, with no additional pain. "Give me the history of this sad business, Pathfinder."

"Ah's! me, sarjeant, it *has* been sad, as you say. That there has been treachery, and the position of the island has been betrayed, is now as sartain, in my judgment, as that we still hold the block. But——"

"Major Duncan was right," interrupted Dunham, laying a hand on the other's arm.

"Not in the sense you mean, sarjeant—no, not in that p'int of view; never. At least, not, in my opinion. I know that natur' is weak—human natur' I mean—and that we should none of us vaunt of our gifts, whether red or white; but I do not think a truer-hearted lad lives on the lines, than Jasper Western."

"Bless you—bless you for that, Pathfinder!" burst forth from Mabel's very soul, while a flood of tears gave vent to emotions that were so varied, while they were so violent. "Oh! bless you, Pathfinder, bless you; the brave should never desert the brave; the honest should sustain the honest."

The father's eyes were fastened anxiously on the face of his daughter, until the latter hid her countenance in her apron to conceal her tears, and then they turned with inquiry to the hard features of the guide. The latter merely wore their usual expression of frankness, sincerity and uprightness, and the serjeant motioned to him to proceed.

"You know the spot where the Sarpent and I left you, serjeant," Pathfinder resumed, "and I need say nothing of all that happened afore. It is now too late to lament what is gone and passed; but I do think if I had staid with the boats, this would not have come to pass! Other men may be as good guides; I make no doubt they are; but then natur' bestows its gifts, and some must be better than other some. I dare say, poor Gilbert who took my place has suffered for his mistake."

"He fell at my elbow—" the serjeant answered in a low, melancholy tone—"we have, indeed, all suffered for our mistakes!"

"No—no—serjeant, I meant no condemnation on you, for men were never better commanded than yourn, in this very expedition. I never beheld a prettier flanking, and the way in which you carried your own boat up ag'in their howitzer, might have teached Lundie, himself, a lesson."

The eyes of the Serjeant brightened, and his face even wore an expression of military triumph, though it was of a degree that suited the humble sphere in which he had been an actor.

"'Twas not badly done, my friend," he said, "and we carried their log breast-work by storm!"

"'Twas nobly done, serjeant, though I fear, when all the truth comes to be known, it will be found that these vagabonds have got their howitzer back ag'in—Well, well, put a stout heart upon it, and try to forget all that is disagreeable, and to remember only the pleasant part of the matter. That is your truest philosophy, ay, and truest religion, too. If the inimy has got the howitzer, ag'in, they've only got what belonged to them afore, and what we could'n't help. They hav'n't got the block-house, yet, nor are they likely to get it, unless they fire it, in the dark. Well, serjeant, the Sarpent and I separated about ten miles down the river, for we thought it wisest not to come upon even a friendly camp, without the usual caution. What has become of Chingachgook I cannot say, though Mabel tells me he is not far off, and I make no question, the noble hearted Delaware is doing his duty, although he is not now visible to our eyes. Mark my words, sarjeant; before this matter is over, we shall hear of him, at some critical time, and that in a discreet and creditable manner. Ah! the Sarpent is, indeed, a wise and virtuous chief, and any white man might covet his gifts, though his rifle is not quite as sure as Killdeer, it must be owned. Well, as I came near the island, I missed the smoke, and that put me on my guard, for I knew the men of the 55th, were not cunning enough to conceal that sign, notwithstanding all that has been told them of its danger. This made me more careful, until I came in sight of their mock fisherman, as I've just told Mabel, and then the whole of their infernal arts was as plain afore me, as if I saw it on a map. I need not tell you, sarjeant, that my first thoughts were of Mabel, and that, finding she was in the block, I came here, in order to live, or die, in her company."

The father turned a gratified look upon his child, and Mabel felt a sinking of the heart that, at such a moment, she could not have thought possible, when she wished to believe all her concern centered in the situation of her parent. As the latter held out his hand, she took it in her own, and kissed it. Then kneeling at his side, she wept as if her heart would break.

"Mabel," he said steadily—"the will of God must be done. It is useless to attempt deceiving either you, or myself; my time has come, and it is a consolation to me, to die like a soldier. Lundie will do me justice, for our good friend, Pathfinder, will tell him what has been done, and how all came to pass. You do not forget our last conversation."

"Nay, father, my time has probably come too—" exclaimed Mabel, who felt, just then, as if it would be a relief to die. "I cannot hope to escape, and Pathfinder would do well to leave us, and return to the garrison, with the sad news while he can."

"Mabel Dunham," said Pathfinder, reproachfully, though he took her hand with kindness, "I have not desarved this. I know I am wild, and uncouth, and ungainly—"

"Pathfinder!"

"Well—well—we'll forget it; you did not mean it; you could not think it. It is useless, now, to talk of escaping, for the sarjeant cannot be moved, and the block-house must be defended, cost what it will. Maybe Lundie will get the tidings of our disaster, and send a party to raise the siege."

"Pathfinder–Mabel–" said the serjeant, who had been writhing with pain, until the cold sweat stood on his forehead–"come both to my side. You understand each other, I hope?"

"Father, say nothing of that–it is all as you wish."

"Thank God. Give me your hand, Mabel–here, Pathfinder, take it. I can do no more than give you the girl in this way. I know you will make her a kind husband. Do not wait, on account of my death, but there will be a chaplain in the fort, before the season closes, and let him marry you at once. My brother, if living, will wish to go back to his vessel, and then the child will have no protector. Mabel, your husband will have been my friend, and that will be some consolation to you, I hope."

"Trust this matter to me, sarjeant," put in Pathfinder. "Leave it all on my hands, as your dying request, and depend on it, all will go as it should."

"I do–I do–I put all confidence in you, my trusty friend, and empower you to act as I could act, myself, in every particular–Mabel, child–hand me the water–you will never repent this night. Bless you, my daughter–God bless, and have you in his holy keeping!"

This tenderness was inexpressibly touching to one of Mabel's feelings, and she felt, at that moment, as if her future union with Pathfinder had received a solemnization that no ceremony of the church could render more holy. Still, a weight, as that of a mountain, lay upon her heart, and she thought it would be happiness to die. Then followed a short pause, when the serjeant, in broken sentences briefly related what had passed since he parted with Pathfinder and the Delaware. The wind had come more favorable, and, instead of encamping on an island, agreeably to the original intention, he had determined to continue on, and reach the station that night. Their approach would have been unseen, and a portion of the calamity averted, he thought, had they not grounded on the point of a neighboring island, where, no doubt the noise made by the men, in getting off the boat, gave notice of their approach, and enabled the enemy to be in readiness to receive them. They had landed without the slightest suspicion of danger, though surprised at not finding any sentinel, and had actually left their arms in the boats, with the intention of first securing their knapsacks and provisions. The fire had been so close, that notwithstanding the obscurity, it was very deadly. Every man had fallen; two or three, however, subsequently arose, and disappeared. Four or five of the soldiers had been killed outright, or so nearly so, as to survive but a few minutes, though, for some unknown reason, the enemy did not make the usual rush for the scalps. Serjeant Dunham fell with the others, and he had heard the voice of Mabel as she rushed from the block-house. This frantic appeal aroused all his parental feelings, and enabled him to crawl as far as the door of the building where he had raised himself against the logs, in the manner already mentioned.

After this simple explanation was made the serjeant was so weak as to need repose, and his companions, while they ministered to his wants, suffered some time to pass in silence. Pathfinder took the occasion, to reconnoitre from the loops and the roof, and he examined the condition of the rifles of which there were a dozen kept in the building, the soldiers having used their regimental muskets in the expedition. But, Mabel never left her father's side for an instant, and when by his breathing, she fancied he slept, she bent her knees and prayed.

The half hour that succeeded was awfully solemn and still. The moccasin of Pathfinder was barely heard over head, and occasionally the sound of the breech of a rifle fell upon the floor; for he was busied in examining the pieces, with a view to ascertain the state of their charges, and their primings. Beyond this, nothing was so loud as the breathing of the wounded man. Mabel's heart yearned to be in communication with the father she was so soon to lose, and yet she would not disturb his apparent repose. But Dunham slept not. He was in that state when the world suddenly loses its attractions, its illusions, and its power, and the unknown future fills the mind, with its conjectures, its revelations and its immensity. He had been a moral man, for one of his mode of life, but he had thought little of this all important moment. Had the din of battle been ringing in his ears, his martial ardor might have endured to the end, but, there, in the silence of that nearly untenanted block-house, with no sound to enliven him, no appeal to keep alive factitious sentiment, no hope of victory to impel, things began to appear in their true colours, and this state of being to be estimated at its just value. He would have given treasures for religious consolation, and yet he knew not where to turn to seek it. He thought of Pathfinder, but he distrusted his knowledge. He thought of Mabel, but for the parent to appeal to the child for such succor, appeared like reversing the order of nature. Then it was that he felt the full responsibility of the parental character, and had some clear glimpses of the manner in which he himself had discharged the trust towards an orphan child. While thoughts like these were rising in his mind, Mabel, who watched the slightest change in his breathing, heard a guarded knock at the door. Supposing it might be Chingachgook, she rose, undid two of the bars, and held the third in her hand, as she asked who was there. The answer was in her uncle's voice, and he implored her to give him immediate admission. Without an instant of hesitation, she turned the bar, and Cap entered. He had barely passed the opening, when Mabel closed the door again, and secured it as before, for practice had rendered her expert, in this portion of her duties.

The sturdy seaman, when he had made sure of the state of his brother-in-law, and that Mabel as well as himself, was safe, was softened nearly to tears. His own appearance he explained, by saying that he had been carelessly guarded, under the impression that he and the Quarter Master were sleeping under the fumes of liquor, with which they had been plied, with a view to keep them quiet in the expected engagement. Muir had been left asleep, or seeming to sleep, but Cap had run into the bushes, on the alarm of the attack, and having found Pathfinder's canoe, had only succeeded, at that moment, in getting to the block-house, whither he had come with the kind intent of escaping with his niece, by water. It is scarcely necessary to say, that he changed his plan, when he ascertained the state of the serjeant, and the apparent security of his present quarters.

"If the worst comes to the worst, Master Pathfinder," he said, "we must strike, and that will entitle us to quarter. We owe it to our manhood to hold out a reasonable time, and to ourselves to haul down the ensign in season to make saving conditions. I

wished Master Muir to do the same thing, when we were captured by these chaps you call vagabonds—and rightly are they
named, for viler vagabonds do not walk the earth—"

"You've found out their characters!" interrupted Pathfinder,
who was always as ready to chime in with abuse of the Mingos,
as with the praises of his friends—"Now, had you fallen into the
hands of the Delawares, you would have l'arned the difference!"

"Well, to me, they seem much of a muchness; blackguards
fore and aft, always excepting our friend the Serpent, who is a
gentleman, for an Injin. But, when these savages made the assault on us, killing Corporal McNab, and his men, as if they had
been so many rabbits, Lt. Muir and myself took refuge in one of
the holes of this here island, of which there are so many among
the rocks—regular geological under-ground burrows made by
the water, as the Lieutenant says,—and there we remained
stowed away like two leaguers in a ship's hold, until we gave out
for want of grub. A man may say that grub is the foundation of
human nature. I desired the Quarter Master to make terms, for
we could have defended ourselves for an hour or two in the
place, bad as it was, but he declined on the ground that the
knaves would'n't keep faith, if any of them were hurt, and so
there was no use in asking them to. I consented to strike, on two
principles; one, that we might be said to have struck already;
for running below is generally thought to be giving up the ship;
and the other, that we had an enemy in our stomachs that was
more formidable in his attacks, than the enemy on deck.
Hunger is a d——le circumstance, as any man who has lived on
it eight and forty hours will acknowledge."

"Uncle!" said Mabel, in a mournful voice, and with an expos-
tulating manner, "my poor father is sadly, sadly hurt!"

"True, Magnet, true—I will sit by him, and do my best at consolation. Are the bars well fastened, girl, for, on such an occasion, the mind should be tranquil and undisturbed."

"We are safe, I believe, from all but this heavy blow of Providence."

"Well, then, Magnet, do you go up to the deck above, and try
to compose yourself, while Pathfinder runs aloft and takes a
look out from the cross-trees. Your father may wish to say
something to me, in private, and it may be well to leave us

alone. These are solemn scenes, and inexperienced people, like myself, do not always wish what they say to be overheard."

Although the idea of her uncle's affording religious consolation by the side of a death-bed, certainly never obtruded itself on the imagination of Mabel, she thought there might be a propriety in the request, with which she was unacquainted, and she complied accordingly. Pathfinder had already ascended to the roof, to make his survey, and the brothers-in-law were left alone. Cap took a seat by the side of the serjeant, and bethought him, seriously, of the grave duty he had before him. A silence of several minutes succeeded, during which brief space, the mariner was digesting the substance of his intended discourse.

"I must say, Serjeant Dunham," Cap at length commenced in his peculiar manner, "that there has been mismanagement somewhere in this unhappy expedition, and, the present being an occasion when truth ought to be spoken, and nothing but the truth, I feel it my duty to say as much, in plain language. In short, serjeant, on this point there cannot well be two opinions, for, seaman as I am, and no soldier, I can see several errors myself, that it needs no great education to detect."

"What would you have, Brother Cap," returned the other in a feeble voice—"what is done is done; and it is now too late to remedy it."

"Very true, Brother Dunham, but not to repent of it. The good book tells us, it is never too late to repent, and I've always heard that this is the precious moment. If you've any thing on your mind, serjeant, hoist it out freely, for you know, you trust it to a friend. You were my own sister's husband, and poor little Magnet is my own sister's daughter, and living, or dead, I shall always look upon you, as a brother. It's a thousand pities that you did'n't lie off and on, with the boats, and send a canoe ahead to reconnoitre, in which case your command would have been saved, and this disaster would not have befallen us all. Well, serjeant, we are *all* mortal, that is some consolation, I make no doubt, and if you go before a little, why, we must follow. Yes, that *must* give him consolation."

"I know all this, Brother Cap, and hope I'm prepared to meet a soldier's fate. There is poor Mabel—"

"Ay, ay—that's a heavy drag, I know, but you would'n't take her with you, if you could, serjeant, and so the better way is to make as light of the separation, as you can. Mabel is a good girl, and so was her mother before her; she was *my* sister, and it shall be my care to see that her daughter gets a good husband, if our lives and scalps are spared; for I suppose no one would care about entering into a family that has no scalps."

"Brother, my child is betrothed—she will become the wife of Pathfinder."

"Well, Brother Dunham, every man has his opinions, and his manner of viewing things, and to my notion this match will be any thing but agreeable to Mabel. I have no objection to the age of the man; I'm not one of them that thinks it is necessary to be a boy to make a girl happy, but on the whole I prefer a man of about fifty for a husband; still, there ought not to be any circumstance between the parties to make them unhappy. Circumstances play the devil with materimony, and I set it down as one, that Pathfinder do'n't know as much as my niece. You've seen but little of the girl, serjeant, and have not got the run of her knowledge; but, let her pay it out freely, as she will do when she gets to be thoroughly acquainted, and you'll fall in with but few schoolmasters that can keep their luffs in her company."

"She's a good child—a dear good child—" muttered the serjeant, his eyes filling with tears—"and it is my misfortune that I have seen so little of her."

"She is, indeed, a good girl, and knows altogether too much for poor Pathfinder, who is a reasonable man and an experienced man, in his own way, but who has no more idea of the main chance than you have of spherical trigonometry, serjeant."

"Ah! Brother Cap, had Pathfinder been with us in the boats, this sad affair might not have happened!"

"That is quite likely, for his worst enemy will allow that the man is a good guide; but, serjeant, if the truth must be spoken, you have managed this expedition in a loose way, altogether; you should have hove-to off your haven, and sent in a boat to reconnoitre, as I told you before. That is a matter to be repented of, and I tell it to you, because truth, in such a case, ought to be spoken."

"My errors are dearly paid for, Brother, and poor Mabel, I fear, will be the sufferer. I think, however, that the calamity would not have happened, had there not been treason. I fear me, Brother, that Jasper Eau douce has played us false!"

"That is just my notion, for this fresh-water life, must sooner or later undermine any man's morals. Lieutenant Muir and myself talked this matter over, while we lay in a bit of a hole, out here on this island, and we both came to the conclusion that nothing short of Jasper's treachery could have brought us all into this infernal scrape. Well, serjeant, you had better compose your mind, and think of other matters, for, when a vessel is about to enter a strange port, it is more prudent to think of the anchorage inside, than to be under-running all the events that have turned up during the v'y'ge. There's the logbook expressly to note all these matters in, and what stands there, must form the column of figures that's to be footed up for, or against us. How, now, Pathfinder; is there any thing in the wind, that you come down the ladder like an Indian in the wake of a scalp?"

The guide raised a finger, for silence, and then beckoned to Cap to ascend the first ladder, and to allow Mabel to take his place, at the side of the serjeant.

"We must be prudent, and we must be bold, too," he said, in a low voice. "The riptyles are in earnest in their intention to fire the block, for they know there is now nothing to be gained by letting it stand. I hear the voice of that vagabond Arrowhead, among them, and he is urging them to set about their diviltry this very night. We must be stirring, Salt-water, and doing too. Luckily, there are four or five barrels of water in the block, and these are something towards a siege. My reckoning is wrong, too, or we shall yet reap some advantage from that honest fellow the Sarpent, being at liberty."

Cap did not wait for a second invitation, but starting up, he was soon in the upper room, with Pathfinder, while Mabel took his post at the side of her father's humble bed. Pathfinder had opened a loop, having so far concealed the light that it would not expose him to a treacherous shot, and, expecting a summons, he stood with his face near the hole, ready to answer. The stillness that succeeded, was at length broken by the voice of Muir.

"Master Pathfinder," called out the Scotchman—"a friend

summons you to a parley. Come freely to one of the loops, for you've nothing to fear, so long as you are in converse with an officer of the 55th–"

"What is your will, Quarter Master–what is your will? I know the 55th, and believe it to be a brave rigiment, though I rather incline to the 60th, as my favorite, and to the Delawares more than to either. But what would you have, Quarter Master; it must be a pressing errand that brings you under the loops of a block house, at this hour of the night, with the sartainty of Killdeer's being inside of it."

"Oh! you'll no harm a friend, Pathfinder, I'm certain, and that's my security. You're a man of judgment, and have gained too great a name on this frontier for bravery, to feel the necessity of fool-hardiness to obtain a character. You'll very well understand, my good friend, there is as much credit to be gained by submitting gracefully, when resistance becomes impossible, as by obstinately holding out contrary to the rules of war. The enemy is too strong for us, my brave comrade, and I come to counsel you to give up the block, on condition of being treated as a prisoner of war."

"I thank you for this advice, Quarter Master, which is the more acceptable, as it costs nothing. But, I do not think it belongs to my gifts to yield a place like this, while food and water last."

"Well, I'd be the last, Pathfinder, to recommend any thing against so brave a resolution, did I see the means of maintaining it. But ye'll remember that Master Cap has fallen–"

"Not he–not he," roared the individual in question through another loop–"so far from that, Lieutenant, he has risen to the height of this here fortification, and has no mind to put his head of hair into the hands of such barbers, again, so long as he can help it. I look upon this block-house as a circumstance, and have no mind to throw it away."

"If that is a living voice," returned Muir, "I am glad to hear it, for we all thought the man had fallen in the late fearful confusion! But, Master Pathfinder, although ye're enjoying the society of your friend Cap, and a great pleasure do I know it to be, by the experience of two days and a night passed in a hole in the earth, we've lost that of Serjeant Dunham, who has fallen, with all the brave men he led in the late expedition. Lundie would have it so, though it would have been more discreet and becoming to send a commissioned officer in command. Dunham was a brave man, notwithstanding, and shall have justice done his memory. In short, we have all acted for the best, and that is as much as could be said in favor of Prince Eugene, the Duke of Marlborough or the Great Earl of Stair himself."

"You're wrong ag'in, Quarter Master, you're wrong ag'in," answered Pathfinder, resorting to a ruse to magnify his force. "The sarjeant is safe in the block too, where, one might say, the whole family is collected."

"Well, I rejoice to hear it, for we had certainly counted the serjeant among the slain. If pretty Mabel is in the block, still, let her not delay an instant, for Heaven's sake, in quitting it, for the enemy is about to put it to the trial by fire. Ye know the potency of that dread element, and will be acting more like the discreet and experienced warrior ye're universally allowed to be, in yielding a place you canna' defend, than in drawing down ruin on yourself and companions."

"I know the potency of fire, as you call it, Quarter Master, and am not to be told, at this late hour, that it can be used for something else, besides cooking a dinner. But, I make no doubt, you've heard of the potency of Killdeer, and the man who attempts to lay a pile of brush ag'in these logs, will get a taste of his power. As for arrows, it is not in their gift, to set this building on fire, for we've no shingles on our roof, but good solid logs and green bark, and plenty of water besides. The roof is so flat, too, as you know yourself, Quarter Master, that we can walk on it, and so no danger on that score, while water lasts. I'm peaceable enough, if let alone, but he who endivors to burn this block over my head will find the fire squinched in his own blood."

"This is idle and-romantic talk, Pathfinder, and ye'll no maintain it yourself when ye come to meditate on the realities. I hope ye'll no gainsay the loyalty, or the courage of the 55th, and I feel convinced that a council of war would decide on the propriety of a surrender, forthwith. Na'–na'–Pathfinder, foolhardiness is na' mair like the bravery o' Wallace, or Bruce,* than Albany on the Hudson is like the old town of Edinbro'."

"As each of us seems to have made up his mind, Quarter Master, more words are useless. If the riptyles near you, are disposed to set about their hellish job, let them begin at once. They can burn wood and I'll burn powder. If I were an Injin at the stake, I suppose I could brag as well as the rest of them, but my gifts and natur' being both white, my turn is rather for doing, than talking. You've said quite enough, considering you carry the King's commission, and should we all be consumed, none of us will bear *you* any malice."

"Pathfinder, ye'll no be exposing Mabel, pretty Mabel Dunham, to sic' a calamity!"

"Mabel Dunham is by the side of her wounded father, and God will care for the safety of a pious child. Not a hair of her head shall fall, while my arm and sight remain true, and though *you* may trust the Mingos, Master Muir, I put no faith in them. You've a knavish Tuscarora in your company there, who has art and malice enough to spoil the character of any tribe with which he consorts, though he found the Mingos ready ruined to his hands, I fear. But, enough said; let each party go to the use of his means and gifts."

Throughout this dialogue Pathfinder kept his body covered, lest a treacherous shot should be aimed at the loop, and he now directed Cap to ascend to the roof in order to be in readiness to meet the first assault. Although the latter used sufficient diligence, he found no less than ten blazing arrows sticking to the bark, while the air was filled with the yells and whoops of the enemy. A rapid discharge of rifles followed, and the bullets came pattering against the logs, in a way to show that the struggle had, indeed, seriously commenced.

These were sounds, however, that appalled neither Pathfinder, nor Cap, while Mabel was too much absorbed with her affliction to feel alarm. She had good sense enough, too, to understand the nature of the defences, and fully to appreciate their importance. As for her father, the familiar noises revived him, and it pained his child, at such a moment, to see that his glassy eye began to kindle, and that the blood returned to a cheek it had deserted, as he listened to the uproar. It was now Mabel first perceived that his reason began slightly to wander.

"Order up the light companies," he muttered–"and let the grenadiers charge!–Do they dare to attack us in our fort! Why does not the artillery open on them?"

At that instant the heavy report of a gun burst on the night, and the crash of rending wood was heard, as a heavy shot tore the logs in the room above, and the whole block shook with the force of a shell that lodged in the work. The Pathfinder narrowly escaped the passage of this formidable missile as it entered, but when it exploded, Mabel could not repress a shriek, for she supposed all over her head, whether animate, or inanimate, destroyed. To increase her horror, her father shouted in a frantic voice to—"Charge!"

"Mabel—" said Pathfinder, with his head at the trap, "this is true Mingo work, more noise than injury. The vagabonds have got the howitzer we took from the French, and have discharged it ag'in the block, but, fortunately, they have fired off the only shell we had, and there is an ind of its use for the present. There is some confusion among the stores, up in this loft, but no one is hurt. Your uncle is still on the roof, and as for myself, I've run the gauntlet of too many rifles, to be skeary about such a thing as a howitzer, and that in Injin hands."

Mabel murmured her thanks, and tried to give all her attention to her father, whose efforts to rise were only counteracted by his debility. During the few fearful minutes that succeeded, she was so much occupied with her care of the invalid, that she scarce heeded the clamour that reigned around her. Indeed, the uproar was so great, that had not her thoughts been otherwise employed, confusion of faculties, rather than alarm, would probably have been the consequence.

Cap preserved his coolness admirably. He had a profound and increasing respect for the prowess of the savages, and even for the majesty of fresh water, it is true; but his apprehensions of the former proceeded more from his dread of being scalped and tortured, than from any unmanly fear of death, and as he was now on the deck of a house, if not the deck of a ship, and knew that there was little danger of boarders, he moved about with a fearlessness, and a real exposure of his person, that Pathfinder, had he been aware of the fact, would have been the first to condemn. Instead of keeping his body covered, agreeably to the usages of Indian warfare, he was seen on every part of the roof, dashing the water right and left, with the apparent steadiness and unconcern, he would have manifested had he been a sail trimmer, exercising his art, in a battle afloat. His appearance was one of the causes of the extraordinary clamor among the assailants, who, unused to seeing their enemies so reckless, opened upon him with their tongues, like the pack that has the fox in view. Still, he appeared to possess a charmed life, for, though the bullets whistled around him on every side, and his clothes were several times torn, nothing cut his skin. When the shell passed through the logs below, the old sailor dropped his bucket, waved his hat, and gave three cheers, in which heroic act he was employed as the dangerous missile exploded. This characteristic feat probably saved his life, for, from that instant, the Indians ceased to fire at him, and even to shoot their flaming arrows at the block, having taken up the notion, simultaneously and by common consent, that the "salt water" was mad; and it was a singular effect of their magnanimity never to lift a hand against those whom they imagined devoid of reason.

The conduct of Pathfinder was very different. Every thing he did was regulated by the most exact calculation, the result of long experience and habitual thoughtfulness. His person was kept carefully out of a line with the loops, and the spot that he selected for his look out, was one that was quite removed from danger. This celebrated guide had often been known to lead forlorn hopes, he had once stood at the stake, suffering under the cruelties and taunts of savage ingenuity and savage ferocity, without quailing, and legends of his exploits, coolness and daring, were to be heard all along that extensive frontier, or, wherever men dwelt and men contended, but, on this occasion, one who did not know his history and character might have thought his exceeding care and studied attention to self preservation, proceeded from an unworthy motive. But such a judge would not have understood his subject. The Pathfinder bethought him of Mabel, and of what might possibly be the consequences to that poor girl, should any casualty befall himself, but the recollection rather quickened his intellect, than changed his customary prudence. He was in fact, one of those who was so unaccustomed to fear, that he never bethought him of the constructions others might put upon his conduct, but, while, in moments of danger, he acted with the wisdom of the serpent, it was also with the simplicity of a child.

For the first ten minutes of the assault, Pathfinder never

raised the breech of his rifle from the floor, except when he changed his own position; for he well knew that the bullets of the enemy were thrown away upon the massive logs of the work, and, as he had been at the capture of the howitzer, he felt certain that the savages had no other shell than the one found in it, when the piece was taken. There existed no reason, therefore, to dread the fire of the assailants, except as a casual bullet might find a passage through a loop-hole. One or two of these accidents did occur, but the balls entered at an angle that deprived them of all chance of doing any injury, so long as the Indians kept near the block; and, if discharged from a distance, there was scarcely the probability of one in a hundred's striking the apertures. But, when Pathfinder heard the sound of moccasined feet, and the rustling of brush at the foot of the building he knew that the attempt to build a fire against the logs, was about to be renewed. He now summoned Cap from the roof, where indeed, all the danger had ceased, and directed him to stand in readiness with his water, at a hole immediately over the spot assailed.

One less trained than our hero would have been in a hurry to repel this dangerous attempt also, and might have resorted to his means prematurely. Not so with Pathfinder. His aim was not only to extinguish the fire, about which he felt little apprehension, but to give the enemy a lesson that would render him wary during the remainder of the night. In order to effect the latter purpose, it became necessary to wait until the light of the intended conflagration should direct his aim, when he well knew that a very slight effort of his skill would suffice. The Iroquois were permitted to collect their heap of dried brush, to pile it against the block, to light it, and to return to their covers, without molestation. All that Pathfinder would suffer Cap to do, was to roll a barrel filled with water, to the hole immediately over the spot, in readiness to be used at the proper instant. That moment, however, did not arrive in his judgment, until the blaze illuminated the surrounding bushes, and there had been time for his quick and practised eye to detect the forms of three or four lurking savages, who were watching the progress of the flames, with the cool indifference of men accustomed to look on human misery with apathy. Then, indeed, he spoke.

"Are you ready, Friend Cap?" he asked. "The heat begins to

strike through the crevices, and, although these green logs, are not of the fiery natur' of an ill-tempered man, they may be kindled into a blaze, if one provokes them too much. Are you ready with the barrel?—See that it has the right cut, and that none of the water is wasted."

"All ready—" answered Cap, in the manner in which a seaman replies to such a demand.

"Then wait for the word. Never be over impatient, in a critical time, nor fool-risky in a battle. Wait for the word."

While the Pathfinder was giving these directions, he was also making his own preparations, for he saw it was time to act. Killdeer was deliberately raised, pointed, and discharged. The whole process occupied about half a minute, and, as the rifle was drawn in, the eye of the marksman was applied to the hole.

"There is one riptyle the less—" Pathfinder muttered to himself—"I've seen that vagabond afore, and know him to be a marciless devil. Well, well; the man acted according to his gifts, and he has been rewarded according to his gifts. One more of the knaves, and that will sarve the turn for to-night. When daylight appears, we may have hotter work."

All this time, another rifle was getting ready, and as Pathfinder ceased, a second savage fell. This, indeed, sufficed, for indisposed to wait for a third visitation from the same hand, the whole band which had been crouching in the bushes around the block, ignorant of who was, and who was not exposed to view, leaped from their covers, and fled to different places for safety.

"Now, pour away, Master Cap," said Pathfinder—"I've made my mark on the blackguards, and we shall have no more fires lighted to-night."

"Scaldings!" cried Cap, upsetting the barrel, with a care that at once, and completely extinguished the flames.

This ended the singular conflict, and the remainder of the night passed in peace. Pathfinder and Cap watched alternately, though neither can be said to have slept. Sleep, indeed, scarcely seemed necessary to them, for both were accustomed to protracted watchings, and there were seasons and times, when the former appeared to be literally insensible to the demands of hunger and thirst, and callous to the effects of fatigue.

Mabel watched by her father's pallet, and began to feel how much our happiness in this world depends even on things that are imaginary. Hitherto she had virtually lived without a father, the connection with her remaining parent being ideal rather than positive; but, now that she was about to lose him, she thought, for the moment, that the world would be a void after his death, and that she could never be acquainted with happiness again.

Chapter XXV.

"There was a roaring in the wind all night;
The rain came heavily, and fell in floods;
But now the sun is rising calm and bright;
The birds are singing in the distant woods—"
Wordsworth, "Resolution and Independence," ll. 1–4.

As the light returned, Pathfinder and Cap ascended again to the roof, with a view once more to reconnoitre the state of things on the island. This part of the block house had a low battlement around it, which afforded a considerable protection to those who stood in its centre; the intention having been to enable marksmen to lie behind it, and to fire over its top. By making proper use, therefore, of these slight defences—slight as to height, though abundantly ample as far as they went—the two look-outs commanded a pretty good view of the island, its covers excepted, and of most of the channels that led to the spot.

The gale was still blowing very fresh at south, and there were places in the river where its surface looked green and angry, though the wind had hardly sweep enough to raise the water into foam. The shape of the little island was generally oval, and its greatest length was from east to west. By keeping in the channels that washed it, in consequence of their several courses, and of the direction of the gale, it would have been possible for a vessel to range past the island, on either of its principal sides, and always keep the wind very nearly abeam. These were the facts first noted by Cap, and explained to his companion, for the hopes of both now rested on the chances of relief sent from Oswego. At this instant, while they stood gazing anxiously about them, Cap cried out in his lusty, hearty, manner—

"Sail ho!"

Pathfinder turned quickly, in the direction of his companion's face, and there, sure enough, was just visible the object of the old sailor's exclamation. The elevation, enabled the two to overlook the low land of several of the adjacent islands, and the canvass of a vessel was seen through the bushes that fringed the shore of one that lay to the southward and westward. The stranger was under what seamen call low sail, but so great was the power of the wind that her white outlines were seen flying past the openings of the verdure, with the velocity of a fast travelling horse, resembling a cloud driving in the heavens.

"That cannot be Jasper," said Pathfinder in disappointment, for he did not recognise the cutter of his friend in the swift-passing object. "No—no—the lad is behind the hour, and that is some craft that the Frenchers have sent to aid their friends, the accursed Mingos."

"This time you are out in your reckoning, friend Pathfinder, if you never were before—" returned Cap, in a manner that had lost none of its dogmatism by the critical circumstances in which they were placed. "Fresh water or salt, that is the head of the Scud's mainsail, for it is cut with a smaller goar*than common, and then you can see that the gaff has been fished*—quite neatly done, I admit, but fished."

"I can see none of this, I confess," answered Pathfinder, to whom even the terms of his companion were Greek.

"No!—Well, I own that surprises me; for I thought *your* eyes could see any thing! Now, to me nothing is plainer than that goar and that fish, and I must say, my honest friend, that, in your place, I should apprehend that my sight was beginning to fail."

"If Jasper is truly coming, I shall apprehend but little. We can make good the block against the whole Mingo nation, for the next eight, or ten hours, and with Eau douce to cover the retreat, I shall despair of nothing. God send that the lad may not run along side of the bank, and fall into an ambushment, as befel the sarjeant!"

"Ay; there's the danger. There ought to have been signals concerted, and an anchorage ground buoyed out, and even a quarantine station, or a Lazaretto*would have been useful could we have made these Minks—ho! respect the laws. If the lad fetches up, as you say, any where in the neighborhood of this island, we may look upon the cutter as lost. And, after all, Master Pathfinder; ought we not to set down this same Jasper as a secret ally of the French, rather than as a friend of our own?—I know the Serjeant views the matter in that light, and I must say this whole affair looks like treason!"

"We shall soon know, we shall soon know, Master Cap, for there, indeed, comes the cutter, clear of the other island, and five minutes must settle the matter. It would be no more than fair, howsever, if we could give the boy some sign in the way of warning. It is not right that he should fall into the trap, without a notice that it has been laid."

Anxiety and suspense, notwithstanding, prevented either from attempting to make any signal. It was not easy, truly, to see how it could be done, for the Scud came foaming through the channel, on the weather side of the island, at a rate that scarce admitted of the necessary time. Nor was any one visible on her deck, to make signs to; even her helm seemed deserted, though her course was as steady as her progress was rapid.

Cap stood in silent admiration of a spectacle so unusual. But as the Scud drew nearer, his practised eye detected the helm in play, by means of tiller ropes, though the person who steered was concealed. As the cutter had weather-boards of some little height, the mystery was explained, no doubt remaining that her people lay behind the latter, in order to be protected from the rifles of the enemy. As this fact showed that no force, beyond that of the small crew, could be on board, Pathfinder received his companion's explanation with an ominous shake of the head.

"This proves that the Sarpent has not reached Oswego," he said, "and that we are not to expect succor from the garrison. I hope Lundie has not taken it into his head to displace the lad, for Jasper Western would be a host of himself, in such a strait. We three, Master Cap, ought to make a manful warfare—you, as a seaman, to keep up the intercourse with the cutter, Jasper as a laker, who knows all that is necessary to be done on the water, and I with gifts that are as good as any among the Mingos, let me be what I may, in other particulars. I say, we ought to make a manful fight, in Mabel's behalf."

"That we ought—and that we will—" answered Cap, heartily, for he began to have more confidence in the security of his scalp, now that he saw the sun again; "I set down the arrival of the Scud as one circumstance, and the chances of Oh! the deuce's honesty as another. This Jasper is a young man of prudence, you find, for he keeps a good offing, and seems determined to know how matters stand on the island, before he ventures to bring up."

"I have it! I have it!—" exclaimed Pathfinder with exultation—"There lies the canoe of the Sarpent, on the cutter's deck, and the chief has got on board, and no doubt has given a true account of our condition, for, unlike a Mingo, a Delaware is sartain to get a story right, or to hold his tongue."

Pathfinder's disposition to think well of the Delawares, and to think ill of the Mingos, must, by this time, be very apparent to the reader. Of the veracity of the former he entertained the highest respect, while of the latter he thought, as the more observant and intelligent classes of this country are getting pretty generally to think of certain scribblers among ourselves, who are known to have been so long in the habits of mendacity, that it is thought they can no longer tell the truth, even when they seriously make the effort.

"That canoe may belong to the cutter," said the captious seaman—"Oh! the Deuce had one on board, when we sailed."

"Very true, friend Cap; but, if you know your sails and masts, by your goars and fishes, I know my canoes and my paths, by frontier knowledge. If you can see new cloth in a sail, I can see new bark in a canoe. That is the boat of the Sarpent, and the noble fellow has struck off for the garrison, as soon as he found the block besieged, has fallen in with the Scud, and, after telling his story, has brought the cutter down here to see what can be done. The Lord grant that Jasper Western be still on board her!"

"Yes—yes—it might not be amiss, for traitor or loyal, the lad has a handy way with him in a gale, it must be owned."

"And in coming over water-falls!" said Pathfinder, nudging the ribs of his companion, with an elbow, and laughing in his silent, but hearty manner. "We will give the boy his due, though he scalps us all with his own hand!"

The Scud was now so near, that Cap made no reply. The scene, just at that instant, was so peculiar that it merits a particular description; which may also aid the reader in forming a more accurate notion of the picture we wish to draw.

The gale was still blowing violently. Many of the smaller trees bowed their tops, as if ready to descend to the earth, while the rushing of the wind through the branches of the groves, resembled the roar of distant chariots. The air was filled with leaves, which, at that late season, were readily driven from their stems, and flew from island to island, like flights of birds. With this exception, the spot seemed silent as the grave. That the savages still remained, was to be inferred from the fact that their canoes, together with the boats of the 55th, lay in a group, in the little cove, that had been selected as a harbour. Otherwise, not a sign of their presence was to be detected. Though taken entirely by surprise by the cutter, the sudden return of which was altogether unlooked for, so uniform and inbred, were their habits of caution, while on the war-path, that, the instant an alarm was given, every man had taken to his cover, with the instinct and cunning of a fox seeking his hole. The same stillness reigned in the block-house, for though Pathfinder and Cap could command a view of the channel, they took the precaution necessary to lie concealed. The unusual absence of any thing like animal life on board the Scud, too, was still more remarkable. As the Indians witnessed her apparently undirected movements, a feeling of awe gained a footing among them, and some of the boldest of their party, began to distrust the issue of an expedition that had commenced so prosperously. Even Arrowhead, accustomed as he was, to intercourse with the whites on both sides of the lakes, fancied there was something ominous in the appearance of this unmanned vessel, and he would gladly, at that moment, have been landed again on the main.

In the mean time, the progress of the cutter was steady and rapid. She held her way mid-channel, now inclining to the gusts, and now rising again, like the philosopher that bends to the calamities of life to resume his erect attitude as they pass away, but always piling the water beneath her bows, in foam. Although she was under so very short canvass, her velocity was great, and there could not have elapsed ten minutes between the time when her sails were first seen glancing past the trees and bushes, in the distance, and the moment when she was abreast of the block-house. Cap and Pathfinder leaned forward, as the cutter came beneath their eyrie, eager to get a better view of her deck, when to the delight of both, Jasper Eau douce, sprang upon his feet, and gave three hearty cheers. Regardless of all risk, Cap leaped upon the rampart of logs, and returned the greeting cheer for cheer. Happily, the policy of the enemy saved the latter, for they still lay quiet, not a rifle being discharged. On the other hand, Pathfinder kept in view the useful, utterly disregarding the more dramatic part of warfare. The moment he beheld his friend Jasper, he called out to him with Stentorian lungs—

"Stand by us, lad, and the day's our own! Give 'em a grist in yonder bushes, and you'll put 'em up like partridges."

Part of this reached Jasper's ears, but most was borne off to leeward, on the wings of the wind. By the time this was said, the Scud had driven past, and in the next moment she was hid from view by the grove in which the block-house was partially concealed.

Two anxious minutes succeeded, but, at the expiration of that brief space, the sails were again gleaming through the trees, Jasper having wore, jibed, and hauled up under the lee of the island, on the other tack. The wind was free enough, as has been already explained, to admit of this manœuvre, and the cutter catching the current under her lee bow, was breasted up to her course, in a way that showed she would come out to windward of the island again, without any difficulty. This whole evolution was made with the greatest facility, not a sheet being touched, the sails trimming themselves, the rudder alone, controlling the admirable machine. The object appeared to be a reconnoissance. When, however, the Scud had made the circuit of the entire island, and had again got her weatherly position, in the channel by which she had first approached, her helm was put down, and she tacked. The noise of the mainsail flapping when it filled, close reefed*as it was, sounded like the report of a gun, and Cap trembled lest the seams should open.

"His Majesty gives good canvass, it must be owned," muttered the old seaman, "and it must be owned, too, that boy handles his boat, as if he were thoroughly bred! D——e, Master Pathfinder, if I believe, after all that has been reported in the matter, that this Mister Oh! the Deuce got his trade on this bit of fresh water."

"He did; yes he did. He never saw the ocean, and has come by his calling altogether, up here on Ontario. I have often thought he has a nat'ral gift, in the way of schooners and sloops, and have respected him accordingly. As for treason, and lying, and black hearted vices, friend Cap, Jasper Western is as free as the most virtuousest of the Delaware warriors, and if you crave to see a truly honest man, you must go among that tribe to discover him."

"There he comes round!" exclaimed the delighted Cap, the Scud at this moment filling on her original tack, "and now we shall see what the boy would be at; he cannot mean to keep running up and down these passages, like a girl footing it through a country dance!"

The Scud now kept so much away, that, for a moment, the two observers on the block-house, feared Jasper meant to come to, and the savages, in their lairs, gleamed out upon her, with a sort of exultation that the crouching tiger may be supposed to feel, as he sees his unconscious victim approach his bed. But Jasper had no such intention. Familiar with the shore, and acquainted with the depth of water on every part of the island, he well knew that the Scud might be run against the bank with impunity, and he ventured fearlessly so near, that as he passed through the little cove, he swept the two boats of the soldiers from their fastenings, and forced them out into the channel, towing them with the cutter. As all the canoes were fastened to the two Dunham boats, by this bold and successful attempt the savages were at once deprived of the means of quitting the island, unless by swimming, and they appeared to be instantly aware of the very important fact. Rising in a body, they filled the air with yells, and poured in a harmless fire. While up, in this unguarded manner, two rifles were discharged by their adversaries. One came from the summit of the block, and an Iroquois fell dead in his tracks, shot through the brain. The other came from the Scud. The last was the piece of the Delaware, but, less true than that of his friend, it only maimed an enemy for life. The people of the Scud shouted, and the savages, sank again, to a man, as if it might be into the earth.

"That was the Sarpent's voice," said Pathfinder, as soon as the second piece was discharged. "I know the crack of his rifle, as well as I do that of Killdeer. 'Tis a good barrel, though not sartain death. Well—well—with Chingachgook and Jasper on the water, and you and I in the block, friend Cap, it will be hard, if we do'n't teach these Mingo scamps the rationality of a fight!"

All this time, the Scud was in motion. As soon as she had reached the end of the island, Jasper sent his prizes adrift, and they went down before the wind, until they stranded on a point, more than a mile to leeward. He then wore, and came stemming the current again, through the other passage. Those on the summit of the block, could now perceive that something was in agitation on the deck of the Scud, and to their great delight, just as the cutter came abreast of the principal cover, or the spot where most of the enemy lay, the howitzer, which composed her sole armament, was unmasked, and a shower of case shot was sent hissing into the bushes. A bevy of quail would not have risen quicker than this unexpected discharge of iron hail, put up the Iroquois, when a second savage fell by a messenger sent from Killdeer, and another went limping away, by a visit from the rifle of Chingachgook. New covers were immediately found, however, and each party seemed to prepare for the renewal of the strife, in another form. But, the appearance of June bearing a white flag, and accompanied by the French officer and Muir, stayed the hands of all, and was the forerunner of another parley.

The negotiation that followed was held beneath the blockhouse, and so near it, as at once to put those who were uncovered completely at the mercy of Pathfinder's unerring aim. Jasper anchored directly abeam, and the howitzer, too, was kept trained upon the negotiators, so that the besieged and their friends, with the exception of the man who held the match, had no hesitation about exposing their persons. Chingachgook, alone, lay in ambush, more, however, from habit, than distrust.

"You've triumphed, Pathfinder," called out the Quarter Master, "and Capt. Sanglier has come himself to offer terms. You'll no be denying a brave enemy an honorable retreat, when he has fought ye fairly, and done all the credit he could to king and country. Ye are too loyal a subject yourself, to visit loyalty and fidelity with a heavy judgment. I am authorized to offer, on the part of the enemy, an evacuation of the island, a mutual exchange of prisoners, and a restoration of scalps. In the absence of baggage and artillery, little more can be done."

As the conversation was necessarily carried on in a high key, both on account of the wind, and on account of the distance, all that was said was heard equally by those in the block, and those in the cutter.

"What do you say to that, Jasper?" called out Pathfinder. "You hear the tarms; shall we let the vagabonds go, or shall we mark them, as they mark their sheep, in the settlements, that we may know them, ag'in?"

"What has befallen Mabel Dunham?" demanded the young man, with a frown on his handsome face, that was visible even to those in the block—"If a hair of her head has been touched, it will go hard with the whole Iroquois tribe!"

"Nay—nay, she is safe below, nursing a dying parent, as becomes her sex. We owe no grudge on account of the Sarjeant's hurt, which comes of lawful warfare; and, as for Mabel—"

"She is here—" exclaimed the girl herself, who had mounted to the roof, the moment she found the direction things were taking. "She is here, and, in the name of our holy religion, and of that God whom we profess to worship in common, let there be no more bloodshed! Enough has been spilt already, and if these men will go away, Pathfinder—if they will depart peaceably, Jasper—oh! do not detain one of them. My poor father is approaching his end, and it were better that he should draw his last breath, in peace with the world. Go—go—Frenchmen and Indians; we are no longer your enemies, and will harm none of you."

"Tut—tut—Magnet," put in Cap, "this sounds religious, perhaps, or like a book of poetry, but it does not sound like common sense. The enemy is just ready to strike; Jasper is anchored, with his broadside to bear, and no doubt with springs on his cable; Pathfinder's eye and hand are as true as the needle, and we shall get prize-money, head-money, and honor, in the bargain, if you will not interfere, for the next half-hour."

"Well," said Pathfinder, "I incline to Mabel's way of thinking. There *has* been enough blood shed to answer our purposes, and to sarve the King, and as for honor, in that meaning, it will do better for young ensigns and recruits, than for cool headed, obsarvant, Christian men. There is honor in doing what's right, and unhonor in doing what's wrong; and I think it wrong to take the life, even of a Mingo, without a useful ind in view, I do; and right to hear reason at all times. So, Lieutenant Muir, let us know what your friends the Frenchers and Injins have to say for themselves."

"My friends!" said Muir, starting—"You'll no be calling the King's enemies my friends, Pathfinder, because the fortune of war has thrown me into their hands? Some of the greatest warriors, both of ancient and modern times, have been prisoners of war, and yon is Master Cap, who can testify whether we did not do all that men could devise to escape the calamity?"

"Ay—ay—" drily answered Cap—"escape is the proper word. We ran below and hid ourselves, and so discreetly, that we might have remained in the hole to this hour, had it not been for the necessity of re-stowing the bread lockers. You burrowed on that occasion, Quarter Master, as handily as a fox; and how the d——l, you knew so well where to find the spot is a matter of wonder to me. A regular skulk on board ship, does not tail aft more readily, when the jib is to be stowed, than you went into that same hole!"

"And did ye no follow! There are moments in a man's life, when reason ascends to instinct—"

"And men descend into holes," interrupted Cap, laughing in his boisterous way, while Pathfinder chimed in, in his peculiar manner. Even Jasper, though still filled with concern for Mabel, was obliged to smile. "They say the d——l would'n't make a sailor, if he did'n't look aloft, and now it seems he'll not make a soldier, if he does'n't look below!"

This burst of merriment, though it was any thing but agreeable to Muir, contributed largely towards keeping the peace. Cap fancied he had said a thing much better than common, and that disposed him to yield his own opinion on the main point, so long as he got the good opinion of his companions on his novel claim to be a wit. After a short discussion, all the savages on the island, were collected in a body, without arms, at the distance of a hundred yards from the block, and under the gun of the Scud, while Pathfinder descended to the door of the block-house, and settled the terms, on which the island was to be finally evacuated, by the enemy. Considering all the circumstances, the conditions were not very discreditable to either party. The Indians were compelled to give up all their arms, even to their knives and tomahawks, as a measure of precaution, their force being still quadruple that of their foes. The French officer, Monsieur Sanglier, as he was rightly styled, or chose to call himself, remonstrated against this act, as one likely to reflect more discredit on his command, than any other part of the affair, but, Pathfinder, who had witnessed one or two Indian massacres, and knew how valueless pledges became when put in opposition to interest, where a savage was concerned, was obdurate. The second stipulation was of nearly the same importance. It compelled Capt. Sanglier to give up all his prisoners, who had been kept well guarded, in the very hole, or cave, in which Cap and Muir had taken refuge. When these men were produced, four of them were found to be unhurt; they had fallen merely to save their lives, a common artifice in that species of warfare, and of the remainder, two were so slightly injured as not to be unfit for service. As they brought their muskets with them, this addition to his force, immediately put Pathfinder at his ease; for having collected all the arms of the enemy in the block-house, he directed these men to take possession of the building, stationing a regular sentinel at the door. The remainder of the soldiers were dead, the badly wounded having been instantly dispatched, in order to obtain the much coveted scalps.

As soon as Jasper was made acquainted with the terms, and the preliminaries had been so far observed as to render it safe for him to be absent, he got the Scud under way, and running down to the point where the boats had stranded, he took them in tow again, and, making a few stretches, brought them into the leeward passage. Here all the savages instantly embarked, when Jasper took the boats in tow, a third time, and running off before the wind, he soon set them adrift, quite a mile to leeward of the island. The Indians were furnished with but a single oar in each boat to steer with; the young sailor well knowing, that, by keeping before the wind, they would land on the shores of Canada, in the course of the morning.

Capt. Sanglier, Arrowhead and June alone remained, when this disposition had been made of the rest of the party; the former having certain papers to draw up and sign with Lieutenant Muir, who, in his eyes, possessed the virtues which are attached to a commission, and the latter preferring, for reasons of his own, not to depart in company with his late friends, the Iroquois. Canoes were retained, for the departure of these three, when the proper moment should arrive.

In the mean time, or while the Scud was running down with the boats in tow, Pathfinder and Cap aided by proper assistants, busied themselves with preparing a breakfast; most of the party not having eaten for four and twenty hours. The brief space that passed in this manner, before the Scud came to, again, was little interrupted by discourse, though Pathfinder found leisure to pay a visit to the serjeant, to say a few friendly words to Mabel, and to give such directions as he thought might smooth the passage of the dying man. As for Mabel, herself, he insisted on her taking some light refreshment, and there no longer existing any motive for keeping it there, he had the guard removed from the block, in order that the daughter might have no impediment to her attentions to her father. These little arrangements completed, our hero returned to the fire, around which he found all the remainder of the party assembled, including Jasper.

Chapter XXVI.

"You saw but sorrow in its waning form,
A working sea remaining from a storm;
When now the weary waves roll o'er the deep,
And faintly murmur ere they fall asleep—"
            Dryden, *Aureng-Zebe*, IV.i.197–200.

MEN accustomed to a warfare, like that we have been describing, are not apt to be much under the influence of tender feelings, while still in the field. Notwithstanding their habits, however, more than one heart was with Mabel in the block, while the incidents we are about to relate were in the course of occurrence, and even the indispensable meal was less relished by the hardiest of the soldiers, than it might have been had not the serjeant been so near his end.

As Pathfinder returned from the block, he was met by Muir, who led him aside in order to hold a private discourse. The manner of the Quarter Master had that air of supererogatory courtesy about it, which almost invariably denotes artifice, for while physiognomy, and phrenology are but lame sciences, at the best, and perhaps lead to as many false as right conclusions, we hold that there is no more infallible evidence of insincerity of purpose, short of overt acts, than a face that smiles when there is no occasion, and the tongue that is out of measure smooth. Muir had much of this manner in common, mingled with an apparent frankness, that his Scottish intonation of voice, Scottish accent, and Scottish modes of expression were singularly adapted to sustain. He owed his preferment, indeed, to a long exercised deference to Lundie and his family, for, while the Major himself was much too acute to be the dupe of one so much his inferior in real talents and attainments, most persons are accustomed to make liberal concessions to the flatterer, even while they distrust his truth, and are perfectly aware of his motive. On the present occasion, the contest in skill, was between two men as completely the opposites of each other, in all the leading essentials of character, as very well could be.

Pathfinder was as simple, as the Quarter Master was practised; he was as sincere as the other was false, and as direct as the last was tortuous. Both were cool and calculating, and both were brave, though in different modes and degrees; Muir never exposing his person except for effect, while the guide included fear among the rational passions, or as a sensation to be deferred to only when good might come of it.

"My dearest friend," Muir commenced, "for ye'll be dearer to us all, by seventy and seven fold, after your late conduct than ever ye were, ye've just established yourself, in this late transaction! It's true, that they'll no be making ye a commissioned officer, for that species of prefairment is not much in your line, nor much in your wishes, I'm thinking; but, as a guide, and a counsellor, and a loyal subject, and an expert marksman, yer' renown may be said to be full. I doubt if the commander in chief will carry away with him from America, as much credit as will fall to yer' share, and ye ought just to sit down in content, and enjoy yerself for the remainder of yer' days. Get married, man, without delay, and look to your precious happiness, for ye've no occasion to look any longer to your glory. Tak' Mabel Dunham, o' Heaven's sake, to yer bosom, and ye'll have both a bonny bride, and a bonny reputation."

"Why, Quarter Master, this is a new piece of advice to come from your mouth!—They've told me I had a rival in you!"

"And ye had, man, and a formidable one too, I can tell ye! One that has never yet courted in vain, and yet one that has courted five times. Lundie twits me with four; and I deny the charge; but he little thinks the truth would outdo even his own arithmetic! Yes, yes; ye had a rival, Pathfinder, but ye've one no langer in me. Ye've my hearty wishes for yer' success with Mabel, and were the honest serjeant likely to survive, ye might rely on my good word with him, too, for a certainty."

"I feel your friendship, Quarter Master, I feel your friendship, though I have no great need of any favor with Sarjeant Dunham, who has long been my friend. I believe we may look upon the matter to be as sartain as most things in war time, for, Mabel and her father consenting, the whole 55th, could'n't very well put a stop to it. Ah's! me; the poor father will scarcely live to see what his heart has so long been set upon!"

"But he'll have the consolation of knowing it will come to

pass, in dying. Oh! it's a great relief, Pathfinder, for the parting spirit to feel certain that the beloved ones left behind, will be well provided for, after its departure. All the Mistress Muirs have duly expressed that sentiment, with their dying breaths."

"All your wives, Quarter Master, have been likely to feel this consolation?"

"Out upon ye, man—I'd no thought ye such a wag! Well— well—pleasant words make no heart-burnings between auld fri'nds. If I cannot espouse Mabel, ye'll no object to my esteeming her, and speaking well of her, and of yoursal' too, on all suitable occasions, and in all companies. But, Pathfinder, ye'll easily understan' that a poor deevil, who loses such a bride, will probably stand in need of some consolation?"

"Quite likely—quite likely, Quarter Master," returned the simple-minded guide; "I know the loss of Mabel would be heavy to be borne, by myself. It may bear hard on your feelings to see us married, but the death of the sarjeant will be likely to put it off, and you'll have time to think more manfully of it, you will."

"I'll bear up against it—yes, I'll bear up against it, though my heart strings crack, and ye might help me, man, by giving me something to do. Ye'll understand that this expedition has been of a varry peculiar nature, for, here am I, bearing the King's commission, just a volunteer, as it might be; while a mere orderly has had the command. I've submitted for various reasons, though my blood has boiled to be in authority, while ye war' battling for the honor of the country, and His Majesty's rights—"

"Quarter Master," interrupted the guide, "you fell so early into the inimy's hands, that your conscience ought to be easily satisfied on that score, so, take my advice, and say nothing about it."

"That's just my opinion, Pathfinder; we'll all say nothing about it. Serjeant Dunham is *hors de combat*—"

"Anan!" said the guide.

"Why the serjeant can command no longer, and it will hardly do to leave a corporal at the head of a victorious party, like this, for the flower that will bloom in a garden will die on the heath, and I was just thinking I would claim the authority that belongs to one who holds a lieutenant's commission. As for the men, they'll no dare to raise any objections, and as for yoursal', my dear friend, now that ye've so much honor, and Mabel, and the consciousness of having done yer' duty, which is more precious than all, I expect to find an ally, rather than one to oppose the plan."

"As for commanding the soldiers of the 55th, lieutenant, it is your right, I suppose, and no one here, will be likely to gainsay it; though you've been a prisoner of war, and there are men who might stand out ag'in giving up their authority to a prisoner released by their own deeds. Still, no one here, will be likely to say any thing hostyle to your wishes."

"That's just it, Pathfinder; and when I come to draw up the report of our success against the boats, and the defence of the block, together with the general operations, including the capitulation, ye'll no find any omission of your claims and merits."

"Tut, for my claims and merits, Quarter Master! Lundie knows what I am, in the forest, and what I am in the fort, and the general knows better than he. No fear of me; tell your own story, only taking care to do justice by Mabel's father, who, in one sense, is the commmanding officer, at this very moment."

Muir expressed his entire satisfaction with this arrangement, as well as his determination to do justice by all, when the two went to the group that was assembled round the fire. Here the Quarter Master began, for the first time since leaving Oswego, to assume some of the authority that might properly be supposed to belong to his rank. Taking the remaining corporal aside, he distinctly told that functionary, that he must in future be regarded as one holding the King's commission, and directed him to acquaint his subordinates with the new state of things. This change in the dynasty was effected without any of the usual symptoms of a revolution, for as all well understood the Lieutenant's legal claims to command, no one felt disposed to dispute his orders. For reasons best known to themselves, Lundie and the Quarter Master had, originally, made a different disposition, and now for reasons of his own, the latter had seen fit to change it. This was reasoning enough for soldiers, though the hurt received by Serjeant Dunham would have sufficiently explained the circumstance, had any explanation been required.

All this time Capt. Sanglier was looking after his own breakfast, with the resignation of a philosopher, the coolness of a veteran, the ingenuity and science of a Frenchman and the voracity of an ostrich. This person had now been in the colony some thirty years, having left France in some such situation in his own army, as Muir filled in the 55th. An iron constitution, perfect obduracy of feeling, a certain address well suited to manage savages, and an indomitable courage, had early pointed him out to the Commander in chief, as a suitable agent to be employed in directing the military operations of his Indian allies. In this capacity, then, he had risen to the titular rank of captain, and, with his promotion, had acquired a portion of the habits and opinions of his associates, with a facility and an adaptation of self that are thought, in this part of the world, to be peculiar to his countrymen. He had often led parties of the Iroquois in their predatory expeditions, and his conduct on such occasions, exhibited the contradictory results of both alleviating the misery produced by this species of warfare, and of augmenting it, by the broader views and greater resources of civilization. In other words, he planned enterprises that, in their importance and consequences much exceeded the usual policy of the Indians, and then stepped in to lessen some of the evils of his own creating. In short, he was an adventurer whom circumstances had thrown into a situation, where the callous qualities of men of his class, might readily show themselves, for good or for evil, and he was not of a character to baffle fortune, by any ill timed squeamishness on the score of early impressions, or to trifle with her liberality, by unnecessarily provoking her frowns through wanton cruelty. Still, as his name was unavoidably connected with many of the excesses committed by his parties, he was generally considered in the American Provinces, a wretch who delighted in bloodshed, and who found his greatest happiness in tormenting the helpless and the innocent, and the name of Sanglier, which was a soubriquet of his own adopting, or of Flint Heart, as he was usually termed on the borders, had got to be as terrible to the women and children of that part of the country, as those of Butler and Brandt*became at a later day.

The meeting between Pathfinder and Sanglier bore some resemblance to that celebrated interview between Wellington and Blucher,* which has been so often and graphically told. It took place at the fire, and the parties stood earnestly regarding each other for more than a minute without speaking. Each felt that in the other, he saw a formidable foe, and each felt, while he ought to treat the other with the manly liberality due to a warrior, that there was little in common between them, in the way of character, as well as of interests. One served for money and preferment, the other because his life had been cast in the wilderness, and the land of his birth needed his arm and experience. The desire of rising above his present situation, never disturbed the tranquillity of Pathfinder, nor had he ever known an ambitious thought, as ambition usually betrays itself, until he became acquainted with Mabel. Since then, indeed, distrust of himself, reverence for her, and the wish to place her in a situation above that which he then filled, had caused him some uneasy moments, but the directness and simplicity of his character had early afforded the required relief, and he soon came to feel, that the woman who would not hesitate to accept him for her husband, would not scruple to share his fortunes, however humble. He respected Sanglier as a brave warrior, and he had far too much of that liberality which is the result of practical knowledge, to believe half of what he had heard to his prejudice; for the most bigotted and illiberal on every subject, are usually those who know nothing about it; but he could not approve of his selfishness, cold blooded calculations, and least of all, the manner in which he forgot his "white gifts" to adopt those that were purely "red." On the other hand, Pathfinder was a riddle to Capt. Sanglier. The latter could not comprehend the other's motives. He had often heard of his disinterestedness, justice and truth; and, in several instances, they had led him into grave errors, on that principle by which a frank and open-mouthed diplomatist is said to keep his secrets better than one that is close-mouthed and wily.

After the two heroes had gazed at each other, in the manner mentioned, Mons. Sanglier touched his cap, for the rudeness of a border life had not entirely destroyed the courtesy of manner he had acquired in youth, nor extinguished that appearance of *bonhommie* which seems inbred in a Frenchman.

"Monsieur le Pathfindair," he said, with a very decided accent, though with a friendly smile. "*Un militaire* honour *le courage, et la loyauté*. You speak Iroquois?"

"Ay, I understand the language of the riptyles, and can get along with it, if there's occasion," returned the literal and truth-telling guide; "but it's neither a tongue, nor a tribe to my taste. Wherever you find the Mingo blood, in my opinion, Master Flinty-heart, you find a knave. Well, I've seen you afore, though it was in battle, and I must say, it was always in the van. You must know most of our bullets by sight?"

"Nevvair, sair, your own. *Une balle* from your honorable hand, be sairtaine deat'. You kill my best warrior, on some island."

"That may be—that may be—though, I dare say, if the truth was known, they would turn out to be great rascals. No offence to you, Master Flinty-heart, but you keep desperate evil company."

"Yes, sair—" returned the Frenchman, who, bent on saying that which was courteous himself, and comprehending with difficulty, was disposed to think he received a compliment—"you, too good. But, *un brave* always *comme ça*. What that mean—ha!—What that *jeune homme* do?"

The hand and eye of Capt. Sanglier directed the look of Pathfinder to the opposite side of the fire, where Jasper, just at that moment, had been rudely seized by two of the soldiers, who were binding his arms, under the directions of Muir.

"What does that mean, indeed," cried the guide, stepping forward, and shoving the two subordinates aside with a power of muscle that would not be denied. "Who has the heart to do this to Jasper Eau douce; and who the boldness to do it afore my eyes?"

"It is by my orders, Pathfinder," answered the Quarter Master, "and I command it on my own responsibility. Ye'll no tak' on yourself, to dispute the legality of orders given by one who bears the King's commission, to the King's soldiers!"

"I'd dispute the King's words, if they came from the King's own mouth, did he say that Jasper desarves this! Has not the lad just saved all our scalps?—Taken us from defeat, and given us victory? No—no—Lieutenant; if this is the first use that you make of your authority, I for one, will not respect it."

"This savors a little of insubordination," answered Muir; "but we can bear much from Pathfinder. It is true, this Jasper has *seemed* to serve us, in this affair, but we ought not to overlook past transactions. Did not Major Duncan himself denounce him to Serjeant Dunham before we left the post; have we not seen sufficient with our own eyes, to make sure of having been betrayed, and is it not natural and almost necessary to believe that this young man has been the traitor. Ah! Pathfinder, ye'll no be makin' yourself a great statesman or a great captain, if ye put too much faith in appearances. Lord Bless me!–Lord Bless me!–If I do not believe, could the truth be come at, as you often say yourself, Pathfinder, that hyprocisy is a more common vice than even envy, and that's the bane o' human nature!"

Capt. Sanglier shrugged his shoulders; then he looked earnestly from Jasper towards the Quarter Master and from the Quarter Master towards Jasper.

"I care not for your envy, or your hypocrisy or even for your human natur'," returned Pathfinder–"Jasper Eau douce is my friend–Jasper Eau douce is a brave lad, and an honest lad, and a loyal lad, and no man of the 55th shall lay hands on him, short of Lundie's own orders, while I'm in the way to prevent it. You may have authority over your soldiers, but you have none over Jasper or me, Master Muir."

"*Bon–*" ejaculated Sanglier, the sound partaking equally of the energies of the throat and of the nose.

"Will ye no hearken to reason, Pathfinder. Ye'll no be forgetting our suspicions and judgments, and here is another circumstance to augment and aggravate them all. Ye can see this little bit of bunting–well where should it be found, but by Mabel Dunham on the branch of a tree, on this very island, just an hour or so, before the attack of the enemy, and if ye'll be at the trouble to look at the fly of the Scud's ensign ye'll just see, that the cloth has been cut from out it. Circumstantial evidence was never stronger."

"*Ma foi—c'est un peu fort, ceci–*" growled Sanglier, between his teeth.

"Talk to me of no ensigns, and signals, when I know the heart–" continued Pathfinder. "Jasper has the gift of honesty, and it is too rare a gift to be trifled with, like a Mingo's conscience. No–no–off hands, or we shall see, which can make the stoutest battle, you and your men of the 55th, or the Sarpent, here, and Killdeer, with Jasper and his crew. You overrate your force, Lieutenant Muir, as much as you underrate Eau douce's truth."

"*Très bon!*"

"Well, if I must speak plainly, Pathfinder, I e'en must. Capt. Sanglier, here, and Arrowhead, this brave Tuscarora, have both informed me that this unfortunate boy is the traitor. After such testimony, you can no longer refuse my right to arrest him, as well as the necessity of the act."

"*Scélérat—*" muttered the Frenchman.

"Capt. Sanglier is a brave soldier, and will not gainsay the conduct of an honest sailor," put in Jasper. "Is there any traitor, here, Capt. Flinty-heart?"

"Ay," added Muir, "lat him speak out, then, since ye wish it, unhappy youth, that the truth may be known. I only hope that ye may escape the last punishment when a court will be sitting on yer misdeeds. How is it, Captain; do ye, or do ye not see a traitor amang us?"

"*Oui*—yes, sair—*bien sûr.*"

"Too much lie—" said Arrowhead, in a voice of thunder, striking the breast of Muir, with the back of his own hand, in a sort of ungovernable gesture. "Where, my warriors?—Where Yengeese scalp? Too much lie."

Muir wanted not for personal courage, nor for a certain sense of personal honor. The violence which had been intended only for a gesture, he mistook for a blow, for conscience was suddenly aroused within him, and he stepped back a pace, extending a hand towards a gun. His face was livid with rage, and his countenance expressed the fell intent of his heart. But Arrowhead was too quick for him. With a wild glare of the eye, the Tuscarora looked about him, then thrusting a hand beneath his own girdle, drew forth a concealed knife, and in the twinkling of an eye buried it in the body of the Quarter Master to the handle. As the latter fell at his feet, gazing into his face with the vacant stare of one surprised by death, Sanglier took a pinch of snuff, and said in a calm voice—

"*Violà l'affaire finie—mais—*" shrugging his shoulders, "*ce n'est qu'un scélérat de moins.*"

The act was too sudden to be prevented, and when Arrowhead, uttering a yell, bounded into the bushes, the white men were too confounded to follow. Chingachgook, however, was more collected, and the bushes had scarcely closed on the passing body of the Tuscarora, than they were again opened by that of the Delaware, in full pursuit.

Jasper Western spoke French fluently, and the words and manner of Sanglier struck him.

"Speak, Monsieur," he cried in English—"*am* I the traitor?"

"*Le voilà*—" answered the cool Frenchman. "*Là-dat* is our *espion*—our *agent*—our friend—*Ma foi—c'etait un grand scélérat! Voici*—"

While speaking, Sanglier bent over the dead body, and thrust a hand into a pocket of the Quarter Master, out of which he drew a purse. Emptying the contents on the ground, several double Louis rolled towards the soldiers, who were not slow in picking them up. Casting the purse from him, in contempt, the soldier of fortune turned towards the soup he had been preparing with so much care, and finding it to his liking, he began to break his fast, with an air of indifference that the most stoical Indian warrior might have envied.

Chapter XXVII.

"The only amaranthine flower on Earth
Is virtue; th' only lasting treasure, Truth."
Cowper, *The Task*, III.268–69.

THE reader must imagine some of the occurrences, that followed the sudden death of Muir. While his body was in the hands of his soldiers, who laid it decently aside, and covered it with a great coat, Chingachgook silently resumed his place at the fire, and both Sanglier and Pathfinder remarked that he carried a fresh and bleeding scalp at his girdle. No one asked any questions, and the former, although perfectly satisfied that Arrowhead had fallen, manifested neither curiosity nor feeling. He continued calmly eating his soup, as if the meal had been tranquil as usual. There was something of pride, and of an assumed indifference to fate, imitated from the Indians, in all this, but there was more that really resulted from practice, habitual self-command, and constitutional hardihood. With Pathfinder, the case was a little different in feeling, though much the same in appearance. He disliked Muir, whose smooth-tongued courtesy was little in accordance with his own frank and ingenuous nature, but he had been shocked at his unexpected and violent death, though accustomed to similar scenes, and he had been surprised at the exposure of his treachery. With a view to ascertain the extent of the latter, as soon as the body was removed, he began to question the captain on the subject. The latter having no particular motive for secrecy, now that his agent was dead, in the course of the breakfast revealed the following circumstances, which will serve to clear up some of the minor incidents of our tale.

Soon after the 55th appeared on the frontiers, Muir had volunteered his services to the enemy. In making his offers, he boasted of his intimacy with Lundie, and of the means it afforded of furnishing more accurate and important information than usual. His terms had been accepted, and Mons.

Sanglier, had several interviews with him, in the vicinity of the fort at Oswego, and had actually passed one entire night secreted in the garrison. Arrowhead, however, was the usual channel of communication, and the anonymous letter to Major Duncan had been originally written by Muir, transmitted to Frontenac, copied and sent back by the Tuscarora, who was returning from that errand when captured by the Scud. It is scarcely necessary to add, that Jasper was to be sacrificed, in order to conceal the Quarter Master's treason, and that the position of the island had been betrayed to the enemy by the latter. An extraordinary compensation, that which was found in his purse, had induced him to accompany the party under Serjeant Dunham, in order to give the signals that were to bring on the attack. The disposition of Muir towards the sex was a natural weakness, and he would have married Mabel, or any one else who would accept his hand, but his admiration of her was in a great degree feigned, in order that he might have an excuse for accompanying the party, without sharing in the responsibility of its defeat, or incurring the risk of having no other strong and seemingly sufficient motive. Much of this was known to Capt. Sanglier, particularly the part in connection with Mabel, and he did not fail to let his auditors into the whole secret, frequently laughing, in a sarcastic manner, as he revealed the different expedients of the luckless Quarter Master.

"*Touchez-la*," said the cold blooded partisan, holding out his sinewy hand to Pathfinder, when he ended his explanations— "You be *honnête*, and dat is *beaucoup*. We tak' de spy, as we tak' *la médicine*, for de good, mais, *je les déteste! Touchez-la*."

"I'll shake your hand, captain, I will, for you're a lawful and nat'ral inimy," returned Pathfinder, "and a manful one; but the body of the Quarter Master shall never disgrace English ground. I did intend to carry it back to Lundie, that he might play his bagpipes over it, but, now, it shall lie here, on the spot where he acted his villainy, and have his own treason for a headstone. Capt. Flinty heart, I suppose this consorting with traitors is a part of a soldier's regular business, but, I tell you honestly, it is not to my liking, and I'd rather it should be you, than I, who had this affair on his conscience. What an awful sinner!—to plot, right and left, ag'in country, friends and the

Lord!–Jasper, boy, a word with you, aside, for a single minute."

Pathfinder now led the young man apart, and squeezing his hand, with the tears in his own eyes, he continued–

"You know me, Eau douce, and I know you," he said, "and this news has not changed my opinion of you, in any manner. I never believed their tales, though it looked solemn at one minute, I will own; yes, it did look solemn; and it made me feel solemn, too. I never suspected you for a minute, for I know your gifts do'n't lie that-a-way, but, I must own I did n't suspect the Quarter Master, neither."

"And he holding His Majesty's commission, Pathfinder!"

"It isn't so much that, Jasper Western; it isn't so much that. He held a commission from God to act right, and to deal fairly with his fellow creatur's, and he has failed awfully in his duty!"

"To think of his pretending love for one like Mabel, too, when he felt none!"

"That was bad, sartainly; the fellow must have had Mingo blood in his veins. The man that deals unfairly by a woman can be but a mongrel, lad, for the Lord has made them helpless on purpose that we may gain their love by kindness and sarvice. Here is the sarjeant, poor man, on his dying bed; he has given me his daughter for a wife, and Mabel, dear girl, she has consented to it, and it makes me feel that I have two welfares to look after, two natur's to care for, and two hearts to gladden. Ah's! me, Jasper; I sometimes feel that I'm not good enough for that sweet child!"

Eau douce had nearly gasped for breath, when he first heard this intelligence, and, though he succeeded in suppressing any other outward sign of agitation, his cheek was blanched nearly to the paleness of death. Still, he found means to answer, not only with firmness, but with energy–

"Say not so, Pathfinder; you are good enough for a Queen."

"Ay, ay, boy, according to your ideas of my goodness; that is to say–I can kill a deer, or even a Mingo at need, with any man on the lines; or I can follow a forest path with as true an eye, or, read the stars, when others do not understand them. No doubt, no doubt, Mabel will have venison enough, and fish enough, and pigeons enough; but will she have knowledge enough, and will she have ideas enough, and pleasant conversation enough, when life comes to drag a little, and each of us begins to pass for our true valu!"

"If you pass for your value, Pathfinder, the greatest lady in the land, would be happy with you. On that head, you have no reason to feel afraid."

"Now, Jasper, I dare to say *you* think so—nay, I *know* you do; for it is nat'ral and according to friendship, for people to look over favorably at them they love. Yes, yes; if I had to marry you, boy, I should give myself no consarn about being well looked upon, for you have always shown a disposition to see me and all I do with friendly eyes. But a young gal, after all, must wish to marry a man that is nearer to her own age and fancies, than to have one old enough to be her father, and rude enough to frighten her. I wonder, Jasper, that Mabel never took a fancy to you, now, rather than setting her mind on me!"

"Take a fancy to me, Pathfinder!" returned the young man, endeavoring to clear his voice without betraying himself— "What is there about me, to please such a girl as Mabel Dunham? I have all that you find fault with in yourself, with none of that excellence that makes even the generals respect you."

"Well—well—it's all chance, say what we will about it. Here have I journeyed and guided through the woods, female after female, and consorted with them in the garrisons, and never have I ever felt an inclination for any, until I saw Mabel Dunham. It's true the poor sarjeant first set me to thinking about his daughter, but after we got a little acquainted like, I'd no need of being spoken to, to think of her night and day. I'm tough, Jasper; yes, I'm very tough; and I'm risolute, enough, as you all know; and yet I do think it would quite break me down, now, to lose Mabel Dunham!"

"We will talk no more of it, Pathfinder," said Jasper, returning his friend's squeeze of the hand, and moving back towards the fire, though slowly and in the manner of one who cared little where he went; "we will talk no more of it. You are worthy of Mabel, and Mabel is worthy of you—you like Mabel, and Mabel likes you—her father has chosen you for her husband, and no one has a right to interfere. As for the Quarter Master, his feigning love for Mabel, is worse even than his treason to the king!"

By this time, they were so near the fire, that it was necessary to change the conversation. Luckily, at that instant, Cap, who had been in the block in company with his dying brother-in-law, and who knew nothing of what had passed since the capitulation, now appeared, walking with a meditative and melancholy air towards the group. Much of that hearty dogmatism, that imparted even to his ordinary àir and demeanor, an appearance of something like contempt for all around him, had disappeared, and he seemed thoughtful, if not meek.

"This death, gentlemen," he said, when he had got sufficiently near, "is a melancholy business, make the best of it. Now, here is Serjeant Dunham, a very good soldier, I make no question, about to slip his cable, and yet he holds on to the better end of it, as if he was determined it should never run out of the hawse-hole, and all because he loves his daughter, it seems to me. For my part, when a friend is really under the necessity of making a long journey, I always wish him well and happily off."

"You would n't kill the sarjeant afore his time," Pathfinder reproachfully answered. "Life is sweet, even to the aged, and, for that matter, I've known some that seemed to set more store by it, when it got to be of the least valu."

Nothing had been farther from Cap's real thoughts, than the wish to hasten his brother-in-law's end. He had found himself embarrassed with the duties of smoothing a death-bed, and all he had meant was to express a sincere desire that the serjeant were happily rid of doubt and suffering. A little shocked, therefore, at the interpretation that had been put on his words, he rejoined with some of the asperity of the man, though rebuked by a consciousness of not having done his own wishes justice.

"You are too old and too sensible a person, Pathfinder," he said, "to fetch a man up with a surge, when he is paying out his ideas in distress, as it might be. Serjeant Dunham is both my brother-in-law, and my friend—that is to say, as intimate a friend, as a soldier well can be with a sea-faring man, and I respect and honor him accordingly. I make no doubt, moreover, that he has lived such a life as becomes a man, and there can be no great harm, after all, in wishing any one well berthed in heaven. Well! We are mortal the best of us, that, you'll not deny; and it ought to be a lesson not to feel pride in our strength and beauty. Where is the Quarter Master, Pathfinder? —It is proper he should come and have a parting word with the poor serjeant, who is only going a little before us."

"You have spoken more truth, Master Cap, than you've been knowing to, all this time; in which there is no great wonder, howsever, mankind as often telling biting truths, when they least mean it, as at any other time. You might have gone farther, notwithstanding, and said that we are mortal, the *worst* of us, which is quite as true, and a good deal more wholesome than saying that we are mortal, the *best* of us. As for the Quarter Master's coming to speak a parting word to the sarjeant, it is quite out of the question, seeing that he has gone ahead, and that too with little parting notice to himself, or any one else."

"You are not quite as clear as common, in your language, Pathfinder. I know that we ought all to have solemn thoughts, on these occasions, but I see no use in speaking in parables."

"If my words are not plain, the idee is. In short, Master Cap, while Sarjeant Dunham has been preparing himself for a long journey, like a conscientious and honest man as he is, deliberately and slowly, the Quarter Master has started, in a hurry, afore him; and, although it is a matter on which it does not become me to be very positive, I give it as my opinion that they travel such different roads, that they will never meet."

"Explain yourself, my friend," said the bewildered seaman, looking around him in search of Muir, whose absence began to excite his distrust. "I see nothing of the Quarter Master, but I think him too much of a man to run away, now that the victory is gained. If the fight were ahead, instead of in our wake, the case would be altered."

"There lies all that is left of him, beneath that great-coat," returned the guide, who then briefly related the manner of the Lieutenant's death. "The Tuscarora was as venomous in his blow, as a rattler, though he failed to give the warning," continued Pathfinder. "I've seen many a desperate fight, and several of these sudden outbreaks of savage temper, but never, before, did I see a human soul quit the body more unexpectedly, or at a worse moment, for the hopes of the dying man. His breath was stopped with the lie on his lips, and the spirit might be said to have passed away in the very ardor of wickedness!"

Cap listened with a gaping mouth, and he gave two or three violent hems, as the other concluded, like one who distrusted his own respiration.

"This is an uncertain and uncomfortable life of yours, Master Pathfinder, what between the fresh water and the savages," he said, "and the sooner I get quit of it, the higher will be my opinion of myself. Now you mention it, I will say that the man ran for that berth in the rocks, when the enemy first bore down upon us, with a sort of instinct that I thought surprising in an officer, but I was in too great a hurry to follow, to log the whole matter accurately. God bless me—God bless me! A traitor do you say, and ready to sell his country, and to a bloody Frenchman too?"

"To sell any thing—country, soul, body, Mabel and all our scalps; and no ways particular, I'll engage, as to the purchaser. The countrymen of Capt. Flinty-heart, here, were the paymasters this time."

"Just like 'em; ever ready to buy, when they can't thrash, and to run when they can do neither."

Mons. Sanglier lifted his cap with ironical gravity, and acknowledged the compliment with an expression of polite contempt that was altogether lost on its insensible subject. But Pathfinder had too much native courtesy, and was far too just-minded, to allow the attack to go unnoticed—

"Well—well—" he interposed, "to my mind there is no great difference atween an Englishman and a Frenchman, a'ter all. They talk different tongues, and live under different kings I will allow, but both are human, and feel like human beings, when there is occasion for it. If a Frenchman is sometimes skeary, so is an Englishman; and as for running away, why a man will now and then do it, as well as a horse, let him come of what people he may."

Capt. Flinty-heart, as Pathfinder called him, made another obeisance, but this time the smile was friendly, and not ironical, for he felt that the intention was good, whatever might have been the mode of expressing it. Too philosophical, however, to heed what a man like Cap might say, or think, he finished his breakfast without allowing his attention to be again diverted from that important pursuit.

"My business, here, was principally with the Quarter Master," Cap continued, as soon as he had done regarding the French-man's pantomine; "the serjeant must be near his end, and I have thought he might wish to say something to his successor in authority, before he finally departed. It is too late, it would seem, and, as you say, Pathfinder, the Lieutenant has truly gone before."

"That he has, though on a different path. As for authority, I suppose the corporal has now a right to command what's left of the 55th, though a small and worried, not to say frightened, party it is. But, if any thing needs to be done, the chances are greatly in favor of my being called on to do it. I suppose, how-sever, we have only to bury our dead, and set fire to the block and the huts, for they stand in the inimy's territory, by position if not by law, and must not be left for their convenience. Our using them again, is out of the question, for now the Frenchers know where the island is to be found, it would be like thrusting the hand into a wolf trap, with our eyes wide open. This part of the work, the Sarpent and I will see to, for we are as practysed in retreats, as in advances."

"All that is very well, my good friend; and now for my poor brother-in-law: though he is a soldier, we cannot let him slip, without a word of consolation, and a leave-taking, in my judg-ment. This has been an unlucky affair, on every tack, though I suppose it is what one had a right to expect, considering the state of the times, and the nature of the navigation. We must make the best of it, and try to help the worthy man to unmoor, without straining his messengers. Death is a circumstance, after all, Master Pathfinder, and one of a very general character, too, seeing that we must all submit to it, sooner or later."

"You say truth, you say truth, and for that reason I hold it to be wise to be always ready. I've often thought, Salt-water, that he is happiest who has the least to leave behind him, when the summons comes. Now, here am I, a hunter, and a scout, and a guide, although I do not own a foot of land on 'arth, yet do I enjoy and possess more than the great Albany Patroon. With the heavens over my head, to keep me in mind of the last great hunt, and the dried leaves beneath my feet, I tramp over the ground as freely as if I was its lord and owner, and what more need heart desire? I do not say, that I love nothing, that belongs to 'arth; for I do, though not much, unless it might be Mabel Dunham, that I can't carry with me. I have some pups, at the higher fort, that I valu, considerable, though they are too noisy for warfare, and so we are compelled to live separate for a while; and, then, I think it would grieve me to part with Killdeer, but I see no reason why we should not be buried in the same grave, for we are as near as can be of the same length, six feet to a hair's breadth; but, 'bating these, and a pipe that the Sarpent gave me, and a few tokens received from travellers, all of which might be put in a pouch, and laid under my head, when the order comes to march, I shall be ready at a minute's warning; and, let me tell you, Master Cap, that's what I call a circumstance, too!"

"'Tis just so with me," answered the sailor, as the two walked towards the block, too much occupied with their respective morality to remember, at the moment, the melancholy errand they were on—"that's just my way, of feeling and reasoning. How often have I felt, when near shipwreck, the relief of not owning the craft! 'If she goes,' I have said to myself, 'why my life goes with her, but not my property, and there's great comfort in that.' I've discovered, in the course of boxing about the world, from the Horn to Cape North, not to speak of this run on a bit of fresh water, that if a man has a few dollars, and puts them in a chest, under lock and key, he is pretty certain to fasten up his heart in the same till, and so I carry pretty much all I own, in a belt round my body, in order, as I say, to keep the vitals in the right place. D——e, Pathfinder, if I think a man without a heart, any better than a fish with a hole in his air bag."

"I don't know how that may be, Master Cap, but a man without a conscience is but a poor creatur', take my word for it, as any one will discover who has to do with a Mingo. I trouble myself but little with dollars, or half-joes, for these are the favoryte coin in this part of the world, but I can easily believe, by what I've seen of mankind, that if a man *has* a chest filled with either, he may be said to lock up his heart in the same box. I once hunted for two summers, during the last peace, and I collected so much peltry that I found my right feelings giving way to a craving after property, and if I have consarn in marrying

Mabel, it is that I may get to love such things too well, in order to make her comfortable."

"You're a philosopher, that's clear, Pathfinder, and I don't know but you're a christian!"

"I should be out of humour with the man that gainsayed the last, Master Cap. I have not been christianized by the Moravians, like so many of the Delawares, it is true, but I hold to Christianity and white gifts. With me, it is as oncreditable for a white man not to be a Christian, as it is for a red skin not to believe in his happy hunting grounds; indeed, after allowing for difference in traditions, and some variations about the manner in which the spirit will be occupied after death, I hold that a good Delaware is a good Christian, though he never saw a Moravian, and a good Christian a good Delaware, so far as natur' is consarned. The Sarpent and I talk these matters over, often, for he has a hankerin' after christianity—"

"The d——l he has!" interrupted Cap. "And what does he intend to do in a church, with all the scalps he takes."

"Don't run away with a false idee, friend Cap; don't run away, with a false idee. These things are only skin deep and all depend on edication and nat'ral gifts. Look around you, at mankind, and tell me why you see a red warrior here, a black one there, and white armies in another place? All this, and a great deal more of the same kind, that I could point out, has been ordered for some 'special purpose, and it is not for us to fly in the face of facts, and deny their truth. No—no—each colour has its gifts, and its laws, and its traditions; and one is not to condemn another because he does not exactly comprehend it."

"You must have read a great deal, Pathfinder, to see things as clear as this," returned Cap, who was not a little mystified by his companion's simple creed—"It's all as plain as day to me, now, though I must say I never fell in with these opinions before. What denomination do you belong to, my friend?"

"Anan?"

"What sect do you hold out for?—What particular church do you fetch up in?"

"Look about you, and judge for yourself. I'm in church now; I eat in church, drink in church, sleep in church. The 'arth is the temple of the Lord, and I wait on him hourly, daily, without ceasing, I humbly hope. No—no—I'll not deny my blood and colour, but am Christian born, and shall die in the same faith. The Moravians tried me hard, and one of the King's chaplains has had his say, too, though that's a class no ways strenuous on such matters, and a missionary sent from Rome talked much with me, as I guided him through the forest, during the last peace, but I've had one answer for them all—I'm a christian, already, and want to be neither Moravian, nor Churchman, nor Papist. No—no—I'll not deny my birth and blood."

"I think a word from you might lighten the serjeant over the shoals of death, Master Pathfinder. He has no one with him but poor Mabel, and she, you know, besides being his daughter, is but a girl and a child after all."

"Mabel is feeble in body, friend Cap, but in matters of this natur', I doubt if she may not be stronger than most men. But Sarjeant Dunham is my friend, and he is your brother-in-law, so, now the press of fighting and maintaining our rights is over, it is fitting we should both go and witness his departure. I've stood by many a dying man, Master Cap," continued Pathfinder, who had a besetting propensity to enlarge on his experience, stopping and holding his companion by a button—"I've stood by many a dying man's side, and seen his last gasp, and heard his last breath, for when the hurry and tumult of the battle is over, it is good to bethink us of the misfortunate, and it is remarkable to witness how differently human natur' feels at such solemn moments. Some go their way, as stupid and ignorant, as if God had never given them reason and an accountable state, while others quit us rejoicing, like men who leave heavy burthens behind them. I think that the mind sees clearly at such moments, my friend, and that past deeds stand thick before the recollection."

"I'll engage they do, Pathfinder. I have witnessed something of this myself, and hope I'm the better man for it. I remember once that I thought my own time had come, and the log was overhauled with a diligence I did not think myself capable of, until that moment. I've not been a very great sinner, friend Pathfinder; that is to say, never on a large scale; though, I dare say, if the truth were spoken, a considerable amount of small matters might be raked up against me, as well as against another man; but, then I've never committed piracy, nor high treason, nor arson, nor any of them sort of things. As to smuggling, and the like of that, why I'm a seafaring man, and I suppose all callings have their weak spots. I dare say, your trade is not altogether without blemish, honorable and useful as it seems to be?"

"Many of the scouts and guides are desperate knaves, and like the Quarter Master, here, some of them take pay of both sides. I hope I'm not one of them, though all occupations lead to temptation. Thrice have I been sorely tried in my life, and once yielded a little, though I hope it was not in a matter to disturb a man's conscience, in his last moments. The first time was, when I found in the woods, a pack of skins that I knowed belonged to a Frencher who was hunting on our side of the lines, where he had no business to be; twenty six as handsome beavers, as ever gladdened human eyes! Well, that was a tight temptation, for I thought the law would have been almost with me, although it was in peace times. But, then I remembered that such laws was'n't made for us hunters, and bethought me that the poor man might have built great expectations for the next winter, on the sale of his skins, and I left them where they lay. Most of our people said I did wrong, but the manner in which I slept that night, convinced me that I had done right. The next trial, was when I found the rifle that is sartainly the only one in this part of the world that can be calculated on as surely as Killdeer, and knowed that by taking it, or even hiding it, I might at once rise to be the first shot in all these parts. I was then young, and by no means as expart as I have since got to be, and youth is ambitious and striving; but, God be praised! I mastered that feeling, and, friend Cap, what is almost as good, I mastered my rival in as fair a shooting match as was ever witnessed in a garrison; he with his piece, and I with Killdeer, and before the General, in person, too!" Here Pathfinder stopped to laugh, his triumph still glittering in his eyes, and glowing on his sunburnt and browned cheek.—"Well, the next conflict with the devil, was the hardest of them all, and that was when I came suddenly, upon a camp of six Mingos, asleep in the woods, with their guns and horns piled in a way that enabled me to get possession of them without waking a miscreant of them all. What an opportunity that would have been for the Sarpent, who would have despatched them one after another with his knife, and had their six scalps at his girdle, in about the time it takes me to tell you the story. Oh! He's a valiant warrior, that Chingachgook, and as honest as he's brave, and as good as he's honest."

"And what may *you* have done in this matter, Master Pathfinder," demanded Cap, who began to be interested in the result—"It seems to me, you had made either a very lucky, or a very unlucky landfall."

"'Twas lucky, and 'twas unlucky, if you can understand that. 'Twas unlucky, for it proved a desperate trial, and yet 'twas lucky, all things considered, in the ind. I did not touch a hair of their heads, for a white man has no nat'ral gifts to take scalps, nor did I even make sure of one of their rifles. I distrusted myself, knowing that a Mingo is no favorite, in my own eyes."

"As for the scalps, I think you were right enough, my worthy friend, but as for the armament and the stores, they would have been condemned by any prize-court in Christendom!"

"That they would—that they would, but then the Mingos would have gone clear, seeing that a white man can no more attack an unarmed, than a sleeping, inimy. No—no—I did myself, and my colour, and my religion, too, greater justice. I waited 'till their nap was over, and they well on their warpath ag'in, and by ambushing them here, and flanking them, there, I peppered the blackguards so intrinsically, like," Pathfinder occasionally caught a fine word from his associates, and used it a little vaguely—"that only one ever got back to his village; and he came into his wigwam limping. Luckily as it turned out, the Great Delaware had only halted to jerk some venison, and was following on my trail, and when he got up, he had five of the scoundrels' scalps hanging where they ought to be; so you see nothing was lost by doing right, either in the way of honor or in that of profit."

Cap grunted an assent, though the distinctions in his companion's morality, it must be owned, were not exactly clear to his understanding. The two had occasionally moved towards the block, as they conversed, and then stopped again, as some matter of more interest than common, brought them to a halt. They were now so near the building, however, that neither thought of pursuing the subject any further, but each prepared himself for the final scene with Serjeant Dunham.

Chapter XXVIII.

"Thou barraine ground, whom winter's wrath hath wasted,
Art made a mirror to behold my plight:
Whilome thy fresh spring flowr'd; and after hasted
Thy summer prowde, with daffodillies dight;
And now is come thy winter's stormy state,
Thy mantle mar'd wherein thou maskedst late."

Spenser, *The Shepheardes Calender*,
"Januarye," ll. 19–24.

ALTHOUGH the soldier may regard danger, and even death, with indifference, in the tumult of battle, when the passage of the soul is delayed to moments of tranquility and reflection, the change commonly brings with it the usual train of solemn reflection; of regrets for the past, and of doubts and anticipations for the future. Many a man has died with an heroic expression on his lips, but with heaviness and distrust at his heart; for, whatever may be the varieties of our religious creeds—let us depend on the mediation of Christ, the dogmas of Mahomet, or the elaborated allegories of the East, there is a conviction common to all men, that death is but the stepping-stone between this and a more elevated state of being. Serjeant Dunham was a brave man, but he was departing for a country in which resolution could avail him nothing, and, as he felt himself gradually loosened from the grasp of the world, his thoughts and feelings took the natural direction; for, if it be true that death is the great leveller, in nothing is it more true, than that it reduces all to the same views of the vanity of life.

Pathfinder, though a man of quaint and peculiar habits and opinions, was always thoughtful and disposed to view the things around him, with a shade of philosophy as well as with seriousness. In him, therefore, the scene in the block house awakened no very novel feelings; but the case was different with Cap. Rude, opinionated, dogmatical and boisterous, the old sailor was little accustomed to view even death, with any approach to the gravity that its importance demands, and, notwithstanding all that had passed, and his real regard for his brother-in-law, he now entered the room of the dying man, with much of that callous unconcern which was the fruit of long training in a school, that, while it gives so many lessons in the sublimest truths, generally wastes its admonitions on scholars who are little disposed to profit by them.

The first proof that Cap gave of his not entering as fully at those around him, into the solemnity of the moment, was by commencing a narration of the events which had just led to the deaths of Muir and Arrowhead. "Both tripped their anchors in a hurry, brother Dunham," he concluded, "and you have the consolation of knowing that others have gone before you, in the great journey, and they, too, men, whom you've no particular reason to love; which to me, were I placed in your situation, would be a source of very great satisfaction. My mother always said, Master Pathfinder, that dying people's spirits should not be damped, but that they ought to be encouraged by all proper and prudent means, and this news will give the poor fellow a great lift, if he feels towards them savages, any way as I feel myself."

June arose, at this intelligence, and stole from the block-house with a noiseless step. Dunham listened with a vacant stare, for life had already lost so many of its ties that he had really forgotten Arrowhead, and cared nothing for Muir; but he inquired, in a feeble voice, for Eau douce. The young man was immediately summoned, and soon made his appearance. The serjeant gazed at him kindly, and the expression of his eyes, was that of regret for the injury he had done him, in thought. The party in the block-house now consisted of Pathfinder, Cap, Mabel, Jasper, and the dying man. With the exception of the daughter, all stood around the serjeant's pallet, in attendance on his last moments. Mabel kneeled at his side, now pressing a clammy hand to her heart, now applying moisture to the parched lips of her father.

"Your case will shortly be ourn, sarjeant," said Pathfinder, who could hardly be said to be awestruck by the scene, for he had witnessed the approach and victories of death too often for that, but who felt the full difference between his triumphs in the excitement of battle, and in the quiet of the domestic circle; "and I make no question we shall meet ag'in, hereafter. Arrowhead has gone his way 'tis true, but it can never be the way of a just Indian. You've seen the last of him; for his path cannot be the path of the just. Reason is ag'in the thought, in his case, as it is also, in my judgment, ag'in it, too, in the case of Lieutenant Muir. You have done your duty in life, and when a man does that, he may start on the longest journey, with a light heart, and an actyve foot."

"I hope so, my friend—I've tried to do my duty."

"Ay—ay—" put in Cap; "intention is half the battle, and though you would have done better had you hove-to in the offing, and sent a craft in to feel how the land lay, things might have turned out differently, no one, here, doubts that you meant all for the best, and, no one anywhere else, I should think, from what I've seen of this world, and read of t'other."

"I did—yes—I meant all for the best."

"Father!—Oh! my beloved father!"

"Magnet is taken aback by this blow, Master Pathfinder, and can say, or do, but little to carry her father over the shoals, so we must try all the harder to serve him a friendly turn ourselves."

"Did you speak, Mabel?" Dunham asked, turning his eyes in the direction of his daughter, for he was already too feeble to turn his body.

"Yes, Father; rely on nothing you have done yourself for mercy and salvation; trust altogether in the blessed mediation of the son of God!"

"The chaplain has told us something like this, brother—the dear child may be right."

"Ay—ay—that's doctrine, out of doubt. He will be our judge, and keeps the log-book of our acts, and will foot them all up, at the last day, and then say who has done well, and who has done ill. I do believe Mabel is right, but then you need not be concerned, as no doubt the account has been fairly kept."

"Uncle!—Dearest Father!—This is a vain illusion—Oh! Place all your trust in the mediation of our holy redeemer! Have you not often felt your own insufficiency to effect your own wishes in the commonest things, and how can you imagine yourself, by your own acts, equal to raising a frail and sinful nature sufficiently to be received into the presence of perfect purity? There is no hope for any, but in the mediation of Christ!"

"This is what the Moravians used to tell us," said Pathfinder to Cap, in a low voice; "Mabel is right."

"Right enough, friend Pathfinder, in the distances, but wrong in the course. I'm afraid the child will get the serjeant adrift, at the very moment when we had him in the best of the water, and in the plainest part of the channel."

"Leave it to Mabel—leave it to Mabel. She knows better than any of us, and can do no harm."

"I have heard this before—" Dunham at length replied—"Ah! Mabel; it is strange for the parent to lean on the child, at a moment like this!"

"Put your trust in God, father—lean on his holy and compassionate son. Pray, dearest, dearest, father—pray for his omnipotent support."

"I am not used to prayer—brother—Pathfinder—Jasper—can you help me to words?"

Cap scarce knew what prayer meant, and he had no answer to give. Pathfinder prayed often, daily if not hourly—but it was mentally, in his own simple modes of thinking, and without the aid of words at all. In this strait, therefore, he was as useless as the mariner, and had no reply to make. As for Jasper Eau douce, though he would gladly have endeavored to move a mountain, to relieve Mabel, this was asking assistance it exceeded his power to give, and he shrunk back with the shame, that is only too apt to overcome the young and vigorous, when called on to perform an act that tacitly confesses their real weakness and dependence on a superior power.

"Father—" said Mabel, wiping her eyes, and endeavoring to compose features that were pallid, and actually quivering with emotion—"*I* will pray with you—*for* you—for *myself*, for us *all*. The petition of the feeblest and humblest is never unheeded."

There was something sublime, as well as much that was supremely touching in this act of filial piety. The quiet, but earnest manner in which this young creature prepared herself to perform this duty, the self-abandonment with which she forgot her sex's timidity and sex's shame, in order to sustain her parent at that trying moment, the loftiness of purpose with which she directed all her powers to the immense object before her, with a woman's devotion, and a woman's superiority to trifles, when her affections make the appeals, and the holy calm into which her grief was compressed, rendered her, for the moment, an object of something very like awe and veneration to her companions.

Mabel had been religiously and reasonably educated; equally without exaggeration and without self-sufficiency. Her reliance on God, was cheerful and full of hope, while it was of the humblest and most dependant nature. She had been accustomed from childhood, to address herself to the Deity, in prayer. Taking example from the divine mandate of Christ himself, who commanded his followers to abstain from 'vain repetitions' and who has left behind him a petition that is unequalled for sublimity and sententiousness, as if expressly to rebuke the disposition of man to set up his own loose and random thoughts as the most acceptable sacrifice. The sect in which she had been reared, has furnished to its followers some of the most beautiful compositions of the language, as a suitable vehicle for its adoration and solicitations. Accustomed to this mode of public and even private prayer, the mind of our heroine had naturally fallen into its train of lofty thought, her taste had become improved by its study, and her language elevated and enriched by its phrases. In short, Mabel, in this respect, was an instance of the influence of familiarity with propriety of thought, fitness of language, and decorum of manner, on the habits and expressions of even those who might be supposed not to be always so susceptible of receiving high impressions of this nature. When she kneeled at the bedside of her father, the very reverence of her attitude and manner, prepared the spectators for what was to come, and as her affectionate heart prompted her tongue, and memory came in aid of both, the petition and praises that she offered up, were of a character that might have worthily led the spirits of any. Although the words were not slavishly borrowed, the expressions partook of the simple dignity of the liturgy to which she had been accustomed, and were probably as worthy of the being to whom they were addressed as they could well be made by human powers. They produced their full impression on the hearers, for it is worthy of remark that, notwithstanding the pernicious effects of a false taste when long submitted to, real sublimity and beauty are so closely allied to nature, that they generally find an echo in every heart.

But when our heroine came to touch upon the situation of the dying man, she became the most truly persuasive, for then she was the most truly zealous and natural. The beauty of the language was preserved, but it was sustained by the simple power of love, and her words were warmed by a holy zeal that approached to the grandeur of true eloquence. We might record some of her expressions, but doubt the propriety of subjecting such sacred themes to a too familiar analysis, and refrain.

The effect of this singular but solemn scene, was different on the different individuals present. Dunham himself, was soon lost in the subject of the prayer, and he felt some such relief as one who finds himself staggering on the edge of a precipice, under a burthen difficult to be borne, might be supposed to experience, when he unexpectedly feels the weight removed, in order to be placed on the shoulders of another, better able to sustain it. Cap was surprised, as well as awed, though the effects on his mind were not very deep, or very lasting. He wondered a little at his own sensations, and had his doubts whether they were as manly and heroic as they ought to be, but he was far too sensible of the influence of truth, humility, religious submission and human dependency, to think of interposing with any of his crude objections. Jasper knelt opposite to Mabel, covered his face, and followed her words, with an earnest wish to aid her prayer with his own, though it may be questioned if his thoughts did not dwell quite as much on the soft, gentle accents of the petitioner, as on the subject of her petitions.

The effect on Pathfinder was striking and visible; visible because he stood erect, also opposite to Mabel, and the workings of his countenance, as usual, betrayed the workings of the spirit within. He leaned on his rifle, and, at moments, the sinewy fingers grasped the barrel, with a force that seemed to compress the weapon, while, once or twice, as Mabel's language rose, in intimate association with her thoughts, he lifted his eyes to the floor above him, as if he expected to find some visible evidence of the presence of the dread being, to whom the words were addressed. Then again, his feelings reverted to the fair creature who was thus pouring out her spirit in fervent but calm petitions in behalf of a dying parent; for Mabel's cheek was no longer pallid, but was flushed with a holy enthusiasm, while her blue eyes were upturned in the light, in a way to resemble a picture by Guido. At these moments, all the honest and manly attachment of Pathfinder, glowed in his ingenuous features, and his gaze at our heroine was such as the fondest parent might fasten on the child of his love.

Serjeant Dunham laid his hand feebly, on the head of Mabel, as she ceased praying, and buried her face in his blanket.

"Bless you—my beloved child—bless you—" he rather whispered than uttered aloud—"this is truly consolation—Would that I, too, could pray!"

"Father, you know the Lord's prayer—you taught it to me yourself, while I was yet an infant."

The serjeant's face gleamed with a smile, for he *did* remember to have discharged that portion at least, of the paternal duty, and the consciousness of it gave him inconceivable gratification at that solemn moment. He was then silent for several minutes, and all present believed that he was communing with God.

"Mabel—my child—" he at length uttered, in a voice that seemed to be reviving—"Mabel—I'm quitting you—" The spirit, at its great and final passage, appears ever to consider the body as nothing—"I'm quitting you, my child—where is your hand?"

"Here, dearest Father—here are both—oh! take both."

"Pathfinder—" added the serjeant, feeling on the opposite side of the bed, where Jasper still knelt, getting one of the hands of the young man, by mistake—"Take it—I leave you as her father—as you and she may please—bless you—bless you, both—"

At that awful instant no one would rudely apprise the serjeant of his mistake, and he died a minute or two later, holding Jasper's and Mabel's hands covered by both his own. Our heroine was ignorant of the fact, until an exclamation of Cap's announced the death of her father, when raising her face, she saw the eyes of Jasper riveted on her own, and felt the warm pressure of his hand. But a single feeling was predominant, at that instant, and Mabel withdrew to weep, scarcely conscious of what had occurred. The Pathfinder took the arm of Eau douce, and left the block.

The two friends walked in silence past the fire, along the glade, and nearly reached the opposite shore of the island, in profound silence. Here they stopped, and Pathfinder spoke.

"'Tis all over, Jasper," he said; "'tis all over. Ah's, me! Poor Sarjeant Dunham has finished his march, and that, too, by the hand of a venomous Mingo. Well, we never know what is to happen, and his luck may be your'n, or mine, to-morrow, or next day!"

"And, Mabel?—What is to become of Mabel, Pathfinder?"

"You heard the sarjeant's dying words—he left his child in my care, Jasper, and it is a most solemn trust, it is; yes, it is a most solemn trust!"

"It's a trust, Pathfinder, of which any man would be glad to relieve you—" returned the youth with a bitter smile.

"I've often thought it has fallen into wrong hands. I'm not consaited, Jasper; I'm not consaited, I do think I'm not; but if Mabel Dunham is willing to overlook all my imperfections and ignorances like, I should be wrong to gainsay it, on account of any sartainty I may have myself about my own want of merit."

"No one will blame you, Pathfinder, for marrying Mabel Dunham, any more than they will blame you for wearing a precious jewel in your bosom, that a friend had fairly given you."

"Do you think they'll blame Mabel, lad?—I've had my misgivings about that, too; for all persons may not be as disposed to look at me with the same eyes as you, and the sarjeant's daughter—" Jasper Eau douce started, as a man flinches at sudden bodily pain, but he otherwise maintained his self-command—"and mankind is envious and ill-natured, more particularly in and about the garrisons. I sometimes wish, Jasper, that Mabel could have taken a fancy to you, I do; and that you had taken a fancy to her, for, it often seems to me that one like you, after all, might make her happier, than I ever can!"

"We will not talk about this, Pathfinder—" interrupted Jasper hoarsely, and impatiently—"You will be Mabel's husband, and it is not right to speak of any one else, in that character. As for me, I shall take Master Cap's advice, and try and make a man of myself, by seeing what is to be done on the salt-water."

"You, Jasper Western!—You quit the lakes, the forests, and the lines, and this, too, for the towns and wasty ways of the settlements, and a little difference in the taste of the water.

Have'n't we the salt licks, if salt is necessary to you, and ought n't man to be satisfied with what contents the other creatur's of God. I counted on you, Jasper; I counted on you, I did—and thought, now, that Mabel and I intend to dwell in a cabin of our own, that some day you might be tempted to choose a companión too, and come and settle in our neighborhood. There is a beautiful spot, about fifty miles west of the garrison, that I had chosen in my mind, for my own place of abode, and there is an excellent harbor, about ten leagues this side of it, where you could run in and out, with the cutter, at any leisure minute, and I'd even fancied you and your wife in possession of the one place, and Mabel and I in possession of t'other. We should be just a healthy hunt apart, and if the Lord does intend any of his creatur's to be happy on 'arth, none could be happier than we four!"

"You forget, my friend," answered Jasper, taking the guide's hand, and forcing a friendly smile—"that I have no fourth person to love and cherish; and I much doubt if I ever shall love any other, as I love you and Mabel."

"Thank'ee, boy; I thank you, with all my heart—but what you call love for Mabel, is only friendship like, and a very different thing from what I feel. Now, instead of sleeping, as sound as natur' at midnight, as I used to could, I dream nightly of Mabel Dunham. The young does sport before me, and when I raise Killdeer, in order to take a little venison, the animals look back, and it seems as if they all had Mabel's sweet countenance, laughing in my face, and looking as if they said, 'shoot me, if you dare!' Then I hear her soft voices calling out among the birds as they sing; and no later than the last nap I took, I bethought me, in fancy, of going over the Niagara, holding Mabel in my arms, rather than part from her. The bitterest moments I've ever known, were them in which the devil, or some Mingo conjurer, perhaps, has just put into my head to fancy in dreams that Mabel is lost to me, by some unaccountable calamity; either by changefulness, or by violence."

"Oh! Pathfinder, if you think this so bitter in a dream, what must it be to one who feels it in reality, and knows it all to be true—true—true. So true, as to leave no hope; to leave nothing but despair!"

These words burst from Jasper, as a fluid pours from the

vessel that has been suddenly broken. They were uttered involuntarily, almost unconsciously, but with a truth and feeling that carried with them the instant conviction of their deep sincerity. Pathfinder started, gazed at his friend for quite a minute, like one bewildered, and then it was, that, in despite of all his simplicity, the truth gleamed upon him. All know how corroborating proofs crowd upon the mind, as soon as it catches a direct clue to any hitherto unsuspected fact; how rapidly the thoughts flow, and premises tend to their just conclusions, under such circumstances. Our hero was so confiding by nature, so just, and so much disposed to imagine that all his friends wished him the same happiness as he wished them, that, until this unfortunate moment, a suspicion of Jasper's attachment for Mabel had never been awakened in his bosom. He was, however, now too experienced in the emotions that characterize the passion, and the burst of feeling in his companion, was too violent and too natural, to leave any further doubt on the subject. The feeling that first followed this change of opinion was one of deep humility and exquisite pain. He bethought him of Jasper's youth, his higher claims to personal appearance, and all the general probabilities that such a suitor would be more agreeable to Mabel, than he could possibly be, himself. Then the noble rectitude of mind, for which the man was so distinguished, asserted its power. It was sustained by his rebuked manner of thinking of himself, and all that habitual deference for the rights and feelings of others, which appeared to be inbred in his very nature. Taking the arm of Jasper, he led him to a log, where he compelled the young man to seat himself, by a sort of irresistible exercise of his iron muscles, and where he placed himself at his side.

The instant his feelings had found vent, Eau douce was both alarmed at, and ashamed of their violence. He would have given all he possessed on earth, could the last three minutes be recalled, but he was too frank by disposition, and too much accustomed to deal ingenuously by his friend, to think a moment, of attempting further concealment, or of any evasion of the explanation that he knew was about to be demanded. Even while he trembled in anticipation of what was about to follow, he never contemplated equivocation.

"Jasper," Pathfinder commenced, in a tone so solemn as to thrill on every nerve in his listener's body, "this *has* surprised me! You have kinder feelings towards Mabel, than I had thought, and, unless my own mistaken vanity and consait have cruelly deceived me, I pity you, boy, from my soul, I do! Yes, I think, I know how to pity any one, who has set his heart on a creatur' like Mabel, unless he sees a prospect of her regarding him, as he regards her. This matter must be cleared up, Eau douce, as the Delawares say, until there shall not be a cloud atween us."

"What clearing up can it want, Pathfinder? I love Mabel Dunham, and Mabel Dunham does not love me—She prefers you for a husband, and the wisest thing I can do, is to go off at once, to the salt-water, and to try to forget you both."

"Forget me, Jasper!—that would be a punishment I don't desarve. But, how do you know that Mabel prefars *me*?—how do you know it, lad; to me it seems impossible, like!"

"Is she not to marry you, and would Mabel marry a man she does not love?"

"She has been hard urged by the sarjeant, she has; and a dutiful child may have found it difficult to withstand the wishes of a dying parent. Have you ever told Mabel, that you prefarred her, Jasper; that you bore her these feelings?"

"Never—Pathfinder—I would not do you that wrong!"

"I believe you, lad, I do believe you; and I think you would now go off to the salt-water and let the secret die with you. But this must not be. Mabel shall hear all, and she shall have her own way, if my heart breaks in the trial, she shall. No words have ever passed atween you then, Jasper?"

"Nothing of account—nothing direct. Still, I will own all my foolishness, Pathfinder, for I ought to own it to a generous friend like you, and there will be an end of it. You know how young people understand each other, or think they understand each other, without always speaking out, in plain speech, and get to know each other's thoughts, or to think they know them, by means of a hundred little ways?"

"Not I, Jasper, not I," truly answered the guide, for, sooth to say, his advances had never been met with any of that sweet and precious encouragement that silently marks the course of sympathy united to passion. "Not I, Jasper—I know nothing of all this. Mabel has always treated me fairly, and said what she has had to say, in speech as plain as tongue could tell it."

"You have had the pleasure of hearing her say that she loved you, Pathfinder!"

"Why, no, Jasper, not just that, in words. She has told me that we never could—never ought to be married—that *she* was not good enough for *me*, though she *did* say that she honored me, and respected me. But, then, the sarjeant said it was always so with the youthful and timid; that her mother did so, and said so afore her, and that I ought to be satisfied if she would consent, on any tarms, to marry me; and, therefore, I have concluded that all was right, I have."

In spite of all his friendship for the successful wooer, in spite of all his honest, sincere wishes for his happiness, we should be unfaithful chroniclers did we not own that Jasper felt his heart bound with an uncontrollable feeling of delight, at this admission. It was not that he saw, or felt, any hope connected with the circumstance, but it was grateful to the jealous covetousness of unlimited love, thus to learn that no other ears had heard the sweet confessions that were denied his own.

"Tell me more of this manner of talking without the use of the tongue—" continued Pathfinder, whose countenance was getting to be grave, and who now questioned his companion, like one that seemed to anticipate evil in the reply. "I can, and have conversed with Chingachgook, and with his son Uncas, too, in that mode, afore the latter fell, but I did n't know that young gals practysed this art, and least of all, Mabel Dunham!"

"'Tis nothing, Pathfinder—I mean only a look, or a smile, or a glance of the eye, or the trembling of an arm, or a hand, when the young woman has had occasion to touch me; and because I have been weak enough to tremble even at Mabel's breath, or her brushing me with her clothes, my vain thoughts have misled me. I never spoke plainly to Mabel, myself, and now there is no reason for it, since there is clearly no hope."

"Jasper," returned Pathfinder simply, but with a dignity that precluded farther remarks at the moment, "we will talk of the sarjeant's funeral, and of our own departure from this island; after these things are disposed of, it will be time enough to say more of the sarjeant's daughter. This matter must be looked into, for the father left me the care of his child."

Jasper was glad enough to change the subject, and the friends separated, each charged with the duty most peculiar to his own station, and habits.

That afternoon all the dead were interred, the grave of Serjeant Dunham being dug in the centre of the glade, beneath the shade of a huge elm. Mabel wept bitterly at the ceremony, and she found relief in thus disburthening her sorrow. The night passed tranquilly, as did the whole of the following day, Jasper declaring that the gale was too scvere to venture on the lake. This circumstance, detained Capt. Sanglier also, who did not quit the island until the morning of the third day after the death of Dunham, when the weather had moderated, and the wind had become fair. Then, indeed, he departed, after taking leave of the Pathfinder, in the manner of one who believed he was in company of a distinguished character, for the last time. The two separated, like those who respect one another, while each felt that the other was an enigma to himself.

Chapter XXIX.

"Playful she turned that he might see
The passing smile her cheek put on;
But when she marked how mournfully
His eyes met hers, that smile was gone,–"
        Moore, *Lalla Rookh*,
        "The Fire-Worshippers," ll. 269–72.

THE occurrences of the last few days had been too exciting, and had made too many demands on the fortitude of our heroine to leave her in the helplessness of grief. She mourned for her father, and she occasionally shuddered, as she recalled the sudden death of Jennie, and all the horrible scenes she had witnessed, but, on the whole, she had aroused herself, and was no longer in the deep depression that usually accompanies grief. Perhaps the overwhelming, almost stupefying sorrow that crushed poor June, and left her for nearly twenty four hours in a state of stupor, assisted Mabel in conquering her own feelings, for she had felt called on to administer consolation to the young Indian woman. This she had done, in the quiet, soothing, insinuating way, in which her sex usually exerts its influence, on such occasions.

The morning of the third day, was set for that on which the Scud was to sail. Jasper had made all his preparations; the different effects were embarked, and Mabel had taken leave of June, a painful and affectionate parting. In a word, all was ready, and every soul had left the island but the Indian woman, Pathfinder, Jasper and our heroine. The former had gone into a thicket to weep, and the three last were approaching the spot where three canoes lay; one of which was the property of June, and the other two were in waiting to carry the others off to the Scud. Pathfinder led the way, but, when he drew near the shore, instead of taking the direction to the boats, he motioned to his companions to follow, and proceeded to a fallen tree, that lay on the margin of the glade, and out of view of those in the cutter. Seating himself on the trunk, he signed to Mabel to take her place on one side of him, and to Jasper to occupy the other.

"Sit down here, Mabel; sit down there, Eau douce," he commenced, as soon as he had taken his own seat; "I've something that lies heavy on my mind, and now is the time to take it off, if it's ever to be done. Sit down, Mabel, and let me lighten my heart, if not my conscience, while I've the strength to do it."

The pause that succeeded, lasted two or three minutes, and both the young people wondered what was to come next, the idea that Pathfinder could have any weight on his conscience, seeming equally improbable to each.

"Mabel," our hero at length resumed, "we must talk plainly to each other, afore we join your uncle in the cutter, where the Salt-water has slept every night since the last rally; for he says it's the only place in which a man can be sure of keeping the hair on his head, he does—Ah's! me; what have I to do with these follies and sayings, now! I try to be pleasant, and to feel light-hearted, but the power of man can't make water run upstream. Mabel, you know that the sarjeant, afore he left us, had settled it atween us two, that we were to become man and wife, and that we were to live together, and to love one another as long as the Lord was pleased to keep us both on 'arth, yes, and afterwards, too?"

Mabel's cheeks had regained a little of their ancient bloom, in the fresh air of the morning, but at this unlooked for address they blanched again, nearly to the pallid hue which grief had imprinted there. Still she looked kindly, though seriously, at Pathfinder, and even endeavored to force a smile.

"Very true, my excellent friend—" she answered—"this was my poor father's wish, and I feel certain that a whole life devoted to your welfare and comforts could scarcely repay you for all you have done for us."

"I fear me, Mabel, that man and wife needs be bound together by a stronger tie than such feelings, I do. You have done nothing for me, or nothing of any account, and yet my very heart yearns toward you, it does, and therefore it seems likely that these feelings come from something besides saving scalps and guiding through woods."

Mabel's cheeks had begun to glow again; and, though she struggled hard to smile, her voice trembled a little, as she answered.

"Had we not better postpone this conversation, Pathfinder," she said; "we are not alone, and nothing is so unpleasant to a listener, they say, as family matters in which he feels no interest."

"It's because we are not alone, Mabel—or rather because Jasper is with us, that I wish to talk of this matter. The sarjeant believed I might make a suitable companion for you, and though I had misgivings about it—yes, I had many misgivings—he finally persuaded me into the idee, and things came round atween us, as you know. But when you promised your father to marry me, Mabel, and gave me your hand so modestly, but so prettily, there was one circumstance, as your uncle calls it, that you did'n't know, and I've thought it right to tell you what it is, afore matters are finally settled. I've often taken a poor deer for my dinner, when good venison was not to be found, but it's in natur' not to take up with the worst, when the best may be had."

"You speak in a way, Pathfinder, that is difficult to be understood. If this conversation is really necessary, I trust you will be more plain."

"Well, then, Mabel, I've been thinking it was quite likely when you gave in to the sarjeant's wishes, that you did not know the natur' of Jasper Western's feelings towards you?"

"Pathfinder!"—and Mabel's cheek now paled to the livid hue of death; then it flushed to the tint of crimson, and her whole form shuddered. Pathfinder, however, was too intent on his own object to notice this agitation, and Eau douce had hid his face in his hands, in time to shut out its view.

"I've been talking with the lad, and, on comparing his dreams with my dreams, his feelings with my feelings and his wishes with my wishes, I fear we think too much alike consarning you, for both of us to be very happy."

"Pathfinder—you forget—you should remember that we are betrothed!" said Mabel huskily, and in a voice so low, that it required acute attention in the listeners, to catch the syllables. Indeed, the last word was not quite intelligible to the guide, and he confessed his ignorance by the usual—

"Anan?"

"You forget that we are to be married; and such allusions are improper, as well as painful."

"Every thing is proper that is right, Mabel, and every thing is right that leads to justice, and fair dealing; though it *is painful* enough, as you say, as I find on trial, I do. Now, Mabel, had you known that Eau douce thinks of you in this way, maybe you never would have consented to be married to one as old and as uncomely as I am!"

"Why this cruel trial, Pathfinder–To what can all this lead–Jasper Western thinks no such thing–he says nothing–he feels nothing–"

"Mabel!" burst from out of the young man's lips, in a way to betray the uncontrollable nature of his emotions, though he uttered not another syllable.

Mabel buried her face in both her hands, and the two sat, like a pair of guilty beings, suddenly detected in the commission of some crime that involved the happiness of a common patron. At that instant, perhaps, Jasper himself was inclined to deny his passion, through an extreme unwillingness to injure his friend, while Mabel, on whom this positive announcement of a fact, that she had rather unconsciously hoped than believed, came so unexpectedly, felt her mind momentarily bewildered, and she scarce knew whether to weep, or to rejoice. Still she was the first to speak, since Eau douce could utter naught that would be disingenuous, or that would pain his friend.

"Pathfinder," she said–"you talk wildly;–why mention this, at all?"

"Well, Mabel, if I talk wildly, I *am* half wild, you know; by natur', I fear, as well as by habits–" as he said this he endeavored to laugh in his usual noiseless way, but the effect produced a strange and discordant sound, and it appeared nearly to choke him. "Yes, I *must* be wild; I'll not attempt to deny it."

"Dearest Pathfinder!–my best, almost my only friend! you *cannot, do not* think I intended to say that!" interrupted Mabel, almost breathless in her haste to relieve his mortification–"If courage, truth, nobleness of soul and conduct, unyielding principles and a hundred other excellent qualities can render any man respectable, esteemed, or beloved, your claims are inferior to those of no other human being."

"What tender and bewitching voices they have, Jasper!" resumed the guide, now laughing freely and naturally–"Yes, natur' seems to have made them on purpose, to sing in our ears, when the music of the woods is silent! But we must come to a right understanding; we must. I ask you ag'in, Mabel, if you had known that Jasper Western loves you as well as I do, or better perhaps, though that is scarce possible; that in his dreams, he sees your face in the water of the lake; that he talks to you, and of you, in his sleep; fancies all that is beautiful, like Mabel Dunham, and all that is good and virtuous; believes he never knowed happiness until he knowed you; could kiss the ground on which you have trod, and forgets all the joys of his calling, to think of you and of the delight of gazing at your beauty, and in listening to your voice, would you then have consented to marry me?"

Mabel could not have answered this question, if she would, but, though her face was buried in her hands, the tint of the rushing blood was visible between the openings, and the suffusion seemed to impart itself to her very fingers. Still nature asserted her power, for there was a single instant when the astonished, almost terrified girl stole a glance at Jasper, as if disputing Pathfinder's history of his feelings, read the truth of all he said in that furtive look, and instantly concealed her face again, as if she would hide it from observation, forever.

"Take time to think, Mabel," the guide continued, "for it is a solemn thing to accept one man for a husband, while the thoughts and wishes lead to another. Jasper and I have talked this matter over, freely and like old friends, and though I always knowed that we viewed most things pretty much alike, I could'n't have thought that we regarded any particular object with the very same eyes, as it might be, until we opened our minds to each other, about you. Now, Jasper owns that the very first time he beheld you, he thought you the sweetest and winningest creatur' he had ever met; that your voice sounded like murmuring water in his ears; that he fancied his sails were your garments, fluttering in the wind; that your laugh, haunted him in his sleep, and that, ag'in and ag'in, has he started up affrighted, because he has fancied some one wanted to force you out of the Scud, where he imagined you had taken up your abode. Nay, the lad has even acknowledged that he weeps often, at the thought that you are likely to spend your days with another, and not with him."

"Jasper!"

"It's solemn truth, Mabel, and it's right you should know it. Now stand up, and choose atween us. I do believe Eau douce loves you as well as I do myself; he has tried to persuade me that he loves you better, but that I will not allow, for I do not think it possible, but I will own the boy loves you, heart and soul, and he has a good right to be heard. The sarjeant left me your protector, and not your tyrant. I told him that I would be a father to you, as well as a husband, and it seems to me no feeling father would deny his child this small privilege. Stand up, Mabel, therefore, and speak your thoughts as freely, as if I were the sarjeant himself, seeking your good, and nothing else."

Mabel dropped her hands, arose, and stood face to face, with her two suitors, though the flush that was on her cheeks was feverish, the evidence of excitement, rather than of shame.

"What would you have, Pathfinder?—" she asked. "Have I not already promised my poor father to do all you desire?"

"Then I desire this. Here I stand, a man of the forest, and of little larning, though I fear with an ambition beyond my desarts, and I'll do my endivors to do justice to both sides. In the first place, it is allowed that so far as feelings in your behalf are consarned, we love you just the same; Jasper thinks his feelings *must* be the strongest, but this I cannot say, in honesty, for it does n't seem to me that it *can* be true; else I would frankly and freely confess it, I would. So in this particular, Mabel, we are here afore you, on equal tarms. As for myself, being the oldest, I'll first say what little can be produced in my favor, as well as ag'in it. As a hunter, I do think there is no man near the lines that can outdo me. If venison, or bear's meat, or even birds and fish should ever be scarce in our cabin, it would be more likely to be owing to natur' and Providence, than to any fault of mine. In short, it does seem to me, that the woman who depended on me, would never be likely to want for food. But, I'm fearful ignorant! It's true, I speak several tongues, such as they be, while I'm very far from being expart at my own. Then, my years are greater than your own, Mabel, and the circumstance that I was so long the sarjeant's comrade, can be no great merit in your eyes. I wish, too, I was more comely, I do; but we are all as natur' made us, and the last thing that a man ought to lament, except on very special occasions, is his looks. When all is remembered, age, looks, larning and habits, Mabel, conscience tells me I ought to confess that I'm altogether unfit for you, if not downright unworthy, and I would give up the hope, this minute, I would, if I did n't feel something pulling at my heart strings which seems hard to undo."

"Pathfinder!—Noble, generous Pathfinder—" cried our heroine, seizing his hand, and kissing it with a species of holy reverence—"you do yourself injustice—you forget my poor father and your promise—you do not know *me*!"

"Now, here's Jasper," continued the guide, without allowing the girl's caresses to win him from his purpose; "with *him*, the case is different. In the way of providing, as in that of loving, there's not much to choose atween us, for the lad is frugal, industrious and careful. Then he is quite a scholar—knows the tongue of the Frenchers—reads many books, and some, I know, that you like to read yourself—can understand you at all times, which, perhaps, is more than I can say for myself."

"What of all this—" interrupted Mabel, impatiently—"why speak of it now—why speak of it, at all!"

"Then the lad has a manner of letting his thoughts be known, that I fear I can never equal. If there's any thing on 'arth that would make my tongue bold and persuading, Mabel, I do think it's yourself, and, yet, in our late conversations, Jasper has outdone me, even on this point, in a way to make me ashamed of myself. He has told me how simple you were, and how true-hearted, and kind-hearted; and how you looked down upon vanities, for though you might be the wife of more than one officer, as he thinks, that you cling to feeling, and would rather be true to yourself, and natur', than a colonel's lady. He fairly made my blood warm, he did, when he spoke of your having beauty without seeming ever to have looked upon it, and the manner in which you moved about like a young fa'an, so nat'ral and graceful like, without knowing it; and the truth and justice of your idees, and the warmth and generosity of your heart—"

"Jasper!" interrupted Mabel, giving way to feelings that had gathered an ungovernable force by being so long pent, and falling into the young man's willing arms, weeping like a child, and almost as helpless. "Jasper!—Jasper!—Why have you kept this from me!"

The answer of Eau douce was not very intelligible, nor was the murmured dialogue that followed remarkable for coherency. But the language of affection is easily understood. The hour that succeeded passed like a very few minutes of ordinary life, so far as a computation of time was concerned, and when Mabel recollected herself, and bethought her of the existence of others, her uncle was pacing the cutter's deck, in great impatience, and wondering why Jasper should be losing so much of a favorable wind. Her first thought was of him, who was so likely to feel the recent betrayal of her real emotions.

"Oh! Jasper!" she exclaimed like one suddenly self convicted —"the Pathfinder!"

Eau douce fairly trembled, not with unmanly apprehension, but with the painful consciousness of the pang he had given his friend, and he looked in all directions, in the expectation of seeing his person. But Pathfinder had withdrawn, with a tact and a delicacy, that might have done credit to the sensibility and breeding of a courtier. For several minutes the two lovers sate, silently waiting his return, uncertain what propriety required, under circumstances so marked, and so peculiar. At length they beheld their friend advancing slowly towards them, with a thoughtful and even pensive air.

"I now understand what you meant, Jasper, by speaking without a tongue, and hearing without an ear," he said, when close enough to the tree to be heard,—"Yes, I understand it, now, I do, and a very pleasant sort of discourse it is, when one can hold it with Mabel Dunham. Ah's me!—I told the sarjeant I was'n't fit for her; that I was too old, too ignorant, and too wild like, but he *would* have it, otherwise."

Jasper and Mabel sate, resembling Milton's picture of our first parents, when the consciousness of sin first laid its leaden weight on their souls. Neither spoke; neither even moved; though both at that moment, fancied they could part with their new-found happiness, in order to restore their friend to his peace of mind. Jasper was pale as death, but, in Mabel, maiden modesty had caused the blood to mantle on her cheeks, until their bloom was heightened to a richness that was scarce equalled in her hours of light-hearted buoyancy and joy. As the feeling which in her sex, always accompanies the security of love returned, threw its softness and tenderness over her countenance, she was singularly beautiful. Pathfinder gazed at her, with an intentness he did not endeavor to conceal, and then he fairly laughed, in his own way, and with a sort of wild exultation as men that are untutored are wont to express their delight. This momentary indulgence, however, was expiated by the pang that followed the sudden consciousness that this glorious young creature was lost to him, forever. It required a full minute, for this simple-minded being to recover from the shock of this conviction, and then he resumed his dignity of manner, speaking with gravity, almost with solemnity.

"I have always known, Mabel Dunham, that men have their gifts," he said, "but I'd forgotten that it did not belong to mine, to please the young, and beautiful, and l'arned. I hope the mistake has been no very heavy sin, and if it was, I've been heavily punished for it, I have. Nay, Mabel, I know what you'd say, but it's unnecessary. I *feel* it all, and that is as good as if I *heard* it all. I've had a bitter hour, Mabel. I've had a very bitter hour, lad—"

"Hour!" echoed Mabel, as the other first used the word, the tell-tale blood, which had begun to ebb towards her heart, rushing again tumultuously to her very temples—"surely not an hour, Pathfinder!"

"Hour!" exclaimed Jasper, at the same instant—"no—no—my worthy friend, it is not ten minutes, since you left us!"

"Well, it may be so, though to me it has seemed to be a day. I begin to think, howsever, that the happy count time by minutes, and the miserable count it by months. But we will talk no more of this; it is all over now, and many words about it, will make you no happier, while they will only tell me what I've lost, and quite likely how much I desarved to lose her—no—no—Mabel, 'tis useless to interrupt me; I admit it all, and your gainsaying it, though it be so well meant, cannot change my mind. Well, Jasper, she is yourn, and though it's hard to think it, I do believe you'll make her happier than I could, for your gifts are better suited to do so, though I would have strived hard to do as much, if I know myself I would. I ought to have known better than to believe the sarjeant, and I ought to have put faith in what Mabel told me at the head of the lake, for reason and judgment might have shown me its truth; but it is so pleasant to think what we wish, and mankind so easily over-persuade us, when we over-persuade ourselves! But, what's the use in talking of it, as I said afore. It's true, Mabel seemed to be consenting, though it all came from a wish to please her father, and from being skeary about the savages—"

"Pathfinder!"

"I understand you, Mabel, and bear no hard feelings, I don't. I sometimes think I should like to live in your neighborhood, that I might look at your happiness, but, on the whole, it's better I should quit the 55th altogether, and go back to the 6oth, which is my natyve rigiment, as it might be. It would have been better, perhaps, had I never left it, though my sarvices were much wanted, in this quarter, and I'd been with some of the 55th, years agone, Sarjeant Dunham for instance, when he was in another corps. Still, Jasper, I do not regret that I've known you—"

"And me, Pathfinder—" impetuously interrupted Mabel—"do you regret having known *me*?—Could I think so, I should never be at peace with myself!"

"You, Mabel—" returned the guide, taking the hand of our heroine, and looking up into her countenance with guileless simplicity, but earnest affection, "how could I be sorry that a ray of the sun came across the gloom of a cheerless day; that light has broken in upon darkness, though it remained so short a time? I do not flatter myself with being able to march quite as light-hearted, as I once used to could, or to sleep as sound, for some time to come, but I shall always remember how near I was to being undesarvedly happy, I shall. So far from blaming you, Mabel, I only blame myself for being so vain, as to think it possible I could please such a creatur', for, sartainly, you told me how it was, when we talked it over, on the mountain, and I ought to have believed you, then, for I do suppose it's nat'ral that young women should know their own minds better than their fathers. Ah's me! It's settled now, and nothing remains but for me to take leave of you, that you may depart; I feel that Master Cap, must be impatient, and there is danger of his coming on shore to look for us, all."

"To take leave!" exclaimed Mabel.

"Leave!" echoed Jasper, "you do not mean to quit us, my friend?"

"'Tis best, Mabel—'tis altogether best, Eau douce, and it's wisest. I could live and die in your company, if I only followed feeling; but if I follow reason, I shall quit you, here. You will go back to Oswego and become man and wife, as soon as you arrive, for, all that is determined with Master Cap, who hankers after the sea ag'in, and who knows what is to happen; while, I shall return to the wilderness, and my Maker. Come Mabel," continued Pathfinder, rising and drawing nearer to our heroine, with grave decorum. "Kiss me. Jasper will not grudge me one kiss; then we'll part."

"Oh! Pathfinder—" exclaimed Mabel falling into the arms of the guide, and kissing his cheeks, again and again, with a freedom and warmth she had been far from manifesting while held to the bosom of Jasper—"God bless you, dearest Pathfinder— you will come to us, hereafter—we shall see you again—when old, you will come to our dwelling, and let me be a daughter to you?"

"Yes—that's it—" returned the guide, almost gasping for breath—"I'll try to think of it, in that way. You're more befitting to be my daughter, than to be my wife, you are. Farewell, Jasper. Now we'll go to the canoe—it's time you were on board."

The manner in which Pathfinder led the way to the shore, was solemn and calm. As soon as he reached the canoe, he again took Mabel, by the hands, held her at the length of his own arms, and gazed wistfully into her face, until the unbidden tears rolled out of the fountains of feeling, and trickled down his rugged cheeks, in streams.

"Bless me, Pathfinder?" said Mabel, kneeling reverently at his feet. "Oh! at least bless me, before we part."

That untutored, but noble-minded being, did as she desired, and aiding her to enter the canoe, seemed to tear himself away, as one snaps a strong and obstinate cord. Before he retired, however, he took Jasper by the arm, and led him a little aside, when he spoke as follows.

"You're kind of heart, and gentle by natur', Jasper, but we are both rough and wild in comparison with that dear creatur'. Be careful of her, and never show the roughness of man's natur' to her soft disposition. You'll get to understand her, in time, and the Lord who governs the lake and the forest, alike, who looks upon virtue with a smile, and upon vice with a frown, keep you happy, and worthy to be so!"

Pathfinder made a sign for his friend to depart, and he stood leaning on his rifle, until the canoe had reached the side of the Scud. Mabel wept as if her heart would break, nor did her eyes once turn from the open spot in the glade, where the form of the Pathfinder was to be seen, until the cutter had passed a point that completely shut out the island. When last in view, the sinewy frame of this extraordinary man was as motionless, as if it were a statue set up in that solitary place, to commemorate the scenes of which it had so lately been the site and the witness.

Chapter XXX.

"Oh! let me only breathe the air,
The blessed air that's breathed by thee;
And whether on its wings it bear
Healing or death, 'tis sweet to me!"
        Moore, *Lalla Rookh*,
        "Paradise and the Peri," ll. 250–53.

Pathfinder was accustomed to solitude, but, when the Scud had actually disappeared, he was almost overcome with a sense of his loneliness. Never before had he been conscious of his isolated condition in the world, for his feelings had gradually been accustoming themselves to the blandishments and wants of social life, particularly as the last were connected with the domestic affections. Now, all had vanished, as it might be, in one moment, and he was left equally without companions and without hope. Even Chingachgook had left him, though it was but temporarily; still his presence was missed at the precise instant which might be termed the most critical in our hero's life.

Pathfinder stood leaning on his rifle, in the attitude described in the last chapter, a long time after the Scud had disappeared. The rigidity of his limbs seemed permanent, and none but a man accustomed to put his muscles to the severest proof, could have maintained that posture, with its marble-like inflexibility, for so great a length of time. At length he moved away from the spot, motion of the body being preceded by a sigh that seemed to heave up from the very depths of his bosom.

It was a peculiarity of this extraordinary being, that his senses and his limbs, for all practical purposes, were never at fault, let the mind be preoccupied with other interests as much as it might. On the present occasion, neither of these great auxiliaries failed him, but, though his thoughts were exclusively occupied with Mabel, her beauty, her preference of Jasper, her tears and her departure, he moved in a direct line to the spot where June still remained, which was the grave of her husband. The conversation that followed, passed in the language of the Tuscaroras, which Pathfinder spoke fluently, but, as that tongue is understood only by the extremely learned, we shall translate it freely into the English, preserving, as far as possible, the tone of thought of each interlocutor, as well as the peculiarities of manner.

June had suffered her hair to fall about her face, had taken a seat on a stone that had been dug from the excavation made by the grave, and was hanging over the spot that contained the body of Arrowhead, unconscious of the presence of any other. She believed, indeed, that all had left the island but herself, and the tread of the guide's moccasined foot was too noiseless, rudely to undeceive her.

Pathfinder stood gazing at the woman, for several minutes, in mute attention. The contemplation of her grief, the recollection of her irreparable loss, and the view of her desolation produced a healthful influence on his own feelings; his reason telling him how much deeper lay the sources of grief, in a young wife, who was suddenly and violently deprived of her husband, than in himself.

"Dew of June," he said, solemnly, but with an earnestness that denoted the strength of his sympathy—"you are not alone in your sorrow. Turn, and let your eyes look upon a friend."

"June has no longer any friend!" the woman answered. "Arrowhead has gone to the happy hunting grounds, and there is no one left to care for June. The Tuscaroras would chase her from their wigwams; the Iroquois are hateful in her eyes, and she could not look at them. No—leave June to starve over the grave of her husband."

"This will never do—this will never do. 'Tis ag'in reason and right. You believe in Manitou, June?"

"He has hid his face from June, because he is angry. He has left her alone, to die."

"Listen to one, who has had a long acquaintance with red natur', though he has a white birth, and white gifts. When the Manitou of a pale face wishes to produce good in a pale face heart, he strikes it with grief, for it is in our sorrows, June, that we look with the truest eyes into ourselves, and with the farthest sighted eyes too, as respects right. The Great Spirit wishes you well, and he has taken away the chief, lest you should be led astray, by his wily tongue, and get to be a Mingo in your disposition, as you were already in your company."

"Arrowhead was a great chief!" returned the woman proudly.

"He had his merits, he had; and he had his demerits, too. But, June, you're not desarted, nor will you be soon. Let your grief out—let it out, according to natur', and when the proper time comes, I shall have more to say to you."

Pathfinder now went to his own canoe, and he left the island. In the course of the day, June heard the crack of his rifle, once or twice, and as the sun was setting, he reappeared bringing her birds ready cooked, and of a delicacy and flavor that might have tempted the appetite of an epicure. This species of intercourse lasted a month, June obstinately refusing to abandon the grave of her husband, all that time, though she still accepted the friendly offerings of her protector. Occasionally they met and conversed, Pathfinder sounding the state of the woman's feelings, but the interviews were short, and far from frequent. June slept in one of the huts, and she laid down her head in security, for she was conscious of the protection of a friend, though Pathfinder invariably retired at night, to an adjacent island, where he had built himself a hut.

At the end of the month, however, the season was getting to be too far advanced to render her situation pleasant to June. The trees had lost their leaves, and the nights were becoming cold and wintry. It was time to depart.

At this moment Chingachgook reappeared. He had a long and confidential interview on the island, with his friend. June witnessed their movements, and she saw that her guardian was distressed. Stealing to his side, she endeavored to soothe his sorrow, with a woman's gentleness, and with a woman's instinct.

"Thank you, June—thank you—" he said—"'Tis well meant, though it's useless. But it is time to quit this place. To-morrow, we shall depart. You will go with us, for now you've got to feel reason."

June assented in the meek manner of an Indian woman, and she withdrew to pass the remainder of her time, near the grave of Arrowhead. Regardless of the hour and the season, the young widow did not pillow her head during the whole of that autumnal night. She sat near the spot that held the remains of her husband, and prayed, in the manner of her people, for his success on the endless path on which he had so lately gone, and for their reunion in the land of the just. Humble and degraded as she would have seemed in the eyes of the sophisticated and unreflecting, the image of God was on her soul, and it vindicated its divine origin by aspirations and feelings that would have surprised those, who feigning more, feel less.

In the morning all three departed; Pathfinder earnest and intelligent in all he did, the Great Serpent silent and imitative, and June meek, resigned, but sorrowful. They went in two canoes, that of the woman being abandoned. Chingachgook led the way, and Pathfinder followed, the course being up stream. Two days they paddled westward, and as many nights they encamped on islands. Fortunately the weather became mild, and when they reached the lake, it was found smooth, and glassy as a pond. It was the Indian summer, and the calms, and almost the blandness of June, slept in the hazy atmosphere.

On the morning of the third day, they passed the mouth of the Oswego, where the fort and the sleeping ensign invited them in vain to enter. Without casting a look aside, Chingachgook paddled past the dark water of the river, and Pathfinder still followed, in silent industry. The ramparts were crowded with spectators, but, Lundie, who knew the persons of his old friends, refused to allow them to be even hailed.

It was noon, when Chingachgook entered a little bay, where the Scud lay at anchor, in a sort of road-stead. A small, ancient clearing was on the shore, and near the margin of the lake was a log dwelling, recently and completely though rudely fitted up. There was an air of frontier comfort, and of frontier abundance around the place, though it was necessarily wild and solitary. Jasper stood on the shore, and, when Pathfinder landed, he was the first to take him by the hand. The meeting was simple, but very cordial. No questions were asked, it being apparent that Chingachgook had made the necessary explanations. Pathfinder never squeezed his friend's hand more cordially, than in this interview, and he even laughed cordially in his face, as he told him how happy and well he appeared.

"Where is she, Jasper?—where is she," the guide at length

whispered, for, at first, he had seemed to be afraid to trust himself with the question.

"She is waiting for us in the house, my dear friend, where you see that June has already hastened before us."

"June may use a lighter step, to meet Mabel, but she cannot carry a lighter heart. And so, lad, you found the chaplain at the garrison, and all was soon settled?"

"We were married within a week after we left you, and Master Cap departed next day—You have forgotten to enquire about your friend, Salt-water—"

"Not I—not I. The Sarpent has told me all that, and then I love so much to hear of Mabel, and her happiness, I do. Did the child smile, or did she weep, when the ceremony was over?"

"She did both, my friend; but——"

"Yes, that's their natur'; tearful and cheerful! Ah's me! they are very pleasant to us of the woods, and I do believe, I should think all right, whatever Mabel might do. And do you think, Jasper, that she thought of me, at all, on that joyful occasion?"

"I know she did, Pathfinder; and she thinks of you, and talks of you daily, almost hourly. None love you as we do!"

"I know few love me better, than yourself, Jasper. Chingachgook is perhaps now the only creatur', of whom I can say that. Well, there's no use in putting it off, any longer; it must be done, and may as well be done at once; so, Jasper, lead the way, and I'll endivor to look upon her sweet countenance once more."

Jasper did lead the way, and they were soon in the presence of Mabel. The latter met her late suitor, with a bright blush, and her limbs trembled so, she could hardly stand. Still her manner was affectionate and frank. During the hour of Pathfinder's visit, for it lasted no longer, though he ate in the dwelling of his friends, one who was expert in tracing the workings of the human mind, might have seen a faithful index to the feelings of Mabel, in her manner to Pathfinder and her husband. With the latter she still had a little of the reserve that usually accompanies young wedlock; but the tones of her voice were kinder even than common, the glance of her eye was tender, and she seldom looked at him without the glow that tinged her cheek betraying the existence of feelings that habit and time had not yet soothed into absolute tranquillity. With Pathfinder all was earnest, sincere, even anxious, but the tones never trembled, the eye never fell, and if the cheek flushed it was with the emotions that are connected with concern.

At length the moment came, when Pathfinder must go his way. Chingachgook had already abandoned the canoes, and was posted on the margin of the woods, where a path led into the forest. Here he calmly waited to be joined by his friend. As soon as the latter was aware of this fact he rose in a solemn manner, and took his leave.

"I've sometimes thought that my own fate has been a little hard," he said, "but that of this woman, Mabel, has shamed me into reason—"

"June remains, and lives with me," eagerly interrupted our heroine.

"So I comprehend it. If any body can bring her back from her grief, and make her wish to live, you can do it, Mabel, though I've misgivings about even your success. The poor creatur' is without a tribe, as well as without a husband, and it's not easy to reconcile the feelings to both losses. Ah's me!—What have I to do, with other people's miseries, and marriages, as if I had n't affliction enough of my own. Don't speak to me, Mabel—don't speak to me, Jasper—let me go my way, in peace and like a man. I've seen your happiness, and that is a great deal, and I shall be able to bear my own sorrow, all the better for it. No—I'll never kiss you ag'in, Mabel: I'll never kiss you ag'in—Here's my hand, Jasper—squeeze it, boy, squeeze it; no fear of its giving way, for it's the hand of a man—And, now, Mabel do you take it,—nay, you must not do this—"preventing Mabel from kissing it, and bathing it with her tears—"you must not do this—"

"Pathfinder—" asked Mabel; "when shall we see you, again?"

"I've thought of that too; yes I've thought of that, I have. If the time should ever come when I can look upon you altogether as a sister, Mabel, or a child—it might be better to say a child, since you're young enough to be my daughter—depend on it, I'll come back, for it would lighten my very heart to witness your gladness. But if I cannot— Farewell—farewell—the sarjeant was wrong—yes, the sarjeant was wrong."

This was the last the Pathfinder ever uttered to the ears of

Jasper Western and Mabel Dunham. He turned away, as if the words choked him, and was quickly at the side of his friend. As soon as the latter saw him approach, he shouldered his own burthen, and glided in among the trees, without waiting to be spoken to. Mabel, her husband and June, all watched the form of the Pathfinder, in the hope of receiving a parting gesture, or a stolen glance of the eye, but he did not look back. Once or twice, they thought they saw his head shake, as one trembles in bitterness of spirit, and a toss of the hand was given, as if he knew that he was watched, but a tread whose vigor no sorrow could enfeeble, soon bore him out of view, and he was lost in the depths of the forest.

Neither Jasper nor his wife ever beheld the Pathfinder again. They remained for another year on the banks of Ontario, and then the pressing solicitations of Cap, induced them to join him in New-York, where Jasper eventually became a successful and respected merchant. Thrice Mabel received valuable presents of furs, at intervals of years, and her feelings told her whence they came, though no name accompanied the gifts. Later in life still, when the mother of several youths, she had occasion to visit the interior, and found herself on the banks of the Mohawk, accompanied by her sons, the eldest of whom was capable of being her protector. On that occasion, she observed a man, in a singular guise, watching her, in the distance, with an intentness, that induced her to inquire into his pursuits and character. She was told he was the most renowned hunter of that portion of the State—it was after the revolution—a being of great purity of character, and of as marked peculiarities, and that he was known in that region of country, by the name of the Leatherstocking. Further than this, Mrs. Western could not ascertain, though the distant glimpse and singular deportment of this unknown hunter, gave her a sleepless night, and cast a shade of melancholy over her still lovely face, that lasted many a day.

As for June, the double loss of husband and tribe produced the effect that Pathfinder had foreseen. She died in the cottage of Mabel, on the shores of the lake, and Jasper conveyed her body to the island, where he interred it by the side of that of Arrowhead.

Lundie, lived to marry his ancient love, and retired a war-worn and battered veteran, but his name has been rendered illustrious in our own time, by the deeds of a younger brother, who succeeded to his territorial title, which, however, was shortly after merged in one earned by his valor on the ocean.

APPENDIX

Cooper's 'Preface to the Leatherstocking Tales' [1850]

THIS series of Stories, which has obtained the name of 'The Leather-Stocking Tales,' has been written in a very desultory and inartificial manner. The order in which the several books appeared was essentially different from that in which they would have been presented to the world, had the regular course of their incidents been consulted. In 'The Pioneers,' the first of the series written, the Leather-Stocking is represented as already old, and driven from his early haunts in the forest, by the sound of an axe, and the smoke of the settler. 'The Last of the Mohicans,' the next book in the order of publication, carried the readers back to a much earlier period in the history of our hero, representing him as middle-aged, and in the fullest vigour of manhood. In 'The Prairie,' his career terminates, and he is laid in his grave. There, it was originally the intention to leave him, in the expectation that, as in the case of the human mass, he would soon be forgotten. But a latent regard for this character induced the author to resuscitate him in 'The Pathfinder,' a book that was not long after succeeded by 'The Deerslayer,' thus completing the series as it now exists.

While the five books that have been written were originally published in the order just mentioned, that of the incidents, insomuch as they are connected with the career of their principal character, is, as has been stated, very different. Taking the life of the Leather-Stocking as a guide, 'The Deerslayer' should have been the opening book, for in that work he is seen just emerging into manhood; to be succeeded by 'The Last of the Mohicans,' 'The Pathfinder,' 'The Pioneers,' and 'The Prairie.' This arrangement embraces the order of events, though far from being that in which the books at first appeared. 'The Pioneers' was published in 1823; 'The Deerslayer in 1841; making the interval between them eighteen years. Whether these progressive years have had a tendency to lessen the value of the last-named book, by lessening the native fire of its author, or of adding somewhat in the way of improved taste and a more matured judgment, is for others to decide.

If anything from the pen of the writer of these romances is at all to outlive himself, it is, unquestionably, the series of 'The Leather-Stocking Tales.' To say this, is not to predict a very lasting reputation for the series itself, but simply to express the belief it will outlast any, or all, of the works from the same hand.

It is undeniable that the desultory manner in which 'The Leather-Stocking Tales' were written, has, in a measure, impaired their harmony, and otherwise lessened their interest. This is proved by the fate of the two books last published, though probably the two most worthy an enlightened and cultivated reader's notice. If the facts could be ascertained, it is probable the result would show that of all those (in America, in particular) who have read the three first books of the series, not one in ten has a knowledge of the existence even of the two last. Several causes have tended to produce this result. The long interval of time between the appearance of 'The Prairie' and that of 'The Pathfinder,' was itself a reason why the later books of the series should be overlooked. There was no longer novelty to attract attention, and the interest was materially impaired by the manner in which events were necessarily anticipated, in laying the last of the series first before the world. With the generation that is now coming on the stage this fault will be partially removed by the edition contained in the present work, in which the several tales will be arranged solely in reference to their connexion with each other.

The author has often been asked if he had any original in his mind, for the character of Leather-Stocking. In a physical sense, different individuals known to the writer in early life, certainly presented themselves as models, through his recollections; but in a moral sense this man of the forest is purely a creation. The idea of delineating a character that possessed little of civilization but its highest principles as they are exhibited in the uneducated, and all of savage life that is not incompatible with these great rules of conduct, is perhaps natural to the situation in which Natty was placed. He is too proud of his origin to sink into the condition of the wild Indian, and too much a man of the woods not to imbibe as much as was at all desirable, from his friends and companions. In a moral point of view it was the intention to illustrate the effect of seed scattered by the way side. To use his own language, his 'gifts' were 'white gifts,' and he was not disposed to bring on them discredit. On the other hand, removed from nearly all the temptations of civilized life, placed in the best associations of that which is deemed savage, and favorably disposed by nature to improve such advantages, it appeared to the writer that his hero was a fit subject to represent the better qualities of both conditions, without pushing either to extremes.

There was no violent stretch of the imagination, perhaps, in supposing one of civilized associations in childhood, retaining many of his earliest lessons amid the scenes of the forest. Had these early impressions, however, not been sustained by continued, though casual connexion with men of his own color, if not of his own caste, all our information goes to show he would soon have lost every trace of his origin. It is believed that sufficient attention was paid to the particular circumstances in which this individual was placed, to justify the picture of his qualities that has been drawn. The Delawares early attracted the attention of the missionaries, and were a tribe unusually influenced by their precepts and example. In many instances they became Christians, and cases occurred in which their subsequent lives gave proof of the efficacy of the great moral changes that had taken place within them.

A leading character in a work of fiction has a fair right to the aid which can be obtained from a poetical view of the subject. It is in this view, rather than in one more strictly circumstantial, that Leather-Stocking has been drawn. The imagination has no great task in portraying to itself a being removed from the every-day inducements to err, which abound in civilized life, while he retains the best and simplest of his early impressions; who sees God in the forest; hears him in the winds; bows to him in the firmament that o'ercanopies all; submits to his sway in a humble belief of his justice and mercy; in a word, a being who finds the impress of the Deity in all the works of nature, without any of the blots produced by the expedients, and passion, and mistakes of man. This is the most that has been attempted in the character of Leather-Stocking. Had this been done without any of the drawbacks of humanity, the picture would have been, in all probability, more pleasing than just. In order to preserve the *vrai-semblable*, therefore, traits derived from the prejudices, tastes, and even the weaknesses of his youth, have been mixed up with these higher qualities and longings, in a way, it is hoped, to represent a reasonable picture of human nature, without offering to the spectator a 'monster of goodness.'

It has been objected to these books that they give a more favorable picture of the red man than he deserves. The writer apprehends that much of this objection arises from the habits of those who have made it. One of his critics, on the appearance of the first work in which Indian character was portrayed, objected that its 'characters were Indians of the school of Heckewelder, rather than of the school of nature.'† These words quite probably contain the substance of the true answer to the objection. Heckewelder was an ardent, benevolent missionary, bent on the good of the red man, and seeing in him one who had the soul, reason, and characteristics of a fellow-being. The critic is understood to have been a very distinguished agent of the government, one very familiar with Indians, as they are seen at the councils to treat for the sale of their lands, where little or none of their domestic qualities come in play, and where, indeed, their evil passions are known to have the fullest scope. As just would it be to draw conclusions of the general state of American society from the scenes of the capital, as to suppose that the negotiating of one of these treaties is a fair picture of Indian life.

It is the privilege of all writers of fiction, more particularly when their works aspire to the elevation of romances, to present the *beau-idéal* of their characters to the reader. This it is which constitutes poetry, and to suppose that the red man is to be represented only in the squalid misery or in the degraded moral state that certainly more or less belongs to his condition, is, we apprehend, taking a very narrow view of an author's privileges. Such criticism would have deprived the world of even Homer.

THE HISTORICAL CONTEXTS OF
THE PATHFINDER

In a letter of 6 April 1839, Cooper's British publisher Richard Bentley urged him to write a naval story set on America's 'own inland Seas', where 'the late unfortunate war gave rise to many gallant encounters'. Bentley's suggestion was a particularly welcome one, Cooper's daughter Susan tells us, because her father had 'for some time . . . wished to lay the scene of a tale on one of the great lakes, and to bring sailors and Indians into the same picture'. Cooper had served as a midshipman on Lake Ontario in 1808/9, and the 'picturesque beauties of the region, the countless islands—all, then, in a wild condition', had left a lasting impression on his memory. But rather than setting *The Pathfinder* during the War of 1812, Cooper turned to an earlier conflict, the French and Indian or Seven Years War (1756–63). That decision enabled him to exploit his naval memories while simultaneously reintroducing Natty Bumppo, the hero of three highly successful novels he had written during the 1820s.

Cooper had read the available historical accounts of the French and Indian War during the writing of the second of those novels, *The Last of the Mohicans* (1826), and as he began his work on *The Pathfinder* he renewed his familiarity with this material. As was his custom, Cooper insisted on the historical accuracy of his romances. In both the 1839 and the 1851 Prefaces to *The Pathfinder*, Cooper affirms his intention to present a faithful picture, 'a passing glimpse, even though it be in a work of fiction, of what that vast region so lately was'. Given that objective, it is worth examining how he used and altered history in *The Pathfinder*.

The French and Indian War

England declared war on France in May 1756, but a struggle for control of the West—specifically the region north of the Ohio—had been escalating for years. In 1753 Governor Duquesne built a chain of forts on the Allegheny and the upper Ohio, including Fort Duquesne at the site of present-day Pittsburgh, to defend French land and trading claims. He thereby asserted France's intention to control the entire West north of the Ohio, a position that ran counter to original charter boundaries and to the claims of newly established land companies. Serious military conflict began with

General Edward Braddock's futile attempt to overtake Fort
Duquesne in July 1755. Braddock's defeat is an important marker
not only because it pushed England to declare war less than a year
later, but also because it significantly affected all-important
Indian alliances.

During the early decades of the eighteenth century, as England
and France began to vie for North American hegemony, the Six
Nations of the Iroquois—Seneca, Cayuga, Onondaga, Oneida,
Mohawk, and Tuscarora—who occupied what is now New York
State, were officially neutral. Tribal allegiances were, however,
highly unstable. After Braddock's defeat, the Ohio Indians—the
Delawares and the Shawnees—joined the French, as did many
Iroquois. The Six Nations' principal goal was to protect their land
and to eliminate European forts and garrisons from Iroquois
territory. Throughout the war, the Iroquois played a double role of
stated neutrality and active participation where and when it suited
this aim. For the most part, allegiances were determined by
geography. The outstanding reason for Indian participation in the
war was their fear of French and British hunger for land; tribes
whose land-rights were infringed by the British, like the Delawares,
fought against them; while those who felt their interests were
served by the British, like the easternmost Mohawks, fought
consistently on their behalf. The Indians, in other words, fought
for the French or the British when their essential tribal objective to
preserve land-rights was served. Competition between the French
and British for Indian support (often a determining factor in
military victories) was intense.

Fort Oswego, located where Oneida Lake discharges through
the Onondaga River into Lake Ontario, was founded in the 1720s
as a trading post. During the war it became one of England's most
important bases. Its strategic location allowed the British to
compete commercially on the greatest of the western trading
routes and gave them a military base from which to rally Indian
support in the heart of New France. By 1756 the French wished to
remove this outpost of trade and diplomacy, thereby eliminating a
possible launching point for campaigns against Forts Frontenac
and Niagara. A power-struggle in the British command, specifically
between General William Shirley and Commissioner of Indian
Affairs William Johnson, inhibited an effective response to this
French threat. Indeed, the garrison suffered from a neglect so
severe that its men reached a point of famine. The fort itself began
to deteriorate markedly; the weak, demoralized, and diseased men
were not strong enough to maintain it. Things were so bad, the

historian Francis Jennings notes, that the 'cannon could not be fired for fear of collapsing the walls from shock'.

Shirley sent reinforcements in March 1756 with Lieutenant Colonel John Bradstreet, but the French were already preparing to cut off the British supply-line from the south. That month a surprise attack on Fort Bull between the Mohawk River and Wood Creek on Lake Oneida deprived the British of a crucial supply station. The French force included Oneida Indians, Canadians, and French regulars, and although reports are conflicting, the attack seems to have ended in a massacre. Bradstreet, meanwhile, was able to get through to Oswego with supplies, but he was ambushed on his return trip. Though outnumbered, he managed to fend off his attackers and returned to Albany. Further misadministration and the breathtaking lack of courage of General Webb, who failed to reinforce the garrison, left Oswego vulnerable; and on 14 August 1756 the fort fell to the French. Even though the garrison readily capitulated, the French military commander failed to avert a massacre after the surrender.

In capturing the fort the French acquired the substantial provisions and equipment Bradstreet had conveyed there. Included in the supplies were six vessels of varied sizes, including a British schooner, and more than a hundred pieces of artillery. Strategically the defeat was probably the worst experienced by the British during the war; it meant the loss of control of Lake Ontario to the French, who used their advantage to strengthen lines of communication to the West. Furthermore, it eliminated the British threat to Fort Niagara and reinforced French alliances with the northern Iroquois.

The tide of war did not begin to turn until 1758, when William Pitt reconstituted the British military command. Pitt appointed aggressive new leaders and won greater co-operation from colonial assemblies. Britain's military turn-around began with Bradstreet's defeat of French forces at Frontenac in August 1758. Mobilizing his forces at Oswego, Bradstreet captured the entire French navy on Lake Ontario. His victory re-established a British stronghold in the region and effectively cut the French lifeline to the West. Deprived of supplies and reinforcements, Fort Duquesne fell to the British in November 1758. Niagara followed in July 1759, and Quebec in September of that year.

Changes in military command, although essential, were not the sole cause of Britain's altered fortunes. Perhaps the most important factor in British success was the realignment of Indian loyalties during these years. The Peace Treaty at Easton in 1758, brought about by constant pressure from Pennsylvania Quakers, supported the territorial claims of the Delaware and Shawnee. Although it was soon violated, the agreement appeared to be a triumph for Indian rights. This apparent 'victory', along with the newly declared neutrality of the Ohio Indians, influenced other western tribes and was the most likely cause of the Indian refusal to support the French at Fort Duquesne in 1758.

Duquesne's fall eroded long-standing Seneca support for the French. By 1759 their loyalty began to shift to the British. Wooed by Johnson, the Seneca joined other Indians in the attacks on Niagara and Frontenac. Although this new alliance was unsteady, it significantly altered the balance of power in the region. At bottom, however, the Indian goal to eliminate European garrisons in the region remained. Senecas fighting for the British wanted the French removed and hoped to oust the British after that goal was achieved. Again, Indian alliances were predicated on preserving tribal territory; and in this case, the British were the beneficiaries of that goal.

In *The Pathfinder*, Cooper presents accurately the Oswego garrison's geographic location and historical function. However, he conflates time and alters events to suit the needs of his plot. Although the novel is set in the late 1750s, in a time after the British defeats at Duquesne (1755) and Ticonderoga (1758), but before Bradstreet's triumph at Frontenac (1758), Cooper presents the Oswego garrison as new to its frontier post and notes, 'it had not been long occupied'. The fort is neither in disrepair nor is its occupying force sick and demoralized. Instead Cooper transforms the British defeat at Oswego into the loss of a fictional outpost in the Thousand Islands, an event no less horrific in detail than the Oswego attack, but much less fateful in its overall impact. Cooper no doubt knew, from his voluminous reading on the war, the details of the Fort Bull and Oswego defeats and used them in creating the Station Island massacre.

The British army was, like the Oswego garrison Cooper draws, a motley group of forces from various nations and cultures plagued by problems of discipline and morale. Major Duncan's irrational distrust of Jasper Western is entirely consistent with the British military command's inability to co-operate with or respect provincial forces. Other early problems included the army's undisciplined state and the notorious corruption of its commanders. Cooper acknowledges these failings in his portrayal of the romantically indefatigable quartermaster, Lieutenant Muir, who betrays his garrison for French gold.

Cooper's depiction of the Indians in *The Pathfinder* is generally accurate but simplified and, in some instances, skewed. Although they were a tributary of the Six Nations, the Delaware were not readily controlled by the Iroquois whom they correctly suspected of involvement in land-frauds perpetrated against them by the British. Cooper retains the legendary Delaware–Iroquois rivalry in *The Pathfinder*, but Chingachgook's British loyalties are disjunctive with the pro-French Delaware position during most of the conflict.

The upper Iroquois and lake Indians were generally pro-French and were reputed to be especially fierce and brutal in warfare. However, Iroquois allegiances were not unchanging and many Iroquois were pro-British. Cooper does not, however, depict the shifts in tribal loyalties, specifically in the late 1750s, but lumps the Iroquois into a single group consistently anti-British. The Mingos, a tribe composed of Senecas and Cayugas who migrated to an area near present-day Cleveland, acquired an identity distinct from their parent tribes and were no longer inhabitants of the lake region. But Pathfinder does not distinguish them from any other Iroquois, even when Chingachgook corrects him. 'No matter', he says, 'Iroquois—devil—Mingo, Mengwe, or furies— all are pretty much the same. I call all rascals Mingos.' A Mingo is, for Natty, 'a creatur' to be put beneath the heel'. The single exception to Cooper's one-dimensional Indian portraits is the villainous Tuscarora chief, Arrowhead. His loyalties constantly shift between the British and the French, but Cooper attributes that duplicity not to tribal land policies but to Arrowhead's Mingo blood.

Cooper's depiction of the Iroquois as inherently evil answered the exigencies of his plot, but it was also consistent with contemporary representations of Native Americans. During Cooper's era, Indians were either noble redmen—whose nobility inhered in their approaching extinction—or bloodthirsty savages. The resultant diminishment of Indian character must surely have eased cultural qualms about the progressive extinction or removal of the eastern tribes. By 1840, the year of *The Pathfinder*'s publication, nearly all of the Indians east of the Mississippi had been removed to reservations in what is now Oklahoma. Cast as agents of evil, the Indians seemed to deserve their fate; their removal appeared not only necessary but—like the 'advancement of civilization' Cooper imagined 'across the whole American continent'—divinely sanctioned.

Marybeth McMahon

EXPLANATORY NOTES

3 *Mohican*: a tribal branch of the Algonquin nation, located primarily in what is now the upper-Hudson Valley of New York State.

8 *Tuscaroras*: the Sixth Nation of the Iroquois confederation, the Tuscaroras were originally located in North Carolina. They were decimated and driven north by white incursions.

10 *Levanters*: strong easterly winds of the western Mediterranean.

camboose: the cook-room of a freight-carrying boat or coaster, generally furnished with a cast-iron stove.

11 *Oneidas*: one of the Six Nations of the Iroquois; they were located in what is now central New York State.

12 *quid*: a piece of tobacco held in the mouth and chewed.

dunnage: boards and wedges used to secure cargo in the hold of a ship.

14 *on soundings*: a vessel is said to be 'in soundings' when it is navigated in water sufficiently shallow for measurements of the depth of water in which the ship is floating to be taken, hence in anchoring grounds.

in an offing: located at sea just beyond anchoring grounds, generally within sight of land.

16 *lie-to*: remain nearly stationary.

22 *ensign halyards*: small lines used to hoist flags.

kid and can: a sailor's mess kit.

23 *Mingo*: specifically a tribe composed of Senecas and Cayugas who migrated to an area near present-day Cleveland; for Natty, a generic term applied to any Iroquois.

Delaware: a confederation of Algonquin tribes, concentrated primarily in the Delaware River Valley. In the French and Indian War they were generally aligned with the French and played a major role in the defeat of General Braddock at Duquesne.

27 *scud*: ocean foam or spray driven by the wind.

29 *Iroquois*: a confederation of Indian tribes located throughout

upper New York state. They were noted for their ferocity. See note on *Six Nations*, p. 346.

30 *tack*: a zigzag course a ship takes to reach a point up wind.

Anan?: colonial slang for 'What?'

34 *Fort Stanwix*: built in 1785 by General John Stanwix near present-day Rome, New York. Strategically located between the Mohawk River and Wood Creek, it was a scene of frequent conflict during the French and Indian War.

49 *hawse*: the part of a ship's bow through which the rope or chain that holds the anchor is passed.

53 *wampum belt*: wampum, a cylindrical shell bead commonly made from a quahog clam, was used as currency by many eastern tribes. When woven into belts it became a significant mnemonic device, recording historical events in intricate designs.

67 *a cable's length in width*: a measurement of 200 yards (183 metres).

74 *Horican*: French name for Lake George, located between Warren and Washington counties in eastern New York State. It was the scene of a number of engagements during the French and Indian War.

93 *the nights are lighted up with the fires of heaven*: Cap is presumably referring to the aurora australis, the southern counterpart of the aurora borealis.

95 *head-land*: a cape; especially a promontory rising sharply from the beach.

lee-shore: the shore towards which the wind is blowing a ship.

leads: a rope with a lead weight tied to the end used in measuring the water's depth.

deep-seas: a lead with an attached line used for measurements in deep water.

103 *capstan-bars*: levers for turning the capstan, a device used to weigh the anchor or hoist heavy sails.

handspikes: crowbars.

113 *cutter-rigged*: a single-masted fore-and-aft rigged vessel.

trampooses: long, wearying journeys from place to place.

Frontenac: a French fort located near present-day Kingston, Ontario. It fell to Colonel John Bradstreet in 1758.

114 *scuttlebutt*: a cask used to hold drinking-water on board ship.

127 *a brig and a snow*: a brig is a two-masted square-rigged vessel. A snow differs only slightly from a brig in that it has a trysail mast above the main lower mast.

136 *halbert*: a weapon carried by sergeants; hence a badge of rank.

137 *Mrs. Grant of Laggan*: Scottish author (1755–1838) of *Memoirs of an American Lady*, first published in 1808.

144 *calash*: a woman's hood.

Ty: Fort Ticonderoga; Muir refers to Abercrombie's defeat there in 1758.

174 *a Powles Hook periagua is a first rate*: Paulus Hook was a point of land on the Hudson near present-day Jersey City; a periagua is a dugout canoe; a first rate is a warship of the highest quality.

crowning a cable: forming the strands of a cable into a loose knot to prevent it from untwisting.

carrick bend: a knot designed to join the two ropes that go around the capstan.

catting an anchor: raising the anchor from the surface of the water to the deck of the ship; catting refers to fixed horizontal beams called catheads on which the anchor was raised.

182 *main boom*: the spar at the foot of the mainsail.

topsail gasket: a rope used to secure the sail to its yard when furled.

kedge: the spare or back-up anchor carried on board ship.

192 *General Braddock*: commander of British forces during the French and Indian War; Braddock (1695–1755) was killed during an assault on Fort Duquesne. His numerically superior forces were ambushed and routed by a combined French and Indian detachment. George Washington, who served as one of Braddock's staff officers, led the survivors in a successful retreat.

201 *Mississagua*: a tribed of Algonquin Indians located in Toronto near the Mississagua River. They were loyal to the French.

202 *belayed the end of the jib halyards to a stretcher in the rigging*: fastened the end of the rope used to hoist a sail to a piece of wood in the rigging used by sailors to brace their feet.

230 *tallowed*: applying tallow to the sounding lead to determine the nature of the bottom.

232 *box the compass*: the ability to recite all the directions of a compass. This was not simply a question of reciting degrees in numerical order from 0 to 360, but of knowing the names of the degrees as expressed in terms of north, south, east, and west. Compass gradations were known by rather complicated combinations of the four terms, such as east by north by three quarters north.

233 *took the bonnet off the jib*: removed a canvas fastening from the jib sail.

241 *Montcalm*: Marquis Louis Joseph de Montcalm (1712–59); commander of the French forces during the French and Indian War, Montcalm was killed at the Battle of Quebec.

242 *Johnny Crapauds*: derogatory term for the French. *Crapaud* is French for toad.

245 *Boreas*: In Greek mythology the personification of the north wind.

248 *Sandy Hook*: peninsula in east central New Jersey about 15 miles south of Manhattan.

259 *throw a lead line overboard and ascertain the drift*: to measure with a lead line the distance a ship sails off her course as the result of being pushed sideways by wind or current.

319 *chevaux de frise*: a piece of timber traversed with iron-pointed spikes or spears five or six feet long. It was used to impede cavalry and foot soldiers; sometimes strung with barbed wire to increase its effectiveness.

320 *which rendered Xenophon so justly celebrated*: Xenophon (*c.*430–354 BC) joined the army of Cyrus the Younger, who desired to dethrone his old brother Artaxerxes II, King of Persia. In a battle at Cunaxa, Cyrus was killed. Xenophon led the Greek survivors through mountainous terrain inhabited by hostile tribes. Military historians credit Xenophon with the development of retreat tactics still useful in mountainous areas.

'spontoon: espontoon, a type of half-pike that was the badge of rank and principal weapon of infantry officers in the eighteenth century.

Lord Stair: John Dalrymple, second Earl of Stair (1673–

1747); a prominent general who served in the Wars of the Spanish Succession and was an aide-de-camp to the Duke of Marlborough.

320 *Duke of Marlborough*: John Churchill, first Duke of Marlborough (1650–1722); commander of the English and Austrian forces at the Battle of Blenheim.

346 *Six Nations*: a confederation of Iroquois tribes composed of the Mohawk, Cayuga, Oneida, Seneca, Onondaga, and Tuscarora. They played a strategic role in the struggle between the French and British for control of North America.

370 *"Anne, sister Anne"*: an allusion to Charles Perrault's version of the Blue Beard story. Blue Beard's wife posts her sister Anne on the castle tower to watch for their brothers, whom she hopes will rescue them.

377 *Fort du Quesne*: French fortification near present-day Pittsburgh; site of Braddock's memorable defeat in 1755.

395 *Wallace, or Bruce*: Sir William Wallace and Robert the Bruce, Scottish military heroes.

403 *a smaller goar*: a reference to the angle at which a sail has been cut.

the gaff had been fished: a length of wood had been attached to a spar to extend the heads of sails not set on stays, done so as to increase speed.

Lazaretto: an isolation hospital for seamen with contagious diseases.

407 *close reefed*: the condition of a square-rigged ship when all the reefs of its topsails have been taken in.

418 *Butler and Brandt*: John Butler (1728–94) and his son Walter Butler (d. 1781) led a band of British loyalists during the Revolutionary War. Butler's Rangers were associated with a series of frontier massacres undertaken by their Indian allies. Joseph Brant was a famous Mohawk chief who fought with the Butlers. His warriors were blamed for the Cherry Valley Massacre in 1778.

419 *that celebrated interview between Wellington and Blucher*: Wellington was the British commander at Waterloo; Gebhard Blücher led the Prussian troops during that battle.

THE WORLD'S CLASSICS

A Select List

SERGEI AKSAKOV: A Russian Gentleman
Translated by J. D. Duff
Edited by Edward Crankshaw

HANS ANDERSEN: Fairy Tales
Translated by L. W. Kingsland
Introduction by Naomi Lewis
Illustrated by Vilhelm Pedersen and Lorenz Frølich

ARTHUR J. ARBERRY (Transl.): The Koran

LUDOVICO ARIOSTO: Orlando Furioso
Translated by Guido Waldman

ARISTOTLE: The Nicomachean Ethics
Translated by David Ross

JANE AUSTEN: Emma
Edited by James Kinsley and David Lodge

Northanger Abbey, Lady Susan, The Watsons,
and Sanditon
Edited by John Davie

Persuasion
Edited by John Davie

ROBERT BAGE: Hermsprong
Edited by Peter Faulkner

WILLIAM BECKFORD: Vathek
Edited by Roger Lonsdale

KEITH BOSLEY (Transl.): The Kalevala

CHARLOTTE BRONTË: Jane Eyre
Edited by Margaret Smith

JOHN BUNYAN: The Pilgrim's Progress
Edited by N. H. Keeble

FRANCES HODGSON BURNETT: The Secret Garden
Edited by Dennis Butts

The Two Drovers and Other Stories
Edited by Graham Tulloch
Introduction by Lord David Cecil

SIR PHILIP SIDNEY:
The Countess of Pembroke's Arcadia (The Old Arcadia)
Edited by Katherine Duncan-Jones

TOBIAS SMOLLETT: The Expedition of Humphry Clinker
Edited by Lewis M. Knapp
Revised by Paul-Gabriel Boucé

ROBERT LOUIS STEVENSON: Treasure Island
Edited by Emma Letley

ANTHONY TROLLOPE: The American Senator
Edited by John Halperin

A complete list of Oxford Paperbacks, including The World's Classics, OPUS, Past Masters, Oxford Authors, Oxford Shakespeare, and Oxford Paperback Reference, is available in the UK from the Arts and Reference Publicity Department (RS), Oxford University Press, Walton Street, Oxford OX2 6DP.

In the USA, complete lists are available from the Paperbacks Marketing Manager, Oxford University Press, 200 Madison Avenue, New York, NY 10016.

Oxford Paperbacks are available from all good bookshops. In case of difficulty, customers in the UK can order direct from Oxford University Press Bookshop, Freepost, 116 High Street, Oxford, OX1 4BR, enclosing full payment. Please add 10 per cent of published price for postage and packing.